THE DRAGONS OF ESTERNES

STEVE TURNBULL

TAU PRESS LTD

DRAGONS OF ESTERNES by Steve Turnbull.

Ebook ISBN: 978-1-913199-05-0

Paperback ISBN: 978-1-913199-06-7

Hardback ISBN: 978-1-913199-07-4

Published by Tau Press Ltd.

Cover by Jeff Brown (jeffbrowngraphics.com).

Edited by Zoë Markham (markhamcorrect.com).

Continuity editing by Adriel Wiggins (www.adrielwiggins.com).

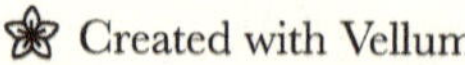 Created with Vellum

Book 1: Rebel Dragon

ISLE OF ESTERNES

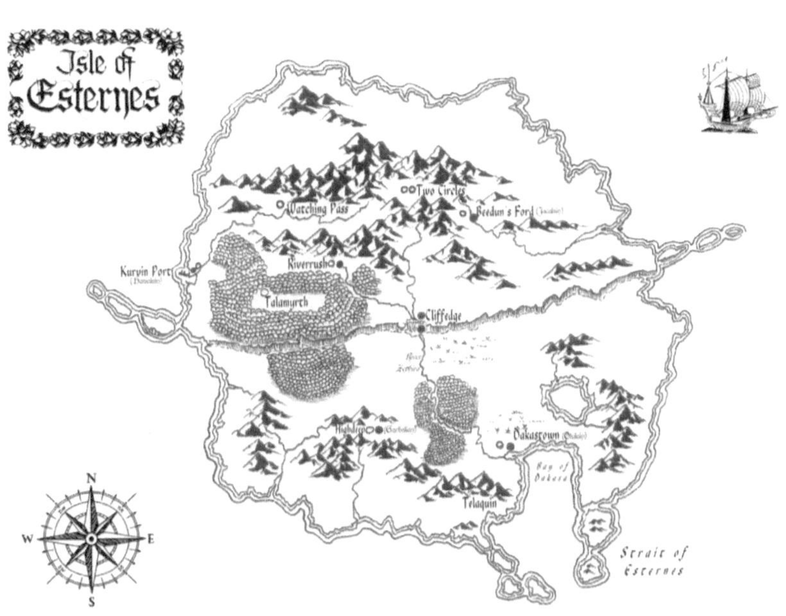

The floorboards trembled beneath her and she came awake with a jump.

The air in the eyrie was cold against her skin, and the light of the smaller moon, Colimar, shone red through the arched window in the tower's stone wall. It was still deepest night.

Must have been a dream, thought Kantees, as she re-adjusted the thin blanket and tried to burrow deeper into the pricking straw. The boards beneath her shifted again and there was a quiet grumble. *Oh, by the Mother's milk. What now? Stupid animal.*

She contemplated doing nothing, pretending not to wake up. Maybe Sheesha would lose interest and go back to sleep. The boards jumped again and Kantees groaned.

"Go back to sleep, Sheesha, it's not even close to morning," she hissed through the cracks. There was nothing to see since the gaps were smaller than her finger-width and there was no light down there anyway. Her reward was to have the boards bumped three more times. Sheesha must be stretching.

While Sheesha might be an animal, he was cleverer than most, even those of his own species. But that didn't stop him behaving like a spoilt child, like little Jelamie, the mistress's youngest. He was always getting into things and places he shouldn't.

Sheesha snuffled at her. The noise he made when he wanted something. Perhaps he'd spilt his water bucket again. He was forever doing that with his tail; it was like he didn't even know he had it.

Maybe it was important. What if Sheesha was ill? If there was a problem with her charge and Kantees ignored it, there'd be trouble.

"And," she said, "if there's nothing wrong, I'll make trouble for *you*."

Kantees climbed to her feet. Her eyes were adjusted to the dark and she could see the mounds of straw and the dark shadow that was the path through them. The hole in the floor to the lower level was a black pit. She picked up the gauntlets and slipped her fingers into the soft leather, then donned the protective hat. Sheesha had never attacked her but it was better to be safe than sorry. The *zirichak* had never woken her in the night either.

Before he had learnt to fly, Sheesha had been very demanding and very annoying. Kantees was glad those days were long past and, what with Sheesha and Jelamie, had decided she was never going to have any children. Even if the master chose someone for her to marry.

Not bothering with the stairs, Kantees grabbed the rope, swung out, wrapped her legs around it and slid to the next level. After all these years she barely noticed the smell—she would be mucking out in the morning—but was almost knocked over when Sheesha rattled over and nudged her in the shoulder. He was almost twice her height

Automatically Kantees reached up and scratched beneath the feathers in the place Sheesha liked the most.

Sheesha pulled back. In the dim light the *zirichak* waddled back —he was far more elegant in the air—brought his hook-beaked head down to Kantees and, with one eye, stared at her.

Kantees had no idea what he wanted. This behaviour was completely new.

"What?" hissed Kantees, as if Sheesha could understand, which was ridiculous because *ziri* were just animals, to be raced by the masters.

Her train of thought was interrupted by the distant sound of an arrow. It was only a momentary whine; it ended with a thump.

Sheesha turned his head and lifted it as if he were looking out of the window.

Taking care not to trip on the hobble chain that prevented Sheesha trying to fly inside, Kantees hurried across to the open hatch. She stuck her head out into a freezing breeze. Squinting, she tried to see.

With only Colimar in the sky, lying close to the horizon, the shadows were long and deep. But at least the sky was clear—if it hadn't been she would have been able to see nothing. As it was, she could make out the shapes of the buildings—she was familiar with them, anyway—but hanging in the air near the wall was something huge like a growth.

She shook her head and looked again. Was she still dreaming? A great bulbous shape, where the light caught it there were bumps and lines that looked, for all the world, like leaves. But leaves as big as a house. It couldn't be a *tekrak*; they never grew that big. But her eyes said it was.

And hanging beneath it, some sort of construction that was hard to make out. And from that, shadowy human shapes were jumping onto the main wall.

An attack?

Sheesha bumped her in the middle of her back, knocking her forwards onto the deep windowsill.

Kantees turned and stroked the huge head, and made settling noises. "It's all right, nothing to worry about."

Nothing for us to worry about. They were heading into the main building. It was nothing to do with her. If the masters wanted to fight, why should she care?

She stared out once more at the massive *tekrak* poised above the wall. No family she knew of had such things. Even now she could scarce believe what she was seeing. Could the *Slissac* have returned to put all the Taymalin to the sword?

The master and mistress, Lord and Lady Jakalain, were decent people even if they had no idea how to bring up children, nor did they treat the slaves badly. Every one of the Kadralin knew how lucky they were, they knew the stories about families that punished their slaves for the slightest crime, and even killed them for pleasure.

Kantees enjoyed her life looking after Sheesha and some of the other *zirichasa*. If the Jakalain were killed, what would happen to her? What would happen to Sheesha?

Perhaps the castle would be taken over by another family who would not be decent.

Mother's milk.

But what could she do? She was here in the Ziri Tower, and by the time she got to ground level and across to the other side it would all be over—and she might well run into a raider. Then she would be dead.

Sheesha prodded her in the back again.

Kantees turned round slowly. She knew Sheesha was intelligent, at least for a *zirichak*, but he couldn't possibly understand what was happening. Surely he did not want Kantees to ride him? For a start, that was a hanging offence and Kantees was quite fond of her life. That also meant Kantees had never flown, although she knew all the equipment and had sat in the saddle holding the reins. Never mind she was a slave.

She looked out of the window again to see more men on the wall now.

But she dared not—it could mean her life. It wasn't fair. Why couldn't someone else make the decision? Why hadn't any of the other *zirichasa* noticed? Why hadn't any armsmen seen what was happening? That was their job.

Because they're dead.

Kantees let out a cry of angry frustration. She turned and pushed Sheesha's head out of the way as she half ran to the tack room. It was too dark to see but she had everything in its correct place and knew where to find the lightest practice saddle.

Sheesha was crouched and waiting with his head down for her to slip the bridle over.

It took a couple of minutes to get the saddle in position and strapped firmly. What a laugh it would be if she took off and then slipped and fell to smash her head open on the rocks. Ha.

The one thing she didn't have was a flying suit. Why would she? There would be almost nothing between her and the freezing air. If she didn't fall, she would probably die of the cold. At least the protective hat would help keep her head warm.

Pulling the last strap tight, she paused. Sheesha dipped his chest so his wings were folded high above them, his claws scratching on the boards. Kantees went to the wall and unhooked the chain that ran from there through the metal collar to the cuffs on his feet. She was a little nervous. He was acting so strangely. There were tales of *zirichak* killing their keepers, but that had never happened here as far as she knew. Those keepers probably had mistreated their charges.

The chain rattled as it went through the cuff. There still hadn't been any noise from outside. What was she going to do when she got out there? She had never been in the main parts of the castle— except the kitchens. She did not know her way around.

For the hundredth time, it seemed, she wondered what she was doing.

Then it occurred to her. Why hadn't the warning bell sounded? It was mounted on one of the side towers and would wake everyone. She opened the great doors that were big enough to let Sheesha fly, then went back to him. She could see by the way he kept dipping his head he was impatient.

She was about to commit a capital crime. She would be hanged for it.

Sheesha squawked and shuffled in his crouched, cramped position. Perhaps she could claim, in her defence, that Sheesha had demanded she ride him. Somehow she did not think that would be very convincing.

She slipped her right foot into the stirrup and brought her left leg up and over. The straps were too long so she shortened them so she could rest her feet firmly. She sat awkwardly and grabbed for the belt that held the rider in position. Sheesha edged towards the door, his great wings moving forwards to hold up his body. Kantees grabbed the reins and pulled them back, not too tight but just taking up the slack along Sheesha's sinuous, feathered neck.

It was then she remembered he always gave a loud trumpet whenever he launched himself into the air. Announcing his emergence into the world, like a challenge.

The attackers would know and they would shoot their arrows, at the very least they would hit Sheesha and that would be enough to kill him.

Sheesha reached the edge and raised his clawed wings to hook them into the frame above the opening. His head poked out and she could see him surveying the air.

Then she was flung back as he dropped into the dark. She tried not to yank on the reins, which were only for guidance. A *zirichak* knew how to fly; the rider only needed to direct the creature left and right, up and down.

Sheesha's wings flicked out but he was diving. All she could see was the small courtyard between the Ziri Tower and the main building. There was a man standing there. He carried an unsheathed sword but she could only see the top of his head.

Could Sheesha tell friends from enemies? Kantees knew he had a sense of smell but how good was it? And another thing, she had been given to understand that *zirichasa* did not fly at night. That was the wisdom passed to her from old Romain. Perhaps he was wrong.

The freezing air shot through her clothes as if they were not even there.

The ground was coming at them. She knew he would pull up. She prayed to the Mother he would pull up. Perhaps they didn't fly at night because they crashed into the ground.

Something changed and her weight was forced into the saddle. The world tilted up slightly and Sheesha passed across the outside wall, still going down but now at a flatter angle. All right, he could fly at night.

They were in shadow now. The castle was built atop one of the foothills that encircled the great mountains that made up the heart of Esternes.

Sheesha was flying level now, the wall of the castle beside them. Every now and then she saw the light of a torch or lamp in the interior through the arrow slits. Then they were past and out into moonlight again, flashing across the scrubland that was only useful for grazing animals.

Where was he going? They needed to do something at the castle … but what?

Gingerly she pulled on the right rein. The response from Sheesha was instantaneous as he banked giddily and the world turned. And there was the rear of the castle, with its walls as high and impregnable as the rest.

Walls easily breached by men aboard a *tekrak* of such enormous size it could carry them in a basket beneath. She shook her head. She had never heard of such a thing.

She focused on the towers. They had already passed the bell tower once on the flight out. It was not as high as the main tower, and it was narrow. With gentle tugs she steered Sheesha to ensure he would fly back the way he had come. She did not want to be on the other side, where the *tekrak* hung.

How could she make him gain height? They were flying only a few feet above the ground. She pulled the reins again and leaned back. Up to now Sheesha had barely flapped his wings. She knew from Romain the wild *zirichasa* soared on the air currents in the mountains and could glide all day without a single beat of their wings if the winds were with them.

But now Sheesha's powerful wings stroked hard and with each downbeat he rose and she was pushed down into the saddle. She was not sure of the best way to approach the tower. It would be best if she was not seen, since she had no desire to become a pincushion for arrows. But the tower itself went high above the level of the walls and Sheesha could not climb vertically. She pulled on his right rein again and leaned forwards. He banked right and flew directly away from the castle.

Kantees looked back over her shoulder. The dark silhouette of the castle with the *tekrak* like a bulbous growth was highlighted against the dull red light of Colimar. She was desperately cold but had to keep going.

She pulled hard on the left rein and Sheesha almost turned over as he banked left. The ground was a long way away. Kantees urged him forwards, goading him with her heels and words. He beat faster and they sped up; she pulled back and he climbed. She judged they were on exactly the right course for the top of the tower.

Kantees reached with her numb fingers for the belt buckle.

They came up over the top of the bell tower from below.

Kantees threw her weight forwards and Sheesha almost fell out of the sky to land on the roof, hind legs first, pulling in his wings to act as his front legs.

Then someone said, "Oi!"

2

*K*antees almost fell out of the saddle and ended up on her hands and knees. She had not realised how cold she was—or how much warmth she had been taking from Sheesha's body. The muscles in her legs ached from the unaccustomed strain, and her inner thighs were rubbed raw.

She hadn't even noticed while they'd been in the air.

"Who are you?"

She lifted her head and, looking under Sheesha's neck, could see a man's legs. He was only a short distance away but probably nervous of the *zirichak.*

"You with the Dunor?"

She wasn't going to say she wasn't. She reached out, grabbed a handful of Sheesha's feathers and pulled herself to her feet. It was dark, and as long as she stayed on this side of Sheesha's neck the man wouldn't be able to tell who she was.

The bell stood in its frame only a short distance away. Next to it lay a body. The longer she delayed, the more likely people would be killed.

"Of course." She tried to give her voice a deeper sound, as if she were a messenger. Not that messengers rode fine beasts like Sheesha, nobody rode the *ziri* except racers, but perhaps he wasn't an expert. No, he'd been relegated to guarding the bell tower. No use for anything else. Though she was not sure how he could have got up here undetected.

That he had done so was enough for her. She took hold of the reins and walked across the roof, keeping Sheesha between them.

"What's the message then, boy?"

"The message?"

She had covered a third of the distance. Sheesha's wings scraped the roof as he moved beside her, taking much smaller strides than he was used to.

"Stop," he said.

She stopped. What could she do? She was no fighter and even if she was she had no weapon. And no armour—barely any clothes at all. Her teeth were chattering. Trying to be clever was just not working and the cold was biting through her skin. Her very dark skin.

"Kadralin slave!"

She dropped the reins and ran for the bell. She did not know how long it would take him to react, or whether he had any throwing weapons. Or worse, a bow.

There had been no rain for a few days but there was plenty of frost on the roof. She was only a couple of paces from the bell when her left foot flew out from under her and she pitched forwards.

The thudding of his heavy feet pounded closer. She turned to see him with his sword raised above his head. It came down. Instinctively she rolled towards him. The blow landed where she had been as she impacted with his legs; it knocked the wind from her and she cried out in pain. He went flying as he tripped over her and his head smashed into the bell. It rang out with a sonorous gong that bounced off the towers and echoed through the courtyard below. Ignoring her screaming ribs, she got to her feet and found the metal striker in a bucket at the side.

She hit the bell again and again.

The soldier pushed himself up, so she hit him as well, whacking his temple with the striker's bulbous head. He let out a groan of pain and slumped back. She trod on his hand and returned to bashing the bell with all her strength.

Sheesha snapped his beak in displeasure at the noise.

"Big strong *ziri* like you? It's only a bit of noise!" shouted Kantees with a laugh. She moved the striker further down the bell and the noise became deeper and louder. She turned to look at the main tower. Lights were being lit and showing at the window. Silhouetted figures stood for a moment looking out and then disappeared fast back inside. She hoped they were readying themselves for battle.

The *tekrak* was big—no, it was huge—but she guessed its complement of soldiers could not be more than thirty at most. And there were many times that number of armsmen in the castle. The attackers could only prevail by stealth, and they no longer had that advantage.

A horn winded from the far side of the castle walls. Torches were being lit inside the huge basket hanging from the *tekrak*. It had windows just like the castle.

Men streamed back along the walls. They were retreating.

The one at her feet tried to crawl away.

"Sheesha! Come!" she called and the *zirichak* thumped and scraped his way over. Long ago, Romain had drawn the bones of the creature for her so she could learn them by heart. Their wings were like hands but with one less finger and much bigger and spread out. When they walked it was as if they were on their elbows with their forearms and fingers pointing upwards. It wasn't elegant.

They had back legs, of course, and sometimes they went up on those alone—usually when threatening or mating.

"If you try to run away, I will let Sheesha eat you," she said and the man froze on the ground. She stopped banging the bell, having succeeded in what she was attempting, and went to Sheesha, walking him closer to the prone guard.

"Throw your sword away," she commanded.

He gripped it tighter.

"Sheesha, speak!"

And the *zirichak* let out an intense squawk, which was a version of the sound he used when complaining but the guard didn't know that. It wasn't Kantees' fault that, despite being told not to teach Sheesha tricks, he learnt things very quickly.

The sword skittered across the roof.

"And your knife."

It went in the other direction.

There was a thunderous roar from across the castle and the Zirichak Tower was lit almost like daylight. The *tekrak* had started its burn. Of course she had seen the swarms of *tekrasa* crossing the skies in spring and autumn. Usually they were mere dots, so high did they float, but at night they descended to earth and their roots dug into the soil so they could feed.

In places where crops grew, the farmers and villagers would come out into the fields to destroy them. Each *tekrak* had a tube at one end, effectively the rear, and they propelled themselves by generating a fire that shot out. It was their magic. They had to be killed because their fire could burn the crops.

The ones that landed in the castle couldn't root anyway, and they were easy to get rid of. But when they took off in the morning the roots came up, their bodies—now bloated with gas—lifted them into the sky, and their fire-tubes drove them away in their swarm.

But this *tekrak* had a fire-tube that shot a flame almost the length of the protective wall. It moved with incredible slowness, a leviathan of the air.

Kantees turned her attention back to the guard. "I want your cloak."

His hands fumbled at his neck.

Sheesha pulled at the reins and shrieked at the *tekrak* as it floated across the courtyard, ropes dangling from the basket. She could even see inside. A man, in the robes of a patterner, sat in the front concentrating. His eyes were closed. Soldiers looked back at her and one barked orders.

The *tekrak* accelerated. Sheesha dragged her up as he rose on his hind legs and beat his wings, threatening the monstrous plant.

"No, Sheesha!" she called at him but he wasn't listening. She clung to the reins. Romain had told her a *zirichak* could not go aloft if someone held the reins. So she clung to them swinging and twisting as Sheesha pulled her off her feet.

The *tekrak* filled the sky and roared overhead. She saw a door open in the side of the basket from which a man with a bow leaned out. The roaring of the massive fire-tube drowned out all other sound. But when she saw him loose three arrows in quick succession, she was terrified he was aiming for her or, even worse, at Sheesha. Then the *tekrak* went over them. And she felt no pain, while Sheesha continued to screech his defiance at the monster.

Heat and flame roared across them. Sheesha squealed and curled up into a tight ball. Kantees thudded to the ground and rolled over.

The wash of heat was gone almost as quickly as it arrived but it left behind a disgusting stench that made the bile rise in her throat. The flame tube lit the top of the tower with its eerie blue light. Raising her head she saw the three arrows, planted in the body of the man she had overpowered.

They could not stop for him, but they would not let him remain alive to reveal any secrets. Hard-hearted as it seemed, she understood the logic.

Kantees went to Sheesha and flung her arms around him, burying herself in his feathers. It was partly to comfort him and give him something familiar. But it also meant she could keep warm, since she did not desire to wrap herself in a cloak now wet with blood.

As she clung to his warmth, a cold certainty crept through her. She was in trouble.

It was true she had saved the castle, they would not be able to deny it, but the fact remained she had ridden Sheesha. And the law was the law. There were so many stories where slaves had done something wrong in an attempt to do the right thing and were punished regardless of the balance.

She had ridden a *zirichak* in defiance of the law. The punishment was death.

But what if they never found out?

The castle was coming alive. Sounds of shouts and arguments floated up from the courtyard. There were armsmen moving on the walls opposite. She did not know if she had been seen but perhaps if she could get Sheesha back into his eyrie they might get away with it.

The trapdoor rattled. Even Sheesha jumped.

"Sheesha, come on," she said and grabbed the reins. With the excitement over, he moved without haste. She yanked at the reins to make him move faster. It didn't work. Once he reached the outside edge of the tower she mounted and dug her heels in.

He spread his wings, hopped up onto the wall, and dropped over the side. This time she was ready for it, and happy since it took them out of sight instantly.

The ground rushed at them. She allowed Sheesha his head and, barely a man's height from the ground, he snapped his wings out into horizontal flight, careening across the ground.

The entrance to Sheesha's eyrie faced the courtyard but if they came in fast from the far side they might not be seen. As she arched him away to the south, she glanced to see if the *tekrak* was still in view but she saw nothing. The bright glow in the sky could just as easily be another star while the false dawn of Lostimal, the second, larger moon, glowed on the horizon. Unlike the dull red of Colimar, Lostimal was white.

She turned to look ahead. The town of Beedun's Ford had already passed behind them, she was not concerned about that. The town would be asleep at this time and would know nothing of the fight at the castle.

Just as she had done before, she brought Sheesha round in a tight turn and headed him back towards the castle. As Lostimal rose, this side of the structure was bathed in its white light, which was inconvenient but unavoidable.

She had been into the town during feast days and the times when she had gone to fetch for the masters, and had thought it was big. Somehow, from the back of a *zirichak* it did not seem quite so large. The Beedun ran through it, splitting off the miners' quarter from the rest. The river was milky—the colour it had as it flowed from the mountains—but now it looked red like blood, reflecting the light of Colimar, though Lostimal would soon take over.

The old ford was in the north, but bridges spanned the river now and was only used by the miners' wagons because either the bridges were too narrow or the cargo too heavy.

And then she was past it and following the rising land. Sheesha beat his wings in deep powerful strokes. She pulled back more and

Sheesha gained even more height. The Ziri Tower was coming at her. She knew the height of the eyrie; she thought she even recognised her window. She pulled Sheesha to the left to stay in shadow and out of the light of Lostimal, at least until the last moment.

Which arrived in the blink of an eye.

As she turned Sheesha round the curve of the tower she came into full view of every person on the walls and in the courtyard. She prayed to the Mother no one would look up at exactly that moment.

Sheesha did not require guidance now. Although he entered the eyrie at a sharper angle than usual and came to a crashing halt inside, thumping into the bales of hay. The hay wasn't for eating since *zirichasa* ate meat, but provided warmth and something to sleep on, like a nest the wild animals would make for themselves.

Kantees unbuckled herself from the seat and slid to the ground. Her legs gave way again and she was freezing but she forced herself to the eyrie doors and closed them. She could not decide whether fast or slow was better. Fast because it got them shut, or slow because they would not attract attention.

Sheesha was already curled up into a tight ball and probably asleep. His breathing was unhurried. More than could be said for hers.

Was that real? Had she really just ridden Sheesha across the sky and saved the castle? It was like being a hero from a story. Except she would be a hero strung up on a gibbet if anyone else knew what she had done. Although that was a very sobering thought, the excitement refused to leave her. And so did the cold.

It was also forbidden to sleep with the *zirichasa*. One reason was that they might decide to eat you in the night. She had never heard of that happening except in Romain's stories. The other reason— probably the real one, she now realised—was that they did not want any *zirichak* to form too strong a bond with their keepers, who were always slaves. And a slave might get it into their head that they could ride.

And she had. She had not fallen off.

"Kadralin cannot fly," Romain had said. "We do not have the skill, and we do not have the command. That is why we are slaves and the Taymalin are the masters."

Not true. She had flown and she had survived—and she had loved it.

She shivered and looked at the compact form of Sheesha. What did it matter if he ate her? After all, in the morning she might be arrested and hanged. Why avoid one risk of death when another was just as likely?

She walked over to Sheesha and petted his neck, saying his name quietly. She leaned her weight on him and as he moved slightly, a space opened up under a wing and she pushed into it. With her head against his chest, hearing his breathing and feeling his powerful heart, she closed her eyes. His wing dropped down to cover her and she slept in his warmth.

3

The next morning the castle was in uproar. From the eyrie, Kantees could hear all the shouting and the arguments. Armsmen marched down to the town. The house patterner, with a retinue, was sent to the Jakalain Circle so that he could send messages.

After tending to Sheesha, who was tired and irritable—just as she was—Kantees descended to the kitchen in the base of the tower. No one looked at her in any way other than the usual. But there seemed no time for talk.

Libbibet, a middle-aged Kadralin woman who ran the servants' kitchen below the tower, was serving as usual and put a couple of spoonfuls of porridge into Kantees' bowl. But instead of her usual expression of merriment and a kind word, her face was serious and her lips pressed together in concerned silence.

Kantees had already decided—after discussing it with the irritable Sheesha, who had failed to offer any advice—that she would pretend she knew nothing. She did not think anyone would have recognised Sheesha in the dark anyway. Even with the light of Lostimal, it only seemed bright because it had been so dark before.

"What's the fuss?" said Kantees.

Libbibet paused, her hand poised with the third spoonful

hanging over Kantees' bowl. She glanced around as if she did not wish to be overheard.

"Lord Jelamie has been stolen away," she hissed. "Raiders in the night."

Kantees was as shocked as the woman. Jelamie was barely seven. He might be a precocious little tyrant, but to be taken from one's family by force? Kantees was doubly shocked because she had seen what had happened, though she did not remember seeing anyone carrying a child.

But she could say nothing.

"Why would someone do that?"

Libbibet leaned forwards conspiratorially. "They say it was the *Slissac* returned."

Kantees had to fight back the words of denial that threatened to burst from her. It had not been the mythical lizard people. She knew it was just the Taymalin. But she could tell no one.

"I wouldn't believe that," she said. "Whenever anything bad happens it's always the *Slissac* that are blamed and no one has seen one for a thousand years or more."

"Children get stolen away in the night by them," said Libbibet. "For their monstrous patterns and ceremonies."

Kantees just shook her head and looked down at the spoon still suspended above her bowl. "Can I have that, then?"

Libbibet slopped it down. "You may scoff all you like." And then she went off into the Kadralin tongue, which Kantees had never learnt because she had been bred and born in slavery and use of the Kadralin tongue would earn any slave a lashing.

Kantees moved away and went to one of the benches reserved for the keepers. Old Romain was there, as was Galiko, who helped look after the older *zirichasa* that no longer flew races. He was simple but had a good heart.

"Where are the others?" she asked as she sat on the bench and put down her bowl.

"Called to the grand hall," said Romain. "To be interrogated until they reveal the truth."

Kantees hid her nervousness with a spoonful of porridge.

"Am I not to go?" she said, thinking that with the house

patterner gone off to the ley-circle, she would not be subject to any magic that might force her to betray the truth.

"Later," was all Romain said.

She nodded and applied herself to her breakfast to avoid further conversation.

"The race in the next ten-day has been cancelled," said Romain. "Sheesha will not be required."

"Is it true Jelamie has been stolen away, as Libbibet says?" she asked.

"It is true," said Romain. "The Lady is distraught and has taken to her rooms. The master is in a dangerous mood and it would not do to cross him."

"Look, Sheesha crapping in the middle of the parade of winners wasn't my fault."

"You embarrassed our masters," said Romain.

She knew better than to talk back but she didn't think a *zirichak* doing its business in a parade was on the same level as having one's child stolen away. No matter how embarrassing it might have been at the time. And she had been punished, although not even Romain with all his experience had any guidance to offer on how to stop an excited animal pooing in public, even if it did offend the sensibilities of some of the more elite of the masters.

Kantees certainly didn't blame Sheesha. He had just come second in an important race and he was excited.

"And they came in the night?"

"Riding a monstrous *tekrak* by all accounts," said Romain.

"Flyer beaten by a flyer," said Galiko. It was barely more than a mutter but Kantees heard it and stared at him. Galiko went on eating his porridge using a tiny spoon he kept with him. He would not use one of the big spoons so it always took him a long time, but no one got angry.

"Why was I not called with the other keepers?" she said to Romain.

"They sleep together. You are separate."

They were all male and had a dormitory off the eyries of the yearlings. She cared for the only racer the Jakalain had; there would be no more unless they bought in new stock or until the yearlings matured. And she was a girl.

The Jakalain had only begun to keep racing *zirichasa* at the request of the heir, their much older son, Daybian. The tower had been there but unused. The boy who had been stolen away, Jelamie, was just the spare to inherit, in case something happened to his elder brother.

"You should present yourself at the hall before midday," said Romain as he got up. He glanced over at Galiko, as he always did, and sighed at the boy's slowness. "Gally!"

The boy beamed. "Romain, sir."

Kantees felt it was impossible to be angry with such innocence, though Romain often was.

"We must winch new hay to the old ones," said Romain, speaking loudly and slowly as if Galiko were deaf and stupid. "Hurry up and finish."

"Yes, Romain."

Galiko went back to his porridge and took another slow spoonful.

The stool Kantees was sitting on scraped as she pushed it back and moved across to sit opposite Galiko.

"What did you mean about a flyer beating a flyer?"

"Gally is stupid. And Gally is slow," said Galiko not looking up from his own food. He took another small mouthful, sucking the spoon clean.

"No, you're not," she said. "Gally is clever and Gally is quiet. And"—she glanced around to make sure no one was close—"if Gally saw anything last night that might get someone into trouble then he has to keep his mouth shut."

His gaze flicked up to meet hers for a moment and then slid away.

"Gally, please," she said quietly. "If you tell them, they will hang me."

He frowned into his porridge. "Kill Kantees?"

"Yes, kill me."

He sat up and put his hand on hers and squeezed it. "Don't want Kantees killed."

"Neither do I."

He grinned at that. "Gally keeps secrets," he said. "Gally keeps lots of secrets."

"Really?" she said. "Like what?"

"Romain loves Kantees," he said.

She imagined, for a brief moment, kissing the face of the old man, laughed, and then realised this was not the time and turned it into a cough.

"Yes, well, Gally," she said. "That's a secret you can keep to the end of time because it's certainly not true."

He squeezed her hand and nodded.

"Never mind, I shouldn't have asked because then it's not a secret." She hesitated. "So, if someone asks about last night and my secret, you won't tell them, will you?"

He shook his head and let go of her hand.

"Promise me, Gally."

"Gally promises, Kantees."

She tried to delay going to the grand hall. Even though she knew it would be better to get it over with. It was like having a splinter, it was uncomfortable but the thought of taking it out was so much worse.

Instead she went back to the eyrie and worked hard doing the chores she had been putting off for many a five-day. Tidying the riding gear, putting aside those items that needed repair. Reorganising the hay bales—exhausting work that made her sweat despite the cold wind blowing through.

But there came a point when it could not be delayed any longer —because otherwise it would be past midday instead of before, then she would have disobeyed, and with that would come punishment. And, quite possibly, the assumption that she was either guilty or knew something.

She gave Sheesha a pat on the neck and he offered the place under his chin for her to scratch. She gave it a little rub, just to show she cared, and then headed for the ladder. The eyrie itself, unlike her loft, had stone slabs for a floor. *Zirichasa* did not like wooden floors. Kantees guessed this was because they nested on the ground. They were big enough that they would have few enemies to worry about.

The ladder went through a small hole in the stone. On the far side was a walled-off area with a wooden trapdoor through which the hay bales were lifted. She had heard the doors crashing shut as each bale went up to the higher eyrie where Romain and Gally worked.

She arrived at the kitchen level and set off towards the main part of the castle. She had been there so rarely it made her nervous.

The guards on the inner gate were more alert than usual, though it was clearly a case of closing the cage after the bird had flown. But they didn't know that. She even heard people calling Jelamie's name. And it looked as if they had sent someone down into the well. After all, it was possible he had just wandered off. It wouldn't have been the first time.

But as Kantees crossed the wide courtyard she glanced up at the wall where the *tekrak* had been tethered. Its fire had blackened the stone of the building with a great soot stain. She glanced up at the bell tower but there was nothing to be seen. They would have found the man with the three arrows in his body.

Someone had rung the bell to warn the castle. One might think it was him and he had been silenced by the arrows. But then it would be realised that he was not a member of the household, and the real guard was there too. Perhaps they would attribute the bell ringing to the original guard, though that made little sense.

No one would imagine that a slave had, in defiance of the law, ridden a *zirichak* to ring the bell and warn the castle.

She started to go down some steps to a small door. Since she was no more than a slave, the idea of going through the main entrance did not even cross her mind.

"Wait," said an armsman. She did not recognise him, but there was no reason why she should. Her life was secluded.

"Sir?"

"What's your name?"

"Kantees, sir." She gestured in the direction of the tower.

"The keeper of Sheesha?"

"Yes, sir."

"Come with me. You're late."

She hesitated for a moment but returned to the courtyard. He waited for her and then headed in through the main door. She stopped before it.

"Sir?"

He turned. "Stop wasting my time and come along."

She swallowed, this was another rule. Not punishable by death but a whipping certainly. The fact that she had been told to do it by someone in authority did not make it any easier. Her early life had been a game of ensuring no rules were broken so that she was not punished. And of protecting others if she could, even if it meant she would be punished instead.

Then again, she had broken so many rules now, what difference did this one make?

She followed her escort. He did not go to the main hall, though she could see its massive grandeur of pillars and balconies through open doors as she passed. As far as she could tell they went the full length of a passage that ran along the hall and then turned right along another one where doors led off into smaller rooms.

Finally the armsman deposited her in a room with huge windows that looked out towards the mountains. Jakalain was a lonely place on the edge of the wilderness. The heart of the island of Esternes was massive peaks and deep valleys where the wild *zirichasa*, as well as other creatures she knew nothing of, flew free. At least, that's what she'd heard.

There was no one else in the room. Behind a table of dark wood stood three chairs, and on its surface lay writing implements—being a slave she could neither read nor write.

There was another chair facing the table.

"Sit there," said the armsman.

"Sit?"

"When the lord enters, you stand up. After he and anyone else with him has sat down, you can sit."

"I'd rather stand."

"You will sit."

He sounded tired. But he had probably been up all night.

"Is there any knowledge of the lordling?" she asked.

His eyes narrowed. "What do you know of it?"

She was terrified her guilt stood out on her face. "Nothing, just gossip in the kitchen."

"Keep your gossip to yourself."

With that he left her alone in the room with the chair that had both a padded seat and a padded back. It looked comfortable but she could not bring herself to sit in it. She had been working in the eyrie and had not cleaned herself up. She was probably soiling the rugs on which she stood; she certainly did not want to dirty the beautiful chair.

Being alone and waiting was terrifying. She felt her heart pounding and she sweated—though that could have been from her earlier exertions. She probably stank, and cursed herself for being so stupid as to engage in hard manual labour before meeting with such important people. But perhaps they expected her to stink.

The armsman had implied that Lord Jakalain himself would be here. It was true that she was often in close proximity to the lords, because she was usually in attendance with Sheesha. But they never spoke to her.

She closed her eyes as a door in the wall beyond the table opened.

4

She gripped the back of the chair with one hand as three men entered. She realised her other hand was shaking and shoved it behind her back. Her mouth went dry and she did not know whether she should look at them or down in respect. She chose down but kept flicking her gaze up, looking for any clues as to what she should do.

She recognised Lord Jakalain. He was pale and dark circles ringed his eyes; he must have been up all night since the alarm. The second man was a patterner, from his robes, while the third was Swordmaster Erang, the chief armsman of the castle.

It was said the patterns of magic could not force a person to perform any act against their will. Did that mean they could not tell whether someone told the truth or not? She did not know. She simply prayed to the Mother that she would not be asked a question where she had to lie in response.

They took their places. The patterner flicked through the papers in front of him and took up the stylus. She stared in fascination as he fiddled with the end of it then found a small pot. He opened it and dipped the stylus in.

She glanced at the other men. Even the Lord Jakalain was watching the patterner, though whether he was impatient or simply

waiting for him to be ready was impossible to tell. The swordmaster
was watching her and she immediately cast her gaze back to the
foot of the table where she could see them but not be looking at
them.

"Sit down, Kantees," said Erang.

She hesitated. "I am sorry, Swordmaster, but I have been in the
eyrie all morning and I do not wish to soil the chair. I beg your
pardon."

"Kantees, is it?" said Lord Jakalain.

She trembled, never having been addressed directly by the lord
before. "Yes, my lord."

"Sheesha's keeper."

"Yes, sire."

"Sit down, Kantees," he said. And where she might question the
swordmaster, she dared not go against the lord himself. She shuffled
to the front of the chair and gingerly placed her behind on it. She
clasped her hands on her lap so that the men would not see them
shake.

"What do you know of what happened last night, Kantees?"
said Erang.

Kantees glanced at the patterner. He was not looking at her but
was writing. It made her feel a little better, that he might only be
there to keep a record of what happened here, not to perform any
magic to divine the truth of her words.

"Kantees?"

"I know very little, sire. I heard the gossip in the kitchen. That is
all."

"Really?"

She stared directly at the swordmaster. "I can tell you what I
heard."

"That won't be necessary," said Lord Jakalain. "We have heard
kitchen gossip a dozen times today."

She dropped her gaze to the floor again. "Yes, my lord."

"More than one person said they saw a *zirichak* flying in the
night."

It seemed as if her heart stopped and she felt as if her very
blood froze within her.

"I saw—" she almost hesitated as her tongue tripped on the lie, "—nothing, sire. I was asleep."

"You were not awakened by the alarm bell?" said Lord Jakalain.

"Sheesha was disturbed by the noise, sire, and upset. I did not go to see but tended to him."

Lies piled on lies. It was as if she were falling into a deep dark hole. But unless someone could claim they had seen Sheesha himself and recognised her on his back, there would be no more lies. She must keep it simple.

But Lord Jakalain was not finished. "You did not see the *tekrak*?"

"I heard stories in the kitchen, sire, but I did not believe them. How could there be a *tekrak* of such size?"

"I saw it with my own eyes, Kantees." He was angry. Lord Jakalain was angry with her.

She threw herself off the chair and prostrated herself on the rugs. "Sire, I am sorry. Beat me for my foolish tongue."

There was a long pause. She heard a chair scrape back on the stone floor and boots walking first away and then growing closer until they went quiet on the rugs. She could sense the man standing above her and she tensed herself for the first blow. She jumped as he caught hold of her shoulder.

"Get up, Kantees," said the Lord Jakalain. His voice was no longer angry, just tired.

She could not make her muscles obey her. His grip tightened and he pulled. She came up on to her knees but she kept her head down.

"I told you to get up." This time there was the iron command in his voice, as if she were testing his patience. She stood but kept her eyes down. Even so, she could see he had withdrawn a short distance.

"Many people saw the monstrous creature, Kantees, but there are many that did not and some remain as sceptical as you."

"I believe you, sire."

A short laugh from the swordmaster told her how inappropriate her comment was. That she, a mere slave, should give her approval to the words of her master. What her master said must be the truth.

Lord Jakalain returned to his seat and murmured something to the patterner who nodded. She wondered what they might be saying. Was it possible she was wrong, and that the patterner was able to tell truth from lies? But still they did not accuse her. And what in truth had she done wrong?

Apart from fly.

She had saved the castle, although she had not been quick enough to keep the lordling from being stolen away. She thought about how she had flown so far away from the castle; if she had spent less time enjoying the sensation perhaps Jelamie would still be with his family. If she had not wasted time with the raider on the tower, things might have been different.

"I am sorry," she said before she could stop herself.

"What do you mean?" said the swordmaster.

"I am sorry I cannot help, sire."

Swordmaster Erang shook his head, once more grimly amused by her presumption, but Lord Jakalain looked at her.

"Thank you, Kantees," he said. "And if you learn anything about the *zirichak* people claimed to see, you will speak to the swordmaster."

"Yes, sire," she said.

The men stood and filed out. The patterner took the papers with him. She must have been the last. They wouldn't talk to Gally because he was a simpleton, so she should be safe. Though it bothered her that Jelamie was taken.

She almost called them back. She almost admitted the truth because she knew a name: the Dunor. That was what the raider had said: *Are you with the Dunor?*

But she had no idea who the Dunor were. Was it a title? Just one person? A race? She had been to many competitions and she had never come across the name.

How could she not tell Lord Jakalain the truth?

But she couldn't. She had ridden Sheesha and the penalty was death. She did not want to die, but neither did she want the boy to suffer, no matter how unpleasant he was.

But another thought ran through her mind, a rebellious thought. She was a slave. The Taymalin had come all those years ago and invaded her people's island. They had become the masters and the

Kadralin the enslaved. Why should she help them? What was the value of that stolen life against hers? Why was it more important?

She knew the answer.

It was because she had a choice. There were many things in her life over which she had no control; that was what being a slave meant. And even though her position as a keeper meant an easier life than most, it could be cut short in a moment.

And it would be, if they discovered what she had done.

Never mind she had saved others from death. She had dared to do what only a Taymalin was permitted.

It was a different armsman that came to escort her back.

He stared at her strangely and insisted on checking her to ensure she had not stolen anything. She did not complain as the man touched her. It was not that he had the right; it was that she had no right to object.

She was the slave. He was one of the masters.

So why should she even consider helping the child of Lord and Lady Jakalain when she herself was nothing more than a possession? Something that could be bought and sold, or discarded when they no longer required her?

No, she thought as she suffered the indignities of a search that went on too long and investigated every part of her. *Since I am nothing but an object to them, there is nothing I can give them.*

5

Over the next few days she tried to ignore what had happened. It wasn't too hard. Since she spent most of her time in Sheesha's eyrie, and the next race had been postponed, she saw no one except those in the tower. There was nothing she needed to do beyond feed and clean the *zirichak*.

Sometimes, though, she would look out across the castle. Things had returned to normal on the surface and they had given up looking for Jelamie in the castle. He had not drowned in the well: they had checked. There was now little doubt he had been taken. Speculation as to why roamed from ransom—though no ransom had been demanded—to being used in some terrible ritual.

This was something Kantees also wondered. It seemed to her that it made no sense. Had the entire raid been mounted to capture a child of limited political value? But if that was the case, why send so many soldiers?

Of course no one else knew what she knew. They had not seen the thirty or more armsmen that had retreated to the *tekrak*.

Information about the monstrous flying plant was now common knowledge, though there were some among the staff who continued to disbelieve it. Romain being one of them, Kantees had to bite her tongue. She could not admit to having seen it.

"Gally saw it," said Galiko at breakfast on the third day after the raid.

"Gally is stupid and doesn't know what he's saying," said Romain unpleasantly. He was once more waiting for Gally to finish breakfast but this morning the youth seemed to be eating even slower than usual.

"Gally saw it," he repeated. "Big as a wall, all fire and smoking and soldiers."

At that moment Daybian walked into the kitchen, flanked by an 'honour guard'.

The sudden addition of guards for all the nobility was not fooling anyone. The Jakalain were scared, and the lord had insisted armsmen accompany every member of his family at all times.

The kitchen went silent in a wave as people realised he was there or noticed others had stopped talking and turned to see who had come in. Not that Daybian was an uncommon sight in the Ziri Tower.

"What's Gally saying?" he said to Romain, and Kantees tensed.

"Nothing, sire, just rambling like the fool he is."

Kantees panicked quietly. If they questioned Gally he was bound to let something slip. She hoped Daybian would find Romain's explanation convincing.

Galiko, like everyone else, had stood as the lordling entered and was looking at the ground, but unfortunately he wanted to defend himself against Romain's accusations.

"Gally saw the fire plant," said the boy.

"Don't listen, young master, you know he's a halfwit. Shut up, Gally."

"Honestly, I don't have time for this." Daybian sounded petulant and irritable as ever. Kantees wondered if he considered his baby brother to be a threat, but with ten years between them she could not see how even he could think it.

"Kantees?"

"Sire?"

"Is Sheesha ready to fly?"

"Keen to, sire, he has been shut up too long."

"Let's get to it then."

So she left her breakfast, barely touched, and hurried up the tower ahead of Daybian's more leisurely pace, though even he had to use the ladder to get into the eyrie. Sometimes Kantees wondered about that. If the castle eyries—most still unoccupied—had been designed for lords to fly their *zirichasa*, why did they not have separate ways in? In the castle there were special passages for the servants so the lords and ladies did not encounter slaves as they moved around.

But not in this tower. Not only that but the Ziri Tower was not made from the same stone as the rest of the castle, as if it didn't belong.

Whatever the reason, she knew she would reach the eyrie with plenty of time to spare to get Sheesha ready.

The *ziri* sensed her excitement as she clambered up and selected the riding tack. Sheesha crouched quietly as Kantees placed the saddle and buckled the straps. She settled the bridle over his muzzle and neck, and brought the reins back to the saddle.

The sound of boots on the ladders announced the arrival of Daybian and his men.

Sheesha shuffled nervously. Kantees saw he was arching his neck and rolling his eyes at the lordling and his men.

"Sire! Your men are unsettling Sheesha."

She moved up to Sheesha's neck and stroked his feathers, breathing gentle and soothing sounds, trying to calm him.

At least when it came to the *zirichak* Daybian was not a fool. He would not be such a good rider if he did not have empathy with his steed. However, the men were not that bright and, though he was the son of the lord, they argued with him. They did not want to go back down and disobey their master.

"Well, you cannot come out with me when I ride. And this eyrie has no other exits but that door into the air."

"But, sire…"

"One of you go up a floor, the other go down. You can guard me just as well like that."

One of them looked across at Kantees. "But what of the slave, sire?"

Daybian's anger at the comment was palpable though he barely raised his voice. "If Kantees wanted to cause me harm, she could have done it a hundred times before now. Now get out before I take the flat of my sword to you."

Finally they gave in. It was easier to give in to the Jakalain present than blindly follow the orders of the Jakalain who was not here. They were not slaves, of course. No one would willingly put a weapon in the hands of the subdued race; they were just paid armsmen.

"Ridiculous," muttered Daybian as he unbuckled his swordbelt and laid it on a hay bale. He stripped off the rest of the finery, then plucked the flying suit from the wall: the leather trousers and jacket that sealed his skin from the wind, and the helmet and special eye protections that he used when he was flying in a race.

Sheesha had settled once the armsmen left. He made a low rumbling sound deep in his throat as Daybian approached, but whether it was because he was pleased to see his master or excited about the prospect of flying after so many days of inactivity, there was no way of knowing. Kantees handed the reins to Daybian with a slight bow and went to undo the chain.

She heard Daybian speaking quietly to Sheesha, making sure he knew who was going to ride him. Sheesha rumbled again. There was no reason that Sheesha should not like Daybian, but the reaction always caused a little twinge of jealousy in Kantees' chest. But, she reminded herself, Sheesha had let her sleep with him.

She undid the chain and ran it through the first and second loops.

"Perhaps you are trying to kill me after all," said Daybian.

Kantees went cold. She looked up to where Daybian sat, poised in the saddle on Sheesha's back. His knees too high, it looked as if he were perching on a table. Kantees swallowed hard, realising she had forgotten to lengthen the stirrups after her ride.

She dropped the chain and rushed over, desperately trying to come up with an excuse that would sound reasonable. In a voice that almost squeaked with her panic, she blurted out her lie. "I am so sorry, my lord, I cleaned the tack and moved the buckles to remove the marks lower down."

Daybian laughed. "Don't worry, Kantees, these things happen."

How casually you joke about such a thing, she thought. *You have never been beaten or lashed.*

And then she cursed herself for being such a fool. The new falsehood was now added to all the others. She quickly lengthened the stirrups to their usual position, then went back to finish removing the chains. Finally, she unhooked them from the loop on Sheesha's leg.

She backed away as Daybian prepared to launch them from the eyrie. Sheesha screeched in delight. Daybian gave him his head and the *zirichak* ran at the eyrie door and leapt from it, his wings snapping open. He dropped for a moment and then powerful strokes lifted him back into sight.

Moments later he slid off to the left and disappeared from view, though another screech from him echoed across the castle.

6

"Have you heard?" said Libbibet as she doled out the breakfast porridge. Her face was drawn in concern.

"Heard what?"

"About Gally?"

Kantees drew in a breath. "What about Gally?"

"The armsmen took him this morning."

"What are you talking about?"

The porridge hung suspended from the spoon like a threat.

"They say he was working with the raiders."

"What?" Kantees almost shouted. "That's ridiculous, he can barely put two words together that make sense."

"You can say that," said Libbibet. "But he knows things about the raid. They'll get the truth out of him."

The porridge slopped into Kantees' bowl but she just put it down and turned, looking for Romain. He was sitting in his usual chair. She headed towards him as Libbibet chided her for forgetting her breakfast.

Kantees sat down in front of him.

"Heard then, have you?" He glanced up at her from his bowl. "To think we had a traitor right here with us."

"Gally's no traitor."

"Lord Jakalain says he is."

And that, for Romain, was that.

"What have they done with him?"

"Locked in the cells, I shouldn't wonder. They'll get what they can from him and hang him."

"How can you sit there and say that? Gally is our friend, he's one of us. He's Kadralin like you and me."

"Sssssh," muttered Romain. "You want to join him? I don't. And now I have to take one of those new keepers from the yearlings to help tend the old ones. Gally was stupid but he didn't complain."

"He wasn't stupid, he was just simple. He *is* just simple."

Kantees stood up. Indecision pulled at her. She needed to find out what was happening with Gally. Perhaps the rumours were wrong. Perhaps there was another reason he had been arrested. Sheesha needed her—but not straight away, since she had already done most of what was needed for the morning and she was not expecting Daybian today.

She looked back at Romain and sat again. "What's Dunor?"

He looked up at her with a frown. "What's what?"

"What's Dunor? Have you heard of it?"

"Dunor?" She nodded but he shook his head. "Never heard of it."

"Are you sure?"

"What's this about?" he asked suspiciously.

She ignored him and got to her feet again. Instead of heading back up the tower, she strode across the kitchen towards the door that led outside and to the main part of the castle. As she walked, she felt Romain's and Libbibet's eyes on her back.

She stepped through into the main courtyard. The day was bright with only a few broken clouds moving steadily across the sky.

What was she doing? She had no idea. She knew she wanted to see Gally but no idea how she could achieve it. There was no reason for them to let her see him. So she stood a few paces into the court-yard filled with people bustling about. All the activities of the castle were going on around her and she was not a part of any of them.

Considering Romain's reaction, she did not think she could even stop anyone to ask where to go. If they knew anything about Gally, they would already have made up their minds as to his guilt.

If Gally was hanged it would be her fault.

"Kantees."

She bowed her head automatically at the sound of Daybian's voice.

"Sire."

"What are you doing here?"

"I'm sorry, sire, I heard about Gally—Galiko."

"Yes, he is being questioned."

"I don't understand. He's just a halfwit. What could he possibly know? More likely he just dreamed something and believes it to be true."

"One would hope your loyalty to your master is as strong as that to your friend."

Loyal to my friend? Yes, I am that. But loyal to my owner? she thought. *I am as loyal as a knife. Romain might be happy with his lot, but I know that I am a slave and that does not please me.*

"As you say, sire."

"You wish to see him?"

"That was my intention, sire, but now that I am here I realise my foolishness. I was about to return to my place in the eyrie."

"Come with me." He strode off to the right to where a number of armsmen were lounging around a barrel.

Unable to argue, Kantees trailed in his footsteps.

The armsmen snapped to attention as Daybian approached. "Where is the slave Galiko being held? One of you can take me."

The most senior, a sergeant, by his armband, bowed. "Aye, my lord. This way."

Kantees did not fail to notice how fast things could be made to happen when one was the son of the lord and carried his authority. But it would be a long time before Daybian was in charge. His father was still quite young and strong.

The sergeant brought them to an entrance in the wall and then down into a tight corridor. As far as Kantees knew, the castle of the Jakalain had never been breached by enemies, certainly not within living memory, but the castle itself was designed for warfare. These narrow passages forced people to fight one at a time.

The walls were etched with patterns said to come alive if an enemy dared to enter. Quite what would happen, no one knew. Kantees doubted anything would; after so much time, the magic would be gone.

She gasped as they entered a room lit by torches and filled with devices to pierce, puncture, squeeze, and rend. It was not that she recognised any of the tools, but she knew what they were for by reputation. A torture chamber. The memories of the Kadralin slaves did not fade, and during the long winter nights they passed around stories about masters who took pleasure in the pain of their possessions. And then they would drink to the continuing health of the Jakalain, who did not do such things.

Unless they want to extract information from a halfwit who has none, she thought. Not true, though. Gally did have information and if he told them, for whatever reason, it would incriminate her. So why was she here, really? Was it for Gally, or for herself?

Both, probably. Gally would be scared. He couldn't possibly understand what was going on.

They passed through the torture room to a series of cells constructed with iron bars. There were a few ragged men and women here, and she had no idea who they were, except that they were Kadralin by their skin. They were all underfed, with their joints stark against their drawn skin, and listless. If they looked up at her at all it was with eyes that barely focused.

Then they reached Gally. He sat on the floor with his back to the other cells as if he did not want to see them. And well he might not. He had such a gentle spirit, the sight would hurt him.

"And here he is," said Daybian with a gesture of his hand as if he were conjuring her friend from a mist.

Unlike the ones who had been here longer, Gally turned at his voice, first taking in the lordling and then seeing her. His face lit up with hope, and her heart broke with the pain of it.

"Kantees." He always stretched the second part of her name almost as if he loved to say it. He reached through the bars and she took his hand.

"Are you all right, Gally?"

"No, Kantees, this is a bad place."

"I know."

Gally's eyes flicked to Daybian and back. "Gally told them," he said.

She felt a cold spear lance through her. But if he had told them about her, then she would not be on this side of the bars.

"What did you tell them?"

"Gally ride the *ziri*. Gally ring the bell."

Kantees closed her eyes and felt her heart pounding in her breast. Tears squeezed out between her lids. He was sacrificing himself for her. Sacrificing himself for her lies.

She looked at Daybian. As a slave she was forbidden to look him directly in the eye, but she did it anyway. "And you believe him? *Him?*"

Daybian shrugged. "It's nothing to do with me. He confessed to a crime and the punishment is death."

"But he's doesn't understand what he's saying. You can't trust what he says."

"As I say, it's none of my business."

"One day you will own this castle and the slaves in it. Would you rather be known as a tyrant who does not care?"

"You speak out of place."

She turned away and dropped her gaze to the floor. "I deserve to be beaten."

"Yes. You do," he said. There was a long pause. "I will mention the concern to my father but I doubt it will make any difference. A *zirichak* was seen and it is believed the rider rang the alarm bell. If it did not come with the raiders, it must have come from here. If Gally did not do it himself, he knows who did. Either way he is committing a crime."

Kantees held her tongue and hated herself for doing it. She wanted to say: *But why would he even admit it unless he was protecting some-one?* And the number of people that he could possibly be protecting was limited to only two: Romain and her.

"Is there anything I can do to make it better here?" she said. If she could not save Gally, perhaps she could at least reduce his suffering.

"There are no rules preventing you from bringing items for him."

"I am a slave, sire, I own nothing. He owns nothing."

"Food is allowed."

She nodded and squeezed Gally's hand. "I'll come back."

"No, Kantees. This is a bad place."

She gave him a smile. "It is a very bad place, Gally, so a visit from a friend is a good thing."

He pulled back his hand and returned to where he had been, with his back to everything.

She wanted to cry again but held it back. The dark eyes of the man in the cell next to Gally caught hers, and he stared at her. She hesitated as Daybian moved past her, and then followed him.

They came out into the daylight. Kantees thought it was strange. After being in the dungeon, she felt it should be night out here as well. And yet the morning was not even halfway gone.

"It is the spring feast tomorrow," said Daybian. "And the patterners say the Mother will feed the earth with her power. Very auspicious. They say."

"It is a Kadralin feast, sire."

"The power of the Mother cannot be denied," he said, "when her milk can be seen to come from … the moons."

She knew he had been going to use a more common term. The power of the Mother descended to the earth when Colimar and Lostimal stood together in the sky. It did not take a great deal of imagination to see them as a woman's breast. That's why the Kadralin called it the Mother's milk.

The ley-circle nearest to the castle was powerful and capable of twisting the nature of the world when the conjunction happened. It was only because Jakalain was in the middle of nowhere that it did not command more importance in the world.

Jakalain had little value to the Taymalin who occupied the Isle of Esternes.

"I had thought to take part in the festivities," he said.

The orgy, she translated. It was true the Kadralin could become quite wild during festivals, and it was common enough for the Taymalin to join in. She could see where this was going, and yet she could not directly refuse even though she had no desire to lie with him. She had no desire to lie with anybody. But when all was said, she was a slave and he was the son of her owner.

"I am sorry, but I cannot attend the feast. I will be tending to Sheesha," she said. "He does not like to be disturbed at night, and it makes him irritable the next day. The noise upsets him."

"I will come up to the eyrie. We will watch the feeding of the earth from there. It would provide an excellent view."

And now I have made it worse, she thought. *He will expect me to be there.*

"As you wish, sire," she said. She would just have to hope that he would get caught up with someone else or decide it was not worth the effort. She shook her head as she walked away. He was a man. The opportunity to lie with a woman, and one that he had just convinced himself desired it, would be the strongest attraction.

She had condemned herself.

7

---

*L*ater that day Kantees scrounged some food from Libbibet and went off to the cells.

Since she was not accompanied by Daybian, she was stopped by the guards. She wished they could be given a lashing for the things they said to her. But she could not respond, or she would have been on the receiving end of the lash—something she had thus far managed to avoid in her life.

However, it was when one of them suggested she might be "available" for the spring festival that she simply suggested he would need to ask Lord Daybian for her use after he had finished with her. That shut him, and the rest of them, up. And she continued with no further molestation.

At least that wasn't a lie, she thought, although if she could think of a way out of Daybian's plan for her, she would take it.

There was a solution, she knew. She could tell the truth. If she revealed that it was she who had ridden Sheesha and saved the castle, then Gally would be safe and she might be able to hope that she would get away with a severe lashing—since the fact she had saved the castle might count in her favour. She sighed. It was hopeless, either Gally died, or she did.

And Jelamie would still be lost.

So instead she could confess to Daybian when he arrived and then throw herself off the tower. That would solve all the problems —except Jelamie, again, but that really wasn't her fault since she had not caused him to be kidnapped. That was someone else's problem.

She came down into the cell and found Gally still facing the corner.

"Gally?" she said. He turned and his face lit up at the sight of her. He climbed to his feet and came to the bars. She passed the packages through.

"It's just some food," she said. "Libbibet said I could bring it for you."

"Thank you, Kantees."

The man in the cell next door was looking at her again. It wasn't that she knew every slave and servant in the castle by sight but she was sure he wasn't one of them. The cut of his clothes was unusual and even his face seemed out of place. His skin was very dark even for a Kadralin—it was like midnight.

She turned her attention back to Galiko. "Have they hurt you?"

He shook his head and focused on the shrivelled apple which was one of the few remaining from last season. The kitchen staff kept the apples on trays in the cellars. They dried up but stayed edible, though mostly they were put into pies. It was still a long time before there would be any fresh.

There was bread, too, and a stone bottle of water.

She moved along the iron bars to get away from the one who watched her, but there really wasn't enough space in Gally's cell.

"What have you told them?"

"Gally kept your secret, Kantees. Gally won't let them kill you."

Once more she felt like crying. "You should have just said you didn't know anything."

He looked at her as if she were talking nonsense. "Master Daybian knew. They said they would hurt me if Gally did not say."

"Daybian was there?"

"Master Daybian came with armsmen."

"Bastard," she muttered. He must have caught the end of the conversation in the kitchen—heard more than he claimed to have.

"But I did not tell the secret, Kantees." He was almost pleading with her to approve of what he had done.

She sighed and smiled. She reached through the bars and put her hand on his shoulder. "You did a very brave thing, Gally."

"Like a hero."

Her smile grew wider. "Yes, like a real hero."

And that settled it. It was impossible to let him suffer for what she had done. Her lies had got them into this mess, so she was going to have to think of a way out of it.

But the only thing she could think of was to run away.

She glanced at the man in the cell next door. He was still staring and her frustration overflowed in a verbal attack. "Why are you staring at me?"

He did not flinch. Not even a blink. Instead, he climbed to his feet. "Greetings to the Lady Kantees." And then he bowed with one hand on his stomach and the other giving a broad gesture. She had never seen anything like it— not directed towards herself, at least. There had been some lord at a race last year who had not had any *zirichasa* to race, but he had bet heavily. His mannerisms had been like this, bold and flowery.

"I think you're mistaking me for someone else, or having a jest," she said. "Now if you don't mind I would appreciate it if you stopped staring at me and left me with my friend."

"As you wish."

He turned his back on her and stepped to the far side of his cell. Kantees was taken aback. She was ready for an argument but he had pulled the wind from her wings.

After a moment she turned back to Gally who had finished the food and was washing it down with the water. She wanted to ask him what the other fellow was in for but she didn't think Gally could cope with the question. His viewpoint was always focused on himself.

"I'll bring some more tomorrow," she said. She hated to go but she had her own duties and she couldn't leave Sheesha for long. "Look, Gally, if they ask you again, why don't you say you've forgotten and that you made it all up."

"Gally must protect you, Kantees. They mustn't hurt you."

"But—" she started, then realised it was pointless. He was so single-minded, once he started on a course it was almost impossible to get him to change. Unless, of course, you could distract him so thoroughly he forgot what he was doing. If they kept on asking him, there was little chance of him forgetting.

She had barely gone five paces when the other man stopped her.

"Kantees."

"Dropped the 'lady' already?"

"I can use it, if you wish."

"I don't."

"I am here to offer my help," he said. "My master sent me because he knew you would be in need."

She turned on him with her hands on her hips. "I don't know what game you're playing, but I can't help you get out of here. In case you hadn't noticed the colour of my skin, I'm just as much a slave here as you. There's no point trying. I can't help you."

"I do not think you were listening."

"I heard every word you said but you seem to have failed to see that you are the one that is in a cell. I am on the outside."

"Yet you are more trapped than I," he said.

Kantees could not think of anything to say so she stood silent, her jaw twitching, until she blurted at him, "I really do not have time for this."

And left.

She hurried across the courtyard, ignoring the jeers of the arms-men. Once through the kitchen she climbed the ladders to the eyrie. Sheesha had messed twice and she spent the time clearing it up, trying to understand what was happening.

Once the shovelling and sweeping was complete she fetched the powder that was intended to reduce the number of parasites on Sheesha's body. She was not sure whether it worked since Sheesha's skin seemed to be home to a constant supply of the horrible little bugs.

Some of which were not so little.

It was an unending task and possibly the one she enjoyed least.

It usually ended with her exploring the base of the feathers, trying to squash (preferably) or grab (if necessary) the little things to remove them. Romain had explained that in the wild the *zirichasa* would preen one another, just like smaller birds did, in order to remove the parasites. For creatures in captivity, the keepers had to do it.

And when she was finished, she had to put up with Sheesha attempting to return the favour, prodding every part of her body, trying to get to her skin around the clothes—perhaps he thought clothes were feathers—and then nipping at her, which was occasionally painful but she was sure he didn't mean to hurt her. Once or twice he had nipped hard enough to elicit blood and a cry of pain. When that happened he would rub his muzzle against her as if apologising.

As she systematically worked her way up his spine between his wings, she realised how much she cared for the beast. And then she felt sad. The only solution she could think of was to run away, leaving a message behind saying that Gally was innocent and only trying to protect her in his childlike way.

Running away meant she would have to leave Sheesha—and she couldn't think of any other apprentice that was ready to look after him.

There were so many problems with that plan—it wasn't even a plan, it was just an idea. In the first place she would have trouble getting out of the castle. Her job was to look after Sheesha. The only time she went out was when there were races.

And there was no way she could leave a message without telling someone because she couldn't write. And there was no one she could trust except Gally, and he would not be able to cope, even assuming they accepted what he said, which wasn't going to happen since he was already under suspicion.

Finally, she had nowhere to go and no way to get there. If she did manage to get out of the castle, a runaway slave would be hunted down in no time at all. There was always one or two every year who decided they would make a run for it. But the Jakalain land was nowhere, and apart from the orchards there weren't even forests to hide in within a tow or three days of travel. She didn't *think* there was. But who would know? People either followed the road, or travelled by patterner's path. And she had never used the roads.

She sighed and lay down along the length of Sheesha's back, letting the warmth from his feathers flow into her. She yawned. The worry of the last few days had meant she was not sleeping very well.

Sheesha moved and lay down too, with her on his back. He let out a gentle grumble that vibrated through her. It made her feel relaxed.

Of course, if she escaped on Sheesha's back she could get away easily and no one would be able to catch her.

She blinked her eyes open and stared at the feathers in front of her face. It was true, she could do that. But that would mean leaving Gally. And then she thought of the crazy man in the cell. What if he wasn't crazy? What if he could help?

No, of course not. He was in a cell. There was nothing he could do.

You are more trapped than I.

His words haunted her. He did not act like someone who was trapped. He seemed totally at ease. And his clothes, in spite of their odd appearance, were of the highest quality. Why was he even locked up?

He was a slave, he had admitted as much himself with the mention of his own master. Yet he did not act like a slave.

8

---

antees looked back up the passageway towards the torture room. This was the third day she had come to this place and it had gained a strange familiarity. All the years she had lived in the castle she had hardly ever set foot inside the main defensive walls. Now she was accustomed to it. The guards recognised her and no longer checked her—though that might have been because of her comment about Daybian.

She was carrying food for Gally again. She did not understand why they kept him locked up. Romain was struggling to keep abreast of the daily chores, and he had even insisted she help him.

Moving hay bales was hard work but she had been doing it since she was young and she was easily as strong as Romain himself. Perhaps that was not saying a great deal, he was getting old. Certainly she was stronger than most of the apprentices.

And the four older *zirichasa*—Romain's charges—liked her. It was not that they were particularly old, but they could no longer race. They seemed to appreciate her attention when she spoke to them and scratched their necks. Daybian had had his father buy them as breeding stock. The male and one of the females—Looesa and Shingul—had been winners in a few races, though not sufficient to make them very expensive.

The apprentices tended the yearlings that were their offspring. Sheesha was not related to any of them as far as she knew.

Romain insisted the apprentices were too incompetent to help and that she must do it. So she spent some time before the midday meal working with him. There was not much to be done. She guessed that Romain probably did none of it when he had Gally to help—and that he chose Gally over any of the others because the simple lad would not question Romain's laziness.

So she was later than she intended.

And Galiko was looking for her through the bars as she came down. Her glance backward confirmed there were no armsmen watching or listening. She was not entirely sure how she felt about the other prisoners. They were criminals of one sort or another. Mostly slaves who had been caught pilfering. Though they might have been wrongfully accused—that was very common.

If they thought she was up to something, they might think it would ease their punishment if they traded the information. But the Taymalin were strict, so she doubted negotiation was acceptable. The slightest hint that any of them knew anything of interest would lead to torture.

However, she did not want to take the chance.

She greeted Gally and gave him the food. Then she leaned against the cage with her back to the other man—she did not even know his name.

"What help can you offer?" she said in a low voice she hoped would not carry.

"You have reconsidered."

"Something needs to be done."

"And you are the one to do it?"

"Stop playing games and answer my question."

"Have you thought of a way out of the castle?"

"Yes, but I cannot leave my friend to the benevolence of my master."

"No, indeed," he said. "The Taymalin are well known for their fatal kindness."

"What's your name?"

"Yenteel."

"Why are you here?"

"My master is interested in you."

"I don't know your master."

"No, but he knows you."

"How is it possible that he knows me?"

"I expect he saw you at the races."

"If your master is that interested, he could just offer Jakalain a price for me."

"Sadly he is not that rich."

"And how did you end up in here?"

"It is difficult to get an invitation into the castle when you are a slave alone."

"That doesn't answer my question."

"Oh, you want the precise details? I propositioned one of the armsmen—a captain."

She blinked. Surely he did not mean what he had just said. She turned and looked at him. "You *propositioned*?"

"I suggested he might like to join me for the night."

Kantees could think of nothing to say.

"The fellow seemed to think I had insulted him and so did not take me up on it, but he did put me where I wanted to be. They considered it a great joke that I would indeed be spending the night at his home. I considered it a great joke as well, that their behaviour was so predictable."

She grinned. "What if he had accepted your offer instead?"

Yenteel shrugged. "I did choose the most handsome one."

"Oh." She shook the mental image loose. "How could being in here be of any help? You did not know I would be coming down here. I did not even know myself."

"It was in the pattern."

Then she really did laugh. "You expect me to believe you can read the world's pattern?"

"You are not required to believe anything if you do not wish to," he said. "Besides, I did not say that I could read it. I only have to know someone who does."

"If I knew the world's pattern I would not squander that knowledge in getting myself put into a prison cell," she said. "Anyway, did the pattern say anything about how you were going to get out?"

"Of course," he said. "You."

Gally had finished eating and just sat watching the two of them talk. She wondered if he was able to follow what was being said. Probably not; that's why he didn't interrupt. He couldn't be part of it. She was not sure even she wanted to be a part of it. The last thing she wanted was to think her actions were being manipulated by someone else.

"Let's say I could get you and Gally out of the castle," she said. "Can you get out of the cell?"

"Yes."

"How?"

"That's for me to know when the time comes."

"Fine, have it your own way," she said. "Can you be ready tomorrow evening?"

"During the feeding, yes."

"After," she said. "I am meeting someone."

It hadn't been a decision as much as a feeling that had been growing on her. The pressure of the missing boy, that Gally was simply being held and neither released nor punished. A feeling had come over her like a day when the clouds were low and it was as if the whole sky pressed down.

The feeding tomorrow would be the best time. The magic would be so wild and dangerous that the patterners wouldn't be able to do anything.

"Kantees?"

She was shocked from her reverie as Daybian came down the corridor. Why on earth was he here? Was he following her, keeping track of her? He was so relaxed, so sure of himself. Arrogant.

Did he know she had been talking to Yenteel? But the prisoner was already on the other side of his cell, looking at the floor, drawing no attention to himself.

And then Daybian grinned at her. "Tomorrow night."

She growled inwardly. He was still planning to take her and no doubt use the excuse of the "wild" Kadralin if there were any consequences. The blame could easily be shifted to those with no responsibility or no choice in the matter.

"When?"

"Unfortunately for us, I must attend the feast and witness the feeding proper with my family. Then I shall come to you."

"What is being done about finding your brother?" she asked and was taken by the genuine heaviness that seemed to come over him.

He shook his head. "It is difficult to know what can be done. The raiders are long gone, and there was nothing to identify the ones that were slain—save that they were Taymalin."

For which we can be grateful, thought Kantees. *If the attackers had been Kadralin every one of us would be suspect and liable for torture.*

"I am sorry," she said even though it was not the place for a slave to feel sympathy for a master. They might not rebel, but they might cheer inside when a master suffered. It detracted from their own pain. But it was true, she was sorry.

Daybian put his hand on her shoulder—almost as one would with a companion, a friend—and gave a gentle squeeze. "No one knows where to look. And there has been no ransom demand."

He dropped his hand and the lascivious grin returned. "Until tomorrow, Kantees."

With that he strode away. Kantees stared after him.

"He will upset your plans," said Yenteel behind her.

"No, he won't."

"You may have to kill him."

She turned and took hold of the bars. Yenteel was there, close, with his midnight skin and brown eyes, taller than she was.

"Whatever I do," she said, "it will not be because of anything you say I should or should not. I will not cause the Jakalain any more pain."

"You are a slave."

"And to act like a master makes me no better than them."

It seemed he had no response to that. He turned away and went to sit in the corner. And whether it was to contemplate on the world's pattern, or to nurse his failure, she really could not care.

She turned back to Gally and he asked her simple questions

about the people in the tower and she answered them to the best of
her ability. She truly did not take much notice of the gossip.

9

In truth she had no reason to stay with Sheesha during the Mother's feeding. It had happened plenty of times before and Sheesha had never given any indication he was upset by the white lights from the sky.

It usually happened at night. Tonight it was overcast, but that did not seem to make any difference to the magic that drove it.

Nobody knew what the feeding was. Leastways, if the patterners did know they kept it a secret. And if the wisdom of the Kadralin had fathomed its mysteries, that knowledge must have been lost when they were enslaved. She hoped the latter was the truth. She would rather it was her people that knew and had forgotten, than the Taymalin's patterners.

She really knew nothing about her own people. She only knew slaves and slavery.

The sky had been dark for a long time. The opposite wall of the castle, where the *tekrak* had landed, was full of people—Taymalin—while the slaves able to do so would be watching from the windows.

Her vantage point was the best, except perhaps for Romain's above her.

The ley-circle was not visible even in daylight since it was behind a ridge, and the clouds were now thick and low.

No sound accompanied a feeding save for the excited screams, shouts, and cheers of the people who watched. She could feel the time approaching. It was a tension in the air. The patterners had already declared that this was going to be a powerful occurrence and everyone who lived close to the circle had been ordered to leave.

The power of a feeding warped the earth. She had never seen it but she was told there were the remains of a castle closer to the circle. What remained of its stone walls were twisted and melted. Strange plants grew nearby, too: abominations. Perhaps it had been stronger once.

Then the world went white.

A column of light came into existence, flooding the world with a brilliance that hurt the eyes. The castle was illuminated in a blaze of pure white, the shadows utter black.

As her eyes adjusted she could see the moving lines within the column as if it were composed of individual strands leading down from the heavens beyond the clouds. And up there, the light emanated from the shape formed by the two moons.

She heard the disjointed chant floating up from below: *"Mother Earth, feed me; Mother Earth, clothe me; as the milk of the Earth feeds her children in the sky, so feed me."*

She joined in and tonight she felt as if it were really true. As if she were being fed by the power of the Mother.

She closed her eyes and the brightness shone through them. She smiled.

And the light winked out.

Below and across the land the revelries began. For some it would become an orgy. For herself, she had to deal with Daybian, but it would take him a while to get here. So she had to be prepared.

And then she stopped. She could not truly believe she was planning to steal Sheesha and the others. But what choice did she have? If she was going to free Gally and Yenteel, even though she felt no real obligation to the latter, she could only do it with the *ziri*.

She hurried up the ladder, past her loft, to the old ones' eyrie. Romain was not here because he had gone off to the celebrations, just as she could have done if she had not had other plans, or been trying to avoid Daybian.

White light flickered momentarily through the gaps in the eyrie door. This happened as well. Sometimes the power was so great, the conjunction of the moons so perfect, that additional bursts of power —leftovers—still erupted from time to time as the moons moved slowly apart.

Looesa and Shingul seemed pleased to see her. They made no objection when she fetched their tack from the walls and slipped it onto them. She sighed. This was a terrible idea. She did not even know if she could get them to follow her to the ground without riders.

But it was the only idea she had. And she had to rely on Yenteel to get out of his cell, release Gally, and deal with any guards though hopefully they would be too busy and it wouldn't be necessary.

"Kantees!"

She jumped. Daybian was below. He was earlier than she expected and must have been in a hurry to see her. His loins must have goaded him. She sighed.

"I am tending to the old ones. I will be down in a moment."

"I'll come up."

"No, please, I'm nearly done. Talk to Sheesha."

She tightened the chest strap on Looesa who now kept nudging her, excited to be going out.

"You have to wait," said Kantees. "I'll be back and then we'll go."

She looked at Jintan, the third of the set. He was significantly older than the other two. He had come as part of the auction lot with them. She did not understand why, since he did not add any value. She shook her head and patted him on the neck, he was very good-natured. He croaked at her and butted her with his nose.

"Not today, Jintan," she said quietly. No one rode him anymore. He was allowed out on a tether only and seldom even then. *He must be losing his strength without the exercise.*

As she climbed down the ladder she heard Daybian murmuring to Sheesha. She smiled. At least he was good with *ziri,* but then

Sheesha wouldn't have tolerated him if he wasn't. They were sensitive creatures.

Daybian was still dressed in his finest and rubbing Sheesha under his chin. His clothing was completely inappropriate for the eyrie. He would get filthy, but it would be up to someone else to clean his clothes so why should he care? Yet if the cleaner failed to remove every stain, they would be the one punished.

The smile she had for him over Sheesha dropped from her face. There was little light in here so he wouldn't see her angry frown. She still had to deal with him and quickly, since the staff on duty would soon return to their posts.

"Have you ever taken part in the revels following a feeding, Kantees?" he asked. She did not have to see his smug grin to know it was there. She could hear it in his voice.

"I watch the feeding from here," she said. "I have no reason to join in with the Taymalin."

"I think you Kadralin have more fun."

She took a deep breath. It was her position, as a slave, to be agreeable and obey her master's every command. But as Sheesha's keeper she had some authority. Her word was followed with regard to his care and development. And Daybian was someone she had to talk to as almost an equal since he was the rider. She knew he liked it when she argued with him, because being male he liked to fight for things—as long as he won.

"You are only interested because you wish for more exercise."

"It is only through exercise that I win races."

"But there is more to life than winning."

"Not for me."

"Always it comes back to you. Is no one else important?"

"You are important to me, Kantees."

"Only because I help you win races."

"But not the important ones, yet."

She sighed. She was tired of his games. "I do not want to be ridden, sire."

There. She had said it. She had denied her master.

She half expected him to be angry and to force himself on her.

But she watched his shadow detach itself from Sheesha's and move towards her slowly.

"Do you not find me handsome?"

"I value my position, sire. What if I were to become with child? I could not look after Sheesha, so could not help you win your races."

"That is a clever excuse."

"Sire," she said. "You can do whatever you want with me and I will not resist. I am your slave."

The shadow turned away and his voice came to her more echoing than before. "I do not wish to force you."

No, he wanted her to go to him willingly, as if she wanted it. "There would be no force required, sire."

"But would you caress me in your passion?"

"I would not resist you."

"And that is the greatest insult of all."

Kantees picked up the shovel she used for shifting Sheesha's droppings. As she took a few steps towards Daybian, he heard her footsteps. She had the strongest feeling that he thought she had relented and was coming to give him the satisfaction he desired.

She swiped him across the head with the shovel and he went down with the slightest cry of pain.

She checked him and made sure there was no blood. She had hit him with the flat part; after all, she felt no malice towards him personally, and she could not afford for him to die. If that happened they really would come after her and keep hunting her until she too was dead.

He was not unconscious but the blow appeared to have knocked his wits from him. She tied him up with spare tack. He might have to spend the rest of the night here but they would find him in the morning when they came looking for her.

His gaze was reproachful as she tied one final thong around his head, holding a rag in position in his mouth. She did not want him alerting anyone too early.

"I'm sorry," she said as she tucked a saddle under his head so he was not too uncomfortable. "I didn't want to do this but you insisted on coming up here tonight."

He mumbled something through the gag.

"This has nothing to do with you," she said.

A short annoyed noise.

"If you weren't being dictated to by what's between your legs, you could still be down there having a nice time."

Something, something, something.

"Well, I didn't want to," she said. "And if you had any sensitivity at all you would have realised that."

Indignation.

"No, you're not."

As she was tightening the final straps, she turned to him.

"In a few years I might have wanted to, perhaps, Daybian." There was a grunt. "I will call you Daybian now, because it doesn't matter. I have broken so many rules already and there are more to come."

This time she was not going to ride unprepared. She collected a set of Daybian's riding gear and pulled it on over her clothes—there was plenty of space. Then she unearthed a bag containing a water bottle and tinderbox from where she had hidden it in the hay.

The time had come.

She went to release the chain that held Sheesha, then squatted down in front of Daybian. His eyes flickered with reflected moonlight.

"I have to explain something so just listen and don't interrupt," she said. "I was the one who rang the alarm bell when the raiders came. Sheesha woke me and insisted I go with him. You can believe that or not, I don't care. Gally saw me and that's all, he's innocent. How could he be anything else?"

She sighed. "I want to put things right. I wasn't quick enough to save Jelamie from being taken, and for that I'm sorry. If I had admitted anything of what happened I would be killed for riding Sheesha. And Gally too perhaps, for not admitting the truth, yet he only did it to save me."

She stood up and went to Sheesha. She put her foot in the saddle and climbed up. After she had tightened the belt and gathered the reins, with Sheesha prancing back and forth ready to go, she turned to Daybian again.

"There is one thing. The raider on the bell tower said something to me before he died. I don't know what it meant but I'm going to find out, and I will rescue Jelamie if he is still alive."

In the dark she could not tell his expression, so she turned and gave Sheesha his head. The *ziri* launched himself from the eyrie.

10

____

The thrill of being on Sheesha's back again was wonderful. But she could not spend any time enjoying it. She wheeled him back to the tower, not caring if anyone saw her. He thought they were going back to his eyrie so she had to force him up to the one above.

The *zirichasa* often called to one another in the tower. Almost as if they were having a conversation. Since Sheesha was the strongest of the four he seemed to have precedence. Kantees did not know how the *ziri* arranged their flocks in the wild, particularly since the yearlings seemed to have no organisation whatsoever.

She dismounted and unchained Looesa, then Shingul. They did not try to leave, but she could only hope they would follow once she and Sheesha were in the air.

She lengthened their leads as far as she could and, still holding them, remounted Sheesha and buckled herself in.

"Come on, then," she said encouragingly as she nudged Sheesha towards the opening. The other two followed as she pulled on their reins, though once Sheesha jumped she would have to let go; otherwise her arm would probably be torn from its socket.

It was the moment of truth.

"Go!" she hissed at Sheesha and, "Come on!" to the others.

Sheesha dived out—she was getting used to that—and wheeled higher in a spiral, which she hadn't instructed him to do but seemed a good idea. On the first turn, Sheesha screeched and the sound echoed across the castle.

Kantees groaned. She had hoped she could start her rescue with no one noticing but there was no chance of that now. Everyone would be looking into the sky, although all they'd see was the great shadow of the dragon against the clouds.

Two more screeches as Looesa and Shingul burst from the eyrie with their leads trailing from their heads. They moved in unison with Looesa slightly in the lead, then wheeled into the spiral and followed Sheesha as he climbed.

Kantees muttered a satisfied, *"Good"*. At least that part of the plan was working as she had hoped. She wouldn't be happy until she was away from this place. And that thought made her falter as Sheesha continued to climb.

She was a runaway slave. She could be killed by anyone and no one would care. Many would be grateful. Even those of her own people would be grateful because she was causing trouble. By her actions she could bring down more trouble on their heads. The masters would be more cautious, their punishments would be harsher.

And it would be her fault.

It was too late to worry about it. She leaned forwards and pushed Sheesha out of his climb. She looked back and found the other two flanking them. They had flown beyond the walls. Below were armsmen on the ramparts, heads craned back staring at the three *ziri*, no more than dark shapes.

They dared not shoot because they did not know who was riding. It might be Daybian. Unfortunately that would change very soon. She leaned over Sheesha's neck and looked down as she brought him round in a circle. The figures below were like beetles crawling across a stone.

The tower allowed her to orient exactly where she was looking: the entrance to the cells.

She recognised Gally from his shuffling gait as he stepped out, with a taller and lankier figure beside him: Yenteel with a bag clutched in one hand. His bag? Perhaps Sheesha's cry had alerted the foreigner.

With a shifting of her weight and gentle words of encouragement she put Sheesha into a dive heading for the main tower and its entrance on the far side of the castle courtyard. The wind swept across her face but the helmet kept it under control and, with her gloves and leather clothing she barely felt the cold on her skin.

She allowed herself a quick glance back, and still Looesa and Shingul were with them. As far as Kantees could tell they were exactly the same distance from one another and from Sheesha's tail as they had been during the climb. She turned back as she felt Sheesha's muscles tensing up. She had not realised how fast they were going and the opposite wall was coming at them fast. Sheesha did not need encouragement in the turn.

The face of the guard at the hall entrance took on a look of horror as Sheesha whipped round in a blast of air which knocked him from his feet.

This was the most dangerous and stupid thing she had done in her entire life.

She reined Sheesha in. His head lifted, he backwinged hard, and they landed with a scrape of talons on stone directly in front of Yenteel and Gally. Behind her she heard the other two touch down together. Yenteel's long, loose hair was blown back and the supercilious grin he had worn in the cells was gone. The shock of the three *ziri* landing in front of him had seen to that.

Good.

She glanced around. Every face in the courtyard was directed towards them. Mouths gaped, some with fear, most with astonishment. Nobody was shouting yet, but she knew that would come.

Gally was backing away. She had expected that. "Gally, help Yenteel mount Shingul! Now!"

He jumped at her command and moved as she directed. Unfortunately, that meant the armsmen's eyes were now directed at Kantees instead of the *ziri*. They were coming to their feet, or standing straighter, hands moving to the swords at their sides.

"Hurry, Gally," she said as he went past. He had not yet queried the fact she was riding Sheesha, and getting someone else mounted was something he had done before, and therefore not outside the bounds of his experience. The next stage would be harder.

She had chosen the older mounts, instead two of the larger yearlings, for several reasons—not least because Gally worked with them so they knew him. She put Yenteel on Shingul because she was the more docile of the two and had sometimes been used to give rides to guests. Not that they ever flew her—either they knew what they were doing and did not need help, or they were given the ride just for the thrill. And sometimes the ride was given to a wife or a mistress to persuade their lords to give money as an investment on the promise of wins in future races.

The armsmen were looking at one another. Clearly they did not want to take on, and possibly damage, such a valuable animal. But they had recognised Kantees, and were moving forwards—slowly and carefully. Perhaps she could have managed with just one more *ziri* but saddles meant they could only carry one person each.

She pulled back on the reins and Sheesha went up on his hind legs, head high, and wings out. He beat them defiantly and screeched again. Here, inside the enclosing walls of the castle, the screech echoed, re-echoed, and redoubled. It was deafening.

The armsmen drew back, though she knew the noise would not stop them for long. Someone shouted. "Ropes! Nets!"

She looked back and saw Yenteel was in place. He did not look happy. Gally had gathered up the reins and put them in his hand, not that he had any clue what to do with them. This was a problem, but if Shingul did not take off with Sheesha, it wasn't her fault.

"Gally, ride Looesa!"

The old *ziri* looked up at the sound of his name, first at her, then at Gally who hesitated and stared at her. He knew he was not allowed to ride. He might not understand that it was a death sentence to do it, but he knew it was forbidden to him.

"Look, Gally, I'm riding. You can do it."

More shouting. A couple of men had emerged from the building carrying a net between them. From the other direction were armsmen on either side of someone swinging a noose with a skill that showed her he knew what he was about.

Not yet, she thought. "Gally! Quick! Get on Looesa!"

Then Looesa called to him, with the same grunting sound Sheesha had used the morning he had woken her during the raid. Gally looked at Looesa. The old *ziri* dropped his whole front body so it was along the ground, making it easy for the lad. The dragon grunted again.

"Looesa wants you to ride, Gally, you wouldn't say no to him, would you?"

The confusion in Gally's face cleared and he grinned. Moments later he was getting into the saddle, having gathered up the reins on his way.

There was a scream from the armsmen to the front and they ran forwards with their nets. Sheesha reared and bellowed again. This time Looesa and Shingul joined in and the courtyard echoed like the mountains with their cries.

"Gally ready!" he shouted sounding excited and happy.

Out of the corner of her eye Kantees caught a movement. The man with the noose had got within a dozen strides of her and the loop of rope was in the air. It flew true. Kantees was buckled into a saddle on the back of a huge creature. She could not dodge.

Sheesha's head whipped round and snapped on the rope. The loop dangled from his teeth. Swinging his head back the other way, the dragon ripped the rope from the man's hands, and a scream of pain from his throat. Staggering away, he pressed his palms under his arms.

Kantees gave Sheesha a kick. "Up!"

The powerful *ziri* went back on his hind legs and as his wings beat down, he leapt into the air. "Looesa! Shingul! Come!" she screamed at the top of her voice though it felt insignificant in the cold air. Yet still, she heard her words echo from the walls.

Each wingbeat forced Sheesha higher, slowly at first, then picking up speed. She allowed herself a glance behind and saw the older *ziri* climbing too, in perfect formation. She sighed with relief. They were going to make it.

They passed the top of the walls and she heard a whistling thrum. Then another. Arrows. They must have decided allowing slaves to escape was worse than damaging the *ziri*. Then a dozen more arrows whistled past. Yenteel cried out in pain.

The sound of arrows dropped away as they passed out of range. But they were still above the castle. They needed a direction, and she had one. It was not much of a choice but it was better than no choice at all.

She leaned forwards so that Sheesha was flying horizontally instead of upwards. Below them the castle looked so small she felt she could reach out and crush it in her fist. But she did not wish to do that. Not right now.

She got her bearings from the river below and set their course to follow where the giant *tekrak* had gone, even though it had left days before.

Once they were established and Sheesha needed no further guidance, she turned in the saddle to look at Gally. He was still grinning. Clearly the idea that the *ziri* had wanted him to ride was still a thing of pleasure to him. She envied him his simplicity.

Yenteel was not in a good way, however. It looked as though the arrow that had hit him had pinned his right arm to his chest. He was holding the reins in his other hand and he was conscious, but that's all she could tell in the dark.

With the blessing of the Mother, she thought, *I will make all this right. Though I have no idea how.*

11

Kantees was not sure how long they had travelled, but the clouds had turned into ragged fragments and the light of Colimar reflected dirty red on their underside as the moon sank below the horizon. The plains below them undulated in dark folds, and they crossed a dozen rivers. To their right were the mountains, looming and threatening as always. But in every other direction, the rolling hills with the occasional wooded area huddled in a valley.

And, once or twice, the light of dwellings. They had flown over a village where smoke drifted from the chimneys of the buildings.

She had no idea where they were or how far they had come but she could not let Yenteel suffer any longer. He moaned occasionally as the *ziri* were buffeted by winds, and besides, her legs were also stiff and sore. Much more of this and she would not be able to walk.

So she let Sheesha descend and choose one of the valleys. It would have wood for a fire, water from the stream, and be sheltered from the elements.

There were holes in her plan, and she was aware of them, but she had focused on getting them out of the castle since nothing else mattered if that could not be achieved. The next problem was food, not only for the riders but their mounts. She had no idea how she would feed them.

Back at the castle they were given the carcasses of animals that they ripped to shreds and gobbled down. Even the bones were consumed after being cracked in their powerful jaws. They were so strong they could easily escape once the group had landed and the riders dismounted.

But perhaps that did not matter. They could continue on foot.

The dark ground came up below them. Sheesha flapped his wings hard and landed with the lightest bump. Moments later there was a cry of pain from Yenteel as Shingul came down.

Unbuckling herself as quickly as possible she jumped down and collapsed into the soft grass as her legs failed to support her. It was damp here. Must have been raining.

Grabbing Sheesha's feathered wing for support she pushed herself to her feet and staggered across to Shingul. Yenteel's face looked ghostly in the dark as if even the colour of his skin had been drained away. The saddle harness was sticky with his blood, but his harsh breathing told her he was not dead.

"Gally, help me," she said. Even with Yenteel unbuckled she did not know how she would get him to the ground without aggravating his wound. Yenteel's tortured breath caught in his throat and he made a noise.

"Don't try to talk," she said.

Then his eyes opened and he stared at her. He tried to speak again. His free arm reached out and grabbed her shoulder. She felt herself beginning to cry and cursed herself. This was not the time.

"Break."

The word was forced from him and she could see the concentration on his face as he made his failing body obey.

"Break?"

His eyes rolled up into their sockets and the lids closed. He slumped. Gally appeared on the other side of Shingul's neck. His face mirrored his concern—he was incapable of any duplicity. He was sad because there was something to be sad about.

"What did he mean?" said Kantees. "Break what?"

"Arrow," said Gally as if it was the most obvious thing in the world.

Kantees looked. Yes, the arrow, but break it where? Then she realised if it was broken between his arm and his stomach they would be able to move him more easily.

"Hold him so he doesn't fall."

Gally took hold of Yenteel's other arm and his leg, while Shingul continued to remain perfectly still, lying flat on the ground so that the injured man could be reached easily. It was astonishing how considerate the *ziri* seemed to be, but this was no time to be thinking about it.

This was going to hurt.

She took hold of the arrow where it pierced his side. His blood made it slick. Then placed her other hand on the shaft further out, beyond where it had entered his arm.

It's only an arrow, she thought. *Easy to break.*

Trying to keep her right hand still she pushed back with the other. Yenteel's fingers twitched as the shaft bent, taking his arm with it. He groaned. She knew she wasn't keeping the arrow rigid and it was moving inside him.

She yelled and shoved hard. The wood snapped. Yenteel moaned as the pain ripped through him. She released her hands and the wood shifted back into position. They had to move him off Shingul's back and that would hurt too.

If only one of them were a healer and could repair the damage that was being done.

But wishing was riding a *ziri*. Except she had done that.

There was still no healer here, the best she could do was hope the damage was not too great and he would recover. She let Gally take the weight since he was strong and he was on the side without the arrow. She pushed Yenteel's leg over Shingul's neck and together she and Gally laid him on the ground.

Shingul sat back on her haunches, leaning on her wing joints, and brought her head round. She sniffed at Yenteel and opened her jaws. For one terrifying moment Kantees thought the *ziri* was going to take a bite out of him, just like one of the animal carcasses. But instead her tongue emerged and she licked him.

Tasting the blood, thought Kantees. She knelt down beside Yenteel and pushed Shingul's massive head away. The man was breathing and though each breath was shallow the rhythm was steady.

She wondered what she should do next. There were horror stories about people who died of injuries when there was no healer nearby. Or were allowed to die of injuries even if there was a healer available. They would lose their blood and die, or their bodies simply ceased to function. Sometimes they would rot like dead meat while they still lived.

She shuddered at the thought. It seemed the damage was not great enough for him to simply die, but he had lost a lot of blood—Shingul was now busy cleaning her feathers of it—so there was the risk he would rot from the inside. And that was the worst prospect of all.

"Gally, take the saddles off the *ziri*."

"No chains."

"I know, but we must trust them not to fly away."

"Romain say Gally not trusted."

"I trust you Gally, and the *ziri* trust you. Looesa let you ride, and put his head down for you, didn't he?"

"I ride Looesa," he said and she could tell from his voice he was smiling.

"Yes you did, as good as a master. Now get the saddles off them, they have flown hard and for a long time. They need to rest."

"All right, Kantees," he said as if she had been scolding him, then went off to where the dark shape of Sheesha watched them.

She turned her attention back to Yenteel. There was not enough light in the sky to see what she could do about the wounds. So they would have to wait until morning.

What could she do?

She fetched her bag and pulled out the stone water bottle. It was heavy but she preferred it to skins. There was a stream nearby, she had seen it as they descended.

"Gally, stay with the *ziri*. I'm going to fetch water."

"Gally is thirsty," said Gally.

Kantees smiled humourlessly and headed for the trees. Behind her there was a grunt from a *ziri* and she heard one of them following her. She wasn't going to argue, she had never been out in the open after dark, and alone, before. She had lived all her life in relative safety, first in the town house and then in the castle tower.

There were animals out here in the wild that could kill you in a moment. Having a *zirichak* at her shoulder would probably dissuade all but the biggest.

The ground got muddy before she reached the river. Then her foot got caught on a submerged root and she almost went over. She was rapidly coming to the conclusion that she did not like the outside. Stone walls, a fire, and a troop of armsmen for protection were much more attractive.

Then her other foot went into cold running water and a bed of soft mud. She took the stopper from the bottle and dipped it below the water. She heard the bubbles coming from it—then the lapping of the water by a giant tongue. Sheesha was drinking. It seemed he had no problem being out in the open at night.

Kantees drank from the bottle first. It made her cold all the way down. Then she refilled it and made her muddy way back to where Yenteel lay. Gally had finished removing the saddles so she told him to lead Looesa and Shingul down to the river to drink.

"And be careful," she said. "It's very muddy. Your feet could get stuck or you might fall over and get it everywhere."

"All right, Kantees. Come on, Looesa. Come on, Shingul." He said it exactly the way Kantees did. This time she did smile and felt happier. He seemed to be coping with the new situation better than she was, but then he didn't have to worry about a dying man, or being chased, or trying to find Jelamie, or being strung up as an escaped slave. No healer could bring you back from *that* journey.

When she was satisfied he was heading the right way, with the *ziri* following him, she turned her attention back to Yenteel. She found one of the saddles and managed to prop his head up. Then she opened the bottle and touched it against his mouth. Nothing. She frowned and tipped it up until the water dribbled down the sides of his cheeks. Still there was no response.

"Come on, Yenteel, drink," she said and peeled back his upper lip with her free hand while trying to pour the water in his mouth.

This time he reacted and she could feel, rather than see, him swallowing. She felt pleased with herself, gave him time to deal with that mouthful of water, and went through the process again until the bottle was empty. She did not think she had lost too much.

Let him take that into his body.

A wave of fatigue ran through her and she almost passed out as she knelt beside him. Sheesha nudged her and she fell backwards.

"What was that for?" she said but Sheesha did not make any noise. And she could not see what he was doing. "We have to wait for the others to get back."

It did not take long before Gally and the *ziri* returned, but in the meanwhile she was getting cold. The tension that had shielded her was wearing off. She had relaxed and with that came the exhaustion.

They had no shelter. She looked across to Sheesha who, as the others returned, curled himself up into his sleeping position. Looesa did the same but Shingul went to where Yenteel lay, placed herself along his length, and covered him with her wing.

In the dark they melded into one mass of shadow but still Kantees stared. Shingul was protecting Yenteel and keeping him warm. Like a mother. Like the mother Kantees had never known. Her eyes became moist once more and she sniffed to clear the sensation.

"Time for bed, Gally."

"My bed is far."

"Yes it is, so you will have a new bed."

"You have a new bed?"

"Looesa is your bed."

"Looesa?"

Kantees found his hand in the dark and led him to where the *zirichak* had curled up. Still huge despite that.

"Ask him if you can sleep under his wing," said Kantees.

"Gally sleep under your wing, Looesa?"

There was no movement.

"Just push a little bit, just there." She took his hand and laid it on Looesa's neck. The *ziri* moved, opened up a little, and lifted his wing. Gally needed no further prompting and carefully climbed inside the space. Shingul adjusted and the wing came down.

"'Night, Gally."

"'Night, Kantees. 'Night Looesa."

The *ziri* grunted. Kantees shook her head in wonderment. It was less as if they were simple animals, and more as if they were friends. Well, of course, she understood that, she had been with Sheesha so long that he was a friend. But the way Shingul was treating Yenteel, whom she had never met, did not make sense.

Sheesha made a low growling noise, not aggressive.

"Yes, all right, Sheesha, I'm coming."

She turned and found him waiting with his wing raised.

"I don't understand," she said quietly but Sheesha was already snoring.

It was fine for him to go to sleep immediately, he did not have her worries. Even though she was so tired it took her a long time to sleep as their options—or lack of them—went through her mind.

They needed to keep moving but Yenteel's injury made that impossible.

One thing at a time was the last thought she remembered having as the warmth of Sheesha's feathers drew her into sleep.

1 2

How big is Esternes?

She woke up with that question in her mind. She had asked it once when she had been at the town house, and been struck to the floor for the impertinence. Her master at that time had not been a rich man, and he was a scholar. They lived by the sea in Dakastown although she did not get the opportunity to go out much. She spent most of her time cleaning.

But just because she was cleaning did not mean that she did not have ears. The scholar was consulted for his wisdom and his astronomical predictions. This was a tricky area because such things were traditionally the province of the patterners. They kept their knowledge to themselves for the most part.

The scholar knew he was walking a fine line but he always managed to keep to the right side of it. He did not trespass on the territory of the patterners. As far as Kantees knew he had never made a pattern in all the time she was with him. It was said that true skill with patterning required one be born with the talent and train with it for years. There were rumours of wild talent, but Kantees could not ask, she could only listen and learn.

Except for that one day when the master had been looking at his maps. Someone had asked him a question and paid their money.

She did not know what the question was, all she was doing was cleaning the grate. And the question popped into her head. She knew that Esternes was an island but she did not know how big. Just as the question popped into her head, it popped out of her mouth. In reply the master had knocked her to the ground.

Her duties then kept her to the kitchen and the garden. Shortly thereafter she was sold.

All for a question.

Romain did not like her asking questions either. He preferred to dictate his wisdom in regard to the *zirichasa* for her to absorb. But she did have questions and sometimes they were things he had failed to mention, so he could be angry at her ignorance but he still had to answer her.

As time passed she learnt everything he had to offer and he simply repeated himself for he seemed incapable of remembering what it was he had told her. When Gally joined them it worked out for the best because it meant that he could lecture Gally who definitely did forget, or completely failed to understand. So Romain could repeat himself as much as he wished.

He ceased to instruct Kantees but she still had questions and there was no one to ask.

The day was bright, the air was cold, and there was dew on the ground. The cold did not bother her but it could not be good for Yenteel. She stepped out from the enfolding wings of Sheesha and stretched. Behind her she heard Sheesha doing the same and the broad shadow of his wings was draped across the ground.

Looesa stood up, and dropped Gally to the ground before stretching. Only Shingul remained where she was, still with her wing across Yenteel.

Kantees sighed. She was still tired but the brightness of the day drove the sleep from her. She found the water bottle.

"Gally, go to the river, fill this, and bring it back."

"I am hungry, Kantees."

"I am too, Gally, but we must look after Yenteel first."

"Why?"

"He is hurt and ill. Fetch the water for him."

Gally grumbled but he went, followed by Looesa, and when

Kantees knelt beside Yenteel, Shingul stood up and went after them. Some birds went about in flocks, Kantees knew, so perhaps *zirichasa* did as well. It was a question she could not answer, just as she did not know the size of Esternes.

Yenteel's colour looked bad in daylight but her concern was the broken pieces of arrow. Perhaps she should deal with this now, before Gally came back. She preferred to protect him from the more unpleasant parts of their adventure.

With her knife she cut away the cloth of Yenteel's jacket and shirt. It seemed a shame because they were of excellent quality. Whoever his master was, he dressed Yenteel well.

The arrow had pierced the lower arm and it was not as bad as she feared. It had gone deep enough to hit a muscle but she did not think it had hit the bone beneath. Looking at the broken arrow she could see that pulling it back out was a bad idea since the break was full of broken bits of wood. It would tear his skin.

Carefully she brought his arm back and away from his body, then placed a knee on his hand and held his arm just above the arrow. She took hold of the broken end and pulled. The fact that Yenteel shuddered with the pain as she drew the wood through his arm pleased her—at least he could still feel pain. He was still in there.

It did not take long before the arrow's flights disappeared into him and then reappeared red with blood. Using the cloth she had cut off she made a bandage around the wounds. They seeped blood a little but it was not serious.

She was shocked when Yenteel's other hand suddenly grabbed her shoulder. His eyes were wide. "When you take it out. You must burn it."

She heard the words but she did not understand them. It must have been clear in her face, as he panted, "Your knife. Make it hot, very hot, when you take out the arrow. Burn the skin shut. Seal it. Otherwise infection and bleeding. You understand?"

His grip was like a *ziri*'s talon digging in to her. She nodded even though she did not know what 'infection' was. "I understand."

He let go and fell back. "Do it now, or I die."

She stared at his face and then at the wound at his side. He had lost consciousness again but she whispered, "I'll try."

Gally was returning and presented her with the water bottle.

"Find wood, Gally," she said. "This is important. We must make a fire as quick as we can. The hottest fire we can."

"I'm tired."

"Please, Gally, don't be difficult. The hottest fire we can."

The *ziri* did not seem at all concerned by the fire that Kantees now had raging. She had built a small wall from earth and filled it with tinder as Gally fetched larger sticks. She got it alight with her tinderbox and kept it going long enough to dry out the twigs, which in turn dried out the branches Gally collected. The wall kept the heat in and the wind out. At least, she wasn't completely useless.

Once she was satisfied, she took a straight branch, tied the knife to its end with Yenteel's boot straps and placed it into the fire.

"We have to take the arrow out, Gally, but we must stop all the bleeding and to do that Yenteel says we must burn his skin."

"That will hurt him," said Gally. "Bad."

"Yes it will, but he told me I must do it. If we don't he will die."

"I like Yenteel."

Kantees wasn't sure she did, she barely knew him, and besides Gally liked almost everyone including those who were cruel to him —simply because he did not understand their taunts and tricks.

"Yes, and that's why we have to do this. But you have to help me."

"Help Kantees?"

"Yes, you have to hold him. It will hurt when I take the arrow out, and it will hurt when I burn him. He will move and you have to hold him still otherwise it will be harder to help him."

It took a few more attempts to convince Gally that all this really would help even though it was like doing a bad thing.

But in the end they could not delay any longer. The fire was hot. The blade wasn't glowing, but it was as hot as she could manage.

She had Gally kneel on Yenteel's shoulders. And she put her knee on his hand again. There wasn't much she could do about his legs, she would just have to be quick. Thankfully she knew that the castle archers did not use barbed heads. It should come straight out, though she guessed there was a hands-length of wood and iron in Yenteel's belly.

She closed her eyes and took a deep breath. She did not want to do this. She might kill him, but if she didn't do it he would die anyway and that would also be her fault.

Her eyes open once more, she smiled at Gally.

"Ready?"

He nodded seriously.

Kantees took hold of the end of the arrow. She had cleaned it of blood and bound it with another bootstrap, so her hand would not slip. She had her other hand on the branch with the knife at its end.

"Three ... two ... one ... now."

The arrow seemed stuck at first; she pulled harder and it came free. Yenteel squirmed and moaned with the pain. The shaft's bloodied length slid out and dark blood flowed from the wound. She dropped the arrow, lifted the knife, and with both hands, prepared to press the flat against the hole in Yenteel's side.

It was such a small hole. She hesitated. Romain would always sew up injuries to the *ziri*. Blood leaked from his side but it did not pump. She always had a needle and thread with her because Romain would check on her.

"Kantees?" said Gally.

She threw the knife away from her and it hissed in the grass, sending up tiny embers.

"Fetch my bag, Gally, by Sheesha's saddle. Quick."

She could sew the two sides together and it would heal as it should. If she burned him it would make a terrible scar and she could not be sure it would heal properly. Then she could bind him around the middle and it would help to hold the wound shut. If he rotted from the inside, it would happen regardless of what method she used to mend him.

Gally returned and she found the needle leather and the thread. It was strong and would not break easily. She had Gally hold him still while she poked the iron needle into him. It was like mending a hole in clothes. The skin was tougher but it worked the same way. And it did not take long. Romain was good for something then.

Yenteel was so far gone that he did not react to the pricking; she wondered whether that would have been true if she had burned him. No, this was far better.

Rummaging through Yenteel's bag she found a shirt. It wasn't clean but it would do. She used it as a pad over the injury and wrapped cording several times around him to hold it in place. It would have to do.

She looked up.

The day had barely progressed. It was not even midday. The sky was clear save for a few slow-moving clouds that seemed intent on avoiding the sun. The air remained cold but it was warm in the light.

She sat back exhausted.

Yenteel was resting quietly and his breathing was steady though still shallow. Gally sat beside him holding his hand.

The *ziri* were lying together with their long necks on the ground but Sheesha had his eyes open, looking at her across his flat snout.

"I've done everything I can," she said as if he could understand her. "It's up to the Mother now."

Then her stomach growled and Sheesha glanced at her midriff accusingly. It made her laugh inside. The *zirichak* pushed himself up with his wings and sat back on his haunches. He put his head on its side to look at her.

"You're hungry?" she said. "It's good for you. Can't have you getting fat."

Sheesha gave a short calling bark and the other two lifted their heads. They looked in the direction of the mountains—shadowy and blue in the sunlight with their tips glowing white.

"No, Sheesha!" Kantees stumbled to her feet. This was his take-off pose.

He glanced briefly in her direction and then launched himself up. The downdraught from his wings buffeted her. Then Looesa went up as well. They wheeled in a spiral gaining height with deep and powerful beats of their wings.

They were beautiful with their feathers shimmering in iridescent blues and greens as the sun's light reflected off them. Sheesha's turn faced him towards the mountains and he shot away with Looesa in a perfect position to the right and behind.

Kantees could do nothing but despair. She watched until the dots they became in the distance were indistinguishable from the dots her eyes invented.

He's gone.

13

She brought her attention back to their meagre camp. Gally still sat with Yenteel, and Shingul still lay on the grass. Was she all right? But she had no reason to think there was anything wrong with the *ziri*.

Why hadn't she gone with the males?

Kantees forced herself to calm. They must be coming back otherwise she would have gone.

Surely that must be true?

Gally was unconcerned but that was hardly surprising, he only worried about the small things. And he worried about Kantees. Keeping the secret of having seen her must have been difficult for him. As far as she knew he did not lie. So to be forced to keep silent must have been difficult.

She went back to where Yenteel lay and crouched down on the other side of him to Gally who was fiddling with something.

"I wanted to thank you, Gally," she said. He did not react but played with what looked like a smooth stone. Perhaps he picked it up at the stream. "I wanted to thank you for keeping my secret about riding Sheesha."

He said nothing.

"If anybody asks now, you can tell them, it's not a secret any more."

"They hurt Kantees?"

"Not for that, Gally," she said. "After what I've done now, stealing the *ziri*, they will punish me for that instead."

"Sheesha not stolen."

She smiled. "What would you call it then?"

"Sheesha helping."

"But Sheesha, Looesa, and Shingul are just animals, Gally," she said. "They just do as they're told." She looked in the direction that Sheesha had gone. "Well, when they want to, anyway."

Gally had gone back to the round stone. The sun glinted on it and she realised it was flat as well as round.

"What's that?"

"Mine. I found it."

"I know but can I have a look?"

"Gally's coin."

"I promise I will give it back," she said. "It looks very pretty, you could just come over here and show it to me if you don't trust me to touch it."

Which was a dirty trick and she felt bad about it the moment the words came out. It was the sort of thing Daybian would say to manipulate people.

Gally looked at her dubiously and then stretched out his arm across Yenteel's body. Rather than take it, Kantees held out her palm so he could decide to give it. It dropped heavily into her hand.

It was a coin and not small. Heavy too. It must be valuable. She had never had money; as a slave she was not allowed to own anything. Everyone broke the rule of course, but with small things that could be hidden easily—though their main currency was secrets.

Back in the tower she had one of Sheesha's feathers. They were supposed to hand them all in to be made into saleable items by people in the town—so they had value. But she had kept that one. Another crime to add to the list she would no doubt be punished for. Death would be too easy. No doubt there would be torture first to make sure she fully understood her crimes.

She shook her head and tried to escape the morbid thoughts.

It was not that she didn't know what coins looked like. She had seen enough of them changing hands in the gambling at the races. But they were always of dark metal and very small, some of them tiny. She had never seen one like this.

It had a man's face on one side. He looked like a Taymalin and he had some sort of circlet on his head, perhaps a king or lord. The other side showed the image of a *nachak* just from the waist up, depicting only its cruel upper arms, its torso, and head. Who would have the symbol of a *nachak*? They were vicious night hunters, so the stories went, and very big.

Not that she knew how big, there were stories that they were the size of a house. Some of the armsmen claimed to have seen them but who knew if they were telling the truth.

She stared at the coin and tilted it until it reflected the sun.

At a guess this would probably be enough to buy a dozen slaves like her. Or enough food to keep her fed for a year. She looked up and smiled at Gally who had a concerned look on his face. She tossed it back; he caught it and gave her a relieved grin.

Then it dawned on her. "Gally, where did you find it?"

He pointed to the river.

"Show me."

The words were hardly out of her mouth when she remembered Yenteel, lying there directly in front of her. She was annoyed at him for being like this. She stood up anyway.

"Shingul?"

The female was facing away from them and towards the mountains, but she lifted her head and bent her neck back to look at them.

"Look after Yenteel, please." She pointed down at his unconscious body.

Shingul grunted in a way that implied she understood, although that was impossible, then went back to watching the mountains. Kantees shook her head. The *ziri* were confusing, on the one hand they could not be more than animals, and yet they seemed to understand.

"Show me the way, Gally."

They set off with Kantees puzzling over the *ziri*. People in the town kept *zatesa* as pets and to guard property. They were quite clever and could be trained or learn tricks. But *zirichasa* were bigger. Did that mean they were cleverer?

They approached the stream. Gally made to go straight through the mud.

"Let's go round," said Kantees pointing to the side away from the woods. A coarse thick grass grew in the mud but she could see the cropped grass closer to the water further along.

Gally stopped and looked obstinate. She had asked him where he had found the coin and that's where he wanted to go.

"Was it on this side of the stream?" she asked.

"Other side."

"That's why you were so wet."

"Fell over."

"I know," she said. "If it's the other side we can go round."

It also looked as if the channel was narrower there. She headed round and, still reluctant, dragging his feet, Gally followed.

The stream here could be jumped easily. It had cut into the ground, running deep and fast, before it opened out and pooled in the area before the trees. She had not noticed before but the ground dropped off on the other side of the trees.

It was then she noticed the grass on this side was ripped up. Something had dug into the ground and torn huge holes into it but only over an area that—*was exactly the size of the giant tekrak*. She walked around the churned-up area. The *tekrak* had come down here, landed and dug its roots into the ground, just like the small ones did.

They had camped here.

She looked round and found three firepits. The ground was disturbed here as well but not in the same way. She was no tracker but it was clear people had made fires and cooked. There were even a few bones about the place. A blanket, damp and torn, lay close to the trees. But if only she had been a tracker she might know how long they had stayed, how far behind them she was.

It was enough to lift her heart.

Something pulled at her sleeve. Gally.

"Gally show Kantees."

"Yes, of course, sorry."

She let him lead the way back towards the stream. It was less muddy on this side, because the land was a little higher, and there was a low bank where the ground fell away to the water.

Gally leaned over and pointed. Then he toppled into the water. Kantees was there in a moment. Gally was on his knees pulling at something in the water, partially covered by the mud; it was a body face down in the water. Gally splashed about, his feet sinking deeper trying to pull the body up.

Kantees laid her hand on his shoulder. "Gally, stop."

"Help him, Kantees. We have to help the master."

"It's too late, Gally. He's dead."

The boy stopped, released the clothing and stood up straight. "Dead?"

"He's been there since the raiders stayed here. A few days. He's dead."

"Sorry, sire." Gally's words were directed at the submerged body.

Kantees gave a sad smile. "I'm sure he'd be happy you tried to save him."

"Gally did try to save him."

"You did."

"But he's dead."

"Yes."

"What do we do, Kantees?"

Good question. He must have come with the raiders, so perhaps there was a clue to who they were on him. The mud had all but claimed him and after a few days in the water she did not relish what his face would look like. She could see one of his hands and that was white, bloated and torn where something had taken bites out of him.

But if there were any clues she needed to know them.

It took a long time to get him out. It seemed that he had been sinking slowly and the mud wanted to keep him. It clung and sucked at him. Both Kantees and Gally were soaked and filthy by the time they forced the water to give him up.

Finally they had him on the higher bank and water seeped from him.

She was surprised that his face was not as bad as she had expected. It was bloated but had not been chewed. In fact all the skin that had been stuck in the mud was untouched. The exposed parts, however, were a different matter.

All manner of tiny water insects and little crawlers—even small fish—made their escape as the body was brought out. Even now she could see he was covered in them. They were probably inside as well.

She wanted to let him dry out in the sun a little, but as soon as he did he would start to smell and that would attract all manner of creatures. They might be able to deal with, or scare off, some of them, but there was a limit.

So she searched him.

He had been rich. The clothes were of better quality than the Jakalain wore. She took his shoes, which would be usable when they dried. With Gally's help she got his jacket off. If he had a money pouch, that was gone. The coin must have been his. She doubted that one coin—that could feed her for a year—would have paid for his clothes.

The only other thing she was interested in was how he had died but there was no indication on his body. No blows that she could see, and no stab wounds. Perhaps they had just held his head in the water until he drowned. But if he had been murdered, why had they taken his money but not his clothes?

She shook her head. The Taymalin had strange customs. Who knew what they were thinking?

Flies were already becoming a nuisance around the body. Kantees looked around a little worriedly. It must be well past midday now, and she was getting very hungry. Something caught her eye and she jerked her head round. She was certain there had been a movement in the trees.

The afternoon was getting warm. He would rot even faster. What little wind there was would be carrying the scent out across the plain. She knew there were no large animals near the Jakalain castle, but they were not near it any more. There could even be *nachasa*.

"Let's go," she said and set off back the way they had come, carrying the coat and boots. If Yenteel recovered he might be able to tell them more.

Once across the stream she glanced back. Half a dozen creatures loped out of the trees and stopped. They were being cautious, checking the skies and all around as they moved, but they were going straight for the body.

That he was going to get eaten did not bother Kantees. It was just nature. She was more concerned about how she was going to deal with her own hunger. Even if she had a weapon, other than a knife, she had no idea how to hunt or set traps.

She might be able to start a fire but she knew nothing of survival in the wild.

14

---

*S*hingul had moved while they had been away and was back with Yenteel, lying alongside him with her wing across his body. Unlike the way she had placed it on his body in the night, this time she had it arched to shade him from the sun.

Kantees went back to the stream and refilled the water bottle after quenching her own thirst. Gally, in the meantime, was going through Shingul's feathers looking for bugs. She could probably leave him to do the simple tasks. He was used to them and they still needed to be done.

Yenteel's skin was cold despite the warmth of the day. She knew that could not be a good sign. He drank the water she offered him in an unthinking reaction, for his body knew what to do even though he did not wake up. He only lost half the bottle's contents, so he took in a good amount.

She untied the bandages and pads covering his wounds. Each of the three wounds was red and leaking a transparent fluid, but the inflamed areas did not seem to have spread so she was happy with that. And although he did not wake, his breathing seemed to have settled to a slower and deeper pace.

She could not be sure but she thought perhaps he might not die.

"Thank you for looking after him, Shingul," she said. The *ziri* raised her head and neck and turned back to look at the girl. Her eyes were wide apart on her head but lidded like a person's, not like some of the smaller creatures.

Kantees' time with the scholar had taught her that there were several classes of creatures but that they could be divided into two main groups: the ones that resembled people in their skeletons, their skin, and their blood, and those that resembled the *Slissac*. The two major divisions had groups within them, but it started to get complicated and she was never able to hear enough to explain it.

She had heard enough to know that the *zirichasa* were on the *Slissac* side but that did not stop her side using them. People rode *kichesa* on the ground, and there were horses too. Though not many of either on Esternes as far as she knew.

Then there was the other complication. While humans—and the *Slissac*, if any still existed—could perform magic through the use of patterns, there were creatures that had magic woven into their very being. The *tekrasa*, for example, with their fire-tubes and the gas in them that let them rise into the air even though they were only plants. Or the wolves that never made a sound yet moved like a single creature as if they were joined in their minds.

She looked at Shingul. The *ziri* had no built-in magic. At least she did not think so, as Romain had never spoken of it. They were clever and understood a lot, but no magic. They simply loved to fly as fast as possible.

A booming call sounded across the wilderness, deep and loud and seeming to go right through her. Shingul raised her head and called back in the same voice. Kantees had never heard them make a sound like that. She did not even know they could.

She stood and, squinting against the brightness, scanned the skies.

Shingul boomed again, this time it was a sequence of three short calls that she kept repeating every few moments.

Then another boom from the sky. Kantees saw a dot that resolved rapidly into two and then they had wings and were gliding down fast. Shingul was looking the same way and stopped her booming.

As the two *ziri* closed in and grew in size she saw that both of them carried something in their claws. And the somethings had legs and heads dangling limply. Her mouth watered and she turned to the fire. It was still hot and the embers glowed. She added more tinder, which was instantly consumed in flames, so she switched to twigs and a couple of smaller branches.

A shadow went over followed by thumps as two dead animals hit the ground: They must have found a wild herd of *kelukisa* and picked off a couple of young ones. She was not experienced with preparing meat to eat, but she knew the basics, and having a stream nearby was useful.

The necks of both animals were broken and there were claw marks in the bodies where they had been carried.

Sheesha and Looesa landed nearby and waddled over, nowhere near as elegant on the ground as in the air. Sheesha picked up the carcass furthest from Kantees and dropped it in front of Shingul who put a wing claw on the body, clamped her jaws on a leg and ripped it off.

Kantees picked up her knife and set to work on the other body.

It took a long time to get enough of the skin off to be able to hack at the muscle. She put one whole leg over the fire, then spent more time chopping one of the other legs into much smaller pieces which she draped on sticks next to the flame in the hope they would cook faster. She set Gally to watch them. He was as hungry as she was but they were not so far gone as to eat raw meat.

She noticed that Sheesha and Looesa allowed Shingul to eat as much of the other as she wanted. Then they finished it off between them. They did not argue but Looesa always let Sheesha take his portion first. Perhaps they had eaten when they had been away.

Was this normal behaviour? She had no idea. Most animals in her experience, and that included other Kadralin, would consume as much as they could before letting another eat, if they had a choice. The *zirichasa* seemed quite civilised—and thoughtful, since they had brought back food for everyone.

The meat was delicious. Perhaps more so because of their hunger.

Kantees kept the fire up and roasted the haunch. She took the remains of the carcass to the stream and set about removing the innards. It was a disgusting process that turned the water all manner of unpleasant colours.

She glanced at where the body of the dead man had been laid. No one had moved him since, and she was glad she was not too close. The *chakisa*-like creatures were still ripping their way through his flesh and innards with little screeches of anger as they fought over some tidbit or another.

There were several smaller ones squatting on their tails making a loose circle, waiting to dash in and grab something. The ones on her side noticed what was happening in the water and investigated. Once they realised there was food here they jumped into the water and gobbled up the parts she was discarding.

Back in the castle it was forbidden to feed the *chakisa* that infested the place, because they ate the bugs and smaller creatures and would not do their job if they were not hungry. These creatures were like them but twice the size.

Kantees did not notice at first, since she was focused on the carcass, but when she looked up they were closer. Perhaps half a dozen of them. And they were watching her.

When her knife went into the carcass and the remains floated away they would leap on them, arguing and snapping with their little pointed teeth. But then they were closer again.

One of them ran a few steps closer, its little feet splashing through the water.

Kantees suddenly felt unsafe. It might be that she could stop one of them, perhaps even two, but six or seven could take her down even if they did not even come up to her knees. Then there was a sound behind her. She turned her head slowly. Another one.

Only a short distance away were the fire, Gally, and three *zirichasa* for whom these things would be barely a mouthful.

She suspected that if she abandoned the food they would ignore her, but she was unwilling to give in to these little bullies. She took hold of the leg of the remains and stood up, which sent them scurrying back a few paces. Since she had stripped out the innards what was left was much lighter.

"Sheesha," she said, not loudly but enough that her voice would carry.

His head popped up and he looked in her direction. The movement did not escape the ones in front of her; every one of those little heads turned towards the camp. They did not move; the threat was too far away to distract them from the food they thought they could get.

Then she heard the flop and thump of a big wing moving.

The little creatures scattered, including the one behind her that zipped past. Their movement attracted the attention of the others eating the dead man. They saw Sheesha and responded by fleeing back into the woods.

Kantees gave a short laugh and dragged the remains back to the camp where she put the rest of it on and in the fire to cook.

"That smells good," said Yenteel in a voice that could barely be heard.

15

antees was surprised at how relieved she was when Yenteel woke up. He gratefully accepted more water and he seemed able to use his undamaged arm. His colour looked better and his skin seemed more alive.

She cut a piece of meat into tiny pieces, so he did not have to chew, and fed them to him.

Shingul moved away and went to the pool with Looesa. They went in and splashed about, almost as if they were having fun although Kantees assumed they were just cleaning themselves. Seeing the *ziri* like this made her realise how little she knew about them, really—how little Romain or any of the other keepers knew.

Having eaten and drunk, Yenteel went back to sleep.

She had hoped to talk to him about the dead body, and she was becoming concerned about pursuit. It was true that no one would be flying to catch them—they would have succeeded already—but, while a *ziri* could fly fast, if they stayed where they were someone would catch up with them eventually.

Especially if they followed the smoke from the fire. Kantees looked in horror at the rising column. It must be visible for miles. She poured what was left of the water onto it, then ran down to the stream to get more.

She paused only long enough to fill the bottle—noticing that Looesa and Shingul were preening each other while sitting in the water and stirring up the mud.

It took another bottle to put the fire out completely. Gouts of steam were rising but they dissipated quickly.

Then Sheesha boomed. Kantees looked where he was looking, back the way they had come, and saw a growing patch of dark against the sky. A booming call echoed back. Kantees shook her head. It was too late. She had been away only a day and it was already too late. Someone had found her.

The *ziri* went into a spiral, descending fast.

Who could ride that well? Who would decide to do it? There was only one answer and she knew it before she even saw his face. Daybian. And he was riding old Jintan. Kantees was surprised the beast could do it. She wished he had not been able.

As the *ziri* spiralled in for a final landing, she fetched her knife and put it in her belt at the small of her back so Daybian would not see it.

Then, before she could think to stop him, Gally ran up to the landing *ziri* and took the reins just as he would have back at the castle. She had thought to call it home, but it was not that any longer.

"So, at least one person here still knows how to respect their masters."

Daybian unbuckled himself and slipped down to the ground. His movements were smooth, with no sign he had been in the saddle too long.

He peeled off his riding gloves. There was a short sword at his waist but he did not go for it. Kantees did not know what to say. She felt crushed and broken, her life now numbered in days.

Sheesha had watched the arrival and now moved so that he stood beside and slightly behind Kantees. It was a comfort to have him there even though there was nothing he could do—he had no understanding of the situation beyond perhaps her feeling of unease.

Daybian's eyes narrowed as he followed Sheesha's movement

but even so he walked forward. The fire stood between them still smoking slightly, she must have missed some embers after all.

"Am I really that ugly?" said Daybian.

Kantees could not help herself. "*What?*"

He shook his head. "No respect at all."

"I cannot commit any greater crime than I already have," she said. "I do not need to show you any respect."

"It might go better for you at a trial if you did."

"Death is death, *sire*." She twisted the last word with as much sarcasm as she could muster.

"Regardless," he said. "My original question still stands."

"I didn't understand it."

"You hit me over the head with Sheesha's shit shovel, just because I wanted to lie with you. I did not think I was so ugly that you would feel the need to do that to escape me."

"Are you so selfish?" she said. "Nothing I did was about you."

"So you don't think I'm ugly?"

"It's not relevant."

"It is to me."

Kantees closed her eyes. She found it hard to believe she was having this conversation. "Whatever the merits of your appearance —" He smiled. "—or the lack of them—" The smile vanished. "—how can I make you understand that I hit you over the head because you insisted on being present when I wanted to escape?"

"You're saying it's a coincidence."

Kantees opened her mouth. The conversation was getting so mixed up she was not entirely sure what the right answer was.

"It was a coincidence that you desired to force yourself on me at a time when I was planning to escape, yes."

"That's all right then."

"Is it?"

"Yes."

"You rode Jintan all the way out here after me because your pride had been pricked?"

"It wasn't the only reason."

"That makes it so much better," she said. "You've come to take me back. I won't go and I will fight you if you try to make me. I would rather die here than be forced to return."

It seemed it was Daybian's turn to look confused. "Not at all."

"I have committed several capital crimes," she said, "including hitting you over the head."

"I believe we have dealt with that issue."

"If you're not here to take me back, and you're satisfied your pride hasn't been injured, why are you here?"

"To help you search for my brother, of course."

At which point Kantees felt faint and leaned back against Sheesha.

"But you can't. You don't have the right to forgive my crimes."

"We'll worry about that later," he said. "That meat smells good, fetch me some, will you? Is the water in that stream clean? And who is that fellow lying on the ground? He doesn't look well."

She did not fetch him any meat—he could get his own, which he did—but she did assure him that the stream was clean enough to drink from, upstream of where she had cleaned out the carcass. That information came with a warning that he should watch out for the big *chakisa*, especially in groups of three or more.

Yenteel woke up again as the sun was descending. He took some more food and water. He was stronger which made Kantees a lot happier.

"Lord Daybian is here."

Yenteel raised an eyebrow. "He has not killed you or taken you back."

Since that was obviously true, and Yenteel had not expressed it as a question, she said nothing more.

"What does he want?"

"To help me find his brother."

"I said he'd be trouble. Do you trust him?"

"Of course not, he's one of the masters. He tried ordering me about as soon as he arrived."

Yenteel glanced across at where Daybian was watching the sun go down and scratching his behind. "He does not strike me as being very bright."

"He isn't," she said. "But he's a good rider, and if you can believe what he says he knows how to use his sword."

"I thought that was what you were avoiding."

Kantees looked daggers at Yenteel, who had the ghost of a smile on his face. "You can feed yourself. You're obviously feeling better."

Then Yenteel said something in a language she did not understand. He had a look of hope on his face which dissolved when she shook her head.

"I don't understand."

"It is your language, Kantees," he said. "Of your people, the Kadralin."

"It is forbidden to speak it."

He made a slight movement that might have been a shrug.

"Why did you come to Jakalain?" she said. "Why were you looking for me? And don't say it was because the world's pattern told you to."

He gave a slight shake of his head. "It is a story that would be long in the telling. We need to be moving on."

"You're not strong enough."

"No, but I am strong enough to make a pattern or two with your help."

"You're a patterner?"

"Everyone can make patterns, Kantees. Everyone does even if they don't think they do. Every movement, every act, every spoken word is part of a pattern."

"But it's not magical."

"Isn't it? When a musician moves their hands on their instrument and it makes a tune, is that not a pattern that is magical?"

"But that's just … doing things right. I've heard plenty of tunes which were not done right."

"And that's the point."

She sighed. Clearly there was no way to argue with him. "What do you need?"

"Fetch my bag. There's some charcoal in a box, and if you can manage to find a cloth that I can draw on, it would help."

She brought the bag and located the box. Yenteel also possessed a white linen shirt so she brought that out and held it up in front of him. He sighed. "It'll wash out, I suppose."

He also wanted something flat to lean on, like a board, but that was harder to come by until Kantees saw Daybian's short sword flapping against his leg. He seemed to be quite content just staring into the distance. Perhaps that was sufficient to occupy his limited mind.

"I need to borrow your sword."

"To kill me?"

She ignored his comment. "Yenteel needs to do a patterning, and he needs something to rest the cloth on while he forms the patterns."

"That slave is a patterner?"

"Yes, apparently he is."

"It's forbidden for slaves to do magic."

"Yes, well, it's also forbidden to hit masters on the head with shit shovels, but you seem to have recovered from that."

Daybian unsheathed his sword. "Do not attempt to run me through with it."

"Much as it would give me great pleasure," said Kantees, "I will restrain myself. I don't hate you personally, Daybian."

"Then you might consider lying with me?"

"Can't you think with your head instead of what's between your legs?"

He grinned and opened his mouth. She cut him off.

"Just don't. Yenteel has already made that joke. It wasn't funny then, and it won't be funny now."

"He thought it too? Then perhaps I will like him after all." Daybian pulled out the sword. It was probably worth about two years' food to someone like her. For him it was just a serviceable tool for killing. It wasn't even of the best quality.

But it did have a flat surface. She took it back to Yenteel who told her to lay the cloth over it and hold it taut while he inscribed symbols. He hummed at the same time. Quite tunelessly.

The designs he made had lots of straight lines forming squares, triangles and other more complex shapes. It was a pattern, but she couldn't see any meaning in it. He took breaks as he worked; the light was failing but he seemed clear about what he was doing.

"Tie it next to my skin under the bandage," he said. "This mark must be over the wound." He pointed just before he passed out.

Kantees made a face but did as he asked. She needed to check his wound anyway.

The fire was going out. There was a shuddering in the air as one of the *ziri* launched into the air. It was Jintan.

"Gally?"

He emerged from the shadows between the others.

"What's Jintan doing?"

"He is going to have a shit."

"How do you know?"

"He was itchy."

"Itchy?"

"Jumping up and down a little bit, Kantees. Did you not want him to go? He would make a mess here and we don't have any shovels."

Kantees had never noticed Sheesha doing that. He seemed content to make a pile in the corner for her to clear up. It occurred to her that in some ways Sheesha was as arrogant as Daybian.

"No, that's all right," she said. "We don't want a mess here. He will come back?"

"Yes, Kantees."

"You keep looking after them then."

"Yes, Kantees, but there is not much to do. Romain will say Gally is lazy."

"Romain isn't here."

"No, Kantees."

Gally turned and went back to the *ziri* who were lying together a short distance away.

"He's a bright lad," said Daybian.

Compared to you? Yes, she thought. "You can have your sword back." She held it out and he took it, sliding it smoothly back into its sheath with a natural confidence that suggested perhaps he really did know what he was doing with it.

"Can you build up the fire?" she added.

"Me?"

Her anger at all the arrogant masters exploded. "Yes, you! You want to come with me, then you do what I say."

"I don't take orders from slaves."

"I'm *not* a slave any more. Out here we're equals. Oh, and in case you're making unwarranted assumptions, I'm riding Sheesha. You can stay on Jintan."

He was quiet for a few moments. "I will admit I do not really know about building up fires. It's not something I have had to do."

"There is wood drying next to the fire. You take some of the branches and put them on the fire. Not too much or you'll suffocate it and we'll run out."

"I see. I will give that a try."

"Good." She was slightly disappointed at how swiftly he had given in. She had been looking forward to shouting at him again.

He turned away and went to the fire. She thought for a moment he seemed sad, but she shrugged it off. Of course he felt sad: she wouldn't let him express his arrogance.

She turned back to Yenteel and carefully untied the cords that held the pad. It was red with fresh blood. Simply drawing the pattern must have been too much effort for him, and he had reopened the wound. She would have to make sure he did not do that again.

That meant more delay. If Daybian could find them, then someone else could. At least at night the smoke would be less visible and nobody would be flying.

She wrapped the patterned cloth around him ensuring the right marks were on the arrow wound. Then she bandaged him up again.

At least she could fly away on Sheesha if it became too much. Except that she couldn't leave them, especially not Gally.

16

When Yenteel woke again, the white moon, Lostimal, was shining in the black. He drank more water and chewed some meat. There was not enough light for her to tell whether he was suffering more than before. His voice seemed about the same.

"You placed the pattern?" he said.

"Just as you said, with the one you pointed out over the wound."

He did not reply immediately but tried to adjust his position and groaned in the effort.

"You can't do that," she said. "If you need to move, tell me. You started bleeding again and this isn't going to help." She glanced at where the wound was but it was impossible to see anything.

"I must do this," he said, his voice straining with the pain he had to be feeling. "I have held you up too long as it is."

"You didn't ask to get shot."

"No, but they gave me that honour anyway."

"We could just wait for you to heal," she said, putting a smile on her face, even though he couldn't see it.

"You're a good liar," he said. "I could have been convinced if I didn't know the truth."

She sighed. "What do you have to do?"

"Work a healer pattern, the one I've drawn on the cloth."

"How can I help?"

"Just hold my hands."

"How long is this going to take?"

"Do you have somewhere you need to be?"

Apart from rescuing someone I don't even care about? A person I have destroyed my whole life for because I told a few lies? Even as she thought it, she knew that was unfair. She had committed the first crime to save a castle full of people who had enslaved her race. She still wasn't sure why. She could have ignored Sheesha. *Couldn't I?*

"I want to know if I'd be better sitting or kneeling."

"Sit."

It was awkward. She ended up facing him, on his wounded side so that he did not have to stretch his injured arm.

His hands were cold. Or hers warm.

She was aware that Daybian was looking, but then why shouldn't he? There was nothing else happening.

Yenteel began a chant. She did not recognise the language but it was similar to the one he had used before to her. So that meant it was Kadralin. Was there no end to the crimes they would commit together? Forbidden language. Forbidden magic. She might not be invoking the pattern but she was certainly helping.

He had shut his eyes and his words came out slurred. She knew that magic required strength and energy. Would he kill himself in an attempt to heal? He had never fully answered the question of why he had been seeking her out.

His master wanted her. What did that mean?

Then her fingers tingled. It was like the feeling when an arm or leg that had gone to sleep began to recover. She worried. There were stories of creatures that fed on the life patterns of others and drained them for their own sustenance. Was Yenteel one of them? Had he been lying? Was this all a ploy so that she would give herself willingly?

She would rather give herself to Daybian.

She giggled. At first she thought it had been out loud but no one said anything. She was confused. The tingling had crept up her arms.

He was eating her alive.

But she suppressed the panic. It made no sense. He had not chosen to be struck by an arrow. He had almost bled to death. What creature would put itself in so much danger simply to have another meal?

There was a grunting noise above her.

Sheesha.

She had not heard him approach. If his head was over them, he must have come in very close indeed. She realised her eyes were closed too, even though she could see lights moving. Golden threads wove in and out. Periodically new ones would appear from the left or right, or top, or bottom, and dance among the strands already there.

Then she realised what she was seeing.

It was the pattern of the healing. Some of the shapes made by the threads were the same as the ones Yenteel had drawn—but much finer and more complex. And so many more of them, as if the drawn pattern was a simplified version.

The tingling had gone through her and reached down into her belly, just as it also went up to her head where it made a ring of prickles as if her hair were standing on end.

Then the pattern seemed to stop moving. The golden light faded from it but somehow she knew the working was not complete. She did not know what to do. Yenteel must have reached the limit of his strength but it had not been enough. She had to do something.

Why? And even as that word filtered through her mind, she knew it was just another part of her. That part that said she should not care about anyone else because no one cared about her. All she had to do was release Yenteel's hands—now cold like ice—and she would be free of him. He would die and she would need to care no longer.

But I do care.

She had no more reason than that. If she did not care, then she was as bad as all the rest with nothing to commend her. Her life would have no meaning.

She opened her mouth to speak but found it so dry she could say nothing. The fibres of gold dimmed towards the blackness that threatened to engulf them.

Something heavy came down on her shoulder.

And with it, a flood of golden brightness that she feared would blind her. The light flowed into her head and down her body, ran along her arms and out.

Yenteel jerked and his hands almost pulled away from hers but she held on. The pattern that had almost faded from view exploded into life. The threads were alive once more, moving and weaving. If she could have shut her mind's eye she would have done it willingly as the power flowed through her and into Yenteel.

It took mere moments, but seemed like eternity. The pattern was complete. Its image vanished from her mind. She slipped her hands from Yenteel's but the weight on her shoulder remained.

Sheesha grumbled in her ear. She turned and saw one side of his massive jaw resting on her shoulder. His mouth was easily big enough to swallow her entire head, while his teeth, barely a hands-breadth from her eyes, were the length of her fingers. The eye on this side was looking directly at her.

"Thank you," she said quietly.

In an effortless motion, Sheesha lifted his head and grumbled again as he stretched his wings.

"Ow! Get off, idiot."

In the silver light of Lostimal she saw Daybian on his hands and knees with Sheesha's wing directly over him. Whether he had ducked to avoid it or been knocked over she had no idea, but it looked comical.

Then she yawned and a wave of fatigue swept through her. She felt as if she had run a thousand leagues. The dark world around her went fuzzy. She rubbed her eyes, but it didn't help. Then she fell back into the grass and forgot about everything.

The sun was above the trees when she woke. There was a blanket over her and saddlebags under her head. She felt comfortable and relaxed. When she realised the headache she expected wasn't there, she settled back into the saddle bags.

Then she remembered why she expected a headache.

The blanket flew off her and she stood up. Sheesha and Looesa were gone again. Jintan and Shingul were splashing in the pool. Beyond them she could see two men; one of them was Daybian, the other was dark and thin. They appeared to be leaning over the body of the man they had pulled from the water.

Where was Gally?

She turned again. He was beside the smouldering fire, putting down fresh branches.

Everything was calm.

Yenteel? She realised that he was not lying beside her, and immediately after, that he was the gaunt fellow with Daybian.

Everyone was up except her. She sat down. The healing must have been successful. She glanced back at the two. Yenteel was using a branch as a walking stick and his injured arm was still in a sling. Well, they had not attempted to fix that.

She considered what had happened. Romain had never mentioned that the *zirichasa* were strong with magic. She was certain he could not have known. They never exhibited anything like that. They did not have fire-tubes like the *tekrasa*; they did not communicate mind-to-mind like wolves—she had to admit defeat at that point, as her examples ran out. She had no idea what other animals might have magic.

Though she had heard a lot of tales, like monstrous *nachasa* the size of mountains. But she had always dismissed those as imaginative stories to scare young children.

But there was nothing told about the *ziri*. Even when she had spoken to other keepers at the races, they boasted about their charges. Of course, she had done it too. But never had any one of them hinted that *zirichasa* might be capable of some magic or other.

Nobody knew.

Nobody except her. And what did she even know? That Sheesha had touched her and given her energy that she could then pass on to Yenteel so that he could complete his patterning? It was vague, and perhaps she had imagined it. It might have been that the power came from her and she had unleashed it by accident.

Yes. If anybody asked that's what she would say. If she told the truth, who knew what terrible things would happen to the *ziri*? People would try to use them for patternings. They would be cut up and sold in markets as cures for this and that.

She shook her head.

Yenteel had said she was a good liar. So that's what she would do.

She needed to relieve herself but decided her hunger needed assuaging first. There was still some cold cooked meat from yesterday which she helped herself to. She felt guilty for a moment, as if she were stealing it because she had not asked anyone. Then she remembered that the only person she needed to ask was herself —or possibly Sheesha, since he'd caught it. However, he wasn't here and she did not think he would begrudge her a meal.

After taking a handful of the meat, she headed across to the other side of the stream to see what they were discussing.

Daybian was holding the coat she had rescued. He and Yenteel had moved away from the body, which had been gnawed down to the bone. The air above it was filled with flies.

"We shall be heading west," said Daybian as she approached.

"I'm sorry?"

Daybian pointed. "We'll go west."

She gritted her teeth. "I see."

Yenteel looked a dozen years older than he had before.

"I must thank you for your help, Kantees." His voice was also weak but better than it had been.

"I am always pleased to be able to help someone who needs it," she said. "But next time I shall be more careful with patterners. I believe you almost killed me as well as yourself."

"But you had enough strength."

"Barely." *If not for Sheesha, we would both be carrion.*

"In that case my gratitude is redoubled." He tried for a sweeping bow but stumbled in the process and caught himself with the stick only at the last moment.

"Why do you think we should go west?" she said to Yenteel, ignoring Daybian.

"I recognise the coat," said Daybian.

"I asked Yenteel."

"But I knew the answer."

Kantees closed her eyes. Perhaps she was more tired than she thought. One thing was certain, her temper was not good. But, damn it, Daybian had no right.

Why wasn't she saying this out loud? She turned to Daybian.

"You are not in charge of this …" Words failed her.

"What?"

She gestured to Yenteel and then back to where Gally worked on the fire. "Us."

"I do not have to remind you, Kantees, that my family owns—"

"*Be careful what you say right now,*" she hissed. "*Or you just might be* walking *back to your family.*"

"—the *ziri*. My family owns the *zirichasa.*"

"I'm borrowing them."

"You've stolen them."

"Yes," she said. "That's right, I have stolen them so they are not yours any longer. They're mine."

"Perhaps we could discuss this later?" said Yenteel.

Just then Shingul and Jintan let out the booming calls that heralded the return of the hunting pair. Daybian turned in surprise to see them stretching their necks up, mouths open to amplify the call.

"Are they all right?" said Daybian. "Are they ill?"

Kantees found her anger evaporating. At least Daybian was honest in his regard of the *ziri* and he was genuinely concerned.

"Did they make that noise yesterday?" said Yenteel. "I seem to recall it from a dream."

"It means Sheesha and Looesa are on their way back," she said. "I didn't know why either, when they did that yesterday." She scanned the skies and saw the dots.

She pointed. "There."

Despite Kantees' concerns about further delay, she didn't argue about staying another night so Yenteel could gain more strength. Besides, it was late in the day and they wouldn't be able to fly for long.

The blanket that had covered her belonged to Daybian and, while the rest of them slept with the *ziri*—not completely comfortable but warm—he chose not to.

Kantees was tired, but even snuggled under Sheesha's feathers and warmed against his body, she had trouble going to sleep.

Everything suddenly felt overwhelming. The world stretched into forever. Her crimes hung round her neck like a millstone. The power of the *zirichasa* was too important. And the *tekrak* had been too big. And where there was one, there would be more. And with them, the people who had taken Jelamie.

Why had they taken him? He was just an annoying child. He wasn't the heir, merely the spare in case something happened to Daybian.

And Daybian was here, in danger of ending the line of Jakalain by getting himself killed in an attempt to rescue his brother who might already be dead. She did not ask for the responsibility of watching over him. He would probably say that he did not require her to do so.

What am I doing? she asked herself again, who knew how many times in the last few days, and she still didn't have a good answer. In the end, all she could think of was that she was trying to do the right thing. But what right did she have to decide what that was?

She had a painful awakening when Sheesha decided it was time to get up. He rolled onto his rear legs and simply stood. Somehow the rolling motion had invaded her dream as a fall from a great height and she only really woke when she hit the ground. Even then, for a moment, she was not entirely sure what was real and what was not.

Sheesha stretched his wings and shook them out so the feathers aligned properly. He bent his neck backwards and his lower back upwards, all the way from the tip of his nose to the tip of his tail, so he was shaped like a cup. He grunted, relaxed, and brought his head round to look Kantees straight in the face. Every time he did this, for this was not the first, was comical as he focused his wide-spread eyes on her. He looked cross-eyed.

And his breath smelled awful.

"Yes," she said. "We're going."

The rest of the camp was not up but Sheesha prodded the other *ziri*. Jintan snapped at him, then ducked his head when Sheesha rumbled ominously. Looesa tipped Gally onto the grass, but Yenteel was spared such abuse. Once again, Shingul had been lying over him to keep him warm instead of having him lie on her.

Kantees went off to the edge of the wood to do the necessary and then headed up to wash where the stream entered the pool. The sun was not high; they would be able to get a good distance today.

Daybian appeared beside her. He had stripped off his shirt to reveal his pasty white skin. If he thought it would make him more attractive to her, he was sadly mistaken. In truth, it had the opposite effect. She stood up as he bent down to splash the water on his face.

"What's west?" she said.

"What do you mean?"

"Why should we go west? You seemed very sure of yourself."

"That fellow"—he waved his hand in the direction of the corpse still lying out on the grass across the stream—"comes from Kurvin Port."

"How do you know?"

"The design on the coat. He's a Hamalain and, from his age, he'll almost certainly be one of the family. They are very rich and influential in the Conclave. I've met Deenya, the sister, and seen Trimiente, nasty piece of work. This is probably Lorima."

"Well, he was one of the raiders."

"Yes." Daybian stood up and looked at her. "This is dangerous."

She couldn't believe it. Was he serious in thinking she didn't know what situation they were in? "Is it that you think all women are stupid, Daybian? Or just slave women?"

He looked hurt. "I honestly do not understand you, Kantees."

"That, Daybian," she said, "is the first intelligent thing to come out of your mouth."

She realised she was just getting angry again, which meant she was getting off the subject. She took a deep breath and calmed herself down.

"I know this is dangerous, Daybian, even if we find Jelamie. I'm still under a sentence of death."

"Why don't you just run away to the mountains, then?"

"Because I'm responsible," she said. "But afterwards, yes, I might just do that."

"Not everything is your responsibility. You're a slave. Your responsibility ends with the job you do."

She closed her eyes again to help suppress the violence that wanted to erupt from her. He really did not understand. To hear him you would think that being a slave was a lovely life, no need to worry about anything. Except being beaten, whipped, raped, or killed at the whim of your master because you were nothing more than a possession. Like a cheap ceramic cup. If you fell and broke into a thousand pieces it might be a shame in the moment, but it did not matter in the long run. Another could always be bought.

"You are such an idiot, Daybian," she said quietly. "You think you know so much."

They returned to the camp and found Gally saddling the *ziri* even though Kantees had not told him to. The meat from two days ago had been eaten but there was fresh from the previous day's kills. She and Daybian ate in silence.

Sheesha and Looesa were good hunters, and considerate enough to bring food back. That surprised her. As far as she knew Sheesha had been bred in captivity and always had been fed dead animals. He had never needed to catch his own. She did not know about Looesa, but he was so tame she could not imagine he had ever had to hunt.

Yet here they were, experts. And the others knew how to call to them—in ways they had never used at the castle.

Perhaps it had something to do with their magic. It didn't matter —she was not going to discuss it with anyone.

Yenteel was stronger and his skin looked healthier than it had at any time in the last couple of days. He would probably want to perform the healer patterning on his arm again, but for now he seemed happy enough with it in the sling.

"Have you given any thought to how we will enter Kurvin Port?" he said.

"You know about Kurvin Port," said Kantees.

"That's where the Hamalain have their dominion."

"I haven't thought about it," said Kantees. "Since I have only just been told. Obviously we cannot fly in but neither can we leave the *ziri* on their own."

"Gally can look after them," said Gally.

She smiled at him. "I know, Gally, and I trust you. But it's not out of concern for the *ziri*, it's about people who might find them."

"Gally doesn't like people." He frowned.

"I know something of the place," said Yenteel. "The mountains come almost down to the sea all around and Kurvin Port itself is in a wide bay with cliffs around it. There are farms on the slopes that supply it."

"That's nice."

"But the cliffs run for leagues along the coast on that side with hundreds of small bays, and many of those have fishing villages."

"Fishing villages may not be as bad as Kurvin Port," she said. "But we still can't fly into them."

"I can," said Daybian.

"But we can't."

As if attempting to forestall another argument, Yenteel cut in. "The cliffs have caves. We just need to find a bay that doesn't have a village, but does have a cave, that's close to Kurvin Port. The *zirichasa* can remain there with Gally while we go into the town."

"I am not clear on our plan when we've arrived," said Kantees. "Just because we know what family the man came from, how does that get us any closer to finding Jelamie?"

"I think," said Yenteel, "we will have to see what happens."

"We can enter the town with you two as my servants," said Daybian. "I can talk to the Hamalain as an equal. I'll report the death of this brother and then we can find out what he was doing raiding the Jakalain."

Kantees watched in amusement as even Daybian realised that wasn't going to work. She looked at the sun crossing the sky.

"That's enough of a plan," she said, "until we can find out more."

There was a short discussion when Daybian still thought he was going to ride Sheesha. But it was the *ziri* himself who settled that by walking up and standing behind Kantees. She could not resist a grin at Daybian's expense.

That Shingul would carry Yenteel was a foregone conclusion, as she seemed to have adopted him. Gally already had the reins of Looesa. Even Daybian did not have the heart to deliberately upset the lad. So he rode old Jintan again.

"He's a remarkably strong *zirichak* for his age," said Daybian as he mounted and gave Jintan's neck an affectionate thump.

Kantees double-checked Yenteel's saddle buckles because he had been almost unconscious the previous time he had flown and she was not sure how he might react now he was truly awake.

"There is no need to mother me, Kantees," he said for her ears only.

"How would you know?" she said. "You have no experience of *ziri*, you do not know what is right or wrong. You are in no position to judge."

Once more, he had no answer but gave her a nod in acknowledgement.

Whether it was something the *ziri* did without thinking she did not know, but they had arranged themselves on the ground in a diamond shape. Sheesha was at the head, Looesa and Shingul ranged to the left and right behind, and Jintan waited in the rear.

She gave Sheesha a little kick. He spread his powerful wings and stroked them downward. He lifted effortlessly. Wingbeat after wingbeat pushed them upward and she thrilled once more at the sensation as the ground dropped away.

Looking behind she saw the others in exactly the same formation as they had been on the ground. She had noticed it before but with the new revelations about the creatures, she saw it with new eyes. The only thing that did not match were their wingbeats.

She let Sheesha choose their flying height once she had pointed him in the right direction—or the best approximation of 'the right direction' she could manage. She still did not know how big Esternes was and the trouble with using a patterner's path—direct travel from ley-circle to ley-circle—was that it gave no indication of the true distance.

In the past, when they had gone to the races, they had always gone by the path. The patterners would chant and inscribe their patterns on the ground to create an invisible gate, you walked into the gate and through the World's Pattern until you reached the gate at the end. The strangest thing about the journey was that you never knew how long it would take.

Even the journey from her old master to Jakalain had been by ley-circle. Her old master had maps but he kept them locked up because they were so valuable.

So, the matter of the size of Esternes was important. How long would it take for a *ziri* to cross it?

The wood where they had camped was swiftly lost to view. The ground appeared flat but it was an undulating surface cut by streams and rivers that flowed from the mountains. Yenteel had said the mountains went to the edge of the sea, so if they followed the mountains they would also reach the sea. Then they could follow the cliffs.

Or they could ask someone.

Villages, sometimes fewer than a dozen buildings grouped together, dotted the landscape. Now that they were travelling in daylight she could see that each village was surrounded by a high fence—which also enclosed areas for animals. Beyond the walls, in almost every case, were herds of *fenichasa* with men, sometimes boys, guarding them.

Just as she looked down, the herdsmen and the people in the villages looked up at the four *ziri* passing across the sky. She wondered what those people thought. Did they see the riders? They must. Sheesha was not flying very high and it was easy enough to see the people down there, so Kantees, Gally, Yenteel, and Daybian must be clearly visible.

Not that it mattered. It would be days before any of these people could pass on a message to someone who mattered even if they wanted to.

Then there was forest.

Almost as if there was a line across the land. Nothing lay below them but trees, and packed so close together only the tops were visible. The undulating green was cut by the occasional wide river. Birds and other flying creatures populated the upper reaches of the trees but what lay below she had no idea.

The sun told her it was getting towards midday. The *ziri* had been flying all that time and must be getting tired. But they were still over the forest, which now stretched from horizon to horizon in all directions except to the north, where the mountains grew out of the green.

She began to look in earnest for a place to land.

None of the rivers seemed to have any islands and she was concerned about what nasty things might live in their waters. Her time with the scholar had educated her enough that she knew no place in the world was free of creatures that would like to eat you.

She would have preferred an open hilltop, so they could at least see when an enemy was approaching, but the trees covered everything.

"Hey!"

It was Yenteel. She turned and saw him pointing off towards the mountains. She peered in that direction and saw what looked like a gap in the trees. He must have been thinking the same thing.

She made Sheesha wheel that way, confident the others would follow. It was a gap, large and circular. Suddenly this did not look like a good idea. As they closed in on it, she could see the trees growing around its edge were twisted and discoloured. The ground itself was devoid of any life. Not a single plant or animal that she could see.

"Ley-circle!" she shouted back and shook her head. "Not safe."

"No feeding!"

She frowned. How could he know that? The feeding at Jakalain had been barely three days ago and it was unlikely there would be another conjunction so close. But she knew from her time at her first master's house that it was more complicated than that; sometimes feedings did happen within a day of each other, though never in the same place. Questions about feedings were frequent and Kevrey would turn most of them away. It was dangerous territory.

She made the decision and put Sheesha into a descent towards the circle. Not the middle, but not too close to the edge. Who knew what pattern-corrupted abominations might be lurking among the distorted trees?

1 8

The fact that Sheesha and the other *ziri* did not seem concerned at landing in the ley-circle gave Kantees some confidence. Perhaps magical creatures would be able to sense trouble.

The surface of the circle was damp soil. It must have rained recently. The Taymalin always put stone down in their circles—preferably the hardest stone they could find, because it resisted the warping in all but the biggest circles. But this one must be unknown to the Taymalin, and perhaps anyone else. She and her companions might have been the first people ever to set foot here.

If anything went wrong they might also be the last. A part of her mind suggested that perhaps they were not the first and the bones of the others were here too, perhaps just beneath the surface. Or blasted to dust by the power of a feeding.

As soon as Looesa had landed, Gally set about removing his saddle and other tack. She almost stopped him but the *ziri* needed to eat and they could not hunt while saddled. So she followed suit with Sheesha while keeping an eye on Yenteel, who was slowly unbuckling himself.

Instead of removing Jintan's saddle, Daybian drew his short sword and prowled around them as if he was looking for trouble. In this she neither blamed him nor wanted him to stop. This was an unsettling place.

It was unnerving to know that, every once in a while, a pillar of white light would descend from the heavens into this space and everything within it would be consumed. No one truly knew what happened. Anything too close was changed and twisted. Yet it was not a malignant force. This was the power of the healers and the patterners, but in such quantity that the patterns of everything within its reach were changed. Or died.

As soon as they were free, Sheesha, Jintan, and Looesa leapt into the air. The closeness of the trees meant they were soon out of sight.

Kantees went to where Yenteel stood, leaning against Shingul's body.

"Do you know where we are?" she said.

He shook his head. "Not precisely. However, this is most likely the Talamyrth, the forest that covers Esternes to the west and south. It would make sense."

"And this ley-circle?"

"I don't know. There are many circles that are not used by people and this one is inaccessible."

"A patterner could make a path to it."

"Only if he knew what he was looking for."

She sighed. "I don't like it." Then she looked at the twisted wall of trees. "And I'm scared of what's out there."

"That is wise," he said.

"Not very encouraging."

"It wasn't meant to be. Only a fool would not be afraid. Even our friend Daybian is not that much of a fool."

Daybian looked up as he heard his name. Kantees scowled at him and he looked away, scanning the trees again.

"What if there's a feeding?"

"There won't be."

"How can you say that?"

Yenteel reached into his bag, glanced once in Daybian's direction, then pulled out a circular device. It had wheels within wheels. He turned it, lining up sections.

"You can't have that," Kantees hissed.

It was Yenteel's turn to look surprised. "You know what it is?"

"I know owning it means death."

"Well, we've already committed enough crimes to be hanged six times over," said Yenteel. "And this tells me there isn't another feeding for several days. Chances are the next one will not be in our lands at all."

"When you say *our* lands, do you mean the Taymalin or the Kadralin?"

"There is not much difference, since the Taymalin occupy all the Kadralin lands."

Kantees looked up towards the mountains. "But not there."

Yenteel turned and followed her gaze, then shook his head. "There is nothing there, Kantees. The centre of Esternes is not habitable by the likes of us. Only the giant *sikechasa* live there, and the prey they feed on."

"I heard our people are free there."

"Tales made to give us hope. More likely you would find the *Slissac* alive and well and crawling about in their holes."

"You have no hope, then?"

"I don't believe in children's stories, Kantees. I believe in what I can sense." For a moment he hesitated. She could see the decision being made on his face, until he said, more quietly, "And I believe in you."

A wave of fear shot through her and she turned away. "I don't want to know."

"Kantees ..." He put his hand on her shoulder.

She shrugged it off, took a step away and turned on him. "Leave me alone."

The sudden movement and her words attracted Daybian's attention and she looked skyward as he strode over.

"What's wrong, Kantees? Does this slave need putting in his place?"

"Shut up. This has nothing to do with you."

She glared at them both. Yenteel with a pleading look on his face, and Daybian both angry and confused. Then she saw Gally looking over.

"Just leave me alone," she said. "This is hard enough without you two confusing things. You." She looked at Yenteel. "I don't want to know why you were at Jakalain and I am certainly not interested in your master's interpretation of the World's Pattern. And you." This time she addressed Daybian. "Stop trying to protect me. You don't own me and I do not want your help."

She turned away and walked a few paces but it took her closer to the maze of trees and she was forced to stop. There was nowhere she could go to be out of their sight. If only Sheesha would return. She could climb into his saddle and leave them behind.

Except she wouldn't. She couldn't.

The other *ziri* would follow Sheesha and she would not abandon these people. Especially not Gally.

So instead she stared into the darkness beyond the exposed trees. Not that they looked much like trees. Their trunks and branches were split with holes through them and, instead of simply growing up to where their leaves could catch the sunlight, they grew in every direction. She followed one branch from where it split off a trunk to where it fed into another one, as if it was one branch for two trees.

Perhaps this was not a bad thing. It meant the confused mass made a barrier against anything large. But then her experience with the *chakisa*-like creatures had shown her that even small could be dangerous in sufficient numbers.

Her skin crawled at the thought of what might be lurking out there. And as she stared, a shadow moved in the dark beyond. A limb of something blocked out a stray light that had managed to pierce the trees, and then revealed it again.

She shuddered.

She did not dare turn her back and, even though she felt a fool, she took steps backwards, keeping her eyes on the spot where she had seen the movement.

We can't stay here overnight. Her shadow was lengthening but she knew without having to check the sky that they still had a good amount of light left.

Something touched her shoulder.

She jumped.

"Sorry," said Yenteel. "You seemed worried."

"Nearly jumped out of my skin, you idiot. You could have just said something."

"The last time I said something you jumped down my throat."

"There's something moving in the dark," she said.

"The place is alive."

"What do you mean?"

"I simply mean this is a forest and there are living things out there. It can't be considered a surprise that there would be things moving in the dark. It doesn't mean they are dangerous to us."

"Something in the forest will be able to kill us."

"That's always true, Kantees. The world is not safe."

"Do you know how much cooked meat we have left?"

"Is that my job? Am I the keeper of the provisions?"

She sighed. "Can you just tell me whether you know or not?"

"I don't."

"Fine."

Kantees turned away from the forest and headed for the pile of belongings. She noted that Gally had already helped himself to a strip of meat and was chewing it. She checked the rest. It was enough for another day, more if they were careful. Daybian might not appreciate short rations but the rest of them would not complain.

Yenteel had spent some time looking into the trees where she had indicated but then joined her. Daybian appeared to have given up patrolling and sat down with his back against Shingul, who did not seem to mind.

"We're moving on as soon as Sheesha and Looesa get back," she said without preamble.

"We should rest them," said Daybian.

"It's not safe here."

"As safe as anywhere else, Kantees," said Yenteel. "We can't know that we'll find anywhere else to set down before dark."

"There is no wood for a fire," she said. "And no way to fetch any through the trees. They are all grown together, with only enough space for a *chakik*. Even if we dared go into that wood, which I do not."

That stopped them. She knew she was being driven by her fear but she had to make them see that they could not stay here.

"I'm sure I could break off some branches," said Daybian.

"Be my guest," she said. "We have no tools so you would have to climb into that. Whatever it is that's there will be able to grab you, or bite you, or sting you, or just eat you whole."

"I am not afraid, Kantees," said Daybian.

"That's because you're too stupid to have an imagination!" she said, and instantly wished she hadn't when the look of hurt crossed his face.

"You think I am *stupid*?"

"No, I—"

"You think I'm stupid," he said. "Now I understand. That's why you wouldn't lie with me."

"*What?* You're still talking about that?" She took a deep breath. "I am sorry I called you stupid. I was angry. I have already told you why I will not lie with you, but if you insist I'll say it again. I am not interested in you. You may have been my master but that still doesn't mean I would wish you to have your way with me. But don't take it personally, it's not you. I don't want anybody."

Yenteel and Gally were staring at her. She immediately felt herself flushing with embarrassment. How had they got onto this subject? Oh yes, Daybian and his inability to think with anything except his loins.

"When Sheesha, Looesa and Jintan get back we will give the *ziri* enough time to eat and digest their food. Then we are leaving."

"And if it's dark by then?" said Yenteel.

"We'll either be dead or we'll be leaving. And that's final."

The *zirichasa* did not seem to mind flying at night so there was no reason they should not do it again. Sheesha would understand.

There was nothing to be done while they waited. They were hedged in by the trees and the ground was bare and uninteresting. Only the clouds above their heads had any degree of variety, so Kantees lay down with her head on a saddle and stared up at the slow-moving shapes against the blue sky.

It was hot but there was no shade. Or rather the only shade that existed—cast by Shingul's body—had been taken by Daybian and then Yenteel. She did not begrudge the injured man since he needed his rest. But she was not happy with Daybian. He did it as if it was his birthright, his privilege. In other circumstances, back at Jakalain, he would be right, but not now and not here.

She dozed off to be woken with a start by Shingul booming into the sky.

The sun had moved and was low in the sky. Had they had trouble finding food? She hoped they had not exhausted themselves. They dropped three animals, two of which were four-legged like the ones they had caught before. The third, carried by Sheesha, was another winged creature, almost half his size. This one had a beak, so was not a *ziri* but just a large bird. It might have good meat. But they couldn't do anything with it apart from cut it up.

Sheesha strutted around after he landed. Kantees smiled. She had seen him do that before when he had almost won a race. The other racing *ziri* did it too. He must be proud of himself. Then she saw the blood on his side.

She ran over to him and pushed the feathers out of the way. A gash in his side was leaking blood. She felt around the wound and dug her fingers into his muscle. The cut wasn't too deep and did not seem to have affected his ability to fly but he was limping a little.

"You idiot," she said to him. "You had to take something that wanted to fight back. Next time just grab a fledgling. Or a shellfish —you love those." All *ziri* did, drove them wild, although they didn't get them much in Jakalain.

She looked at the sun and back at the wound. And felt her plans coming crashing down.

"Yenteel, can you heal this?"

He came over and examined the damage, and then Sheesha. "We haven't got anything big enough to mark the pattern."

"We can't stay here."

"Then you must make Sheesha fly," he said and then looked at the other *ziri*. Looesa and Jintan were already curled up while Shingul tore chunks out of one of the carcasses. "But while I may not be as experienced as you with *zirichasa*, they look tired."

Mother's milk. He was right, of course. She just didn't want to admit it.

"I can try to put up a ward," he said. "But it would have to be big and I don't know if I have the strength to activate it."

"I can help," she said.

He nodded but still seemed unsure.

"How much power does it need?"

"It would need to be big enough to enclose everyone," he said, "and last all through the night."

"I thought ley-circles were the sources of power," she said and he stared at her.

"They are."

"We're standing in a big one."

"Yes," he said and looked down then grinned. "We are."

"What do you need?"

"I have to be able to draw an exact pattern in a circle."

"Where do you need to draw it?"

"In the ground."

Kantees looked up. "Daybian, lend Yenteel your sword."

"I will not. You called me stupid."

"Stop behaving like a child. He needs to be able to create a pattern that will protect us through the night."

"So now I'm a child?"

"*Kisharuk's curse!* Just give him your milk-sucking sword!"

She stalked off to where Gally sat staring at the trees.

"Bad things in trees, Kantees."

"I know, Gally. Yenteel needs your help to draw a big circle so he can make a pattern that will protect us."

"You said we fly away," he said.

"I did say that, but Sheesha got into a fight and he has a nasty scratch. So we have to stay."

"Gally will help."

"Thank you, Gally. Be quick."

Kantees did not know how long it would take to make the circle but she was sure that whatever was in the trees would come out the moment the clearing was as dark as it was in the forest. Perhaps sooner.

19

The sun was brushing the top of the trees on the west side of the circle. And Yenteel was busy working with the sword, scratching patterns into the dry soil.

She wondered how accurate he needed to be. He had spent several minutes trying to find the centre of the ley-circle itself, though he had done that by eye. The point he chose looked right to her though it may have been off a little, and there he made a hole in the ground to mark the place. Not only did nothing live in the ley-circle, there were no stones. As if everything had been pulverised to dust.

Meanwhile Kantees had untied one set of reins to use in drawing the pattern. Gally held one end in the hole while Yenteel stretched it taut and used the sword to mark the first circle. Then they did it again but with the reins shortened by the length of his forearm. The next stage was to mark off twelve equal segments between the two circles, which was a matter of trial and error.

After that it was just Yenteel making patterns, using the sword as a stylus, in each of the segments. Although he was working with large symbols it seemed to take forever as the sun descended.

She tried to pretend it was her imagination when she saw movement in the trees on the west side, in the deepest shade. But Gally noticed and pointed. Kantees looked at Daybian, who was staring in the same direction. Then he glanced at Yenteel with his sword, obviously wishing he had it instead.

Only the *ziri* seemed unconcerned because the three who had gone hunting were now asleep, but Shingul did seem to be keeping an eye on the movement. Perhaps they were being cautious too. Creatures of their size did not have many enemies but Kantees would be upset if they chose to fly away in the event of an attack.

She hoped it wouldn't come to that.

And what would happen if they were inside the protection but Sheesha decided he had been provoked and wanted to fight again? In some ways he seemed to be a typical male, though she liked him a good deal more than Daybian, and even Yenteel.

She was aware it was pointless worrying over things she could not control. But knowing that did not help at all.

By the time Yenteel was on the penultimate segment, the sun's light was only brushing the tops of the trees. The movement in the trees was constant, though she could not see what was there. It was as if the shadows themselves had come alive.

If they were going to trust the pattern they needed to get inside it now.

"Daybian, fetch your sleeping blanket." He opened his mouth to speak. "Don't argue, please, just do it. Gally, collect all the tack together. We need to get it into the pattern."

While that was happening, she went to Sheesha and gently woke him by repeating his name into his ear. Just like any person, Sheesha did not like to be woken suddenly. That had been a painful lesson to learn and she rubbed her cheek unconsciously.

The big *ziri* woke the other two. There was a flurry of shadows and a skittering noise she had not heard before. Clearly the sight of four big *zirichasa* wide awake was upsetting to their observers. Sheesha gave a low growl in the direction of the trees.

"Lay the blanket over the lines in the last segment," she said to Daybian. "Then we need to move everything inside. Try not to step on the lines."

She knew they should have done that earlier but she didn't want to crowd Yenteel. There wasn't going to be a great deal of space with four people, four *ziri*, and their gear.

The first attempt at getting Sheesha into the pattern was a disaster. In the air he was perfection, but on land he was clumsy and immediately dragged the blanket across the ground, obliterating the markings.

Kantees went numb staring at the gap. Having been about to start on that last segment, Yenteel stopped and stared at the damage. Then up at Kantees.

"I can still see the lines," he said, though his voice was strained.

"Gally! Get the tack back on the *ziri*. Just enough to fly them. Daybian, you keep moving everything else into the pattern."

She pulled Sheesha across to the saddle and threw it on his back.

The shadows were moaning.

As she fastened and tightened the buckles round his body, Sheesha growled and hissed at the shapes in the dark. She did not stop to see if it had any effect but had to yank his head down to get the bridle in place.

"I've finished," called Daybian.

"Fly Sheesha into the pattern. Hurry."

Daybian ran over to her and grabbed the reins. He pulled himself up.

"Don't touch the lines," she said.

He held her gaze for a moment and nodded.

The blast from Sheesha's wings blew her off balance and for a terrified moment she thought it might have scrubbed the pattern, but it looked undamaged. Yenteel was working on the final segment, having scratched the marks afresh through the places where they had been obliterated.

Gally had Jintan ready.

She wasn't sure what to do. Gally was no rider. He just sat on the *ziri*'s back and let it follow the rest.

"Do Looesa," she said and hurried to Shingul just as Daybian brought Sheesha down lightly into the pattern. Kantees shook her head. How could they all fit into the space? Daybian was off in a trice and got Sheesha to back up to the edge of the markings, then lie down with his tail circled around him.

Kantees made the mistake of looking into the shadows. As the sun went down her eyes had adjusted and now she could see what watched them. They looked like men. If men were covered in hair. And they were getting into the ley-circle by climbing over the wall of interconnected trees. Some of them carried clubs and they were heading slowly towards her and the pattern.

She tore her eyes away from the scene and back to the job in hand.

There isn't enough time.

"Kantees, I'm ready!" shouted Yenteel just as Daybian leapt out of the pattern and ran for Jintan. Gally was tightening the reins on Looesa, but froze as he saw the figures coming slowly towards them. She heard him cry in fear. By then, Daybian was into the saddle and kicking the old *zirichak* into the air.

"Gally! Go to Yenteel. Now!" She put everything she had into the command. He looked at her. She pointed forcefully.

"But Kantees…"

"Go!" He went, at a run.

Kantees stared. There was no time to get Shingul's tack buckled on.

"Kantees!" shouted Daybian from above. "Leave them. They can fly."

But where would they go? They needed to rest somewhere safe. Assuming Yenteel could get his pattern to work. She saw Jintan coming down in the middle of it. She had to admit Daybian was an excellent rider, despite all his other—many—faults.

"Yenteel, do it." She forced her voice to calm. "Come on, Shingul."

Kantees sprinted across to Looesa and jumped into the saddle. No time to buckle in. The figures were close and the noise of their moans, which seemed to be resolving into some sort of chant, increased.

Looesa snapped at them. In answer, one of them swung a club. The *ziri* evaded it easily, but there were more coming.

"Up, Looesa! Come on, Shingul!"

Looesa stretched his neck upwards; his wings beat hard and he lifted into the air in spurts that drove them from the ground. She clung to the reins. Gally had done his job right and they were firm. She glanced back. Shingul had lifted from the ground. A club buzzed past her head.

She almost cried out in anger and frustration. Damn these things! Why weren't they as stupid as … Daybian. A blue glow flooded the ley-circle. The inscribed pattern lit up. She prayed that either it did not reach as high as her, or that Yenteel's conjuration was not yet complete.

With a movement of the reins she guided Looesa over the glowing light and tried to make him drop vertically. There was little enough room below; *ziri* did not land straight down unless there was no space. As far as Looesa could see he had plenty of room despite the creatures closing in on all sides. He flew beyond the confines of the pattern. She pulled him round.

They liked to gain height using spirals, so why not land the same way? It would have to be a very tight spiral.

She pulled the right rein hard in and leaned her weight over to the right, unbalancing Looesa. He turned into it but she kept it tight and he descended, almost turning on his right wingtip. Kantees hoped Shingul was following.

Below her Yenteel was kneeling on the unmarked dirt just inside the inner circle of the pattern, with his hands palms-down by the final segment he had drawn. She could not imagine how much pain his injured arm must be in. Sheesha and Jintan were standing and snapping aggressively at the incoming figures while Daybian was being jerked between both their reins, one in each hand, as he kept them from leaving the pattern.

The glow intensified suddenly and a wall of blue erupted around them. Looesa's wing caught on it. He lost all forward motion and fell the remaining distance to crash down in front of Sheesha's head. Another pile of feathers landed directly on top of Daybian.

All noise from outside ceased but there were plenty of angry squawks and shouts from the animals and humans inside. Kantees slipped off Looesa's back onto the hard earth facing the wall of blue light. She could see through it, as if it were blue glass, but it did not distort what was beyond.

The creatures had stopped a short distance away.

Worried, she got to her feet and went across to where Yenteel knelt. She went down beside him. There was a look of concentration on his face.

"It's working, Yenteel."

He said nothing.

"Will it hold?"

Again he said nothing, almost as if he did not hear her. She reached out and put her hand on his bare forearm. Instantly she felt her essence draining, just as it had done before when he had healed himself.

They could not survive the night if he had to keep it going. Surely he had said that it would use the power from the ley-circle? But as she thought about it, he had not said that. Did he expect her to be able to provide magic?

She called out to Sheesha and almost at the same moment his head came down beside her. She put her other hand on his neck and felt his power. So much of it. Like a bottomless well. And she was the conduit. It flowed through her into Yenteel.

The look of desperation on Yenteel's face relaxed and the blue light increased in strength. For a moment she felt a greater power even than Sheesha. Then Yenteel pulled his hands from the wall of blue.

She gasped in fear that it would collapse. But it stayed.

And then Sheesha was just Sheesha. She let go of Yenteel's arm and he put his other back in its sling. The creatures beyond the wall did not seem to want to come too close. Perhaps there was just too much light for them here.

She reached out and touched the blue wall. It was neither hot nor cold and she could not see what she was pressing her finger against. The surface was unyielding but perfectly smooth.

"We did it," she said and looked round. They were all here, all the people and all the *ziri*. "Thank you, Yenteel."

He grinned as he touched the wall himself and ran his fingers from side to side across its surface.

"I've never done one this big," he said as if he was in awe. "I wasn't even sure it would draw magic from the ley-circle itself."

"You knew what to do," she said. "If it wasn't for you, we would be dead."

"And me," said Daybian.

"And Gally," said Gally.

Sheesha grunted.

2 0

When dawn crawled into the sky the creatures seem to melt away with it. Although it was easy to see them crawling across the upper branches of the trees and out into the darkness beyond.

The *ziri* had slept—and snored—just as Gally, Yenteel, and Daybian had.

But Kantees only dozed. She would drift off and then come awake as the thought of the horde beyond the insubstantial wall crept into her dreams. As the night wore on it became hot and stuffy in their protected space, as if the air itself were turning stale. That stopped her sleeping too. There had been a time when she had been locked in a box with no air. It was not something she recalled with any clarity but it came into her nightmares.

The coming of daylight was a relief even if she felt so tired she could drop off again. And the air was such she hardly felt as if she could breathe.

The ward itself seemed as strong as ever and it went up until it blurred into the sky. If she had not got Looesa and Shingul inside it when she did, they would have been trapped outside, and forced to find somewhere to spend the night in that forest.

She wondered about the manlike things. Were they people who

had been distorted by the power of the feeding? She was curious but it was a mystery she was happy to leave unsolved.

One of the *ziri* shat and the stench filled the space.

"Yenteel," she said, shaking him. "Do you know how to stop it? We need to get out, we need fresh air."

It took longer than she expected for him to wake up. At first, he did not seem to remember where he was.

Finally she got him to the wall.

"Do what you have to do," she said. Behind her the *ziri* were waking and stretching their necks so their heads were up high. That seemed to rouse them. They dipped their heads but every now and then would stretch up to breathe.

Yenteel had his hands against the wall but nothing was happening.

"Yenteel!"

She knew she was panicking but her lungs weren't taking in air. Daybian was still lying on the ground, not having stirred despite all the activity.

"It should stop," panted Yenteel. "I put my sigil into the pattern."

"What are you saying?" said Kantees and realised she was clenching and relaxing her hands over and over. The panic made her icy inside even though she was sweating.

"I can't stop it."

Kantees looked over at Daybian's body. He must have succumbed already. Gally was sitting up but looked confused. Sheesha was stretching up and breathing deeply. Whatever was in the air must be down here and not up there. If they had something to make the air move, it might help.

"Sheesha!" she called and when he looked at her, she flapped her arms. It must have looked ridiculous. Yenteel probably thought she had lost her mind.

"Sheesha!" she called again, more insistently. And beat her arms. He looked at her with an infuriating lack of understanding. The other *ziri* looked too. It was Shingul who stood up on her back legs and, despite the lack of space beat her wings. A breeze of fresher air wafted down to Kantees and with it her panic faded.

"Yes! Shingul, that's right!" Like a maniac Kantees flapped her arms harder and faster. Shingul copied her and air began to circulate. As if he was not to be outdone by some female, Sheesha did the same. Soon the space inside the walls was filled with beating wings and the air freshened noticeably. Kantees' tiredness left her and Gally started to laugh. Yenteel seemed to pull himself together and tried the wall again.

This time it flickered but still did not fall.

He shook his head. "I don't have the strength to reach the pattern."

On the floor, Daybian coughed and breathed deeply. Kantees knew this was temporary; eventually even this new air would be used up.

"Have you ever heard of something like this before?" she said.

"Never but I did not study in the halls of the patterners."

Of course not, he was Kadralin. If only she had been willing to stretch Sheesha instead of waiting. If only she had not been persuaded by the assurances of a man who knew nothing of the place they were in. If only she had trusted her own judgement. And now they would be killed by their own protection.

It was the milk of the Mother itself. It was not evil but so powerful it could destroy without intention.

Daybian was standing now and seemed to have understood their predicament. He pulled out his sword and struck the wall. It did nothing except hurt his hand, but he did it again anyway. And again. Kantees ducked beneath Shingul's beating wings and laid her hand on his.

"Stop."

She could see the depth of fear in his eyes. She looked at the flat blade of the sword and the end, blunted and scratched from its use yesterday as a writing tool.

She grabbed Daybian by the wrist. "Come with me."

She dragged him across the circle to Yenteel. "Can you cast the same ward on the sword?"

Yenteel frowned. "I don't ..."

"This pattern." She gestured around them. "Can you put it on the sword and do whatever you do to trigger it?"

"I suppose so."

"Do it," she said. "Now."

"Charcoal will not write on steel."

"We have water."

"They won't mix."

She hesitated for only a moment and then went to Yenteel's bag and fetched his eating bowl, then took out her knife. Kneeling beside the bowl, and after only a moment's contemplation of the pain to come, she sliced the blade across her palm. Both the men made a noise of surprise, and then Daybian knelt beside her.

As her blood dripped into the bowl, he cut himself too.

Then Yenteel joined them and his blood flowed, too. After he judged they had enough, Yenteel crumbled one of his charcoal sticks into the pot and stirred it up with the knife, pummelling the lumps as he found them. The mixture thickened. Using the knife as his stylus, Yenteel inscribed the pattern around and along the sword blade.

The air was getting hotter again, and the *ziri* had given up beating their wings. They were all tired.

The process of inscription did not take very long and when Yenteel took hold of the sword hilt, Kantees put her hand on his. "Activate the ward and perhaps we can push the sword into the wall. Then you can do what you need to stop it."

Yenteel did not argue. Moments later a blue fire licked across the length of the blade. This time, it was powered by only the strength of Yenteel himself.

Together they pressed the point against the wall but still it did not want to move.

"This is my sword," said Daybian and added his hand to theirs. He pushed and the steel slid into the blue.

Moments later the wall evaporated as if it had never been, and they fell forwards across the pattern inscribed into the dusty ground.

The fresh air revived them and even though no one said anything, Kantees knew they all wanted to be away from this place. After some water and the last of the meat, having ensured the *zirichasa* were properly buckled for the journey, they took to the skies, heading west again where clouds were piling up from their grey undersides to the brilliant white tops.

Kantees was not happy. She had nearly killed them all twice over. First, with the bad decision about staying at the ley-circle, and then nearly suffocating them with the pattern she helped Yenteel create. One side of her said she could not have known that either choice was a bad one. But that was the point: She had no idea. How could she make any decisions if she did not know all the facts?

The forest streamed below them. An unending carpet of green. Then the sky filled with the clouds and a strong wind buffeted the *ziri*. They were being knocked backwards and forwards, and occasionally they would fall. As if the air was gone from under their wings.

And finally, to add insult to injury, the rain came. Not a drizzle but a downpour that soaked her through in a moment. Sheesha slowed down. Kantees knew from experience that the water just rolled off the *ziri* feathers, but it could not be easy flying through this. The air grew cold and she shivered.

The intensity of the rain increased and the world became a cocoon of grey around them. She could see neither the clouds above nor the forest below, nor anything to either side. She urged Sheesha to descend and he obeyed. A glance behind showed the others following in formation. Peering through the rain, she got the idea that Jintan was labouring. He was the oldest, after all. Would he give up or would he keep flying until his strength gave out and he simply fell from the sky?

She could not allow that to happen.

She pushed Sheesha into a sharper dive. They had been flying at the height the *zirichasa* seemed to like, which meant they were not too far from the ground—but high enough that a fall would be deadly. Still, it would not do to come down so fast that they ran into something.

She eased Sheesha back a little so the dive was less steep. The buffeting from the wind decreased as they came down.

The rain was a constant hiss in her ears but now she thought she heard something else: a rhythmic roar, not a perfect regular pattern, but one that came and went. There was a shout from Yenteel. She could not make out the words but instinctively she pulled up Sheesha's head.

The roar seemed to be behind them now.

Below them, she could see the darker grey she took for the top of the trees. And the speed with which it was moving surprised her. From the feel of the wind—and rain—on her face she had assumed they were travelling quite slowly, but the ground was rushing past.

"Too far!"

That's what Yenteel's new shout sound like. Too far? What did that mean?

She looked over her shoulder at him. He was making a big gesture with his good arm, as if he wanted her to turn round. She would have to find somewhere to land so they could talk. Had he seen such a place back there?

Pulling back on the reins again, she tried to slow Sheesha even more but he did not respond. Instead he just descended.

The tops of the trees looked wrong as they grew closer. They did not resolve into leaves and branches. The grey was a moving mass of water. The sea! And barely a *ziri*'s wingspan below them. Fear gripped her again. The Isle of Esternes bordered a sea that was so huge they might travel for days across it before encountering an island or any other land.

Yenteel had known. The sound she had heard must have been waves crashing onto the shore. The good news was that it meant they had not travelled far beyond the coastline, but she could see nothing. How could she be sure they were heading in the right direction?

The waves—more correctly, the swell—was running in towards the land. That was why she thought their speed was greater than it was. Sheesha had refused to go any slower because he would have fallen out of the sky if he had. But that meant they could follow the swell back to land. It might not be the most direct line but it should work.

She pulled Sheesha up until they were at a more comfortable height and started the turn. Not too abrupt, because the others had to follow. Yenteel had ceased to shout at her which was a relief.

Once Sheesha was moving with the swell beneath, she let him have his head and he made strong strokes for the shore.

The rain continued to pour down and it was still impossible to see anything ahead. Yenteel had said the whole coastline was cliffs, which meant they would either have to climb fast or land on the beach. As long as she was prepared, that would be fine.

It wasn't long before she heard the booming of the waves. She reined Sheesha in once more. What would they land on—a sandy beach, or rocks?

A dark shape loomed out of the greyness ahead below them. She peered down, expecting to see a rock in the water but its lines were smooth curves. A sharp end curved round to the other where it was cut off. A boat!

Another, bigger, dark shape emerged.

Kantees gasped and kicked Sheesha into a climb though he was already doing it. They scraped over the top of a mast. Then boats were everywhere, there was barely an open stretch of water. They crossed a spit of land against which the sea beat its endless drum.

The rain thinned and they burst through into light under a grey sky.

Boats lined the quay, and on the stone streets people went to and fro, hundreds of them, thousands even. Houses stacked up in a great curve from left to right. Streets went up the cliffs behind in zig-zags where houses had been placed on every precarious point.

All their earlier planning of what they would do when they reached Kurvin Port evaporated like rain on a hot stone. The people of Kurvin Port turned and stared at the four massive *ziri* and their riders, who had arrived out of the sea mists.

21

They would never be able to enter the town in secret now. She turned round as far as she could so she could see Yenteel and Daybian. She was willing to take any idea now that she had messed up again. Three times in two days she could have got them killed.

Yenteel looked to be at a loss. Daybian was scanning the tops of the cliffs, and after a moment he pointed up and to the right. She looked and saw an enormous building, constructed from a reddish stone, dominating the entirety of Kurvin Port.

He could not be serious. She shook her head.

"Yes!" he shouted. "Only choice!"

She didn't want to trust him. He was one of the masters and he wanted to put them straight into the palm of the Hamalain. Without a doubt, that place was their home. The centre of their trading empire.

But he was right, they had little choice. The *ziri* were tired, and Jintan certainly could not fly much longer. If they made an attempt to go inland or along the coast, they would easily be caught. She understood what Daybian was thinking: make it look as if this was their intention, to be bold.

It was not a plan she liked, but it was the only option if they wanted a chance at finding out the truth about the raiders.

In the time it had taken her to come to this conclusion, they had passed across the coast and were climbing the steep slope. Two rivers descended from the top and bridges curved across their waters everywhere they intersected with the roadways.

It was a tremendous demonstration of engineering skill—no doubt used by the Hamalain to prove to their people they were both powerful and magnanimous. The people who lived here, perhaps even the slaves, would feel they were blessed.

She shook her head as more people came out into the thoroughfares and looked up at them as they climbed. The numbers were overwhelming. It was like a mountain of faces.

Kantees urged Sheesha to make the turn as they continued to mount the slope. Soon they reached the ridge and she could see that the town had spread into the next bay as well as extending back across lower hills with more houses of the rich.

She focused on the Hamalain house. There were gardens which they could land in but the Hamalain had a Ziri Tower, made of a different and darker stone to the rest, just like Jakalain. She could see faces looking out from the eyries. And some *ziri*. Screeches went up from the tower to be answered by those from the four they rode. She could feel Sheesha's voice through her knees. It resonated with power and she smiled at the apparent subservience of the responses from the tower.

She would have liked to land in the tower but there was no way of knowing which eyries were unoccupied. If they landed in the gardens they would have little time to get their story straight. The top of the tower at Jakalain was a landing place, so if the design here was the same as there, they could use it.

They were already over the grounds of the Hamalain estate, so she set Sheesha to climb and began a slow spiral up and around the tower.

As she had hoped, the top was flat. Gratefully, she brought the *ziri* in to land.

Daybian was unbuckled and off Jintan as fast as he could move.

"Kantees, listen, you must defer to me. If you don't, they'll have us all strung up."

"I realise that."

"Oh," he said. "You do?"

"I am not an idiot."

He frowned at her implication. "And you cannot say things like that in the presence of anyone here. Word will get back."

She nodded.

"Silence is probably the best option," he said and turned to the others. "Gally, you'll look after the *ziri* like you always do, and do what Kantees says."

"Gally always does what Kantees says."

"Yenteel, you had better be my secretary."

"And what story will explain why we are here?" said Kantees. "With almost nothing but the clothes we stand up in."

They all stood silent as the sound of shouting drifted up from below.

"Shipwreck in a storm," said Yenteel. "We escaped on the *ziri* and only just made it to land."

"I have never heard of *ziri* being taken on a boat," said Kantees. "We travel by patterners' path."

"An island without a big ley-circle," said Yenteel. "But a new source of *zirichasa*. We were coming back."

A trapdoor in the floor rattled.

"Will Gally say the wrong things?" said Daybian.

Kantees gave him a look of disgust. "He is simple-minded, *sire*, it doesn't matter what he says. We can simply deny it."

Armsmen flowed from below. Kantees gathered the reins of Sheesha and Looesa and pulled them back towards the edge. Gally had the other two.

Daybian strode forward with an air of entitlement that made the armsmen falter. Yenteel followed with a similar confidence, but a few steps behind.

"I am Lord Daybian of Jakalain. If this is the estate of the Lords Hamalain I request that I be brought into their presence so that I may apologise for taking advantage of their hospitality in this unorthodox manner."

There was only one problem with this plan, thought Kantees. One of the brothers in the house of Hamalain wanted to attack Jakalain. Daybian's announcing himself like this was a sure way to get him—and the rest of them—captured or murdered.

However, the armsmen treated him with more respect and he was allowed to descend with Yenteel, leaving Kantees and Gally on the roof with the *ziri*.

And then it started raining again. She was not entirely sure the day could get much worse.

Kantees was quietly pleased when the day improved. Having established that neither she nor Gally was armed, nor did either of them carry any weapons among their meagre supplies, the guards allowed her to talk to a Kadralin man called Ferel. He was officious and clearly unwilling to consider even the slightest possibility that her charges were of any quality—although she saw the way his eyes lingered on Sheesha.

However, they did have two empty eyries so she was able to bring Sheesha into one and the other three into the other. This arrangement was apparently the way things were done here.

"The dominant male always has his own eyrie," Ferel said. Kantees absorbed that information. Romain had never mentioned anything about dominant males. Perhaps she could learn things here. Did the people here know the *zirichasa* possessed the power of the ley-circles in abundance?

Somehow she doubted it since she herself had only discovered it by accident.

She had met slaves like Ferel before. He was the kind that liked to think they were special in some way and therefore above the others. Romain, for all his many faults, knew where he stood in the relationship between the masters and the slaves. On the inside, Ferel thought he was a master, but that was an attitude that could easily get one killed.

Kantees said nothing. She listened, agreed, and learnt, just as she had always done with Romain.

Getting the *ziri* into the eyries was a little tricky since she and

Gally were no longer able to ride. No one mentioned the fact they had arrived on *zirichak*-back. Perhaps it would be ignored. She wasn't sure.

In this instance, however, they stripped off the tack and Kantees went down through the tower to Sheesha's allocated eyrie. Then called to him. After examining the eyrie thoroughly, he settled down to sleep. She stood at the exit for a moment looking out. This side of the tower stood on the edge of the cliff and below her was not only the height of the tower but the drop-off from the clifftop past the houses to the very distant ground below. She shivered and went back inside.

She went through the same process with the other three. Looesa first to get him settled and then the other two to join him. Gally came down and for the first time in a ten-day, he seemed happy. The life of adventure was not something he tolerated easily. He preferred things to be steady and predictable. This might not have been their original eyrie but it was close enough for Gally. Romain might not be here, but Ferel could tell him what to do.

If she could have left him here with the Hamalain she would have done. If it had been her alone she would have mounted Sheesha and flown away. Avoiding masters, ley-circles, and shadowy creatures, she would have gone up into the mountains to find her people.

But it was not just her. She might not like Daybian but somehow he had become her responsibility, even if she had managed to nearly kill all of them so many times. She was the one who had got them all into the protection of Yenteel's ward. She was the one who had given them the way to escape from it. She might have got them out over the sea, but she had given them the right direction to come back.

She leaned against Sheesha. They were safe for the moment at least. And she fell asleep.

22

It was still raining outside when she woke up but it was not dark. She realised she was very hungry and imagined Sheesha probably was as well.

She went through into the back and looked at the trapdoor and ladder. She was going to have to go down at some point in order to eat and arrange for food so it might as well be now. But perhaps she could take Gally for support. He might not be useful, but he would be on her side—and that meant a lot.

The eyrie for Looesa, Shingul, and Jintan was two levels down. She found him shovelling *ziri* dung.

"Already?" she said with a smile.

He frowned. "Gally thinks Shingul has an upset tummy. The poop is very horrible."

Hardly surprising, she thought; Shingul had been eating wild food and who knew what was in it that might be bad for *ziri*. Still, she had not noticed any problem in Sheesha.

"Are the others ill?" she said.

"No, Kantees, but they have not pooped."

"We shall ask Ferel," she said. "Leave the pile somewhere off to the side. He can take a look at it." He certainly seemed better informed than Romain.

Gally had finished shovelling.

"Come on, let's find Ferel and see about some food for ourselves and the *ziri*."

"Gally is hungry, Kantees."

"Me too."

The construction of the tower seemed to be identical to the one at Jakalain, which she found odd. It wasn't just that it was a tower with eyries, but the placement of all the trapdoors, ladders, even the design of individual eyries seemed to be the same.

Just as she had seen when they arrived, the stone of the Ziri Tower was different to the rest of the Hamalain palace. It was not the red-pink stone but something darker and greyer. And older. A rebellious thought crossed her mind: What if the towers had been built by the Kadralin before the Taymalin invaded? What if this was the work of her people?

Such thought was sacrilege, of course. The Taymalin insisted the original people had been nothing more than warring tribes roaming the island. They claimed to have brought peace.

She sighed. That had been hundreds of years ago. Even if the stories they told were lies, it was really too long ago to do anything about it.

What it meant was that finding the kitchen and dining area was easy. Though her confidence at being able to find her away around was crushed when the eyes of a dozen strangers were directed in her direction. And Gally's. She searched for Ferel's face but she didn't see him; there was an older man who looked as if he might have some authority.

"Excuse me," she said.

The man looked up from the plate of tiny fish with some sort of root vegetable.

"You the ones from Jakalain."

It sounded more a statement than a question.

"Yes, I am Kantees, this is Gally."

"What do you want?"

"We hoped we would be able to feed our *ziri*," she said. "We flew far and they have not been able to eat properly in a while."

"On a ship, were you?"

"Yes, there was a storm, I think it sank."

The man eyed Gally. "Your boy doesn't say much."

"He is simple-minded but a good worker and the *ziri* like him."

"Gally looks after Looesa and Shingul and Jintan," said Gally.

The man's eyebrows rose ever so slightly, then came back down. "And you get the dominant male?"

"For seven years."

"Surprised he didn't eat you." He grinned at her, although Kantees wasn't sure if he was smiling at his joke or the thought of her being eaten.

"Sheesha is kind enough to put up with me," she said carefully. Being a keeper of the *ziri* was a job where it did not matter if one was man or woman.

"Race, does he?"

Trick question. They were only supposed to have picked him up from the island but she said she had been with him for seven years. She had already endangered them all, but perhaps she could rescue it.

"Only mock races, he has been training."

The man grunted.

"Do you think it will be possible to spare food for them?" she said again, trying to get back on track.

"And Kantees and Gally," said Gally. "Gally is very hungry."

"Hope you like fish," he said. "Just about all we get."

"Who should I speak to about the food?" said Kantees.

"Payla, over there, about your own," he said. "And me about your *ziri*. Wouldn't let one of them starve. Temekin's the name. I'm in charge of stores."

"Thank you," she said and pushed Gally in the direction of the food.

Temekin stood up and leaned in to her. "You and the others were riding."

She nodded as she looked into his face to see whether he approved or not.

"That's a death sentence."

She still could not tell if he was happy with the idea.

"Better dead later than dead soon," she said.

He nodded and then spoke even quieter. "Is it good?"

"It is the most wonderful thing I have ever experienced," she said.

His face took on a forlorn look which he replaced almost immediately. "Ever? You must still be a virgin then."

"And planning to stay that way, Temekin," she said. "Until I meet someone who's a better ride than a *ziri*, even an old one like our Jintan."

"I'd be willing to take that test."

"No offence, but I won't be looking for someone retired to the eyrie."

Then he laughed out loud and clapped her on the shoulder. "I like you, Kantees of Jakalain. I'll make sure your *ziri* get a good feed."

She thanked him, then chased after Gally who was staring at the containers, under the eye of an annoyed woman.

"Gally doesn't know this food," he said. "What will Gally like?"

"I'm sorry—Payla?"

"What's wrong with him? I tell him what will be good but he doesn't listen."

"He has the mind of a child, but he's good with *ziri*," said Kantees wondering why she had to keep excusing Galiko's behaviour. Why couldn't people just accept him for what he was? "Is there anything that's particularly sweet?"

She pointed at a plate with a white meat mixed in with a vegetable she didn't recognise.

"I'm sorry, Payla, we come from Jakalain, it's inland so we don't have a lot of fish or…" she trailed off not knowing how to describe the vegetable without insulting their host.

"Seaweed."

"Seaweed?"

"It's a plant that grows in the sea. After it's harvested, we dry it, soak it in honey, and eat it."

Kantees glanced at Gally. He hadn't reacted to the description. So she took a small amount of it and tested it. It was crunchy and very sweet. Delicious.

She offered a little to Gally. He opened his mouth warily and tasted. His face lit up in a grin.

"We'll take two of these," she said.

"Good choice," said Payla. "You wouldn't like the other one. Octopus."

Kantees had no idea what an octopus was but she was sure Payla was right. It didn't even sound nice.

The building might be the same, but the furnishings and customs were different. She did not want to make any mistakes so she found them a table off to the side that was otherwise unoccupied.

The food was strange but not unpleasant. Gally watched her before he dug into his own.

After they had eaten they climbed the tower and found the four *zirichasa* had been fed. Kantees could not tell what the food was, though it seemed to be some sort of large fish. She had no appreciation of the different types and assumed that Temekin knew his business. The *ziri* had no problem wolfing it down, except Shingul.

Ferel had declared she should be kept restrained so that she could not give whatever malady she had to the others, and that she only be fed small amounts of fish.

And at that point Kantees had nothing left to do. Back at Jakalain there were always tasks needing attention but not here, since there were others to do it. Being at a loose end made her uncomfortable.

She went to the exit from the eyrie and looked out. The rain had started up again, making it hard for her to see the town below. All she could make out were grey rooftops. Having nothing to do gave her the opportunity to worry about Yenteel and Daybian. Their story was like a house built of straw; to be honest, the only thing that gave it any validity was the fact that everyone in the town had seen them arrive from the sea.

"Kantees."

She recognised Yenteel's voice. He was panting as he awkwardly climbed up through the trapdoor, his arm not yet healed. He had been using it to help climb but slipped it back into the sling as soon as he could.

"How goes the plan?"

"Things are moving too swiftly," he said and did not sound very happy about it.

"Do they believe the story?"

"I don't know, but they are offering to send Daybian back to Jakalain using the patterner's path."

"But we can't trust them," she said.

He shook his head. Sheesha's stomach grumbled as he digested the fish.

"What if they were after Daybian all the time and I interrupted their attack?"

"They weren't after Daybian or Jelamie," said Yenteel.

"You are not going to say they wanted me." She felt the anger rising in her. She was nothing, just a slave who was good with the *ziri*. There was nothing about her that any family of the Taymalin could want.

"Not saying it does not make it any the less true."

Kantees turned away and went to stand with Sheesha. He was half asleep and did not mind when she checked the gouge in his side left by the fight. It was healing normally.

"If they had wanted me they would have attacked the tower," she said. "Or just offered to buy me. They wouldn't have been the first."

"It's possible they did not know exactly who they wanted, perhaps they just assumed it was the heir because he was Taymalin."

"I don't see how anybody could mix up a Kadralin slave with a Taymalin lord. And, in case you hadn't noticed, we're not even the same sex."

"But he is good with the *ziri*, is he not?"

For all his faults. She nodded.

"As you are."

"What have the *zirichasa* got to do with it?"

"That's something else you don't like to discuss."

"Reading the World's Pattern? Prophecies?" She almost spat the word. "We're slaves, Yenteel."

"It doesn't matter how it happened," he said. "The Hamalain and I turned up at the same time looking for someone who was good with *ziri*. I, however, had the advantage of not being blinded by preconceptions of who might be the right one."

She had no answer. She could not argue that the raid and the arrival of Yenteel had coincided.

"So why did they take Jelamie?"

Yenteel shook his head. "Because he was available?"

"But there was no ransom, they could have traded him for Daybian."

Even as she said it she knew it wasn't true. Daybian was far more important to the family than his younger brother. The lord and lady would have made the decision to lose the spare rather than put the heir at risk. So why take him at all?

She had a feeling that Daybian would not approve of that—he was here looking for his brother. *Oh, wait.*

"Daybian did not get his family's approval to come after Jelamie and us."

"He hasn't said that but no, I do not think they would have allowed it. Certainly not on his own, on the back of a *zirichak*, and an old one."

"There's nothing wrong with Jintan," she said almost absently, as if defending the *ziri* was an automatic reaction. She shook her head. Yenteel was making sense and she hated him for it. What he didn't know—and she was not about to tell him about the magic— was even more convincing.

"I don't believe it. It's just a coincidence," she said finally, hoping she might convince herself as well as Yenteel. She took a deep breath and tried to put it from her mind, there were more important matters to deal with. "How soon do they want to send him back to Jakalain?"

"They had offered to do it today."

"That's quite a rush," she said.

"Daybian demurred. And has bought us another night."

"But you think they were after Daybian?"

"Yes."

"They wouldn't let him go back to Jakalain then."

"No."

"If he was on the patterner's path, they would be able to take him anywhere they pleased."

"Quite so."

"And they think he barely escaped a shipwreck."

Yenteel pulled a face. "Perhaps. Either way they can be reasonably sure no one at Jakalain knows where he is."

"We do."

"Yes. If they remove Daybian, they will dispose of us as well."

Kantees dug her hands into Sheesha's feathers as if she was trying to draw strength from him. Where was his magic when she needed it?

"I don't know what to do," she said. "We haven't learnt anything and we're no closer to finding Jelamie."

Was there even any point in carrying on?

"Is that why we're here?" said Yenteel.

"Of course it is," she said. "Why else would I put myself at this much risk?"

"I really don't know. It seems a very strange thing to do, trying to save the life of a child you don't even like."

She turned on him. "What do you want from me, Yenteel? Do you want me to say that I am trying to make up for the wrongs I've done? Or perhaps that I was once young and in a place I did not understand where people did not treat me well, so I understand what he may be going through and want to stop it?"

"Well," he said. "Which is it?"

"Neither. Both. Honestly I do not care. I'm doing it because I'm doing it. Because if it wasn't this I would just be running with my tail between my legs. At least if I do this I can show those at Jakalain that even a slave is a human being. Someone who can choose to care for someone who might not even deserve it."

Yenteel fell silent.

It had grown dark outside. The sound of the sea carried up the cliffs and into the tower. There was a calm comfort in it. She had forgotten that sound from when she was very young. Even though she had lived so close to the water, all she really knew of it was the sound coming in through the window in the attic where she slept with the others of the household.

She supposed she had been happy then, after a fashion. The work had not been hard and she had been able to listen and learn. Though now she regretted not being able to read and write. There was so much learning in books. Perhaps, if they got out of this alive, she might persuade Yenteel to teach her.

Except he would no doubt go back to his master—she would not go with him no matter how much he pleaded. He could have Daybian instead.

"We should leave first thing in the morning," said Yenteel.

She nodded. At least this time they would not have to face the armed guards. Daybian and Yenteel could come up the tower and they could just mount the *ziri* and leave. Unfortunately they had absolutely no idea where they should be going next.

"What does it mean that we found the Hamalain dead in the pool?" she said suddenly. "The *tekrak* would have been able to cover the distance to here before we caught up with it. It could travel through the entire day without getting tired."

"I am more curious as to how it was controlled," said Yenteel.

"There was a patterner in the room beneath it," she said, surprised he didn't already know. "It was him giving the instructions to the creature."

"How do you know?"

"I saw him. They flew directly at me and then over."

"You did not mention that before."

"You did not ask."

"What else have you not told me?"

"I believe that is an impossible question to answer," she said. "The important thing is the name the raider said."

"The Dunor. Yes, well I have no idea what that is."

"We could ask the Hamalain," she said.

"I know you are not serious."

Am I not? she thought.

"The raider you spoke to," he said. "What sort of person was he?"

"None too bright and not well informed since he assumed I must be a raider as well, even though I arrived on Sheesha. Just like any of the armsmen in the castle, I suppose. Happy as long as he has something to eat, a flagon of ale, and somebody to tell him who to kill."

"Very well. Let us assume he was typical of the raiders, perhaps even one of the better ones since he had been assigned to look after the bell tower alone." Yenteel thought for a moment. "So the Hamalain who was in charge—I think it might have been the brother Lorima."

"That's what Daybian said."

Yenteel gave her a long look. "What I said about things you haven't told me."

"You were recovering from the arrow—the one I saved you from, without burning the wound."

"I believe I have thanked you for that."

"I don't think you did, perhaps it was something you haven't told me."

"Thank you for saving my life."

"What about Lorima then?"

"He's not here, away on a business trip apparently. And also overdue to return."

"So you have been making enquiries."

"Yes. The patterner would have been one of the Hamalain's own since they would not trust anyone else. No one has seen a giant *tekrak* around here so they must have acquired it, and the men, elsewhere."

"You're saying they were mercenaries," said Kantees.

"I am."

"And that they might have rebelled after the failure of the raid and decided to keep the *tekrak* and the patterner for themselves."

"It fits what we know."

Kantees considered. "Would they also keep Jelamie?"

"They might. You say he is a little wild and uncontrollable?"

"I said he's spoilt," said Kantees. "His mother had given up on having another child. There was even talk that the father might acknowledge one of his bastards just to ensure there was continuity if something happened to Daybian. So when she became pregnant again and had Jelamie ..."

"She spared the rod."

"She would not gainsay him a single wish." Kantees was surprised at her own feelings over the matter. "And now he runs riot around the castle."

"So perhaps he amuses them."

"We can only hope that is the case," said Kantees. "Whatever the truth, they will not treat him as well as his mother."

She let it go at that. They could both imagine what unpleasantness could be forced on the boy.

"I must be getting back," said Yenteel. "Be ready in the morning."

"We still do not know which way to go."

"Let us think on it," he said and was gone.

Sheesha grumbled at the noise but was snoring within moments.

The dampness of the air made it cold and Kantees snuggled for warmth and comfort under Sheesha's wing.

23

"This is a completely disgusting place."

Kantees opened her eyes at the harsh voice but could see only feathers and daylight. But what she could hear were many feet on the wooden floorboards of the eyrie. Sheesha grumbled—he wasn't scared, but he was annoyed. He lifted a wing and she climbed out.

Six armsmen held crossbows pointed in her direction. Instinctively she took a few steps to the side so they were not pointing at her *ziri*.

In the middle of the men, slightly behind, was someone who could only be one of the Hamalain brothers. He even resembled the man they had found, at least in the nose. However this one was much larger—fatter. Though clearly not so fat that he could not climb the tower, but if he expanded much more that option would not be available. His clothing was of the finest quality, of course, but still practical in the form of trousers, sturdy shoes, and coat, fastened up.

She realised she had forgotten herself and immediately knelt with her head bowed. Since she had no job to be about, and the lord was here in Sheesha's eyrie, she had to pay deference to him and follow his orders.

"Seneschal."

She heard the sounds of another man moving forward, and by lifting her head slightly she could see another pair of shoes. Also of high quality.

"Ask it where my brother is."

"Lord Trimiente wants to know what's happened to his brother."

Inside Kantees laughed. Clearly Trimiente was one of those who would not speak to a slave directly because to do so would taint him. She had had conversations like this before at the races. It was completely ridiculous.

"I do not know anything of the lord's brother."

The blow knocked her to the floor and left the side of her head aching. It was not that she had not expected it but usually it came after a repeat of the question. It would seem Lord Trimiente's patience was limited.

Kantees lifted her head to look at Sheesha who was very still. His eyes were on her. She willed him to do nothing.

The next blow slammed her head into the floorboards.

"No one told you you could get up. What do you know of Lord Lorima?"

"I do not know who that is."

The next blow landed in her side. He must have kicked her. It hurt but she had borne worse. It was just bruises, they would heal soon enough.

The seneschal's voice was in her ear. "You're thinking you can take a beating. I know. And it is true this is for show. So the lord can see you being beaten, but when we start the torture you will suffer terribly before you die. Tell us what we want to know."

"Since I am to die whether I tell you or not—even if there were something—it makes no difference if I speak or stay silent."

She felt him move away and his heel came down on her spine, knocking the wind from her, and it felt as if something broke. Through the pain there was a low growl so deep it was felt rather than heard.

"Shoot the beast," said Lord Trimiente.

"No!" The word caught in Kantees' throat and she coughed. "No."

The seneschal was back at her ear. "You care so much about the beast? Then if you do not tell his lordship what he wants to know I will have the animal strung up. Its feathers pulled out one by one. It will be flayed alive and you will be forced to watch."

The image of Sheesha being tortured formed in her mind and Kantees sobbed.

"I will tell you."

She was yanked into a sitting position and the ache in her back flared into incandescent pain. She felt the blood drain from her face and hands. The armsmen still had their crossbows aimed at Sheesha, and the seneschal was looking at her with an intensity she had never experienced. She could barely think.

"Well?"

"I will tell him."

The seneschal slapped her across the face.

"Isn't it right he should hear the words from the person who found his brother's body?"

Lord Trimiente must have been listening. "Bring it here."

Kantees could barely walk so the seneschal had to support her for the ten paces it took to approach the lord and collapse at his feet.

"Tell him."

"Let him ask me," she said. "I will be dead before the day is out. What harm is there?"

She could not see the exchange of looks between the seneschal and his lord but whatever there had been was sufficient. It was Lord Trimiente's voice she heard next.

"Where is my brother?"

"He is dead perhaps ten leagues from Jakalain."

"You're lying," said the lord but she knew from his voice he believed her.

"I found him myself face down in a pool where he had been drowned. My lord Daybian recognised him."

"So you came to seek your revenge."

"Revenge for what, lord? Your brother with his mercenaries

raided our castle and though they were routed still he took something precious to Lady Jakalain, her second son Jelamie."

"Nonsense, he did not want the child."

"Nevertheless that is what happened and Daybian set off in pursuit, but we were days behind. We came to a place where the raiders had camped and there I found the body of your brother."

"I believe you, slave."

A strange certainty came over Kantees. The certainty that she would die. It seemed to drive the pain from her and she breathed slower, more deeply. Then she whispered in a voice so low, no one could hear the words. "I don't care if you believe me."

"What?" said Lord Trimiente.

Again almost a whisper. "I don't care if you believe me."

She heard Sheesha move, a shuffling of his feet and wings.

"What did you say, slave?"

"I said I don't care if you believe me."

She pushed herself to her feet even though pain tore at her muscles.

"How dare you!"

"I dare because I am already dead and I hadn't even realised it. You can't do anything to me!"

With that she turned and, fighting her protesting body, she pounded towards the open exit of the eyrie.

And flung herself into the emptiness.

2 4

She wondered how long it would take for her to hit the ground. Since the tower stood at the edge of the precipice overlooking the town, she had further to fall than simply the height of the tower. Perhaps it would take forever, because now that she was falling she felt as if she weighed nothing, like the feathers of the *zirichasa*. It was as if she was flying. She stretched out her arms and the air streamed across her skin.

She felt guilty. She had done precisely what she said she would not do, and abandoned everyone she knew; everything she believed in. But even the guilt was blasted away by the wind of her fall.

A seabird shrieked.

Then there was a touch. And she was sucked to the side and pressed into feathers. She opened the eyes she had closed against inevitable death. *Zirichak* feathers, familiar ones. She felt his muscles move as he spread his wings and she was pressed harder into his body. He would not let her die.

Now that she could see, the houses below seemed very close and growing fast. But Sheesha bent his wings against the air and, though they still fell together at a speed that took her breath, their course bent away from the closest structures and they fell fast towards those at the base of the cliff.

But Sheesha held his wings firm and slowly their fall transformed into level flight at a speed she barely comprehended. They
shot out across the sea, clearing the tops of the masts so fast she had
but a moment to contemplate them before they were gone.

Then she felt Sheesha's magic: the golden glow within. It poured
out and enfolded her. They were not slowing down. The sea below
flashed past. The brighter crests of the swell became a blur. Sheesha
was not beating his wings; instead they moved backwards until he
was like an arrow piercing the world. Yet she could not feel it,
cocooned within the magic.

This was it. This was their magic. This was what they did. No
wonder they wanted to fly fast. It they could travel fast enough, they
became arrows of the sky.

And she was the one who had brought it forth in Sheesha. If she
had not thrown herself out, he would not have chased and
caught her.

So she clung with her arms hooked over the front of his wings
next to his body.

Then she thought of Gally, Yenteel, and—may the *Kisharuk*
curse him—Daybian. He would be so jealous. If he survived
the day.

"We must go back, Sheesha," she said quietly and she knew he
could hear her. Perhaps not hear, but he knew what she wanted.

And suddenly Kantees found herself tumbling through the air
again. And falling. She caught a glimpse of Sheesha like a ball of
feathers. The magic had gone, vanished like a candle being snuffed
out. The air had struck her like a solid wall ripping her from Sheesha's back.

She hit cold salty water and went under. She kept her eyes open
though it stung, and clawed her way back to the surface in a panic.
She did not know how to swim.

From the air the swell in the ocean had not looked very big, but
now water towered over her and brought her up to its crest and then
down into the trough again. She tried to shove away the panic that
gripped her. People swam all the time. She knew they could do it.
Anybody could do it. She desperately tried to convince herself as
her head went under and she got another mouthful of water.

Where was Sheesha? Was he all right?

A shadow went over her. A giant pair of wings. He must not get soaked. He could tolerate some rain but if he was thoroughly wetted he would not be able to fly and they would both drown. Better he flew back to shore than try to rescue her.

She rose to the top of the next swell and Sheesha flew over the top of her with his legs down as if he was going to land. She knew he was not that foolish but what did it mean? She dropped down into the next trough.

In his next pass over he timed it wrong and she was at the low point. His talons splashed into the wave. She tried to shout at him to go but her mouth filled again and she just coughed. She was getting tired as she fought with the sea, and the panic was rising again. Yes it was true that she had tried to kill herself only a short time before. But she had survived and learnt so much.

She did not want to die now.

As she rose on the leading edge of the next swell she saw him coming in again, this time he glided in along the ridge of the wave itself. With perfect timing he intercepted her just as she reached the crest. His talons were again dragging through the surface and one went each side of her.

With a last effort she pushed herself upwards and hooked each arm around one leg above the claw. His wings beat and she lifted with him. They beat once more and she left the water. Again, and she was her own height above it, but looking backwards all she could see was Sheesha's sinuous feathered tail with the broad fan at its end.

He did not seem to be trying to gain much height but went round in a circle. She could see nothing but the ocean to the horizon in all directions. She did not know how long he could fly in such an unbalanced way—or how long she could hold on. There was no knowing how far they had come from the coast at the speed he had been flying.

Perhaps it was hopeless and they were both going to die anyway.

But Sheesha, after making his complete circle, set off, gaining a little height. She knew the *ziri* had excellent eyesight, far better than any human. Perhaps he had seen something she could not.

Wherever he was going, it did not take long, though she could not see where he was heading. He turned in the air again and spiralled down. The turns he made did not reveal anywhere to land —it was still water everywhere around.

She looked straight down. There was something poking up from the surface of the water. It wasn't very large and appeared perfectly round although the waves went all the way across the top of it from time to time. It did not look like rock and she did not think this was a good idea.

But she had no choice in the matter as Sheesha spiralled in for a landing. When she was a short distance above it she let go and fell. Her feet slipped on the smooth wet surface and she landed heavily. Sheesha made one more turn to make sure he knew where she was and with a flurry of beating wings landed gently.

The first thing Kantees realised was that their refuge was not fixed. It was floating and rose and fell with the water, but more sluggishly as if it was very big. This meant that every now and then its dipping down coincided with a wave, and that was when the surface became completely covered.

On the first occasion Kantees' feet were dragged from under her and she was almost swept away. However that showed her that this object floating in the ocean seemed to be a ball shape and the surface curved slowly beneath the waves.

Nor was it stone. What the outside reminded her of, most of all, was the shells she had cleaned in her first master's study. This was rougher and there were other shells clinging to it. She walked unsteadily to Sheesha who would flap into the air a little every time a big wave came over.

In a moment of stability she put her arms around his neck. "Thank you."

He brought his head round and nudged her with his snout. She took it for an acknowledgement.

"We have to get back as quick as we can," she said.

She looked at the sun. It seemed that very little time had passed since they had left Kurvin Port. She shook her head. It was confusing. So much could happen in such a short time and it seemed like forever. Yet it was nothing.

They were no safer here than they had ever been. There were plenty of things in the sea that could eat you. Her old master had smaller samples of monstrous creatures pulled from the sea by fishermen in their nets.

She had no desire to meet their larger brothers.

Kantees waited until one of the big waves had gone over the top and then climbed on Sheesha's back. This time she sat between his wing pinions with her legs down. She could grip him that way and could see. If necessary she could lean forward onto his neck.

With no further prompting from her, as their temporary refuge hit the top of a swell, Sheesha leapt into the sky beating his wings hard to quickly gain altitude. Kantees looked down. A short distance from the huge ball were five creatures floating on their backs. The scale was difficult to judge but she thought they might be about half her height. They had four legs, although their front pairs were folded like arms as they lay there watching Sheesha and Kantees climb into the sky. Their bodies were covered in fur and they had tails, big powerful ones. As the *ziri* climbed upwards they turned together and dived, heading towards the ball.

Shocalin, she thought. Legends. Yet it seemed they too were real. Intelligent as any man and renowned for their wisdom. Though, since they were only a legend how would anyone truly know how wise they were? People had thought her old master, Kevrey of Tander, was wise but she knew that trick: he said things that meant nothing—or everything—and let people draw their own conclusions. He might have been more knowledgeable than most but it did not make him wise. Perhaps the *Shocalin* were assumed to be wise because they said nothing.

It did not matter. It had nothing to do with her. She should simply concentrate on what was coming, and what she needed to do next. Rescue her friends and find that stupid boy, always sticking his nose into places where it did not belong.

They had to return to shore. She had no idea how far they had come so it might take all day or longer for them to return at normal flying pace. Neither did she know if it was possible to repeat what they had done before—perhaps avoiding the mess at the end. Particularly if the end happened over land instead of more forgiving water.

Sheesha did not object to being sent higher. So she had him climb while heading in what she believed to be the right direction. The sea spread out beneath them, getting wider and wider. She saw a large fishing boat off to what she thought was the south but there was no sign of any land.

For one short moment she considered going to the boat and asking for directions. The thought of it made her laugh but it was not a serious idea. She knew that sailors were superstitious and there was always the risk they might try to shoot at her before she got to them.

She did not know how high she needed to go but the air was growing cold so she thought it was probably enough. The prospect of sending Sheesha into a dive back towards the water scared her, but she did not think it needed to be as precipitous a dive as when she had been falling.

He did not need to catch her this time; she just needed to be able to hang on.

"This is it, Sheesha, you're going to fly fast again."

She leaned forward. He spread his wings and went nose down into the dive. Their speed increased quickly. Soon the blast of the wind was threatening to knock her off so she leaned forward and put her arms around Sheesha's neck.

Faster and faster.

Without being told, Sheesha increased the dive angle and pulled his wings in. They were dropping like a stone. Kantees had her eyes shut against the blast. She just had to trust he would not let them crash into the sea.

Then it started. She felt the warmth boiling from him, the power, and the golden light behind her eyelids. The wind stopped and she opened her eyes. Once more they were flashing across the surface of the sea. She leaned back and Sheesha climbed. In moments they were as high as they had been before, and ahead, on the horizon, there was a dark mass.

Land, she thought and then said out loud, "Slow down."

She half expected her words to be ripped from her lips but she and Sheesha were indeed surrounded by a shell of magic that protected everything within.

This time, she got the feeling Sheesha was being more careful. Since they were enclosed, and quite high, it was difficult to tell if they were slowing down but suddenly the air ripped through. Kantees was knocked back but her legs, hooked over Sheesha's wings, saved her. And Sheesha himself did not lose control. Instead he snapped out his wings and glided, as their speed reduced.

The mass of darker ground ahead resolved into cliffs with the mountains of Esternes in the distance. It was late afternoon when they crossed the shoreline. The only problem now, since she could not see Kurvin Port, was which direction she should head along the coast.

Unfortunately she really was going to have to ask for directions.

There was smoke rising from a bay and she decided that would be as good as any place. Once more she hoped she was not too late for the rescue. Last time she was too late to stop Jelamie from being taken. This time her companions might be dead. It depended on how the remaining Hamalain had taken her sudden escape. They might simply have killed them all in a fit of pique. Or set about torturing them. She did not know whether Sheesha's golden magic was visible—and, if it was, whether it had been observed.

One thing at a time. She could not help them—or avenge them —if she did not know which way to go.

Sheesha glided along the coast. The tide was in and waves thundered against the rocks as they went from bay to bay. It must be quite a large fishing village, she thought, because there was a considerable amount of smoke rising.

They rounded the final headland. There were boats bobbing in the bay. A pier stretched out into the water, and there were about a dozen houses. Of which all but one were smouldering ruins.

2 5

She circled the village once. The cliff behind was not as high as in Kurvin Port, nor were buildings built up the hill. A path led from the village up to some fields at the top of the cliffs.

She had Sheesha land at the top of cliff, and dismounted. She wanted him to stay there but she had no way of enforcing it. So she just said, "Stay here, I'll be back," and headed down the steep and rough path.

Looking up she saw Sheesha had poked his head over the edge to watch her. She stumbled on the trail and grabbed at the cliff while her stomach turned somersaults.

How can I be afraid of heights? she thought as she steadied herself by holding on to a clump of coarse grass growing out of a crack in the rock. *Maybe I'm just afraid of falling.*

She went on, this time not taking her eyes off the path. Although it was uneven, in particularly steep sections rocks had been placed to make steps. They were rounded stones, however, and were not a great help. Even so it did not take long for her to reach the flat area of the bay.

As she had been focusing on the path she looked up with surprise to see a group of men and women. Most had the pale skin of the Taymalin, though wrinkled and weathered by exposure to the sky and the sea. There was one with darker skin, though still not the shade of a true Kadralin. A by-blow of some mating between the two: a half-breed that some called Jutolin. There were plenty of them in the world, and both Kadralin and Taymalin treated them badly.

This man wore clothes similar to the rest. None of them were rich, of course.

"Who art?"

"I am of Corlain—" She had heard the family name years ago, a family not on Esternes but far to the south. "—travelling to Hamalain. What happened here?"

The man looked terrified and glanced at the others around him. If he was looking for some sort of sign, she didn't think he got one. "*Tekrak*."

She decided to play innocent. "It's the wrong season for *tekrasa*."

He shook his head and the other people shuffled their feet. "One *tekrak*."

She looked at the burning buildings. "One *tekrak*? Why did you not chop off its fire-tube and pierce it through?"

He hesitated, perhaps thinking she would not believe him. "One *tekrak* bigger than a house with men riding inside."

"Men inside a *tekrak*? You have been drinking."

All the people shook their heads now. They were on his side and he gained courage. "No, one *tekrak* bigger than a house and with men in a house it was carrying."

The trouble with playing dumb was that she could not ask whether there had been a child with them without giving away the fact that she knew about it.

"There has never been a *tekrak* so big."

"So it was we thought. But the Old Mother says different. She says it is the *Slissac* returned."

Kantees wondered who the Old Mother might be. It didn't matter. What mattered was the quandary she was now in. The state of the buildings meant that this had happened recently. So the raiders could not be far away, but the longer she delayed in getting back to Hamalain the more likely she would find Yenteel, Gally, and Daybian dead.

She shook her head. This was not a quandary at all. She must rescue her friends first and with the four of them they had a better chance of rescuing Jelamie than she did alone. The speed of the *tekrak* was no match for a *ziri*, even one without magic, even if the *tekrak* didn't have to rest. And she was still unsure whether she wanted to reveal the truth to the others. Or to anyone—unless they had seen something when she escaped.

She hesitated. She needed to get back but what other secrets might the Hamalain have? Where had they found such a monstrous *tekrak*? How had a Taymalin patterner learnt to control it? How had it even occurred to him that it could be controlled? Perhaps these were important questions to be answered after all. The scholar she had served would have wanted to know. He did not like mysteries. "Knowledge is the beginning of wisdom" was one of his favourite sayings.

"Where is the Old Mother? I would like to talk to her."

The small crowd parted and the half-breed beckoned for her to follow.

He led the way between the smoking buildings. If any effort had been used to put the fire out, nothing was happening now. Most of the fishing boats were out on the water and she could see their dark shapes as the villagers fished.

"What did they want?" she said. "The men who came?"

"They took our food," he said and then choked. "And they took our daughters."

Kantees sighed. "I'm sorry."

"Will you take word of our loss to Hamalain?" he said.

"I will tell them what happened. They will take revenge on these people."

He stopped and turned. "We do not want revenge, mistress of the *zirichak*, just our daughters back."

If they have not been murdered after being raped, she thought, but did not say. There was no need, the people in the village knew why the girls had been taken. Kantees found her palms were itching. She wanted to be away, and she desperately wanted to find these raiders and let Sheesha tear out their throats one by one. There was nothing in them that was redeemable.

She knew she could not take on every woe of the world and put it right, but here the needs of these poor people coincided with her own. She would do what she could to help them.

"How many girls?"

"Five, including my Jakanda."

She did not ask how old. She did not want to know, but that they had taken the daughters meant they wanted young ones who would be too scared and too weak to fight back. Those men were base cowards.

They had left the village now and walked along the pebbled beach close to the waterline. There was a cave mouth and carved steps leading up to it. They were ancient and worn, with dips in the centre where uncounted feet had climbed through the uncounted years.

Patterns were carved around the entrance. Kantees was not curious about them, for she did not want a patterner's skills even if they could be useful. She supposed that, given the right patterns, she could control Sheesha's magic just as the *tekrak* was controlled. But she did not want that. Sheesha's power was his own. He was free to give it or not. She had no right to force it from him.

A short tunnel, with a trickle of water running along it, led inside to a large room. It was lit by a couple of candles and as her eyes adjusted she could see there was not a single surface where a pattern had not been inscribed.

The Old Mother was not that old. Kantees guessed her to be barely into her middle age and she got up without any difficulty when Kantees entered. She was Taymalin by her look.

"What is your name, Kadralin?" barked the woman.

"I am Kantees," she responded instantly, unable to hold it in.

"And you ride the *ziri* even though it is forbidden."

Kantees was not impressed. "If you know already everything about me then tell me what I want to know and I'll be on my way."

The woman grinned and gestured to the chair. "I saw you fly over and it made me curious. What is a Kadralin girl doing riding such a fine beast that could only come from the towers of a Taymalin castle?"

"It's a long story."

"I have time."

"I do not."

The woman shrugged. "What do you want to know?"

"I was told you said the *Slissac* had returned."

She shook her head. "What I said was that the *Kisharuk* stirs and the tools of the *Slissac* are abroad."

"The *Kisharuk* is a myth told to scare the children of the Taymalin."

"You think so?"

"Even if it was real, it's got nothing to do with us."

"If it was real," said the Old Mother, "do you think it would make a distinction between Taymalin and Kadralin?"

Kantees frowned and tried something else. "What tools of the *Slissac*?"

"The giant *tekrak*."

"The *Slissac* made it?"

The woman nodded and then drank from a cup she had at her side. "We are skilled with material things. But where we make machines, the *Slissac* moulded the patterns of living creatures to do their bidding."

Kantees shook her head again. "You can't do that."

"And you are so wise in the ways of patterns you can say that?"

"When Taymar escaped from the *Slissac* with his people, they would have known how to do it. But as you say, we make things, the Taymalin don't mould patterns."

"Perhaps that was a skill they were not taught. Would you teach slaves how to defeat you?"

Kantees looked away. This woman had an answer for everything, but none of it was satisfactory; after all, she was just a woman in a cave. What could she know?

"Kantees, it does not matter whether you believe me," she said. "I have answered your questions and, as you have said, you have things to do."

Kantees stood up and felt that she had been very selfish. "Is there anything I can do to help?"

"Just do what you have to do."

"I need to get to Hamalain," she said. "Which way is it?"

The woman pointed and then dropped her arm. Kantees desperately tried to determine which way that was in respect to the coast. She kept it in her head as she stepped back through the tunnel and into the light: to the northeast.

"Sheesha!" she called as soon as she was on the beach and could see his wings poking up over the edge of the cliff. His long neck poked up. "Come on!"

The *zirichak* launched himself over the cliff and snapped his wings out. In moments he was gliding over her head at speed. He whipped into a turn that also killed his speed and landed on the beach.

She turned to the man. "What is your name?"

"Welyn."

"I promise I will search for your daughter and try to bring her back to you."

If I don't, I'll be dead.

She climbed on to Sheesha's back and settled herself between his wings. "When the giant *tekrak* left, which direction did it go?"

The man pointed in the other direction to Hamalain, which made sense because if they knew where they were they would not want to go that way. They would probably make their way along the coast raiding as they went. Until they were stopped.

She launched Sheesha into the air and set him on the course along the coast, encouraging him to make the best speed he could—without using the magic.

Once more she seemed to be heading into trouble to perform the impossible. That appeared to be the entire story of her life, now. So perhaps she had better learn to enjoy it.

The chances of her ending up dead were increasing all the time.

2 6

The Ziri Tower at Hamalain came into sight like a finger pointing accusingly at the sky. And she had no plan. The sky was overcast, but the clouds were high and visibility was good, which meant she could be seen easily as she approached. It was not close to evening, so if she wanted to enter when it was dark she would have to wait. She did not think she could afford the time.

Trying desperately to think of how best to get into the castle, she put Sheesha into a climbing spiral. There was no way she could use the magical speed that he could achieve; he would simply overshoot. And besides, she did not want to reveal that—assuming the Hamalain did not know already.

Then she heard the strange, deep hoot of a *zirichak*. It came from the far distance but was unmistakable. She knew it must be Shingul or one of the others, because she had never heard a *ziri* utter that sound until this journey. Any *zirichasa* that lived in a tower did not use it.

She peered towards the tower itself but could not make out anything. Sheesha, however, was not looking that way. He had pulled out of the spiral and his neck was pointing inland at Kurvin Port. There was no dust trail but she could see three wagons on the road, carrying *ziri*—one in each. Sheesha immediately headed that way but Kantees leaned back and pulled on his neck feathers.

"No, Sheesha, wait."

She stared down and saw armsmen surrounding the carriages, and men who might be Yenteel, Gally, and Daybian. Out in front, riding horses not *kichesa*, was a group of men she did not recognise.

They must be heading for the ley-circle of Kurvin Port, intending to walk the patterner's path to somewhere—and it would not be to Jakalain, of that she was certain. Despite it being the place of her slavery, right at this moment, even Kantees would be happy to be back there. As long as they weren't planning to put her head in a noose.

She looked along the roadway they were following. It ended at a circle—except the circle was a hole in the ground. She recognised it from the few times they had raced at Hamalain. Ley-circles were often not on the surface. They might be below it, and many were underwater. The capital city of Canvor in Faerholme, far to the south on the mainland, was famous for having a powerful ley-circle that lay below the level of the lake by which it stood, which meant the city could only be approached by land and thus never be surprised.

Hamalain's was below the ground. She could see the road led to a ramp and down.

Sheesha was becoming more insistent. He wanted to go but she managed to hold him in check. The group would reach the ramp quite soon. She urged Sheesha to turn and fly around to approach the circle from the other side.

The best moment for attack would be just before the pattern for the path was woven. She had travelled enough times by the path she knew it would take a little while to complete the pattern but beyond knowing it would be "soon" she had no real idea.

The riders at the front of the group dismounted and walked down into the tunnel. The *ziri*, however, were taken down on the carriages. It was unlikely they would transport the wagons as well, so there would be a short time while the *zirichasa* were unloaded.

The *ziri* would not have their saddles or reins, so everyone would have to ride without. Daybian would be fine once he had finished complaining. Gally would not like it but would do as she said, and Yenteel—well, he would just have to put up with it.

Kantees counted to fifty, slowly, after the wagons disappeared to give them a chance to get down to the ley-circle proper. She leaned forwards and Sheesha, no longer restrained, went into a dive.

The angle was not sharp so his speed did not reach the point at which the magic became active. She did not know how deep the circle was and she wanted to arrive with as little warning as possible. The nature of the ley-circles made them indefensible close up. It was only possible to build walls at some distance out from them, and it seemed the Hamalain had not even bothered to do that.

She remembered one city they had gone to on Esternes that had created massive fortifications around their circle. The circle itself was not large but the city was the centre of mining. Metals were constantly being shipped out and luxuries brought in. The family that owned the place, the Garbalain, were richer even than Hamalain and clearly they feared attack.

Sheesha arrived over the hole, driven through the rock by the Mother's feeding. It was deep, perhaps almost half the height of the Ziri Tower. And that meant she had arrived too soon. She had forgotten how much time it took to get down to its base, via the cavern.

From off to one side, in the direction of the road, came shouting —and it was not friendly. Armsmen were already hurrying her way. She groaned. This time she really could get them all killed.

"Down, Sheesha, quick."

The *ziri* turned into one of his descending spirals. He seemed to understand the need for speed and was descending at a tight angle. One of the armsmen had a bow and he was drawing an arrow as Sheesha and Kantees went below the level of the ground.

She looked down to where dozens of candles, mounted on massive candelabra, lit the space. Three men, patterners by their robes, were talking and pointing at the ground. Discussing their patterns, no doubt.

She half expected arrows to rain down on her and Sheesha as she looked up to see the armsmen's heads silhouetted against the grey sky. But they did not shoot.

Instead she heard them calling down, warning the men below of the descending *zirichak*. The patterners looked up when she was almost halfway down. The width of the circle was barely sufficient to accommodate the breadth of Sheesha's wings.

The words "Take cover" floated past her as a warning to those below. The armsmen were holding their fire for fear they might hit the patterners. Kantees urged Sheesha to descend faster and he did something she had never seen.

He stopped circling and put out his wings, bent upwards. Together they almost fell towards the ground. Small wingbeats and adjustments to the angles kept their motion under control but they were going down vertically. Moments later they hit the bottom.

An arrow splintered on the ground next to them.

There was a single large arch which was an entrance to a tunnel. It was very rough and the edges looked melted. She leapt from Sheesha's back. "Come on!" she yelled as two more arrows barely missed them. Just one through a wing could prevent him flying.

In his ungainly way, he followed as she jumped through the opening—it was easily big enough for the *ziri* but the ground was uneven. She wondered how often they had to remake the entrance after a feeding had distorted the rock. Once inside, it was impossible for the archers above to hit them. In the tunnel she noticed an acrid and unpleasant smell that bit into her nose and throat.

The tunnel, and its rising floor level, was well lit with lanterns fixed to the walls. This far in, the magic would not touch them so permanent features could be placed safely. She knew she needed to move quickly, otherwise the patterners would give too much warning and she would be captured. Moments later there was a bend in the tunnel and beyond it she emerged into an open space. A staging area. The carts were being unloaded at the other side.

But the panting patterners were already shouting a warning, their voices echoing round the stone walls of the chamber.

"Daybian! Yenteel! Gally!" she yelled. "Shingul! Looesa! Jintan!"

And Sheesha roared deafeningly. Kantees felt as if the noise shook the very stones around her. She would not have been surprised if the daggers of rock hanging from the ceiling dislodged and fell.

Across the middle of the space, the towers of stone one expected to see had been destroyed and removed, leaving only lumps. But around the walls it was like a construction of some mad architect with multi-coloured columns—some ribbed, some smooth—reaching up from the floor to the ceiling.

Sheesha's roar did have one effect. The air was filled with the screechings of thousands upon thousands of *sikechasa*—which explained the smell—that exploded into the air like a storm, wheeling and turning, filling the whole space with their noise and fluttering. Yet not a single one of them touched her as she ran across the stone floor.

Men were shouting, some in fear, others in anger. She could hear someone trying to give orders to get things under control. There was a sharp *crack* from one of the carts: the shattering of wood. She glanced round to see Daybian smashing his forehead into the nose of a guard who seemed more fearful of the wheeling *sikechasa* than of the prince until the pain made him lose interest in everything else.

Yenteel and Gally were on the ground. Gally lay face down, whimpering in terror while Yenteel tore at the cords around his wrists with his teeth. The *sikechasa* were escaping through both tunnels and the air was clearing of them.

One of the carts collapsed as its axle snapped. Looesa stretched upwards and the binding ropes slipped from him. Behind Kantees, someone screamed and then went silent with a cracking of breaking bones. She chose not to look but focused on Daybian.

He was trying to get the knife from his prone assailant.

She pushed him out of the way. "Let me!"

Since her hands were free she was able grab the fellow's blade from his belt in a trice. She turned and grabbed one of Daybian's wrists to keep him still while she sawed through the leather thongs. One went, then another, and the cords fell away from him.

"Help Yenteel and Gally," she said into his ear. "I'll get the *ziri*."

He didn't argue. He didn't even pause but grabbed the armsman's sword and went. Looesa's jaws were clamped around the arm of one of the soldiers, who was whimpering in terror. Kantees looked away, she did not want to see.

Shingul was struggling in the cords that bound her wings to her body, the feathers protecting the flesh beneath from the coarseness of the ropes. Kantees could not imagine how much power Looesa had been able to bring to bear to snap his cart. That power now made the poor armsman scream as an accompaniment to sounds of bones crunching and flesh ripping.

"Lay still, Shingul," Kantees said quietly and the beast stopped struggling immediately. Kantees attacked the cords binding her neck. One at a time she hacked through them until they were loose enough for Shingul to raise her head.

As Kantees moved to attack the ropes on her body, Shingul's neck doubled over on itself, zipped over Kantees' shoulder, and snapped at something that screamed and then went silent. A sword clattered to the floor beside her.

Kantees concentrated on the ropes while Shingul's head hissed and weaved above her. Finally enough were gone and Shingul lifted herself up. She roared the way Sheesha had. Kantees could feel her anger like a wave of heat.

She looked up to see Yenteel and Gally working on Jintan's bonds. She could not help there. Daybian ran an armsman through with the sword and, as he turned and pulled the weapon from the man's belly, she saw the grim concentration on his face.

Then he noticed her watching him. She fully expected him to grin—but instead he lifted his sword before his face in salute. A *ziri* crunched something or, more likely, someone behind her.

And it was abruptly quiet.

2 7

"This respite will be momentary," said Daybian, his voice calm and low.

Kantees had never seen this side to the man before. He was deadly serious, so unlike the cocksure princeling she knew.

"We must go," he said. "They will return in greater numbers."

"Perhaps they will flee," said Yenteel. "I would, and not return."

Even Kantees knew that was wishful thinking.

"Gally does not like it here. Gally wants to fly away."

"Yes," said Kantees. "You give us wise counsel."

He grinned although she was sure he had no idea what her words meant.

At that moment Sheesha's head turned towards the main entrance and he growled. The other three followed suit. The enemy were coming.

"This way," said Kantees and headed at a jog back towards the ley-circle. "We can fly out."

From up the tunnel the sound of boots on stone grew like distant thunder. She and her companions ran faster but had barely reached the exit when the armsmen exploded from the other tunnel with a shout.

Kantees paused at the entrance to make sure Yenteel and Gally went through.

"Keep going, it only goes to the circle," she said. The armsmen were taking up position behind the shattered carts and debris. The whirring of an arrow startled her, but it was going away from them. Turning to see Daybian nocking another, she blinked. She had not even seen him pick them up.

The second arrow whistled away as Sheesha brought up the rear of the *ziri*.

"You go," said Daybian. "I can hold them off for a short time."

Kantees could see the five arrows at his feet. A very short time. An incoming arrow shattered as it hit the wall above the exit.

"They're as bad as me," said Daybian.

"Don't get yourself killed," she said.

He fired. Four arrows. "So you *do* care about me."

"As much as I care for any sad and pathetic animal. Oh!" An arrow grazed her arm, drawing blood.

"Love to chat," said Daybian. He fired. Three arrows. "But you have some other sad and pathetic animals to look after."

She turned away from him and hurried down the tunnel, feeling like she was never going to see him again. And for some reason, that made her chest hurt.

She picked up the pace. He only had a couple of arrows and while they might be cautious crossing the cave it wouldn't take them long. But all she and the others had to do was get on the *ziri* and fly out of here.

When she got to the bottom of the tunnel she had to push her way through four *ziri* and two humans crammed by the door.

"What's wrong?"

"Archers," said Yenteel and pointed up.

She cursed herself for an idiot. Of course. They weren't stupid; they would have surmised the plan and put men on guard.

"To the *Kisharuk* with them," she said and ran out into the circle.

There were three sets of candelabra. Before an arrow hit the ground she knocked the first one over, she had come out so fast and unexpectedly. She reached the second and that went over, too. Most of the candles went out as they hit the ground. The archers couldn't hit what they couldn't see. But they would have realised what she was doing and if they had any sense they would be aiming for the third one, waiting for her to appear.

She didn't stop moving but breathed a prayer to the Mother and then screamed as she ran at the third. Pain ripped through her leg as she struck its heavy metal stem and knocked it down. She fell in the other direction but kept rolling despite the pain, hoping to disappear into the shadows available.

She did not die.

Not yet.

But there was no time. Daybian would be out of arrows by now but he would stay there, pretending he was still able to shoot, to slow them down. He was an idiot too. They were well-matched in that way.

"Come out, quickly. Stay to the sides."

Yenteel and Gally emerged. Light came down from above, of course, and Kantees found it hard to believe that the people up there could not see them easily. But no arrows flew. They would be waiting for the *ziri* to come up, when they would be easy targets.

And they were right to do so; there was no way they could miss a bunch of giant flapping dragons. For a moment she contemplated returning to the cavern, but in that space the *ziri* would not be able to fly and could be picked off easily.

"Look," she said to the other two as Sheesha strode out into the circle. "We can ride without a saddle and reins." Sheesha stooped and she flung a leg over his neck. "We sit where the saddle would be and hook our legs under the wings like this."

"How can you guide them?" said Yenteel.

"You lean forwards, back, left, and right. They understand what's needed but mostly you just have to give them a direction and let them do it. You don't have to control their every movement."

She looked at Jintan. She expected he would just follow the rest, leaving Daybian behind.

"There will be archers at the top," she said. "Sheesha and I will go first and draw their fire."

"I'm sorry I have no pattern I can work to help," said Yenteel.

"Nobody has a pattern for this," she said.

But we are on a ley-circle, she thought. *It may not be the most powerful in the world but beneath us lies the power of the Mother's milk.*

She leaned forwards and put her arms around Sheesha's neck. In the distance she could hear fighting. They had reached Daybian. Very soon they would be here.

"Sheesha," she said quietly to him. "The power is here. Can we not use it, my love?"

She imagined she felt the power of the *zirichasa* and imagined the milk beneath them that did not lie quiet. It was a roiling lake, bubbling and steaming gold, desperate to be free. The raw power from which patterns were made, waiting to be shaped. Why not shaped by the *ziri*?

"Up, Sheesha!"

He burst into the air and stroked hard upwards. Faster and faster. The light grew.

And turned golden.

It was almost as if they jumped directly into the sky. She knew she should have fallen but there was no sensation. The light blinked away and for a moment they were falling. Kantees hung on as Sheesha regained control. They were above the hole, at least the height of the Ziri Tower.

Without a word from Kantees, Sheesha screamed and dived.

The well of the ley-circle was surrounded by armsmen, not a great number but plenty enough to shoot *ziri* in a barrel. But they were not peering into the well. They were staring up at Sheesha as he roared from the sky directly at them.

Kantees could barely look as the first half-dozen were knocked into the well. And, while Looesa and Shingul made their way from the depths, the archers ran from the winged monster, their weapons forgotten as this sky-demon that had shot from the well, bathed in golden light, came roaring at them.

Not a single arrow was fired.

Kantees saw Looesa and Shingul emerge into the light but Jintan was not following.

Kantees oriented herself and pointed back along the coast. "Yenteel! Follow the coast until you come to a village that is burning. Wait for us there."

He nodded and awkwardly managed to get Shingul turning.

Sheesha needed no encouragement to dive back into the hole. Kantees came down slowly, she did not want to collide with Jintan on the way up.

The words "Jintan, up!" echoed from below and Kantees grinned in relief. Daybian was too stupid to die.

Then there was a cry of pain—not human. "Jintan! Come on, you can do it."

"Daybian!" shouted Kantees.

"Come on, Jintan, old warrior!"

"Daybian!"

Kantees couldn't see anything. She urged Sheesha lower but he was reluctant. What could he see that she could not?

"Ah! Get off me, you brute." Daybian.

All she could hear was hissing and snapping which ceased abruptly. An arrow arched up and over Sheesha before falling back. She could have snatched it from the air if it had been closer.

"Daybian!"

"I'm all right, Kantees. Jintan ..." His voice broke off. "Don't come down. Too many."

Then there was another thud and he said nothing more.

Kantees held in her grief.

"Sheesha, go."

Strong wingbeats carried her up and out.

2 8

She was crying for Jintan, not Daybian—she didn't even like him much. The world was a damp blur and she barely knew the right direction. But Sheesha did. Did Sheesha grieve for Jintan? She could not tell, but if she worried for someone else she could push her own sorrow away.

This time she had succeeded in getting one of them killed.

The others, especially Daybian, would say that it was not her fault. But she was in charge, although she was not entirely sure how that had happened. Perhaps if she had been willing to let Daybian lead they wouldn't have got into this situation. *Perhaps*.

And now Jintan was dead. He was old, of course, but that was not the reason his body lay at the bottom of the well getting cold. She was. If she hadn't been so foolhardy this morning—was it only this morning? If she had not tried to kill herself and leapt from the tower, then Sheesha would not have saved her and she would not have been carried away by him.

Daybian would have been taken off to wherever the Hamalain were taking him. Perhaps they would have taken her as well. She did not want to admit that Yenteel was right. If they had followed *that* course she, Gally, and he would be dead and the *ziri* would be living in the Hamalain tower.

Instead they were all alive save for one *zirichak*.

That did not make it all right. She cared more for the *ziri* than any of the people, except perhaps Gally. The loss of Jintan hurt her like a thousand torments.

But this was no time to be maudlin. She needed to focus. They may have lost Jintan and Daybian but she had a good idea of where the *tekrak* was and where it was heading. While it was clearly possible to make a *tekrak* fly at night, it was still a plant and she doubted it liked to travel in the dark. Plants wanted light, and especially sunlight. That was why they flew as high as possible when they travelled the skies in spring and autumn—to stay above the clouds—and why they landed at night. To feed and to rest.

And they were now just a day behind it and its handlers (or was it its crew?), and the *ziri* could fly faster than a *tekrak*. The only question was which direction the enemy had taken.

The wind had dried her tears. She took Sheesha up so that she could see further. Hopefully, his superior eyesight would spot the other two soon. They needed her direction.

The smoke of the burned village came into view and she set Sheesha to descend. She heard the deep, hooting calls of Looesa and Shingul as they caught sight of Sheesha. It made her smile. Below she could see them on the top of the cliff with their wings outstretched, two figures standing near to them.

And at what cost had she rescued them? The armsmen would tell their masters how the *ziri* had shot like a golden arrow from the ley-circle and at such a speed they could not possibly have fired on it. Then the Hamalain would know that their search had been successful, even though they had lost their brother. Just as Yenteel no doubt did. He could be smug in the knowledge that he had chosen the right person to attach himself to.

But, she thought, *it's not me. It's Sheesha.*

"Gally rode Looesa without a saddle, Kantees," was the first thing he said to her after she slipped from Sheesha's back to the ground. She put her arm around his shoulders and gave him a hug. "And you were like a flower!" He grinned widely.

She frowned. "A flower, Gally? I am not like a flower."

"A yellow flower growing very fast."

Then she laughed. Of course. "Yes, I suppose I was."

"I am also interested in how you became a flower," said Yenteel, and he was not smiling at all. "Very interested indeed."

"Where is Jintan?" said Gally.

Kantees froze. How could she explain to Gally? She looked at Yenteel and the look on her face must have told him everything.

"Daybian?" he said.

"I'm sorry, Gally, but Jintan was hurt by the armsmen when he tried to escape with Daybian."

"Is he killed?"

Kantees was not sure whether he meant Jintan or Daybian.

"Daybian is alive, I think." She stopped with the lump in her throat threatening to steal her words. "Jintan was killed." Her voice came out in a croak that could barely be heard.

"Poor Jintan," said Gally. "Gally thinks he would have liked to be like Sheesha's flower."

Kantees turned away to face the sea. Her throat hurt, and the grief was like heavy clouds in her eyes. She did not trust herself to speak without sobbing and she did not want to do that in front of Gally and Kantees.

As she faced away from them, trying to get control of herself, a group of the villagers appeared over the top of the cliff. She recognised Welyn, and wondered why he was chosen to speak to them. Was it because their skin colour was the same? Did people really care out here, even though Welyn lived among them and had even had a wife and child? People were strange.

She was more surprised to see the Old Mother. For some reason Kantees had it in her head the woman would stay in her cave, weaving patterns to ensure a good harvest of fish, and healing the sick.

So Kantees swallowed her grief and brushed the tears from her eyes, and when they arrived she introduced them: Welyn first, and then the Old Mother.

"She's not old," said Gally.

"My name is Lintha," she said to Gally. "I am not old, but I am older than you. So you can call me Mother."

There was something about her that made Gally stare and then realise he was staring, for which he had been punished in the past, and he looked away.

"Old Mother," said Yenteel. "I am honoured to be in the presence of one so revered and wise."

She looked slightly amused. "I suspect you are a man with a sly tongue."

Yenteel did not smile but looked her in the eye. "Everything I have is at your disposal. Even my tongue."

Kantees was shocked and outraged on the woman's behalf, but she just laughed.

"If I require your service, I will send for you. But I doubt there is anything you can do for me."

"I am well travelled and have learnt much. I am happy to be a teacher as well as a student."

At which point Kantees became confused. From what Yenteel had said back at the castle, she assumed he preferred the company of men. Yet here he was, flirting with the wise woman of the village.

She interrupted. "We have important matters to deal with."

Yenteel had the decency to look embarrassed.

"You intend to go after the raiders?" said Lintha.

Kantees nodded. "They have the son of the Jakalain, and your daughters." She glanced at Welyn's face as she said it; he mirrored her own grief, though she could not imagine what it must feel like to lose one's own flesh. She had no one but the *ziri*.

"If you are able, then we will be forever in your debt."

"You are Taymalin and we are nothing but runaway slaves. You will owe us nothing."

Lintha smiled. "You think I am Taymalin because my skin is pale? My father was as dark as Welyn, and he was the leader of the village for most of his life. Just as Welyn is now—why do you think he is the one who speaks with you? My mother was dark too, but her mother had been of the Taymalin—as much as we care about such things—and I take from her. It is only in the cities that those in power make distinctions based on skin. We cannot afford to. Our blood is the same colour and our sweat tastes the same. It is only by our blood and sweat that we live."

Kantees was not sure what to say. She felt she owed them an apology, but to give one would reveal the depth of her own prejudice—inherited from the masters. So instead she went back to the point.

"Can you help us?"

"We can give you food and a place to sleep for the night that is out of the wind."

"And the *ziri*?"

"There are caves large enough."

"I would sleep with the *ziri*," she said. "And so will Gally."

"I'll take a bed," said Yenteel.

Lintha gave him a sidelong glance. "We will see what can be arranged. Our houses are barely habitable and it will take a while to put them back in order. The fishing must always take precedence."

The wind had increased and was blowing the feathers of the *zirichasa* every which way.

And then rain hit them. Freezing cold, from off the sea.

Kantees, Gally, and the three *ziri* were housed in a cave that was used for storage and stank of fish. But it was deep and well out of the rain. Dry wood was brought for them to build a fire. The cave became smoky but not so bad that they couldn't sleep.

Yenteel, as he had said, did not sleep in the cave. Kantees suspected he might be with the Old Mother, and shook her head. It seemed inappropriate somehow and still a little confusing. So instead she worried about Daybian. She hoped he had not been killed, but she was determined to find him anyway. Then she would avenge or rescue him, whichever it happened to be.

Then she thought of Jintan, and cried into Sheesha's feathers.

29

reakfast involved bread and eggs. Kantees was grateful it wasn't fish, though she suspected fish was brought out for meals most of the time. The fields at the top of the cliff did not look as if they provided more than a meagre supplement for the main product. The bread was old and hard, since the ovens had been destroyed in the fires, but the eggs flavoursome.

Yenteel joined them when she and Gally had almost finished, but he did not want any of their food. He looked tired. Kantees shook her head slightly, and went back to finishing the mess of eggs on the stone that served as a plate.

"Did you receive any divine inspiration as to where we should go?" said Kantees in a tone that was more cutting than she had intended when the words were in her head.

But Yenteel did not seem to notice. "Along the coast."

"Gally likes the eggs."

Yenteel spoke before Kantees had a chance. "That's good, Gally, make sure you eat them all up, too."

Kantees frowned at him. Did he think he was going to usurp her authority over Gally as well? She was almost tempted to tell him about the *ziri* magic. Just to show him she was still in charge.

It was almost as if he read her mind. "Are you going to explain about what you and Sheesha did yesterday?"

"I don't know what you mean."

He turned and looked at her. He might have been tired but she felt as if he was attempting to pull the very thoughts from her mind. Honestly, she didn't know why she was being so contrary. Only that she was irritated with him.

"Magic, Kantees."

"No."

"Yes, it was magic. I felt it. You said you don't know any patterns."

"I wasn't lying."

"We are all aware of how accomplished a liar you are. Please do not prolong this."

"I'm not lying," she said. "I don't know patterning. I don't want to know. You can keep your precious secrets."

"It's not my secrets I'm concerned about, it's yours. You and Sheesha shot out of that well like an arrow from a bow," he said. "We would have ended up like one of those urchins in the sea if you had not been able to get out."

She knew about urchins. She had seen them with and without their spines at the scholar's house. Then her eyes widened, as a realisation came upon her: the vast ball she and Sheesha had landed on. It had been like an urchin's shell.

It was crazy. How could an urchin have grown that big unless it was an abomination? Did that mean that a *nachak* as big as a mountain might truly stalk the heart of Esternes? Everything she had thought were legends became revealed to her as she travelled.

"What?" said Yenteel.

She realised she had become silent and withdrawn into her thoughts, even though he had been talking to her.

"I'm sorry, Yenteel. I should have told you but I barely even believed it myself even though I was there and saw it happen." Because, when you are a slave, secrets are the one thing that you can keep and no one can steal them away.

"Tell me what?"

She shook her head. "First you must explain something. When

you were in the cell you said you would have spent the night with the soldier if he had wanted—rather than having him lock you up."

"I did say that."

"I believed you."

"It was not a lie."

"Then tell me you did not spend the night with Lintha last night."

He smiled. "But, Kantees, I did lie with the Old Mother last night."

"I don't understand. I know that some men prefer the company of other men. I thought you were one of them, yet"—she threw her hands up—"last night?"

"Have you never observed beauty in another woman?"

"Yes, but that's not the same. All women are more beautiful than I ..." She hesitated. "Except Hogoma. And that's not her fault."

"Did I meet her?"

"You would remember. But it's not the same, Yenteel."

"Not precisely, no," he said. "But have you ever felt attraction to a man?"

She knew the answer only too well. "I don't know what you mean."

"Do lies always come so readily to your lips?"

She sighed, and lied. "Yes, I have."

"Then just imagine that you might also feel that for a woman as well as a man."

"I don't."

His smile changed to a mischievous grin. "Are you lying to me again?" She frowned and he laughed out loud. "I am only teasing you."

"So you would lie with a man or a woman?"

"I believe I have said so," replied Yenteel.

"Do you want to lie with me?"

"What a fateful question," he said. "Consider if I were to say no, then you would be affronted and upset. You would think there was some fault with you. Yet if I were to say aye, you would be threatened and disgusted. And try to push me away. There are some questions, Kantees, it is not wise to ask."

"So you don't want to?"

"And there you have it. I cannot even be equivocal because you instantly jump to the negative. This is a conversation, Kantees, that neither you nor I can win. Let us return to the real question, shall we?"

She was annoyed he had not answered her, regardless that she understood the logic of why. She took a deep breath and tried to put it aside.

"I was not lying when I said I did nothing. It was Sheesha that did it."

Yenteel glanced across at the *ziri*. Kantees followed his gaze. Sheesha was leaning over a rock pool staring into it intently, his whole body still—not relaxed, but rigid as if he was holding himself ready. His head lashed down into the water, which erupted in a great splash. He came back up with something wriggling between his razor teeth. Then he sneezed and his prey disappeared back into the pool.

Sheesha shook himself to get rid of the water, which sprayed from his head and neck feathers. He looked around for his lost meal but couldn't see it.

"Sheesha did the magic?" said Yenteel.

"People do magic, animals *are* magic," said Kantees.

"And nobody has discovered this before?"

Kantees shrugged. "I don't know. Perhaps it was forgotten."

Yenteel nodded. "Things do get forgotten."

She looked out, past Sheesha, at the sea and to the horizon. "It happened yesterday." *Was it truly only yesterday?*

"Yes, I am curious about yesterday too. How was it you escaped?"

She hesitated. She had been in such a strange place in her mind when Trimiente had questioned her. "I ..." She wanted to lie, wanted to say that she had leapt onto Sheesha's back to fly to freedom. But if that had been the truth, she would never have discovered the magic.

"I tried to kill myself by throwing myself out of the tower." The words came out all in a rush and tears ran down her cheeks. "I'm so sorry. They were threatening Sheesha, they would have hurt him. It was the only thing I could do to save him."

Yenteel moved closer and put his arm around her shoulders. She tensed at his touch but then dropped her head onto his shoulders and sobbed.

"That was very brave," he said after a while.

"It was stupid," she said. "I deserted you all."

"If you did it to save Sheesha, then that is brave. It may not have been the most intelligent thing to do, but it was not cowardly."

He let her cry more and then said, "However, you are here crying on my shoulder so somehow you managed not to die. That sounds like an interesting story."

So she told him how Sheesha had come down after her, and prevented her from being dashed against the rocks and houses. And how he had sped away as his magic took hold. She told him about the giant urchin shell and the *shocalin*. Yenteel was impressed at that.

After she had described the return journey, he listened to how she had begun the rescue, at which point he knew the rest.

"But how is it Sheesha could fly fast so quickly in the rescue?"

"The circle," she said. "It was the same as when you used the one in the forest for your pattern. I thought perhaps Sheesha could use it, and he did."

"Using the power from the forest ley-circle was your idea," said Yenteel.

"But it worked."

"Yes, and you suggested it to Sheesha, didn't you? Just as you did me?"

"Don't be foolish, *ziri* don't understand language."

"So how was it you explained your idea to him?"

Kantees opened her mouth to answer and then closed it again. It had not occurred to her, everything had happened so naturally.

"Do you think the others can do it?" said Yenteel.

"The other *ziri*? I don't know but every *tekrasa* can fly and has a fire-tube, doesn't it?"

He nodded. "If it truly is part of their nature then they would all be capable." He looked at Looesa and Shingul. "But perhaps they lose the ability with age."

"Sheesha did not seem exhausted by it," said Kantees. "But it was only for a very short time, I suppose." And then she stood up as if she wanted to put an end to the conversation. "We should go. We have Jelamie and five girls to rescue."

"Have you given any thought to that?"

"I have not," she said. "But let us find them first."

3 0

Kantees sent Gally to find Welyn and inform him they were leaving. He returned with a group of villagers and the Old Mother.

Welyn gave them a couple of sacks filled with dried and smoked fish with some bread. Kantees was genuinely grateful though she was more concerned about feeding the *ziri*, or at least giving them an opportunity to feed that did not lose them too much time.

Lintha gave Yenteel several pieces of rolled-up bark and a kiss on the cheek. "They are for mist and for rain," she said, "and another for wind; you may find them useful when your other magic lets you down."

Yenteel seemed touched. Kantees assumed they must be patternings. He must have been a good lover, she thought. Or Lintha hadn't had it for a long time—it probably wasn't good to indulge with the villagers themselves. She told herself off for being so harsh. Lintha did not deserve bad thoughts.

"Come on," she said impatiently. "The sun is climbing."

The *zirichasa* lay down so the three riders could climb on easily, and then stood up on their hind legs. Kantees gave a short wave and gave Sheesha a little kick.

A flurry of wings brought them up to the level of the cliff.

Kantees gave Sheesha a direction along the coast away from Hamalain. The villagers were lost to sight almost immediately. Kantees debated how they should proceed. Staying low along the coast did not seem best. They wanted to be able to approach the *tekrak* without being seen. So it was a choice between going out to sea, or going high.

She glanced up. It was fully overcast but the clouds were not low and it didn't feel as if it would rain today.

If she were a raider, she would be more concerned at being followed or attacked by land. The sea would not be considered a threat. So if their assumptions were correct and the raiders were following the coast, it would be best to be over the sea. *And* high.

Sheesha curved out over the water, gaining height, and the other two followed in their perfect formation. Kantees looked behind. She missed seeing Jintan there. She missed having Daybian to complain about.

One thing at a time, Kantees.

She had vowed to save Jelamie, even if it was only a promise to herself. She had promised Welyn she would save his daughter if she could. Or have her revenge. He had not asked for that but she would not leave any of these men alive if it was within her power to bring about their deaths. She had no love for Lorima Hamalain, but they had killed him in cold blood. And these men had shot their own soldier to make sure he could not reveal their secrets.

On the night everything changed.

If it had not happened she would still be in the eyrie at Jakalain with Sheesha, preparing him for the races while dodging Daybian's advances. Something that she would not have been able to do forever. Eventually he would have lost his patience and forced her. But now, she would never be able to do it again. Ever. Was this better or worse? Or was it just different?

But something inside her said that he wouldn't have forced her. It was what he had said himself. If she did not want it, but let him anyway, he did not want it. She would probably have given it to him out of pity. He was not bad for a Taymalin master. Even if he was arrogant. She smiled. It turned out that he had been good with his weapon after all. It had been a very different Daybian fighting in the cavern. A man that she might respect.

Perhaps when she rescued him she would apologise. And he would wonder what for, and she would tell him all the nasty thoughts she had had about him. And he would laugh, because it would be all about him. She changed her mind; apologising to him was a very bad idea.

Sheesha flattened out at a height that gave them a clear view of the coastline and a good distance inland. They could see perhaps seven or eight leagues in all directions. It was invigorating. Out to sea she could see a fishing vessel and wondered if it was the same one as yesterday. If it was, it might give her some idea of how far Sheesha had travelled in that short time. But it might not be.

She allowed her gaze to wander to the coastline ahead of them. It reminded her of a broken biscuit from which bites had been taken at intervals—large and small—and the crumbs scattered in trails out into the ocean. Further along the coast she could see much larger dark lumps curving out from the cliffs and ending in a much larger landmass.

The world was big, she thought, and there was so much to know. She had no idea what those islands were called. Up until a moment ago she had not even known they existed. Did people live on them? If they did, were they free Kadralin? Or Taymalin? Or perhaps even *shocalin*. Did *shocalin* live on land, or only at sea? Did they make their homes inside giant urchins? Of course, that assumed she was right about the creatures she saw being *shocalin* and that they were living inside the shell.

She shook her head. There were more questions in this world than there were answers. She could never know it all. Whether it was about the world around her or the world within. More questions than she knew how to answer.

The afternoon wore on and she ran out of thoughts. She did not have to keep her eyes on the coast the whole time. It seemed to move so slowly she could just glance at it now and then. They passed a dozen tiny fishing villages crowding the cliffs as the mountains closed in tighter to the sea. The cliffs themselves became taller.

They needed to stop. The *ziri* needed to eat. She scanned the coast carefully. Out of the high hills rushed a huge waterfall. The river had created a lake at the top of the cliff but its water leaked down through the rock itself and sprayed out into the sea.

Buildings huddled on the heights, and there were small boats on the lake instead of the ocean. Herds of *fenichasa* and other animals were dotted about chewing on the greenery. She contemplated moving on to a place where they would not be observed but the day was growing late and after their recent experience she thought perhaps they might not be in danger.

At a touch from her knee, Sheesha curved inland and lost height.

She wondered whether she should have consulted with Yenteel but it was almost impossible to have a conversation when flying, and the *zirichasa* seemed disinclined to fly out of their formation. She looked over her shoulder at Yenteel and pointed at the lake. He smiled, so she guessed he thought it was a reasonable decision.

The *ziri* were flying directly at the houses at considerable speed when Kantees realised she might have made a mistake. They had been spotted by somebody and now people were running back and forth among the buildings. Moments later one man with a bow appeared, then another behind him.

Kantees leaned hard to the right and Sheesha veered off. But *Kisharuk* curse her if she was going to let them be forced away by ignorant villagers whose first response was to attack. She kept Sheesha turning until he went into a landing spiral.

They touched down near the drop-off between the cliff and the lake. The ground trembled beneath her feet when she jumped down. A small stream of water ran through what looked like an old riverbed, overgrown with plants. The lake itself had a maelstrom at this end where water fed down into the tunnel below and out from the cliff. The vibration in the ground must be the river forcing its way through the rock.

At the far end of the lake, where the water tumbled from the mountains, a mist filled the air. It was a beautiful place, she thought, except for the men with weapons hurrying in their direction.

"I'll do the talking," said Yenteel.

"Just as you like," she said. "But, to be clear, I do not want to be killed. So don't aggravate them. I came down here because this looked like a good place to feed the *ziri*."

Yenteel did not acknowledge her but walked towards the men with his hands held out to show he was not armed. They did not look friendly.

"Get back on Looesa, Gally," she said. "I am not sure these people will be friends."

"Sheesha wants to eat a *fenichak*," he said.

She stared at him. With everything that had been happening she wondered whether he had learnt how to read their minds. Not that that seemed likely. It wasn't hard to know what a *zirichak* wanted: a place to sleep, a chance to fly fast, and food. They were often fed *fenichasa*, so to their thinking the ones around here were a likely meal.

Her choice of landing place was looking worse by the minute.

She looked across at Yenteel. She couldn't hear what they were saying but the men had lowered their weapons and were talking. At least that meant they weren't going to get shot. Not yet, anyway.

She turned and walked towards the cliff. The grass went right to the edge but she wasn't intending to go too close. It might be treacherous. Then Sheesha's wing came down in front of her and his head curved round as he tried to look at her with both eyes. She smiled at him.

"I wasn't going to jump, Sheesha," she said. "Not this time."

He made a grumbling noise in the back of his very long and deep throat. She leaned against his wing and looked out to sea. There were islands down there. Not big ones, but even the smallest was covered with trees and undergrowth.

"I bet there's food you can eat on those islands, Sheesha." She pointed. "Why don't you have a look? These villagers are too scared of you eating theirs."

And Sheesha looked where she was pointing. He snorted and launched himself off the cliff in a long glide, followed by Shingul. She turned to see why Looesa hadn't gone too but Gally was on his back.

"You can get down, Gally. Looesa can go with Sheesha to get some food."

As Gally slid from the *ziri*'s back, Looesa made a very ungainly run at the cliff edge and launched himself off. For all they were awkward on land, the *zirichasa* were beautiful as they swooped across the intervening water and circled the first of the islands.

"Kantees!"

She tore her eyes from the *ziri* and saw Yenteel beckoning to her. She walked over, not in a hurry, as she had no real interest in what these people had to say.

"This is Bolda," he said indicating the middle-aged man with the bow who stood in front of the others. The men were of various ages, young and old. All looked stern—apart from the youngest who was eyeing her the way young men often did, with his eyes directed at her chest instead of her face. She was used to it.

"Bolda wants to know what you did with the *zirichasa*."

"I sent them to the islands down there to feed," she said to Yenteel, and then addressed Bolda directly. "I guessed you were concerned for your herds."

"You *sent* them?" he said.

"I suggested it."

"You talk to the *ziri*?"

Kantees shrugged. She wasn't going to explain that it wasn't like that. She said things and sometimes Sheesha understood what she wanted, and sometimes he didn't. Let them think she could make herself understood all the time.

"They were hungry and needed to feed."

"Will they come back?"

"Of course."

"We have children here."

"They don't eat children." Wild ones *might* if they were hungry, she supposed, but Kantees was reasonably sure that Sheesha wouldn't. "Especially if they've just eaten."

Yenteel interrupted. "Bolda knows something about the *tekrak*."

"You've seen it?"

"It's one of the reasons they were cautious about us," said Yenteel.

"The man can speak for himself, can't he?" She looked pointedly at Bolda.

"The monstrous thing flew over at midday."

"Which way was it going?"

Bolda pointed further along the coast.

"At midday?" She looked at the position of the sun, behind the light cloud. "We can't be far behind it."

She almost wished she hadn't sent the *ziri* to feed. If she had known before, they could have mounted up and gone after it.

"Why do you seek it?" said Bolda in a cautious voice that almost suggested he didn't want to know.

"They have kidnapped and most likely despoiled children, destroyed one village we know about, and have murdered. I intend to have revenge upon them." She said it in a matter-of-fact way, which was the only way she knew how to deal with what they had done without letting out the anger she held in her heart.

"Did they murder your kin, Mother?"

Kantees hesitated both at the question and his choice of honorific for her. "No, not my kin."

"But you declare a blood feud?"

Was that what it was? She nodded. "It must be done."

"Their crimes are against both Kadralin and Taymalin," said Yenteel. "There are no others who would stand for both, save for Kantees who commands the *zirichasa*."

Her heart froze at Yenteel's words. What pattern was he weaving? Was he attempting to trap her in a legend? Trying to make her into something she wasn't?

She wanted to deny it and make him take the words back, but it was too late. She could see it in the eyes of the men who stood there, see the idea take hold and worm into their minds. She could almost see the way she grew in their eyes—or perhaps it was the way they shrank. Before they had been defiant and willing to fight or even kill her to protect what was theirs. But Yenteel had made them slaves to an idea.

There was nothing she could do now. She would deal with these raiders and then she would turn her back on Yenteel. If she chose to leave there was nothing he could do to stop her. That would stop him doing any more harm. These people did not need someone else to become slave to. There was too much of that already in the world.

They were all looking at her as if they expected something. She glanced at Yenteel, and she could almost see his grin although his face showed nothing of it. It wasn't on the outside but he was triumphant within.

"We need to rest," she said finally. "But have to remain here so the *ziri* know where to find us when they return. And then we'll leave."

"I will send someone with food and water," said Bolda.

She knew better than to insult him by refusing. The group turned away but left two guards.

Kantees lay down on the grass and closed her eyes. She wanted to shout at Yenteel but it would have to wait. He settled himself cross-legged facing her not too far away.

"I hate you," she said in a conversational tone that she did not think would carry to the villagers on guard. "You people say that you only follow the World's Pattern, but the truth is that you bind the world to your own will. You twist it into the image you want."

"I won't deny it."

"Good."

"But that's not the whole story. My master is working for a future for us all."

She propped herself up on her elbows. "What about my choice, Yenteel? What if I don't want this future your master envisages?"

"Then you will prevent it from happening."

"I don't have that sort of power." She lay back again and stared at the mottled cloud shapes above her. She was glad the sun wasn't shining. It would annoy her on a day as depressing as this.

"Power is a strange and fickle thing," he said. "Sometimes it's just a matter of saying the right words at the right moment. Those who try to grab power find it impossible to hold, and it slips through their fingers. Their mistake is in thinking power is something that can be taken. That's not how it is. The Hamalain—even the Jakalain who are less tyrannical—their power is maintained only by force. It is easy for them to lose it, should they slip for only a moment."

"You're going to tell me what it *is* like, I suppose?"

"True power is in giving. It is the willingness to give."

"So you manipulate these poor people into thinking I am some sort of goddess who they can worship and follow?"

"A nudge in the right direction. There may come a time when you need all the help you can get."

Kantees stood up and walked away from him. She went back to the cliff edge and stared out and down at the islands. She couldn't see Sheesha or the others but that probably meant they were on the ground, eating.

She looked up at the sun again. Time was getting on and they needed to get moving. But the *ziri* would need time to digest before they could move on again.

And they needed a plan.

31

"I want one of your children," said Kantees to Bolda as she ate some of the food the villagers had brought. More fish, naturally, but this time with *kilikash* mashed up on the side melted with *fenichak* cheese. She was surprised how good it was. The *ziri* had returned and were resting while they digested their meal.

Bolda frowned at the question, thinking the worst. Kantees hoped her idea might help to dissipate those Yenteel had planted earlier.

"Why?"

"The child needs to be brave and small to enter the camp of the raiders. They don't have to *be* young but should *look* young. And preferably I'd like a girl."

"But why, Mother?"

Kantees cursed inwardly; this was having the reverse effect because she was asking for something outrageous.

"Ulina," said one of the other men, sitting behind Bolda. "She is crazy and has no family."

Bolda liked that idea. He nodded and the man who had spoken jumped to his feet and went back towards the village.

"What do you mean, crazy?"

"She climbs where no one who valued their life would climb," said Bolda. He pointed at the cliff. "She went down to the sea there because she had found the eggs of a nesting bird on the edge and dropped one."

"But it would be broken," said Kantees.

Bolda shrugged. "She would not say why. But she went down and returned." Then he pointed behind himself at the waterfall that thundered from the mountains. "She climbed to the valley from which the water pours."

Kantees stared. It was higher than a Ziri Tower. "Did she say why she did it?"

"Because she wanted to see."

The conversation lapsed as she, Yenteel, and Gally finished the food that had been brought. She thought she might need a rest to digest the *kilikash*, which now sat heavily on her stomach. It had been good, though. She said so and that pleased Bolda more than it should.

The girl arrived at a run. She was dressed in a smock that had been sewn and patched so much it seemed most of the original material had been replaced. And it was dirty, as were her bare feet. Under the dirt and ragged shift she was pale as any Taymalin and so thin she might have been a spirit barely occupying physical form.

"I am Ulina, Mother, and I would like to ride the *ziri*."

Something about her and the way she spoke made Kantees smile.

"Greetings, Ulina. If you want to ride the *ziri* then you must call me Kantees."

"Why?"

"Because that is my name."

If Kantees had been concerned as to whether Ulina would be as clever as she needed the child to be, that worry was blown away by the quick, brown eyes that took in everything. "You have three *ziri* and there are three of you. What will I ride?"

"You will ride Sheesha with me."

"Then I can go." It was not a question.

Kantees laughed. "Yes, it seems you can. But this will be dangerous and you may be killed. We may all be killed before the sun sets tomorrow."

Now came Ulina's turn to laugh. "Every day we may die. I do not fear death."

"But do you welcome it into your heart?"

"I do not! Because each day is new and there are new things in it. I want to see everything."

Kantees stood up. "Very well, Ulina, I will accept you on this journey, and when it is done you can come back and tell everyone what happened."

"No."

"No?"

"I don't want to come back. I have discovered everything there is to know about this place. I want to see new things. I will only come if you will take me with you forever, Kantees of the *Ziri*."

Kantees looked at Yenteel, who was sitting nearby. Not only had his words worked their patterning on the mind of Bolda and probably those of his men, but it had already spread to the village.

He raised his eyebrows and smiled. "There is nothing more powerful than ideas, Kantees. They burn like fire through wheat fields. And they cannot be extinguished."

"But they can be lost and forgotten, Yenteel," she said and turned back to Ulina. "I promise that I will take you with me, Ulina, until you grow bored with me, or one or other of us is dead."

"Blood bond!" said Ulina. Kantees sighed. Her palm was still tight from where she had cut it to make the paste for the patterning back in the forest. Perhaps she could get away with a small cut on the thumb in this case.

She knelt and pulled out her knife. It was none too sharp after all the use it had had and needed some time with a sharpening block. But Ulina plunged her hand into the neck of her smock and pulled on the chain that hung there until out came a tiny sheath from which she drew a tiny blade.

There were patterns on its surface.

Kantees was aware of these patterned knives but had never seen one; it could cut steel and never needed sharpening. They were worth a thousand slaves. She wondered what the child was doing with it and looked at Bolda, who shrugged.

"She had it with her when she wandered into the village." He gave the impression he wasn't telling the entire truth. But it didn't matter, it explained why they were happy for her to go on this trip. She wasn't really one of theirs.

Kantees pricked her thumb so a drop of blood oozed from it. She handed the tiny blade, shorter than her little finger, back to Ulina who did the same and they pressed their thumbs together.

"There," said Ulina. "Now you must keep your promise."

"I would have anyway."

But Ulina ignored that and put her blade away.

"How old are you?" said Kantees. The girl looked to have perhaps seven or eight years but she seemed older. Ulina shook her head.

"She was three years at most when she turned up here. That was seven years ago."

"Seven boring years," said Ulina.

"Better you take her," said Bolda, "or one day she will anger someone too much. As it is she will die an old maid."

Kantees turned her back on them and went to the *ziri*. She stroked along Sheesha's neck feathers, blue and gold. He was beautiful. And he didn't argue the way people did. The way *she* did.

"Are you ready?" she said.

In response, Sheesha pushed back onto his hind legs, stretched his wings to their full extent, and pushed his head into the sky. He relaxed and shook his feathers back into position. He was ready.

Kantees looked over her shoulder. "Time to go."

If this worked the way she hoped, they would find the *tekrak* on the ground and would be able to put her plan into action. Ulina wasn't vital to the plan but it would help if she could do what was asked of her. Kantees was sure she would at least be willing to try.

Ulina appeared at Kantees' hip, looking up at Sheesha's head and neck.

"He's big."

"He could eat you in one swallow."

"Then I would not be able to come with you."

"But you would be with me. In his tummy."

Without being asked, Sheesha put his head and neck down so Kantees could mount.

"Sheesha, this is Ulina, she's going to be riding with me."

Sheesha grumbled.

"What did he say, Kantees of the *Ziri*?" said Ulina.

"He said he is very strong and won't even notice you."

Kantees put her leg over the *ziri*'s neck, then lifted Ulina up and in front of her. There was a little adjustment to be done but Ulina was so small she could sit between Kantees' legs and still be partly on the wings.

"You can hold on to his feathers," said Kantees. "But don't pull them hard. He won't like it and they will just come out anyway."

With that she gave Sheesha a little squeeze with her thighs. He went back on his haunches and launched himself upwards. Kantees realised she had forgotten to check on the others but a quick glance showed her both Gally and Yenteel were with them.

Ulina laughed as each wingbeat lifted them higher. Kantees turned the *ziri* along the coast and he kept climbing.

"Keep your eyes open for the *tekrak* on the ground, Ulina."

"I will."

The clouds had cleared and, in the east, the mountains were bright against the darkening sky. Kantees was not sure what she was feeling as they travelled along the coast again with the sun descending into the sea. She was excited they would finally catch up with the raiders, but the excitement was mixed with dread and apprehension.

Without Daybian it would be just her and Yenteel against so many armed men. She thought she knew what she needed to do but it depended on many things she did not know, or could only guess.

The sky darkened as the sun burned into the horizon. She hoped that the moons would not appear too soon. They needed as much dark as possible.

Stars emerged as the sky went black and still they flew. The temperature dropped. Kantees put her arms around Ulina, partly to keep the girl warm but also to stay warm herself.

The *ziri* were not bothered by the dark, just as she thought. It was always assumed they wanted to sleep at night because that's what their owners and keepers did. The *zirichasa* were happy to oblige but it seemed night-time sleep was not a requirement.

The sea was one shade of dark, reflecting the stars, but the land was a deeper dark with the occasional fire, or houses lit from the inside.

"Kantees of the Ziri," said Ulina, and she pointed.

Kantees followed the direction the child was pointing and saw the open campfires highlighting the great round body of the *tekrak*. Her heart jumped, her breathing quickened, and fear crept through her fingers.

The time had come.

*B*right Lostimal had stayed below the horizon so far but Colimar had risen, casting its wan red light across the land. Perhaps it was for the best; they needed some light, but not too much.

Kantees and Gally stood with the three *ziri* on the edge of the cliff. From below the breaking waves roared their constant thunder. Yenteel and Ulina were making their way inland towards a low ridge. The raiders' encampment was out of sight over the top.

They had doubled back a good distance and then flown in low across the sea, finally rising up to land at the top without being seen in the dim red moonlight. That part of the plan had gone well enough, but there was nothing to disrupt it. If Ulina failed, the raiders would be on their guard.

"But what if they stay awake all night?" Kantees had said to Yenteel.

"They are arrogant men and they have alcohol," he replied. "They will drink themselves into a stupor."

"They will have men on guard."

"Who will also be drinking, because they are raiders and mercenaries who have no paymaster but themselves."

"They will be wreaking their lusts on the girls."

Yenteel could not deny it. "That is why we are here, Kantees. We cannot save them from the past, but we can save them from the future."

And he had said it in such a pointed way that she could not help but think of his words about his master, and her. In what way was her interference any different from someone who wanted to save the world?

She did not want to save the world—just the girls. She had seen plenty who were mistreated, women of any age who bore the marks of men who owned them in one way or another. It was not fair and those that did it should be punished.

But she was risking the lives of Yenteel, Ulina, and Gally just to do it. Did she have that right? Ulina certainly didn't understand.

So she had tried to explain.

"My master told me to obey your instructions," said Yenteel.

"Even to death?" She had become exasperated with his attitude.

"He did say it could happen, but then nothing in this world is certain, Kantees. I could be eaten by a wild *zirichak* tomorrow." Then he smiled, and she wanted to hit him.

"It's an adventure," said Ulina. "Today I flew higher than anything I could climb and saw the world."

"But the raiders will hurt you if you are caught."

"Any pain will be theirs."

Kantees gave up. She needed them for this to work the best way that it could. Without them, it was doubtful she could succeed at all.

But after they had gone, it was Gally who was her biggest problem.

"Gally will go with Kantees."

She did not know what to say. She did not simply want to forbid him because it did not seem the decent thing to do. She wanted him to at least understand enough to make the decision himself.

"I must make the golden flower with Sheesha, Gally." She did not know if the others could do it. And as it was, she would be asking Sheesha to do something so very dangerous she might kill them both before they even reached the raiders. "You must stay here with Looesa and Shingul so they are here when Yenteel and Ulina return."

"Gally knows all die, maybe."

She sighed. "Yes. We may not come back."

"Gally knows you must do the good thing."

She smiled with tears in her eyes.

"You have enough food to stay here two nights, Gally. If no one has come you can fly back to the burned village and stay with them. Lintha will look after you."

"Yenteel likes Lintha."

"He does. And Lintha will be sad if we don't come back. But Gally, stay two nights and then go to Lintha. You understand?"

"Gally knows."

And that was the best she could do.

She looked up at Colimar. Yenteel was knowledgeable about the stars as well and he gave her instructions. And the time had come.

She gave Gally a kiss on his cheek. "I will return as soon as I can."

"Goodbye, Kantees of the Ziri."

She suppressed her frown and did not tell him off for using the name. She wanted him to be as happy as possible.

Now she was hoping Looesa and Shingul did not get it into their heads to follow Sheesha. They had no reins or tethers, so there was nothing Gally could do to stop them, but it would spoil everything if they did.

Thankfully, as she urged Sheesha into the air, the other two remained on the ground.

She had Sheesha dip down to the sea so they would not be observed, and only started him into a climb when they were a good distance out. It was strange, she thought, how she never felt unsafe when she was on his back, even though she had no saddle and no buckles. Riding this way seemed natural.

As he spiralled up, she saw the raiders' camp. The fires were lower now. She thought she could hear singing—raucous and tuneless. It was pierced by a child's scream. She shivered as it penetrated her heart like a knife. What if that was Ulina? They would not hesitate to torture her.

And even if it wasn't her, it could be Jakanda, or one of the others.

She must stay with the plan. But what if Yenteel had been captured too?

On the next of Sheesha's spiral turns the camp looked different, as if it was fading out. The fires were blurred and indistinct. On the next turn it was clear the mist had risen. Yenteel had not been captured; he had used the first of Lintha's patterns. Now that the mist was firmly in place, it was as if it had a long tail that stretched from the camp all the way to the cliff and down into the sea. It wasn't localised around the camp but spread out in the valley, filling it up to the ridges on either side and spilling over.

That was her signal.

Without another word from her, Sheesha dived. She leaned forwards onto his neck and wrapped her arms around it. This was the third time and she was used to it, and she even felt a confident calm from Sheesha himself.

The magic within him boiled up and overflowed. This time she tried to stay in control, not just be a passenger. The golden glow flowed around them. Sheesha's wings folded back. She aimed at the river of mist. It took the merest fraction of time and they were into it.

The mist around them glowed with gold while silence still enfolded them. Half a heartbeat later they shot back out into the night.

Sheesha slowed immediately and his wings flashed out to beat against the sudden blast of wind as they came to a halt. He spun in the air.

It was as if a knife had sliced through the mist and torn it apart along its length. The top and side of the *tekrak* had been exposed. Yenteel should have stopped the pattern but it would take a while for the mist to dissipate, if it did at all.

With the magic gone, she could hear uproar in the camp but could see very little. Until a raider came running from the mist, screaming in terror. He shouted something about demons and magic. Then he looked up to see Sheesha. And he saw his death.

Kantees jumped from his back. It was a longer drop than she expected, and she fell heavily on her ankle and collapsed to the floor. Sheesha dropped like a stone onto the raider and cut his scream short.

She got to her feet. Her ankle was not broken but perhaps a little sprained, so she hobbled forwards. Two men came from the mist just in time to see their compatriot ripped in half.

Their shock at the sight was short-lived as Sheesha pounced. His long neck snaked out and snapped at the head of one while he brought his tail round and knocked the second off his feet and then stomped him with a hind leg and crushed him with a talon.

The mist was clearing faster than Kantees expected. Perhaps the magic was the only thing holding it in place. She desperately wanted to know if Ulina had managed to get the children free but she dared not call out.

The noise in the place was increasing. Lostimal, as Yenteel had said it would, was lifting behind the mountains and light was growing.

She wanted to kill all the raiders but right now she would be glad to be gone from there. She could not fight.

"Who are you?"

The speaker was a man in need of a shave and missing half his clothes but he seemed comfortable with the sword in one hand and the knife in the other.

Strands of mist wove in and out of the bushes and trees as if they did not want to leave. They took turns hiding and revealing the man as he walked towards her.

He took in her simple clothes and grinned. "Never mind. It doesn't matter who you are, your pattern ends here."

Kantees heard a movement behind her. The man stopped and his eyes went up.

"You need to know my name, so you can tell whatever demon claims your pattern what it was that killed you," she said. "I am Kantees of the Ziri, and I will have revenge on you in the name of those you have hurt."

Sheesha roared. It was less thunderous than it had been underground, but frightening nonetheless.

"So, raider, murderer, ravisher of children, who are you?"

"I am Ofindah, captain of armsmen, and slayer of Kantees."

He moved in a relaxed motion, bringing his arm up swiftly and releasing the dagger from his hand. She blinked. Everything happened in slow motion. She wanted to get out of the way, but Sheesha was behind her and she dared not move in case he was hurt.

The blade struck her in the shoulder, and for a moment she thought he must have thrown badly. Then the pain flashed through her and she went down on one knee with the shock of it.

"So much for your revenge, Kantees of the Ziri."

A child screamed but it was not a scream of pain. Ulina materialised from the curling mists and climbed the man like a tree. Her tiny patterned knife sliced across the side of his neck. He shrugged her off as if he had not felt the injury—just as Kantees had not felt hers—and Ulina landed hard with a cry that *was* of pain.

Kantees leaned against Sheesha's wing and forced herself back onto her feet.

In Ofindah's eyes she saw the realisation that something was not right. He raised his hand to his neck and touched it. The shadows meant Kantees could not see clearly, but he brought his hand back and stared at the fingers.

She could feel the dagger grating against her bones as she staggered forwards. The pain kept her focused.

The raider swayed but still clung to his sword and raised it as she approached. She ignored it.

"Do you feel it, Ofindah?" she said. "Your pattern being rubbed out?"

He opened his mouth as if to speak but only blood spilled from it. His eyes glazed over.

Despite the pain, she forced herself to remain standing so that her face would be the very last thing he saw. The sword slipped from his fingers and clattered to the ground. His eyes rolled up into his head and he crumpled.

Kantees did not feel at all well. Her legs went weak and she fell to her hands and knees.

I cannot stop now, she thought. *That's only one.*

Someone small got under her arm and helped her stay on her feet. Ulina.

The bulk of the *tekrak* loomed to Kantees' left. In the light of Lostimal she could make out its great curved roots digging into the soil. It did not have the basket under it; they must remove it at night.

She staggered forwards again with Ulina at her side and Sheesha at her back. A man came running from the mist, saw her, and then looked up at the *ziri*. He fled the way he had come. Another *ziri* roar came from in front of them.

Looesa and Shingul had not stayed put. Gally would be upset.

The mist ahead glowed red with a fire's embers.

"The carriage, Ulina?" Her words did not seem very clear.

"I got the others out," said the child. "Like you told me."

"Jelamie?"

"Only peasant children, Kantees of the Ziri."

"Don't," she said, but could not get the rest of the words out. Ulina would not understand what she was talking about. She desperately wanted to pull the dagger from her shoulder but she knew that could make the wound worse. She could bleed like Ofindah until she had lost so much blood she would die of it. *Jelamie?*

She had made a promise to herself. She had told her promise to Daybian. She would find his brother.

If he still lived.

The sounds of men screaming and dying had stopped now. And as they made their way through the mists, they saw nothing to tell them many men had died. She hoped they were all dead. She hoped they had all suffered and had been terrified in their last moments. She wanted them to have understood what their victims had suffered.

She heard a sob. At first it sounded like one of the dying men, but when it came again she knew it was someone young. Ulina had said the villagers' children had been freed, hadn't she? Kantees was having trouble concentrating. The pain distracted her.

The sound seemed to come from the *tekrak*, now behind her.

She tried to say the boy's name but her voice did not seem to want to work anymore. It was almost as if she was too tired to speak. So instead she forced herself to go back, which confused both her companions. Then Ulina must have heard it too, because she almost dragged Kantees towards the sound.

The fire-tube of the huge flying plant was as broad as Ulina was high. The silver light of Lostimal gleamed off its curved surface. The ridges of the leaves from which it was composed were shadowy lines.

She could smell the noxious gas the *tekrak*'s body contained as it leaked between the leaves.

A small foot hung from the tube.

When Kantees reached out to touch it, it was pulled in immediately.

Kantees concentrated on her throat. "Jelamie," she croaked. "It's Kantees, from Jakalain."

The boy wailed.

3 3

The patterner had been found hiding behind a chest in the carriage. He had been as mistreated as the rest but perhaps, as an adult, he could make more sense of it.

Yenteel had come down when the fighting had stopped and he was sure the *ziri* had won. He made no pretence of bravery but put his limited healing skills to work on Kantees' injury. She kept Ofindah's knife on her belt, in the sheath she had taken from his dead body.

They would not bury or burn the dead raiders, but rather would leave them to the elements and the animals. There were too many anyway, and they deserved no such respect.

Three of the children, Jelamie among them, did not say anything but stared with wild eyes at the *ziri*. The patterner would not talk about what had happened. He just shook his head when Kantees asked. But he did explain the boy had not been the target of the raid; that was his elder brother, and they had not even known Jelamie was aboard until late the following day. After they had killed Lorima Hamalain. The patterner either did as he was told or he would suffer. He chose to obey.

The raiders had decided to keep Jelamie as a pet—though they mistreated him and forced him to sleep in the *tekrak*'s fire-tube. It amused them, seeing him trying to rest with the fear that if he over-slept he might be incinerated.

As dawn approached, the patterner spoke to Kantees. She was very tired but had found it impossible to sleep.

"I will lose the *tekrak*," he said. "Unless we can move it over to the carriage."

"I don't understand."

"When the sun shines on its leaves, it will ignite its fire-tube and take off. We have to move it to the carriage where I can make it wrap its roots around the structure. Then it will obey."

"Why not let it go?" Then she stopped and with her good hand grabbed him by the collar. "Where did you get this monster and how did you learn to control it?"

He shut his mouth and looked at her in fear, as if she were one of the raiders. Her shoulder ached and she knew she was just tired. She released him.

The glow of dawn was lighting the sky behind the mountains. She could simply release the *tekrak* but then they would be many people and just three *ziri*. Or she could let this man control it and they could all ride. He knew things she needed to know—perhaps where they had taken Daybian, or at least a clue she could follow.

"Very well. What must we do?"

She put Ulina in charge of the girls and Jelamie with instruc-tions to clear out the carriage of anything they did not need. She had taken a look inside and concluded it was a disgusting mess. The patterner explained how the glyphs for control were etched into the roof of the carriage itself, but that meant the *tekrak* must be manhandled into position. Once in place, it would not let go until the magic was released.

It took many of the raiders to hold the monster down each morning while they moved it. Now they had three humans and three *ziri*. Kantees was not sure how Sheesha and the others would feel about holding ropes.

She set Gally to making loops in the cords that hung from the net thrown across the *tekrak*'s body. The net itself was not tied to the creature but she needed no explanation for that. Leaving aside the risk of puncturing its body, the net stretched as it strained. There was no way of holding it in place.

She went to the elongated front of the monster. It was hard to understand how it could navigate without eyes or ears, or even a sense of smell. But it did: probably another manifestation of its magic.

Sheesha came willingly when she called to him, and at her word Looesa and Shingul came too. She had noticed how they followed Sheesha's lead and copied what he did, so she wanted them to watch—hoping only that Sheesha did not protest.

The *ziri* wore their tack easily enough but that was what they were trained for. This would be different. There had not been time to be clever. She had Sheesha duck his head and she slipped the loop over it, then brought it down his neck to his body. His wings were partly spread because he had used them to walk over.

Kantees pushed him down so he was lying prone. He turned his long neck to watch what she was doing. He was biddable and trusting, but curious. She hoped she was not about to betray that trust.

Now that he was prone, he automatically brought his wings in next to his body. Kantees only wanted the loop to go over one of them, but she made it as big as she could. She glanced again at the sky. The sun would be here soon. She pushed the loop back along his body on one side and, pulling hard, managed to get it over the hooks and claws of the wing's leading edge, just as Sheesha thought she was trying to get him to stand again.

His wings stretched and the loop lay diagonally across his body. He pulled at it experimentally.

"Just wait, Sheesha," she said with an outward calm she was not feeling inside. "Wait. Let's get the others into theirs, shall we?"

She went to the side of the huge *tekrak* and called to Shingul while Gally led Looesa round the other way. As she had expected, Shingul was a little jumpier and kept looking at Sheesha, but he remained calm so she did, too. Kantees went through the same process, which was easier the second time—and perhaps because Shingul was smaller.

When she was done, Kantees ran to where Gally was working, only to find that he had already succeeded. Both he and Looesa had smug looks. She laughed, then jumped as the *tekrak* creaked. She spun around. The roots were coming out of the ground. They had been barely in time with the ropes.

But now was the real test.

She hurried back to Sheesha in case he needed calming, but he was merely watching the movement of the plant with half an eye. Quite disinterested. She supposed this might be because it wasn't edible.

But, as the roots came up, the great green ball of leaves creaked again and lifted. Gally and Yenteel had been assigned ropes at the far end, near the fire-tube but not in line with it. Kantees did not have a rope but she thought she might be able to push from this side. She wanted to be able to see everything and guide them. Or calm the *ziri* if that was needed.

She worried about what might happen if one of them panicked and decided the rope was a trap. This was a tremendously dangerous thing they were doing. The *ziri* could hurt themselves, or hurt someone else. Men could understand—the *zirichasa* simply trusted. And it was her they put their faith in.

She saw light under the *tekrak*. The biggest roots had drawn up, with soil and plants dripping from them like water. The ropes and net stretched. Soon there was enough space for the children to go under it, though they were standing off to the side and watching with no excitement. They had seen this before.

"Gally! Yenteel! Start to walk towards the carriage!" They obeyed easily enough but the *ziri* were not looking happy. The ropes pulling across their bellies was not something they were used to.

"Sheesha," she said in a sharp tone. "Come on." And she started to walk towards the body of the *tekrak* in slow, small steps—it wasn't a great distance but she wanted Sheesha to get the idea they were going somewhere. The big *ziri* grunted and she saw the rope over her head slacken as he moved after her.

"Shingul! Looesa! Move!"

They looked at her. They looked at Sheesha, who grunted again. They hesitated.

"Looesa, go to Gally!" And she pointed. Thankfully *ziri* were brighter than *zatesa*, who were good for guarding and being pets but would have just looked at her pointing finger. Looesa knew who Gally was and turned his head. "Gally, tell him to come. Yenteel, call to Shingul, ask her to come to you."

They did as she said and the *ziri* walked. Luckily, again unlike *zatesa*, they were big and preferred to move slowly—at least on the ground. So they didn't rush.

Kantees breathed a sigh of relief. If it worked now, it could work in the evening. She imagined the horror on Daybian's face if he'd seen this. Using the racing *zirichasa* as beasts of burden! She smiled to herself.

They got the *tekrak* in position and the patterner, in his chair at the front of the carriage, muttered to himself and chanted. The roots came alive once more and wound themselves around the ironwork.

The loose ropes were tied off on stakes already driven into the ground. Otherwise, the carriage would lift. Then Kantees and Gally released the *ziri*. Sheesha proceeded to investigate the plant and its roots as if it had now become something of interest. He even poked his head inside the carriage and sniffed the patterner.

"Gally and Yenteel, you ride in the basket with the children. I will fly with the *ziri*."

"You shouldn't ride the *ziri*, you're just a slave."

Kantees turned and stared at Jelamie. Those were the first words he had spoken. She wanted to be angry with him, but it would not be fair. He was still a child, and he had been sorely used by these men.

Instead she went down on one knee although it hurt her shoulder to do so. Yenteel had only had time to do a simple pattern that mended the worst.

"You would be right, Jelamie, if I were still a slave, but I am not. On the night of the raid I freed myself so that I was able to ring the warning bell and bring out the armsmen to fight the raiders."

He looked confused. The idea that slaves might free themselves did not fit with his understanding. But he was too young see a flaw in the argument. He just felt it was inherently wrong. But for Kantees herself it was a revelation. She had said the words simply to placate him, but the truth of them struck her: She had freed herself because freedom was something you claimed as your right. It could not be given because that validated slavery itself.

"And if I had not freed myself I could not have come on the *ziri* to rescue you."

"You came for me?"

"Of course. What other reason could I have?"

And that, at least, was the complete truth. She decided not to mention that Daybian had also been on the journey. Explaining that his brother was captured and possibly dead would not do the boy any good at all. No, she would not burden him further, and she would tolerate anything unpleasant he said.

"Come on, it's time to go," she said and held out her hand. He hesitated for a moment, then raised his pale fingers to her dark ones. Then he threw himself into her arms, weeping.

Pain shot through her shoulder but she bit down on her lip to keep from crying out. Instead she enfolded him and held him. Her own eyes filled with tears.

First they would take the girls back to their village. That would take a day. Then they would fly the monstrous beast close to Jakalain and she would take Jelamie to his parents, though she would not linger. They would soon have her in irons and destined for the noose if she gave them half a chance—freedom might be claimed but it was easily lost if one was not careful. She would have Yenteel write a letter that Jelamie could deliver explaining the situation.

And then?

Then she would make the patterner tell her what she needed to know and find Daybian.

And after that, Kantees of the Ziri? asked the voice in her head.

"We'll see," she said out loud.

~ End of Book 1 ~

Book 2: Outlaw Dragon

ISLE OF ESTERNES

1

The white light of Lostimal shone across the undulating plains and the dim red glow of Colimar filled in the shadows. Beneath the bulk of the *tekrak*, they had made their camp a day's walk from the castle of Jakalain. Gally, Yenteel and Ulina had remained there with the patterner Tenical, and the two older *zirichasa*, Looesa and Shingul. Kantees carried the boy back to his home on Sheesha's back.

It had seemed strange going back there. The familiarity of the place on the one hand, balanced against the changes she had suffered. She had not promised Lord and Lady Jakalain she would return their abducted son but she felt responsible, and was glad she had done it.

However, in returning Jelamie to his parents, Kantees was careful not to give them any chance to apprehend her. They would have strung her up as an escaped slave and thief given a chance since she had flown off on their valuable property, taking another slave and an escaped prisoner with her.

She had given Jelamie the letter that Yenteel had written— Kantees could neither write nor read—and the boy had promised he would deliver it. He was certainly more subdued than he had been before his adventure. She had not liked the spoiled brat he had been, but she was not sure the new Jelamie was better. He had suffered badly at the hands of the mercenaries.

Letting Sheesha ride the winds at his own pace, Kantees had overridden the *ziri*'s desire to go to his own eyrie, and landed on the top of the Ziri Tower. She had slipped off Sheesha's back and knelt to give the boy a hug which he accepted willingly. The clattering of approaching armsmen drove her back into the sky immediately. She wondered if the boy would ever recover from his experiences; she hoped so, as long as he did not forget and go back to being the old, unpleasant, Jelamie.

The camp came into sight, the curve of the *tekrak* highlighted on one side by the fire. Sheesha went into his usual spiral descent to land. There was no need to guide him. There was no booming welcome from the other *ziri* at this time, unlike during the day. Perhaps they were just asleep, or perhaps at night the call might attract foes from the darkness.

Kantees dismounted and thanked Sheesha for letting her ride— neither she nor the others used any kind of saddle or even reins, so it really was up to the *zirichasa* whether they allowed people to fly them. But Sheesha seemed to enjoy it, and the others did not object.

"Any problems?" asked Yenteel, sounding barely awake.

"None."

He went silent and turned over. Kantees sat down by the fire and stared into its embers. Riding Sheesha, even in this mild weather, was not the warmest activity and she needed better clothing. She still wore what she had escaped in—rough trousers and a top that was long enough to be a smock. It was not that she wanted expensive clothes, which was fortunate given her circumstances, but just a linen undershirt would be nice to keep the roughness from her skin.

Or clothes like Daybian wore. She had lost the set she had stolen at Kurvin Port when that obnoxious Lord Hamalain had come to arrest and torture her.

She hesitated as she remembered Daybian's face in the cave. The serious Daybian. The man who had saluted her. Not the boy with the clever comments who thought the entire world revolved around him. And she remembered his words as his *ziri* had been killed. When he told her to save herself and the others.

The embers in the fire crackled. Sparks flew up.

She took a deep breath. She needed sleep and a clear head in the morning. There were decisions to be made. She settled down in the cool air without even a blanket.

There was a mist lying on the plain when she woke. She was damp through, and cold. Gally and the child, Ulina, were trying to relight the fire. Kantees looked around but could only see the shadowy bulk of the *tekrak*. The giant plant had refused to fly on a wet day before, which suited her fine since she wanted to talk to Tenical.

If she could find him.

The *ziri* were huddled together against the weather. Neither the patterner nor Yenteel were in sight. She set off around the body of the *tekrak*.

Then she heard Yenteel. From his tone he seemed to be trying to persuade Tenical of something. She paused to eavesdrop but could not make out the words.

"Yenteel!" she called into the mist.

"Here, Kantees."

She could already see their shapes and, as she walked up to them, they resolved into more detail. It seemed odd to her that Yenteel, his face black as a moonless night, could be talking to a Taymalin in such a way. Tenical's face was the pale shade of all those who enslaved her people.

"Why won't the *tekrak* fly today?" she said.

Tenical shrugged. "Some days it does not. Perhaps because there is no sun, perhaps because its gases are not pure enough to lift it, perhaps because it has not got enough to burn in its fire-tube."

"Have you thought about what I said?"

"I told you, Kantees, I do not know what the Dunor is."

She sighed. He might be telling the truth but she had no way of knowing. He might be an accomplished liar, just as she was. "What about where the Hamalain have taken Daybian?"

"He might still be at Kurvin Port," said Yenteel as if he was defending the Taymalin.

Kantees frowned. She did not need his interference.

"They want information," she said. "They will assume he has it."

"The golden light," said Tenical.

"What?"

"I am not blind, Kantees. That pattern you used to make the golden light around Sheesha that scared Ofindah's men before you attacked."

She paused, not her pattern at all but Sheesha's own magic. "Yes. Very good. They think he knows how to make that."

"Does he?"

"No."

"Then they will torture him to his death. Unless you think he will reveal that it is you who knows the pattern."

"He can't," she said, "he's never even seen it. Where would they take him?"

"I have already told you I don't know."

"Do you know *anything*, Tenical of the Hamalain? Because if you know nothing then what good are you?" She knew her anger was wasted but it was all so frustrating. "Who taught you to control the *tekrak*?"

"Other patterners at the place I was sent."

She took a deep breath and tried to calm herself. "How could you not know where you were instructed if you had to fly the *tekrak* back to Esternes?"

"But we did not. They opened a patterner's path."

"To Hamalain?"

"No, it was another circle in the north of the island. We flew it round the east and came to Jakalain from the other direction."

"For the sole purpose of capturing Daybian?"

He nodded.

"Who told you he was the one?"

Tenical shrugged and shook his head. "I just did as I was instructed—I have nothing in common with mercenaries."

She stared at him.

"Kantees, you saved my life and it is in repayment I help you. But I am still a Hamalain and I cannot betray my people."

"By helping me, Tenical of Hamalain, you have already betrayed them and if you think otherwise you are a fool."

He had no answer.

"The other ley-circle?" she said.

"It's in the Watching Pass."

Kantees looked at Yenteel but he only shrugged.

"Do the Hamalain have their patterners there all the time? And please don't say you don't know."

"They do maintain patterners there all the time. I spent time there working with them. They dig stone that burns from the ground in that area, and it is used in the fires at Kurvin Port."

Kantees remembered her previous master, Kevrey, had received a supply of the stone that burns. "Very good. This is what we shall do. We will take the *tekrak* to the Watching Pass and we will tell them you are to return to the place where you were trained. If we are lucky that will be the place they took Daybian. If not, we may be able to find out. And perhaps they will also know what the Dunor is."

Both Tenical and Yenteel opened their mouths to speak but she silenced them by raising her hands. "You will take the *tekrak*," she said, looking at them. "With Gally, Looesa and Shingul. I have an errand to run and will take Ulina with me so that she is not under your feet."

"You expect us to be able to handle the *tekrak* with just three of us and two *ziri*?" said Yenteel.

"It might be hard," she said. "But Shingul and Looesa can hold it down with you and Gally to guide this beast."

I hope.

"Gally stay with Kantees."

She closed her eyes. It was what she had expected but it was still somehow disappointing when he uttered the words.

"Gally needs to help Yenteel and Tenical."

He shook his head and then pointed at Ulina.

"Ulina is too young, she is coming with me." Kantees prayed that Ulina wouldn't decide to join in and complain that she was quite old enough. She had been the one who'd killed the leader of the raiders and it did not seem to have bothered her. That in itself was worrying since at the village where they found her they'd been very pleased to hand her over, claiming they had no idea where she had come from.

But Ulina said nothing.

"Kantees takes Ulina but leaves Gally?"

Now he really was upset. She knew she could just insist but it wasn't fair to him.

"Ulina can't look after the *ziri*," she said in exasperation.

"Gally looks after the *zirichasa*," he said indignantly.

"Exactly," she said. "And if Gally comes with Kantees who will look after the *ziri*?"

"Kantees looks after Sheesha. Gally looks after Looesa." He trailed off as his simple logic provided its own answer. Yenteel rode on Shingul but Yenteel would be staying behind.

Kantees said nothing as she watched him working it out.

"Gally stay with Yenteel."

"Yes, I need you to look after the *ziri*," she said. "Just like you always do because you are their friend."

He nodded. Still not happy but defeated by his own argument.

"There's one more thing, Gally," she said. "Do you still have that coin we found on the Hamalain?" She wasn't hopeful, it had probably been pocketed by one of the armsmen when they'd arrested Gally in Hamalain.

He reached into his clothes and pulled out a rag. The gold glinted when he unwrapped it.

"How?" she said.

"Gally ate it so soldiers not have it."

Ah. She eyed it suspiciously, and then considered what he must have been doing every time…

The thought was too unpleasant to contemplate.

"I need to take it with me."

"It is Gally's."

"Yes, I know." *But I need money.* "I will bring you presents from Dakastown. Something even better than the coin."

"Better?"

She nodded and he handed it over. Thankfully in the rag.

2

The mist started to lift at lunchtime and the *tekrak* stirred. They all worked to get the creature in position above the great basket. Kantees explained the situation to Sheesha, as she always did, although she knew he couldn't really understand her. He seemed to get the idea from her tone, though.

When she and Ulina climbed into the space on his back between his wings, the other two *ziri* made no effort to follow. Somehow they understood too.

Tenical was fighting to keep the *tekrak* on the ground while they said their swift goodbyes. They would take the beast back the way it had come, following the mountains to the east coast then heading north. That way Kantees would be able to find them.

Yenteel had taken her to one side earlier to ask where she was going.

"I am going to find my old master in Dakastown to ask him about the Dunor."

"On the back of a stolen *ziri*?"

"We have to drink the milk we're served, Yenteel."

"I should be coming with you."

"I know, but it wouldn't work. The *tekrak* is too slow."

He laughed at that. "It can cover three or four times the ground that mounted men can manage."

"And with Sheesha's magic I can be in Dakastown by evening and back tomorrow." She hesitated. "But for one small problem."

"What's that?"

"I have no idea how to find Dakastown."

"It's on the southern coast."

"Yes, I know that much, it looks out onto the Bay of Dakasa. But do you know where that is?"

Yenteel rummaged around for a piece of charcoal in his bag and then sketched a shape that was a very rough diamond on the side of the basket. "We are roughly here in the heart of Esternes." He shaded the top. "These are the mountains." He shaded the bottom left and pointed to a spot on the left. "That's Talamyrth and this is Kurvin Port. Down here at the bottom—there's a chain of islands leading to the mainland—is the bay and Dakastown is there."

"When's the next feeding?"

Yenteel glanced across at Tenical, who was working his patterns in the gondola, before pulling out the metal disk, a hands-breadth across. Around the edge were regular markings and writing. One half of the edge was shaded dark and the other bright. Inset into the main body were other rings with their own markings which could turn independently of one another. Yenteel fiddled with it, finding a point on the rim before turning the inner rings.

"There will be one tomorrow afternoon." He turned it again. "And in a little over a five-day."

"Where?"

"I don't know."

"Then what use is it?"

Yenteel looked up at the sky. "Lostimal and Colimar are far apart when they are in the sky here, so the next feeding must be in a very distant place."

"And the one after?"

"Closer, but not here."

"The patterners would not like someone like you having that."

Yenteel put it back in his bag. "They do not like anyone having such things—except themselves, of course."

She looked at the hastily drawn map. "So I should go south?"

"You need to find the Zephira River." He drew in a line from the central mountains, skirting the forest and then down and across to the bay.

She nodded. "Dakastown is on that river. I know."

"If you head south and east you might find it before Cliffedge," he drew another line across the middle of the map," or perhaps after it. Either way, find the river and follow it."

She took the map and pushed it into her bag. Not that it would be much help on the journey itself.

"And how will you find us, Kantees, when you return?"

"Head north to the mountains and skirt them to the east. I will do the same. I should be able to catch up with you."

He smiled at her. "Be careful."

A surge of nnoyance went through her. "Of course. After all, we wouldn't want to accidentally kill Kantees of the Ziri."

"That's not what I meant."

"Are you sure?"

"I may be following my master's orders, Kantees, but that doesn't mean I don't care about you."

"Well, you can keep your caring to yourself, Yenteel. Just make sure you don't get into trouble."

"What could possibly happen in a day?"

The *tekrak* floated into the sky with Looesa and Shingul on board—it was easier than having them fly around the whole time and it did not seem to bother them. It must be almost the same as being in an eyrie to them.

The young girl settled in front of Kantees on the *ziri*'s shoulders.

"Are you ready, Ulina?"

"I am ready, Kantees of the Ziri."

"Just Kantees."

"As you command, Mother."

Kantees closed her eyes and counted to ten. She was not entirely sure that Ulina wasn't doing it deliberately to annoy her. Instead of saying anything, she gave Sheesha the signal.

He leapt into the air and spiralled up as she got her bearings. The real world was not as simple as the map Yenteel had drawn. For one thing, the mountains did not cut off in a straight line, and in the real world they were perhaps ten to twenty leagues away.

It was another cloudy day and a strong cold wind was coming down from the mountains. But with Gally's coin they had money and she was going to buy both Ulina and herself a more suitable set of clothing. She knew the traders who dealt with *ziri* racing in Dakastown.

She had been back more than once but only using the patterner's path, and she had never seen her old master, Kevrey of Tander, even at the races.

They had reached a good height and she set Sheesha in the best approximation of south-east that she could manage. The opposite direction to the *tekrak* that was still visible as a dark patch with an orange fire to its rear leaving a dirty smoke trail.

"Ulina, Sheesha is going to do the *ziri* magic."

"The golden light?"

"Yes. You just need to hold on while he goes faster. The most important thing is to be careful when we stop, as it's easy to fall off then, but I will warn you before we do."

"Yes, Mother."

She sounded a little nervous as well as excited so Kantees did not comment. She nudged Sheesha. "Go fast, my love."

Sheesha pulled in his wings and dived.

Ulina screamed. At first Kantees thought the child was scared, then realised it was excitement. Even Kantees laughed to herself as Sheesha careened faster and faster towards the ground. She trusted him.

When he was a short distance from the ground he flattened out and the magic happened. The golden glow grew around them and the wind blowing their hair ceased as if they were inside a yellow glass bottle. The ground became a blur.

"Oh, Kantees!" said Ulina.

"Keep an eye out for a big river."

The first couple of times they had flown like this, she and Sheesha had been over the sea, which did not really show the speed.

The third time had been a short flight upwards. But this was differ-ent. It was easier to focus on the terrain farther away that did not appear to move so fast.

Woods, small ranges of hills, tilled fields, a town or two, they all flashed by and were gone.

How big was the Isle of Esternes? How broad from side to side, from end to end? How fast were they going? How long would it take? She had confidently said it would only take a day to get there and back but in truth she had no idea.

Sheesha flew like an arrow from a bow but what if she wanted to change direction? She could see the dark line of hills on the horizon.

Gently, in case something went wrong, she leaned back—the way she would if she wanted Sheesha to climb. Moments later she could see they were rising. She moved back to where she had been and the climb seemed to stop.

She looked along Sheesha's neck that was like a poker pointing straight ahead. Behind she could see his wings were held tightly against his body and his tail, too, was straight. He truly was an arrow of the sky.

With the sky overcast she had no idea how far the day had progressed, and without any knowledge of where they were she could not judge how far they had come. It made her nervous and she worried about Sheesha. In normal flight he moved his body; his wings would beat, of course, but his neck undulated as he moved, as did his tail.

But moving like this it was almost as if he was lifeless.

And the more she had these thoughts the more worried she became.

"Hold on tight, Ulina." Kantees hooked her legs under the wings.

"Sheesha, let us stop," she said quietly. The golden glow faded and they were blasted with wind. Sheesha back-winged hard until he could glide.

Instantly Kantees could smell burning. They were over a wood nestling in the lower reaches of the hills she had seen that ran as far as she could see in both directions. Smoke was rising from constructions she first took for huts, but if they were then they were all on fire because the smoke was intense, leaking from every part of them.

Charcoal burners.

"Sheesha is tired," said Ulina.

Kantees looked up. What did the girl know of *zirichasa*? But she was right, Sheesha's head was drooping and he barely moved his wings.

Never mind that she was worried about where they were, she should have been concerned for him. She cursed her stupidity. Patterners always tired after engaging with powerful patterns. Yenteel had nearly killed himself in trying to heal himself. If it had not been for Kantees and Sheesha he would be dead.

Why did she think it would be different for a *ziri*?

She looked for somewhere to come down. Sheesha would probably appreciate an easy landing but the place was all trees. She spotted a bare hill to the left and brought Sheesha round. He gathered her intention and, with just one beat of his wings to gain a little height, glided toward it.

There were shouts from below, but she could not see who it was and whether they were friendly. There was no point worrying about that right now, Sheesha was moving faster than a man could run. They would have time to prepare for a welcoming party after they landed.

Sheesha did not even circle once to look at the terrain he was landing on. He simply came down heavily, almost jolting Kantees and Ulina from between his wings. And then he lay flat with his wings outstretched.

3

antees leapt from his back as Ulina slid off the side. She rushed to his head; she had never seen him like this in all their years together. Even after a tough race he would still be able to stand and make threatening growls at the others.

But when she reached him and put her hand on his round snout she had no idea what she should do. It wasn't as if he could tell her what was wrong. Kantees rummaged in her bag and pulled out the water bottle. She wet her hand and wiped it on his nose above the mouth. His jaw opened slightly and his thick tongue slid out to wipe away the moisture.

She did it a second time and, in the moment he licked, she poured water on to his tongue.

He slurped.

"Open your mouth, you big lump," she said.

With his tongue still out, almost as broad as her waist, his jaw opened and she emptied the water into it.

"I should have landed near water," she said.

Sheesha grunted. So, he was thirsty and probably hungry. If he had enough water—

"Kantees of the Ziri! Mother!"

Damn the girl. Kantees stood and looked along the length of the *ziri.* Ulina stood there, facing three men who dwarfed her. Ulina had her arm outstretched and was holding her knife. It did not look much, being about the length of her finger, but it was magic and would slice cleanly through anything. That in itself was worth a thousand times as much as the gold coin—not that Kantees would ever try to take it from the girl.

Unfortunately, the men would not realise what they were facing. All they saw was a little girl with a tiny knife. That Ulina was a little girl was true but Kantees had seen her kill a man with no hesitation and no remorse. If these men gave her cause to fight them they would regret it, and so would Kantees.

"Ulina! Do not hurt them," she said.

"They will not hurt Sheesha!"

To their credit the men did not laugh, but perhaps they weren't listening. They were looking at Sheesha, laid out on the hill, the length of seven men nose to tail and even more across the wings.

Kantees looked down at him; even she had never seen him spread out like this. He must be intimidating to those who did not know him. Though not to her, particularly with his eyes shut. From the way he had drunk the water she thought he was probably all right. Just tired and hungry. Not just tired: exhausted.

She had to skirt around his wing and the length of his body—his legs were splayed out inelegantly—and along his tail. She reached Ulina and put her hand on her shoulder.

"Put down your knife, Ulina."

The men were dusty black with the smoke from their charcoal stacks, but beneath that layer they looked like Taymalin.

"I am Kantees of the Ziri," she said, hating herself for using the name. Damn Yenteel for his manipulations, but the truth was she would get the most help if they thought she was important. Names have power. "And this is my protector, Ulina."

Of the three it was a smaller and older man that spoke first. "I am Klobish." He turned and pointed to the other two. "Franek and Ut." The latter had a strange mottled scar on his face and neck.

"The *ziri* is tired," she said. "We have ridden far. He needs water and meat."

"Water we have in plenty. There's a stream yonder." He pointed back past her. "Meat we have but for ourselves, and what we can share with thee. We cannot feed a beast such as this." Then he shivered as a thought visibly crossed his mind.

"He does not eat people," she said. Although she suspected that to be a lie since Sheesha and the others had killed a lot of men in the past few days—and would probably have been happy to eat them too. "Unless I command it."

That seemed to have an effect.

She thought she needed to say something else to round it off, but she had run out of ideas and was tired herself. Riding the *ziri* may not require much energy but simply sitting while he flew at such speed was tiring enough.

A glance at the sky told her it probably wouldn't rain.

"We will rest here while the *ziri* recovers enough to go down to the stream. Then he will hunt."

The men still waited. Oh, *Kisharuk* curse them, they wanted a blessing—that's what came of using a fancy name and riding a monster. "May the blessings of the Mother go with you." That sounded right and it seemed to suit them, as they retreated back down the hill.

Kantees sighed and sat down by Sheesha's tail where the feathers fanned out in their blues and golds, tipped with white that looked almost silver.

Ulina still clutched the tiny dagger in her hand as she watched the men retreat.

"It's fine, Ulina, they won't hurt us."

The girl did not answer, her body as tense as a drawn bowstring.

"Ulina. Sit."

Almost as if she had not heard Kantees speaking, the child turned. "I do not like them."

"They are harmless," said Kantees. "We should worry more for Sheesha." So saying, she got to her feet. Sheesha needed her. "Let's find the stream they mentioned."

Kantees paused for a moment at the *ziri's* head and told him they were going to get him more water. He did not stir. She knew he did not understand the words but she hoped it would make him feel safer while she was gone.

She laughed to herself. The idea that she might make him feel safe. He was vastly more dangerous than she was. Even Ulina was more dangerous than her. After all, she had sworn she would kill the raiders herself, but it was Ulina and the *ziri* who had done it, not her. She was full of big words and little action. But then she had always been a good liar.

She looked suspiciously at the woods as they approached. Trees could harbour creatures that killed but there seemed to be a foot-worn path coming from round the side of the hill that led off beneath the branches. They followed that and stumbled on the stream not far in. Birds were singing and there was the constant buzz from insects. It was probably a lovely place when the sun was shining, but she did not feel up to appreciating its beauty.

Several stones had been placed in the mud at the water's edge to create an area where a person could kneel and collect water without stirring up the dirt. Kantees would have been happier with water from a well. There was no telling what might have died upstream. Well, it was unlikely to affect Sheesha.

She pulled out the water bottle and wished she had something bigger.

This was not a problem she had considered. And that was a failing—one of her continued failings. How many times in the preceding ten-days had she made incorrect assumptions that had nearly got them all killed? And had succeeded in getting Daybian captured and Jintan murdered?

She shook her head and plunged the bottle into the water, watching the bubbles rise.

There was the rustle of leaves above and something thudded to the ground beside her. She threw herself to the side, almost losing the water bottle in the process, and fetched up sitting in the muddy water against a tree root.

Something big and leathery, leaking blood, lay on the stones.

Where is Ulina? The girl was gone. Kantees panicked. "Ulina!"

Something moved above her. The branches shifted and broken

leaves drifted down. *Something in the trees!* Ulina's face poked out, upside down from the greenery.

"Kantees, I got it!"

Ulina loved to climb. Kantees knew this. A closer inspection told her that the creature on the floor was a big *sikechak*, the same sort of thing that had been in the cavern next to the ley-circle at Kurvin Port.

As far as Kantees was aware they tasted awful. Though you could live on them. They preferred to sleep by day, so Ulina must have caught this one napping.

The girl's face disappeared up as her legs came down through the leaves and Ulina dropped and landed on the stones.

"Why are you sitting in the water?" she said.

"I fell over."

The answer apparently satisfied Ulina, who picked up the *sikechak* by one leg and held it up. "I got it for Sheesha." Then she frowned. "Will he like it?"

Kantees gave a half-smile; she was not pleased with what the girl had done but the result had been good. She wasn't Ulina's kin so she had no right to tell her how to behave or what was right and wrong. Then again, if Ulina did have any kin the chances are she would never see them again. Which meant that perhaps the task did fall to Kantees after all.

"Sheesha will be very pleased," she said. "But you should tell me what you're going to do."

"Why?"

"Because everything we do affects those around us, even if we think it doesn't."

Ulina stared at her for a moment and then nodded. "I under-stand." Then she headed back the way they had come, dragging the *sikechak* behind her so its head bounced on every bump and root.

Kantees pulled herself dripping from the water. It was a good thing the weather wasn't cold. She had water everywhere it was uncomfortable to have it, and there was no way to dry it except removing the remains of her clothing—which she was not about to do with those men around—or wait for it to dry on her, which might end up giving her sores.

Looking after Sheesha was more important than whether her skin hurt. So she headed after Ulina.

When they got back to him Sheesha had moved and was now curled up. But he lifted his head as they approached. Getting him to drink the water now that he was more alert was more trouble than it was worth, particularly since he was far more interested in the fresh meat.

Kantees did not enjoy watching *ziri* eat carcasses, so she looked away as he crunched through it, though it was barely more than a light meal for him. Ulina was, however, fascinated and watched the entire process. Once he had finished Kantees succeeded in getting more water into him and wiped his bloodied snout.

"You're a messy eater," she said, to which he grunted.

"He understands you, Kantees," said Ulina.

"Don't be silly, he's just an animal."

Ulina gave her a hard look. "You know that's not true. Yenteel said you are a liar. I don't think you should say things that aren't true."

It's the only way I can survive, said the voice in her mind.

"You're probably right, but when you are a slave it comes naturally. It's a hard habit to break. But," she said, "that is only true when what you're saying *is* a lie. Sheesha is very clever but he is still an animal. If he understands anything it's just the way I say things. He can tell if I'm angry, happy, or sad, and then responds."

Ulina screwed up her face in an expression that did not hide the fact that she did not believe this for one single moment.

"If he understands me, why doesn't he understand you?"

"You're Kantees of the Ziri," said Ulina as if that settled any argument.

"I'm just Kantees."

She looked at the sky. Her schedule had already collapsed. Even if Sheesha recovered soon and went hunting, they wouldn't be able to ride before dark.

And she still had no idea how far they had come, how far they had still to go, or even where they were.

4

It rained in the night. Kantees and Ulina climbed under Sheesha's wing for warmth and shelter, though they were both already wet through.

Sheesha had gone hunting into the low slopes of the hills to the south, and from the top of the hill they had been able to watch him. Kantees had assumed he would soar through the air and then stoop on his unsuspecting prey. It may have been that he was too tired to do that because he landed and spent some time motionless, looking almost like a tree stump at this distance—even if it was a very brightly coloured one.

Then he moved, so fast it was difficult to see, and snatched something from the ground which he chomped a couple of times, then raised his head skyward to allow it to slide down his throat. He did this several times before moving to a new location.

Whatever it was he was eating they couldn't see this far away. Certainly nothing very large.

He returned via a stop at the stream. Rather than sleep on top of the hill, exposed to the wind, Kantees had them go down the slope. She had been woken not only by the falling rain in the pitch black of the night but also rivulets coming down the hill and seeping into her clothes.

Which was how they ended up tucked in with Sheesha.

The morning was overcast and Kantees itched to be away, but they needed some breakfast and Sheesha had gone off to eat more of whatever he had found on the slopes. So instead, Kantees and Ulina headed down through what was left of the trees looking for the men. She had been wrong about the thick forest the day before. Perhaps it was thicker elsewhere but here barely one tree in ten had been left standing by the colliers as they chopped them down to turn them into charcoal.

They found a small hut made of piled stones, the gaps plugged by clay. The door was small and covered by a cloth. Kantees called out but no one responded. There was a track worn by many feet— or perhaps one pair of feet many times—leading further across the chopped-down trees.

She could see smoke rising not too far away and heard someone coughing before she saw him. He was busy applying clay from a bucket to the outer walls of what could have been mistaken for another hut. He glanced at them approaching, then scanned behind them and the air above looking for Sheesha. He coughed again.

"Rain's the *Kisharuk*'s piss," he said as he dug another handful of clay from the bucket and slapped it over a hole that had been leaking smoke.

Kantees did not know how to respond to such a greeting. "We're trying to get to Dakastown."

He did not turn but remained focused on his task. "Dakastown, is it?"

"Yes. Do you know the way?"

"South. Good market for charcoal is Dakastown."

"How far?"

He shrugged. "We just make the charcoal." He coughed again. The smoke from the pile was acrid and made Kantees' throat tingle. What must it be like having to breathe it all day, every day?

"How does it get to Dakastown?" she asked. "Patterner's path?"

At that he burst out laughing. "Think you we can afford a pattern-er's path?" His laugh degenerated into another bout of coughing. "No, Mother, we sells it to the river men and they sells it to the harbour men and they sells it to the metalworkers whether it's in Dakastown, or

Cliffedge, or wherever it may end up." Now he did turn to them. "My charcoal burns hot and smelts the iron that makes all the pretty things for the rich folks in Dakastown. What do you do, Mother?"

Ulina stepped forward. "This is Kantees of the Ziri; she has brought vengeance to those who dishonoured Taymalin and Kadralin. And when she flies her Sheesha, he is a golden arrow in the sky."

The man stared at the girl and scratched his head. "I don't know anything about that."

He went back to plugging the holes the rain must have made in his clay-covered construction. Kantees knew nothing about how charcoal was made, but he must know his business.

"How long before this is ready?"

"It'll burn for a five-day," he said. "And the wood turns to black. Then we crack it open and let it cool. But that's the difficult time, can't let it catch aflame otherwise it will all be ruined and worthless."

Kantees frowned. "But you said it burned for a five-day."

"Different sort of burning, Mother."

She was expecting him to say more but he didn't, so she accepted it. A different sort of burning when it was encased in clay and, she thought, could not breathe. She nodded to herself, remembering how they had almost run out of air inside of Yenteel's magical protection.

The man had been very talkative. Perhaps working in the forest alone, save for the others doing the same job, made him less cautious. She was not sure if he was going to be upset, or simply impressed, but her silence left him space to continue.

"Where do we find the river men? They must know the way to Dakastown."

"Yes, Mother, they'll know," he said, turning and pointing to the north. "There's a track the carts use. You follow that and it will take you to the town then you ask the river men the way."

Kantees smiled and gave him a blessing again.

When she turned away the smile dropped from her face. She hated this deception. She was not important, yet wherever she went she got treated as if she was special—all because of Sheesha. It made her angry.

She strode back towards the hill with Ulina having to run to keep up.

"What's wrong, Kantees?"

"Everything."

"I don't understand."

"Please stop defending me to everyone, Ulina, you're just making it worse."

It took Kantees a few moments to realise that Ulina was no longer following her. There was no sound of her feet squishing in the muddy ground, and no sound of her breathing. Kantees stopped and turned.

The girl was standing twenty paces behind.

Kantees waited.

Ulina did not move but stared at Kantees. The rain started again and Kantees swore. As she imagined the collier did too.

So Kantees retraced her steps and went down on one knee in front of the girl so their faces would be at the same level. Either Ulina was crying or the rain was getting on her cheeks. Or both.

It surprised Kantees because she had gotten the idea that Ulina never cried. This was a girl who could kill a grown man.

"Why are you crying, Ulina?"

"You don't want me. You are like the people in the village. Nobody wants me."

"I didn't say I didn't want you," said Kantees. "And I made a promise." She held up the hand that had spilt the blood for her oath.

"Grown-ups always lie to children and Yenteel says you are a very good liar."

Kantees smiled without humour. "Yes, it is true, I am a good liar but I did not lie to you."

Ulina burst into sobs breaking up her words. "How can I know?"

Words stuck in Kantees' throat. There it was, her lies that came so easily and could sound so convincing, they mocked the truth when she spoke it. And that meant there was nothing she could say that could possibly mean anything.

Instead she knelt back on her heels, despite the squelching of the mud, and held open her arms. She did not reach for Ulina, but waited.

The girl trembled as she cried and the rain fell on them both. Kantees desperately wanted to set off. Yenteel, Gally and Tenical would be expecting them back today and that was not going to happen. There was no way of knowing whether Yenteel would be able to deal with Gally if he became upset. He could be very diffi-cult sometimes.

Like Ulina. Like Kantees herself. There was a truth if she needed one.

Then Ulina moved forward into Kantees' arms. And she enfolded her and held her tight.

Kantees heard the sound of wind through giant wings, followed by a sodden thump as a wet *ziri* landed behind her. Sheesha grunted and his head came down on Kantees' shoulder, knocking her over into the mud and taking Ulina with her.

Ulina giggled through her sobs but Kantees did not feel like laughing. She was cold and wet. Ulina's distrust had cut her as deep as the girl's little knife, and it was entirely justified.

"We have to get going," said Kantees, but she could not move with the weight of Sheesha still resting his head on her shoulder.

"Sheesha wants a hug too," said Ulina, and she squeezed out from under Kantees, putting her knee into Kantees' stomach as she did so. Kantees bore the pressure without comment. Though Ulina's mood seemed to have lifted, she guessed the happy facade might be fragile.

Sheesha licked Kantees' cheek, leaving it drier and cleaner but stickier.

No longer caring about the mud, Kantees rolled over on to her knees and used Sheesha's head to lever herself up into a standing position. She was caked in dirt. *It will dry and fall off.*

"Come on," she said and clambered awkwardly on to Sheesha's neck. Ulina came up and let Kantees lift her into place. The acrid scent of the charcoal burners drifted across to her. And Sheesha sneezed. They were almost thrown from him as his entire body flexed.

"Let's get away from here," said Kantees. "Sheesha, up!"

The great beast spread his wings and gave them a shake to remove the excess water. His downstroke lifted them but Kantees could tell he was having some difficulty. But she did not know whether that was from his previous tiredness or the rain. Probably both. She had already decided she wasn't going to strain him. Since they were already late, trying to make up the time was pointless.

She knew the route Tenical intended to take, she would simply follow that until Sheesha caught up with the *tekrak*.

But for now she guided Sheesha, with his laborious wingbeats, above the track the collier had indicated. There were dozens of burning charcoal stacks scattered through the woods in groups, with men working on them patching the damage from the rain. As they flew, they left the smoke behind and entered an area where yew trees grew among the stumps—but she could see the remains of charcoal burners between them. And then there was an area where the foliage had grown up and hidden the ground. It was as if they were travelling through time. This had been the route of the colliers over the years. Moving through the forest, destroying the trees for their charcoal, only to move on and have it grow up behind them.

She shook her head. Trees did not grow fast and by now they must have travelled further back along the collier's progress than her own birth. Certainly Ulina's.

The track they followed was a line drawn into the past.

Then the forest came to an end to be replaced by open pasture with huge beasts cropping the grass. She did not recognise them, with their long reddish pelts glistening wetly, but she had tasted the meat of the *lukisa* and guessed that was what these were. Their hair was woven into cloth while their skins were tanned and used for many things. The beasts, as long nose to tail as Sheesha snout to tail fan, paused in their munching and looked up at the predatory wings of the *ziri*. Kantees doubted that one *ziri* on its own could take down even one of these. They must weigh at least ten times more.

It continued to rain but Sheesha did not seem to be having too much difficulty. Kantees and Ulina were getting a bath from it, however, and the mud ran off them in dirty rivulets, and it was cold. She smiled to herself. Through all the winters she had spent in the Ziri Tower at Jakalain, all she had was the hay and a single blanket to keep her warm.

Even when they had travelled to the races it wasn't much better. Sometimes worse, depending on the season and where the race took place. Some days and nights she had almost frozen. If only she had known then Sheesha would have allowed her to sleep in the cocoon of his feathers.

Unfortunately, he could do nothing about the rain.

The track crossed a series of streams where wooden bridges had been put in place. They were old by the look of them but in good repair. She tried to see ahead but there was nothing but the greyness of the rain, and the hills to the left which they were following.

She realised that, without even being asked, Sheesha had stayed low and flew to one side of the track so she could see it. He did seem to understand her needs, even when she did not speak them out loud.

They passed another herd of *lukisa*, about fifty of them, looking bedraggled. This time she spotted the herdsman hunched under a waterproof skin with his three *zatesa*. They watched Sheesha with even more care than the *lukisa* did, but then it was their job to protect the herd. Enough of them could probably take down a *ziri* if given the opportunity, but Kantees had no intention of landing, and she was not sure three would be enough to defeat Sheesha.

She had no idea how much ground they had covered but she thought it must be at least five leagues. They crossed another wooded area and off to the right were more stacks burning wood to make charcoal. It occurred to her that the men who worked these woods must be in a far better position than the ones she had met, being closer to the town. But this wood was nowhere near as extensive, and just beyond it were a series of small fields with lines of cultivated plants.

Then they passed a village—housing the farmers for the fields, she assumed. Up in the hills of Jakalain the soil was not fertile and could neither support much in the way of plants nor feed herds of *lukisa*.

The village fell behind and there was more grazing land, soon replaced by another village. Then all the grazing land was gone and it was only fields. People looked up and pointed. Children ran screaming to their mothers. *Kichesa* pulling carts took fright and Kantees had Sheesha gain altitude so they became more of a ghostly dark shape in the clouds, rather than a hunting monster. The track was a line across the terrain below them.

Finally, buildings higher than a single storey came into view and in moments they were passing across the bustling streets of a trader town cut in half by a broad river. Perhaps it was the Zephira and they could follow it all the way to Dakastown. But they needed provisions and somewhere dry. Perhaps she might even buy clothes here. Though, for all it seemed a busy place, it was still in the middle of nowhere. Not like Dakastown.

The problem now was how she was going to get Sheesha on to the ground without being shot at or causing a panic. She stared glumly at the muddy roadways streaming with water, and the buildings with water sluicing off their roofs.

That was going to be a trick.

5

They crossed the river. The far bank had fewer buildings and there were fewer people on the streets. Kantees turned Sheesha to head upstream. The deluge of rain hid them from view except for anyone directly below, though at the same time it stopped them from being able to see much.

A set of large buildings she took for warehouses passed beneath them. There seemed to be no one moving around them so she took a chance. Sheesha went into a sharp spiral dive and they seemed to fall from the sky. The space below was open and surrounded by fencing where it did not face onto the main building, but Kantees guided the *ziri* towards the corner nearest the building. At which point he accelerated his descent with his wings angled up.

They landed and he absorbed the jolt with his back legs.

Kantees jumped down with Ulina. There was a raised wooden platform attached to the building with an overhang from roof, and she pulled Sheesha into it, though he seemed not to notice that his tail was still out in the rain until Ulina ran around and shifted it bodily. Sheesha twisted his neck round until he was looking directly at the child holding his tail. Kantees smiled. She had often noticed how he seemed to have no understanding that the tail he saw was the same thing he could feel. Almost as if his tail did not belong to him.

A growl from behind interrupted her. She turned to see two very large *zatesa* stalking towards them with slow steps. She cursed herself for not realising the place would have protection. There might even be a guard.

But Sheesha's head swung back and he stretched it over her head while spreading his wings. Suddenly he was enormous. And then he roared at the *zatesa*. It was if they shrank in size; their bellies hit the ground. Sheesha kept his wings spread and dropped his snout to sniff at the two.

"Don't hurt them, Sheesha," she said. "They're only doing their job."

A low growl rumbled in Sheesha's throat, growing in volume. Kantees suddenly remembered Ulina and turned to see where she was. The girl was beneath Sheesha's left wing looking at the *zatesa*. She did not look afraid and her tiny knife was once more in her hand. Though it would be of little use if they chose to attack.

Looking back Kantees could see that making trouble was the last thing on their minds. They had flattened themselves against the ground, though their larger hindquarters were up in the air. Sheesha was still sniffing them as if undecided whether to eat them.

Then he licked one and then the other, pulled in his wings and neck, and sat down with a thump that shook the floorboards. He grunted.

Kantees did not take her eyes off the *zatesa* as she backed up next to Sheesha in case they decided to attack after all. Instead, one of them sat up and used its long tongue to clean itself. The other one lay down on its side, but in such a way as to keep Sheesha in view. Kantees was astonished. She had not felt Sheesha use any magic, yet what she had seen *looked* like magic. These animals would be trained to kill intruders. She had seen ones similar on her race visits.

There had been that smug keeper she had met who had explained in repetitive detail how the *zatesa* respected authority and if you could dominate them they would do whatever you wanted. The Ziri master back at Hamalain had said Sheesha was a dominant male. These were all things that Romain, her mentor at Jakalain, had never mentioned. She doubted he even knew.

So if Sheesha was a dominant *ziri* perhaps that transferred to the *zatesa*. The question was, would that dominance extend to her as well? Could she get past them to get out and make her enquiries?

Kantees looked around. The rain was still coming down heavily but was a little less torrential. The fences around the yard were high and looked solid. They would need to be in order to keep the *zatesa* in. There was a door into the building but that was too close to the *zati* for her to try it. She went, cautiously and keeping an eye open, to another one nearer; large double doors for moving goods in and out, she guessed.

It was firmly locked. Ulina's knife might be able to cut through the lock but Kantees did not think that would be necessary. They just needed to get over the fence.

"I can climb out, Kantees," said Ulina. "I can find out what we need to know."

Kantees turned to look at the girl and shook her head. "I can't send you on your own."

Ulina raised her eyebrows in a way that reminded Kantees of Yenteel. "You did not hesitate to send me to help the children when we attacked the raiders."

"I hesitated," said Kantees.

"But you sent me."

For some reason Kantees was certain that was a completely different situation, although she could not really explain why.

"Towns are more dangerous than raiders."

"What is it we must know?" asked Ulina.

Kantees closed her eyes and sighed. "Is the river the Zephira? And even if it isn't, do we get to Dakastown by following it? Also, how many days by boat does it take to get to Dakastown?"

"Does the river go to Dakastown and how long does it take," repeated Ulina.

"Yes."

"Shall I bring food?"

"Not unless someone gives it to you out of kindness. Do not steal anything, Ulina, there is no need to put yourself at any more risk than is necessary."

"But I'm hungry."

"We'll find something further downstream when we leave here. A place like this is dangerous, we must find somewhere smaller."

Ulina looked unconvinced but finally nodded. She ran to the fence and scaled it in a moment, where Kantees would have been struggling to reach the top. Ulina disappeared and the last thing Kantees heard of her was her feet squelching into the mud when she landed.

Sheesha shook himself, showering Kantees and the *zatesa* in rainwater, then settled down to sleep. She hoped he would not be hungry too soon, concerned the meal he had eaten earlier would not be enough for very long. But there was little she could do about that now, unless he decided to eat the *zati*.

Once he had stopped shifting his position in order to get comfortable, she sat down with her back to his chest, feeling the slowing *thump-thump-thump* of his heartbeat. The warmth of his body seeped through her and the gentle rhythm lulled her into a doze.

The growls of the *zatesa* woke her where the noise of men did not. For a moment she was terrified that whatever pattern Sheesha had cast on the *zatesa* had worn off and they were going to attack. But as she opened her eyes—to a rainy vista little different from before—she saw that the yard's guardians were on their feet looking the length of the yard to the gates at the end. They were not threatening her or Sheesha.

Then she noticed the voices. Men shouting to one another, looking for something.

Sheesha was still asleep. Kantees jabbed her elbow into his neck to wake him up.

The *zatesa* jumped from the raised platform and stepped out into the rain. The drops splashed off their tight reptilian skin. Their muscles moved powerfully. They always looked a little ungainly because their rear legs were so much bigger; unlike a *ziri*, they were built for moving fast across the ground.

Kantees wondered how long she had dozed but there was no way to tell, except for the fact the light was not fading so it was still some time in the afternoon. Where was Ulina? Had she had enough time to get the answers they needed?

Now Kantees wondered whether she had done the right thing. They could have just followed the river anyway, they would have reached the sea eventually. Had she put Ulina into danger unnecessarily? Did she really need to know?

"It came down near here!" A voice cut clearly through the rain-filled air.

It was not Ulina they were after. It was Sheesha.

The *zatesa* had reached the gate and were pacing in front of it. Kantees could hear their growling. That should dissuade the searchers. She could even hear some men muttering nervously.

It was at that moment Sheesha decided he needed to evacuate his bowels. It was not that he was noisy about it as he waddled out into the rain and went to the fence. She was also sure that, when he stretched, he did not become visible above the fence.

It was the smell. She had spent most of her life working with that stench and barely noticed it, especially since he had done it far from where she was sitting. He was considerate that way. But for someone not accustomed to it, it was pungent, disgusting, and if you knew your animal dung, distinctive.

She heard a voice say "*Ziri*" and was on her feet, running for Sheesha, immediately.

One of the *zatesa* snorted. She didn't look and trusted that Sheesha would continue to overawe them as he did anyone who was not used to him. He saw her coming but did not have time to dip his neck when she arrived. She grabbed a handful of feathers and pulled herself up, flinging her leg over.

The *zatesa* erupted in growls followed by an almost musical tone produced through their muzzles. The two of them together made a discordant roar. It was such a horrible sound it set her teeth on edge.

Beyond the fence, arguing broke out. One person saying they had to get in, more than one saying there was no chance they were going to face two angry guardian *zati*.

Kantees had been about to fly, but realised if she did the men would know for sure she was there and might try to bring Sheesha down. The man who knew the *ziri* smell was outnumbered for now, but Kantees was sure he, whoever he was, would not give up and she could not afford to give them time to organise.

As far as she could tell there was no pool of magic in this place, not even a small ley-circle. This town existed only because of the river, charcoal and trade. If there was no circle it meant they couldn't get a message out quickly, but it also meant Sheesha couldn't do one of his tricks—like the short burst of speed he had achieved back at Hamalain.

That left brute force, and Sheesha did not lack for that.

The gate looked solid but the fence had long stretches of wood between the supporting posts, which did not look strong.

Kantees hesitated. She had not made any plans with Ulina about what to do if either of them ran into trouble. She cursed herself once more; she always seemed to be making mistakes, and every one of them could result in death.

But she could not wait. They had to move now. She gave Sheesha a little kick but leaned forward so he would get the idea not to take off. The voices were all coming from the right of the yard. So she aimed Sheesha at the left and urged him forward. He was confused at first, fully expecting to take to the air, but he was obedient to her request.

He stopped when they reached the fence. Glancing round, Kantees saw the *zatesa* following, looking unsettled and still hooting intermittently. They seemed keen to follow Sheesha and that was what Kantees wanted.

She nudged the *ziri* again, and after a moment's confusion he jumped up like some massive bird hopping from the ground to a branch. He landed on the fence and his wings whipped out for balance.

A cry of horror in front made her peer round Sheesha's neck at a man—just some trader or other—staring up at the monster perched above him.

The fence creaked. Sheesha flapped his wings and Kantees heard the cracking of wood beneath them. The man fled. He had not even screamed. But someone off to her right shouted. "Here! The dragon!"

The fence collapsed with a great splintering and cracking as it shattered beneath them. Sheesha dropped forward and landed awkwardly in the lane.

She heard the hue and cry as the men came running from the other side of the yard.

Where were the *zatesa*? She looked and they were hanging back. That wasn't part of the plan. "Come on!" she yelled at them. "You're free!"

Half a dozen men pounded round the corner with mud flying up at every stride. They had weapons: just tools, but hammers and pitchforks were bad enough. One of them had a bow, she guessed he was the one who had recognised the smell. He was also dressed for travel.

For the briefest moment she thought perhaps he was after them specifically. But that made no sense. Nobody knew they were coming here, she had not even known herself. It must be a coincidence—no matter how inconvenient.

She had hoped the *zati* would leap out into the lane to stand there majestic and menacing—maybe even chasing the oncoming attackers. Unfortunately, they were more circumspect and sniffed at the broken fence.

There was no time to waste. She urged Sheesha round to face the men, then pulled on his neck feathers. He reared up and stretched his wings. His head snaked down and he growled. The men came to a skidding halt.

"Come on," said the traveller. "It's just a girl on a racer!"

He charged on, hoping, perhaps, to bring the others with him. However, it seemed that Sheesha's growl had finally activated the *zatesa*, who leapt over the broken wood to stand in the lane.

The man with the bow came to a stop.

Kantees yelled as Sheesha moved forward, picking up speed as his taloned feet splashed in the muddy lane. He added his warning hoot to her cry and the *zatesa* joined in with their discordant howl.

The men—even the traveller—turned and fled. A couple fell in the rush, splashing into the sodden ground, desperately flailing to get themselves back on their feet and not to be the ones at the back of the fleeing mob.

The *zatesa*, with their sinuous bodies undulating, gave chase.

"Kantees!"

She turned at the sound of Ulina's voice—and so did Sheesha, his long neck holding his head high to find the source of the sound. The girl was back on the other side of the yard, perched on the fence.

Without being instructed Sheesha turned his bulk in the narrow lane and went back through the gap he had made, then half-hopped, flapping his wings for extra speed and lift, across the open space.

Ulina squealed and Kantees could see she was fighting something behind her, on the other side of the fence. As they got closer she saw a hand. Ulina was scrabbling at her neck for her little knife while beating at the hands that had grabbed her clothes.

Sheesha arrived at the fence and snaked his head over to look down at whoever was on the other side. There was a cry of fear and the hands holding Ulina let her go. She fell forward from the top of the fence and landed on her hands and feet at the bottom.

There was the snap of teeth but it was not accompanied by the sound of flesh and bone crunching—Kantees was grateful, she was not entirely happy with the amount of death and mayhem caused so far. She reached down and caught Ulina's outstretched hand. She pulled the girl up, facing the wrong way, but they clung to one another as Sheesha turned again.

"Go, Sheesha!" she said.

His wings beat and she was pushed down into their working muscles as they lifted all three into the air.

As they climbed, the sound of shouts, screams and discordant hooting reached her ears. She hoped the *zatesa* wouldn't kill anyone. As long as someone could get a door between them, they would be fine.

She steered the *ziri* to the river then to the right. She no longer cared if they were seen. She urged Sheesha to fly faster as they moved downstream along the river.

They had made a successful escape, but if this was even a sample of what could happen in a populated place, they would need the blessings of the Mother to be able to survive in Dakastown.

6

She let Sheesha climb to a good height but had no desire to push him any faster. The air was still full of rain. She was exhausted and still cold and damp. Ulina was no better and just clung to Kantees without changing position.

Kantees looked up at the underside of the grey clouds. Clouds came between the sun and the ground. Sometimes the clouds were in layers and rain only came from the lower ones.

She looked down. Ulina had told her she had found an old boatman down by the water. He had seemed happy to talk and said the river was the Zephira, and that by boat it took a five-day to travel all the way to Dakastown if you had a full cargo and made no stops except at night. Coming back, it was at least a ten-day depending on the wind. But there was the Prince's Gantry at Cliffedge that took a day on its own. The name sparked a memory in Kantees, but she couldn't place it.

She could see boats on the water even now. There was not much wind and the ones coming upstream were using oars—probably manned by slaves, both Kadralin and any Taymalin who had fallen foul of the law.

The river stretched out, wandering in wide bends, never in a straight line. And there were lakes and marshes either side along its banks.

She looked up once more. She wanted to be out of the rain.

Sheesha stroked harder and they climbed through the rain. The clouds must have been further away than they looked and it took a while before the rain became mist as they pushed up into the grey. The ground disappeared and it got darker. The clouds soaked her. She worried about Sheesha; would he become too wet?

But he did not stop the strong beating of his wings, which she could feel through her rump rather than see, carrying them up and up. The grey of the clouds turned white and they burst through into brilliant sunshine.

Kantees felt her heart would break with the beauty of the world above the clouds. The sky was unbroken blue with the brilliance of the sun blazing down on them. And below were the clouds, a terrain of brilliant white like hills and mountains. She breathed in deep. The air was cold but the sun still warmed her.

She turned Ulina round so she could see the beauty too, but held her tight, not for any fear of falling—because who could feel unsafe on the back of a *zirichak*?—but because she wanted to feel her close; as if the wondrous cloud landscape made her heart overflow with love, and the dampness of Sheesha's wings made him shimmer with iridescent colour.

This was perfection. And the eye of the Mother was on them.

Low down in the south-east, directly along their path, Lostimal appeared in the day as it sometimes did. It was in its three-quarter phase and at its centre was Colimar. The feeding occurred when the moons were directly overhead, the only time that Lostimal and Colimar were the Breast of the Mother feeding the land with her milk. But they were in conjunction at other times, and when they were low on the horizon like this they resembled an eye. Kantees offered a prayer to the Mother, thanking her for her blessing.

Sheesha's speed increased. Kantees had not instructed him but he was his own master. Under the gaze of the Mother he drew in his wings and the golden magic surrounded them. Kantees could feel the difference between now and how it had been the previous day.

Today Sheesha was drawing the power from outside himself—perhaps from the Mother herself—instead of exhausting himself.

She knew she had learnt something important as they arrowed through the sky.

But once again it was difficult to know whether they would travel too far. Up here above the clouds it was even more difficult to determine how fast they were going. If Sheesha took the power from outside himself did he move more quickly?

If he took strength from a ley-circle did that mean he could not travel far using that power? If he was being fed by the Mother directly now—as she thought he must be—could he travel longer and without tiring?

Then there was the fact that the conjunctions of the moons did not last long because Colimar moved more quickly than Lostimal. She looked up and peered through the golden light. It was as if the Eye of the Mother was looking to the right and no longer directly at them.

She urged Sheesha to slow down. She did not want him tiring the way he had yesterday.

He was obedient and this time he managed the transition from swift flight to normal smoothly, which was just as well since they were so far above the ground. He extended his wings and they glided.

Ulina had said nothing the whole time but Kantees could feel her heart pounding as she held her close. They had travelled so far that the clouds below them were now broken with gaps between. The sight through those gaps was as astonishing as the tops of the clouds had been when she first saw them.

Greens and browns of the landscape, and thankfully the wide river still in view, but there was something up ahead she could not quite make out.

At her urging Sheesha went into a dive. Not steep but enough to let them lose height and come through one of the gaps. Behind them the lands of Esternes were still hidden in the grey of rain. Below were forests but ahead there was a line across the landscape.

The river ran along to it and then disappeared over the edge. It was a cliff that ran across the centre of the land.

Sheesha crossed the line of the cliff. The fall was tremendous and the escarpment ran across the landscape as if someone had cut the rock of the earth and pushed the section up. There were dozens of waterfalls but even from a great distance they could hear the thunder where the Zephira fell. A cloud of water spray filled the air, where it struck the land below and formed itself once more into a river and continued to the south-east.

A great town that seemed to be split above and below stood on the banks of the higher and lower rivers; it had to be Cliffedge. Now, as Kantees looked down at it, she understood the Prince's Gantry.

At the top of the waterfall, and at its base where the spray filled the air, channels had been cut to form a network of canals and wharfs where boats queued and waited to be taken up or brought down on the Prince's Gantry.

And there it was: a huge construction of metal, wood and stone with arms standing out from the edge, from which hung two baskets —so huge they could carry an entire boat. At this moment one was at the top, another at the bottom. Its design was easy to understand, but of a magnitude that was hard to comprehend. With both baskets full they would be winched so that the one rose while the other fell. Even at this distance as she circled around, the ropes were visible as black lines against the cliff. They must be an arms-length in diameter.

She wondered how much magic must be used to make the entire structure strong enough to carry the boats, as well as make it rise and fall. And how brave and foolhardy both the sailors in their boats must be, as well as the men who worked the machine.

She shook her head. It was not a thing she needed to worry about. Even if a basket fell from the top to the bottom, she doubted the trade would ever stop. It could not afford to. But what she and Ulina needed was a place to stay and somewhere they could get some food.

She thought about the coin in her bag. She needed to exchange that into smaller currency so they could spend it.

Once more she stared at the split town of Cliffedge. This time she looked at the buildings; both halves of the town had a large barracks set slightly off to one side. The defence of the place was taken very seriously. If she landed above, in the light, she would attract more attention than going down into the dripping and shadowy mists at the base of the cliff.

She set Sheesha into a descending spiral.

Entering the mists at the base of the great waterfall was similar to flying through the clouds to reach the blue of the sky, something she found herself longing for, because instead of light they were heading into dark. Even though it was not yet night and there was grey light above, in the damp mists it was shadowy with only the constant roar of the waterfall in her ears.

Sheesha touched down.

Kantees slipped to the ground and her feet squished into mud. Ulina landed beside her and, to Kantees' astonishment, a small hand slipped into hers and gripped her fingers tight.

It was hard to orient herself but Kantees had aimed Sheesha for a point near a road that led out of the mist. Following it should take them into the lower town. From above the buildings had been visible, but here it was all shadow. Assuming they had landed in the right place, and with the falling water thundering off to her right, Kantees set off with Ulina still holding her hand.

Kantees glanced back to see that Sheesha was following.

There was no way of knowing what reception they would get but she was tired of trying to keep Sheesha away from people. It hadn't worked out very well, so perhaps if she just acted as if everything was normal—that having a massive *zirichak* walking along behind was not unusual—perhaps they might make better progress.

She found the road, slightly raised from the surroundings and composed largely of stone so the water drained. Kantees turned towards the waterfall.

Windowless buildings loomed out of the grey. At first she thought they must be storehouses, but when she reached the front of the first she could see a picture of different types of bread next to writing she could not read. Something inside made her angry; why should she not be able to read just because she had been a slave? She wasn't a slave any longer. She would learn as soon as she had a chance.

This place would do as well as any other.

She climbed the steps, followed by Ulina, and tried the door. It seemed to be locked. Now she was close she could smell the baking and it made her mouth water. She knocked hard. She could not be sure but she thought she heard a sound from inside, so she took a step back.

A door slammed inside and then locks were turned on the one she faced. She glanced back, Sheesha seemed very interested in what was going on.

"You stay here, Sheesha." She paused. "Try not to scare any passers-by."

She shook her head and looked down at Ulina staring back up at her.

"I hope he doesn't get into trouble," said Kantees.

"Sheesha knows what you want," said Ulina.

"And I know what he wants. We'd better buy something for him as well as ourselves."

The door opened and a man stood there. "It's late. We're closed."

"We need food," said Kantees.

"I have nothing for beggars."

Then his eyes went from Kantees to something behind her. She heard Sheesha make a little growl in the back of his throat.

"We're not beggars," said Kantees. "I am delivering this *ziri*. I have money. We've been travelling all day and need food."

The man only had eyes for Sheesha, and Kantees could tell from the way the man's eyes moved that the *ziri* was moving his head to the side and round Kantees.

"Can we come in? Sheesha won't hurt you, if he can have something to eat too."

The man backed away and gestured to them, his eyes still on the monster behind her. Kantees and Ulina followed him.

"Stay, Sheesha," Kantees said again, more for the effect on the man than a need to reinforce her instructions. After all, the big *ziri* wouldn't fit anyway.

Inside the door was a short passage with barely enough room for the three of them. The man pointed behind her and for a moment she thought he was still bothered about Sheesha but then he wiggled his finger and she shut the door. The space was very dark and she would have thought it to be some sort of trap if the man had not been in there with them.

There was the sound of another door opening and warm dry air wafted in, carrying the heavenly scent of baking and sweet bread.

7

A woman Kantees took for the wife of the baker stared at them from behind a counter. She had a cloth in her hand resting on the surface she had been cleaning.

"We're closed," she said, almost as if the words came out of her mouth without thought.

"Special circumstances," said the man. His tone suggested fear and the woman frowned at Kantees and then down at Ulina, who did not, Kantees thought, ever give the impression of being a sweet girl.

"I'm sorry," said Kantees. "We insisted. We're travelling south to Dakastown and haven't eaten all day."

"We don't do charity except for the Taymalins," said the woman.

"I can pay."

"We're closed."

Kantees shut her eyes. Why did everything have to be so hard? She opened them again and was about to speak when the man beat her to it.

"They have a *zirichak* outside."

The woman frowned at him. "What's that got to do with it?"

"It scared me."

"Look," said Kantees, pulling out the coin and tossing it on to the counter in front of the woman. In the light of the candles the gold glinted. "I don't mind paying more, a special rate; I don't even mind if the bread you have is stale."

"Stale?" The woman's head jerked up from where she had been staring at the coin in front of her. "We don't sell stale bread."

The sight of the gold seemed to have persuaded her. She put down the cloth and ordered her husband into the back to fetch a selection of goods.

"Have you got a basket?"

"Only my bag."

"How much do you need?"

"Enough to get to Dakastown."

"We can't give you enough for a five-day, you wouldn't be able to carry it."

"Less than a day, we are riding the *ziri*."

If the bakers knew that riding a *ziri* was forbidden to slaves they did not mention it. Cliffedge had no Ziri Tower, they did not hold races, otherwise Kantees would have been here before.

"But we are also heading back north so we would like as much bread and as many pies as we can carry," said Kantees. "And if you can give us change for the coin that would help."

She looked down at the coin and Kantees could almost see the woman calculating. She picked it up and weighed it in her hand, then studied it. "You come from Kurvin Port?"

Kantees nodded. "Hamalain."

"I don't know that we can give you enough in change for this."

"I'm tired, Kantees," said Ulina. "Do we have to go on tonight?"

It was true they would not get a great distance before they had to rest for the night, and it would be another night in the open sleeping under Sheesha's wing.

"Can we pay for the night as well?"

The woman shrugged. "You can sleep here, I suppose."

"But our *ziri* needs to come in out of the rain."

"It's not rain, sweetie, it's the fall."

Kantees nodded. "But do you have a place we could stay with the *ziri*?"

"If you don't mind sleeping in the storeroom. Kantees, is it?"

"Yes, this is Ulina, and Sheesha is outside."

"Is it dangerous?"

"He," said Kantees. "Only dangerous to people who threaten him or me."

"Or me," said Ulina.

"We will do our best not to threaten, then. My name is Martorie, my husband is Tarl."

She called him out of the back and explained they did not need to prepare the food now because the guests would be staying the night.

"I still can't give you enough change for the coin," said Martorie.

"I'll just take what you can give," said Kantees.

"We'll have no change for anyone else."

Kantees felt very tired. It really wasn't her problem. Either the woman was going to help them or not. They could solve their own difficulties, she was going to be overpaying so much they could deal with it.

"Why is the town in the mist and not outside it? Wouldn't it make your life a lot easier?"

"Patterner's magic won't protect anyone outside the fall."

"Why not?"

She shrugged. "No one told us why; the patterners keep their magic to themselves like they do everywhere. They just tell us their magic won't protect us outside the fall, so we stay inside the fall like we always have."

Kantees didn't argue, but it seemed a ridiculous explanation. What sort of protective magic were they using anyway? Protection from what?

"If you want to bring your *ziri* around to the back of the building Tarl will let you into the storeroom. We'll heat up some food and bring it through."

Kantees thanked her and told Ulina to stay while she fetched Sheesha.

"No, I'm coming with you."

"You'll just get wet again."

"I'm coming." She tightened her grip on Kantees' hand.

Kantees looked down into the child's eyes and realised Ulina did not trust her and thought she might just fly away. The idea had not crossed Kantees' mind but there was no point trying to tell Ulina that, she wouldn't believe it.

Instead Kantees smiled and nodded. "Of course. You can help me."

It was not long before they were in the storeroom, dusty with the brown flour that coated everything and turned into a crust on anything damp. Kantees, Ulina and Sheesha soon had patchy congealed lumps all over them.

But it was warm and dry. Martorie brought them a couple of blankets along with a tray of food piled high. She had stopped short at the door when she saw Sheesha.

However, she overcame her initial shock—perhaps because at that moment Sheesha was busy investigating the feathers under one wing—and delivered the bread and pies. They were not stale but were going hard. It didn't matter.

Kantees peeled off her clothes and had Ulina do the same. Kantees wrapped the child in her blanket and then wrapped the other around herself, tucking it in above her bust to hold it in place. Not that she had much in that area. She had noticed men preferred women with big bosoms so she couldn't fathom why Daybian had been so attracted to her, but then she knew he was an idiot when it came to such things.

There was nothing they could do about the damp on Sheesha, and he seemed unconcerned about caking his bright feathers with lumps of flour.

A wave of tiredness came over Kantees. She had been focused all day on their goal, first at the charcoal burners and then flying above the clouds. She smiled at the memory. Then shook her head and glanced at Sheesha. Now he was investigating his rear end in that unconcerned way animals have.

It didn't matter to him that he flew faster than an arrow.

Kantees yawned. She moved a sack of flour and rested her head on it. Her scalp had started to itch as her hair grew out. She should get it shaved, she thought.

8

They were loaded with food. The bread would become hard in a day and the pies would not last much longer, but it was more than they had had for a long time.

After flying for a while through the bright morning, they had landed on an island in a place where the river widened. Kantees had sent Sheesha off to find some food while she and Ulina cleaned themselves and their clothes, still coated in a sticky layer of damp and caked flour, in the sluggish water.

The sun had decided to appear today and it helped to dry them thoroughly, more than they had been in a couple of days. Kantees thought about what the baker's wife had said about the magic and shook her head. She could not imagine what sort of protective patterns might be woven into the mists—let alone what they protected against.

The couple had been vague on that, they simply did as they were told.

It was just another exercise in power as far as Kantees was concerned. The patterners claimed there was a spell and the people believed them even though it meant they ended up living in the middle of mist that never lifted and soaked everything. Not that they seemed unhappy.

By the time Kantees and Ulina had finished cleaning and drying themselves, Sheesha returned and landed lightly in the glade that lay alongside the river on this side of the island. He preened himself and settled down for a sleep. Kantees got the strong impression he had eaten well, just as they had with their bread rolls and meat-filled pies all wrapped in a greased but edible material to keep them dry.

While Sheesha slept, she and Ulina walked across to the other side of the island to where trees overhung the water. They disturbed a gaggle of creatures that looked like *sikechasa* but were bigger. They moved like a flock of birds but dove in and out of the surface of the water. Kantees had no idea what they were but they did look like they would make a fine meal—if she were able to hunt, but she did not have that skill.

"You know how to hunt, Ulina. You got that *sikechak* in the charcoal woods?"

"I know how to kill, Kantees."

The child had opened a door to her past but that was not a journey Kantees wanted to make. Ulina's bloodthirsty habits and wicked knife could stay her secret.

There was a boat sailing south with the river. It had a pair of red triangular sails bowed out in the wind and, with the current, seemed to be making good speed. On the vessel's deck, a couple of men were tending to ropes, and another climbing down the mast while one at the back controlled the tiller. Kantees could see their cargo in boxes piled high between the masts. There were probably more below.

This vessel would have come down the Prince's Gantry. Perhaps the ship and crew had made that trip many times—more than likely. It was a terrifying thought. Kantees did not mind being higher than the clouds on the back of Sheesha, but the thought of dangling from ropes in a huge basket holding such a heavy boat made her fingers curl in fear.

One of the men waved at them. Kantees froze. In some strange way she had imagined that she and Ulina must be invisible; they watched the world pass by but the world could not see them. Then she raised her hand and returned the gesture even though it was tight and small.

"Do you know that man?" asked Ulina as the vessel slid silently past only a stone's throw away.

The man was still looking at Kantees and she had a sudden flash of recognition: The charcoal town. The hunter. A surge of fear ran through her and she went cold.

"I don't know him," she said. Even she could tell her voice was strained as she said it.

"Don't lie to me, Kantees."

Was she really that transparent? She was supposed be a very accomplished liar. Clearly not this time.

The man was smoking a pipe and he grinned at her. So close she almost felt he might leap into the river and swim to them. But he did not move, just gave her another wave as the vessel slipped away downstream.

"You know him."

"No," said Kantees and almost said no more, but Ulina's words from before came back to her. "I mean I don't know who he is, but I do recognise him. He was in the town when the mob came after us. He was leading them. He was the one who knew where we were."

"What does he want?"

"I don't know."

But he had tried to make the crowd attack, and whatever his purpose was it had not been friendly then. There was no reason to suppose his intention had changed.

"Come on," she said, turning back to make the two dozen paces across the island that would return them to Sheesha.

He was asleep.

Kantees glanced at the sky. The hunter must have been travelling fast as well. But if he was on that boat and the wind and the current were with them perhaps it would be fast enough. There was a great deal of trade on the river and she had seen for herself how full the wharfs at the top were. The mechanism probably ran all night as well as all day.

The boat could have sailed in after her in the late evening and been carried down during the night. They had already been here some time before they'd seen it.

How much time would they have at Dakastown before he

arrived? If she had any idea of the distance between Cliffedge and the charcoal town they had left yesterday afternoon she could determine how fast Sheesha flew.

She looked at the *ziri* lying comfortably and at perfect peace on the bed of damp leaves.

If he would only wake up now perhaps they could reach Dakastown by day's end. They had money in a more useful form and some spare clothes the baker's wife had produced for them, which were more respectable than the tatters they wore now. Kantees did not want to change until they were closer.

A plan formed as she sat down to eat another pie.

Sheesha woke at about midday and they loaded him up—he did not complain about the extra bags—and they took to the sky once more. The weather was still overcast but it did not feel as if it would rain. Kantees took Sheesha up through the clouds and they bathed in the sunlight, even though the air was cold.

Kantees allowed Sheesha to increase his speed and they moved smoothly into the realm of *ziri* magic. As they flashed across the hills and valleys of the brilliant white clouds she caught glimpses of the land below.

The river was not hard to follow, as it continued to widen and reflected the brightness of the sky above it. Sheesha responded to her movements to change direction as the course of the waterway turned somewhat to the east.

As they sped on, the clouds ahead piled up in higher and higher ranges, like mountains of fluff. And they became darker. Flashes of brightness flickered within them. Kantees urged Sheesha to slow and they descended once more, but this time into torrential rain.

Though it was still daylight the world had grown dark and the wind blasted the rain at them from all sides. Ulina nestled back into Kantees gripping her loose, and soaked, clothing.

If only they could remain above the clouds forever in sunlight.

They could not see far through the downpour. Kantees set the tired *ziri* into a descent spiral. Gliding allowed him to preserve his strength, although he needed to adjust all the time as the wind buffeted them. She was careful. Dakastown was on the coast and she was aware they might have overshot their target once more. They could be over the sea instead of land.

For a moment she thought they had done just that, as a body of water was revealed below them—and then she panicked as she realised the spiralling meant she had no idea which way they had been travelling and could not retrace their route to return to land.

But the water below did not move like the sea. There were no waves, and plants in huge clumps protruded from the surface, suggesting it was not very deep. It was either a marsh or the edges of a lake. There was a light in the distance—even though Kantees had no idea which direction that was. A light meant people.

She turned Sheesha that way. The illumination seemed to be low, close to the level of the water, but it shone out as they approached. It had a greenish hue, unlike anything Kantees recognised.

She peered into the gloom trying to make out whether there was a building or a boat but there was not a shadow of either. Something nagged her from the depths of her memory as the light grew ever closer. Sheesha hesitated in flight as doubt filled her.

Three things happened at once.

The light went out as a huge spout of water erupted directly in front of them. Sheesha had no time to dodge and his head disappeared into it. But he sheared off to the left, losing height as he did so.

Ulina screamed.

The torrent of water subsided and half a dozen lights flashed on around them.

Kantees groaned as she tried to force the tired *ziri* to climb as fast as he could. More geysers shot upwards around them, one from each of the glowing green lights. One hit Sheesha in the wing and he lost height again.

Dakastown! Kantees realised. It had that name for a reason, she just hadn't been thinking. These waters were filled with *dakasa* and she had fallen for their lure. She was beginning to panic. The waters all around were lighting up to the point she could see the moving shapes of the almost transparent creatures beneath the water. There must be hundreds of them. Sheesha couldn't avoid every geyser of water and each one caused him to lose height. He was holding his own for the present, but he was already tired and she could feel him weakening.

If they couldn't escape they would die.

Sheesha needed more strength.

Dakastown had a ley-circle. A big one. It seemed to glow in the distance.

Another huge burst of water caught Sheesha in the middle and she and Ulina were soaked. Kantees did not know how he could keep flying.

Kantees reached out to Sheesha and directed his attention to the ley-circle. Its golden power flowed effortlessly into the weary *ziri*. Sheesha wrapped himself in its power just as he had in Kurvin Port and shot forward like an arrow. Behind them the waterspouts erupted, but the three of them were gone before the creatures even noticed.

The patch of lights disappeared behind them.

The power of the ley-circle became a guide. Kantees turned Sheesha and they followed the thread of golden power towards its source. Moments later they were over dry land and Kantees had Sheesha release the power. He back-winged and brought them to a shivering halt above a wood. In the distance she could see the glow of lights from the seaport through the haze of the rain, and beyond it the bay.

Sheesha dropped down into a small open space between the trees. Kantees hoped the fact that Sheesha was a big male *zirichak* would keep any predators away from them. Or he would warn them if something big came their way. Here the rain was no more than a light drizzle but Kantees still wished it would stop. She was tired of being wet all the time.

It was then she realised Ulina was crying and not trying to get off. Awkwardly, Kantees got herself down on to the ground and tried to persuade the girl to dismount. But she just kept crying.

Kantees was at a loss. She knew the *dakasa* were scary but they had survived, hadn't they?

"Jump down, Ulina."

The girl remained resolutely on the *ziri*'s back.

Kantees removed the various bags. They were wet on the outside but it seemed the containers from the lower part of Cliffedge were designed to keep moisture out. The food was still edible.

But Ulina did not get down, even when tempted with a pie.

"Sheesha cannot get himself dry when you are on his back," said Kantees. That at least seemed to produce a response. Ulina looked up, and Sheesha chose that moment to bring his head round and look at the girl on his back.

"I'm scared," she said. And it seemed to Kantees that Ulina was talking to Sheesha and not to her. Sheesha brought his muzzle to a point barely a hands-breadth from Ulina's face. He was so big he could probably have swallowed the girl in a single bite, and just as Kantees was noticing that, Sheesha opened his mouth. Kantees gasped in horror as if her thought was going to come true. Sheesha's tongue snaked out and he licked Ulina's face.

"Ugh!" she cried and pushed his snout away. Sheesha grumbled and then nudged her.

"He knows you're scared, Ulina. He won't let anything happen to you. There are no monsters here."

Finally making up her mind, Ulina brought her leg over and slipped into Kantees' waiting arms. They were both treated to a shower of water as Sheesha shook himself. The water flashed off his feathers, which shimmered in the dim light. He then lay down and was asleep in moments.

That's that for the day then, thought Kantees. *Another delay.* She sighed and munched through one of the pies.

9

She woke before dawn, shook Sheesha awake and packed up before waking Ulina. The rain had stopped but a dampness still hung in the air.

The idea had come to her in the night. It was an audacious plan but she was tired of skulking and hiding. There were risks of course but, if things went to plan, they could be finished and out of Dakas-town before nightfall.

Kantees hesitated. She was aware that none of her plans had worked out the way she had intended so far, but that had been because she was dealing with too many things she did not know or understand.

The beauty of her new plan was that it dealt with things she did understand.

She dressed in her new clothes and had Ulina do the same. They still looked like slaves but that was just as it should be. They no longer looked like ragged runaways and that was important.

She knew that Sheesha wanted to hunt; he must be very hungry after yesterday's exertions, but the other part of the plan meant that he would also get fed.

She loaded up the *ziri*, who grumbled, and mounted with Ulina. Sheesha lifted from the ground and Kantees found the power source that was the Dakastown ley-circle. She had Sheesha take the power and they shot away directly towards it. Once upon a time, she knew from her previous life, the circle had been at ground level, but there had been an earthquake that had levelled Dakastown almost completely over a hundred years ago. It had caused the ground to sink and now the ley-circle was the height of two men in the air.

This had not presented a major problem and the patterners had created a movable deck of wood. It was taken away during a feeding to prevent it being destroyed. Kantees had travelled to Dakastown for the races and knew the layout.

It took Sheesha no time at all to traverse the distance, and he landed with a gentle thump and scraping of talons. Quickly, before anybody checked, Kantees dropped to the wooden deck and pulled Ulina after her, along with the bags and containers.

"Identify yourself!" cried a voice from beyond the edge of the deck.

"Forgive me, master, I am a *ziri* slave from the house of Jakalain. I bring my charge, Sheesha, for my master Lord Daybian to ride."

There was movement at the edge of the circle and Kantees dropped to her knees and put her face to the wood, pulling Ulina down too. "Do what I do," she said quietly.

With her head down she could not see what was happening, but it sounded as if at least two, perhaps three, sets of feet climbed on to the planking and made their way forwards.

Sheesha hissed. They stopped.

"There are no races scheduled."

"Forgive me, master, I am only a slave and obey as I am instructed."

Kantees hated this obeisance. It had been barely a ten-day since she had run away from Jakalain, and it was a habit she was keen to lose.

There was muttering between the men. "No patterner's path was opened."

"Forgive me, master. I do not know of such things. The patterners of Jakalain did the will of our lord and I was sent." She hesitated and then added, "How else could we be here?"

It was a risk. A comment that could get her beaten but she

hoped that they would be tired enough to think that someone had made a mistake.

One of the men gave a whistle three times in quick succession and Kantees heard swords being sheathed. Protection of ley-circles was taken seriously, especially when an arrival was unexpected. But, after a fashion, Sheesha himself was his own validation: only the nobility owned *zirichasa*, so if one arrived in a ley-circle it must have been ordered by someone of noble blood, and could not be questioned by the likes of these men.

The sun broached the horizon and Sheesha's feathers glistened in its light.

There was further muttered discussion and finally Kantees was invited to descend to ground level, bringing her assistant and her charge.

Ziri racing was popular in Dakastown and there were holding areas, owned by the Otulain family and provided for the animals of visiting nobility before and after they had travelled. Kantees knew them well enough—as did Sheesha.

They did not require any guidance but the eyries were not staffed since no race was planned. These temporary residencies for *zirichasa* were not like a Ziri Tower, although they were given the name eyrie. Instead they were single storey, round stone structures with an open space in the centre allowing a *ziri* to fly in and out. There were suitably-sized rooms for the *ziri* and accommodation for the keepers. Far superior to what she was used to in the tower. Dakastown—and the Otulain family—was serious about its racing.

Kantees demanded, and got, food for them all, though it took a while to arrive and the sun was high before she felt she could leave.

"Stay with Sheesha, Ulina."

"I want to go with you."

"Someone must remain with Sheesha, and I have to find out about the Dunor."

"Will they let you out?"

"I will tell them I must deliver a letter."

"I'm sure they will believe you, Kantees," said Ulina. "You are a good liar."

Kantees sighed. She suspected Ulina would never let her forget their argument, and the fact that Ulina did not know whether Kantees could be trusted at all. Well, she must simply demonstrate she was trustworthy, though the constant need to tell falsehoods did not help her position.

"If there's any trouble," said Kantees, "let Sheesha fly you. Travel up the river and I will find you."

"Unless you are dead."

"Wait a five-day." And what then? The child could not be expected to fly Sheesha to find Yenteel and the *tekrak*. She would have to make sure she was not dead, otherwise all Ulina's limited trust would be gone.

Kantees also gave Sheesha a good talking to and explained that he must protect Ulina. Not that she expected him to understand but he rested his head on her shoulder, which she had come to learn was a sign of his affection—even though he had no idea of his weight and tended to crush a person to their knees if they weren't prepared.

She knew she was wasting time. She needed to get out; if all went well this should take less than a day. Unfortunately, nothing they had done thus far had gone to plan. So, with her bag of what remained of the pies—the staff would continue to feed Sheesha and Ulina—she set off into the town.

The bustle of people along the cobbled streets, mingling with the carts and animals, was a shock and for a while she was disoriented. She had known it once, though as a young house slave she was not allowed out. For so many years she had been alone in the Ziri Tower, with only the occasional race to extend her experience of people. Even then she was always required to be close to Sheesha. Never on her own.

The closest to this had been Kurvin Port, but even then they had not walked the streets, only seen it from above.

Now she was alone in the crowds that batted her one way and another, and it was only as she allowed herself to be carried along by the flow of people that she realised she was not sure where she was going.

Her master's house had been set halfway up a slope and it was from the rear windows that she could see the sea. She reached a square and the current of people grew less intense. The road and buildings dropped away towards the water and a statue of Taymar stood at its centre on a marble pedestal. The figure looked out to the water.

Kantees stood down the slope from the statue herself and looked out across the roofs. The bay was so big you could not see from one side to the other, but it provided a wonderfully calm surface upon which hundreds of vessels fished. The south-east of the bay met a range of high hills, the *Telaquin*, which became a line of islands threading out into the sea towards the coast of the mainland. From the windows at the back of her old master's house, the *Telaquin* were almost directly ahead. And from here they were to the right.

That meant she must go to the left and make her way around to a point above the main harbour on which Dakastown stood. She was wary of entering the back streets so she kept to the main ones. She was sure that as she got closer to the right place she would remember.

She was wrong.

10

Kantees stood in the middle of a street she did not recognise. It was paved in smooth white stone with thin lines of red running through it. The walls that ran along each side of it were constructed from the same material and she found the way the road dwindled into the distance to be almost hypnotic. At intervals were pillars topped with foliage, and from them hung large ornate lanterns.

This was not a road she knew.

When she had grown up here there had been estates on either side reaching up to the ridge above and down towards the sea. There were buildings up the slope, but instead of the lines of homes crammed one against the other these were the houses of the rich, set apart from one another with delicate paths criss-crossing lawns of flower beds tended by Kadralin gardeners.

She crossed to the other side and looked over. Parkland greeted her eye. Every building that had been here, right down to the water's edge where the sea lapped the beaches, was gone. It was as if her memories had been ripped from her, and if they were an anchor in the past she was now afloat and drifting without oar or tiller.

Leaning on the wall she looked down. Rich people walked there, and there was nothing for her. Her old master was gone.

She knew what must have happened: the Otulain had decided to remodel their town.

Her fingers curled into fists and she slammed them down on to the wall. "Why is it never simple?" she shouted to no one in particular.

She took a deep breath. If her master had been a butcher or a tailor it would have been simple, she would simply ask where their street had been moved. But she could not ask where Kevrey of Tander had gone; he had never been popular, and the patterners in particular did not like his trade in information.

But if she could not find him who else could she ask about the Dunor? That name thrown at her by a minor raider on the top of the bell tower at Jakalain. If only he had kept his peace then she would not have heard the name and would not be chasing across the world to find out what it meant.

"Are you lost?"

Kantees was on her knees in a moment and staring at the ground. The cultured tones of the speaker could only mean that this man, whoever he was, was a high-caste Taymalin. She needed to remember her place. And remember that Sheesha and Ulina were waiting for her.

Whoever he was, he became tired of waiting for her to respond. "Do you have your tongue still?"

"I beg your forgiveness, master. I will leave."

"I asked if you were lost. You seemed … frustrated."

"It is nothing, master. I will leave." She twisted round as if about to head back into the town.

"Not until you answer my questions."

Kantees closed her eyes. This was exactly the kind of trouble she wanted to avoid but she had been stupid. So surprised by this new street, she had allowed herself to become the object of someone's attention.

"I am sorry, master. I was looking for somewhere. I must have come the wrong way."

"Perhaps I can help, where did you want to be?"

Now Kantees was confused, Taymalin did not offer help to Kadralin slaves. The man must have another motive, most likely he wanted what Daybian had wanted: her body. Though Daybian claimed he would not have taken what was not freely offered, which was good except he could not understand why she did not want him.

"I beg your pardon, sire, please, I will just leave."

"I do believe you're avoiding the question."

To compound the issue, she heard the sound of iron-shod hooves clattering on to the road from the direction of the town. At least three horses. Of course they were horses and not *kichesa*, the highest born of the Taymalin preferred these new mounts.

"Levin, what are you doing with that slave?" cried a woman's voice. She seemed amused.

"Mistress Deenya, the girl is lost and I was putting her on the right road."

"The road to your bedchamber I have no doubt."

"You wound me, madam." If he were truly hurt, he hid it behind the laughter in his words.

"And if those words could wound *you* then I believe you would have been long in your grave, Levin."

From the sound of his voice, Kantees thought he must be looking at the new arrival, having turned his back on her; she lifted her head slightly to see if she could at least get an idea of the people she was dealing with.

"She is trying to see whether you are worthy of her."

Mother's milk! Damn the woman.

"What is your name, girl?"

Kantees swore under her breath again. "Mina, mistress."

"And your master?"

"Kevrey of Tander." The words just fell out, she needed to lie and his was the first name that came to mind. She cringed.

"Ha! That old fool?" said the woman. "Why are you here?"

"Indeed," said the man. "If my memory does not fail me I believe he lived hereabouts before the new palace was built—"

"Still being built," she said. "The place is a hovel."

"—so why would you be here, Mina?"

This time the answer flowed out of her so easily she almost believed it herself. "I beg your pardon, my lord, my lady. My master owed a debt to the Jakalain and chose to have me indenture there for several years. I am only just returned and came to where I know he used to be, only to find it transformed into this beautiful place."

"Jakalain," she said derisively. "Those yokels."

"Very good, Mina, and now you have answered all my questions."

"I wouldn't take her to your bed, Lev, she's probably as filthy as they are. You'll never get the smell off your body."

Kantees' anger was building but she held it in check. These people could be death to her. Besides, she had no intention of going to his bed, she would never be able to wash away his stench either.

"I am honoured by your concern, Mistress Deenya," he said.

Kantees could see well enough that she did not miss his sweeping bow to the woman. Could it possibly contain a hint of disrespect? Perhaps, since Mistress Deenya did not seem a pleasant woman. Kantees was not familiar with the other families and did not know whether she was an Otulain—or this Levin either.

She was saved any further embarrassment as Mistress Deenya and her two attendants moved off along the lane. "This road is ridiculous," she called back. "Why couldn't your father have built his new palace at this end so we didn't have to ride all the way along here just to get to it? It's so windy."

There was barely a breeze.

The one called Levin did not reply but watched her go. Once the sound of hooves had dropped to the merest echo, he turned back to Kantees.

"Well, Mina, the palace is currently looking considerably less attractive than it did just a short time ago. Since your master has moved, I will show you where he has gone, shall I?"

Kantees was torn. A guide would be very useful but the last thing she needed was a Taymalin—and an Otulain at that, possibly the heir—in attendance when all she wanted was to ask about the Dunor and get out.

"In fact, you do smell," he said casually as they walked back towards the town.

"I am sorry, my lord, I have been travelling a good while." She put more distance between them and dropped back. He stopped.

"I wish you to walk closer so I can talk to you."

The last thing she wanted. "Yes, my lord."

"You smell of *ziri*."

"I was required to work with them, sire."

"I thought I recognised you." Kantees felt her heart plummet, could this get any worse? "How is Daybian?"

Kidnapped and taken by the Dunor while he was covering my escape. "He was well when I last saw him, sire." And that wasn't even a lie, though he had been in the middle of a battle. Thankfully he did not ask her any further questions but only spoke of the changes to the town in the last few years. Dakastown was the main trading centre between the mainland, across the Strait of Esternes, and the interior of Esternes itself via the river. It had commerce in plenty and the Otulain were wealthy.

Levin carried himself with the confidence she had seen in a few of the high-caste Taymalin. So comfortable in their position they did not need to condescend to those who were below them, and in them was a willingness to speak with and even learn from anyone. It was not an unpleasant trait, but sadly lacking in the majority of the masters.

And, when all was said and done, she was still a slave—at least as far as he was concerned—and that someone might be the property of another did not concern him. It was the natural order, to his mind.

As they moved deeper into the town the number of people grew and it became necessary for Kantees to walk behind Levin. A position she certainly preferred.

They crossed the road by which she had entered the town and headed round into the low hills on the other side. Rivers and streams poured from each valley and the main thoroughfare crossed each in sweeping arches. This was all new and, unlike the road to the palace, it thronged with people and animals.

Levin made good progress, as if he were a ship cutting through the waves; the people parted before him. Animals, however, took no notice of his rank and those he needed to walk around.

Finally, they took a side street going uphill. Kantees was relieved they were not heading down, because that would have meant her old master had lost what little rank he held in the town's society. Downhill meant that the sewage of those above descended to the houses below, while uphill meant good air and light.

The shops on either side were a mixture of scribes, lawyers, and map-makers doing a good trade by the number of people there—all of them in good quality clothing, even the ones that were obviously sailors.

She peeked in through the window of one of the map-makers as they passed. On an easel, looking out, was a detailed map of—well she did not know where, and even if she had been able to read they moved by too fast.

How big was Esternes? Big enough that a *zirichasa* flying at the speed of an arrow would take perhaps two days to travel from its middle to its southern coast. A trip that might take a boat perhaps three or four times that.

And then Levin stopped at a door. The windows were shuttered and it looked unoccupied. There was a wooden sign beside the door, unlike most shops which had a picture or small statue to represent their trade. This one had nothing but words. Which she could not read.

"Here he is," said Levin. He stared at the shutters and then stepped back to look at the upper windows. Kantees glanced up, one of them was open. Levin rapped on the door.

They waited. Nothing happened. Levin knocked again, this time louder.

Kantees desperately wanted him to decide it was not worth waiting but he seemed as intent on getting a response as she would have been.

"Lazy excuse for a trader."

"He thinks you're the bailiff, my lord," came a voice from behind them. Kantees turned, but although there were several people looking in their direction from the other shops, it was impossible to tell who had spoken.

"Kevrey of Tander! This is Levin of Otulain. I demand entry."

The sound of something being knocked over, and a voice

swearing came from above. Then a head haloed with unkempt hair poked out, looked down at them and then disappeared back inside. Silhouetted against the sun, Kantees was uncertain whether it had been her old master.

Words floated down to them. "Patience, my lord, you cannot hurry wisdom."

That definitely was Kevrey. She sighed in relief. It had taken more days than she had counted on but at least she was here now and could get an answer to her question. Assuming that he knew it. That had been nagging at her. What if he didn't know?

She shook her head. He *must* know. He had always known everything. Or he made up something convincing. She sighed again. If there were any place that she could lay the blame for her skill at subterfuge, it was the tongue of Kevrey of Tander.

It took a while but finally there was the sound of bolts being drawn back, and with a final click of a key the door opened into a dark interior. The smell that wafted out made a *ziri* eyrie seem a bouquet of flowers. She recognised the smell of stale alcohol, and that was just from Kevrey himself. Other smells included rotting meat—something else she was familiar with—and a musky odour hiding behind something intensely sweet. The contrast did not make the overall effect any easier to tolerate; on the contrary, it emphasised the unpleasantness of it all.

His clothes looked as if they were the same ones he had been wearing when she had been sold to Jakalain, now threadbare and considerably more soiled.

On the positive side, the appalling smells and sight might drive Levin away.

Levin glanced at Kantees then back at Kevrey, who seemed to be having difficulty focusing against the light. He was thinner than he had been, his face now so gaunt and pale he looked as if he might be on the brink of death.

Unexpectedly, Kantees felt a wave of sorrow go through her. He had been like a bright star when she had been here before. He had been so active, angry or happy he always had life. This person who stood before them was like an animated corpse.

"Kevrey of Tander?"

Her old master squinted at Levin and his eyes watered.

"It is my old master, sire, perhaps if you will permit me?"

It was bold, and in most situations would have brought her a beating, but she slipped in front of the lord and pushed the door back gently. The old man gave her a watery stare.

"Hello, master, it's Mina. I have returned after all these years at Jakalain."

If his wits were gone he could expose her here and now. On the other hand, if he had lost his way, it would be easy to explain his confusion as being the product of his dotage.

"Mina?"

"Yes, master, you sent me away to Jakalain. I have returned to you."

She gently took his hands from the door and he allowed himself to be taken inside, though he stared at her face as if he was trying to place her.

She guided him to the left into the main downstairs room, which should have been the shop. There were tables and cupboards and drawers, similar to the room he had used for greeting guests before. But there were none of his things. No maps, papers, no books, no measuring devices, no looking glass. As empty as it must have been on the day he moved in.

There was a pair of chairs, and she set him down into one of them, then went to the window to open the shutters and get some fresh air and light into the place.

The locks did not want to move at first, as if they had not been opened in a long time, but she won out in the end. The light poured in and revealed a room that had not been dusted in a great while, and a grate that had held no fire in an age.

Levin of Otulain stood at the door and watched. As she threw back the final shutter he spoke. "He does not seem to know you."

"It has been many years, sire." She turned to the old man. In the daylight he looked worse. His skin was not just the pale pallor of the Taymalin, it possessed a tinge of yellow. His eyes were bloodshot and he blinked in the brightness.

Kantees felt a strange emotion that she could not place. Not sorrow, though it seemed to be its kin in the way it held her heart as if it would break. He was so thin.

She knelt before him and took his hand in hers. It was cold like death. "Master Kevrey, do you not recognise me?"

This was not how she had wanted to greet him. She had wanted the man she had left all those years ago, confident in his power and his knowledge. Not this wandering fool. And her lies had placed her in a difficult position if he remembered her name—

"Kantees?" His voice was frail too.

"As I said, it seems he does not recognise you."

"Yes, I am—was—Kantees. They call me Mina now." She held her breath. It was not unusual for masters to change the names of slaves, if they happened to wish it. She was trying to convince two people at once in different ways. "But please call me by that name if it is your wish."

She did not look at the lord at the door. Perhaps he had not heard what Kevrey said.

"Kantees of Jakalain?" said Levin. "Of course."

11

_K_antees went as cold as the hand she was holding.

"Daybian spoke of you," he said. "He was quite taken with your skill with his prize _ziri_, what was his name? Sheesha. Excellent beast."

Kantees stayed where she was, there was no point trying to run, there was nowhere to go. He commanded the room and the exit.

Mother's milk! Once more her lies had betrayed her. Why had he come with her? Now she knew: Kevrey had recognised her, perhaps not precisely but something in her had stirred his memory and piqued his interest.

"Master," she said, drawing Kevrey's attention back to her. "I must ask you a question. I can pay for the answer."

"Don't ignore me, girl!"

Kantees was tired of acting like a slave. She had had so many years of it and she had freed herself. This pretence was just another lie and she would do it no more. She climbed to her feet and turned to the door, facing Levin like an equal. She looked him in the eye.

"Sire, I have come a long way to ask my old master a question. If you will give me but a moment to do this thing. Then I will give you my full attention."

His eyes narrowed. She was not sure what that meant but when he gave a curt nod she turned back to the old man in the chair. She knelt once more so that he did not have to look up at her.

"Master," she said again. "I am Kantees. I am the slave who asked a question of you. I am the one you sold to Jakalain in disgust since I would not keep to my place." She glanced at Levin. "Sadly, I did not learn the lesson you tried to teach me and I still do not know my place. But I have a question I must ask now, it is very important."

"I remember you, Kantees. I remember you always pried into those things that were not yours to know. You listened at the door. I remember your bright eyes and how you devoured the knowledge I laid out for you."

"You knew?"

He coughed, though it might have been a laugh. "Of course, I knew. Do you think for one moment there was anything that happened in my house I did not know about?"

"Oh." Kantees frowned. Her entire world turned on its head. If he had been deliberately providing her with opportunities to learn —what did that mean? "Why?"

"I was curious to see how much you were able to understand. Being merely Kadralin."

She jumped back as if she had been stung. Anger welled up. "We are not animals," she hissed, barely able to prevent herself from shouting. "We are not to be taught tricks. I am a person!"

In spite of the dangerous tone in her voice, her old master allowed a smile to cross his face. "It was I who learnt a lesson, Kantees."

She did not trust herself to speak further so she just stared at him, waiting for him to condemn himself further out of his own mouth. She wondered if she could kill the old man before Levin stopped her. *How dare he!*

"Are you curious to know what lesson you taught me?"

She said nothing.

"That I was an arrogant fool." He sighed and looked away. "And this is where my hubris has brought me." He gestured around.

"The Kadralin have their own knowledge, old man." *What you would not have given in your younger days to learn what I know of the* ziri.

"We do not need yours, or the corrupted wisdom of the *Slissac*. We built the Ziri Towers, we lived in these places before we were dispossessed. We have our own knowledge and we do not need yours."

She heard Levin adjust his feet. Outside life continued as it always had. Inside the world was turning, spinning and changing.

"I know the name of my enemy," she said. "Which is also the enemy of the Taymalin, but I do not know what it is. That is what you must answer."

"But you do not know why I sent you away."

"Because I dared ask a question. You thought you could get rid of what you'd made by throwing me away. Instead you threw me into a fire where I have become tempered and sharp."

Kantees hesitated. She was saying all these things, as if they were true. And saying them in front of Levin, who might kill her for their utterance. It was crazy—and yet, in her heart, she knew they were the truth. At last she felt as if the words coming from her mouth were not lies. Though they would form the rope that would hang her, or the blade to cut out her heart.

"No." The old man sighed once more. "I sent you away to protect you."

"Ha."

"I cared for you, Kantees. I had given you a world of knowledge and made you inquisitive. I gave you the tools to think. But those things would kill you if they became known and—" he hesitated, "—events were coming to a situation where they might have been discovered. I sold you to Jakalain to get you as far away from the Dunor as possible."

Kantees could not have been more surprised if the old man had exploded in a cloud of golden dust.

Something brushed against her shoulder. And an arrow blossomed in Kevrey's chest.

He looked up into Kantees' eyes. His lips moved and his voice scraped through his throat as he fought to breathe. "My bed."

For just a moment she saw something she did not understand, then the light faded just as something crashed into her side, knocking her across the room. A heavy weight landed on top of her.

"Stay down," shouted Levin in her ear. He was moving again, as fast as he had brought her out of the light.

Kantees stared at the body of Kevrey. Two more arrows sprouted from his chest. *Why? He's already dead.*

And then she burst into tears as if they had been waiting behind her eyes for just this moment. She rubbed at them. There was no time for this. She would have to mourn him at another time, though part of her claimed she did not need to mourn him at all. He was just another Taymalin who had used her. He had thought she was no more than an animal to be trained.

But he had learnt. She shook her head. He should not have needed to learn. That the Kadralin were people just like the Taymalin was not something that required teaching. It was in the heart of any man who saw beyond the colour of someone's skin. Sheesha had more compassion than the Taymalin in their arrogance.

The first window shutter slammed shut.

"Taymar's teeth!" Levin said as he crawled to the second window. "Damned if I'm going to die for an educated slave." He pulled that closed too.

"I am not a slave," shouted Kantees. "Weren't you listening?"

"Yes, I was listening to the rantings of an old man who had fallen for his slave."

"I was barely ten years old!"

Levin shrugged. "Makes no difference to some."

"He was protecting me from the Dunor."

"Rumours and nonsense."

A second shock. Did everyone know about the Dunor except her? "You've heard of them?"

"Of course I have," he said. "A cabal of Taymalin seeking to create an empire? Or was it to bring back the *Slissac*? Or perhaps to raise the *Kisharuk*? Take your pick. It's all nonsense."

"What nonsense? Who do you think wanted him killed now? Who probably wants me dead?"

"I should let them."

"What makes you think you'll be spared, Levin?"

"You will address me properly, slave. Mina, Kantees, whatever your name really is."

"I'll call you by your name, Levin. I am no slave."

"Really, who freed you then? Daybian?"

"I freed myself!"

"Just a runaway then."

Kantees glanced at the window trying to guess what the assassin would do next. She doubted he would want to leave them alive. Well, if he was sent by the Dunor then her life was definitely forfeit. No reason to leave a loose end like Levin around.

Who were the Dunor? It seemed Levin did not know much after all. It was just a joke to him.

Another arrow struck the shutter.

Kantees frowned. Why would someone shoot an arrow against a closed shutter?

A wisp of smoke curled through a gap, highlighted in the sunlight.

"He's setting a fire," Kantees said and clambered to her feet.

Levin looked, hesitated for a heartbeat, then ran for the door. "Farahalek!"

It was Kantees' turn to be incredulous. She had heard of the assassins, they were the sort of story the Taymalin masters told their children to scare them into obedience. But they were just a story. Then again, she would not have believed in a giant *tekrak* if someone had told her a turn of Lostimal ago.

She was barely to the door when the world behind her erupted in fire and she was deafened by a thunderous roar. A wave of heat went across her back and slivers of shattered wood ploughed into her exposed skin. The shockwave knocked her into Levin and they both fell again.

Kantees thought of Ulina. She had to get back to the circle for the sake of the girl; she had to get away. Levin might not know much, or even believe, but it was enough to know that they were a group of powerful people who, right now, were intent on her destruction and anyone around her. If only Sheesha was here now.

If wishes were ziri, slaves would fly.

But almost immediately Levin was up again. If Kantees could admire these Taymalin men for anything, they seemed to thrive on battle. Daybian had been the same. It must be their training, always the warriors—always the conquerors.

He headed towards the back, apparently unconcerned as to whether she was following him. Of course not. But Kantees looked up at the stairs, tight and curving round abruptly. She glanced once more at Levin's disappearing back and headed up the stairs. As she grabbed the rope that comprised the rail she saw blood on her hand. She could not feel the pain yet, that would no doubt come.

She rounded the second curve and came out into a small alcove that led directly into the room above the front. She stopped. The window was open and the shutters back. Black smoke filtered up from below, both outside and through the floorboards, and she could hear the crackle of burning wood. Across the room was the bed. If she had been a high-born Taymalin lady she might have been disgusted by the dirt and the smell—now masked by the burning wood. But she was not. She had spent years shovelling the shit of a *ziri* and before that she had dealt with Kevrey and all his mess. It was familiar to her, even though the location was different.

Outside there were shouts of "Fire!" and someone was beating a piece of metal with a hammer in alarm. The houses were so closely packed that a single fire unchecked could easily consume a dozen buildings. She imagined the alarm might hamper the movements of their assassin but she did not want to take any chances.

She got down on her hands and knees to crawl across the room. The floorboards were smooth and worn, though not as much as those in Kevrey's old house had been. She reached the bed and glanced at the windows. The smoke was thicker and she fancied she could even feel the heat from below. She needed to hurry.

If Kevrey was hiding something where would he put it? She stripped the single blanket from the pallet. It would not be that, nor would it be in any obvious place where any slave or thief might be able to pilfer it. Kevrey was clever. And let's pretend that he expected her to return at some point.

She stared. She pulled the pallet away. It was cheap and filled only with straw. Kantees wondered how he had fallen so far. Why had he stopped trading in knowledge? That was his income and the thing he enjoyed. He would not have been able to live without his books and his maps. Beside the bed was a jug, containing a liquid. A quick smell revealed it to be something alcoholic. She did not recognise it.

The frame of the bed was wooden, and there were slats across that supported the pallet. The ones in the middle were bowed where they had supported his weight for so long. The smell of burning was getting stronger, and when she glanced at the window again, she was shocked at the amount of smoke that now obscured the light. And now she was certain that she could feel the heat from below. Time was limited.

Perhaps it was not the bed at all, something else?

She looked around. But *no*. This was Kevrey, if he said "bed" then that was precisely what he intended. Something about the bed. It had a leg at each corner and two more: one on each side in the middle. They were a different colour of wood. She pulled the bed up on its side. The base of every leg was clay, hard and with a shine except where the dirt had been ground into it. She pulled out her knife and levered off first one and then the other of the middle legs.

Just wood. Solid wood. She sighed and shook her head. Then coughed as the smoke bit into her throat. She was about to give up when she heard someone else coughing. She turned as a dark figure stumbled out of the stairwell.

"Levin?"

"Are you insane? We have to get out of here."

"Just go!"

"Not without you."

"You're an idiot."

"I'm not the one dismantling a bed in a burning building."

"I'm looking for something."

"He doesn't have any treasure."

Kantees turned back to the bed. Her eyes were watering and it was much hotter in the room. There was not much that could be heard above the predatory growling of the fire beneath them. Red light glowed up through the cracks and every now and then a wisp of flame came through.

It's here. I know it is.

She could barely make out the bed now through her tear-filled eyes and the smoke. With a sudden realisation, she attacked the clay feet of the other legs. First one then another came free. Just wood. Then the third. She coughed as it fell off and at first she didn't notice that there was a hole.

"I'm going," said Levin and she heard his footsteps retreating.

She could not get her hand into the hole so she had to turn the frame back. Nothing fell out. She got down to floor level and found she could breathe more easily there. She jammed her fingers into the hole and felt around. Something brushed her finger; she almost ignored it but there it was again. She managed to pincer the cord between two fingers and pulled gently. It slid between her fingers.

"Mother's milk! Come *on!*"

She adjusted her position so she could get her fingers further in and tried to curl the cord round one of them. This time she got better purchase and, reluctantly, the cord allowed itself to be dragged out. The moment she could see an end she grabbed it properly and pulled hard. A package fell out. It was the size of her fist, wrapped in coarse cloth and tied with string.

There was no time to look at it. She grabbed it up—it was heavy —and shoved it inside her top and crawled towards the way out. Only to see Levin coming back.

He was coughing badly.

The floorboards were hot beneath her, the glow from below constant and growing in strength. She grabbed his arm and yanked him down to her level.

"Easier to breathe," she said, her voice rasping.

"Going to die—anyway," he said between attempts to draw a breath.

Kantees did not want to die just yet. She peered round through bleary eyes. The windows showed only as brighter areas through the smoke. They were a floor up, and it would be a desperate person who threw themselves out in the hopes of survival. Not to mention crossing a floor that might collapse and drop them through into the raging flames below.

There was an orange glow from the direction of the stairs now. Levin had not come back for her, just for his own life. It's strange how we cling to life even when all hope is gone, she thought. But perhaps that's because we never really give up.

There was a dark patch near where the bed had been. She blinked away the tears and tried to think. The smoke was even making that hard now. Levin was on all fours and keeping his head to the floor, though clear of the cracks.

What did the dark patch mean? Fireplace. It was the fireplace. Made of stone, not wood. She giggled but it turned into a cough— the irony of being saved from a fire by a chimney.

She did not trust herself to speak, it was all she could do to stop herself from coughing, so she just tapped Levin on his head and moved off towards the fireplace. The stone was still cool beneath her fingers. She pulled the grate out and pushed it away.

She was not sure if Levin understood what she intended but he grabbed the grate from her, and above the cracking of wood and roaring of flame she heard it crash across the floor.

Was it any worse burning to death stuck in a chimney than waiting for it out here?

She didn't care. And stood up. The smoke was bad and rising up the flue. She braced herself against the sides and tried to find hand-holds. There were some but not many. However, she found she could push herself up as long as she maintained the pressure against the sides.

The heat seemed to reduce a little but the smoke was thick, making it very hard to breathe. She couldn't stop herself from coughing any longer and felt that her lungs were being torn out. But still she climbed. Beneath her she could hear Levin coughing. Kantees kept pushing.

Above her the dark smoke grew paler and thinned. Breathing became easier.

"Kantees!" She heard Levin wheezing below her. "Kantees, I'm stuck."

Perhaps that was why the smoke had become thinner. It couldn't get past him. He was much larger than her. She stopped with her face up into the cool and fresh air. She could just leave him. She owed him nothing. Except without him she would not have found her old master.

Or perhaps she would, but not have been attacked.

She shook her head. There was no way of guessing what might have been and it had no value. All she had was now, and the future, while Levin's future was limited. Even if they escaped on to the roof there was still a good chance they would die. Even if the assassin—the Farahalek—wasn't still waiting to finish them off.

Kantees reached up to the light and the fresh air. Her fingers curled around the top of the chimney stack.

"Grab my foot!" she called down to Levin.

"Just go!"

"Do you want to die? Reach up and grab my foot."

Fear ran through her as a hand brushed against the sole of her foot and then grabbed at her ankle. It felt as if she would be dragged down into the inferno below. She had to force herself to hold her foot in place.

"Pull yourself up!"

There was no answer but the grip tightened. Her toes were pushed into a small gap but threatened to rip free as he pulled harder and his grip tightened. She dug her fingers into the stonework above, wishing she could just get away.

She shrieked as her toes gave way and her foot dropped, pulling her hands free. She jammed her elbows to the sides and scraped them raw as she brought herself to a stop.

He was no longer holding her ankle. Was he there at all?

"Levin?"

He coughed. Not dead yet then.

Using her other foot, she managed to lever herself back into the position she had been in before but found a better position for her other foot. The heat from below was increasing; she did not dare imagine how hot his feet must be.

"Try again."

"Get …out." His short command was punctuated by coughing.

"Just try again!"

He did not argue, perhaps he understood that he was protecting her from the worst of the heat, giving her fresh air to breathe. The thought prompted her to notice that the air was perhaps not as fresh as it had been. She looked up to see streams of smoke, ash and red embers shooting skyward from around the chimney. They might be too late.

The hand clamped on her ankle again but this time she felt surer of her position. She braced herself as he pulled. The thought that she would have bruises on her foot floated through her mind.

Levin gave a cry that seemed barely human and grated in his throat as he pulled himself up. The pressure went from her foot although he was still holding it.

"Up." The word was barely recognisable.

Realising he must be free, Kantees climbed again and within moments pulled herself up so she was sitting on the edge of the chimney. The roof was burning and had already collapsed in places. The serenity of the bay and the ships on the water seemed unreal against the inferno that raged around her.

Levin's hand appeared. She grabbed him by the wrist and pushed his palm against the edge of the stonework. It gripped and he pulled himself up and out. He gasped a breath of air and then another.

Heat was now pouring up from below and the flue was lit by a red glow. Levin's clothes were blackened and smoking. They were still not free. Kantees looked behind. From where they were to the ridge tiles was the space of a single stride, but the roof was on fire.

But it seemed that the roof on the other side was not yet burning. Perhaps this house was divided from the one behind by a stone wall.

Levin turned himself around on the chimney top and she barely recognised him as the same person. His hair was askew and filled with ash. His face and hands, where they were not cut and bleeding, had been caked in soot from the flue itself.

He stared at her and she realised she must look much the same.

"This way," was all she said. Making sure the package was still inside her shirt, she climbed up on to the edge of the chimney.

It is only a single step, she told herself. But if she fell short she would drop into the conflagration and feel the pain of being burned alive. If she went too far she would fall down the roof on the other side; perhaps not as bad but she did not know what was there. They might drop from this second storey to the ground and die that way. *At least it would be quicker.*

With that cheery thought she took a deep breath and half-stepped, half-jumped across the gap. Her foot landed on the curved ridge tile and slipped straight off. She felt herself falling backwards and terror grabbed her heart. But her momentum carried her forward and her behind landed on the far side. The relief that she was not going to burn up was replaced by the fear of falling as she slipped at increasing speed down the slope towards the end of the roof.

She forced herself to roll over and tried to dig her toes into the tiles at the same time, grabbing anything she could with her fingers, tearing the skin from them on the rough surfaces.

Above her she saw Levin silhouetted against the sky. He teetered on the ridge. She prayed to the Mother he would not fall into the fire. She would not wish that on him no matter who he was.

She continued to slide. She was not gathering speed but nor was she stopping until her toes caught on the guttering. Something broke and fell away but she stopped moving. She flattened her entire body against the roof and lay her cheek against the cool tiles, panting for breath.

The roar of the burning house still reached her ears but it was quieter and she could hear a child crying somewhere. She looked back up at Levin. Somehow he had succeeded in lying down and was making his way down feet first.

It took a moment to realise she was looking at his feet, not boots, blackened though they were. The lower part of his leggings were burned and the material cracked and broke as he made his way down to her. He was off to her right, which was in the direction of where this section of roof intersected another, and there was a gully where perhaps they might be able to get better purchase. Making sure she did not get in his way, she moved sideways with her feet pressing into the gutter, which moved and cracked ominously but did not give way.

When she reached the gully she rolled over again and sat up with her feet pressing into the tiles on the opposite roof. Levin caught up with her and did the same.

Flames poured skyward from the house but it did not look as if the fire was spreading, at least not in their direction.

Kantees looked at Levin's feet. They were blistered and black; not all of that was soot, some of it was burned skin. She looked away. Something cracked and groaned in the building from which they had escaped. She looked up once more just in time to see the top of the chimney collapse out of sight.

She felt as if she ought to say something but could not think of anything. Then she felt Levin's hand on hers and he squeezed it. Strangely she did not feel either offended or threatened by his touch.

"Thank you." His voice sounded as cracked and broken as his feet looked. He must have breathed in a great deal of smoke. She had been lucky to get away with so little harm.

Though now they were away from the danger, the damage that had been done to her was beginning to make itself known. The scratches, the burns and the scrapes began to clamour for attention. Kantees wished that Yenteel was here with his healing patterns. She missed him even though he was very irritating, the way he kept implying she was someone special.

But from what her old master had said before he died—before he was murdered—that was precisely what she was. Someone special. Kantees of the Ziri.

"He'll be sure we're dead," said Kantees.

Levin coughed and spat something black from his mouth. "Until I turn up alive."

"Perhaps he won't know."

"The Farahalek will know."

"Will he try to kill you again?"

Levin paused. "I don't know."

"Does he even know who you are?"

Levin shrugged stiffly. "He may but I would not be able to keep the story a secret if I return to my home in this state."

Kantees fell silent. She knew what she should do but she did not want to do it. The last thing she needed was someone else with her to slow her down. She was already very late. It was true that she had wanted more information as to the nature of the Dunor, but to know they were a secret cabal of Taymalin was good enough. It meant she had some idea of what she was up against, and the more she thought about it the worse it got.

"You'll have to come with me." The words came from her mouth almost unbidden. It was what she knew she ought to do, not what she wanted to do.

"I don't think I will. This morning has been all the excitement I need for several years."

"Daybian has been kidnapped by the Dunor. I—" was all she could manage before stopping. She did not want to ask a Taymalin for help. She needed Yenteel for his patterns, the *tekrak* and its patterner to gain access to the ley-circle that would take them to where, she hoped, Daybian was being held. But she remembered the warrior that Daybian had become when he had needed to, despite all his fooling around. And she could see the same thing in Levin now. He could be useful both for the fighting and simply because, beneath the soot, his skin was white.

But, most of all, she needed Sheesha.

"I would like your help in rescuing him."

"The Dunor have him?"

She nodded.

"And you would risk your life to rescue him?"

She nodded again—she owed Daybian a debt. And Levin owed her.

"Then I will come with you."

The finality of the statement did not, however, help them in their current predicament.

"We need to get to the circle," she said.

"I cannot arrange for the patterners to make a path."

"I came on a *ziri*."

"You rode a *zirichak*?"

"I did. I am not a slave."

"Sheesha?"

She nodded.

"You stole Sheesha?"

"Let us not go into my crimes," said Kantees. "Otherwise you will have no choice but to strangle me here and now. That, however, will not save Daybian. So, you must either overlook my misdeeds, or we can proceed no further."

He sighed and then a pained look came over his face as if his body had somehow been protecting him from his injuries until now.

Kantees looked around. The drop to the yard between the houses was not too great. She could do it easily enough but she was less sure of Levin.

"We have to get moving," she said and looked into his face. He stared back as sweat broke out on his brow as if he were holding back the pain by sheer force of will. There was a rain butt below them. The water should be fresh enough.

"Let's get down."

She reached the ground without too much difficulty—though her ankle, where Levin had gripped it, now throbbed. He moved more slowly and very carefully. He let himself down on his arms as slowly as he could; when they gave out he fell the final distance with a cry of pain as his feet hit the cobbles.

Kantees caught him and helped him sit. She tore cloth from his tattered clothing and set about cleaning his feet. They were much worse than they had seemed, she doubted he would be able to move on his own.

She let him clean his own face, hands and arms while she rinsed herself in an attempt to look at least partly acceptable. The clothes given to her by the baker's wife were now ruined. In truth, Levin's did not look much better, but you could still see he was high-class Taymalin.

Kantees could not decide whether that was a good or a bad

thing. Perhaps good because he could prevent them being questioned, as long as people did not recognise *exactly* who he was.

She wrapped his feet in more rags ripped from her own clothing. She caught him staring at her legs. *Not feeling so bad then.*

"Can you walk?"

Using the edge of the water butt for leverage, he pulled himself to his feet. He started to sweat again. *What possesses a man to hide the pain?*

"Lean on my shoulders," she said. He hesitated for a moment and then gave in to the obvious agony and together they shuffled across the courtyard while smoke continued to pour into the sky behind them.

"We need transport," said Kantees. "Otherwise it will take us the rest of the day and all of the night to get to the circle."

"My *ziri*," he said through clenched teeth.

She remembered Waileth, a female not as fast as Sheesha, but younger and very acrobatic. Bluer in her feathers than Sheesha, with purple tips. Was it strange that she knew the *zirichasa* better than people?

Unlike Kurvin Port, where the Ziri Tower was perched high on a ridge, here it was on an island in the shallow lake inland from the main town. Where they had encountered the *dakasa*. Perhaps it had been connected to the mainland by a land bridge at one time, now it was easiest to reach if you were already on a *ziri*.

"We still need to get to the circle to fetch Sheesha—" and Ulina, "—to fly us in. And still need some transport to get you there."

By this time, they had made their way through an alley to a main street where the passers-by behaved as if there was no fire and simply went about their business. Here, higher up, the businesses were primarily traders, anyone with more than a couple of ships in their fleet carrying goods from Esternes to the mainland.

"Have you got money?" she asked.

"What need have I to carry money?"

Kantees sighed. Their dishevelled clothing was already drawing attention.

"Sit down there." She guided Levin to a stone water trough in front of a shop. A small cart drawn by an old *kichek* with faded colour in its scales.

Inside the shop, selling simple but hard-wearing fabrics, she found the cart driver in his leather cloak and hood talking to the shopkeeper, who glanced at her as she entered, and frowned.

Kantees gritted her teeth as the driver also turned. One of his eyes was misty yet it seemed to be that one that studied her.

"What do you want?" said the shopkeeper impatiently.

"I am sorry, gentle-folk, to interrupt, but I am with the master." She half turned and gestured to the almost ragged figure of Levin. "He is the worse for wear—" she paused for a moment to let the suggested meaning sink in, from the slight grin on their faces they understood what she implied, "—and must travel this day from the ley-circle. He needs to make haste but can barely stand."

"What's this to us?"

"Good sirs, he spied your cart and would trouble you for a ride. For which he will pay." Only the last statement had been a lie. Kantees was not sure whether deliberately misleading someone counted as a lie but she had tried not to. It was poor Gally's money she would be paying with.

Gally! She had not bought him a present. If she left Dakastown without something special—something that in his simple eyes would be more valuable than the gold coin she had borrowed, his heart would be broken— and it would be another lie to add to her list.

"So, the sot wants to escape being seen like this by his family?"

"It would not be my place to say, good sir."

"And how much is he willing to pay?"

"A short journey like this? Perhaps a beggar's tooth?" A quarter of a penny, enough for a good drink, it was bound to go higher but she needed to start low.

The shopkeeper glanced at the driver. Kantees realised she did not know whether the driver was independent, in which case she would end up paying both.

"My man would not harness his *kichek* for that. Half a crown."

Kantees resisted a spiteful comeback but it was an outrageous amount for a journey that would be done before dark. "You could shoe a horse for as much, or feed your *kichek* for a moon-turn. A penny."

"Ten-penny."

"Three."

"Seven."

"Five."

"Six."

Kantees hesitated, she was going to split the difference but then he would just split it again or suggest some ridiculous condition such as only carrying Levin and not her.

"For the both of us on the cart. Done."

The shopkeeper nodded. If she had been a man, or white, he would have shaken on it. She was not offended. The price was still too high but it would do and did not deplete her funds too much. She could always demand it back off Levin when they were safe, and he had recovered.

Just a short time later they were on the cart and heading across the city and away from the smoking remains of her old master's house. Sitting in the back with Levin, the driver had helped him up, but if he had wondered at the state of him and the smell of the fire, he said nothing. Kantees was just glad they were moving.

At the *ziri* houses next to the circle they climbed down from the cart. Levin suppressed a cry of pain as his feet hit the ground. She let him put his arm over her shoulder.

"Sorry, Kantees."

"It's not far." Kantees gave the driver another half-penny. "No need to share that with your master," she said.

He nodded. "Go in the Mother's peace."

Kantees jerked her head up in surprise. He did not look Kadralin.

"Rest in her arms," she said.

The man smiled.

"Thank you," she said.

He turned the cart by leading the *kichek* in a tight circle. "You are welcome, Kantees of the Ziri."

Kantees stared after him as the cart moved away, its iron-shod wheels sparking occasionally on the cobbles. How could he possibly know who she was? Levin had used her name and here they were at the ley-circle *ziri* eyries. She frowned. That stupid name.

Levin interrupted her train of thought with a groan.

He was sitting at the side of the road looking forlorn. She shook her head. He wasn't going to die, why did he have to act as if he would? She had her own pains and aches to deal with, did she let it stop her?

"Come on."

She helped him to his feet and half-carried him through the arch and into the interior. The light outside was fading and it was dark. Further in they came to the door and she hammered on it.

"Ulina! Let me in."

There was a long pause before the bolt at the bottom was drawn back, and then the one at the top. Kantees frowned, how could Ulina have managed that? For a moment she panicked. There was no way she could fight back with Levin leaning on her so heavily.

Then the door opened a crack. Ulina seemed to fall out in front of her and threw her arms around Kantees. At least one arm went round. There was a cry from both Ulina and Levin as the girl's other hand struck something tender.

Something large moved behind the door, lit from behind by a fire, and Sheesha's big head wormed its way through the narrow gap then pushed the door open with a crash. The huge *ziri* rumbled and pushed his head against her face, almost toppling them all over.

"For the sake of the Mother will you let me get him inside! Sheesha, stop pushing and help."

The big muzzle shifted to the man and snuffled him.

"Levin, put your arm on Sheesha's neck." *And get off mine.* Levin was not unconscious but she guessed the pain must be demanding all his attention. She wished she knew the healing patterns like Yenteel, because with the addition of Sheesha's power, and that of the nearby circle, she could have fixed both of them in no time.

Sheesha seemed to understand what was needed and Levin's weight was transferred. The *ziri* waddled very slowly into the interior, leading Levin to the fire. Kantees went down on one knee and hugged Ulina.

"I'm sorry I was so long."

"You smell of fire."

"Yes, I was in a fire."

"Who is that man?"

"His name is Levin, he saved my life and I saved his."

"Does that mean you love him? Daybian won't like that."

"What? No, and it doesn't matter what Daybian thinks. Besides, you've never met Daybian so how would you know?"

Ulina shrugged and pulled away. She took Kantees by the hand and led her inside. Kantees shut and bolted the door, bottom and top.

"How did you make Sheesha lift you up to do the top bolt?"

Ulina shrugged again. "I asked him to—" then she laughed, "—he let me sit right on his head." She pointed to the top of her own head.

Kantees said nothing more as they went through into the central open area and to the fire. Much to Kantees' surprise, and perhaps chagrin, Sheesha had arranged himself so that Levin could lean against him. She said nothing but dug out some food and ate it while she cut some fruit into small chunks for Levin.

He was awake but he just stared at the fire, although he did eat what she gave him. And drank a lot of water. Kantees found some clothes in a wardrobe in the keeper's room, then washed herself down in an effort to get rid of the smell. She took the bundle from her master's house and laid it to one side. Now that she was no longer in a rush, she noticed how heavy it seemed for its size. She found she had a strange lack of curiosity, the package reminded her of him and the way his life had drained away in front of her ... it hurt.

She didn't have a change of clothes for Levin but she washed his feet again and then cleaned his hands and face. Ulina stared but said nothing. The soles of Levin's feet were a mass of blisters; some had broken and were bleeding.

Colimar stood in the sky, its red light barely enough to provide any additional illumination. Kantees preferred it when Lostimal was there. The white purity of the Mother instead of the baleful eye of Colimar. She held the package in her hand. This was not the right light to see what he had left for her.

It wasn't going to be anything good. The man had twisted her and destroyed her life by making her think and giving her a curiosity that someone like her should not have. Then she shook her head again. Why not?

By what right did the Taymalin claim that the Kadralin must remain ignorant? By the gift of Taymar, the one who gave them the right to take whatever they saw as theirs.

She felt like throwing it into the embers of the fire as it slowly died. It was bound to be something to complicate her life even more. If that weren't enough, she now had this Levin to take care of.

She should just leave him here. Let his family find him, let *them* protect him from the Farahalek and the Dunor.

She was tired and her body ached. She had blisters too. Typical of a man to claim all the agony for himself. Daybian was the same.

And every time she had that thought she was reminded of the *other* Daybian. The one who had honoured her with a salute as he threw himself into battle. The one who had offered his own life to help her escape, even though he owed her nothing.

And then there was Levin, who had saved her by recognising the threat of the arrows while she had stared, dumbstruck, at her dying master. The man who had been willing to give up his own life when they were in the chimney.

"Not that you had any choice," she said out loud, looking at Levin, who seemed to have fallen asleep. Not even Ulina questioned her comment. She was curled up on the other side of the fire. Even Sheesha was asleep.

"I am the only one awake," she said to the red moon. "And that is always the way of it."

She did not feel safe here. It had been a very long time since that had been any part of her life. It seemed that she was the only one who cared enough to worry about what might happen. But as she stared into the glowing red of the fire, like an echo of the small moon, her eyes closed and she slept.

"Taymar's teeth!"

"Stop whining."

Sheesha grunted as Levin's weight came down on his back. As if the big *ziri* couldn't carry the weight of another person. They weren't carrying any pies now, they had finished the last of them that morning. They left behind the torn remnants of clothes that no longer served any useful purpose.

Kantees did not like to leave a mess. In fact, she would rather not leave at all. This morning she had woken with a headache and could not breathe through her nose. Levin was full of bravado but as soon as he had tried to stand his face had been filled with agony again. He tried to disguise it, just like men do, but it was too much even for that.

She had washed his feet once more. They really needed an ointment or oil to rub in but they had nothing of that sort.

She had Ulina fetch their meagre belongings. Kantees made sure she had the package. Then they loaded themselves on to Sheesha's back.

Which was why Levin had complained so much. She had made him sit back farther than he wanted and there really wasn't much support for him, or anything to hold on to—except Kantees when she climbed up in front of him.

"Hold my waist," she said, then had to suppress a shudder as his hands grasped her. Ulina climbed up and sat in front of Kantees.

Would Sheesha be able to carry them all? He spread his wings and she felt the muscles moving beneath her. She smiled. There was something in his power that gave her confidence. It was not the magic he held within, but the raw physical energy.

The downstroke was strong but his body barely moved, his legs only staggering a little. Kantees did not want him to use the power from the ley-circle even though it lay only a tantalisingly short distance away in case someone saw them.

Sheesha settled himself for a moment and then sprang forward as he brought his wings down again fast. He took another hop, and after a blindingly fast upswing he beat again and she felt herself pushed down into his back.

The far wall came at them. Beat after powerful beat pushed them upwards. Sheesha banked to the right to avoid the wall and each stroke lifted them higher. They cleared the roof and were out into the cold morning air. It blew away her headache. Sheesha continued to climb in a spiral, showing them first the town and the sea, then the river and its thousands of streams across the muddy delta. Finally the hills that rose on either side.

The fields behind the town were laid out in a great bowl. Kantees fancied that perhaps once this had been a lake until the river had finally escaped directly into the sea and drained it.

They turned again. Boats headed out across the bay; some were fishing, while bigger ones carried goods to the mainland. If Sheesha gained enough height, they might even be able to see it, but that was not their purpose.

The third time they came around to face the river, Kantees spotted the Ziri Tower and headed Sheesha in that direction. They had not decided on any plan but what they had to do was simple enough.

A *ziri* approaching the tower would not attract too much attention, particularly at this time of the morning when most would be at their breakfast, if not still in their beds. And unlike those attached to castles, this place did not possess a significant military force. They did not need it being stuck out in the middle of the water and would just be more mouths to feed.

Sheesha covered the distance in a very short amount of time, and after the difficult take-off he seemed to be able to fly well enough with the extra weight. She hoped landing would not be troublesome for him.

They flew around the tower once and Levin pointed out the eyrie for his *zirichak* Waileth. It was not too far from the top but the outer door was shut. She was not surprised. They would have to land on the top of tower as they had at Kurvin Port and make their way down to the eyrie.

Sheesha came down heavily and immediately lay down on the rooftop. Muscle strains were not uncommon in racing *ziri*, although Sheesha had never had one as yet.

Ulina slid off in the direction of the central section of the roof as Kantees lifted her leg over and dropped off on the wall side. She stared over the edge and listened out for shouts, but it seemed no one had noticed them. She prayed to the Mother that it was so.

Levin was less able to climb down. He got his leg over but clung to Sheesha's neck as he let himself down. He said nothing as his burnt and blistered feet touched the roof but could not suppress a grunt.

"Ulina, see if the door is unlocked. Here, Levin, let me help."

If he had any concern that accepting help from a woman, and a runaway slave at that, was demeaning he had lost such pride the day before, willingly putting his arm across her shoulders, although she was sure he was trying to avoid putting too much weight on her.

The air smelled strange to Kantees, not only damp but there was something fetid about it. Probably the marshes below and the *dakasa* waiting to capture anything foolish enough to wander into their water.

Kantees and Levin made their way round to the door which now stood open. Kantees noted the way the metal had been sliced clean through. It had been locked and Ulina's little dagger had dealt with it. How could an abandoned Taymalin girl possess a dagger so valuable, and so powered with patterns that, even in the hands of a child, it could cut through iron as if it was little more than clay?

It was the kind of question that Kantees was not sure she wanted the answer to. Never mind the bloodthirsty way the child could kill and seem so unconcerned.

"Wait with Sheesha," she said to Ulina. "When I call, fly down with him into the eyrie." The girl nodded seriously and let them go.

The stairs were awkward but they managed them with her going first and Levin resting his hands on her shoulders. She had stopped shuddering at his touch but it was not a sensation she wanted to prolong.

They would have to go past the eyrie with the elder *ziri*, and then the one with the dominant male. Levin had an elder brother who rode that one, Kantees had seen them in the races, but it knew Levin and would not get upset if he passed through. She hoped that it would not have a problem with her.

If they encountered any of the keepers, Levin was their master. Kantees gritted her teeth, she was not happy being around slaves anymore. She wanted to tell them to break their chains—to just leave, there was nothing to stop them. The Taymalin were so arrogant in their superiority they would not understand what had happened if the slaves simply stopped being slaves.

But then, what would the Kadralin do? Run and hide? Kantees shook her head, this was not anything she needed to think about. She must simply focus on Daybian, she owed him and she would do her best to rescue him.

After that, she would seek her people in the heart of the Esternes, where the Taymalin did not rule. She refused to believe Yenteel's claim the heart of Esternes was just uninhabitable mountains, they *had* to be there.

The ladder was a problem; there was no way she could help him. He gave her a look of helplessness but managed to grab hold and put his feet on the rungs. He kept adjusting their position until he was apparently satisfied, he'd found the one that hurt the least. Then, with terrible slowness, he descended and disappeared from sight while Kantees worried about them being discovered.

"Tegon!"

His shout shook her from her thoughts and she peered into the hole. What was he doing?

"Tegon! Come here!"

There was movement in the eyrie below. "Master?"

"Tegon, go down below and have Kuli prepare Waileth, I am taking her out."

"Yes, master."

Kantees could tell from the way this Tegon answered that he was very confused about why his master was coming down the ladder, and also why Levin was in such a bad condition. But a slave could not question a lord.

She heard someone descending a ladder quickly.

"Kantees," Levin called up. She looked down.

"Go back up, wait for me."

She was reluctant to do as he said but she could not fault his new plan. If she was there it would look very strange—much more than it already did. At least for now it was just their master doing something that was normal. And by the time he managed to climb down his *ziri* should be prepared. If she was a slight chance they might disobey, fearing their master was somehow being coerced.

But she did not want to leave him. She was not even sure she could trust him.

Taking a deep breath, she pulled back and returned to the roof. What if he did decide not to go with them? What difference did it make? She did not want him anyway, he was just another responsibility that she didn't need. If he stayed behind and the Farahalek decided he needed to be killed it did not matter to her.

Except she found it did matter. She had made herself responsible for yet another person—yet another Taymalin master. She seemed to be collecting them. She wanted to be back with Yenteel and Gally, even if the former was irritatingly self-confident and Gally could be, well, just irritating. Except that wasn't his fault, the Mother had made him a simpleton.

Ulina was sitting on Sheesha's back and looked up in surprise as Kantees emerged.

"He's doing it on his own," Kantees said by way of explanation.

Ulina slid forward to allow Kantees room to climb up behind, but instead she went to Sheesha's head and put her arms around him. She buried her head in his feathers and breathed in the light scent of his body that was reminiscent of autumn leaves.

What if Daybian was dead? What if all this was pointless? If she had just gone to find her people instead of rescuing Jelamie she would not have had to deal with all of this.

In the distance she heard the door of an eyrie being slid back. She could just fly away now. Levin didn't know where she was going and he would not be able to follow.

But she knew she would not, they knew about Levin so he was in danger too. There was no escape. She had learnt of the Dunor and she had sought them out, only to find that they wished to find her and perhaps kill or use her because of what she knew. Her eyes became damp as she thought of Kevrey. He had sent her away; not to punish her, but to protect her.

Yet they had come for her anyway—even though they thought they were looking for Daybian. And in that act, they had set her feet upon this path. Those who believed in prophesies were doomed to die by them.

She heard wingbeats and moments later she recognised the colours of Waileth emerge into the dull light with the figure of Levin on her back, now properly dressed for riding. He gave her a wave and flew above the tower, maintaining a circle above it.

Kantees mounted Sheesha and gave him a gentle nudge. Instead of launching into the air, which would have been difficult in the confined space, he hopped up onto the rampart and allowed himself to fall over the edge, just as he had that night when Kantees had ridden him for the first time. There was a man at the base of the tower looking up at them.

Waileth screeched as Sheesha accelerated towards the ground and then whipped out his wings and soared upwards without a single beat.

"Show off," she said, but the words were ripped from her mouth by the speed of their flight.

They needed to go north. But following the river until they were well away from Dakastown would take them roughly in the direction they needed to go. Perhaps Levin had a better idea of the shape of Esternes than she did.

The shock of recognition hit her. The man at the base of the tower. He was the one who had been on the boat and had waved. The one in the town on the Zephira who had egged the crowd on.

He was here? How could he have known where they would be even when she had not until the previous day? She shook her head. Of course he would know, where else would you expect to find a *ziri* except in a Ziri Tower? Well, he was too late.

Sheesha levelled out and Kantees glanced back. Just as she expected, Waileth had fallen in behind him. He was a dominant male and would lead; Waileth would follow.

15

The day continued grey but at least it wasn't raining. Kantees kept them flying until they were clear of the twisted channels of the river and it followed just a single narrow course through the low hills beyond. She judged it would take a minimum of a day for someone to reach that distance, even in a boat with the wind behind them. The man could not follow now.

They set down on a small plateau bare of life except for a few bushes fighting to grow in the thin soil, their roots digging into the cracks in the rocks.

Sheesha ignored Waileth but she placed herself so she was in his line of vision. His response was to preen himself.

"They behave differently when it's not a race," she said.

"The female runs from the male until she catches him," said Levin. He was sitting on the ground wearing his riding clothes. He even had boots, though she imagined they must hurt since his feet had swollen. He did not complain, and it must be easier than walking in bare feet.

Kantees glanced at him, wondering whether he might be referring to her in some unsubtle way, but he was not looking in her direction and did not seem prone to the insinuations—and outright suggestions—that Daybian enjoyed. He was looking at his *ziri*.

"How can you ride without tack and saddle?"

Kantees shrugged. "It's easy enough. Besides, what you do makes them as much slaves as us. I prefer to let them have the choice as to whether to carry us."

"You think Waileth would not carry me if she had a choice?"

"Perhaps she would, but do you give her that option?"

"She may be smaller than your Sheesha, but she could kill me just as easily as he could."

"So she has a choice?"

"I think so."

Kantees was silent for a while.

"We have to go north to catch up with my friends," she said.

"The ones on their way to rescue Daybian?" he said. "Even if you'd been away a ten-day they won't have got far."

Kantees wasn't sure whether she should tell him about the giant *tekrak*. He probably wouldn't believe her, so it was simpler not to mention it.

"Have you ever flown all the way to Jakalain?" she said.

"Of course not, why fly and wear out your *ziri* before a race?"

"It took me three days to get here from there."

He just nodded and she realised he had no idea of the distance either. At normal flying speed it might take twice that long—since Sheesha could not maintain the magical speed for long. She could not quite bring herself to broach *that* subject either. That was perhaps even less believable than a giant flying plant.

She did not even know if Waileth was capable of it. If she wasn't, this journey would be interminable.

She looked over to where Ulina was sitting on the edge and throwing stones out into the void. There were several large *sikechasa* wheeling in the distance but she thought the presence of the much larger *ziri* would keep them away. They would not want a fight.

"We had better get moving," she said and got to her feet. "I'm going to follow the river to Cliffedge and then we'll go north-east to the mountains."

"I've never seen Cliffedge," he said. She held out her hand and pulled him awkwardly to his feet. "I've heard it's very interesting."

"Yes."

He was walking better in the boots but she still let him put some of his weight on her.

"Levin?"

"Yes?"

"If something strange happens when we're flying, don't be too surprised."

"What kind of thing?"

"Never mind what kind, but if it does, trust your *ziri*. Trust Waileth."

"Of course," he said, and she could hear a tone of amusement. "I always trust her."

"That's good." She had no idea whether the magic would work with another *ziri* as well, or if perhaps they had to do it individually. There was also the problem that if Waileth was left behind Kantees might not be able to find them again.

Levin clambered awkwardly into the saddle on Waileth's back and buckled himself in. Almost automatically, Kantees checked his buckles and the tightness of the straps.

"If we get separated," she said, "there's a baker in the mists on the road into Cliffedge Below. If you give them my name they will let you stay there—" *if they don't hate me*, "—just wait for me there."

"What aren't you telling me?"

"You wouldn't believe me."

"That is not encouraging."

"We'll be going above the clouds."

"You and the child aren't dressed for it."

"We'll be fine."

Kantees patted Waileth's neck and walked over to Sheesha, who removed his head from under his wing where he had been working through the feathers.

"Ulina! We're moving."

The girl ran over and Kantees lifted her into position before climbing up herself.

Sheesha launched smoothly into the air. He had eaten well yesterday and should be ready to fly fast. Waileth would be well fed so Kantees did not need to worry about her either. But if this worked, they would both be very hungry by the afternoon. They must waste no more time getting back to Yenteel and the others.

They headed upriver under the heavy cloud, climbing steadily. The greyness engulfed them and Kantees worried that they might lose each other before she even tried to go fast. But, when they broke free into the sunshine, Waileth was exactly where she had been before: a little back and to the right.

There was more to *ziri* magic than just flying fast.

The sun turned the top of the clouds into fluffy white mountains but she climbed further so they had a straight run. She had taken the bearing on the position of the sun as they came out of the cloud and was confident she could maintain the correct course.

They had done it before.

She reached out to Sheesha and encouraged him to draw on the power within. He no longer needed to dive to make it happen. It seemed that he grew in knowledge and experience just as she did.

But she was still worried about Levin and Waileth. As flecks of golden light sparked around Sheesha she glanced back. *As long as he doesn't take fright.*

Levin was staring, not at Sheesha but at Waileth. Kantees allowed herself to smile. It was happening to her as well. There was a bond in the flying *ziri* that made them act as one. She had seen it in the way the Jakalain *ziri* had followed Sheesha. And now it worked with Waileth and the magic.

The golden light became a sheath around them, and the wall did not curve around behind Sheesha but extended out and encompassed Waileth as well. As if both were in a bubble, though their relative positions remained precisely the same.

Even if Waileth had not experienced it before it was clear that she knew, by instinct, what to do, as her wings folded in and the two of them shot through the air.

That was the other reason Kantees wanted them to be above the clouds: she did not want them to be observed. Whoever the man following them was, she felt strongly that he should know as little about what the *ziri* could do as possible.

Kantees turned her head from the spectacle of the clouds shooting away beneath them, as if it were those that were moving and not the *ziri*. She looked at Levin. He had the reins in a grip like death and stared ahead as if he was in shock. Kantees allowed herself a smile but she had probably looked much the same on her first journey as she escaped across the sea from Kurvin Port. Though, she remembered, she had been more concerned with the fact she had tried to kill herself.

She whistled. The air inside the golden bubble did not move. It was captured just as they were, and that meant sound was not ripped away.

Levin jerked round to look at her. She gave a little wave—Levin shook his head slightly as if in wonderment—then studied Waileth. Because Sheesha's head was in front she had never seen what he looked like when he flew like this. Waileth's neck was straight out like a poker. Her mouth was shut and her eyes open unblinkingly. There was a golden light behind them as the golden magic boiled out of her and held the air away from them as they arrowed through the sky.

It was impossible to tell how tired the *ziri* were. And that was a concern.

Kantees looked at the sun and adjusted their course. Ahead of them the clouds were building even higher, and in one particularly mountainous pile that stretched upwards she could see flashes of light that she took for lightning.

She did not want to slow down but neither did she want to attempt a flight through a storm like that. The only clear air was away to the left and that was not a direction she intended to go.

Taking care to make the adjustment slowly, she sent Sheesha into a gentle dive. But no matter that she had made it a shallow angle, they dived straight into the cloud. The water did not touch them this time.

Flying down through the cloud at high speed made her nervous. She could not see anything but the darkness beyond the grey. *What if the cloud extended to the ground? What if they ran into the cliff of Cliffedge?*

They broke through the cloud layer. It wasn't raining. They were still far above the ground and the great cliff that cut through Esternes was just a dark line on the horizon, she was astonished at how much distance they had covered. Even at normal speed they could reach it quickly. She twisted round again.

"We're going to slow down," she called to him. "Hang on tight, the first time we did it, I fell off." She realised from his expression that wasn't very encouraging. "But we've had lots of experience since then. It'll be fine."

Kantees looked ahead and saw that the cliff was now clearly visible. Though the river was quite a way to their left.

"Let's slow down, Sheesha, my love," she said quietly. "But gently, Waileth has never done this before."

The golden light surrounding them thinned, Sheesha spread his wings, and a quick glance told Kantees Waileth was following his lead. The magic shredded suddenly and dissipated. The wind struck them like a wall but Kantees was ready for it. A look back showed that Levin was still in his seat. He was strapped-in anyway.

Kantees had Sheesha slow and go into a landing spiral. Levin would probably have some things he needed to say after all that.

The area they were coming down on was marshy and Kantees recoiled at the thought of lurking *dakasa*. However, there was a hill standing high above the pools and rivulets. She headed for that and they came down on a sloping side covered in long grass. If the sun had been shining it would have been quite pleasant.

Ulina slipped off and Kantees followed. She went to Waileth and helped the silent Levin undo his buckles, then caught him as he came down. Kantees set about stripping Waileth of the tack. If the *ziri* wanted to feed, this was a good opportunity to let them do so.

She made sure the tack was untangled and dropped the saddle in the grass.

Levin had been watching her as he sat in the grass. Neither of them said a word until Kantees sat herself near him. In the distance, above the dark edge of the cliff, there were flashes of lightning

"Well?" he said at last.

"*Ziri* magic."

"Waileth wouldn't obey me."

Kantees could understand that would scare him the most, to be always in charge and then, in the most terrifying of moments, have that torn from him.

"You wouldn't have believed me if I'd told you."

"No," he said. "And if you had tried, I would have taken my chances in Dakastown instead." He sighed.

Down the slope from them Sheesha was preening again while Waileth was not even looking in his direction. It seemed that the patterning they used did not directly affect how they related to one another. He was still trying to look good to attract the female. Just as well there wasn't another male around. It could get nasty, although Sheesha had generally been well-behaved, but perhaps that was because he was already the dominant male of the Jakalain *zirichasa*.

"The pattern is in their nature," said Kantees.

"How is it you discovered it?"

"It was an accident." She was not going to explain how it happened. "It doesn't matter."

"Does Daybian know?"

"No, I found out after he had been taken."

She did explain how the Hamalain had tried to capture her and the rest of her friends. The escape from the ley-circle and Daybian's capture.

"Deenya is a Hamalain," said Levin.

Kantees looked at him, not understanding what he had said, then she realised. "That woman from Dakastown?"

He nodded. "The Hamalain comprise two brothers and a sister. Lorima, Trimiente and Deenya."

"Lorima's dead."

"Yes. Did you kill him?"

She bristled. "No. I found him murdered by the mercenaries he'd hired. They were not happy the raid on Jakalain had gone badly and unprofitably. I suppose."

"And you went after them because of Daybian's little brother?"

"What's so strange about that?"

"You're a slave, why should you care?"

"I'm still a person, you milk-puke." She got up and stormed further up the slope. *And if I'd listened to Sheesha earlier, perhaps he wouldn't have had time to sneak into the gondola.* It's hard to trust when the world betrays you, but Kevrey had not betrayed her after all. He had been protecting her.

From the summit of the hill she could see leagues in most direc-tions across the flat marshland here at the bottom of the cliff. To the north, the cliff itself was still a couple of leagues away, but it towered upwards and blocked the sky. Waterfalls spilled off the edge and only the larger ones reached the ground. The small ones turned into mist and blew away.

To the west was the fog that filled the air around Cliffedge Below. The gantries of the great lifting engines poked out like branches from the top of the cliff. The marsh surrounding them was threatening. She did not know if *dakasa* lived this far inland, but if they did this was a perfect location for them. She glanced at the *ziri*, not wanting them to feed here. It was too dangerous.

It was only a short hop to the top of the cliff. Could she persuade Sheesha to go up there? But a shadow passed over her as Sheesha headed away from the hill with Waileth in tow. They must be hungry, and she hoped they would find something easily. The watery wasteland did not look as if it was home to much game.

There was something down by the water's edge at the bottom of the hill, and she frowned before realising it was Ulina.

She panicked as the image of the child getting dragged into the water by pale tentacles invaded her mind. She ran and shouted to her to get away from the water.

16

antees stumbled the last few steps to where Ulina was staring at her as she came yelling down the hill. Kantees grabbed her by the wrist and pulled her from the water's edge. She stumbled over a rock and collapsed, holding the child tight.

As the echoes of her own voice fell away across the calm, motionless water with the coarse grasses and reeds poking up through them, it all became silence.

"What's wrong, Kantees?" said Ulina. "Why are you crying?"

"It's not safe," said Kantees, her voice hoarse from the shouting. "It's not safe. You have to be careful."

"What isn't safe?"

"What's wrong?" echoed Levin. Kantees could hear his uncertain paces as he made his way down the hill.

"*Dakasa!*" she said.

"They do not live inland," he said. "Only in the sea or nearby where the water is salty."

His voice was calm but held a hint of strain. Whether that was the pain of his feet or concern for Kantees' sudden panic she couldn't be sure. But it didn't matter, even if that were true. There were always dangers in the wild. She had seen them.

"You mustn't run away like that," she said to Ulina.

"I wasn't running."

"You can't just wander off."

"Why not? Will you tie my feet, Kantees? Hobble me like a *kichek*?"

Kantees pushed herself up into a sitting position but still held Ulina, though the girl started to squirm.

"The world is not safe."

"I have my knife."

"Sometimes your knife will not be enough."

"Then I shall die."

And there it was again: the echoes of Ulina's life before. The place Kantees did not want to go.

With a groan of effort Levin sat down beside them on the grass. He put his hand on Kantees' shoulder. She shrugged it off but relaxed her grip on the girl, who immediately slipped away from her and went to a boulder to sit. She was not near the water's edge.

"The world is full of danger, Levin."

"It is," he said. "I only have to look at my feet."

"In a deserted ley-circle in the middle of the Talamyrth there were abominations like men who tried to kill us," she said. "Perhaps they had been men once but they were distorted by the power of the Mother."

Levin said nothing.

"When I first discovered the *ziri* magic, I fell into the sea and might have drowned but for a giant shell as big as Jakalain that floated in the water. And even so, Sheesha was barely able to rescue me. When we reached Dakastown the *dakasa* in the mere, near the tower, tried to bring us down with their water spouts." She turned to him. "But always the greatest danger is the people. White people, like you. Trying to kill me, trying to capture Sheesha, stealing children and torturing them."

She turned and faced back across the watery wasteland. "Tell me I should not be afraid for myself and those I have become responsible for?"

She thought that perhaps he had an answer, because he was silent for a long time.

"I do not claim any great wisdom," he said finally. "But I do not think you can live your life in the fear of what *might* happen."

"So you just ignore it?"

"I do not ignore danger, Kantees. But it is not my master."

"It is not easy for a slave to have no master."

"Ex-slave."

Anger boiled up inside her. "How dare you! You don't know *anything*. I was driven to become masterless because I cared about what happened to the Jakalain. The raiders would have ignored me because I was a slave. I committed crimes—by Taymalin rules—to save them and they would kill me for doing the right thing."

"Did you need to steal Sheesha?"

"I had already ridden him. I was as good as dead. He was the only way I could escape."

"You did not think that perhaps the Jakalain might bend the rules for you? That justice was more important than blind adherence to a set of codes?"

Kantees said nothing and watched the thin waterfalls disperse into clouds of mist along the tall jagged rocks of the cliff.

"And how does it feel to be masterless, Kantees?"

"I am afraid all the time," she said. "But that is no different than before, it's just a different type of fear."

"It's the price of freedom," he said. "You think that we Taymalin enjoy every moment of our power?"

"Of course you do."

"My father has the weight of twenty thousand lives on his shoulders. The decisions he makes may kill people, not just yours but mine too. You are responsible for what? Half a dozen lives? How does that compare?"

"Because I care about them."

"By what right do you judge whether a man you have never met cares about those in his charge?" It was his turn to be angry. "You think the price of caring about your people is too high? Perhaps you should also consider not everyone would want to pay it."

Her anger returned. "Everyone should have the choice!"

He paused. "I think you are probably right," he said. He

adjusted the position of his feet on the grass to get more comfortable. "Did you know the Kadralin on the mainland are not slaves?"

She stared at him. "You're lying."

He shook his head. "No. Oh, they are not in charge, of course, mostly they are servants. But if they choose to leave their service, they can. There are Kadralin who are not servants at all and trade from place to place. They are free."

"Then—" she could barely get the words out, "—why are we slaves?"

"Honestly, Kantees, I have no idea. It's just the way it is."

"That's not good enough."

"I didn't make the rules, Kantees."

She got up and stalked back up the hill. She saw Ulina following her, though at a distance as if she was not really obeying her instructions.

Once she reached the top she looked across the darkening landscape. There were lights growing here and there. Some were the warm, yellow light of fires, though nothing too close, for which she was grateful. But others were the pale green glow that she associated with the *dakasa*. Not in the numbers that had shown in the delta, but still plenty.

As the world grew darker around them she thought about what Levin had said. It was difficult, she did not want to give him or his kind any benefit of the doubt. But the truth was that she had never truly been mistreated. The Jakalain and Kevrey were good people. It seemed that perhaps Levin was as well. Though she could not know whether that applied to the rest of the Otulain family.

But her people were free on the mainland?

Her thoughts were interrupted by the arrival of Sheesha and Waileth. They settled down for the night.

17

$\mathcal{N}$othing attacked them in the night. Kantees slept soundly under Sheesha's wing with Ulina, who seemed to have forgotten the upset from earlier.

Levin did not sleep under Waileth's wing. He had spouted some nonsense about possibly being killed by the *ziri* moving, and instead, slept out in the damp and the cold. Kantees would not have been surprised if he caught some illness, but come the morning he seemed his usual self—as much as she knew what that should be like.

"How are your feet now?" she asked, seeking to mend their disagreement of the evening before.

"They still hurt, Kantees," he said gruffly, though that might simply have been because he was not fully awake and had not yet broken his fast.

"We have nothing to eat," she said. "We can either waste time getting something from upper Cliffedge—" she had no desire to return to the mists of the lower town, "—or push on to the north."

An idea had sparked in her mind as she had fallen asleep. It seemed a crazy thing to do but she felt the responsibility Levin had spoken of, as well as wanting to shake off the feeling that everything she did was a lie.

"I am hungry," he said.

"Me too," said Ulina.

"I..." Kantees trailed off and then gathered her courage and started again. "I thought we might stop at Jakalain."

"Even though they might lock you up and hang you?"

Ulina squeaked in horror. "I will not let them."

Kantees gave her a smile then turned back to Levin. "I thought about what you said."

"I shouldn't talk so much, it gets people into trouble."

"They deserve to know what's happened to their son."

"You don't even know."

"At least I have some idea."

"What if they are in league with the Dunor like the Hamalain?"

Kantees gathered up their meagre things and gave Sheesha a nudge to make him settle back on his haunches so they could ride. Then she remembered they would have to go through the rigmarole of getting Waileth's riding gear sorted out.

"I do not believe my old master would have sold me to them if he thought they were part of the cabal. He sent me there to be safe from the Dunor."

Levin was sitting on the floor struggling to get a boot on. He gave a frustrated cry and lay back.

"I am not worthy of you, Kantees," he said, looking straight up into the sky and clutching the boot to his chest.

"What are you talking about?"

He sat back up and tossed the boot over to the saddle. "I want to order you to help me."

"I am glad you did not."

"You wouldn't have done it anyway."

"That is true."

"I can't use a saddle without boots."

That was the truth; his feet would suffer badly if he put them into the metal stirrups without something to protect them. And she was unwilling to leave the saddle behind—she was not even sure Waileth would accept Levin without the saddle.

"Would you like me to help you?" she said.

"I would," he said. "If you do not mind."

Kantees collected the boot and brought it back. She examined his feet. "We should probably wash them again. No, wait." She jumped up and went to the saddle bags and rummaged through them. "Ha," she said and pulled out a small clay pot.

"What?" he said with concern on his face.

"Beeswax."

"That's for the leather."

"It will soothe and protect your feet."

"Very well, but I will do it."

"Don't be ridiculous. I can get it done faster, and besides, I've been using it for years. I know how to make leather shine with it."

"I do not want my feet to shine."

Kantees knelt at his feet and grinned at him.

"You were joking," he said.

"I was joking."

She took hold of one foot and unwrapped the makeshift bandages. They stuck and she peeled them off as carefully as she could. Many of the blisters had now broken and the cloth was stained with yellow circles.

"Ulina, please, will you fetch some water?"

Ulina stood up. "Yesterday you did not want me near the water for fear of *dakasa* or other creatures."

Kantees took a deep breath. "I was afraid for you," she admitted. "And I am still. But I will trust you and your knife. Take care and do not linger."

The girl grabbed up an empty water bottle and headed down the hill at almost a run—which put Kantees' heart in her mouth in case the girl tripped and fell against a stone. But Kantees forced herself to remain silent. She turned away so that she was not following the child's every movement.

Levin was smiling. But it was not the condescending smile she would have expected from Daybian. It seemed genuine.

Kantees felt embarrassed, feeling she had to explain herself. "I am still terrified something bad will happen."

"It might, but that's life."

"I am trying not to let my fear rule me."

"I'm sure that's not easy."

She frowned, feeling that his words were some sort of criticism, but it had not been spoken as if to hurt. It was as if he understood how she felt. So she just nodded.

There was an awkward silence interrupted explosively by a *ziri* farting.

"Sheesha!"

"I think that was Waileth."

Kantees gave a short laugh. "They are sitting close together."

Sheesha lifted his head and sniffed the air, then curled round to investigate Waileth's rear end. She snapped her teeth at him and he jerked back.

Levin laughed. "A word to the wise, Sheesha, never draw attention to a lady's misdemeanours."

Sheesha grumbled as if he were replying and Kantees laughed.

Ulina returned a short while later and Kantees set about cleaning Levin's feet and applying the beeswax. Kantees rewrapped them—tighter than before—in the same old bandages, but she did not have a lot of choice. There was not much of her own clothes, or Levin's tattered shirt, left to make new ones and they would not be noticeably cleaner.

She hoped the beeswax would help to protect from any infection.

The boots went on easier with the tighter bandages and with Kantees to hold them while Levin pushed. Once on his feet, he was able to walk much better than he had in previous days.

Kantees saddled Waileth, barely having to think about it as her hands knew exactly what to do.

"Waileth likes you," said Levin.

"*Ziri* are just children, they appreciate a firm hand and clear guidance." Kantees hesitated, and the confidence and genuine friendship that seemed to have built between them allowed her to say, "Just as it is with men."

Levin smiled. "I take it that you will be in charge again for this journey? And I will merely be the passenger?"

"It seems to be the way it is," said Kantees. "Although Sheesha is the one who's in charge."

"You guide him," said Levin. "To make the *ziri* fly with magic is something I would like to learn."

Kantees trembled at his words. The idea that the Taymalin might fly the *zirichasa* at magical speeds was disturbing in itself, but worse: this was the only thing she had that was hers and hers alone. What he said made it feel as if he had already stolen it from her.

Levin mounted Waileth without assistance. And that was another threat: he no longer needed her.

She shook her head trying to dispel the thoughts. It was just another aspect of her concern, this time fearing something in the future that had not even come to pass—and could not harm her.

With her own bags and Ulina, she climbed aboard her beautiful Sheesha. She could feel the life in him, and it made her stronger. If Levin had never felt the heart of a *ziri* the way she did, then he could never learn what she knew. This was not about patterns, this was touching another living creature with more than one's senses. This was more than just magic.

At her word, Sheesha beat his wings hard and Kantees' heart leapt as her *ziri* launched himself from the hill. She almost shouted with delight as his powerful wings drove them upwards. A quick glance behind showed Waileth was already in her assigned position and following Sheesha's every move without the slightest guidance from her rider.

As he said, he was just a passenger.

They flew west along the cliff, climbing steadily. The sun was at their backs as the day grew lighter. Sheesha took them through the mist of a waterfall that could not reach to the foot of the cliff. She admonished him for making them wet, but she did not really mind.

Her eye was caught by a movement on the cliff-face and she saw *fenichasa* moving across the seemingly vertical surface. Jumping from rock to rock, eating the plants that grew in the crevices.

Birds roosted and flew.

The screech of a *sikechak* echoed out as a warning and a threat. Sheesha's voice echoed back in a dangerous scream. It was repeated by Waileth. They did not hear the challenger again.

Then they burst above the plain of the upper plateau. Unlike the boggy lands below, up here there were farms, fields and livestock.

The line of the cliff went off into the far distance in front and behind, cutting the land in two. Kantees remembered that she had planned to head along the line of the cliff to the coast and then head north to intercept Yenteel and the *tekrak*.

But her plans had changed.

The mountains in the heart of Esternes were not yet visible, but Kantees knew which direction she needed to go. She had thought she might wait until they had gained more height before allowing Sheesha to go fast, but she was impatient to see what her decision would bring.

She found she desperately wanted to return to Jakalain now. So she urged Sheesha forwards. His wings beat stronger and they accelerated. Then the magic started. The golden light embraced them and it was if the ground rolled away beneath them while they remained completely still in the sky.

Under her instruction, Sheesha climbed effortlessly, with Waileth behind. They passed clutches of farm buildings and the occasional town. They were low enough that they were visible but Kantees thought perhaps they moved too fast and were too unusual for anyone to recognise them for what they were.

From the height they reached, Kantees could see a dark line on the horizon in the west. She shivered, that must be the Talamyrth. If she never visited that forest again it would be a thousand-day too soon. But that probably meant they were not pointing sufficiently to the east.

Sheesha adjusted his direction even as she thought it.

The mountains grew up blue to the north. She turned again, slightly more eastward.

Then she felt the magic. The power of the Mother's milk beckoning to her from almost directly ahead of them. This was no minor ley-circle. She could almost taste it and Sheesha drew its power into himself and moved yet faster. As if he wanted to go home.

Kantees' skin tingled with the power she could feel that flooded through Sheesha. Such power. She closed her eyes—and she could see it. There it was like a bubbling lake of molten energy, yellow and red and blue with a stream pouring from it into Sheesha.

They were approaching it very quickly.

Kantees blinked her eyes open and called for Sheesha to slow down. It was almost as if he obeyed only reluctantly. But he did as she asked and they came to a rapid halt high above the castle of Jakalain.

The air was suddenly cold as if they had been plunged into a freezing lake.

Without her requesting it, Sheesha circled, maintaining his height. Kantees realised she had not thought any of this through. She had decided to come to Jakalain but without any clear idea of what she was going to do.

"Oh well," she said out loud. "If I'm going to die I'm going to be bold about it."

"I will protect you, Kantees."

She gave the child a squeeze and directed Sheesha down towards the Ziri Tower. Kantees gave a grim smile. Her people had made that tower. The Taymalin had stolen it, just as they stole anything they fancied. But the truth of the *ziri* had been kept from them and all they did was use them to race, which she now recognised was a corruption of the true nature of the *zirichasa*, who would, given a choice, rather fly together.

She could not decide whether she was surprised that the hatch to Sheesha's eyrie was open. She could imagine that Daybian's parents would leave it like that in case their son returned riding his *ziri*.

Jelamie would have given them the letter Kantees had Yenteel write for her, explaining how Kantees had rescued him. And he would have told them the story too, as much as he was willing to at least. The letter had also explained how she was seeking Daybian.

Unfortunately, her arrival might make them think their son had returned. And in the time she'd been gone she had done nothing practical to find their son. She had wandered off to Dakastown to have a single question answered. They might not think she had kept her word.

On a sudden impulse, she turned Sheesha away from his eyrie.

He squawked in confusion and protest. "No. We must land in the courtyard."

Where the bows of the armsmen could kill her in a moment.

She checked quickly that Waileth was behind her as they made the final descent.

People—servants and slaves—ran from the central space. Armsmen appeared on the high walkways and wall. Some with bows. Sheesha landed in the centre. Kantees slipped from his back and stood beside his neck. She felt Ulina's hand press into hers—the child had never been in a place like this. Perhaps.

She heard the shuffling footsteps of Levin as he came up on her other side, just as the main doors were flung back as the Lord and Lady Jakalain hurried out without any pomp or introductions.

They expected to see their son.

They hesitated at the top of the stairs as they realised the ragged man standing beside Kantees was not the one they hoped for.

Then a young voice shouted, "Ulina!"

1 8

*J*elamie pushed past his parents and ran down the stone steps and across the courtyard. Ulina did not move from Kantees' side. Jelamie slowed to a walk and one of the armsmen hurried towards him, looking back to see whether he was supposed to stop the boy.

Jelamie stopped and the armsmen came up beside him protectively.

"Where's Daybian, Kantees?" said the boy.

Kantees said nothing but looked beyond him to his parents, who continued forward at a measured pace. It was odd, she thought to herself, she had never really looked at them before. Even the last time they were here she had been in a hurry to leave before the armsmen got it into their heads to shoot the criminal Kadralin.

"Where's Daybian?"

"I haven't found him yet," she said to the boy, and then to the parents, "I'm sorry."

The Lord Jakalain had dark hair and a beard that was kept neat, as was appropriate. But the black was turning grey in places. Daybian resembled him but the father was thinner. Though perhaps that was due to the worry. His Lady had lighter hair and Kantees

349

suspected she dyed it to keep the grey away. The colour was too consistent. Whatever the case, she did not look like she slept well.

"Tell me why I do not have you shot on the spot, slave."

Kantees' blood boiled but she controlled herself. "By your rules that is your right, Lord Jakalain. However, since I am your best hope of finding your son, perhaps that would be unwise."

She heard a shuffling behind her and saw their gaze shift to her right.

"Lord and Lady Jakalain, I am Levin of Otulain. Please excuse me if I do not bow."

"Lord Levin." Lord Jakalain gave a short bow and the Lady nodded. "We are surprised to see you here but you are welcome to our house."

The Lady added, "Are you in need of a healer?"

"I would be most grateful for that, Lady, though I would take counsel with your husband first. And some food. Perhaps."

Kantees could tell from his tone that he was smiling. She, however, was not pleased that control of the conversation had passed to him by default. He was not in charge of their party.

"Yes, we do need to talk," she said. "All of us. Together. In private."

There were murmurs and the armsman beside Jelamie looked sternly in her direction. A criminal Kadralin talking out of turn and demanding she be in counsel with their master. But that was not the whole problem, it was that the other slaves would see the way she was behaving and might take it into their own heads to stand up for themselves.

"Yes," said Levin. "Kantees knows more of this situation than anyone. And if not for her I would be dead."

If it were not for me, you would be safe in your castle still believing that the Dunor was a figment of someone's imagination.

She turned her attention to Jelamie. "So young Lord, are you happy to be home?"

"I am happy, Kantees," he said. "But I miss flying in the *tekrak* and the people here think I am imagining it, even though many saw it that first night. They say I am making it up, will you tell them the truth?"

"I will tell them but I do not think they will believe a runaway slave, do you? If they won't even believe you."

"That is a problem."

The armsmen closed in around them as if unsure whether they were escorting them or arresting them. Sheesha growled, and Waileth followed his lead.

Kantees turned to the big dragon and put her hand on the side of his big head. "It's alright, Sheesha, they won't hurt us." She glanced up at the Ziri Tower. "Why don't you take Waileth up to your eyrie and I'm sure Romain and the other keepers will bring you lots of food."

She took a step back as Sheesha gave a short bark in Waileth's direction and took to the wing. The downdraught from the two of them taking off was enough to make Kantees stagger.

Levin was staring at her. "How did you do that?"

"What?"

He gestured at the retreating *ziri*.

"He seems to understand what I'm saying most of the time. Don't you talk to Waileth?"

"Of course, but I don't expect…"

"You never gave her a chance to show she understands. You say something and then force her by hand and foot anyway."

Levin went quiet and thoughtful. He glanced once more at the *ziri* as they approached the open hatch of the eyrie then disappeared inside.

"Will Waileth be all right? Males can be funny about their eyries."

Kantees smiled. "Yes, they can but I'm sure she'll be fine."

They turned and headed across the stones to the main building. Ulina stayed by her side and Jelamie did not seem to be able to make up his mind whether he should be with his parents or Kantees, so remained in a position between looking backwards and forwards.

They passed through the main doors. Only the second time she had ever been inside. The first time was when she was being interrogated about the raid on the castle that she had foiled. And she had lied to save her own skin—though now she wondered whether Levin was right that they might not have punished her after all.

It was obvious to her that punishment would have been wrong, but she did not find it easy to ascribe justice to the acts of the Taymalin. They were just invaders and slave masters as far as she was concerned.

She was not happy about changing her viewpoint. After all, they still had slaves.

The three of them were brought to the same room where she had been questioned. It was much smaller than most of the rooms on the ground floor and ideal for an intimate discussion. When she had been here before it had been set up with one chair facing three. This time there were settees and armchairs, and a fire burning in the grate even though the weather was not too cold. It made the room pleasant to be in.

Kantees had hoped they could get to the point quickly but there was food first—not that she objected, it had been a while since she had eaten properly. There was no attempt at conversation. Levin sat on a comfortable chair with his feet raised while Ulina brought him things to eat. The Lady Jakalain was not present; only the Lord, though they were joined a short while later by Swordmaster Erang and the patterner who had been at her interrogation.

The Swordmaster looked at her askance and then ignored her. The patterner spoke briefly to Levin, perhaps about his injuries since he departed again to return a short while later. Kantees could only suppose he had gone to make some arrangements to heal Levin's feet.

Time was getting on and Kantees was becoming impatient when Lord Jakalain asked them to sit. Unlike before, the chairs were drawn into a circle. Only Ulina was excluded, although she sat on the floor next to Kantees once more in a way that suggested she was providing protection. If the child was offering to protect Kantees, then she would accept that protection without hesitation.

"It has been barely a five-day since you delivered our youngest son to us, Kantees," said Lord Jakalain. "I did not expect to see you so soon. And I had hoped you might have news of Daybian, if not actually returning him to us."

"My lord," she started, and then stopped. There were lies in her past and if she were to proceed with the truth those lies must be undone. "My lord, the last time I was in this room I did not tell the truth of the events of the night of the raid."

Erang leaned forward ominously as if he were ready to draw his sword and run her through. Ulina got up on her knees as if she would be able to stop him. Erang looked at the girl and frowned. Kantees pressed her hand on to Ulina's shoulder and made her sit back on her heels.

"That night I was the one who rang the bell. I flew Sheesha to the tower and fought with the raider who was there."

"You?" said Erang.

"Sheesha woke me and—" she sighed, "—insisted I ride him."

Erang was clearly unconvinced, but Lord Jakalain looked at Levin. "Is this possible?"

"I have noticed that Sheesha is a very clever *ziri*, my lord," he said. "He would not understand that Kantees was not permitted to ride him but he would understand an attack and might choose the person closest to him to help."

Lord Jakalain looked back at Kantees, his silence encouraging her to continue.

"When I landed on the roof the raider spoke to me, he asked if I was with the Dunor."

"Ridiculous!" said Erang. "My lord, must we listen to this nonsense?"

However, neither the lord nor the patterner showed the same degree of scepticism. The patterner was looking thoughtful.

"Why did you not say this at the time?" asked the lord.

"With respect, sire," she said, "you would not have believed me and you would have had me imprisoned, if not hung, for the crimes I committed."

"Damn right," said Erang.

"You saved the castle," said the lord, "I do not think I would have had you killed."

Kantees looked at Levin and he gave a slight smile. Perhaps Taymalin justice might not have had her killed but they would still have deprived her of what little freedom she had regardless of what she had done for them. It was impossible to talk to them. They could not see the way they were, even when they uttered the words.

She was saved any further explanation as Lord Jakalain moved on.

"Lord Levin?"

"Sire?"

"May I enquire how you fit into this?"

"Of course, sire. I found Kantees in Dakastown; she was looking for her old master, Kevrey. He had moved since my father had part of the old town pulled down to make way for a park. I'm sure you've seen it."

Lord Jakalain nodded.

"I decided to assist her but at Kevrey's shop we came under attack. Kevrey was killed and the house set on fire. We barely escaped with our lives."

Erang was frowning. "In the few days since she returned Jelamie you are suggesting this runaway made it all the way to Dakastown and back?"

Kantees panicked and stared at Levin, willing him not to say anything about the *ziri* magic. They mustn't know…

Levin relaxed back into his chair. "Swordmaster, a *ziri* can cover a great deal of ground, and between Otulain and Jakalain we do possess some of the finest beasts for racing. If, however, you are suggesting that I am lying…"

Kantees closed her eyes and thanked the Mother for Levin's self-control. If it had been Daybian he would almost certainly have blurted out the truth. She glanced back at Levin and there was a slight smile on his face that suggested he took pleasure in making the Swordmaster squirm. Silly male games.

"No one is questioning your word," muttered Erang.

Levin acknowledged him with a nod.

Lord Jakalain turned his attention back to Kantees. "However, I am curious as to why you sought out your former master when I expected you to be searching for my son."

"Because of the mention of the Dunor, sire," she said quickly. "I had never heard of them but I knew, if anyone knew the truth, it would be Kevrey because he dealt in information and knowledge."

"And what did he reveal to you?"

"Nothing." Kantees felt the tears welling up once more even though she had never imagined she could feel such close kinship with a master. "He was murdered before he could tell me."

"Farahalek," said Levin. "No doubt hired by the Dunor to silence him."

Kantees had the feeling that Erang wanted to claim the Dunor were merely a figment of someone's imagination, but it would mean going against his own master as well as Levin. She looked at the patterner, who had said nothing all this time. He was looking at her with more interest than she liked. She averted her eyes and checked on Ulina. The girl was fiddling with her sleeve. Probably bored with all the grown-up talk.

"How did the Farahalek know that he needed silencing?" asked Lord Jakalain.

"I think I was being followed," said Kantees.

"Yet you were on a powerful *ziri* that can outstrip the fastest horse or *kichek*?" said Erang, not hiding his scorn.

"I was following the river, Swordmaster," she said carefully. "A *ziri* must rest, hunt and eat just as any person. A boat on the river may be slower but it need stop for nothing."

"Were you followed here?" asked the patterner suddenly; he sounded a little nervous.

Levin answered. "A boat travelling upstream cannot go as fast and as soon as we reached Cliffedge we headed here instead. Even if someone attempted to follow, they could not have done so without their own *ziri*."

"Unless they took a patterner's path," said Erang.

"They did not know where we were going," said Levin. "We had not decided ourselves until we reached Cliffedge."

"But your arrival here was noticeable," said Erang, and he turned to the patterner. "Are there any shipments to go out by the circle today, Master Hokart?"

"I do not believe so."

Erang turned back to Lord Jakalain. "Sire, while I do not believe in this talk of the Dunor, we cannot take any chances if the Farahalek are involved. If there are any spies in the castle, they will send word to their masters and it will not be long before everyone knows that Lord Levin and the slave arrived here and received your counsel. That will put you and your family at risk."

Levin interrupted. "What do you mean, spies? We are not at war."

Erang pursed his lips and looked at Lord Jakalain.

"Do what you must, Erang. Let us do our best to keep this quiet." Then the lord looked back at Levin. "Of course we are not at war, there is little profit in it. We all have our own lands which we rule as best we may, but that does not mean we trust one another. And," he said with a glance at Kantees as if he was not happy admitting this in front of one of the lower orders, "there are those families, such as the Hamalain, who are looking to take advantage. There are other ways of taking control of a family beyond simply making war."

He stood up and everyone followed suit except Ulina, but nobody took any notice of that.

"Lord Levin, let us get your wounds mended as best we can. We will outfit you more appropriately for your journey with Kantees. While I do trust her intent, I would be happier to have a Taymalin such as you with her."

Kantees seethed once more—they insisted on talking about her as if she was not here—but she held her tongue.

"As you wish, my lord," said Levin.

"Likewise, Kantees," he said. "We will have you equipped with as much as you need in order to find and return my son. I will determine what needs to be done here in case whoever is paying the Farahalek decides to have them visit Jakalain."

19

It was the strangest feeling in the world to be waited on by servants—not slaves—who only a short time before she had seen as her social superiors. They were Taymalin, she was Kadralin, and that fact did not escape them either.

They did not talk to her. They supplied what she and Ulina needed by way of a bath of hot water and clothes to replace the tatters they were now wearing. One of them—the youngest, a girl not much older than Ulina—remained behind but the others left.

Kantees slowly stripped off the remnants of her clothes, placing the package they had recovered from her old master's house on the chest of drawers near the window. She stared at it for a long while. It was probably nothing important.

She told herself that but knew she was lying. Kevrey had hidden it for a reason. He had told her of it because he intended her to open it. But that was the point, he'd still been trying to manipulate her, just like Yenteel. So she pretended she had not had enough time, or that it had not been the right time. It remained wrapped.

Ulina seemed at home with the bath and enjoyed washing herself. Kantees had not bathed often and was not entirely sure she liked it. But she let the water cover her body and tried to enjoy it.

The soap was a new concept but, again, Ulina was familiar with it and Kantees copied what the girl did.

As the water cooled they climbed out, leaving behind a scum of filth. Kantees found she liked having clean skin and decided it might be something she indulged in again, perhaps not leaving it too long.

The clothes included riding gear but also some coarse but well-made smocks, skirts, shirts and some heavier outdoor clothes. There were two sets for Ulina as well. They were a little large but would be fine for a good year as long as she did not grow too fast.

And there were boots. Kantees had never owned boots. The feeling as they encased her feet and tied up the sides was very odd, but they made her feel tall and strong. It was not unpleasant.

Kantees packed the spare clothes into her bags.

Then caught sight of herself in the mirror. Reflections she had seen, in water and metal. Her old master had a mirror in his bedroom but that was just a small one in a wooden frame. This one was half her height and stood on its own mount. It was clearly very expensive because the glass was smooth and the reflected image so clear.

It still took her a moment to accept that what she saw looking back at her was just herself, and not another person in the room. Her short hair was like a black brush. Clad now in oiled *kichek*-leather she looked like any *ziri*-rider she might see at the races. And yet, her skin was too dark. It did not fit the clothes.

Ulina moved up and Kantees exchanged glances with the mirror-child.

"It is a mirror," said Kantees.

"Of course it is," said Ulina.

Kantees shook her head. The Taymalin lived in such luxury while the servants had so little, and the slaves had nothing at all.

The young maid answered a knock on the door. It was Levin. He looked much better; there was colour in his cheeks that had not been there before and his clothes had been replaced. He was once again the lordling he was bred to be. But he did not intimidate her, they had been through fire together.

"May I enter?"

"Of course." She bit back the word *sire*. He was not her master.

He was not her superior. She was the one who commanded the *zirichasa*. Then the words echoed back to her: "Kantees of the Ziri". She shook her head; she would not fall into that trap.

Levin stepped through the door with barely a hitch in his step. The healing must have been done and in such a way that it had not drained him in the process. It was a skill Yenteel should certainly learn.

Levin looked her up and down, then nodded. "I prefer this Kantees to the tattered one."

"What about me?" said Ulina.

He appraised her the same way. "Yes, a clean Ulina is a better Ulina."

Kantees watched him as his eyes fell on the package. "You haven't opened it."

"I was waiting for the right time."

He nodded. "I understand." He surveyed the bags. "Is this everything you're taking?"

Kantees frowned in surprise at the easy way he had moved from the package.

"Aren't you curious?"

"That's why I asked if this was everything."

"You know what I mean."

"It's yours, Kantees, it's not up to me when you decide to open it."

Her frown deepened. "I don't understand you."

"I thought my meaning was plain enough."

"You nearly died for that." There was a light dusting of soot on the wood where the package had shed some of its heritage.

"So did you, and that changes nothing."

Kantees went over to where the package lay, seemingly insignificant.

"I could open it now."

"I will leave if you wish."

"No," she said quickly. "No, I would like you to stay." *There might be words, and I cannot read.*

"You may go."

At his words Kantees spun round, and realised he wasn't talking to her—or Ulina—but the maid, who did as she was told. Kantees could not quite explain the feeling of guilt that came over her. She knew why Levin had done it, the girl would probably be told to report everything she had seen or heard, but that was not her fault. That was the Taymalin.

But perhaps she was a spy for the Dunor? Kantees was not sure that made any sense, and she did not think she could go through her life imagining that everyone she met was untrustworthy.

Even Levin.

She examined the string tied around the cloth. It was sealed with wax but the heat from the fire that had engulfed the house had melted it. If there had been any glyph on the seal it was gone. She pulled the string until it snapped out of the wax and revealed a knot. That too was thick with melted wax.

"Ulina, can you cut this?"

Kantees held the strings as Ulina's tiny, and lethal, patterned blade sliced through the knot as if it were water. Levin watched and made a little noise. Kantees glanced at him but he didn't seem to want to say anything, instead his eyes were riveted on the blade.

As they should be. That little knife with its matching sheath was worth a dozen *zirichasa*.

Kantees brought the package back to the top of the chest of drawers and pulled the string off and laid it to one side. She hesitated, then unwrapped the material gingerly. The covering fell away, exposing something black that reflected the light from the window in its large facets.

"What is it?" said Levin.

"I don't know."

Kantees stared at it. It was a featureless cube of black material with its corners cut off. She reached out and touched it with a finger. It wasn't cold like metal, it was more as if she had touched stone. Lifeless and inert.

She picked it up and turned, showing it to Levin, then turned it to examine every side. It was all the same with not a single mark on it.

"Have you ever seen anything like it?" she asked. She felt let-down.

Levin shook his head. "I've seen some ornamental pieces like that. Tirnian, I think. They usually have patterns inscribed on the surface. Talismans for luck mostly, sold to the gullible."

Kantees did not think her old master would have been gullible enough to hide a luck charm and protect it with his life. It certainly hadn't been lucky for him—or them, since they'd had it.

"Perhaps it's something else," she said.

"There aren't any patterns inscribed on it."

"No." She held it up to the light and examined each surface to see if anything was visible that couldn't be seen normally. "Nothing." She sighed, wrapped it up again and put it in her pack. "Perhaps Yenteel will know what it is."

The journey from the room in the castle across the courtyard then up the Ziri Tower was one of the strangest Kantees had ever experienced. She led the way, followed by Ulina and Levin, then Lord Jakalain with the Swordmaster and several armsmen.

That she was leading the way was bad enough, but as she entered the lower areas of the tower there were people she knew, both servants and slaves. They passed through the kitchen area and Kantees looked at where Libbibet was bossing the kitchen staff. The place went silent and Kantees could see the moment of confusion before Libbibet recognised her. There was no friendship in that moment.

Kantees understood. She had stolen away with the best *ziri;* not that Libbibet cared about the racing beasts, but she cared that Kantees had set the place in uproar. That a slave had run away, broken out two slaves from the cells, and probably caused difficulties for everyone else because the Taymalin would be angry and worried others might follow.

At that moment, Romain appeared at the door ahead of them. Kantees knew he would have dearly loved to shout at her. Not only had she stolen his precious *ziri* but she had taken Gally with her. He had been Romain's whipping boy and convenient excuse for any errors. But with such important people behind her, he could say and do nothing.

Except ignore her, as he spoke to Lord Jakalain directly. "The *ziri* have been fed and are saddled, master."

"Very good, Romain. Lord Levin—" Kantees turned with Levin, "—I hope our care for your *zirichak* is up to the standards of the Otulain. We will take our leave here and bid you well for your journey."

"Thank you, Lord Jakalain. I know from Kantees' skill that she was taught by the best here."

The Lord glanced around and then beckoned to Kantees. She sighed, knowing that this would look very strange to the people she had once worked with, but she dutifully crossed to her ex-master, who drew her to one side.

"Kantees, I am putting a great deal of trust in you, and believe me, I would not do so if it were not for Lord Levin."

"Yes, sire."

"Bring Daybian home to me and I will forgive your every crime."

Kantees restrained herself and made no comment about being held as a slave with no will of her own. "I have promised I will do it."

The man grunted an acknowledgement, hesitated and placed his hand on her shoulder. "I cannot claim to understand you, Kantees. If it were me who had escaped my chains I do not think I would return."

"I am trying to make amends for my lies, sire. And to keep my promises, but once that is done it will be the last you know of me."

He nodded and let his hand slip from her shoulders. "My wife wishes you well and she sends…" He stopped and pursed his lips as if he did not wish to utter the next words. "She sends the blessings of the Mother. And I offer you the blessing of Taymar."

"Thank you, sire," said Kantees. "I accept your blessings in the spirit they were offered." *Though you can keep your Taymar and drown him for all I care.*

He said nothing more and looked across at the others. She took that to mean her private discussion was at an end, so she turned and went back to Levin and Ulina. And the frowning cloud that was Romain.

"This way," she said as she picked up her bags and headed for the lower tower steps. The Swordmaster followed them.

The horde of keeper apprentices watched silently as Kantees went through and up the first ladder. She could feel their eyes boring into her back. They were all slaves—like Romain—what did they make of her and her escape? Did they dream of stealing a *ziri* and flying away?

This is what scared the Taymalin, and scared Romain too, no doubt. She had made life at Jakalain uncertain.

They passed the lower eyries as they climbed. The younger *ziri* moved quietly across the stone floors as they passed, and eventually reached the place where Kantees had slept for so many years. She felt something in her throat as a sadness came over her. The old smell of centuries of *zirichasa* and the smell of Sheesha himself.

He gave a welcoming cry as she climbed up. Waileth snuffled too. The place was so familiar that seeing the second *ziri* here was strange, but clearly Sheesha was willing to tolerate her. Kantees shrugged; he was old enough to mate and if Waileth accepted him that was fine. Although Waileth being gravid was not what they needed at this time.

Kantees put her bags down and started to unbuckle the tack that Romain had put on Sheesha.

"What are you doing?" said Romain as he arrived up the ladder and stomped across the floor.

"I fly without," said Kantees.

"Like a savage!"

Kantees stopped what she was doing and glared at him. "What did you say?"

"Riding like a savage. I might have expected it from you."

"What savages? And how do you know how they ride?"

The Swordmaster had made it up the ladder and moved in behind Romain. It was getting crowded. Sheesha growled at the two men.

"Everyone knows savages ride without a saddle."

"You never said that to me," she said. "And what savages? You mean Kadralin? You mean our people?"

"They are not my people."

Kantees let her annoyance slide away. "No," she said, "no, they really aren't your people. You have abandoned them."

But it meant she was right. The Ziri Towers had been built by the Kadralin before the Taymalin came, and they had ridden without saddles. It pleased her. Then her mood dropped as she realised there was something she needed to tell Romain.

"Jintan is dead."

The Swordmaster perked up at that, as if it somehow gave him the justification to go against his master's orders.

"How?"

"You know Daybian stole him away to follow me. We travelled to Hamalain, to Kurvin Port."

"There was trouble at their ley-circle," said the Swordmaster. "That was you?"

"Daybian had been kidnapped by the Hamalain, Swordmaster Erang, as you know from the letter I left," said Kantees, clearly and slowly so that he would be sure to understand. "I was trying to rescue him. He fought bravely when I had released him from his bonds—you would have been proud, he must have learnt your lessons very well. But as we were trying to escape, Jintan was shot. That is how Daybian was captured."

Romain looked genuinely upset. Certainly not about Daybian, but he had worked with Jintan for so many years. It was something that Kantees did at least understand and she was glad to see that Romain did have a heart.

"The others?" he asked.

"They were well when I left them," said Kantees. "I do not think they have been in any danger." *I hope not.*

In the silence that followed, she finished removing the saddles and reins from Sheesha. She hung them up in the correct place on the wall, then put the bags across Sheesha's neck and climbed up when he ducked down for her. Ulina climbed up too while Levin got himself into the saddle on Waileth.

There was nothing more to be said. She glanced at Levin and he nodded. Kantees gave Sheesha a command and he walked to the hatch of the eyrie and in a smooth motion launched himself out.

He did not allow himself to fall but gave a couple of powerful strokes that carried him upwards and across the keep.

Kantees glanced behind at Waileth and then at the rapidly shrinking hatch of the eyrie.

She sighed. Now all they had to do was find the *tekrak* and hope there had been no trouble.

2 0

I t was mid-afternoon when they left Jakalain and headed north-east. Kantees had considered staying at the castle longer but, while they had been treated well enough, they had also been moved along quickly. Fed, clothed, healed and taken back to their *ziri*.

They were not welcome there. Kantees had no illusions, there was unlikely to be any place in Esternes where a Taymalin lord would welcome a runaway slave, let alone one who had earned a reputation.

But that was behind her now. They needed to find the *tekrak*. Her instructions to Yenteel had been simple enough. Head north to the mountains and then skirt them to the east—away from the Talamyrth.

That had been a five-day ago. The *tekrak* was slow but it was still faster than a horse or *kichek* and did not need to slow down to ford rivers or cross hills. They would not catch them today, so she did not hurry and allowed the *ziri* to fly at normal speed. As the sun approached the horizon, they found a suitable place to set down where two rivers joined, making it impossible for anything to approach them on two of three sides.

They made a fire and settled in for the night.

Kantees found her feet to be very cold when she woke. She had moved in the night and they stuck out beyond Sheesha's wing. The sun was not up but there was a dim light in the sky that edged the feathers.

She sighed and listened to the sound of the water from the two rivers. A constant but infinitely varied sound. Something in the sky caught her eye. She reached out to push away the feathers and saw a golden light passing across the stars at a great height.

Kantees caught her breath. A *ziri* riding the pattern. It was heading away from the mountains behind them down to the south and east. She kept her eye locked on it because it was no more than a short golden line slicing like an arrow through the blackness.

So, she thought, *that is what Sheesha and I look like when we are high in the sky.* If it were daylight they would probably be invisible to the ground—never mind if there were clouds.

But who could it be? She was sure she knew the answer. It must be her own people, the Kadralin who had never forgotten the old ways, who lived in the heart of Esternes.

When I am finished with this, she promised herself. *When I am done with this journey, I will find my people and join them. I'll take Ulina and Gally with me.*

She climbed to her feet, pushing against Sheesha's body to lever herself up, and stepped out onto the damp grass. She shivered and looked across at Waileth. It seemed Levin had succumbed to the idea that he could sleep with his *ziri* and there was no visible sign of him, but she could hear him snoring quietly.

Breathing the cold air deep, she tried to shake off the lethargy of sleep. She went to her bag and pulled out a pie from Jakalain. She took it to the bank overlooking the confluence of the two rivers and watched the water as it churned and clashed before moving off into the new channel, wider, deeper and faster.

She took Kevrey's gift from inside her jacket, laid it on the grass and looked at it. The stone it was made from was completely black but its surfaces reflected the brightening sky. It was just a lump of polished stone.

Why hadn't he thought to leave some instructions with it? *Because he had not expected to be killed.*

He had become a fraction of what he was when she knew him. It had looked as if he stayed drunk as long as he could afford alcohol. And that he had sold almost everything to satiate his thirst. She looked into the distance and frowned, then searched the sky for the line of gold, but it was long gone.

She was nothing but a runaway slave on a fruitless mission to rescue a lordling belonging to a race she despised.

Not all of them.

She hated the responsibilities that had been piled on her. Escaping slavery was supposed to make her free but she felt even more weighed down than she had before. Hemmed in by promises she could not break. Promises that would end in her death before she was able to fulfil them, or any of the dreams that she had.

"Don't think too hard," said Levin. He stood beside her but she did not look up.

"I almost wish I had ignored Sheesha and stayed an ignorant slave."

"Almost."

"There is nothing good about being a slave, Levin."

"I can't imagine it."

"No, but I don't have to," she said. "And my life was not difficult. I had Sheesha."

"The *ziri* compensate for a lot," he said.

"What in your life needs compensating for?" She did not keep the sarcasm from her voice.

"I am the spare, Kantees. My only purpose in life is as the replacement if something bad should happen to my elder brother. But it is to him that all the attention is given. He is the one who gets the best *ziri*, the best tutors, the best choice of consort. I have no value unless he dies."

"Do you want him to die?"

"Of course not, he is my brother and I love him."

Kantees, skilled liar that she was, detected the stench of false-hood in the words uttered so quickly and so smoothly. "But?"

"I do not want him to die, Kantees. The thing you hate so much about being free? That is the thing we all fear and hate. You chose it without realising what road you were taking, but my brother had it thrust upon him." He paused. "I do not want that responsibility, Kantees. I do not want to be responsible for all the lives of Otulain. I like only having to race the *ziri*."

She stared out across the grass-covered landscape of low rolling hills descending away from them. "But responsibility catches us up in the end anyway," she said.

And, she thought to herself, even a slave has responsibility even if they are not supposed to. You have to take care how you deal with the others. You look after them even if it is only in a small way. She helped Gally so he would not be punished by Romain. She made it her duty. Her responsibility, even though she was not always successful.

"I don't think it's possible to live without responsibility," she said finally. "The things we choose to bind us are the things that make us free."

"Kevrey made you into a philosopher."

She could tell from his tone he was smiling. "Is a philosopher a weapon?"

"Ideas are."

"And philosophers make ideas?"

He crouched down beside her. "Philosophers? Yes, I suppose so. Storytellers. Bards and their songs."

"Whose idea was it to enslave my people?" she said. "Here on Esternes?"

"The driver of the cart back in Dakastown called you by name."

"You heard that?"

She shivered.

"Kantees of the Ziri."

She shrugged. "It doesn't mean anything."

His hand came down on her shoulder and she did not shake it off. Instead, she turned and looked at him. His face was close to hers and she could feel his breath when he spoke. "It means revolution, Kantees."

"I don't use that name. I don't want it."

It was puzzling the way she did not feel threatened by his touch, so unlike the way she'd rebelled against Daybian's advances.

Words she was not expecting formed on her tongue and were expelled through her mouth almost as if she had no control of them. "Would you like to kiss me?"

"What?"

Again the words came to her as if from somewhere else. "If you would like to kiss me, I would not mind."

He frowned. "No."

She frowned. "No?"

"I mean, you are a very attractive woman, Kantees. I'm sure many men would like to kiss you."

"But not you?"

He looked at his hand on her shoulder as if he had not realised it was there and pulled it away. Not abruptly, but with a certain finality.

"I'm sorry, Kantees, if I have been forward and implied something I did not intend."

"You *don't* want to kiss me? Why not?"

"I am happy to kiss you if that's what you want."

"But you don't want to."

He looked helpless and confused. Kantees could feel the anger boiling up in her, fighting with her own confusion and self-doubt.

"Because I'm Kadralin."

"No!"

"You've been with many Kadralin women but you don't want me?"

"Not at all. I haven't been with any Kadralin women."

"I heard what Lady Deenya said to you back in Dakastown."

"It wasn't true."

"So it *is* because of my skin?"

"No," he said in exasperation. "I haven't been with any Taymalin women either." But his voice caught on the word *any*.

"You're lying to me, you *have* been with a Taymalin woman."

He sighed. "I don't understand how we arrived here."

"Explain to me why I should not be insulted?"

"Because I did not start this, Kantees, you were the one who demanded I kiss you."

"I did not demand."

"But you were upset when I refused, how is that not a demand?"

The realisation she was behaving just like Daybian swept through her but somehow she just could not stop. "Have you ever lain with a woman?"

"Once."

"Once?"

"Once," he repeated and then sighed again. "It was not my idea and I cannot say I enjoyed it."

"You didn't?"

"Must I repeat everything I say before you will believe it?" Levin glanced back at where the two *ziri* were still asleep, or at least feigning it. Ulina had not appeared.

"You need to explain yourself."

"Surely that is my own business and not yours?"

Kantees stopped. She wanted to say that he owed her for his refusal but that would not have been the truth. "I'm sorry, Levin. You're right. It's none of my business."

His hand came down on hers. Which just confused her again. She looked into his face, still close, still just as sweet and perhaps sad.

"Kantees, it is my duty to be able to produce offspring. We must be capable of continuing the line, there must always be an Otulain going forwards into the future. If there is not, the family name will die and we will be nothing more than a memory. The name is every-thing; our personal desires and wishes are not important."

"You're saying they made you lie with this woman so that you could have a child?"

"Oh no, I could not have married her, she was a whore."

"Oh," she said. "Then why?"

"To make sure I was capable."

Sometimes she felt like she should perhaps cut out her own tongue so that the words did not come spilling out. "And were you?"

He looked away and took his hand from hers.

"Oh," was all she could say as a mountain of guilt landed on her. She found his hand with hers and squeezed it. "Levin," she said, "if you want to lie with me at any time, just let me know."

A strange smile came over his face. "You're offering yourself to me?"

She frowned again. "Yes, clearly that is what I just did."

"Why?"

"I know that sometimes when there is something that you *must* do and the weight of responsibility is on your shoulders, it can be difficult." The look on his face suggested her explanation was not enough. "I just want to help you."

He gave a small sad laugh. "I think perhaps that is the kindest and stupidest thing anyone has ever said to me."

"It was certainly kind but I do not think it was stupid."

"Are you experienced in the ways of love, Kantees?"

She hesitated, wanting to divert the question but honesty seemed important in this moment. "Less than you," she said quietly.

"What if you were to get with child?"

She shrugged and then smiled. "Women have their ways, Levin."

"And you know these ways of women?"

"I've heard of them but I do not know what they are. Besides, perhaps you are incapable of siring a child."

"That is not very encouraging."

The sound of a *ziri* burp drifted to them across the grass.

"Sheesha!"

"I think it was Waileth."

"You can tell the difference?"

Levin shrugged. "My *ziri* is a lady, she is more delicate in her tones."

Kantees laughed and was glad for the opportunity to change the subject.

She gathered up Kevrey's stone, put it inside her tunic and got to her feet. "Let's get moving," she said. "We have enough light. The *ziri* are still full from yesterday. The sky is clear and we shall find the others today."

"What are we looking for?"

"A *tekrak*."

"It's not the season for them, and besides, we would never spot it from a significant height."

"Trust me, Levin, we'll see this one."

One thing Kantees had noticed in her pattern flights with Sheesha was how far away objects appeared to move slowly. It was not something she understood but it seemed to be a magic that pervaded the world. Close objects moved quickly past, far ones crawled.

Which was convenient for them as they climbed high above the hills keeping the mountains to their left, because from a good height they could watch for the *tekrak* and not worry about missing it. Sheesha accelerated until the magic grew and expanded to embrace them.

It was almost normal now. She still found it astonishing and wonderful—but unsurprising. She smiled. It seemed a person could accept anything. She turned and looked at Levin. He was still wonder-struck, staring down and around. As she watched, he reached up to touch the golden light, but it retreated before his fingers.

That's interesting, she thought. *It expands to ensure we stay inside. What if someone fell off?*

She didn't imagine the magic would protect someone who became completely disconnected from a *ziri* in the formation. Would the magic work for more *zirichasa*? How many? Did the magic only come from Sheesha or did Waileth make it too? They had travelled faster to Cliffedge with the two *zirichasa*, and that was important.

She shook her head. Perhaps she would have a chance to find out one day. Perhaps she would find her own people and they would know.

"Keep an eye out for the *tekrak*, Ulina," she said.

"I am," came the curt reply. She was looking to the left so Kantees focused on the right where the low hills spread out. There were clusters of houses surrounded by fields that gave way to untended lands where the huge *lukisa* roamed in herds. There were not many trees, just the occasional copse here and there. Similar to the land that surrounded Jakalain.

Far to the east the air became hazy, along with the dark of what Kantees took to be another forest like the Talamyrth. Their experiences in that place made her wary, and she would not attempt to cross one that large again unless she knew it was safe.

She took in the view ahead but was sure the *tekrak* was not there. She turned her attention to the mountains, certain her people were hidden in the valleys there—hadn't she seen the *ziri* flying high and fast this morning coming from the mountains?

But from what she could see the valleys did not look hospitable. The nearby ground was green and probably made excellent grazing, but further in the steep sides of the grey cliffs came together forming high ridges. In the distance the higher peaks were topped with white, which she took to be snow. Sheesha had taught her that air became colder the higher you went. She sighed. There was no point trying to judge from here. She would have to look. When she had time.

Sheesha gave a sudden cry and changed direction abruptly. Caught unawares, Kantees fell back, though her legs hooked under the wings saved her from falling. Ulina seemed unmoved by the experience.

Kantees looked back to ensure Levin was still with them only to find that Waileth was in precisely the same relative position, as if the course change had not even happened. Levin gave her a wave. He was firmly buckled in to the saddle. Waileth could fly upside down and he wouldn't fall off.

She looked forward trying to see what Sheesha was doing.

At that moment the magic faded and they were blasted by the wind. Sheesha was ignoring her. He screamed again; it was a call she had never heard before. All she could see ahead was smoke behind the rounded slope of one of the bigger hills.

Instead of gliding, Sheesha drove himself forward with powerful strokes. The only time he had acted like this before was the night they had rung the alarm bell.

The hill grew closer and Kantees saw the shape of a *ziri* fly out from behind it and into view. A bright arcing shape flew up. An arrow with a burning tip. The *ziri* snapped it from the air then dropped it.

In a wave of recognition, she realised it was Looesa. Now, instead of wanting to hold Sheesha back, Kantees leaned forward, pushing into Ulina. The top of the rounded bulk of the *tekrak* came into view with smoke swirling around it. From behind she heard Levin swear. She turned her head. Waileth was still in formation.

Kantees tried to make Sheesha head towards the slope on this side. If there was a fight, Kantees wanted to be on the ground, with the bags and Ulina. They would be no good in a battle on Sheesha's back.

Sheesha resisted, still heading directly to where Looesa was climbing and turning as another fire arrow shot from the ground. Whoever was attacking was hidden by the curve of the hill. Kantees could not imagine Yenteel, Gally and Tenical were putting up much of a fight. They were not warriors.

Neither was she.

"Sheesha, you need to let us off," she said quietly as if her voice would carry to those who were attacking her friends. At her words Sheesha adjusted his course again and arrowed towards the ground on this side of the hill. He back-winged ferociously, driving her into his spine as he touched down on the grassy surface. Ulina slipped off in a moment. Kantees lifted her leg over and dropped, pulling the bags with her.

Almost as if he had not stopped, Sheesha launched himself off the hill with a tremendous kick. She watched as he curved round and away, beating his wings to gain altitude. Waileth, who had not landed and still had Levin on her back, manoeuvred smoothly into position behind him again and followed his climb. Levin pulled a short bow from among his bags and looked as if he were trying to string it. It seemed he had given up trying to control Waileth.

Sheesha was still climbing and it looked as if he was planning to go over the hill. Kantees searched around for some stones to fill her pockets and pulled her knife from its sheath. She was not going to throw herself into a fight with anyone armed with fire arrows, but if she could add to the confusion, while those who could fight dealt with the problem, then she would.

It was at that moment she realised Ulina was missing.

She looked up and saw the girl, crouched and heading around the hill, but also climbing to give herself a better position, perhaps. Kantees dared not call out for fear of attracting unwelcome attention in the child's direction.

Kantees shuddered at the memory of Ulina slitting the throat of the mercenary leader, Ofindah, with her tiny knife before he even realised he was being attacked. He had been arrogant and Ulina had come at him from behind as the man threatened Kantees.

But she was still a child.

Kantees abandoned the search for stones and with her knife in hand she raced after Ulina. She stumbled along the slope of the hill, angling down to come at the attackers from a different angle and, with the Mother's blessing, distract them.

The thing that concerned her the most was that they had no plan, but then how could they plan when she had no idea what lay beyond the bend in the hill?

In only a few moments the *tekrak* came into view. She had forgotten how massive it was, with its huge body composed of giant overlapping leaves that retained the lifting gas that kept it in the air.

It was tilting precariously. Its fire-tube roared with flame as it tried to get away from the ropes strung between it and the ground. There were at least eight of them, hooks at the end of the three solidly attached to the gondola, while the others were stuck in the root system above.

Kantees stared worriedly at two fire arrows embedded in the leaves, still burning. If they managed to get through to the lifting gas the whole creature would go up in flames in the blink of an eye.

She couldn't see anyone in the gondola. It was like a pin cushion with ordinary arrows sticking from it. The others must be inside and lying on the floor to avoid getting shot—unless they were already dead. Kantees pushed that thought away.

Her eye was caught by one of the embedded fire arrows which, without warning, dislodged itself from the leaves, flew sideways and then dropped straight down.

Yenteel, or more likely Tenical, must be alive. They were the only two she knew who could work a patterning and she did not think Yenteel was so skilled.

Then Looesa flew over her head screaming. He came down low, skimming the grass, and disappeared from sight round the hill. Shingul followed. Kantees was so happy they were both unharmed, at least so far.

There were yells from the other side. Kantees kept her head down and moved forwards.

Another fire arrow went up and penetrated the body of the *tekrak*. She had always been told they were unfeeling plants yet the surface where the arrow penetrated quivered and moved.

There was a boulder close to where the attackers seemed to be, so Kantees crawled to it, then carefully raised her head just as Sheesha and Waileth came over the brow of the hill above her.

The attackers were difficult to make out as their clothes blended with the grass and bushes around them. Looesa and Shingul had passed the group and were making a long loop in the distance away from her.

As Sheesha and Waileth streaked down from behind the men, she saw Levin let fly with his bow into the group. There was a cry. Kantees saw immediately how bad this would be. The men reacted quickly as the two new *ziri* went over them—the one with the rider became the focus of their attention. Arrows flew after him.

Kantees desperately wanted Sheesha to veer off and make Waileth go with him. Why didn't Sheesha defer to Levin on Waileth's back? Why was he still in charge?

Sheesha must have sensed the danger. Without any warning he folded his wings in tight, along with Waileth, and they dropped out of the sky like stones—with Levin hanging on for his life. The wings flicked out and she heard Levin grunt in pain.

The arrows shot harmlessly over the *ziri*. This time.

Where is Ulina? She looked up the hill. Kantees shook her head. She did not like the idea of Ulina attacking armed men. She knew the child was a violent force of nature but surely there were too many men for even her to deal with. She might get two of them, but those that remained would kill her in no time. Meanwhile, the *ziri* might be able to harass and distract the men but they didn't seem to be able to stop them, and eventually the attackers would bring the *tekrak* down, which seemed to be their intention.

If only they had a plan.

She glanced up again. Four *zirichasa* were now in a diamond formation, Sheesha at the tip, turned across the sky. They would be coming in fast within a dozen heartbeats. A man bellowed in pain and anger just beyond the ridge. *Ulina.*

Kantees stared at the ropes holding the *tekrak*, then at her knife. It was far too blunt to cut through the cords fast. But Ulina's knife could slice through in moments despite its size. Looking up again, Kantees paused for a moment, watching the *ziri* curving in towards them from the other side. *Sheesha, you need to come in low,* she thought.

Moments later the formation dipped towards the grass and disappeared from her view. Kantees sprung from behind the boulders. She was so far back from the main group she had to take several strides before she could see the men.

Five of them, four with bows and two of those with flame arrows. Smoke rose gently from a small fire. Kantees sprinted across the grass, her feet slipping momentarily on the moist ground. They did not look in her direction.

The man without a bow headed away from the main group, uphill. He must be after Ulina. The others were preparing to fire at the *tekrak*. Surely they must be aware of the incoming *ziri*, and even if they weren't they would only have to glance to their left.

She needed to get the ropes off the *tekrak*. Once it was free they would be able to escape.

"Over here," she shouted. Five heads turned as one. Their faces were grim and they did not look surprised. The man heading away from the group, she saw now, had a thick beard, and he turned away and continued back up the hill. Kantees could not spare the breath for the curse she wanted to utter. He was the one she needed to engage. Three bowmen turned back to the *tekrak* but the fourth raised his bow and drew back the string in a single motion. He let fly at her as if he were flicking dirt from his sleeve.

A blade of gold exploded behind the men and shot across the sky. For the tiniest fraction of a moment Kantees saw four *ziri* surrounded by the bubble of golden magic and then she was thrown to the ground by the violent blast of wind that accompanied them.

Something stung her cheek.

Although she had never been on the outside of the effect she at least knew what she had just witnessed and recovered quickly.

Poking her head up, the men were nowhere in sight. They must have been driven to the floor just as she was. Another cry of pain rent the air. Kantees gathered herself up and flung herself towards the group again.

The *tekrak* bobbed on the end of its bonds. One of the hooks had ripped a chunk of leaves from the main body. Kantees had a passing thought as to whether it hurt the plant but her plan was more important. She knew Ulina was somewhere close but could not see her.

"Ulina! Cut the ropes!"

She repeated her words as she bore down on the men. Unfortunately, her words seemed to spur them into action. Perhaps that was not a surprise since she wanted to thwart their plan, whatever it might be.

The first man on his feet was the one who had shot at her with his bow. He was still clutching it as she careened into him with her blade held out in front of her. He sidestepped but not fast enough. Her shoulder struck his and she felt the blade digging in. Without thinking, she grabbed his arm and clung to it as he fell back under the impact. She was forced in the other direction but used his arm to keep herself upright and pulled him round, off-balance.

She lost her balance and stumbled. He was now behind her but still she clung on as she turned. There was no plan in her mind and she was terribly aware of the other three men rising from the grass around her.

Ulina ran across her field of vision, heading for the ropes. Kantees was grateful the child had heard but knew she herself would be cut down with so many enemies, so many men, around her. Her impulse was to let go but she stood more chance of surviving if she kept the man turning.

She was now facing downhill and the *tekrak* was above her.

"Kantees!"

She recognised Gally's voice immediately and almost cried out. She must protect him at the very least. Maintaining her grip on the attacker she launched herself into a dive down the steep slope. She pulled the man over the edge of the drop-off. She did not care whether she lived or died. She meant to take him with her wherever she ended up.

A whipping sound cracked through the air. Men shouted behind her. As she and her opponent turned through the air she saw the sky and four *ziri* descending. Men shouted and the arm she clung to pulled at her. She held on.

He hit the ground first and she crashed on top of him. The impact drove the breath from her and she felt a pain in her ribs. Instinctively she released his arm and rolled away, trying to force air into her lungs. Pain lanced through her chest. The shouts of the men turned to screams of pain that cut off quickly.

Kantees managed to breathe.

She was lying with her head downhill and she watched as the *tekrak* moved away from the hill with ropes dangling from the body and gondola. Upside down she saw Gally's round face next to Yenteel's thin features. Both staring down at her. She wanted to shout at them to hide but no words came. Even breathing was hard.

Every moment she expected the man she had attacked to leap on her and spit her with a sword or an arrow. But that moment did not come. Her breathing became easier and the pain became a dull ache. Perhaps she was not dying.

2 2

----

*S*he jumped as a figure loomed over her.

"Are you going to lie there all day?"

Levin. She tried to move but her head-down position on the slope, and the aches that threatened agony when she tensed her muscles, kept her where she was.

"I can't move." Her voice came out in a rasp.

"You have a scratch on your cheek," he said, and then, to her embarrassment, studied the rest of her body. "I see no other injuries. You're not bleeding."

The silence was broken by the sudden roar of the giant *tekrak*'s fire-tube. Levin looked up as the shadow crossed the sky above them. He shook his head. "I understand why you did not try to explain it. How can that be?"

She said nothing and he turned back.

He knelt beside her. "Let me help you," he said. "I'll lift you into a sitting position and then we'll turn you."

"I think that will hurt."

"Or you could just stay there."

She took a deep breath, which made her ribs hurt, and nodded. She braced herself against the pain as he put his arm behind her neck and pulled her up into a sitting position. She bit down on the agony. How could she not be injured and be in this much pain?

There were *ziri* moving about further up the slope, silhouetted against the sky, while the *tekrak* manoeuvred itself and settled towards the ground. Closer, there was the man she had fought. He lay with her knife buried in his stomach, the blood on his clothes already drying and turning brown.

Levin saw where she was looking. "You got him." He seemed impressed. "There's not many that could go one-on-one against a Farahalek and live to tell the tale."

She looked at him as if his words did not mean anything, but he was still looking at the body.

"Someone wants you and your friends very dead." He sighed. "Unfortunately, that now includes me. If I had known what it meant to be mixed up with you I think I would have left you on your own in Dakastown."

"If I had known," she said, "I would have been happy that you did."

He shrugged. "What's done is done. It's good to know that even a gang of assassins cannot stand against angry *zirichasa*."

"Ulina?"

"She is unharmed." This time she knew he was uncertain, as his eyes searched for the girl but she was not in sight. "If I read the situation right, she killed two of them before she cut the ropes."

Kantees nodded, although he was not looking at her. "Can you turn me?"

"Sorry." He took hold of her legs and twisted her around until she could sit normally without support. Although now she was looking downhill and away from the *ziri* and the *tekrak*. Levin was kneeling to her side and looking up.

"How does a *tekrak* get to be so huge, Kantees?"

"Even the patterner, Tenical, does not know," she said. "They taught him the patterns to control it but nothing more. So he says."

"Can you trust him?"

"I have had no reason to doubt his loyalty so far."

"That is not truly an answer."

"I do not truly know the answer. It is possible he is leading us into a trap, but what choice do I have if I am to rescue Daybian?" *Assuming I'm even right about where he is.*

Levin nodded and stood. He held out his hand to her. "Can you walk?"

The prospect did not please her but she took his hand and he pulled her to her feet. Pain lanced through her but it seemed it only happened when she used the muscles in her lower chest. She pressed her fingers into her clothes and found an area that was sensitive.

She looked at the dead Farahalek, the position of the knife handle aligned with where she hurt. So, killing him had been an accident. She had fallen onto him and driven the knife in. A fatal accident.

Leaning on Levin, she let him guide her along the slope, climbing slowly. There was an unpleasant smell drifting down to them.

"You might not want to look," said Levin.

The bodies of the remaining attackers were ripped to pieces. Sheesha and the other *ziri* were preening. Just like they did after eating a kill. It occurred to Kantees that she was, perhaps, safer than she thought she was.

Ulina was sitting a short distance away wiping her little blade on the grass. The *tekrak* touched down and its roots writhed. Gally and Yenteel jumped down from the gondola. Kantees touched Levin on the arm. "They could do with some help."

"With that?"

"Just help." She caught his concerned look, though whether it was because of the giant plant or for her she could not tell. "I'll be fine."

He let go of her tentatively, ready to catch her if she could not stand without him. She managed to stay on her feet. Sheesha's head slid under her other arm and she closed her eyes and clung to his neck. She wanted to bury herself in his feathers.

Assured of her safety, Levin picked his way through the bodies and stood a short distance from Gally and Yenteel. Kantees wondered how he felt about working alongside two slaves—but then he did not seem bothered by her. And it wasn't because he was attracted to her. She had got that message very clearly. He was not interested, and for that she was grateful. Her offer was genuine but she hoped he would never take her up on it.

Yenteel had spoken, though Kantees could not hear what he said. Levin went round to the other side of the gondola, probably to grab the ropes there.

"Thank you, Sheesha," she said quietly and scratched him just the way he liked it. She knew she ought to thank Ulina as well, though she wondered if it was wrong to encourage the girl's violence.

Farahalek. They had killed five assassins. The *ziri* had done most of the work, distracting them and then tearing them to pieces. Ulina had got two, and Kantees had taken the other—with nothing but luck on her side. In truth it had all been pure luck from beginning to end. They could not count on that happening again. She just needed to find Daybian, free him, and then she could disappear. She had no desire to be hunted by assassins for the rest of her life.

This was no fight of hers. If the Dunor wanted to take over the Taymalin world what did it matter to her? She was not involved.

Above her, the root system of the *tekrak* writhed and released the gondola. It dropped at one end on the slope and rolled sideways. They should have wedged it first. But it came to rest without falling any further. It took only a few more moments to drag the monstrous creature a short distance further and, under Tenical's instruction, make it come down and engage its roots. She wondered whether it took extra effort to make it do that in the day when it would normally be flying—or perhaps its injuries encouraged it to dig in and feed.

She shrugged. It was another thing she had no need to know. Once they had rescued Daybian she would leave them behind as well.

Gally dug a mallet from a pocket and drove a stake into the hill. He wrapped the rope around it and tied it off. He then hurried to Yenteel and did the same, finally disappearing from sight to do the ropes on the other side.

Yenteel turned and hurried down the hill in her direction, his face split by a wide grin. "You're late, Kantees."

"I think I was just in time."

Yenteel looked down at the bodies. "I'm sure we could have dealt with them."

There was a damp red patch on his shirt. "You've been hit."

"Already repaired," he said. "There was little enough to do while Tenical tried to get the beast loose from the ropes." He took in her injuries. "You, however, are in need of assistance."

"Bruises is all."

At that moment Sheesha decided to shift his position and pain shot through her chest. She couldn't keep it from her face. The humour went from Yenteel's.

"Lie down."

Clinging to Sheesha's neck Kantees went down on her knees— the slope ensured that was not too far. Yenteel helped her turn, though the pain lanced through her at every move. Tears formed in her eyes, although she did not feel as if she were crying. Yenteel cradled the back of her head and she let herself drop back, grateful that she did not have to tense her muscles any longer.

"Where is it hurting?"

She pointed in the direction of her lower ribs on the left. Without waiting for permission Yenteel pulled her clothes up and down, and the cold air drifted across her skin. It was not unpleasant. She watched Yenteel's face as he studied her flesh. She thought she ought to be embarrassed but she was too tired to even worry.

"This may hurt," he said quietly. It didn't, at least at first. She could feel his fingers pressing gently on her stomach and then on her right side. His fingers were smooth and she realised he must have done no hard labour in his entire life. Lucky him.

His hand touched her just below her breast. "What are you doing?"

"Checking the extent of the damage."

"What damage?"

Then it hurt, like needles driven into her flesh, and she was so surprised she cried out.

"That damage."

She tried to lift her head to see but the very act was torture. "What is it?"

"You're very badly bruised."

"Bruises don't feel like that."

She grunted as he did something else to her.

"I think at least one of your ribs is broken."

"Can you fix it?"

"I expect so," he said. "But how did it happen?"

She glanced in the direction of the man she had killed. "I fell on him. I must have pushed my knife into him with my chest."

Yenteel gave a short laugh. "That's one way to do it."

Darkness blocked out the sky. Kantees squinted and realised it was three people, all leaning over her: Ulina, Gally and Levin.

"Gally and Ulina, get a fire going," said Yenteel. "Away from these bodies."

He stood up and faced Levin. He put out his hand. Levin's hesitation was obvious but then he clasped hands. "I am Levin."

"Yenteel." He looked back down at Kantees. "Another lordling? You seem to collect them."

"I must be just lucky."

"We need to have a talk, Kantees," said Levin.

Yenteel held up his hand as if to ward him off. "Not until she's been healed."

Sheesha chose that moment to bring his massive face down to Kantees' and lick her.

"I'm all right," she said as convincingly as she could. "You go and hunt with Looesa. Leave Waileth and Shingul here to protect us."

The *ziri* nudged her face gently and moved away around the hill. Moments later he was airborne with Looesa falling into formation behind him.

"That's what I want to talk about," said Levin.

"And I said, later," said Yenteel and glared at him. Levin was higher up the slope but Yenteel was taller than him by a head. "She needs to be moved away from this—" he indicated the bodies, "—and healed. Then you can talk to her as much as she can stand."

After a moment's hesitation Levin nodded. "How do you want to move her?"

"There are poles in the gondola we can use to make a litter for her to lie on, we'll carry her." Levin set off immediately.

"I can walk," said Kantees.

"I don't know how badly your ribs are broken. You think this hurts? How bad do you think it would be if a broken bone pierced your lung?"

Kantees went quiet.

It took some time before they had the litter prepared, and longer—including several painful moments—before they got her round to the other side of the hill where Gally and Ulina had built the fire.

She had stopped talking since Yenteel's warning, and she could see almost nothing as she was on her back looking at the sky except the bulk of the *tekrak*. So she watched the clouds moving swiftly across the distant blue. Lostimal loomed large and bright, making one of its day time appearances. She knew the movement of the two moons was entirely predictable and Yenteel's device for predicting feedings.

Did knowing when a feeding would happen make it less wondrous?

When Yenteel returned he brought burnt sticks from the fire and set about placing patterns on her skin, where the damage was worse. He tried not to cause pain but he could not prevent it completely. Her sharply drawn breaths caused him to stop and mutter an apology.

Once the fire was built, Yenteel sent Gally and Ulina to fetch water. Kantees would have been worried if it was Gally alone, but there was not much that could withstand the child's wicked little blade. The thought did not give her comfort.

She wondered what Levin was doing.

Her drifting thoughts were interrupted by Yenteel.

"I'm ready to begin," he said quietly. "Are you?"

She did not want to speak so she gave the barest of nods. He nodded back with a reassuring smile. She closed her eyes and tried to relax, feeling the dull ache in her chest. She knew he knew how to do this, he had done it himself when he was at death's door—though it had needed Sheesha to provide the power to finish the task without him killing himself.

Yenteel's gentle chant filled her ears and her skin prickled, but not with pain. A golden light filled her vision behind her eyes as the power was moulded to the pattern of her body—the way it should be. Her ribs felt as if they burned, but again without pain. Yenteel's hands moved on her skin and pressed in.

That hurt!

Something moved. Shifted. Clicked.

Yenteel's chanting continued. In her half-dream state she wondered if the chanting was necessary. She did not chant when the *ziri* flew so very fast that the magic took them.

With her mind separated from her surroundings, she could not put a dam on her curiosity and the questions layered themselves one on top of the other. Why did no one know what the *ziri* could do? What was the *ziri* she had seen in the sky? Who were the Dunor and why did they want to kill her? What was the strange thing he had given to her?

Then her body filled with warmth and golden light, and she slept.

2 3

---

*T*he first thing she realised when she awoke was that she was cold and damp. Finally, she discovered she was hungry. Very hungry.

She sat up before she remembered that she should be careful. Her ribs on the left felt tight but did not hurt. The walls of the gondola surrounded her. Open to the elements, the roots of the great plant wound into the frame and the world beyond was grey with rain, which the body of the *tekrak* protected them from.

At the front sat the dark form of the patterner, Tenical, making his patterns to guide the monster. To the left she could see the darker grey of mountains. They must be heading north still, depending on how long she had been asleep.

There was a sound behind her and Gally appeared at her side. He sat on a bench and offered her a hunk of bread and a cup. He was grinning. She smiled in return; she had learnt long ago that his smiles were infectious—perhaps because they were untainted by the guile of most people.

"Thank you, Gally."

"Yenteel said Kantees want food when you wake."

"He was right."

"We have birds, Kantees," Gally said brightly. Kantees felt confused.

"Birds?"

"See, pretty birds." Kantees was already looking out into the space around the *tekrak* but Gally wasn't pointing there, he was pointing at a cage inside the gondola. And he was right, she could see moving flashes of gold and blue. They looked like the feathers of a *zirichak* but tiny—and when *ziri* hatched they were already bigger than these, but had no feathers.

But something else was bothering her. She looked towards the rear where Ulina and Yenteel sat, and frowned.

"Where's Levin?"

The smile disappeared from Gally's face. Kantees panicked. "Where is he?"

Gally pointed past her out towards the mountains. She turned her head and saw a diamond shape of *ziri* curving across the nearest slope.

She did not want to accept what she saw. Sheesha was at the head of the formation, with Levin on his back. It felt like a betrayal.

"Sheesha let him," said Gally in answer to her unspoken question. It seemed even Gally was not happy with the situation.

"Why?" she said to no one in particular.

"You can ask him when we land," said Yenteel. "But I watched him very closely. He did not force Sheesha—not that I can imagine any way he could—he asked politely. I think he's been trying that trick of yours."

"And?" Kantees could not keep the frightened desperation from her voice. How could she bear it if a Taymalin stole her knowledge? Like they always did.

Yenteel shrugged. "Nothing. Either Sheesha doesn't want to, or there's something about you. You're still Kantees of the Ziri."

She was torn. On the one hand she wanted to chastise him for using the name she hated, on the other she was grateful that she was important to the *ziri*. At least enough that they would not use their magic for just anyone.

And she should not be upset about Sheesha letting Levin ride.

After all, he was trained to take any rider. The formation swung in towards the *tekrak* and Levin waved to her. He was smiling. Her return wave was not enthusiastic but she did not frown. He was still using a saddle.

The day wore on and they covered a considerable amount of ground. She spoke briefly to Tenical, who explained they were following the original plan of skirting round the east then north side of the central mountains.

"Where did those birds come from?"

"Those raiders had them, they're *melinasa*."

Kantees looked blank.

"They're used for carrying messages—" and at Kantees' continuing look of confusion, "—you write a message and attach it to their leg, or use a harness. They can perceive specific patterns from great distances and can be trained to travel to them."

"Why not just use a patterner's path at a ley-circle?"

"Because ley-circles are few and far between, and sometimes you might not want others to be able to intercept them."

"Can we use them?"

He shook his head. "We don't know the patterns they've been trained for so they will travel to wherever the Farahalek intended. However, they are also delicious when roasted."

Kantees spent some time watching Levin working with the *zirichasa*. He tried various manoeuvres to see how the formation was maintained. To Kantees' eye, the *ziri* were perfect. They were all much the same size, although Sheesha was the biggest and they kept up with him and matched his every move.

She guessed Levin must have tried to achieve the great speed earlier in the day when she was asleep. He did not try it now.

The rain diminished, although the clouds were still wrapped around the peaks of the mountains. Eventually Levin simply flew along with the *tekrak* as it followed the foothills.

It was still light when they set down and Kantees felt strong enough to help with tying up the *tekrak*. Levin landed and lent a hand as well. There were few trees or bushes on the mountain slopes, but they had brought wood with them and built a fire close to the giant plant.

"How is it?" Kantees asked Tenical, nodding at the tear in the creature's side where the broken leaf covering was turning brown.

"It seems none the worse," he said. "New leaves grow out all the time and replace old ones which flake off. It was not badly damaged and it does not feel pain."

Kantees did not comment on the tremors she had seen during the fight, but she did not think he was right.

Levin came to sit by the fire while Gally attended to the *ziri*.

"I'm sorry I couldn't ask you," he said. "But Sheesha seemed willing enough to let me ride him. He is an impressive animal." He smiled. "I wish he had been mine."

All of Kantees' bad temper evaporated at his words, and now she felt guilty for even thinking them.

"It seems Kantees of the Ziri is the only person for whom Sheesha will do his magic."

Her bad temper was back in a moment. "Don't call me that."

"Yenteel said you didn't like it."

"I don't. I'm not that person."

"What person is that?"

She frowned at him. "I'm not a hero, or a leader. I don't want to be part of any story. I just want to live my life without anyone dictating how it should be." She took a deep breath. "I did not free myself from Taymalin slavery—*your slavery*—just to be caught up in a different one."

"I did not create the slaves."

"Your life is what it is because of slaves. People like me, Gally and Yenteel."

"I don't think it's right."

"What have you done about it?"

Levin went silent for a long while and stared into the flames. "You're right, but you are also wrong."

"I am not interested in your justifications, *sire*." Her final word dripped with sarcasm.

"You are right, I have done nothing about a system that I do not agree with." There was a momentary hesitation as if he were about to say something else, but he stopped himself. "But you're wrong about being a leader. Every person here is following you. And we have heard your name being whispered by the common people. If you wanted to escape into anonymity you are already too late. You were too late when you stole Sheesha."

Kantees stared at him. She wrapped her arms around her knees. Her throat hurt and her eyes dripped tears. "I don't want this." Her voice came out in barely more than a croak as she felt her plans crashing around her. "I only want to find a home."

Levin reached out and placed his hand gently on her shoulder. "I cannot stop what is happening. I do not have that power, I doubt anyone does, but I will help you in any way that I can." He glanced around at the others going about their chores—or simply staying away from the fire as she and he talked. "And that is the same for everyone here, I think."

"Why?" she whispered.

"They trust you and believe in you."

"I have nearly killed them so many times. I don't know what I'm doing."

He shook his head and smiled. "They are still alive and they are still here. You have not led them astray."

"I lost Daybian."

"And now you're going to fetch him."

"I'm always scared."

"Me too," he said. "Only a fool would not be afraid." He gave her shoulder a squeeze and let his hand drop. "I had a teacher once, I treated him very badly but he was always patient with me despite everything. He used to say that most people live their lives without attempting to achieve anything, and it seems like they are happy, but when they are gone there is nothing to show they ever lived. But then there are those who make decisions and force them to come to pass. They may fail but they pick themselves up and try again. He said that was the mark of a true hero: someone who made life obey them, instead of obeying life."

She looked at him and wiped the tears from her face. "I hope he said it better than that."

Levin gave a short laugh. "He did but I didn't listen well enough."

"You're saying I'm a hero because I twist the world's pattern to my own desires?"

"That's probably a better way of putting it."

She shook her head. "That's where it doesn't work because I didn't choose any of this."

Levin got up and stretched. "And I think you are deluding yourself, Kantees of the Ziri. Are you really trying to say that nothing that has happened has come from your choices?"

"That is what I'm saying. This is nothing to do with me."

"I'll give you some time to think it over, Kantees, but if you can give me even one thing that has happened that is not from a choice you have made then I'll accept what you say. Not before."

Her chest still ached but she got to her feet without his help. He was taller than her but she was able to hold his eye. "I don't need to think about it. It was against my judgement that we landed in a powerful ley-circle in the heart of Talamyrth where we were attacked by half-men, and nearly died of suffocation because a ward Yenteel created could not be taken down."

"I have not heard this story," said Levin, "but the Talamyrth is known for the evils within its borders. But tell me this: If you had told your companions that you refused to land there, what would have happened? Would they have deserted you and done it anyway?"

Kantees hesitated.

"No," said Yenteel from a short distance away. "Even Daybian would have acquiesced if Kantees had insisted we go on."

"But the *ziri* were tired, they needed to rest," she said.

"So you made a choice," said Levin.

"But then, of course, I am to blame. I always knew that."

Levin smiled again. "It's not blame, Kantees, it's leadership. Responsibility."

And with that he walked away, leaving her fuming powerlessly as she tried to think of something that was not her doing, her choice. And every time she thought she had something, his argument would sneak in under her defence and her decision was always there, lurking in the background.

It was as she suspected: Everything was her fault.

But they followed her anyway. Very foolish of them.

2 4

Three days later Kantees felt as if she was being driven mad by boredom. The *tekrak* made steady progress but it was so slow it felt like nothing. Kantees could have travelled all the way to their destination and back several times with Sheesha's magic.

She had even toyed with the idea that it might be possible to include the monstrous plant in the golden light, but of course there was no way to get it up to the necessary speed for the magic to begin. Nor any way to persuade Sheesha to include the creature in his magic, even assuming it was possible.

There was so little to do that she was driven to the black stone of Kevrey. She pulled it out and examined it again. It continued to reveal nothing of its secrets to her. She showed it to Yenteel.

"Have you seen a stone like this before?"

Yenteel took the stone and turned it over in his fingers. "Where did you get it?"

"My old master, Kevrey, had it hidden. He told me where it was as he died. I thought it might be important but I can make nothing of it."

"Where did you get that?" She jumped at the harsh tone of Tenical, who sat in his usual place among the cushions in the prow of the vessel, guiding the *tekrak*. It seemed it did not need constant attention but he remained at his station in case of emergencies. The attack of the Farahalek had upset him.

"It's mine," she said defensively.

"I doubt that," he said. "Do you even know what it is?"

"It's mine because it was given to me by my old master in Dakastown. And no, I do not know what it is, but you do so why don't you tell me?"

Tenical hesitated and the look on his face suggested that perhaps he felt he had already said too much.

"You cannot take it back, patterner. Levin said it looked like a trinket from Tirnia but that it would have patterns on its surface if it was. It's made of rock and yet it is perfectly shaped and perfectly smooth. This much I know and it is nothing at all. Yet you recognised it instantly from the merest glance. Tell me what it is."

Kantees felt the gondola move and heard Yenteel coming up beside her. "I am also very interested in what you think this is," he said. "And unlike Kantees, I am willing to force the answer from you."

"You will not," said Kantees. "Whatever Tenical has to tell, he will do of his own free will. I will not make another person a slave, otherwise I become Taymalin even though my skin is black."

Tenical turned to face forward and his hands moved across the patterns in front of him. The *tekrak* changed direction slightly, giving a mountain spur more room.

The patterner turned back to face Kantees.

"It's a focus of power, a reservoir of Mother's milk. Called a *chilafrah* in the old language," he said. "The talismans of Tirnia are a corruption of their design, not that any of them work. They are simply delusions for the hopeful and the hopeless. But what you hold in your hands is real."

Kantees looked down at the black stone in her hand. "But what does it do?"

"I have told you."

"I know that name," said Yenteel. "I thought they were a myth of the *Slissac* or, at least, lost with them. It is like a cask for ale, Kantees, but it holds power."

Kantees stared at the lump in her hand. "This?"

"If it is what Tenical claims."

"You doubt me?" said Tenical with a hint of irritation.

Kantees turned it over. The shape looked the same from all directions, it had no up or down. "You still haven't told me what it does."

Tenical simply tutted and turned away.

"If you have the skill," said Yenteel, "it can be used to make patterns. It is like the scrolls given to me by Lintha. They hold their power within them which is released when activated."

"Scrolls," muttered Tenical. His tone indicating contempt for such patternings.

"It was one of those scrolls that made the mist when we rescued you," said Yenteel. Tenical did not respond.

Kantees sighed. "It is of little use to me."

Yenteel stared at her.

"What?" said Kantees.

Yenteel put his hand over the *chilafrah*. "What you hold in your hands is worth a thousand *ziri*."

"Then I shall sell it," she said. "I cannot use it and there is nothing for me to use it for if I could."

"Keep it secret," said Yenteel. "If it was widely known you have it, everyone from the most ineffectual cutpurse to the armies of men will be happy to kill you to get something that valuable."

Kantees closed her eyes. "Everything just gets worse."

That night they camped between two peaks next to a fast-flowing river that tumbled down a ravine towards the lowlands in the north. Yenteel showed her on his rough map that they were approaching the west coast of Esternes along the north side of the central mountains. There was another vast forest, though this one was of pine trees with minimal undergrowth, unlike the Talamyrth to the south.

Levin had spent most of the day on Sheesha's back. Kantees did not complain since the *ziri* came to her as soon as the saddle was removed and licked her face. Sheesha was still her *ziri*.

"How long before we get there?" she asked Tenical and Yenteel, while Levin stood nearby warming himself and Gally fussed over the *zirichasa*.

They discussed it for a few moments and then Yenteel said, "Not tomorrow, but the next day, probably early. Perhaps by midday."

"And what is our plan?" She looked at Tenical.

"We were sent to capture Daybian of Jakalain."

"When you should have been after me."

Tenical shrugged. "I was simply driving the carriage. Lorima Hamalain was giving the orders until the mercenaries killed him. I did not want to follow him to whatever paradise awaits us, and they needed me."

"Unfortunately they already have Daybian," said Levin. "Otherwise I could have pretended to be him."

"What do the patterners at the circle know of the comings and goings?"

Tenical shook his head. "I do not know."

"Is it likely they would know anything?" She was thinking of the way she had pretended to arrive in the ley-circle at Dakastown. There had been no real surprise, people just assumed they hadn't been informed.

"At this end it is unlikely. They told me only as much as I needed to know."

Kantees frowned at Tenical. Getting him to talk was like extracting a splinter, slow and painful.

He must have understood her impatience and annoyance because he continued without prompting. "But there were guards at the other end, they were alert and there were many of them."

A new thought occurred to Kantees. "How many of these giant *tekrasa* did they have? And how many patterners were being trained like you?"

Tenical pointedly shut his mouth. Levin shifted to place his hand on his sword, and Ulina pulled her tiny knife from its little sheath around her neck.

"Stop it!" she said. "Put those away. Nobody will be forced to speak."

Levin looked at her defiantly but removed his hand from his sword. Ulina hesitated longer but returned the blade to its sheath.

Kantees turned her attention back to Tenical.

"Many," he said finally.

"How many?"

"I don't know how many *tekrasa* but there were twenty patterners in my cohort. I was the most successful," he said. "Some were simply scared and others could not grasp how to use the patterns."

Kantees held up her hand. "And how many *tekrak* travelled the patterner's path?"

"Perhaps one or two each day."

Almost to herself Kantees said, "And yet there has been little or no talk of them."

"Preparations for war," said Levin. "The Taymalin must be warned."

"The Dunor *are* Taymalin, Levin. Why should I care if your people kill each other?"

"Because if you did not care you would be as bad as those you hate," he said gently, echoing her own thoughts. "Kadralin slaves and peasants will be used as frontline troops. Nobody wins in a war, Kantees."

"We will rescue Daybian, then you can warn your people."

"And if I am killed?"

"Then I will warn them."

We might all die, she thought, *but we will pretend that cannot happen.*

"So, what is our best way in?" she asked.

They discussed their choices until the fire burned low and the stars were sharp points in the sky until they had a plan that would get them in, but they had little idea of what awaited them at the other end of the path. Whether subterfuge would get them to Daybian, or secrecy, swiftness or violence, they had no way of knowing.

And if the Dunor were really preparing for war, violence would be a road to certain death.

Kantees did not find it encouraging, but what choice did she have? She had made a promise.

2 5

*K*antees barely spoke to anyone throughout the following day. Some of that was because she had chosen to ride Sheesha and it was impossible to converse with Levin even though he remained so close behind.

The edge of the inland mountains turned to the south-east but they were still too far from the coast to be able to see the sea.

Being once more on Sheesha's back brought life back into Kantees. She did not realise how much she had missed it until that moment when Sheesha launched himself from the ground and his powerful wingbeats carried her upwards. The sloping grasslands and screes dropped away and there was only the cold air singing in her ears.

The other *ziri* fell into their usual formation with Waileth on her right, Looesa on the left and Shingul to the rear directly behind. She wondered how they decided on the pattern and how they maintained it regardless of how much she had Sheesha climb, dive, and turn.

She kept him flying normally. There was no way of knowing how much strength he would need tomorrow. It was bad enough that they would somehow have to persuade the patterners to allow *ziri* through as well as the *tekrak*. And then they would have to get back.

But that was for tomorrow.

She took the *ziri* into the mountains. She had convinced herself she was not looking for her people, at least not yet, but if she happened upon them in the hidden valleys it would not be a bad thing. After all, she had seen the golden streak in the sky and she knew what that meant.

"Kantees!"

She turned to look at Levin when he called out. They were just crossing a cliff from which a thin waterfall fell. So tall that the base was shrouded in mist, and where that thinned out she could see the rocks. There seemed to be no matching river flowing away.

Levin was still in his saddle. It seemed he was unwilling to trust his mount sufficiently to become a partner in flight, preferring to stay a master. Typical Taymalin.

But then Sheesha turned his head as well. Without wrenching Waileth's head with the reins, Levin moved out of the formation. Waileth turned and flew directly away to the side. Smoothly, as if it were planned, Shingul beat her wings harder and moved up into the place Waileth had occupied. No, not quite the same, slightly further back and out. She turned about to stare at Looesa, he had moved back and out as well.

Sheesha's interest waned and he looked ahead once more.

Kantees stared at Waileth's shrinking form, which turned so she matched Sheesha's direction once more. Then Levin turned her head back in and they approached steadily. There came a point where Shingul dropped back and Waileth took her place once more.

There was a plateau ahead, high and frosted over, and while no trees grew on it there was a hint of green. Kantees directed Sheesha to it and they landed.

Confused as to how she was feeling, Kantees slipped off Sheesha's neck and strode over to where Levin was undoing his straps.

Through clenched teeth she could only say, "What did you do?"

"I wanted to talk to you after the fight with the Farahalek, but I could not find the right time. I didn't want to when the others were present."

"What did you do?"

"I changed the pattern."

"You changed the pattern."

"Yes."

Kantees watched as he finally slipped off the *ziri* and his boots crunched into the coarse and frosty grass. She could not think of anything to say. It was as if she had fallen and was too dizzy to stand.

"How does Sheesha know what you want, Kantees?"

"What do you mean?"

Levin shook his head. "I don't understand you. You're not stupid, and you want to know the answers. Yet when it comes to the relationship you have with Sheesha you just ignore what's obvious to anybody who has been around you for any length of time. Sheesha knows what you want and he does it."

"He's clever."

Levin glanced past her, at the gold and blue monster. "Yes, he is. I've never met a stupid *zirichak* but he is cleverer than all of them. Perhaps that is why he's their leader."

"He senses my movements on his back," she said. "You wouldn't understand because you insist on using a saddle. I want something and I make a movement, he feels it and does what I want."

Levin reached his arm up and around Waileth's neck covered with its glistening orange feathers. It was so natural it was as if he did not even think about it. He put his head on one side, reminding her of how a *zatek* looked when it was trying to understand human speech. She suppressed the smile that tried to reach her lips.

"What about when we fought the Farahalek?" he said. "How is it that Sheesha chose to launch himself at such speed so low over the assassins that they were confused and we could attack and beat them?"

"Luck," she said, but so weakly she was not even convincing herself.

"Tell me you didn't think of it before Sheesha did it."

"I didn't…"

Levin said nothing but his eyes reminded her of her old master when he was chastising her.

It was true. She knew it was true. And all the times before when she had thought a thing and Sheesha had done it. Though in almost all cases she had been on his back there were too many for it to be any kind of coincidence. Too many for it to be simple interpretation of her body movements.

There was a magic between them. Just as Sheesha had a bond with the other *ziri*, so that he could guide them and arrange them in a particular formation around him.

"You are not wrong," she said very quietly.

"You are Kantees of the Ziri, in truth."

She wanted to protest but found she could not. It was almost as if she had always known, from that very first moment when she had seen Sheesha. Touched him.

"But I don't know *his* mind," she said.

"Why must it work both ways?"

"That doesn't seem fair."

"You care for him, he knows that."

She turned away from them and walked to the cliff-edge. The ground became rougher and more unstable. She stopped and looked out. The valley below curved away to the right and there were mountains in every direction. Their white caps glistened and a wind she could not feel ripped away the snow on their peaks in white streamers.

The sound of Levin's boots came up beside her.

"You worked all this out just by watching me with Sheesha." It was more a statement than a question. "Has anyone else noticed?"

"Yenteel, I would imagine. He was the one who named you, wasn't he?"

"He hasn't said anything."

"I believe Yenteel has his own plans, perhaps discussing them with you is not among them."

"I trust him."

"You have known him longer than I have."

"But you're not wrong," she said again, and glanced at him standing beside her.

He turned his head and smiled. "I've been right twice in such a short time. I am honoured."

She frowned and then smiled. "Am I really that bad?"

He shook his head. "I don't know where you get the strength to carry on. I can follow you but I do not believe I could lead these people."

She looked back at the wide expanse beyond the cliff. "What did you mean when you said you changed the pattern?"

"It doesn't make sense for the *ziri* to follow blindly," he said. "They are not like wolves, tied together in a pack so tightly they cannot bear to be alone."

Kantees had never encountered wolves but she knew what he was talking about and she realised he was right about the similarity and the difference. Wolf packs were bound by a pattern so completely that if one were killed the others felt it. They were more like a single animal, like a hive of bees. If wolves could have such magic then why not *zirichasa*? Only their bond was temporary.

"You dominated Waileth, became her leader once more. How?"

He shrugged. "We do it all the time when we race, don't we? Otherwise all the *ziri* would follow the dominant one. Once I remembered that, it was easy enough to put myself into that frame of mind and command Waileth to follow my lead instead of Sheesha's."

"He didn't like it," said Kantees.

"But you didn't mind."

"I was surprised, but no, Waileth is yours. I did not mind you breaking free."

"So Sheesha followed your lead and let Waileth go."

"I was glad in a way."

"Glad?"

She smiled at him. "It meant I wasn't responsible for you and Waileth as well as everybody else." She paused. "I don't want to be responsible for everyone."

"We've discussed that already."

She sighed and nodded. "So does Waileth understand your unspoken commands?"

"Unfortunately not. And nor does Sheesha as far as I can tell. That talent is all yours, Kantees."

Kantees turned and headed back towards Sheesha. The mountains loomed higher towards the heart of Esternes. Perhaps, in the depths of the mountains, there were those who had the same talent. Her people. She would find them.

After they had rescued Daybian.

2 6

At a height where Sheesha would be a dot against the blue, Kantees looked down on the ley-circle they had come so far to reach. The *tekrak* was still half a day out and she had come ahead to scout the area.

This circle was located on the surface, which pleased her, and backed by the rising slopes of the mountains. If they could get back through it, they would be able to retreat into the valleys and hide.

A short distance from the circle was a small town, barely more than a village, except there was some sort of fort on the other side of the river flowing from further up the valley.

Tenical had not mentioned that, but she was not entirely surprised. The ground around and between the wooden buildings, both within and outside a palisade, was churned up. There were *kichek*-drawn wagons moving and men busy on the buildings.

She had never seen a war, but she could see these were being constructed as barracks and that could only mean armsmen. Slightly further up the valley she saw oval shadows that she had taken for trees, though she now recognised them as *tekrasa*, seventeen of them. She knew just one of them could carry thirty men—she had seen it with her own eyes so many moon-turns ago. Over five hundred armsmen in that group alone and there was no telling how many more were being grown.

It was hopeless. How could they possibly get in, find Daybian and escape with him?

But no matter how hopeless it was, she had no choice. The idea of simply flying away did not even cross her mind.

She turned Sheesha and headed back along the valley. Gally also troubled her. She did not want to take him because of the risk, but she knew he would protest. After all, she had already left him behind once, and she doubted whether he trusted her any more.

But how could she take him into a place that he would not understand and put him in danger?

The alternative was not much better. She had spotted a small, isolated valley on her way here. She could probably persuade him to stay with Looesa and Shingul. It ought to be easier getting in without two extra *ziri* and a boy.

Except she might never return and he would be left to fend for himself. She did not think the *ziri* would abandon him but they might, and there was only so much food she could leave for him. Would the *ziri* feed him too?

The argument tore her one way and then the other, all the way back to the *tekrak*. She could not leave Yenteel. She needed Levin, and Tenical was essential. Ulina would be useful but Gally was simple and would not understand the risk.

The plan could work with him but she did not need the added worry. As Sheesha came in to land along the approaching path of the *tekrak*, she had managed to convince herself she would persuade him to stay behind.

Seeing her ahead, Tenical instructed the *tekrak* to descend and it dipped down towards her, coming to a gentle halt. Yenteel threw down a rope and Gally climbed down it. He hammered a stake into the ground and tied the rope swiftly.

The *tekrak* floated above and the rope creaked as it stretched and strained bringing the floating plant to a halt.

Gally dropped the hammer beside the stake and glanced at her.

She smiled. Why not? He had learnt these new skills for handling the *tekrak* and performed them very well.

"Kantees?" She blinked at him. This was one of the few times he had initiated a conversation between them. She saw him glance up at the gondola. Yenteel was looking out and gave Gally an encouraging nod.

Gally walked towards her almost deferentially. "Kantees?"

"What is it, Gally?"

"Do not leave Gally behind."

She opened her mouth but no words came out. She looked up at Yenteel, wondering if he had put Gally up to this. She looked back at the round face and wide, sad eyes.

"I don't want you to get hurt."

"Gally will protect you and look after the *ziri*. Gally can help with the *tekrak*. Kantees saw Gally tie the rope. Gally knows how."

"But I will be so sad if you are hurt."

"Gally will be sad too but Gally wants to help. If Gally goes with Kantees, Gally can protect."

His eyes were pleading with her and his voice almost broke. The suppressed emotions tore her even further apart—his desperate need to help, and the pain it would cause her if he died because of his willingness. Every word widened the chasm in her until she felt as if she would fall apart where she stood.

Waileth glided down and landed a short distance away. Levin removed his helmet and watched her as if he knew what was happening. They must have been discussing it behind her back. What did they think she should do?

What was the right answer?

Then she remembered her old master Kevrey. He had not been talking to her. He seldom did. But now she realised that she had been present in many meetings he had with his customers. More meetings than it seemed she should. So she could listen, and learn.

A high-born Taymalin had come asking Kevrey what magic he could use to make the right decision for his daughter's forthcoming betrothal, as there were two suitors and they were of roughly equal value. The question was, which should be chosen?

It was not the sort of thing Kevrey liked to be consulted on, but when one is known for possessing knowledge it was the kind of enquiry that came up. And Kevrey would answer, but he refused to charge for it, because it meant he had committed the visitor to a specific decision, and if it went bad Kevrey did not want the blame.

The problem was that, for some questions, there was no right answer.

In the case of the suitors her master had said, "If they are equal choose the one most equitable for your daughter." When there was no obvious right or wrong, he'd suggest choosing the one that felt the best.

"Gally," she said. He flinched and she realised she had said the word sternly. She smiled, reaching out to put her hand on his and soften her tone. "Gally, it would be an honour for you to join us in our adventure."

It took him a long moment to decipher her words, and then it was clear he did not believe them—or thought he had misheard. "Gally can come?"

Her smile broadened. "Gally must come. I need you with me."

Again the pause. Then it was almost as if he swelled with pride. And hugged her. Over his shoulder Kantees could see Levin, who smiled and nodded.

She detached herself from Gally and called up to Yenteel. "Are we ready?"

"You need to be up here, but yes, we are ready."

Kantees looked at Levin. This was the part of the plan she was least happy about. They would be trying to take the *ziri* through with them. She hoped the patterners at the gate would not argue. They had the *tekrak* on their side: anyone flying one must be part of the Dunor force, and it was unlikely the patterners would know every high-caste Taymalin who was a friend to them.

Yenteel and Gally were merely slaves, but she must play herself.

With some difficulty, she climbed the rope and hauled herself into the gondola. Climbing ropes was not a skill she had ever required. Below them, Levin, with Gally's help, transferred his saddle to Sheesha. He climbed aboard and buckled himself in.

Finally, Gally untied the rope, knocked the stake out of the ground and, carrying it and the hammer, made his way up. Far quicker than Kantees had managed.

Tenical changed the patterns and the fire-tube erupted, pushing the *tekrak* forwards.

Ulina simply sat and watched. She too had a task in this plan, although it was not killing. Kantees considered how ludicrous it would have been to leave Gally behind when she was taking a young girl along. Except for the little fact she was certain that, whatever happened to them, Ulina was the one best equipped to survive. Small enough to hide and ruthless in a fight.

It took the *tekrak* a long time to reach the valley but as soon as it was in sight Yenteel came over to her.

"It's time."

She nodded. This was the part she had been dreading: from this point on she would have no control over what happened. She became the victim as Yenteel tied her legs and hands, then—after a moment's pause—put a gag on her.

He had not tied the bonds so tight they cut off circulation or hurt, but they were firm enough to pass inspection. And she was completely trapped. Terror swept through her as she tried to move and her helplessness became even more apparent. Without intending to, she struggled against the ropes.

"Don't," said Yenteel. "Panicking yourself will not help."

Kantees would have dearly loved to tell him where he could stick his soothing words. That he was right just made it worse. She forced herself to become immobile and the panic faded to a nagging anxiety.

The *tekrak* turned north and into the valley. Yenteel moved to the side, looked over and then forwards.

"Well, we're committed now," he said. "They've seen us." He went to the rear and looked up. "Levin is in position above us. Those *ziri* look impressive."

They had discussed whether she should be blindfolded as well. She had put her foot down, and insisted she needed to see what was happening even if she could do nothing about it. But the truth was different because stuck here in the middle of the gondola she could see nothing of significance, only the hills sliding slowly past on either side.

It was frustrating and her wrists and ankles ached because of the way she had struggled.

If this did not go the way they had planned she would suffer badly. But Ulina was still there, sitting a short distance away. The child was the only one able to ensure Kantees regained her freedom.

The roaring of the fire-tube ceased and there was no sound but the creaking of the ropes. The *tekrak* descended. Gally gathered up a neatly coiled rope and stood at the side. Four shadows passed them on the right as Sheesha, Waileth, Looesa and Shingul flew down and past them.

This was dangerous. *Zirichasa* were not used as beasts for transport—they were only for racing. It was important that the name of Kantees of the Ziri had been spoken here. The name she hated would be the key to getting them in. They had captured her and her *ziri* to bring to the Dunor.

Gally threw the rope over the side and climbed out to descend it. She had seen him do it many times now but it still made her heart pound: *what if he fell?*

But he didn't.

The tops of wooden buildings a short distance away came into view. The *tekrak* stopped and, if all was well, should have landed in the ley-circle ready for the path to be opened.

She heard Levin raising his voice, angry. Yenteel got up and came over to her. "Sorry, Kantees," he said. He pulled her roughly to her feet and manhandled her to the side of the gondola. The ropes cut into her skin.

Below them she saw Levin with three patterners. They did not look happy and neither did he.

"That's Kantees of the Ziri," he shouted. "That's the one the Dunor have been looking for, not that sop from Jakalain. Now, do you want your masters to know that you kept their true prize from them?"

Kantees could not believe he would use such a weak ploy. But their options were limited. She had an idea and fixed her eye on Sheesha. What if Levin was right? What if she really could influence the *ziri's* actions? She tried.

Sheesha screamed and reared up, wings outstretched. The other three followed suit. The patterners jumped back and kept retreating. Kantees had seen Levin jump but he managed to hold himself together even with four angry *ziri* behind him.

"Get that path open, right now!"

---

*S*omeone went to fetch the chalk and burners.

Yenteel looked from the scene below to her face. He stared at her as if trying to read her thoughts, to see if the little show from the *ziri* had been something to do with her. Or she could just be imagining it in him.

Kantees settled Sheesha, who immediately sat back on his haunches and preened himself. The others followed suit. Kantees could not deny it, Levin was right, the *ziri* looked on her as their leader. If only she could understand how this worked.

"Looks like we're past the first turn," said Yenteel, making an awkward reference to *ziri* racing. From a standing start, the rider who reached the first turn in front stood a good chance of winning —assuming they had the staying power for the whole race.

The patterner novices returned quickly and set up the burners around the circle; the three patterners set to work marking out the designs needed for the path.

She had been through this process a hundred times with Sheesha. He would not be concerned walking the patterner's path, and she knew the other *zirichasa* had done it too.

Gally had taken a patterner's path and she had not had time to warn him. She doubted it would be any concern to Yenteel, even if he had never done it before. He would see it only as something of interest. Ulina? Kantees had no idea, but little of the world seemed to disturb the calm of the child.

Yenteel helped her back to the bench. "It might be easier if you lie on the floor," he said. "I could make you comfortable."

She glared at him.

"More comfortable, anyway."

She wanted to say no, to be alert for whatever happened. But the preparations for the path could take a while, and it was difficult sitting when she could not adjust her feet or move her hands easily. Reluctantly she gave an abrupt nod.

Yenteel found her blanket and rolled it up to support her head, then helped her lie down. "Better?"

She grunted her assent through the gag. Better perhaps, but still not good.

A patterner's path was a strange thing, invisible until you entered it —only the patterner who created it knew its boundaries. From what she had learnt from her many journeys and listening to patterners talking, each was unique. It was like a tunnel cut from the World's Pattern joining two ley-circles. The skill of the patterner who formed the path determined its length, not the real distance as a *ziri* might fly. The size, too, was dependent on skill but also what was desired. A change in the pattern could make one wide or tall or small.

She did remember one terrible journey where it had taken nearly half a day from one end to the other. Sheesha had become quite upset. Kantees might be experienced in making these journeys but they still scared her. The walls and floor of a patterner's path consisted of intricate and moving light but between the threads there was just empty nothing. An abyss of utter night into which she felt she might fall if the path should fail.

She knew that, in the walls, she was looking directly at the World's Pattern where it had been pushed and bent to the will of the patterner. That power in itself was terrifying, but what it was doing to the world seemed more so.

She hoped that these patterners were skilled and the path would be short.

It was possible that she dozed. She certainly had no idea how much time had passed when the *tekrak's* fire-tube burst into life again. From her position on the floor she could see even less, but it was easy enough to watch the clouds cut off by the start of the path. She watched the daylight as long as she could and then it was nothing but the abyss and patterns.

She heard Gally's voice. He was moaning quietly. They had not thought to warn him or be with him. Then there was Yenteel soothing him.

She could not see Ulina and there was no sound from her. Not that Kantees was expecting it. Levin should be walking the *zirichasa* through, probably in front so that he was not affected by the burning gas from the *tekrak*.

In their planning they had also discussed how the time of day would affect their arrival. Tenical was unsure how much of a time difference there was between the two locations. Those for whom it mattered—sailors and patterners—knew the world was round like a ball, and that the sun and the moons went around it. It meant that as the sun turned about them it was a different time of day in different places.

Kantees had never experienced it, since all the places she went for the races were not far apart. But the weather could be completely different, going from cold Jakalain to some place where the sun's heat bore down relentlessly.

But if the place they were journeying to was more advanced in time it might be evening by the time they reached it. Or early morning. Tenical had said that it was a large island and that the weather was warm. More than that they did not know.

She stared at the lights that moved just beyond the gondola. No patterner had ever told her not to touch the walls, and it would have been a strange rule since they must walk on it. She had reached out and run her fingers along the boundary of the path and the World's Pattern. She had felt nothing. There was resistance when she had tried to push against it, but there was no other sensation. No heat, no cold, it was neither rough nor smooth. She could not feel it at all.

She had never tried to touch it again.

And then they were out. The boundary to the real world slid from the front to the back and she breathed warm air, heavy with moisture and strongly scented with flowers. The sky wasn't dark but it was clearly either dawn or late evening.

Now came the second test.

This time they were forced to throw out all the ropes and, as far as she could tell, there were men below to hold the *tekrak*, perhaps even tie it off. She could not hear Levin and was reluctant to reach out to Sheesha since she had no idea what was happening, as that might cause problems.

Yenteel came and stood in her field of view but faced away from her.

"It's evening," he said quietly. "Clearly a place that is much warmer than your island of Esternes. No telling what biting insects and other nasties they have here." That was a cheering thought. "Levin is talking to the guards. They are cautious but relaxed, which is not surprising. After all, who would know to come here except someone who sides with the Dunor, and who would have one of these ridiculously huge plants except one sent out by the Dunor?"

She saw him turn his head towards the front. "Looks like they want to talk to Tenical. Gally they've already dismissed as being a dull-witted slave. Ulina caused some interest but a girl-child is no threat." How little they knew. "Oh, and me. I must go and pretend to be another stupid slave."

He moved out of her line of sight.

Moments later she heard the clatter of something banging against the side of the gondola and boots thumping up wooden steps. Armsmen peered over the side and then clambered on board. They glanced at her trussed up on the deck—Kantees realised she still had the blanket as a cushion for her head. Hopefully it would not matter.

They made crude comments about what they would like to do

with her but their only action was to check she really was tied and gagged thoroughly. They were not gentle about it. Then they searched the gondola but did not find anything. Levin had the *chilafrah*.

Presently, Yenteel came back and the armsmen climbed back down to the ground.

"One small problem," he said. "They insist on taking you off and putting you in their holding cells here at the ley-circle while the rest of us will stay in the gondola. They have a staging area set apart for *tekrasa*."

Kantees wanted to ask what would be done to feed the *ziri* but it was impossible. There was more stomping on the steps and Levin climbed on board followed by four armsmen, one of them a sergeant.

"There she is," he said. "She better not be hurt, and she'll need untying."

"You don't need to tell me my job."

"No damage, the Dunor need to understand what she does."

"You said she's not a patterner."

Levin laughed harshly. "Can't even read. But it doesn't matter. She's like an animal with a single power. What would you expect from a runaway Kadralin slave?"

Even though she knew Levin didn't mean it, Kantees glared at him. There had been enough comments like that at Jakalain from the staff and soldiers to make it hurt.

"Looks like she wants your balls for soup," said the sergeant.

"I caught her, and I get to take her to the Dunor."

The sergeant nodded. "That's been agreed, but our rules say anyone arriving late in the evening gets locked up until morning."

"Well, you'd better get going with her, we need to get this beast tied down and feeding before it goes to sleep."

The men picked her up easily, one at her head and the other her feet. The fact that an odd hand grabbed at her breast or between her legs went unnoticed to everyone else. Or ignored. They might have to leave her undamaged but that did not mean they couldn't touch the merchandise.

They did not drop her on the way down the steps, though it felt precarious. There was a short walk to a stone building. Doors were unlocked and relocked. By the end of it she was lying on a pallet behind iron bars that occupied one wall. The rest of the walls were stone and there was a single window high up. No glass and also barred.

They did not untie her as Levin had requested. She squirmed to get comfortable and wondered what she would do when her personal needs became too strong.

Although they had hoped this would not happen, the thought that she might get separated had been included in their planning. But this was not something she was in control of, and the only thing she could do now was wait.

She tried to sleep.

2 8

$\mathcal{H}$er cell was suddenly a great deal colder, and the light from Colimar made a barred red patch on the wall opposite where there had been none before.

The night time sounds of this place were unfamiliar. In Jakalain the winter nights were quiet except for the wind and rain. Summer beasts made more noise. While in Dakastown, as far as she could remember, it was the sea birds that dominated both day and night with their constant crying. And, when the wind was in the right direction, the constant rolling of the waves.

She could not hear the sea here, not above the cries, squawks and squeaks of unnumbered beasts, of a size it was impossible to estimate. Wherever they had been brought she knew they must be very far from Esternes.

But those had not been the sounds that awakened her.

"Kantees."

A small high-pitched sound. Ulina.

"I am still tied," Kantees tried to say but the gag muffled the words.

There was no further word from the child but the light of Colimar was blocked by a shadow as a piercing metallic sound sliced through the air. Kantees shivered, though whether it was the pitch of the sound grating against her skin, or the fear that they might be discovered, she was not sure. Perhaps both.

The sound went away and then restarted. Twice more until there was a crunch nearby. A small hand came down on Kantees' wrist, there was the slightest pressure and the wrist bonds fell away. Moments later her ankles were free too.

Ulina did not rush her as Kantees pushed herself into a sitting position using her hands, which had lost all their senses. She didn't dare attempt to walk yet. Kneeling beside Kantees, Ulina gently sliced through the cord of her gag. Kantees found even her tongue was numb.

As the circulation returned to her extremities pins and needles set in, then a dull aching pain.

"How much night remains?" Kantees asked.

"The guards have been long enough in their bunks to be well asleep but we have not lost much."

Kantees nodded. *Good.* She stood up with care, her feet were recovering but she did not feel confident on them yet. She looked around the cell. It was big enough to house twenty men at a push. The window Ulina had come through was far enough off the floor to make it difficult to reach, but there was a rope dangling from the sawn-off bars.

While she was aware of the magical sharpness of Ulina's little blade, it did not cease to astonish her how potent it truly was.

Imagine an arrow with a head that could pierce any hide? Or a sword so sharp no armour could withstand it? She shook her head. Perhaps it was as well such things did not exist except in stories.

"You go first, Ulina." She gestured at the rope and the child scrambled up so fast there was time to only draw a single breath.

Kantees did not feel so confident but the rope was knotted to make foot and hand grips easier, and she was no weakling. So it may have taken a little longer, but she soon squeezed through the gap Ulina had made and let herself down the other side to land on a path of soft soil.

The red moon was still the only light and its glow painted the path with the colour of blood, and the leaves of the plants that grew all around were black. The night creatures were louder out here, the air filled with scents. Some were sweet like perfume, while others reminded her of Sheesha's dung pile.

Ulina seemed confident about where she was going so Kantees just followed. Her extremities continued to regain their feeling and the prickling and pain subsided to a dull ache. She exercised her jaw, though it continued to feel as if the rope and the gag were still there.

They left the vicinity of the prison buildings, following first one path and then another between stands of tall black trees with dense shadowy undergrowth. Kantees smelled the *zirichasa* before she saw them. The paths Ulina had been following had been comfortably wide and lit by the red moon. Now she slipped away into the dark between the trees where it did not even look as if a real track existed.

Somewhere ahead a *ziri* snuffled. Relief spread through Kantees as she recognised Sheesha. She had not realised how bad it had been for her separated from him until that moment. It was as if a binding around her mind had been cut free. She reached out to him.

"Sheesha?" said Levin's voice quietly. "What is it?"

The dark tunnel through the undergrowth disappeared behind, and Kantees stepped out into a paved forecourt backed by a stone-built building of two storeys. The *ziri* lay comfortably around the space, a fire highlighting their feathers. One long neck was raised and the head turned in her direction. Sheesha.

First one figure and then two more stood up by the fire. Levin, Yenteel and Gally. She assumed Tenical remained with the *tekrak*. She was glad about that; she did not fully trust him. This rescue was for her and the people who chose to accompany her. For Tenical it had always been the lesser of two evils, and the repayment of a life debt.

He might consider that paid in full now. He could always claim Kantees had coerced him.

She went to Sheesha and hugged his neck. She felt his head behind, crushing her inward. He was as pleased to see her as she him. She could have stayed there forever, but there were things that must be done.

After unwinding herself she stepped up to the fire.

"What do we know?"

Yenteel opened his mouth to speak when the sound of a bell ringing insistently broke through the night-time noises. It was quite far distant, but coming from the direction of the prison where Kantees had been held.

"It seems they may have discovered your escape," said Yenteel.

Waileth, Looesa and Shingul woke up.

"Do we know where Daybian is being held?"

Levin took hold of her arm. "Let's get mounted."

"I need to know where to go."

There were shouts in the distance, increasing in number and reflections of torchlight reflected on branches and leaves.

Levin drew breath. "There's a castle further up the river."

"How long to get there?"

"Not long."

"Can we get in?"

"That's why we're here."

Kantees closed her eyes. They were attacking a castle they did not know, in a land where they would find no succour. *So be it.*

"Let us fly."

The sound of *ziri* wings pounding the air made her feel strong as they rose into the air. Around them the uproar was increasing, and as they gained altitude they could see the groups of armsmen crossing and criss-crossing the paths with their torches, looking for her. A larger group was making directly towards the building they had just left.

Kantees knew what she intended.

In the far distance, on a rise above a dark plain the castle stood ominously. Her heart pounded when she saw it; it resembled Jakalain in the shape and size of its walls. She did not know what that meant. She hoped it might mean the design was similar inside.

But that was not her immediate target. She wheeled Sheesha round and headed back the way they had come in. Shouts went up from below as their dark shadows went across the sky. Colimar might help them see in this blackest of night but it also meant they were visible to their foes. But that was the way she wanted it.

Kantees could feel the power of the ley-circle as they approached. She urged Sheesha faster and he obeyed. His wings pounded the air and the others strained to keep up.

She heard arrows whining through the sky.

Without warning, two monstrous black forms rose up ahead. Beneath them were two gondolas filled with armsmen clutching bows and aiming in their direction.

"Now, Sheesha!"

She did not know if they were close enough but she prayed it would be the way it had been at Kurvin Port.

It was.

Golden power enveloped them and the formation of *ziri* launched like an arrow into the dark. Somehow they avoided striking the *tekrasa*, and moments later were streaking at almost tree-top level away from the camp. And away from the castle.

Kantees could feel Sheesha's power. He was drawing his energy from the ley-circle at least for now. They had not practised any complex manoeuvres while travelling at pattern speed but she needed them now. They could not afford to get too far from their target.

She instructed Sheesha to turn. As she expected, the effect was not immediate but he banked slowly and, as she saw with a quick glance, the others turned with them. The *ziri* made a wide arc in the sky, and though she tried to keep their height low she was desperately aware that the last thing they wanted was to run into a hill or a tree.

Peering through the golden curtain that surrounded them, she saw the distant hill with the castle. Perhaps twice as far as it had been, but since they had been moving for so little time they would be able to make it there before the alarm was properly raised.

With their course directly towards the massive building, Kantees allowed Sheesha to increase speed. The ground was close but because it was dark she barely saw anything as their golden lightning cut through the air.

She barely had time to think of how best to manage their

approach before the castle was heading for them like a stone dropped from a cliff. She ordered Sheesha to slow. The glow faded shortly before they reached the walls. Kantees powered Sheesha up and over the main curtain wall. The inner wall was slightly taller, and there were armsmen rushing to their posts one way or the other.

"Yenteel, we need defences when we hit the ground!"

He said something but she could not make out what it was.

The design of the castle was similar to Jakalain and she could see the entrance to the cells. The main building had few lights but more than she was happy with. Armsmen were emerging from doors both in the courtyard and on the walls.

This would not be like Jakalain. Here they were the enemy and no quarter would be given.

And that was all the thought she had time for before the *ziri* came to a back-crunching landing on the flagstones.

29

*K*antees almost threw Ulina off Sheesha's neck and slipped down beside her.

"Kantees, let the *ziri* fight!" Levin's voice penetrated the sudden quiet.

It took her a moment to realise he was making sense. Even though she was worried for their precious feathers. "Make sure they don't get hurt," she called back before rushing towards the door to the cells.

She passed Yenteel, who was busy with something from his backpack, though she didn't recognise it. Gally followed her and came up behind as she reached the door. Ulina already had her little knife out and was cutting at the door lock.

"Ulina, just cut the wood around the hinges." Kantees pointed to the other side of the door. At Jakalain there were bolts on the inside of the door, just cutting the lock would do no good.

"My knife is too short to go through all the wood."

"Just do it, Ulina. Make it weak enough."

She turned away from the door and looked out at the courtyard. It was hard to see clearly. The shapes of the *ziri* towered like monsters over the armsmen who had come out into the courtyard before they realised what was attacking them.

Every now and then a *ziri* head would dip like lightning and there would be a scream. In among them, she saw Levin moving back and forth. His sword flashed. More torches were coming alight behind the windows and she could even see shadows of people looking out. Here she was in the heart of the Dunor and all she was doing was rescuing her friend.

But he and Levin together would be able to warn the Taymalin of the threat they were under. Get Daybian away from here and she would have done her duty.

"Done," said Ulina. Kantees turned to see Ulina jumping down from the wall beside the door. She laid her hand on Gally's arm. "Break down the door, Gally."

"Is that the good thing that must be done?"

"Daybian is most likely held in the cells."

"Like me and Yenteel. Like you."

"That's right."

Gally stared at the door for a moment and then threw his entire body at it. His shoulder crashed into it. The wood shrieked and splintered, then collapsed inward. It did not fall down but hinged on the lock side. Light spilt from inside, almost blinding her. Kantees knew surprise would prevent those inside acting immediately but even in the act of taking a breath she was slower than Ulina.

The girl was already inside. Kantees swore and followed even though she had no weapon, with Gally hard on her heels.

She burst into the room to see the first of Ulina's new victims collapsing to his knees. She did not have time to take in what the girl had done as a brute of an armsman headed towards her with a short sword in his hand.

He was not armoured, and from what Kantees could see of a table and chairs knocked to the ground they were still preparing to fight. The man swung at her wildly. She ducked beneath the stroke and closed on him. After years of shovelling Sheesha's shit, moving bales of hay and carcasses of meat, she was no weakling, but nor was she a match for an armsman.

But men had vulnerabilities. She flung her arms around him, smelling the stale beer that hung about him, and drove her knee between his legs. The contact was solid. He groaned, she felt his arms tense and he let out an agonised moan. The sword clattered to the ground. Kantees pushed back and away from him. She had no desire to kill him, she was not Ulina, but she grabbed up the sword. The hilt was slick with his sweat.

Something slammed into her back and knocked her breathless into the wall. She had no time to raise her arms and her face scraped the raw stone. Someone else cried out and she turned as Gally punched another of the armsmen in the gut. He folded and threw up.

Kantees wasn't seeing clearly but she knew the small blur must be Ulina heading further into the cells. There was unlikely to be any active torture at this time, or so she imagined. Even torturers needed to sleep, didn't they?

Keeping her hand against the wall for balance, Kantees followed Ulina further into the cells. If the design was the same as Jakalain it would have its confession area next and the main selection of cells beyond that. Barely ten strides brought her into the torture chamber with its vicious tools. There was no one here.

If they were going to put Daybian on the rack they would have done it as soon as he arrived, and that was—how long? She could not even remember, two ten-days? They would have either given up or he would be dead.

She prayed to the Mother he had survived.

"Gally! Fetch Yenteel, we may need him."

There was a grunt from behind her.

Kantees wondered if Ulina's little knife might cease to work if she kept using it to slice metal. Did patterns wear out? She had no idea, but Yenteel could open these locks, and even if he was not needed for that, his skill as a healer would be.

She passed through the empty room where even the brazier of hot coals provided only the slightest warmth, then moved further.

Ulina stood by one cell staring inside. Kantees hesitated. The child was a whirlwind, and yet here she stood still and simply looked. What could be so bad that it gave her pause? Kantees came up to her and put her hand on the child's shoulder. She gathered her courage and looked through the bars.

At Daybian sleeping on his side with his head cushioned by his arm. As if there was nothing to concern him. His clothes were dirty, and a little ragged, but in the dim light he looked unharmed. The usual arrogant fool that he always was.

"Daybian," she said quietly. He did not stir. Kantees lifted the short sword and poked it through the bars. She could reach his leg. She jabbed it. "Daybian!"

He jerked into wakefulness but disoriented. He rubbed his leg absently as he stared through the bars. His gaze slid from Kantees to Ulina and back to Kantees. Realisation hit him as if he had been doused with water. He jumped to his feet.

"Kantees, what are you doing? This is a trap for you!" Then he swayed and grabbed at the bars to steady himself. "Got up too fast."

"How can it be a trap?" she said. "How could they know?"

"That thing you did at the Hamalain circle."

There was a scream from outside. Yenteel came powering down the corridor. He stopped short as he saw Daybian standing there as if nothing was wrong.

"He looks fine."

"Yes," said Kantees. "Can you unlock the door?"

"You let her come," said Daybian turning on Yenteel. "Why didn't you stop her?"

Yenteel pulled a pouch from his pocket. But Ulina held up a bunch of keys.

"Better," he said, and checked through them until he found one he liked and slipped it into the lock. It clicked open.

"We need to get out of here," said Kantees.

"What army did you bring?" said Daybian as he stepped out, adjusting his tattered jacket as if it made any difference to the way he looked.

"No army," said Kantees. "Just the *ziri*. Come on." She turned away and jogged back up the corridor. Ulina scooted past her at a full run.

"Let me go first," said Daybian as they reached the antecham- ber. The sounds of screeching *ziri* grew and faded. Air blew in from the outside and whistled round the room.

"You're not even armed."

Daybian grabbed a knife from one of the bodies. "I am now."

Kantees put out a thought to Sheesha to collect them from the door. "Just wait, the *ziri* will be here in a moment." Right on cue Sheesha's massive head poked in.

Daybian looked at the four of them. "Did you get another *ziri*?"

"Yes, but it's got a rider. You take Shingul. Yenteel and Gally ride Looesa together again. Now, go!"

They tumbled outside into a maelstrom of wind that ripped across the courtyard, churning up debris and hurling it at the walls. The constant roar tore any words from their throats. The *ziri* were waiting to be mounted. Kantees caught sight of Levin pounding across the courtyard towards them. He looked as if he was shouting at them but Kantees could hear nothing but the wind.

Looking up she saw armsmen clinging to the parapet, unable to let go and use their bows. She knew Yenteel was not a great patterner and could not imagine where he had conjured this from— if it was him at all.

Then, without the slightest slackening, it was gone. The silence was deafening. Pieces of wood clattered to the ground. "Mount up!" she commanded. She was glad to see Daybian willing to leave and he was on Shingul's back in a moment. At least he was happy enough riding bareback.

It took Levin slightly longer to get ready. There were shouts from above, and the armsmen in the courtyard—realising finally that the storm was gone—were heading towards them at a run.

Kantees delayed as long as she dared, but when the first arrow shattered on the stones beside her she drove Sheesha and the others into the air. She knew she was too far from the ley-circle to launch the *ziri* to pattern speed but she took them up as fast as she could. They passed the parapet and she kept going up.

As soon as they were beyond bowshot range she turned the *ziri* back towards the ley-circle.

"Yenteel, do you have any idea where we are?"

"Based on the positions of the stars, the temperature and the change in time, somewhere off the southern coast of Karane. Closer to Mirriasmia than anywhere else, but not that much. Hundreds of leagues, I think."

Mirriasmia? She knew of it, she'd heard of the Thousand

Mouths. She doubted they would regain access to the ley-circle and persuade anyone to make a path before they were overcome by the forces of the Dunor.

Which left them with only one option: they must fly until they could find another ley-circle and patterners to take them home. But they must pick up Tenical first.

She did not push the *ziri*. It was going to be bad enough, later, trying to fly across an expanse of ocean where they had no idea how long it would take.

They flew on towards the ley-circle. Tenical should be there. If they could not pick him up he was going to try to get back to Esternes where he could disappear. Even if he was completely honest with the Dunor, the chances were they would torture him to ensure he was not lying. It was not an idea that appealed to him.

Kantees hoped he would be there, she did not relish waiting and searching for him when this entire place was trying to kill them. Lostimal was rising and its white light drowned out Colimar's red. Bright fires appeared and disappeared ahead of them, and it took Kantees a moment to realise: the air between them and the ley-circle was filling with *tekrasa*, dozens of them.

Sheesha and the other *ziri* angled upwards. They could easily outmanoeuvre the flying plants, but there were so many of them it was going to be difficult to avoid them all. Some of the masters of those *tekrasa* had realised her intentions already and were gaining height.

Kantees let the *ziri* slow even further and closed up the formation.

"Levin, you need to break free. We'll keep these plants busy while you pick up Tenical."

"Levin?" said Daybian. "Otulain?"

"Greetings, Jakalain. You are now thoroughly indebted to me for rescuing you."

"Is that your poor old Waileth?"

"My excellent beauty is as good as Shingul, sausage brain."

"Will you two stop?" shouted Kantees. "You can do this after we've escaped."

Levin gave her a bow, as best he could strapped into the saddle. "I will rendezvous with Tenical as we discussed." There was a pause and Sheesha shuddered as Waileth broke formation. The other two changed positions.

"What's going on?" said Daybian, perhaps realising that he was not in control of his mount.

"It would take too long to explain," said Kantees. "For now, just hold on tight. This is not going to be easy."

3 0

The white light of Colimar glistened on the edges of the leaves and veins that made up the *tekrasa;* even at night the deep green shone like a forest.

Among some of the gondolas she could see fires being lit. They would be for the fire arrows. There was no way the creatures could hope to match the speed or manoeuvrability of the *ziri* but they were pushing into positions surrounding the ley-circle, probably to protect it.

If any *ziri* attempted to land there, or anyone tried to create a patterner's path, the archers could rain death upon them. Unfortunately, that had been part of the plan to pick up Tenical. They had hoped—though it had been very unlikely—that they would rescue Daybian without setting off an alarm. In that event they hoped to escape the way they had come in.

Tenical would know they had been unsuccessful and now simply waited to be picked up. Though seeing the wall of *tekrasa,* would his courage hold? Or would he attempt to escape on his own?

There was no longer any time to think. Kantees launched Sheesha and the others in a long arc that spiralled in towards the ley-circle. She kept an eye open for arrows and it was not until they had reached the far side of the protection wall that the first ones buzzed about them. The accuracy was not good, but if hundreds were fired in their direction, some would strike.

In a moment, she ordered Sheesha to turn directly towards the ley-circle and dive.

The patterners controlling the *tekrasa* must have received training because they had formed a pattern in the air. It gave Kantees the impression of a reed basket, where each plant represented a crossing point of the woven threads.

It meant there were wide gaps between them, but all directions were covered and the gaps were all the same size.

The *ziri* swooped low and fast across the treetops then slipped through one of the gaps. There were *tekrasa* to the left and right of them and one directly above. Only trees below. The buzz of arrows increased and then cut off.

The bulk of the *tekrak* passed overhead and they emerged into the interior of the *tekrak* "basket". Kantees at once realised her mistake. Suddenly they could see every gondola hanging from every *tekrak* that formed the structure. And that meant every archer could see them and they were a target.

With horror, she realised that Levin would stand no chance if he dared enter this killing space.

Kantees wanted to use the power she felt tugging at her from the ley-circle but that would mean revealing her hand too soon. The air filled with the thrum of bowstrings. Before the storm of arrows arrived, she turned Sheesha almost on his tail, praying to the Mother that the others would follow fast.

She dived below the tree line and between the trunks so the leaves would hide them. Sheesha threaded his way through the trees like an embroidery needle. She heard ripping sounds as arrows tore through the treetops, as well as the occasional *thunk* as one buried its point in something more solid. She held her breath against the sound of a *ziri* in pain but nothing came. They burst from the trees and launched upwards, with only a small fraction of the archers able to track and fire at them now.

Kantees acknowledged the skill of whoever it was that had conceived the killing basket. And then she imagined it being deployed around a castle of the Taymalin. They would be able to bring it to its knees in just a few days. No place open to the air would be safe, and if they had anything more potent than archers they might even breach the inner walls without needing a ground force.

The thought was terrifying. Clearly the Dunor were ready to move and she was providing them with an opportunity to test themselves against a real opponent.

She turned the formation and followed the perimeter just out of arrow range as she studied the *tekrasa*. The ones higher up kept igniting their fire-tubes. The wind was probably stronger up there and they had to adjust their position.

A *tekrak* was not designed for manoeuvrability. All it did, when left alone, was launch itself into the air in the morning and follow its path across the sky with the others. She knew it was able to adjust the direction of its fire-tube a little, just enough to change course when it needed to—though how it knew what to do was anybody's guess.

Even when it was being used to carry people in its gondola, the way Tenical had been using it, there was still a single direction to fly throughout the day with very few changes in course.

What these men were trying to do with them was against their nature. Forcing them to fly at night, making them hold a position with delicate adjustments.

Kantees shook her head. This was not what *tekrasa* did, it didn't matter how huge they were. This was breaking their patterns.

Kantees sighed. Their *tekrasa* formation must be disrupted and she suspected there was only one way to do it. It did not appeal.

She whispered to Ulina as she turned the *ziri* in for another attack. But this time she had a plan.

Under Kantees' instruction, Sheesha turned in towards the ley-circle once more. He dived to follow a road that provided partial tree cover as Kantees tried something new. With an effort she pictured the *ziri* flying one behind the other. She could feel the resistance but then something changed and they altered their positions, with Shingul to the rear.

There were armsmen on the road but they fled or dived for cover as the massive *zirichasa* streaked between the trees. As they flew under the lowest *tekrak*, Sheesha launched into an almost vertical climb with Kantees hanging on desperately. Ulina lay against her chest. They flashed past the gondola and then the body of the *tekrak*. Ulina stood up with her feet on Kantees' stomach and launched herself into space. Kantees stared in horror as the child disappeared into the dark.

Sheesha turned in the air and flattened his course, taking him towards and under the next gondola in the pattern.

If only they had been well-equipped with weapons, thought Kantees, they could have given these *tekrak* something to think about.

The rain of arrows did not materialise, as she had suspected, but staying close to the *tekrasa* the armsmen were reluctant to fire in case they struck their compatriots.

Sheesha turned away and out of the *tekrasa* pattern. Kantees looked back to see the one nearest the ground looking very wrong. The gondola was lopsided and hanging down while the *tekrak* was pointing upwards. The fire-tube burst into life.

Ulina had cut the ropes at one end. They had been in such a rush to get the creatures into the air they had not bound the roots properly. It took time to weave the patterns properly, Tenical had always complained about it when she tried to rush him.

Then the gondola simply fell away and Kantees could see the roots writhing. Something must have interrupted the patterner— perhaps just the fact that he was in danger of falling. The gondola crashed through the trees and flames licked up from the on-board fire.

Released of its burden, and the patterner's control, the free *tekrak* shot upwards and struck the gondola of the one above, knocking it to the side and forcing it to roll. Taken unawares, men fell. But Kantees did not miss the tiny figure leaping into space just before it struck and landing on the top of the next beast over.

Kantees brought the *ziri* round. It would not take the armsmen long to see where the trouble was coming from, but Kantees was happy to let Ulina remove another one.

The first *tekrak*, perhaps in reaction to what it must consider to be danger, ignited its fire-tube and launched itself across the centre of the *tekrak* basket formation, the roots on the one it had struck were closing up. The upper structure of the gondola snapped and broke. This one fell much further and Kantees heard the screams of the men.

She closed on the one Ulina was now attacking. Once more Ulina sliced away the ropes and the gondola swayed dangerously. Kantees brought the *ziri* in close, expecting a wave of arrows, but the armsmen were either staring at the crashing gondolas or looking in terror at their own that was behaving as if it might go the same way.

Ulina threw herself off the top of the *tekrak* as Sheesha flew below. Kantees caught her and dropped her into her sitting position.

"Stay on course," shouted Daybian.

Kantees glanced back at him and saw him hefting the short sword he'd picked up. His eyes were fixed on the front of the *tekrak*. She nodded, though he was not looking. Kantees ensured Sheesha maintained his course and she watched as the sword arced through the air.

It did not spear the patterner, but the hilt struck him hard on the back. A shudder went through the *tekrak* as he lost his concentration.

Sheesha dived away to the right and the others followed. Moments later the third gondola broke free and crashed earthward. Three *tekrak* burned their fire-tubes across the ley-circle towards the wall of attackers on the other side.

Kantees, however, watched a *ziri* flying low and slow along the ground close to the ley-circle. It stopped and a man ran from the bushes. He climbed aboard and the *ziri* turned to make its way towards the gap they had broken in the wall.

On the far side, the *tekrasa* still under control had broken ranks to get out of the way of the freed plants burning towards them.

Waileth climbed to join them, beating her wings hard with the additional weight.

"Do you know which way we need to be heading, Yenteel?" Kantees called.

He pointed in a direction that was close to the ley-circle. Good enough.

Kantees felt Waileth rejoin the formation and they adjusted into a diamond shape. Kantees took them up a short distance and then turned towards the ley-circle. This would still be dangerous, as there were plenty of *tekrak* with armsmen who had not panicked, but nothing as bad as it might have been.

"Here we go!"

The *ziri* formation dived as one. Their wings pounded the air, building their speed. As they flashed into the gap made by Ulina, Kantees reached out to feel the power of the ley-circle.

"Now, sweetheart," she said gently to Sheesha. "Let us go very fast and very far indeed."

Instantly they were wrapped in a velvet envelope of gold. In a fraction of a heartbeat they burst through the other side of the *tekrak* wall. Kantees turned them upwards and they mounted the sky in a single breath.

The silver world lit by Lostimal was stained gold. Rivers reflected moonlight and flickered below them. Perhaps the place they had been brought to was not an island, but in their northward flight the ocean was not far.

Kantees adjusted their course closer to the direction Yenteel had indicated as they flew far and fast from the Dunor.

~ End of Book 2 ~

ISLE OF ESTERNES

1

Mist undulated beneath them. Or was it clouds? Was there even a difference?

They had long since slowed to normal flying speed because they were far from any ley-circle and the *zirichasa* were getting tired. They had been flying for too long.

Kantees shook herself. The difference between coming down through cloud, as opposed to mist, was that the latter would result in them ploughing into the sea. And that would be the end.

But they were all tired and thirsty; the sun had been on them all day.

She wasn't even sure they were heading in the right direction any more. But Yenteel was. Whenever she queried him, he consulted one of his devices and just pointed. "North and west."

Yenteel was a strange one, and she still had no real idea what his intentions were. He tagged along and helped with his limited magic, but he was the one who had come searching for her in the first place. Ultimately he was the reason she was here on the back of a stolen *ziri* having rescued Daybian from the clutches of a cabal of the Taymalin elite. She was not sure how she felt about that.

North-west was all very well, but how far did they need to go? They could not keep this up.

Perhaps if they just glided.

Her thought, by whatever magic tied her to her mount, became Sheesha's action. He stretched out his wings with a slight arch in them. The other *ziri* followed his lead as they always did. She glanced over at Waileth who carried Levin and Tenical. If they had had a chance to redistribute the weight she would have… no, there were too many of them and too few mounts.

Perhaps little Ulina with Levin, and Tenical with her. It might have been slightly better since Sheesha was the strongest. There was no way they could change now.

"Kantees!"

She turned to see Yenteel waving urgently to attract her attention, it was hard to make yourself heard in the air Once he had her attention, he pointed directly upwards. She looked to see the two moons, bright Lostimal and the smaller blood-red Colimar, hanging there, with only a short distance between them.

"A feeding?" she called.

He nodded furiously.

"Which way?"

He shrugged. Kantees sighed. What use was knowing when there would be a feeding if you did not know where it was going to be?

The moons beckoned her again. If there was going to be a feeding there had to be a ley-circle nearby, the *ziri* could draw power from it and fly fast, perhaps to the coast. Then again, just because the moons aligned, did that mean there must be a ley-circle at that place?

She did not know and it was too complicated a question to ask mid-flight.

Colimar moved a great deal more quickly through the sky than Lostimal and when they stood together in the sky the power of the Mother fed the earth with her milk. Kevrey of Tander had been obsessed over the question of whether the ley-circles fed the moons, or the moons fed the earth through them. She had been taught it was the latter.

She had travelled through them along the patterner's path. She had seen countless feedings and observed what the power of the milk could do to plants, creatures and even the stones.

Which, for Kantees, surely meant that there would be a ley-circle here. Somewhere. She looked up. The red disk of Colimar was touching Lostimal. They must be very close but all she could see was the mist.

She ordered Sheesha down and he glided into a spiralling descent. The others followed suit without being given any instruction, trying to hold the formation they naturally adopted. The other riders were looking up too. The air bristled with energy. Kantees prayed to the Mother they were not directly in line with the feeding. Nothing good ever came of that. The power of the feeding destroyed the patterns that composed all things, even being close to the feeding caused terrible changes, sometimes creating abominations.

It seemed the greatest power could cause the greatest harm. White light flickered to the side of them, perhaps a league away and towards the afternoon sun. Kantees turned and kept them gliding that way. A feeding did not last long but she did not want to be too close when it was at its height.

The brilliant white light flickered again. She brought her hand to cover her eyes as the power flashed on and stayed. Kantees urged to Sheesha to fly faster and he obeyed without hesitation. She felt the power surging and Sheesha taking it into himself as if he were a reservoir. She did not know if the other *ziri* did this as well. But it didn't matter.

The Mother's milk was now a vast pillar of solid brilliance. Sheesha was moving faster still. Kantees adjusted his direction to go around it.

Below them the mists boiled, churned up where they contacted the pillar of light. Through the roiling fog, Kantees could see the sea and the feeding going deep beneath the surface, dimming and turning blue as it went. Waves beat against the light and simply vanished. There was no backwash or rebounding wave as you might get if you splashed your hand in a water trough. It was almost as if the light was not there and the waves went through it but she knew that could not be truth.

Sheesha moved beneath her. He flexed his muscles and she knew he was ready to fly fast but something else caught her eye, deep in the water.

On that first day when she had discovered the magic of the *ziri* and flown out across the sea from Esternes, she had fallen in but had been saved by a huge ball-like thing in the water. As big as the castle at Jakalain, though it lay with just the top at the surface and the rest submerged.

Beneath the waves here, there was another one. She had no concept of scale but the brightness of the feeding illuminated it on one side and this one was completely submerged. It hung a short distance from the light.

When Sheesha had succeeded in rescuing her from that ball she had seen two *shocalin* in the water near it. They were legendary creatures supposedly wise and as sophisticated as people, though they lived in the water. And now here was another of these balls floating beside a feeding. Just as Kadralin and Taymalin both attended the feedings, even if it was in different ways.

The light of the feeding flickered once more and then disappeared. The world looked darker until her eyes adjusted. A thunderous roar erupted from below them as sea water poured into the space left by the light. A geyser rocketed upwards and soaked them all through.

"Go," said Kantees to Sheesha. Golden light burst around the entire group and they shot away. Sheesha folded in his wings and the other *ziri* did the same. Below them the mists reflected gold as they passed and the sun faded into insignificance in the beauty and power of their flight.

2

They crossed the coast and came a league or two inland to a place where a stream emerged from a wood, so that they had fresh water. From the air, Kantees had judged it to be less than a league across and the trees were not densely packed which she found reassuring. She had had enough unpleasant encounters with things that lived in forests.

The *ziri* settled quickly, worn out after such a long flight, even if magic had carried them part of the way. Gally and Kantees tended the mounts, just as they had back at Jakalain. Letting herself go through the motions that had become habit over so many years was relaxing.

Then as the afternoon became evening, they discussed what they should do next and tempers frayed.

"We can't pay for a patterner's path," said Levin, "because we have no money."

"We are three thousand leagues from home," said Kantees. "We can't fly all that way."

"Well, we could," said Yenteel.

"It would take a hundred days even if we didn't stop to hunt and rest," said Kantees. "We have to take the path."

"You think there's a city near here with a circle?" Levin addressed Yenteel.

"If we follow the coast we're bound to find one eventually," he said.

"So you don't know."

"It's a matter of certainties and probabilities."

Levin shook his head. "Either you know or you don't."

"We saw a village on the way in," said Yenteel. "If there are people, there will be towns. Somewhere there will be a big ley-circle and people will have built their homes around it. That's how you Taymalin do things."

"And the Kadralin are different, I suppose?"

"Of course. We live *with* nature; you simply use it."

Kantees stood up and walked away from the group. Gally had gathered wood. The fire was pleasant, the sky was clear and it wasn't cold yet. Perhaps it wouldn't get cold here. She knew that the weather stayed warmer the further south you went. It was another one of those facts she had picked up from her first master.

In those far gone days, she had thought she was being clever, sneaking titbits of knowledge. It turned out he had been educating her and she had not even known. But even so, she had very few skills that were useful. She couldn't even read. It was not as if she wanted to be here. Now that she had rescued Daybian, as she had promised she would do, all she wanted was to get back to Esternes and search for her own people in the mountains.

But they were stuck so far from there. Yenteel knew roughly where they were but Kantees had little idea of the world's geography.

"Do you mind if I join you?"

She jumped, she hadn't even heard Daybian approaching. It could have been anyone; it could have been some creature from the woods set to kill her. She shivered and glanced back at the shadows beneath the leaves and the moving lights of glowing insects.

"It's like the Talamyrth," said Daybian.

He hadn't said a great deal since his rescue—not that he had had much chance. But he seemed subdued, not at all like his usual self. Which could only be an improvement.

"No abominations trying to kill us," she said.

"Or suffocating protection spells."

She smiled, then realised he couldn't see it in the dark. She knew this was the point at which she should ask him what had happened to him. But she didn't really want to know.

He stood there beside her without speaking.

They were far enough inland there was no sound from the sea. But the night was not silent. Insects sawed and squeaked, hummed and buzzed. Every now and then there was a cry from some animal, then something the size of her head would flutter past.

"I—" she started and then stopped again. She did not like Daybian but he had sacrificed himself so that she could get away. "I am sorry about Jintan."

"He was a good *ziri*," said Daybian. "He was never fast enough to win any races but he was always willing."

"I never saw him race."

"You wouldn't have been impressed."

She did not respond. It felt like a criticism. Worse than that, it felt like a just criticism.

"I'll get you home, Daybian. I promised your parents I would. Like Jelamie."

"You found him? Taymar be thanked."

"Yes, not long after…" She broke off, not wanting to go to that place. "He had been badly treated by the mercenaries but he seemed all right by the time we returned him."

"You brought Jelamie back, just as you promised, and then you came after me. It seems you spend all your time rescuing the male line of Jakalain," he said.

"You helped me."

"I did. But I was captured, you were not. I wouldn't have known where to start without you."

"I'm no leader, Daybian," she said feeling suddenly hot and angry. "Do not try to give me that mantle. I won't wear it."

She heard him laugh quietly.

"Don't laugh at me."

"I'm not, really. But, Kantees of the Ziri, it may be a rag-tag group but you are our leader whether you like it or not."

She said nothing. She hated the name that Yenteel had invented for her. It was a strange sort of magic that had carried the name throughout Esternes.

Yenteel had ruined her life.

"And my leader too," he said. "Even though you refused to have a tumble with me in the hay of Sheesha's eyrie."

She smiled and looked down at the dark grass. "You are insufferable, Daybian of Jakalain."

"I know."

"I was worried about you," she said. "But it seems you are perfectly all right."

"You were worried about me? So you do care?"

"I only care that your parents might think I had brought back a substitute rather than the real thing."

"Good."

"What?"

"I may be back to being my insufferable self, but you are back to being irascible," he said. "Yenteel was worried."

"Yenteel can bury his head in a pile of *ziri* shit."

They both laughed at that. Then he stopped abruptly.

"They know about the *ziri* magic, Kantees. They thought it was me at first but then they got the detailed reports of what happened at the Kurvin Port ley-circle. Then they knew it was you."

"Levin's tried, he can't do it, and I told him everything I know," she said. "But he is able to make Waileth break formation. And I'm sure you could." She did not know why she was trying to placate his hurt pride. She changed the subject. "I found out who the Dunor are."

"So did I."

Kantees closed her eyes and berated herself for being stupid. Of course he had, he was there.

"They're in league with Tirnia," he said. "The emperor is powerful and rich; he will move against the west if he can, and what better way than if the houses are already fighting one another?"

"Then I suppose we must get away as soon as we can."

He laid his hand on her arm to stop her from turning away. "Don't touch me, Daybian."

He pulled his hand away. "I do not know this patterner, Tenical, can we trust him?"

"He controlled the *tekrak* that was sent to abduct you, but he fell foul of the mercenaries as well. I saved his life at the same time as Jelamie. He owes us his skill, though he does nothing from the goodness of his heart. He's from Hamalain, he worked for the Dunor but knows he cannot return because he helped us. He is here because he has nowhere else to go. Though without a *tekrak* to control I do not know what value he will be."

"Can he make a patterner's path?"

They returned to the fire where the argument was still in full swing without coming to any conclusion. And it was getting louder. She could not see Gally or Ulina, they must already be sleeping. The light from the flames flickered across the faces of Yenteel, Tenical and Levin.

"I think you will only have to raise your voices a little bit more to be heard in Esternes and then someone will come to fetch us home," said Kantees. They fell silent. "Tenical, can you create a patterner's path?"

"It's not that simple."

She put her hands on her hips. "I did not ask if it was simple, I asked if you can do it."

"It's not like dropping a plank over a stream to cross it. It takes concentration and you must know the pattern of the circle you're trying to reach."

"So, you know how to do it?"

He looked up at her from where he sat beyond the embers. "Yes, I know how."

"That means we can find a circle, you can conjure the path, and we can cross back to Esternes."

"You don't understand," he said. "I only know one circle in Esternes."

"We only need one."

"But it's Watching Pass."

Kantees shook her head. "That doesn't matter, we'll be coming out of it and flying away as fast as we can." Tenical did not look convinced but he didn't argue. "All that remains is finding one to start from." She looked at Yenteel. "I don't suppose you have a forbidden device capable of locating ley-circles?"

"I have never even heard of such a thing."

There was a movement from Tenical. Kantees looked at him. "Is there such a thing?"

"No."

She let it go. She wasn't sure she believed him but even if there was a device that could locate ley-circles, they did not have one.

"How big does the circle have to be for you to make a path?"

"The more potent the circle the easier it is. If I try to use a weak one we could be on the path for many ten-days"

Yenteel leaned in towards Tenical. "Does anybody know why circles are different in size and potency?"

"No."

"It doesn't matter, Yenteel. And you should stop baiting Tenical, he's helping us."

"As you wish, Kantees of the Ziri."

She glared at him then took a deep breath. "Well, we have a plan then. We'll follow the coast, ask at a village to find out where the nearest ley-circle is. Once that part is done we will determine how we may best arrange it for Tenical to make the path. And then we are back in Esternes."

"You make it sound simple," said Levin.

"I didn't see you helping," said Daybian.

"At least I didn't get myself captured."

"Shut up, both of you," said Kantees. "The *ziri* have better manners. I'm going to sleep now and I expect the rest of you to do the same. We need to be fresh in the morning."

"What about a watch?" said Levin. He had never adopted the practice of sleeping under his *zirichak*'s wing like the rest of them.

"Sheesha will warn us," said Kantees and headed to where the big animal was curled up in its feathers. He lifted his wing when she pushed at him and she dug inside, finding Ulina already asleep. Kantees curled up and breathed in Sheesha's scent as the wing came down and she went to sleep almost immediately.

3

———————

The sun glowed through a misty dawn. Only the peaks of low hills to the north were visible, and the sky was blue only directly above their heads. In every other direction it was just grey.

Kantees had to let the *ziri* go off on a hunt first thing because they had not eaten properly for a couple of days, but then neither had the any of them. In the past at least one of the *zirichasa* would have stayed behind, but on this occasion they all went. Gally gathered the riding gear that Levin used and set about cleaning it. He was happiest when he was doing those tasks he had grown up performing.

Yenteel took Ulina down to where the water pooled and reeds grew up in the bank. Kantees went with them, leaving the three Taymalin to glower at each other. They had their specific skills but were as useless as she was at living in the wild, but she was willing to learn.

Ulina wouldn't lend Yenteel her little knife but was happy to use it to slice through the thick reeds and help trim them into half a dozen simple spears.

"Just being cautious," he said.

Once they returned, Kantees tended the fire. The embers were still hot so despite the damp in the air, and the layer of wet covering everything, it wasn't long before the flames were licking upwards once more.

Yenteel and Ulina returned with a dozen silver-bodied fish.

"That was quick," said Kantees.

Yenteel glanced at Ulina. "It wasn't me," he said. "The girl has a very sure eye and a steady hand."

Kantees poked the fire with a stick and sent up a cloud of sparks. They all knew there was something odd about Ulina and her murderous skills. All except Daybian, she realised, and then wondered whether she should warn him. It didn't seem right that she might have to warn a grown man against the cold way a child could deal death.

She did not think he was at risk. Ulina was not random in her violence, thus far it had always been aligned with Kantees' needs. She and the child had made a pact, Kantees had promised the girl she could stay, but Ulina had not promised anything in return. Protection was not what she needed, it was care.

Thankfully Yenteel seemed to know what he was doing with the fish. He had apparently gutted and cleaned them back at the river.

Something moved in the mist. Kantees stood up so suddenly the dark shape skittered away and was lost.

"Levin! Daybian! Tenical?"

They emerged from the mist. Gally was still by the fire but looked up at her worried tone.

"Gally is here, Kantees."

"There's something in the mist," said Kantees. "Stop cleaning, get on your feet."

"Not finished, Kantees. Gally wants to finish and make it shiny for Lord Levin."

"Lord Levin doesn't mind, Gally," said Levin. "Do as Kantees says. She knows what's best."

Daybian had lost the sword he'd picked up at the island but he picked up one of the branches they had cut for the fire in one hand and a reed spear in the other. Levin had his sword. Tenical just drew closer to the fire. He looked up at the sky where the sun was now a bright spot well above the horizon.

"Shouldn't this mist have lifted with the day?" he said to no one in particular.

Daybian kept looking round at the moving shapes. "Are those big *chakisa*? Or very tiny *nachasa*?"

"This is not the time to be funny. I couldn't tell but they're bigger than the ones back in Jakalain," said Kantees.

"Bad beasts bit the Lord that Gally found," said Gally. "They ate him!"

"Tenical, Yenteel, can't you do something?"

The mist seemed to cling now and it was still cold. Ulina came up and grabbed hold of Kantees' shirt, but she had drawn her little dagger and was holding it with a steady hand. Tenical didn't say anything, he was not a brave man. Kantees was not sympathetic.

"We need to build up the fire," she said.

Levin moved forward suddenly and swiped with his blade. Something screeched in pain but Kantees could see nothing through the mist, she even thought it might be getting darker. Above them the blue they had been able to see was turning grey.

With Ulina's help they piled all the wood on the fire, but made sure to leave space for it to breathe.

Out in the mist a bird-like chirrup sounded. Then another. The sound did not echo but fell flat within the dank mist. The chirrups sounded from behind and to the sides.

"We're surrounded," said Tenical, his voice wavering and uncertain. He backed as close as he could get to the fire without burning.

Daybian reached back and replaced his branch with one that was burning. He pulled another from the fire and handed it to Levin.

"Thanks."

Kantees stared into the convenient grey mist. "People can do magic," she muttered. "Animals *are* magic."

The chirruping was increasing in speed and intensity, it was enough to drive you mad if you listened to it long enough. The animals were doing this. They were making the fog—so thick now even the fire seemed to be dimming while Levin and Daybian were just grey shadows.

She saw the shape that was Daybian duck and then rise up as

another shadow emerged through the fog. They impacted and Daybian heaved upwards. It was difficult to tell what trajectory the incoming shape had been on, but now it flew up over the fire, over Kantees and Ulina, and landed with a thud—and a sudden exhalation of breath—on the grass. Moments later it squealed and the chirruping hesitated.

Kantees could no longer see it in the dark but it had been hurt and the others had noticed too.

The chirruping started up again. Slower now but building. Kantees wiped the dampness from her face. On a whim she tasted it. Nothing, it was just water.

Whatever these beasts were, it was clear they surrounded their prey and could create a fog so the victim could not see. Frozen in place, too afraid to move because it was surrounded and blinded, it would become dinner in no time at all.

A perfect trap for creatures that did not think.

"Ulina, take my hand." Their fingers intertwined. "Put your dagger away. Stay with me."

"But I cannot defend you."

"It'll be fine. Levin, Daybian, close in together, I'm coming to you. Say something so I don't miss you." The fog was so solid now that almost no light was getting to them. "Gally, look after Tenical, both of you come close. Stay together."

"What do you want me to say?" said Daybian. "I was always the most incompetent at extemporising a poem and I can't hold a tune—"

He stopped as Kantees grabbed his arm. "Gally? Levin?"

"I'm here," said Levin in her ear.

"Gally has Tenical, Kantees."

"We're going to run," said Kantees. "Fast, and all together. Ulina, get on my back."

The girl climbed up then clung to Kantees' neck with her legs wrapped around her middle. She weighed so little that, with the tension and excitement, Kantees barely noticed at all.

Kantees reached out and grabbed Daybian's coat. "Gally and Tenical, hold on to Yenteel, and hold hands." It took a moment but they finally connected. "Levin, you go first. Use your sword. Daybian, you hold on to him."

"Anyone not holding someone else?" Silence. "Go."

Daybian's coat was almost ripped from her hands as he started off, but she clung on and moved, seemingly dragging Yenteel with her, knowing that Tenical was at the rear. To be honest she considered him the least useful.

For a few moments they wobbled together through the mist. She wanted them to run but it was impossible to go fast when they could not see the terrain and they had to keep a firm hold.

They hurried through the chirruping beasts, time slowed, the creeping fear that she had been wrong seeped into her. Then she heard Levin whoop and the scream of a beast. The chirruping faltered as she burst out into bright sunshine. She released Daybian's hand and stumbled forwards. Gally still clung to her back but within three or four steps they were all out of the fog. Another animal screeched in pain. There was a thud and she turned to see Daybian lifting his still-burning branch from the back of a four-legged creature that resembled a small wolf except its fur was covered in black and red blotches of colour.

The head had a wide mouth and a lot of teeth. But the intense noise of their attack had faded and as Levin and Daybian laid into the creatures—at least two dozen of them—they turned tail and fled into the fog. Ulina slipped from her back and had her dagger out but nothing came their way.

The fog itself thinned quickly and evaporated into nothing. Leaving their camp just as it had been as the sun was coming up. The beasts must have disappeared into the woods.

Kantees shook her head. "I am not camping beside trees ever again. There's never anything good that comes out of a wood."

"I'll fetch the food," said Yenteel and went back towards their camp with Daybian and Gally.

Levin turned to her. "How did you know what to do?"

"We're not animals," she said. "We don't have to wait frozen in fear, in the dark. We can fight back. We can move."

She sat down where she was and lay back so the sun could warm her.

Until a shadow fell across her face and she looked up. Tenical.

"I am sorry I could not help."

"It doesn't matter," said Kantees and closed her eyes again. She didn't need him pouring out his remorse. She simply was not interested.

But the shadow persisted. She opened her eyes again.

"What do you want me to say?"

"When I failed before people were not kind."

"I'm not kind," she said, "but you are doing a good job of flogging yourself. You don't need me to do it for you."

He didn't go away but stood there blocking the sun. She sighed and got to her feet so she could at least look him in the face properly.

"What do you want me to say?" she repeated. "Do you want me to say that you failed and that you do not deserve to have any dinner?" She turned away. "Is there any chance we could break our fast, Yenteel, are those fish still alright?"

He looked up from the new fire he was trying to start. "Some insects got at them but they're edible."

Kantees turned back to Tenical and shook her head. "Without you we couldn't have rescued Daybian. You've done as much for us as we have for you. It would have been useful if you had been able to help us with those … things, but Ulina didn't help, neither did Gally, or Yenteel."

He bowed to her in the way of the Taymalin. "Thank you for your gracious kindness, Kantees of the Ziri."

"Don't call me that. There's nothing special about me."

He met her eye and raised a brow. "How long will you deny a truth that is obvious to everyone else?"

"As long as it takes for everyone else to stop deluding themselves," she said.

Ulina came up holding a piece of fish in a large leaf. "Yenteel wants you to have the first piece," she said.

"Does he?" said Kantees. "Am I testing it in case it's poisonous?"

A shocked expression crossed the child's face and she stared at the fish. Then she broke a piece off the side and stuffed it into her mouth.

"Ulina, no!"

But it was too late. The girl swallowed the fish. Kantees grabbed the leaf off her just in case she decided to try more of it, if it didn't kill her this time.

"Tastes good," said Ulina. "Would a poisonous thing taste nice?"

"Probably," said Kantees.

"What's wrong?" said Yenteel. "Wouldn't Ulina give you the fish?"

"I suggested it might be poisonous," said Kantees. "So she ate some to test it. And that's your fault, Yenteel."

"My fault? How?"

"Because you're the one who called me Kantees of the Ziri. You're the one who's trying to turn me into something I'm not. And that makes people sacrifice themselves. And *that* makes it your fault. Did you ever think of that?"

"People make their own decisions, Kantees."

"You feed them lies and manipulate them. If they do something crazy because of it then you are the cause."

He looked at the ground but she could tell by the way he held himself he was not giving in. He looked back up at her. "Who has the ability to communicate their desires to the *ziri*? Who can make the *ziri* fly faster than an arrow?"

She kept her mouth stubbornly shut.

"Name me one person who can do that who is not *you*, Kantees, and I will gladly take back the name I have given you."

"You have to agree it's a legendary name," said Daybian who, it seemed, had wandered up behind her. "Better than Kantees of the Shit Shovel."

"It's not me," she said weakly. "It's Sheesha."

"Just let me know when you find someone else who can do it," said Yenteel and he stalked back to the fire. "The rest of the fish is going to be overcooked now."

With the argument apparently concluded Tenical and Daybian moved away to talk to Levin, leaving Kantees with Ulina, and Gally lurking behind her. Kantees went down on one knee in front of Ulina.

"Are you feeling alright?"

"I don't think it was poisonous, Kantees."

"Don't ever do that again, Ulina," she said gently. "I swore I would look after you and I can't do that if you're going to taste my food in case it's poisonous."

"You didn't swear to protect me, Kantees," said Ulina. "You said you would stay with me until I wanted to leave or one of us died."

"Gally will protect Kantees and Ulina."

Kantees looked into the face of Galiko, so sweet, innocent, open and honest. Where she was deceitful and unwilling to let anyone get close to her.

"Thank you, Gally, but if I am truly Kantees of the Ziri, then it is I who should protect you."

"I am not dead, Kantees."

She smiled. It was a sad smile, but it was genuine. Gally could always make her smile. Ulina took a step forward and put her arms around Kantees who returned the gesture. And then Gally grabbed them both and squeezed. As his weight bore down on them Kantees felt herself overbalancing and she crashed to the side with Ulina still in her arms and Gally on top of them both.

From nowhere laughter exploded from her and she could barely breathe. Ulina was giggling and Kantees could feel the thump-thump of Gally's breathless laugh. Kantees let go and rolled away from them, still laughing.

A shadow moved across her. "That looks like fun, can I join in?" said Daybian. He was holding something in his hand.

"You Taymalin have no sense of humour," she said through the mirth.

"Oh, really?" he said and squatted down beside her. "No sense of humour?" He moved suddenly and she found her mouth full of fish. The shock of it made her breathe in and the fish went deeper. She choked on it and rolled over, coughing and spitting it out.

A blur of something went past her as she coughed again and pieces of fish hit the grass.

"Ow! Ow!" There was a short pause and then another cry of pain from Daybian.

She heard Levin laugh.

Her throat ached but seemed to be clear of fish. Looking up, she saw Daybian lying on the ground face down. Ulina was standing on his back with one foot on his neck. Kantees was glad to see she did not have her little knife in her hand.

Gally was beside her and helped her to her feet. She coughed again but nothing came up.

She thought of a dozen things to say to Daybian but none of them were polite and, it seemed, none of them needed to be said. Ulina looked in her direction and Kantees gave a little wave to indicate she should get off him.

Daybian gave another grunt of pain as Ulina did something to his neck with her foot, then she stepped off. Kantees leaned on Gally even though she did not really need to, just so he felt useful.

"You need—" She stopped, her voice was grating and it hurt to talk, but she wasn't going to let him get away without some comment. She cleared her throat. "You need to work on that sense of humour, Taymalin."

She went to the fire and sat down. Yenteel offered her some more fish.

"I've had enough," she said.

4

"I'm sorry," said Daybian.

The *ziri* had returned and now needed to rest after gorging themselves on whatever it was they had found. With them back, Kantees doubted they would have to worry about any further attacks from the fog-making creatures. None of them had ever heard of such a thing, let alone have a name for them.

It was strange encountering something like that. She was reminded of wolves but these creatures were smaller and they made noise, which wolves did not. Wolves moved like a single entity, always as if they had a single mind. She did not get that impression from these creatures. The only real similarity was that they clearly hunted in packs. 'Fog-wolves' was the name she decided on.

But even that seemed strange. It was not like the old names they usually used. They had no old name for these. But then, neither did wolves.

"Are you listening? I said I was sorry."

"Yes, I heard. I accept your apology."

"You know I didn't mean to hurt you."

"No, of course not."

"Am I forgiven?"

"Honestly Daybian, I don't care. You did something unintentionally stupid, and I paid the price. How is that different from anything you've done before with your life?" She regretted saying it the moment the words left her mouth.

She could feel the words cutting in to him and the pain they caused.

"I'll go."

"No, wait."

"You have more insults for me? Yes, of course, Kantees of the Ziri, allow me to stand here while you cut my heart out. Better still, hand me the knife and I'll do it myself. Will that be satisfactory?"

Kantees closed her eyes and sighed. "I am the one who should be apologising to you."

"May I suggest, instead, that we put it all behind us and start fresh? I'll stop apologising to you and you can do the same?"

"Yes," she said. "That seems like a good plan."

"Good."

Kantees took a deep breath. It was all very well talking about putting it behind them. The act of doing so was something else completely. But she would try.

"I have a plan for getting through the ley-circle at Watching Pass," she said.

"You do?"

"It's the same thing I did when I was at Dakastown, but in reverse."

"Is that where you met Levin?"

"Yes."

Daybian hesitated. "Do you like him?"

"Like him?"

"You know, *like* him."

"He's got more sense than you," said Kantees. "I like that in him."

"Oh."

Kantees gave her head a slight shake, she knew what this was about. With Daybian it was always about him. "But no, not in any special way."

"Good."

"I still have no interest in you either."

"I'm sure I'll be able to change your mind on that."

"You won't."

"We'll see."

"Yes, we will. Nothing is going to happen between us, Daybian, not soon and not ever. It would be best if you accepted that." She took a deep breath, she needed to get off this subject. "I want to go over this plan and I want you to tell me what's wrong with it. Can you do that?"

"Criticise something you've said? Yes, I think I know how to do that."

They were on their way again. Yenteel had landed at a fishing village and asked the way to the nearest ley-circle. The villagers, it turned out, had no idea but they did know the nearest market town.

"I could barely understand a word they were saying," said Yenteel when they stopped a short distance further on, and not beside a wood. "And it was mutual."

"But they were Kadralin," said Kantees. "I saw them."

"Language changes," said Yenteel. "My master warned me about that. From what he said, it's a miracle we could communicate at all."

"And who is your master?" said Kantees. "That is something you've failed to mention over the last few ten-days."

"I am not permitted to tell you."

Kantees knew there was no point trying to force the information from him but that did not stop her from getting angry again. All they did was try to manipulate her. At least no one would have heard of "Kantees of the Ziri" this far from Esternes.

She did not push their mounts. She could tell Sheesha was still very tired after their escape from the island.

To the north, there were mountains, she could not tell how far they were but only the upper slopes and snow-capped peaks were clearly visible. The lower reaches were lost in a haze of blue.

It was so hot. There had been five-days in Jakalain when the sun had made the stone of the castle too hot to touch but those periods never lasted very long. But this was the kind of place where the sun was hot all the time.

The grasslands beneath them undulated gently and rivers wound through the terrain like bright blue ribbons. Trees were few except where they clumped into woods along the rivers. But it was not a wilderness. The plains were teeming with life. Herds of unidentifiable grass-eaters cut swathes through the waving grass. They resembled the *lukisa* but had horns. The group flew over a lake where the shallow waters were white with birds.

There was plenty for a hungry *ziri* here but no cliffs, or Ziri Tower, to make an eyrie.

They kept the sea in view to the southwest but did not try to follow it as the coast thrust out for leagues and then curved back in to form bays where rivers poured into it.

"There!" shouted Yenteel suddenly. Kantees realised she had almost fallen asleep, not that Sheesha would have let her fall. She looked where he was pointing. Several leagues ahead, a pinnacle of rock lanced from the ground as if it was some sort of giant needle piercing a green cloth.

"Now that would be a place for *ziri* to live," Kantees said to no one in particular. The tower they were approaching was considerably taller than a Ziri Tower, though.

"Is that where we are heading, Yenteel?"

"Taymar's Shaft."

Kantees stared at him across the gently moving wings of the *ziri*. "You're not serious?"

"That's what they called it, more or less," he called back with a grin on his face. "And there's the town at its base."

It took a while longer before they could make out the buildings on the ground, spread out across the plain. Then she felt the power. Or rather, Sheesha felt it and she knew it was there through him.

She turned and shouted to the others, "There's power here, can you see a ley-circle?"

She scoured the terrain as they drew closer to the spire but there was nothing. No circle on the ground, no hole driven into the earth where one might have been below. She looked again at the tower, there were patches of green on it where plants had taken hold but there was no mistaking it, the tower was not natural. Its curve was perfect and the surface smooth.

The height was astonishing. A hundred man-heights? Two hundred? And gently tapering to the tip—except there was no tip. It was cut off. Without thinking of the others, she urged Sheesha upwards and the *ziri* responded to her unspoken desire.

The others simply followed because they had no choice.

They climbed to the peak. And the feeling from Sheesha told Kantees everything she needed to know. This was the circle. She glanced into the sky. The sun was almost overhead but she squinted and saw no sign of the two moons. Sheesha landed on the smooth stone and Kantees slipped off his neck, landing both feet on the surface.

The others touched down a few moments later.

There was a wind but it was not strong, it blew with a constant pressure, and did not gust so seemed safe enough.

The top was perhaps fifty paces across at its widest and a perfect circle. Patterns had been inscribed into the surface in concentric circles. They reminded her of the protective circle Yenteel had created, which gave her some concern but, unless someone activated them, they should be safe. Tenical was studying them intently already.

Gally brought the *ziri* together into a tight group. His eyes kept flicking towards the edge, first one way and then another.

Daybian and Levin stood a good distance apart, staring into the distance. She ignored them, doubting they would have anything useful to say about this spire. So she walked over to Gally.

"If you sit down, Gally, you'll feel safer," she said gently.

"Gally liked the Ziri Tower," he said. "Gally doesn't like this tower."

"I know, but sit down, or lie down. It will be better."

Gally did as he was told. He still did not look happy but he was less restless. The *ziri* crowded round him and also lay down so Gally was in the middle of them. Kantees could not decide whether they were intentionally helping him, or just following his lead. It didn't matter, the result was the same.

She noticed Yenteel waving her over.

She crossed the lines of patterns. "There's no feeding due for a two-day," he said. "So we're definitely safe."

Kantees wondered, not for the first time, what value there was in a device that could say *when* a feeding might happen, but not *where*. She was quite sure there was little chance they would be in the immediate vicinity of two feedings within just a few days of each other.

"But this *is* a ley-circle?" she said, while certain that it was she was keen to have some corroboration.

"It is," said Tenical, who was now on his hands and knees, tracing the complex patterns with his fingers. "But it's not a big one and it's not up here."

"But I can feel it," said Kantees, then wished she hadn't. Both Yenteel and Tenical turned to look at her.

"You can feel a ley-circle?" said Yenteel.

"No," she said. "No, I misspoke. I can't feel it, but I know when Sheesha can feel it."

There was a querying noise form the *ziri* who poked his head up at the sound of his name.

"Yes, Sheesha," she said. "You're very clever." He grunted and lay his head down again.

"Why did no one know of this ability in the *zirichasa*?" said Tenical.

"Kantees is the only one who can do it," said Yenteel. "So it's never come up before."

"What do you mean this isn't the circle?" said Kantees, keen to change the subject before Yenteel called her *Kantees of the Ziri* again. "There are ley-circles in the air, like the one at Dakastown"

"There are," said Tenical. "But most of them are on the surface, and so is this one. It's below us."

"Then why build a tower? And why hasn't it been destroyed by a feeding?"

Tenical shook his head. "I can't say why it's been built, but your other question is easily answered. These patterns protect it."

Yenteel said nothing but Kantees could see he was hanging on Tenical's every word.

She shook her head. "That makes no sense. Why would anybody do that? Someone would have to be here to activate the patterns, and if someone was here during a feeding they would be killed, or changed."

"Probably," said Tenical in an abstracted way that suggested he was no longer listening. His attention had gone back to the patterns.

"Kantees!" shouted Levin from the far side.

What now? She looked over and, for one terrifying moment, thought Daybian was gone. Then she realised the lump at the edge of the tower was Daybian lying down and looking over the edge. She headed across but did not go too near.

"We found ropes," said Levin.

"I found ropes," said Daybian.

"There are some ropes," said Levin, "stretching all the way down to the town. Someone's climbing up."

"Three someones," said Daybian.

"How long before they get here?"

"A while," said Daybian. "It's a long way, and on a rope ladder too." He twisted his head round. "I could cut the ropes."

"Let's not annoy them more than we already have," she said. "We can just fly away."

This tower had not been part of the plan. They were being distracted. She headed back to Tenical.

"Can you make a path with this circle?"

"Not from up here. It seems as if it should be powerful enough but that power is down below. There doesn't seem to be a way inside from here, apart from these holes."

Kantees hadn't noticed them but now Tenical pointed them out the patterns were perforated with holes barely big enough to insert a finger. "What are they?"

Tenical looked at her. "I have no idea." He stood up. "If a feeding struck the circle, the rock's pattern would be disrupted and would cease to exist." He gestured at the circles. "These patterns are not like anything I've ever been taught. I have no idea what this tower is, or what it could be for." His last words came out almost in a state of desperation, as if his lack of understanding caused physical pain.

"Or who built it," said Yenteel.

Kantees glanced at Daybian and Levin, now both lying on the edge looking over. She turned back to Yenteel.

"It can't be," said Tenical.

Yenteel shrugged. "Do you have a better suggestion?"

"We left them behind."

"This tower is not new. It could have been here a long time before we arrived."

"I cannot accept it."

"What are you talking about?" said Kantees.

Yenteel turned his dark face towards her. "*Slissac*."

Her old master had pictures of *Slissac* hidden away. Tall and thin, the females as straight-bodied as the males. Cruel faces with hard lips. The reptilian race, masters of patterning, that had enslaved the Taymalin thousands of years ago, from which they'd finally escaped and made their way to this land, and made war on the Kadralin. And enslaved her people in Esternes.

She wasn't quite sure when that had happened but she allowed herself a grim smile. The Taymalin deified the one who led them out of slavery, and named themselves after him. Yet they could not resist committing the *Slissac*'s crime, as if they were somehow better than the Kadralin.

"Yenteel, do you have a far-seeing device?" called Levin from the edge.

Yenteel hurried over rummaging in his bag. Kantees followed leaving a concerned Tenical staring down at the patterns at his feet.

"Put the loop around your wrist before you look," said Yenteel. "My master would be very upset if you were to lose it."

Levin did as he was told. "Someone sit on me so I don't go over, I need both hands for this." Yenteel sat on one of his thighs. Kantees remembered what she had learnt about Yenteel's likes and dislikes, and wondered whether he took particular pleasure in the action. Not that she had noticed anything previously.

"You were right, Daybian."

"I told you."

"Right about what?" said Kantees.

"They're very well-armed and moving swiftly despite the climb."

"Kantees!" It was Gally. "Look!"

She spun round and saw he was pointing up.

"Tekrak," she said quietly.

And something else.

5

Half a dozen black shapes had detached themselves from the *tekrak* above them and were coming down fast. She couldn't make them out against the bright blue sky, except their silhouettes seemed to have wings.

The fire-tube of the *tekrak* was still burning and left a trail of thin black smoke across the sky. The patterner in control of it must have been driving it hard. She knew it wasn't natural because, apart from its size, she could see the gondola hanging beneath it.

How much time did they have?

Not enough.

"Gally! Get the *ziri* ready to fly."

She looked up to find there were now even more shapes coming down, she even saw one of them leap from the gondola. A human shape—with wings.

There was the sound of a sword being drawn behind her. A glance showed her that Levin was prepared. Daybian had nothing more than a knife.

"Ulina! Protect Daybian."

"No," he shouted back. "Protect Kantees."

Idiot.

The four *ziri* were up and stretching their wings. Kantees bit her lip and looked at Sheesha, he turned his head and one big eye looked back at her. She pointed at the figures coming down at them. Sheesha gave a screech and launched himself off the pinnacle and disappeared downward; the others followed.

"Yenteel—" She stopped, she had no idea what to suggest as he turned to face her. "Do something useful."

He touched his forehead. "Yes, Kantees of the Ziri." He pulled his bag open again.

Tenical grabbed her arm. "You sent the *ziri* away? How will we escape? Oh—" Ulina's patterned knife was at his belly. The child was staring directly into his eyes. He let go of Kantees.

"There was no time," she said. As if to prove her point a shadow curved overhead and tumbled into the stone. She thought she heard a crack as a bone broke. He did not get a chance to cry out as Levin slashed his blade into the man's neck. The weight of the blow knocked him to the ground and he did not move.

Yenteel rushed over and grabbed an arm of the body, dragging him towards the edge.

"No," shouted Daybian. "This way." He pointed to the place where they had been watching the attackers coming up. Yenteel changed direction and with Daybian's help they heaved the body over.

Kantees checked above. The others were coming in slower. This one must have been headstrong and thought he would make a name for himself by landing first. Instead he would become an object lesson. She squinted up; there were too many of the men coming in to count, but she knew the gondolas did not hold unlimited numbers.

"There's more climbing the tower," shouted Levin.

"Cut the ropes," shouted Kantees. *Where are you, Sheesha?*

The first wave of perhaps ten were much closer and would land in moments. She could see their weapons glinting in the sunlight.

"Tenical, make the path!"

"I can't, we're too far from the circle."

"We're directly above it! Try!"

Four *ziri* flashed through with the sun glinting red, blue and gold from their feathers. They screeched in unison and the sound was deafening. They ripped through the descending attackers. Waileth, Looesa and Shingul grabbed one each in their claws. The screeching of the *ziri* was joined by the cries of the men as the dagger talons cut into them. Sheesha took one man in each claw, and squeezed. Kantees saw blood spurt from their wounds. Then he let go and they dropped.

That was half of the first group.

Of the rest, one missed the pinnacle and fell past. He must have been distracted by the *ziri*. The first one to land was in front of Kantees. He was as white as any Taymalin, and grim, his sword ready to take her life. Then his face changed to one of pain and surprise. He fell to his knees as blood leaked from his ankles. Ulina stepped over him and sliced through his neck with her knife.

Daybian wrested the sword from the armsman's hand as he died. "That's better."

There was no time to dispose of the bodies now. Levin bludgeoned one in the head with his sword as the man came down. Somehow he managed to stay on his feet as he landed but Levin slammed into him and he tumbled over the edge.

Whatever Yenteel had been looking for in his bag, he found it. Kantees couldn't see what it was but cried out his name as another man came down almost on top of him. Yenteel ducked and rolled away towards the edge.

A head appeared beyond the edge of the tower behind Tenical who was concentrating and oblivious. Kantees ran past and kicked the head as if it was an apple. The man did not lose his grip and though she had torn the skin from his forehead he just grinned at her. His eyes flicked at something behind her head.

She ducked left and hit the ground, rolling away as one of the winged attackers came down where she had been. There was not enough room for him to land and he went over. From her prone position Kantees kicked the man clinging to the edge in the eye, he cried out but wouldn't let go. She kicked again and again until he was no longer there.

She rolled on to her back and looked up just as the *ziri* went through again and picked off another six. Looesa had decided he could do the same as Sheesha. But there were still too many.

"Give me the *chilafrah*."

Kantees looked round to see Tenical glaring at her, his face strained. "What?"

"The gift from your master. If you want a path, I need it."

Daybian and Levin stood against four attackers, they were doing well enough but there was blood on Levin's shirt and there were more attackers descending, never mind those that were on the way up.

Ulina was motionless nearby; her hand clasped the dagger and both were coated with congealing blood.

"Kantees! The *chilafrah!*"

"It's in the bag on Sheesha," she shouted back, unable to keep the anger from her voice.

"Kantees!" That was Gally. She rolled over and got to her feet ready to protect him but Gally was not hurt. He stood in the open holding her bag. Behind him one of the gliding attackers was coming directly at him.

"Gally, give Tenical my bag." She tried not to shout at him, though she could not imagine how he was coping with all the mayhem. She just needed him to move to the side. These attackers did not seem to be able control their descent very well. But Gally was slow, he took time understanding her words. He took time finding Tenical in the chaos. He *took time* getting his big body into motion. Kantees suppressed a cry.

Ulina ran at Gally. What he lacked in speed, she had in abundance, she was so light and so young. Gally barely even noticed, so focused was he, when she jumped up at him, pushed off his bent knee then launched herself from his shoulder directly into the path of the oncoming bird-man.

It did not matter what reactions the descending attacker had. The knife was buried in his neck before he knew what hit him. But he had not been over the pinnacle and when his body lost its strength he slumped and the wings no longer carried him forward. Both he and Ulina vanished over the edge.

Kantees suppressed her scream, desperate not to disturb Gally as he lumbered across to Tenical.

"Everyone down!" shouted Yenteel. "On the floor. Grab the edge if you can! Gally, lie down now. There's a good boy."

A gust of wind hit Kantees, she staggered for a moment. A second stronger gust pushed her towards the far edge.

She threw herself down and dug her fingers into the grooves of the patternings in the stone. Wind whipped across her. She wanted to know what everyone else was doing, wanted to ensure they were all right, but the blast was increasing in strength. What seemed to be a piece of tree bark jammed itself under her chin as she held her head down.

The wind noise increased until it was screaming across the open top of the spire. She couldn't hear anything else. She moved her feet slightly until they too dug into grooves. It was the best she could manage as the blasting wind streamed around her trying to lift her from the stone and carry her over the edge.

Then it died away and was gone. Shaking, she lay there nervous that it might return. And terrified she might lift her head and discover she was the only one still alive, alone on the pinnacle.

"A little help?" said a plaintive Daybian.

Kantees pushed herself to her feet. The piece of bark remained stuck to her face momentarily and then fell back.

"You caught it. Good," said Yenteel. "I wasn't sure whether the patterning would continue if it went over the edge."

"Really," said Daybian. "My fingers are going numb."

Yenteel was squatting near the edge, his clothes disarrayed. She turned to the sound of Daybian's voice. She could see Tenical and Gally, and beyond them, Levin. No Daybian, until she spotted two sets of fingers gripping the edge. She dashed over as Levin knelt down and took hold of one wrist. Then he reached farther and yanked Daybian up.

Kantees looked up. There was no sign of any of the attackers or the *tekrak*, they had been blown away.

Ulina? Sheesha?

Kantees scanned the sky in all directions. Nothing. Then a streak of golden light in the distance, and growing by the moment. So this was what they looked like when others saw them. She frowned, they were very obvious. Conflicting emotions tore at her, the joy at seeing Sheesha coming back and the loss of Ulina.

"Tenical. Make the path. Yenteel, help him if you can."

"No *thank you*?" said Yenteel.

"I'll thank Lintha, next time I see her."

"You think she would have given me those patterns if I hadn't satisfied her in the night?"

"I'm sure you can be very proud of your performance," said Kantees. "But right now we need to get away from here. They'll be back."

The *ziri* broke out of the golden light and in perfect formation the four of them touched down. Ulina, still bloody, dropped from Sheesha's back and ran to Kantees, who went down on one knee and threw her arms around the child.

"I thought you had died."

"Sheesha caught me."

"Of course he did."

She released the girl from the hug but held on to her hand. Kantees went to Sheesha and buried her face in the feathers at his neck. "Thank you," she said quietly.

"Kantees." Levin and Daybian were standing behind them. Levin's arm had been put in a makeshift sling made from his shirt; Kantees experienced a wave of guilt for being too wrapped in her own possible loss to check on them.

"What?"

"How did they find us?"

She hesitated and then nodded. "I was stupid. They knew we would make for a ley-circle and they could make paths to all the nearest and carry word."

"If it hadn't been for Yenteel letting off wind," said Daybian without the hint of a smile, but a dirty look from Yenteel. "We would be dead."

"On the positive side," said Levin. "We now know how they are planning to deploy attacks from the giant *tekrasa*."

"But we have to get the message back to Esternes."

"That's where we're going," said Kantees, slightly confused, then the light dawned. "You think they'll be waiting for us at Watching Pass."

"Tenical is a Hamalain," said Levin. "At best they will think he knows the circles at either Kurvin Port, or Watching Pass. They only have to prepare defences there."

"But we can't stay here," said Kantees. "And we must take a patterner's path to be in time."

"That's the way of it," said Daybian.

"What can we do?" said Kantees.

"We were hoping you would have the solution to that."

"Me?" Kantees felt embarrassed that she sounded weak but why did they think that she would have the answer? Two Taymalin lords expected her to have a solution to the problem and deferred to her for it. A runaway Kadralin slave.

Kantees looked at Tenical; she wouldn't disturb him because he was focused on the patterning. Carving a route through the World Pattern to join two distant locations together. He was holding the *chilafrah*, the gift from her old master. Worth a thousand *ziri*, Yenteel had said. Perhaps more.

She looked at the *ziri* and then back at Tenical. She knew a patterner could walk their own path which meant he did not have to maintain it from here while they went through.

When the *tekrak* went through, it flew. Of course, because it couldn't walk, but the patterner controlling it made it fly. Could *ziri* fly along a path? When she touched the sides of the path she felt nothing. She was touching the essence of the world and there was nothing to be felt.

But it supported you if you walked on it. Usually they made the *zirichasa* walk through a path.

Why not fly?

As long as it was big enough. The Dunor might be waiting for them at the other end, but if they came through at full speed?

"We'll fly through," said Kantees abruptly.

"No," and, "You can't," said Daybian and Levin simultaneously.

"Why not?"

"Because…" said Levin, but he had no answer.

"Because that's not what we do," said Daybian.

"And that's why we have to do it."

"It's dangerous," said Levin.

"Why?"

"It's ready," said Tenical.

Kantees looked but the path was invisible, of course, only Tenical knew its borders.

"Is it wide enough for the *ziri* to fly?"

"You're not serious?"

Her face conveyed the sincerity of her intention, and her unwillingness to have another bout of argument.

"It's wide enough."

"Do you have to keep hold of my *chilafrah?*" said Kantees, nodding towards the lump of stone in Tenical's hand. Tenical looked at it and then reluctantly handed it back. It was warm. Kantees put it back in her bag.

"You should put that somewhere safe," said the patterner.

"When you find somewhere safe, Tenical, let me know," she said. "How long will the path be maintained?"

Tenical shook his head. "I'm not sure, but longer than usual. There's something strange about this circle, I think it's the patterning. It seems to intensify the effects."

"Good thing for us," said Yenteel. "Or Lintha's pattern might have been a gentle summer breeze."

"Let's go," said Kantees.

The *zirichasa* launched by dropping off the sides of the pinnacle and, following Sheesha under Kantees' guidance, flew at a sedate speed towards the location Tenical had indicated. They flew in line, nose to tail.

Kantees hoped the *ziri* would not be upset by the sudden transition into the strangeness of the patterner's path but she trusted Sheesha to keep them together.

She expected there to be some sensation as they crossed the boundary but it was no different than flying from day into night, just more abrupt. Sheesha made a surprised noise but Kantees soothed him and told him what a strong and brave *ziri* he was. His confidence transferred itself to the others.

There was no way of knowing how long the path would be but

in flight they would travel it much faster than walking. She felt Ulina's grip on her waist. She encouraged the *ziri* to go faster and he did as he was told.

Since they could not penetrate the walls of the path she had no concern about them going off course. *A little faster, Sheesha.*

They exploded into fresh air and the deepest night.

The circle was surrounded by fires that lit the ground and the trees, and a dozen *tekrasa* floating around the ley-circle, forced to fly in the dark.

"Go fast, my love," she whispered into Sheesha's ear.

The cries that went up from the defenders were cut off as the air about the *zirichasa* turned golden.

6

_K_antees turned them west and north towards the coast, but away from Kurvin Port, and had Sheesha climb to a height well above the mountain tops they had seen in this area on their previous journey in the other direction. The sky was cloudy and there was very little to see except the velvet black, filled with dampness.

Somehow this place had the right smell. She knew she was home, even if she had no real place to call home. They rose through clouds that made the darkness even blacker and emerged into moonlight. They needed to lose any possible pursuers. They might be slow but they were persistent and the golden trail of the _ziri_ was something people would notice.

She asked Sheesha to slow down and in a few moments they were blasted by the freezing night air.

The _ziri_ glided, lazily stroking the air with their wings when they needed to climb. Kantees closed her eyes. She had done it. _They_ had done it. They had rescued Daybian from the heart of the Dunor. It was what she had promised and now she was free.

"What time is it?" she yelled to Yenteel.

"After midnight but not a lot," he called back. "We should set down."

"Not until we can see," she said. "Might fly into a mountain."

"Perhaps we could see the lights of a town, or a village."

"Give it some time," said Kantees. "We only going down if there's no choice."

Ulina's grip around her waist had loosened which meant she must have fallen asleep.

Kantees encouraged Sheesha to climb again, reasoning that they should be able to spot gaps in the clouds more easily if they went higher.

"Are we going to hide on Colimar?" called Daybian from the back of Shingul. She looked over her shoulder at him and saw him pointing at the moon.

"Going up so we can see down."

"I'm sure that makes sense to you."

"Well, yes it does," she said to herself.

Her plan bore fruit only a short time later as they reached a kind of border in the clouds where the solid surface beneath them broke up, leaving just shreds from there to the coast. Colimar was behind them and did not reflect on the sea but instead it was a great flat expanse of dark against the mottled ground beneath them.

It seemed they were long past the mountains, because the ground beneath them undulated gently and was interlaced with rivers running down from the high hills.

Here and there, as they slowly descended, they could see lights from fires marking villages and towns. Kantees was reluctant to make human contact and leave someone behind who had witnessed their passing.

She allowed Sheesha to turn more north so the sea was to their left. An outcrop of hills protruded from an area of plains to the east. The hills were ringed by woods, which she did not like, but the hills themselves were free of trees. There were no human lights near them so Kantees steered Sheesha in that direction. The *ziri* had been gliding soundlessly the whole way down from the clouds. And as they came over the hills, Sheesha looped around them so they could be viewed from all sides.

The only signs of life were sleeping *kelukisa*, similar to but smaller than their *lukisa* cousins, and in the dark they resembled small groups of grey rocks. They were not a threat and if they were living on these hills there could be no real danger.

But Kantees still did not want to take any chances and had Sheesha finally land on one of the inner slopes so that they could not be seen from beyond the hills.

She slipped down from Sheesha's neck, took a few steps in the damp, close-cropped, grass, and stretched.

"Kantees," said Yenteel quietly. "Ulina's asleep."

Kantees lifted her down while Yenteel got out a blanket which they wrapped around the sleeping child. Kantees put her down on the grass with her bag as a pillow.

Colimar shone down, it was showing only half its face but the light was still bright enough to see by.

Kantees looked down at Ulina; asleep she was the child she should be.

"You know she's Farahalek, don't you?" said Yenteel.

"I don't want to know."

"She's trained to kill."

"We wouldn't be here without her."

"It's inhuman."

"You mean to manipulate her and turn her into something she wasn't meant to be?"

He had the decency to shut up.

A wave of exhaustion swept over her. She picked up Ulina again and turned to where Sheesha was curling up. She crawled under his wing and buried herself in his warm feathers. She was asleep before she had a chance to remind herself how tired she was.

She awoke to a downpour. It was dry beneath Sheesha's wing but she could not stay there. She gave it a little time to see if the rain was going to let up but it had clearly decided it was going to stay for a while. Good Esternes weather.

The *ziri* were all still curled up, although she could see them peeking out from beneath their feathers. Gally's feet stuck out under

Looesa's wing. Tenical was sitting on a stone huddled against the rain.

"You're in time for the midday meal," said Yenteel beside a smoky fire on which she could see a small pot bubbling.

He must have noticed her scouring the hills around them.

"We're safe, Kantees, at least as safe as we can be out here. You chose a good location. Levin and Daybian have already scaled the tallest hill—" he indicated the one opposite them, "—and confirmed we are fully surrounded by trees. They also found some collapsed buildings farther over on the edge of the woods. They thought it looked like a farm, though you can't trust a Taymalin aristocrat to find his behind with both hands."

"I heard that," said Daybian.

"Though there's nothing wrong with their hearing."

"You managed to get the fire going," she said, crouching beside him. Whatever he was cooking up in the pot smelled delicious, and she put her hands closer to the fire even though it wasn't a cold day, despite the rain.

"I put some tinder aside last night, it was touch and go getting it going this morning, but I've had plenty of practice."

"I'll try to remember that."

He gave her a side-long glance but did not comment.

Daybian and Levin came up to the fire, water dripping from their hair.

"How long are we planning to stay here?" said Levin.

Kantees stood up. "You can go whenever you like," she said, then realised how bad that sounded. "I didn't mean I want you to go, but—"

She realised everyone who was up was now looking at her. She hadn't meant to say this so soon. "But there's no reason for us to stay together. I'm going into the mountains to look for my people. You two," she glanced awkwardly at Levin and Daybian, "should warn your people about the Dunor. Perhaps you should take Tenical as well."

"Are you planning to go into the mountains alone?" said Yenteel.

"No, of course not. Gally and Ulina will come with me on Sheesha."

"And I?" he said.

"You can go back to your master and tell him you failed." She looked into his eyes. "Yenteel, I am not the person you think I am. Nor will I become the one you want me to be." She looked up at the two Taymalin. "Is that plan all right for you?"

Daybian ignored him. "I don't think you should break up the team, Kantees."

"We're not a team, Daybian, that's just your imagination."

"You saved my life."

"Now you can go home and save Jakalain, so that you can become its Lord."

"I'm not in line for the seat of power," said Levin, "what reason do I have to go? My family will side with the Dunor, I have no doubt, and I'll never sit on the Otulain throne."

"Then help Daybian; if he returns alone with some crazy story no one will believe him."

"That's true," said Levin.

"Sadly, it is," said Daybian. "But then I'd be able to return to help you, Kantees."

"You and I will never share a bed, Daybian."

He held up his hands. "I did not even mention it."

"I know how your mind works, but look," she said. "I can't take you into the mountains. Gally and I, even Yenteel, are Kadralin, and Ulina is just a child. They won't kill us." Then she looked pointedly at the other three. "Your pasty faces will be your deaths, and give me trouble."

Levin was the first to nod. Then he knelt on one knee in the mud. "If you are ever in need, Kantees of the Ziri, I pledge myself to your aid."

Daybian followed suit. "Me too."

Kantees felt the tears in her eyes but was sure they would be hidden by the rain. "Don't call me that." But she choked on the words.

It did not take a great deal of time for them to prepare to leave. The rain reduced to a light drizzle that was somehow more irritating than steady rain. She tried not to care as they waved and launched into the air, but she could not help watching until the grey shapes were indistinguishable from the clouds.

"It would have been handy to keep the patterner," said Yenteel.

"I don't trust him," she said promptly, "and he's Taymalin."

"I didn't think you trusted me."

"I don't like what you do but I don't think you'll betray me," said Kantees. "But even if I tied you to a *ziri*, you would have come back."

"I would."

Kantees nodded. "We may as well get going."

"Do you have any idea where?"

"Into the mountains."

"There are a lot of mountains."

"Somewhere the Taymalin haven't gone."

"And how will you know that?"

Kantees felt the heat rise in her cheeks. "I don't know, Yenteel. All right? Is that what you wanted to hear? I have no idea how to find *our* people." She thought it important to emphasise that they were his people as well.

The rain stopped but everything, including the *ziri*, was soaked through. Instead of setting off, Kantees built up the fire, and the four of them crowded around it for warmth. Their clothes steamed.

"It's an interesting problem," said Yenteel after a while. He dug out a stick from the fire and traced a large shape. "Let's say that's Esternes. Dakastown is here." He made a hole at the bottom of the shape. "Jakalain there and Kurvin Port over here." He ran a jagged line across the middle. "And that's the cliff that divides the upper and lower parts."

"Someone was following me," she said.

"When?"

"On my way to Dakastown."

"But you were *ziri*-back."

"I know but there were places I was delayed, and he always seemed to know where we were. I lost him after Cliffedge but he caught up again at the Ziri Tower in Dakastown."

"Taymalin or Kadralin?"

"His skin was white," she said; she hadn't forgotten what the wise woman Lintha had said about skin colour. After all, if Daybian had taken her and she caught, what colour would the child have been? Not that she'd had any intention of letting that happen. She felt no attraction for him. In truth, she had never felt that sort of attraction to anyone. Yenteel more than made up for that imbalance since he apparently had no preference.

"Did he try to harm you?"

"I thought so when we first encountered him stirring up a mob of townsfolk to go after us but, after that, he seemed to be just following." She hesitated. "Perhaps I was wrong about his intentions."

"Stirring up a mob against you? I don't think someone could do that by accident."

"I suppose."

"But you haven't seen him since?"

"No."

"We won't worry about him then." He returned to his drawing and etched out an area to the east of Kurvin Port that extended to Jakalain, almost the whole way across Esternes. "And that's the mountains. It took us a four-day to fly from Jakalain to the west coast, so that's perhaps a hundred leagues. And the mountain range at its widest perhaps thirty leagues."

Kantees stared at his map and her heart sank.

"It's impossible," she said.

"Difficult," said Yenteel. "Time consuming perhaps, but not impossible."

Kantees looked at him expectantly. He sounded as if he knew how to do it but all he did was stand up and move away from the fire.

"How then?" she said, her voice tinged with annoyance.

"You are Kantees of the Ziri," he said. "You work it out."

"Don't call me that."

"It's a clue," said Ulina.

"What do you mean?"

Ulina eyed Yenteel before turning her head to Kantees. "He thinks you can use Sheesha."

"And Looesa," said Gally even though he probably had no idea what they were talking about. "We can see the map."

Kantees shook her head and stared at the scrapings Yenteel had made in the mud.

"They aren't going to be round the edges," she said. "And from what we've seen of this end of the mountains there are a lot of Taymalin."

She looked over to where Yenteel was standing. He didn't seem to be listening but he had the device that calculated feedings in his hand and was looking up at the clouds.

"Everyone thinks the mountains are just that, all the way through," said Kantees. "But the Kadralin wouldn't be able to live if it was only mountains, there would have to be deep valleys to grow food and keep livestock."

"Or plateaus," said Yenteel.

"The mountains might just be a ring and there might be a place to live in the middle," said Kantees. That was the moment she understood what Gally had said. "And if we were flying high enough we could see a wide area just like the map—and if Sheesha and Looesa were able to fly fast, we could scout the mountains in a day."

"A few days," said Yenteel. "They would have to rest and feed."

"But if the people who lived there saw us, they could send a sign."

"They might."

The sun came out in the afternoon and it was warm in its light, but there was still a cold breeze. The hills hid them from the rest of the world and it would have been an inviting place to stay, if she did not have somewhere else she wanted to be.

She checked her bag and made sure the *chilafrah* was in it. The only thing she had to show for all that she had been through. That and the fact she had been manipulated all her life. But that ended now. There was nothing anyone could do, no leverage anyone held over her. Yenteel could say what he wanted, she did not have to listen, and any effect he had on people was nothing to do with her any more. She had no more need of the Taymalin world; once she found the Kadralin that would be the end of her journey.

If they are there.

She shook her head to clear it of such thoughts. That was Yenteel, and Daybian, and Levin. She knew she was right. They were there, in the mountains, and they were free.

But if they are free why haven't they taken their lands back?

"I'm not listening to you."

Ulina looked at her and frowned.

Kantees put a smile on her face. "Not you." She made a point of checking what Yenteel and Gally were doing. Her smile became genuine when she saw Gally checking Looesa's feathers and working down to his legs. It had been a long time since she had checked Sheesha for mites and parasites, he hadn't scratched excessively so she didn't think it was a problem.

But she hadn't checked.

Yenteel had climbed to the top of the hill again and was looking out across the plain south to the mountains.

"What do you see?" she called up to him.

The sunlight reflected from the buckles on his belt and pack as he turned. "Nothing."

"Good."

He came down the slope in long strides. "Is it?"

"It means we can leave and not be observed. Yes, that's good."

"I'm wondering what the Dunor are up to."

"That's not my problem anymore," she said with a finality that stopped him from saying anything further.

And it's not, she told herself but the thought hung in her mind. *Why do I feel guilty about it then?*

"Just as well the Taymalin can deal with it," said Yenteel.

"Yes. We've delayed long enough, Yenteel, let's go."

The *ziri* ducked down to allow them to mount. Ulina put her arms around Kantees. It was a comforting feeling, she liked knowing that the girl trusted her.

The two *zirichasa* leapt into the air with their wings beating hard to gain altitude. She glanced over at Looesa, he was strong. He could manage.

They wheeled round until Kantees headed them out across the marshes. To where the mountains rose in the blue distance. With Looesa to the right and slightly behind Sheesha.

Kantees had decided they would not fly high and fast. That way they would attract too much attention; if they flew low and at their usual speed it might take longer but they would only be visible to someone close by, and it seemed that few lived here. As long as they stayed clear of any major towns and ley-circles no one would see them pass

Mid-afternoon they passed a small group of houses sited on the shores of a lake. Smoke rose from a chimney. They were only over it for a short time but she saw small boats moored in the shallow water and a small area of cultivated land with someone moving among the plants. She could not tell if they were Taymalin or Kadralin but, as Lintha said, perhaps the difference was not great enough to matter.

As they headed into evening the land rose until the mountains became a wall.

They needed to find somewhere for the night. The number of trees was also increasing and she was keen not to spend the night near any wooded area. Kantees asked Sheesha to climb; now they were away from the flat and open lands she felt more confident.

From the greater altitude she searched for a safe spot but as the sun went down shadows filled the valleys and it was difficult to see what was below them. She turned them east to go along the edge of the range, probably following a similar route to Daybian and Levin.

Kantees spotted a wide valley cut by a river that tumbled down from the heights and thought they might be safer in the mountains. She turned them to follow the river's course.

"There's a road!" shouted Yenteel. She looked back and then followed his pointing finger. She stared down and realised he was right, in the dying light there was a ribbon of paler stone that ran along the edge the river. It pleased her because she felt it meant they were heading the right way.

There was a place where the river crashed beneath them through a deep gorge. They followed its tumultuous course up past rapids and waterfalls. The road had disappeared off to one side but reappeared as they came out on to a green plateau with fir trees clinging to the mountain's sides. The river widened here and split as it went around an outcropping of rock. The curved lumps of stone looked like a huge pile of *ziri* droppings. But it was protected on all sides by the river and did not possess a single tree, just some sparse bushes.

A short time later they had landed and found a place on the shore where they could stand easily. The place was not silent with the constant splashing of the water and, in the distance, the low thunder of a waterfall. But it was still peaceful.

While the light still lasted, they took a short hop across the water to collect wood for a fire and soon had it blazing. Kantees relaxed with her feet warming and her back against a boulder. This was how she had imagined her life would be—even though Ulina, Gally and Yenteel had not been part of her dream.

The screech of a *sikechak* brought her awake. It was cold. The fire was just embers and the sky was clear. The great leathery predators flew in the mountains. The biggest ones, it was said, dwarfed a *ziri*.

The snowy tops of the mountains she could see were highlighted with red. Colimar must be behind her. It had the light to tint shadows with blood but not enough to make the world properly visible. The small red moon in the sky alone was considered to be an ill omen but she did not believe in such things.

A moving shadow to the right caught her eye. She turned her head but it was gone. Then she saw it again, soaring above the water of the river. Then it dived and vanished. She held her breath until it erupted from the surface and heavy wingbeats drove it upwards, the water splashing from it reflecting red.

Was it a *sikechak*? She did not know, but it was very big. Sheesha grumbled in his sleep. Kantees got up stiffly and, after scanning the dark in a fruitless search for the flying creature, persuaded Sheesha to lift his wing and she tucked herself in beside Ulina.

"Do *sikechasa* dive for fish?" she said to Yenteel as they ate some warmed-up salted meat.

"That's not something I've heard of," he said.

"What about hunting at night?"

He shrugged.

"I saw one dive last night," she said.

"There are diving birds," he said. "But I've not heard of a *sikechak* doing that."

"I know," she said. "I lived on the coast."

"How big was it?"

"Half the size of Sheesha, perhaps. It was dark."

"But you saw a *sikechak* diving for food in the dark?"

"I wasn't dreaming."

"I didn't say you were," he said and swallowed the meat he had been chewing. "The world is full of wondrous things."

"Most of them are trying to kill us."

"Dakastown—" he started but she interrupted him.

"I know about *dakasa*, I was brought up in Dakastown, and the ones in the lake behind the hills nearly brought Sheesha down."

"But you lived to tell the tale."

"Fog-wolves, circle-warped abominations, wolves, giant *kichesa*, not to mention *nachasa*."

Yenteel held up a finger. "To be fair, we did not encounter a *nachak* when we were in the south."

"I'm sure they would have turned up given a chance," she said. "Let's not forget flying soldiers leaping from giant *tekrasa*."

He laughed. "Yes, those too. But they weren't flying, just gliding. I think those wings they wore had been patterned to bring them down gently."

They both fell silent. Kantees could not help but imagine a dozen *tekrasa* above Jakalain raining down soldiers on the fortifications and killing everyone within.

I don't care.

Except that she saw their faces: Libbibet, Romain, Jelamie, the Lord and Lady, Swordmaster Erang, even the patterner Hokart. And she tried harder not to care.

There's nothing I can do.

Something the length of a man lying down, and sinuous, moved through the water just below the surface. It went past, upstream, and was lost in the ripples and waves.

"Did you see that?" she said.

"Eel," said Yenteel. He glanced at her confused face. "Like a snake but lives in water."

"I know. We need to be careful."

"I expect it was one of those your *sikechak* was after last night."

He was probably right. One of those could feed them for a five-day. But not the *ziri*.

"How far do you think we are from the Watching Pass?"

Yenteel looked at the sky, it was overcast; he looked at the mountains, and the river. "I have no idea."

"None of your devices will tell us?"

"I have a device that tells us which direction we're heading, I have one for far-seeing, and there's the one that can calculate when a feeding happens."

"Nothing else?"

"Isn't that enough?"

"Where did they come from?"

"My master, of course."

"The master you refuse to tell me anything about."

"That's right."

"Is he a patterner?"

"I am not sure that you understand the meaning of *anything*."

"Why is it important?"

"I refer you to my previous comment."

She stood up. "Fine. Have it your way."

"Thank you," he said. "I will."

Kantees tested the wind with a damp finger. There was none. "I think if we get the *ziri* to take us across to the road we can walk while they hunt."

"Why would you want to walk when you can just wait a while and then fly?"

"Because I always feel like I'm wasting time when we're waiting for the *ziri*."

A short time later they were standing on stone slabs that led away in both directions. The *ziri* were already out of sight. Kantees wondered how they would find their prey in this place, but wild *zirichasa* lived in mountains so they must know where to find what they needed.

In comparison to being *ziri*-back, walking was slow, though it did give more time to examine the landscape. A great deal more time. Far too much time in her opinion.

The stones that made up the road had well-defined edges and corners, though they were clearly very old and some had shattered. Straggly plants grew in the gaps between them, and there was obviously no traffic to keep them from taking over.

"We might be the first to walk this road in a thousand years," said Yenteel.

Ulina spent some time jumping from stone to stone, and Gally copied her.

The river was wide and slow-moving here. Kantees thought she saw shapes moving across the surface. And that reminded her of the *shocalin* she had seen in the sea. But this was not like that, the sea-going *shocalin* were large and furry with big eyes. All she could imagine here were gigantic snakes. She hoped they didn't have any strange patterning that allowed them to swim on land, or lure their victims into the sea.

She sighed, her life had been so confined, first in the house of her old master, and then in Jakalain. She had learnt how to make a fire when she was young, of course, but that was inside with dry wood, being able to do it outside was always an achievement for her. She was unwilling to admit the truth that she needed Yenteel, as well as Ulina as her bodyguard since she had no skill with weapons. Galiko was the only one more disadvantaged than she and that was an unfair comparison since he had been born without the ability to learn.

Without these people around her she would be dead.

The valley in which the river ran curved to the left and the road followed it along the right bank. Each step revealed a fraction more of the vista. Cliffs climbing up on either side, snow-capped peaks behind, the water stretching out wide and flat and only disturbed by the eels.

A screech met her ears and for a moment she thought it was the returning *zirichasa* but the wheeling silhouettes between the far peaks were not feathered. It was impossible to tell how big the *sikechasa* were at that distance. But somehow she knew they must be large. Certainly big enough to carry off a small child like Ulina, or perhaps a young woman like herself.

"There's a building," said Yenteel. She turned her head and saw he was using his far-seeing device. She turned again to see where he was looking and could just make out a stone house the same colour as the stone of the cliffs behind it.

8

It took them a long time to walk the distance. Kantees was beginning to wonder where the *ziri* had got to. Even worry a little though she found it hard to imagine that two powerful *zirichasa* could fall victim to any creature—even a giant *sikechak*.

The shape of the building resolved as they grew closer. Squat at only two floors, and rectangular in overall shape, it sat a short distance from the water and there was a clear path from the main doors, up some steps, down to the water's edge, and even a short distance into it. Bushes clung to the sides of the building as if sheltering there and dark holes pitted the roof.

The windows were strange and mismatched. On the lower floor they were small squares and rectangles set deep into the thick stone but for the floor above the windows were tall, thin and grouped in fives. And there were many of them stretching right across the front and the side that they could see, as if the builders had wanted to let as much light in as possible.

If there had been any glass or other covering on the lower windows it was gone. But many of the windows of the upper floor still reflected the sky. Though not all. The main door was double width and constructed of solid wood. There were dark patches spread randomly across it and one place where it looked as if the wood had been scorched by flame. Kantees told herself it didn't mean anything.

They mounted the stone steps.

"Do you think it's safe?" said Kantees.

"I see no sign of life," said Yenteel. "Do you?"

She shook her head and turned back to the building to see Ulina halfway to the roof. Kantees stopped herself from crying out, just in case the building was occupied. The windows were not the child's target as she bypassed them and headed over the eaves and on to the roof tiles. She dislodged something and it fell to the ground with a thump. Just a clod of earth from the gutter.

"Let's try the door," said Kantees. "If there is someone here we can distract them."

But the door would not budge, no matter how hard they pulled, even when Gally replaced Kantees to provide more strength.

The scraping of a bolt being drawn surprised them all, Kantees backed away and then realised Gally was in front of her. She grabbed him by the arm and pulled him behind her.

The door scraped as one side swung open and came to a grinding halt. Ulina poked her head out.

"It was locked," she said.

"Is it empty?"

"Nobody is here."

Kantees turned and scanned the sky as Ulina ducked back inside and Yenteel went through the gap. There was no sign of the *ziri*.

"Gally, will you wait out here so you can wave to Sheesha and Looesa when they come back?"

"Yes, Kantees."

"That's good, we won't be long and if you need us just call out."

"Yes, Kantees."

She turned and went sideways through the gap.

"Kantees?"

She stopped. "What?"

"Can I sit on the steps? My legs are tired."

"Of course." She glanced at the lake. "Just don't go near the water."

"Yes, Kantees."

The interior was dark but her eyes soon adjusted and the dark shapes of Yenteel and Ulina resolved themselves. The place was a mess with mouldering remains of what had probably been furniture lying broken on the floor.

Yenteel was staring at the stone floor as Kantees caught up.

The light from the windows highlighted the shards of a broken, human skull. What she had taken for wood was scattered bones.

"Somebody lost a fight here," said Yenteel.

"But the doors were barred from the inside."

"Whoever killed him could have escaped through the roof."

Kantees turned and went to the nearest window. Shattered glass glinted on the floor. "Or in and out through the window."

"Whatever it was," said Yenteel, "it was a long time ago."

Kantees jumped as she thought she saw, out of the corner of her eye, a shadow pass one of the windows. She went to the door and looked out. She did not want to scare Gally but she wanted to make sure he was still alright. He was seated on the steps, turning his head as he scanned the sky.

She looked out across the water. It was calm and the sun glinted off it. Small waves lapped against the shore. Everything was quiet. Even the *sikechasa* were silent.

From here she could see the far end of the lake now, where the river tumbled down into it from a higher valley where the mountains pressed together.

Where is Sheesha?

There was a screech from the side of the building. The outside. *Ulina!* Kantees squeezed out and ran along the front, dodging bushes. Something moving on two legs shot out from the corner heading towards the water. Ulina was right behind it. The light glinted off her tiny dagger.

Kantees did not pause to shout at Ulina to stop but launched herself down the slope in pursuit of both, though she had nothing to fight with even if she managed to catch up.

She was taller, her legs were long, and she had an instinct to protect Ulina—even if the girl stood a far better chance protecting herself—and caught up fast.

They broke through the bushes and Kantees saw what they were chasing. Not much larger than Ulina, it had two arms and legs like a person, but its overall colouration was green and grey, though Kantees was not sure where its skin stopped and some sort of loose clothing, if that's what it was, began.

Kantees crossed the roadway and passed Ulina in long strides. She hit the pebbly beach with a regular crunch underfoot as the creature reached the water only a few feet ahead of her. It did not slow down but leapt upwards to make a long low dive. It hit the water with barely a splash and vanished beneath the surface.

Unable to bring herself to a halt in time Kantees stumbled into the water, up to her knees. It was numbingly cold. She stopped and stared out trying to see where it had gone but there was nothing but the steady stream of small waves lapping against her legs and on to the shore. Not that she could follow it anyway.

And the ripple that moved crosswise to the rest.

Kantees saw it but for a moment it did not register. She dragged one foot back and planted it on the shifting pebbles. She did not turn round but kept her eyes glued to the oncoming shape just below the transparent surface.

She stepped back again. The water was now just at her calves. The next step and the next step. They were getting easier as she moved up the beach. But the wave was now streaking toward her through the water.

And she was out, stumbling backwards across the uneven and shifting ground. But the thing kept coming. Then Ulina was running past her, ready to take on the beast but Kantees would not allow it. Her hand lashed out and she grabbed Ulina by the wrist. Kantees threw herself to the side, whipping Ulina round and towards her. As the eel shot up on to the beach, Kantees rolled away, shielding the child from the wide snapping jaws big enough to take a hand off, all the way to the elbow.

But the eel did not care that it was on land and slithered after her—*at least it doesn't have legs*—Kantees kept moving, pushing Ulina away and then sliding across the smooth stones after her. A steady thump-thump approached and got louder.

Kantees saw a piece of wood swing hard, heard a splintering crash, and saw the sinuous head of the eel snap up and back, rising into the air and falling back onto the pebbles. Followed by Gally pounding the pole in his hands again and again into the creature.

"Gally, stop."

He did not hear.

"Gally! Stop! It's dead."

Then all she could hear was him panting, his breathing coarse in his throat.

Kantees clambered to her feet and pulled Ulina up. "Come on, Gally. Get away from the water."

Far out on the river she could see more movement and she did not want to be here when the water creatures came for their revenge.

They stumbled up the beach. Kantees was exhausted and trembling. Just as she had been that time that seemed so long ago on the bell tower at Jakalain. The night when all her troubles started.

"Yenteel!"

He must have been oblivious to the events because he simply stuck his head out of the door as if nothing had happened.

"We're leaving now."

"But I found something."

She glanced back at the water. In one place, not too far away, the water was churning and boiling.

"We're in danger. We have to go *right now*."

There must have been something in her voice. He did not argue but popped back inside for a moment and returned with his bag.

Kantees stared at the river. They needed to get away from it as soon as they possibly could. The road simply followed it but there looked to be a path leading away and up the side of the cliff.

"That way."

From a ledge halfway up the cliff, they watched the creatures milling around the building; some climbed up on top and waved weapons at them. The water was filled with the shapes of eels moving about and crossing one another.

"*Ustecalin*," said Yenteel. "I thought they were a myth."

"Why would you think that?"

"Nobody's ever seen them."

"Whoever lived in that house certainly saw them."

"Gally has seen them," said Gally very seriously.

"And you saved my life, and Ulina's," said Kantees, ignoring the look on the girl's face that implied she would have been perfectly safe. But she did not spoil the moment for Gally, who grinned.

"Gally is a hero."

"You are," said Kantees but the thought of him rushing into danger scared her. "You were a good hero today, but don't be a hero again, Gally."

"Gally saved Kantees."

"Yes." There was nothing she could say that would not crush him. She would just have to make sure he was not forced into that position again.

The sun was going down but Kantees did not want to stop. "We need to be far away from the water."

They kept moving. When they found rough steps leading up a particularly steep section they knew that this was not just some animal track they were following. It took them until the sun had disappeared behind the mountains before they emerged on the ridge between the valley with the river, still glistening below them, and the next.

They passed over the top of the ridge and the path led down the other side but as the light was fading it became harder to see.

"We need to stop, Kantees," said Yenteel.

She scanned the sky. "Where are the *ziri*?" Every time she thought about them, the fact they were not here and should have been, her heart pounded and fear crept through her, numbing her fingers.

"They'll be fine," said Yenteel. "Sheesha's probably found a nice girlfriend to mate with."

"And Looesa?"

"He's acting as chaperone, and that's why nothing's happened."

Kantees knew she should smile but her head hurt.

They found a place surrounded on three sides by rocks, but there were no raw materials for a fire. They were forced to simply lie on the ground using their packs as pillows. It reminded Kantees of the eyrie; she tried to force the idea away but all she could think of was Sheesha.

She slept badly and the cold seeped through her clothes in the time before dawn. The others were still sleeping so Kantees got to her feet quietly and walked out on to the hillside. Below her, not as deep as the valley they had come from, was an open green plain dotted with *lukisa*. They were probably big enough not to be concerned about *sikechasa* except perhaps the biggest.

The path led down into the valley and she could see it winding away into the distance. There was a river in this valley too, but it was much smaller than the previous one and wound in great curves across the valley bottom. A group of *lukisa* stood in the water in one place, a movement caught her eye in the grass near to them. More than one movement. Wolves on the hunt.

She watched in fascination as the creatures prowled forward so slowly it was almost as if they weren't moving at all. There were ten of them in a wide half-circle. The *lukisa* were becoming restive. The wolves exploded into action, all at once, chasing in on the single nearest beast. The group turned to flee but they were not fast enough as the wolves all leapt on the same hapless beast. Kantees looked away as the river water darkened.

"Wolves," said Yenteel. "We had better be careful."

"They won't be hunting for a while after this," said Kantees.

"Very good," said Yenteel. "We'll turn you into an experienced traveller yet."

"I learnt in my master's house in Dakastown."

"I see, well it's good knowledge to have wherever you learnt it." He paused for a moment. "Is there any food?"

"Why are you asking me?"

"Well, you being the leader, it's important you know this sort of thing."

She punched him in the arm.

There was no food. They packed their bags and headed down the path as it sloped gently into the valley. The wolves could be seen devouring the remains of the *lukik* they had brought down.

"Perhaps we could scare them off and see what they've left," said Kantees.

"You want to steal a meal from wolves?"

"Just an idea."

"Once the hunters have finished with it," said Yenteel, "they'll drag the rest off to the caves the pack is living in."

"Do you know how to set traps?"

"I do. If there are wolves and *lukisa* there will be smaller animals."

"Birds," said Gally and he pointed to a clump of trees further down the river. Kantees turned to look. It was a whole cloud of birds—it was hard to tell how big the individuals were—swooping and circling. They must have been brightly coloured as blues, reds and greens flashed between and around the branches.

"Something's got them upset," said Yenteel. A distant clamour of squawks and screeches slowly grew. Even the wolves paused in their eating to look.

"Are they good to eat?" asked Kantees.

"Perhaps, but you'll get torn apart before you manage to cook one, even if you could kill it without being pecked to death."

"Oh." Kantees looked up and scanned the sky again. She felt as if her heart was breaking, she had never been away from Sheesha for so long. "I felt safer with the *ziri*," she said.

"And they could have brought us something to eat," said Yenteel. "But this is nothing, it's been barely a half-day since our last meal. I once went without for a five-day."

"Why?"

"Long story."

"We have time."

Yenteel glanced at Ulina and Gally. "It's not a story that's appropriate for younger and more innocent ears."

Kantees closed her eyes and shook her head. "The world is too dangerous for me," she said. "When I looked after Sheesha in his eyrie I didn't have to worry about anything except the next race."

"Or whether a certain lordling of our acquaintance would force himself on you. Or if you'd get sold to someone who didn't treat you well. Or whether you would be beaten either for a good reason, a bad reason, or even for no reason at all."

"Shut up."

He did.

Something was nagging her. It started as an itch at the back of her neck but intensified as they continued to follow the path with the open land downhill on their right. By the time they had descended to the grassland, the itch had turned to an ache. But still not enough to worry about, she just wanted to get some food, or find Sheesha and, of the two options, the second was the best.

They reached a bend where the path curved away to the left, keeping on the edge of the grass and winding between bushes. The pain intensified and she felt as if she was drowning.

"My head aches," she said touching the back of her head. As she turned towards Yenteel, her legs gave way and her knees bent under her weight as if they had no strength. The ground came up fast but she could barely feel it as she passed out.

She opened her eyes and blinked. Yenteel, Gally and Ulina were all looking into her face. Gally grinned but the concerned look of the others remained.

"What happened?" said Yenteel.

"What do you mean?"

"You went down like a stone-struck *sikechak*."

The memory came back. "Oh yes." Then she noticed her hands and cheek were stinging. There were grazes and tiny cuts on her palms.

"You said your head ached."

"Thanks for reminding me," she said because at his words the throb at the base of her skull returned. "It's not as bad now."

"I think we should be more concerned as to why you have it at all."

"People get headaches," said Kantees.

Ulina held out a water skin. The cold liquid was refreshing but it only emphasised the emptiness of her stomach. The headache did not reduce in strength, instead it seemed to become more distinct.

"How long was I out?"

"Long enough for Ulina to go down the path a way and find a stream to refill the water."

"Too small for fish," said Ulina.

"Did you see where this path goes?"

"Farther," said Ulina.

Kantees looked up at the peaks that surrounded them. She got the idea that each of them was a person staring down at her, a crowd of them looking over each other's shoulders, just at her.

"Kantees?"

"What?"

"I said do you think you can walk?"

"Of course I can." She pushed herself up and a wave of dizziness came over her. She thumped back down. "Perhaps."

Yenteel held out his hand, as did Gally. She hesitated, then took each hand and they levered her to her feet. She hung on as her head felt as if it was going to fall off.

"How's the headache?"

"It's alright," she said.

"Kantees, please, the truth, not what you think you want us to hear, or the way you want it to be."

She sighed. The world was becoming more stable. "It's no worse than when I was sitting down. I just feel a bit dizzy."

Sheesha! She felt lost without him.

Yenteel picked up her bag. "We'll take it slowly. You lean on Gally. Ulina can bring up the rear so nothing can surprise us and I will follow the path in the front."

And we'll cover less distance in an afternoon than a ziri would do in a couple of breaths.

She leaned on Gally.

"I will look after you, Kantees," he said with real concern in his voice. It almost broke her heart.

Yenteel moved off and Gally turned to follow, bringing Kantees with him.

She took one step forward and screamed as her head felt as if it was going to explode. Instinctively she turned in to Gally and threw her arms around him so she would not fall over again. She did not want to pass out, she was not weak!

The pain faded back to the dull ache.

"Kantees! Talk to me!" Yenteel's voice seemed to come from a great distance and she realised she had done exactly what she had not wanted to. She had lost consciousness while clinging to Gally and he had stopped her from falling over. In fact it seemed he had not moved at all as she was still looking over his shoulder at the valley.

"Yenteel," she said. "Please don't shout."

"What happened?"

"I turned to follow and my head hurt," she said. It felt as if her jaw was loose and she was not forming the words properly but Yenteel seemed to understand.

He was silent for a while and Kantees felt the clouds in her head drifting away. Her eyes were tired. She pushed herself gently away from Gally but kept her hand on his shoulder for support. His face was filled with confusion and concern.

"I'll be alright," she said to him. "We just need to understand what's happening."

She glanced down at Ulina. There was a tear on the child's cheek; the moment Kantees stared at it the girl brushed it away with the back of her hand. *She thinks I'm lying. Perhaps I am.*

"Do you feel ill?" said Yenteel.

She tried to focus but the throbbing in her head drowned out everything else. "My head hurts."

"Let me check."

He disappeared from her line of sight and she felt his hand on her scalp. In the last few ten-days her shorn hair had been getting longer. She didn't like it and it needed to be cut off.

"I can't see anything wrong," he said. "Can you point to where it hurts?"

She was loath to let go of Gally in case she fell over again but managed to point.

"Does it hurt when I press?"

She felt him pushing at her skull and then below the edge of it into her spine.

"It's just the same," she said. "It doesn't get any worse."

"Can you turn your head?"

Kantees made sure she had a firm grip on Gally's arm and shoulder and slowly turned her head one way as far as she could and then back the other way.

"No change," she said.

"How about nodding?"

"You're running out of ideas," said Kantees with a weak grin, which he couldn't see because he was still behind her. Gally saw it though and he beamed his innocent smile back at her.

"Just do it."

She put her chin to her chest and then looked up to the sky. A wave of dizziness hit her and she convulsively gripped Gally as she felt she was going to fall again, but the ache in the back of her head did not get any worse.

"No change in the headache," she said, glad to get her head back on the level. "But that one made me dizzy."

There was no response from Yenteel but he moved back to where he had been so she could see him.

"I don't know," he said, "when did it start?"

"The headache?"

"Yes."

"Yesterday."

"You didn't say anything."

"I didn't think it was anything," she said. "Besides it wasn't very bad, just a slight ache. And it didn't hurt at all when we were climbing the ridge."

It felt right.

"What?" said Yenteel.

"Nothing."

"You thought of something."

"It doesn't matter, it wasn't anything."

Yenteel took a couple of steps forward and put his face right in front of hers. "What aren't you telling me?"

"It's ridiculous."

"Just tell me."

"I thought it felt right."

"What felt right?"

"I don't know." She wanted to scream at him but felt too weak.

"Yes, you do."

She shook her head silently, her lips pressed shut. For the first time ever she thought he looked angry. At her.

To her relief he stepped back again. He looked up the path in the direction from which they had come, then along the way they would go. His eyes narrowed as he turned round completely and faced across the valley.

"Take a step back, Kantees," he said without turning.

"What?"

"Backwards, take a step back. Keep holding on to Gally."

"Why?"

"Because if you won't tell me, I'll have to do this the hard way."

Kantees shrugged, made sure she was holding on to Galiko, who smiled encouragingly, and took a small step back.

The pain in the back of her head swelled ominously, she took in a sharp breath and stepped forwards again. It subsided.

"Try sideways."

"Which way?"

"I don't think it matters."

After her previous experience she took a very small step to the left, and as her body followed her foot the pain increased. She moved back. The same in the other direction.

"Worse?"

"I'm stuck here," said Kantees in a voice that was somewhere between a whine and a whimper.

"Step forward."

"What's the point?"

He turned on her. "The point, Kantees, is that we are conducting an experiment and we only know that it hurts more in three of the directions you could go. There's one more to try. So, if you don't mind I would like you to take a step forward."

She took a deep breath and held it as she inched forwards. Gally moved back but still supported her. She gave him a smile. He grinned back.

The pain did not increase. She moved forward more. Still nothing.

Yenteel nodded. "Looks like we're going that way." He pointed across the valley.

"I don't understand."

Yenteel gave a short laugh. "Neither do I, Kantees," he said. "But we have no food so we can't stay here and if the only direction we are able to use is that one, then that's the one we'll use." He looked thoughtfully at the green stretching out in front of them. "Besides, we might be able to catch something on the way."

10

The first part of the walk was the worst, and the slowest. With her movement so limited Kantees clung to Gally and shuffled forward through the long grass. Memories of the nasty *chakisa* they had met shortly after they had escaped Jakalain kept coming back to her. No one had been hurt but the beasts were persistent and if enough of them jumped you they would kill you one small bite at a time.

This was just the sort of place she expected to find them; she could imagine them liking the long grass where they could attack without being seen.

But her fears did not materialise and, by midday, they had reached the river. The course they were forced to take brought them to a place almost exactly between the location the wolves had attacked the *lukik* and the trees with the cloud of multi-coloured birds. But now that they were down in the grass they could see neither.

The ground turned wet and muddy before they emerged on the river bank. The water was moving swiftly and was wide, but it didn't look too deep.

"Can we wade across?" said Kantees, then looked at Ulina. Even if Kantees, Yenteel and Gally could, Ulina would easily get swept away. Not for the last time Kantees scanned the sky for any trace of her beloved Sheesha. And not for the last time she was disappointed. She knew Sheesha would be able to find them, they had hardly covered any distance in the last day, but if Sheesha was never coming back…? She pushed the thought aside again knowing it would return to haunt her at any moment when she let her mind wander.

"Do we have any rope?" she said. "Perhaps a boat?"

Yenteel gave her a funny look. "How's your head?"

"The same, the ache is there but no pain."

He turned back to the river. "I studied this at length yesterday. I'm sure it's wider than it was."

"Meltwater," said Kantees. "The snow and ice in the high mountains is melting as spring is coming in. River levels rise and they can flood."

"More of your book learning."

"You know I can't read," she said. "But I have ears and I lived in the shadow of the mountains most of my life."

"I don't understand what your Master Kevrey was trying to do if he didn't teach you to read. There is no greater weapon than the ability to read and write."

"Obviously I am not that type of weapon," she said.

"I wonder if he knew about your ability with the dragons."

"He liked to bet on the races," she said. "But I never even saw a *ziri* close up, until I ran into Sheesha—" *And that moment had been terrifying and wonderful* "—and this isn't getting us across the river."

"No." Yenteel turned and stared at the rushing water.

Kantees sighed. She was useless in this state, if the only thing she could do was walk forwards. Perhaps the ache in her head was a little reduced. It was hard to tell.

"Stay still, Gally, let me test the pain once more."

She took a deep breath and braced herself then took a tiny step backwards. The pain did not increase. "Ha!"

She took a bigger step back, still no change. But the third step brought an increase in intensity still not enough to cause her to collapse, but a warning. At least it was better, probably because she was walking in the right direction, whatever that right direction was leading them to. She thought about the fog-wolves.

"Yenteel, what if it's a trap?" she called to him.

"What?" he said distractedly.

"This thing in my head, what if some creature has made a pattern that forces me to walk towards them so they can kill and eat me. Or eat me before I'm dead."

"It hasn't affected the rest of us."

"But we already know that I have some sort of contact with Sheesha, if not the other *ziri*."

"Well, if that's the case we're with you and can help you."

Kantees let the matter drop and tried moving sideways. That now seemed to be quite easy and even ten steps in each direction did not make her head any worse.

"I can move around more freely," she said having released Gally from being her support and walking down to the water's edge where Yenteel still stood.

"That's good."

"What about a pattern?"

"I don't have anything for this situation. It's mostly just healing and that protective pattern. We've used up Lintha's gifts. Besides—" he stretched and yawned, "—there's no additional power here that I can see."

"Why don't we just walk across?"

"Look at it, Kantees, that's a lot of water and it's very fast flowing. It would be so easy to get knocked off your feet and carried away downstream. I might manage it, Gally would probably be fine, but you would find it very difficult and Ulina would stand no chance at all."

The idea that had been forming in Kantees' mind crystallised. "So we just all go together."

Yenteel frowned with a lack of understanding.

"If we all go together, Ulina on my back to give me extra weight, we hold hands, no, we use your belt and Gally's to make sure we can't be separated. Gally and you walk down stream and stop me from getting washed away. We move slowly. Just like Gally helped me today. If any one of us loses their footing the others can hold them."

He stared at her. "That is very clever."

The mechanics of arranging the group was less easy than her simple description. The belt idea worked but only if they looped them around their wrists and held hands. The belt would catch them if they let go. Yenteel and Gally linked arms then Ulina did her climbing trick and clung to Kantees' back.

They stood there as if they were one six-legged beast. Then carefully they moved in tiny steps into the water.

It was freezing. Kantees had not considered that, though knowing the water was flowing from the high mountains she should have realised. But it was not a great distance to the other side, they could make it.

The icy water worked its way up her legs as they went deeper. Before it reached her knees she almost couldn't feel her feet.

"The water is very cold," said Gally.

"Yes it is," said Kantees, feeling that simple agreement was the best answer.

Then the pressure began to build up on her thighs and lower body.

"Only one of us move at a time," she said and found her teeth almost chattering. She had been colder in the winter nights in Shee-sha's eyrie but at least she had been dry and had hay to crawl into. Yenteel shuffled to his right, under prompting Gally did the same, then it was Kantees' turn. And round they went.

Each time she lifted her feet Kantees felt as if her legs would be ripped away from beneath her. Even with Ulina helping to hold her down the two of them together were not a great weight. Kantees tried to angle her body as if she was almost lying, and the force of the river washed the water up and over her back, making Ulina even wetter but she could hold her feet down better.

Something touched her leg and she cried out.

Yenteel and Gally looked at her in horror, perhaps thinking she might collapse in pain. But whatever had touched her disappeared in the swirls and currents. "S-s-sorry," she said and this time her teeth did chatter. She clamped them together.

Yenteel, Gally, Kantees; Yenteel, Gally, Kantees. They kept moving across, their progress slow but steady. Kantees had lost all feeling in her legs. But, with the help of the others, kept herself upright.

Yenteel, on his turn to move, suddenly dipped to the right and almost went under. Kantees saw Gally's muscles tense and Yenteel lifted.

"Big hole."

Without discussion they moved a little upstream and then kept moving.

It felt as if she was a legless thing in the water and that she had never been anywhere else. Her entire body was numb. She could not feel the hands of the people she was clutching. Finally, the ground sloped up and step by tiny step they made their way up and out.

Then they were on the other bank, cold and dripping. Even Ulina was soaked through and her usually pale skin was like white parchment. Even though she was exhausted Kantees forced herself to her feet, staying aware of the ache at the back of her head she tried to sort out a fire.

This side of the river had a high bank but it was not difficult to climb. She collected kindling and piled it up on the grass. The movement brought feeling back to her legs and feet though now they were crying out in pain as the sensation returned.

She stopped and scanned the sky hoping for a sight of the *ziri*, as usual there was nothing. But there was a mist up-river. For a moment she panicked thinking it might be fog-wolves, but then realised it was too big. And getting bigger.

Not getting bigger—getting closer. She felt the thunder before she heard it.

Something coming? A stampeding herd?

The shape of the mist became more distinct and she saw roiling clouds shooting upwards. A tree appeared and disappeared into the mist. The thunder grew. Kantees staggered to the edge of the bank.

"Get up! Climb! We have to get away from the river. Now! For the sake of the Mother! Now!" She kept shouting. Ulina obeyed first and fastest. Yenteel was on his feet and dragging the bulk of Gally up. Gally saw the oncoming mist and heard the roar and moved swiftly too.

They breasted the top of the bank. With a last look of loss at her pile of firewood Kantees and the others ran into the long grass away from the river as a mountain of water thundered along the channel, pouring out across the opposite bank which was on the same level as the river, but spilling over in great waves on to the higher side.

The tree she had seen tumbling through the water earlier buried itself in the ground directly in their path. Then they were inundated and Kantees was pulled off her feet.

It was the throbbing in her head that woke her, followed closely by the pains that seemed to be coming in from all over her body. She was lying face down on grass and could feel stones poking into her. The clothes on her back and legs seemed dry and hot, but underneath it was cold and damp.

She pressed down and lifted herself up into a kneeling position. A rustling from nearby made her turn her head to see but the light of the sun was too bright and all she could make out was an unfocused green swathe. Kneeling didn't make any part of her hurt any worse so she guessed she had not broken anything.

After a short time, her vision cleared but all she could see was the green which went off into the distance and the mountains beyond. Turning to the left and right she couldn't see anything she recognised. Almost without making the decision she pushed herself to her feet. The grass near her moved, not with the wind but something too short to be seen, causing the tops to move as it pushed its way through. She hoped it wasn't those *chakisa*.

It was as if the area had been hit by a great wind with flattened trees and bushes. Others torn from the ground and lying with their roots to the sky. She turned all the way round. The river was behind her. It looked as calm and serene as it had before except it was now almost a lake and extended away across the lower level on the other side.

As she watched, the carcass of a *lukik* floated slowly past, one leg out of the water. That would have kept them fed for days. Her stomach grumbled in protest.

Where were the others?

Surely they would have been deposited somewhere nearby? But there was no sign. Perhaps she had been lucky and dropped quickly while they had been carried much further. She turned and looked at the ridge on the other side of the river. She searched for some sign of the path they had come down but she saw nothing she recognised. But that didn't mean anything, there was no reason for her to be able to recognise anything.

The only thing that suggested she had not been carried very far was the pain at the back of her head. It was not protesting that she was going the wrong way. Unfortunately it was still there and she was loath to test it by searching for the others.

But what choice did she have? She would not be able to survive alone here in the wild. She must find them regardless of what the pain in her head wanted.

She went over to the fallen tree, sat on the trunk and checked her bag. She still had her flints, and the *chilafrah*. A fire seemed the right thing to attract attention—and to keep away unwanted animals. The only problem was that everything had been soaked by the flood.

11

It took until the sun was well down in the afternoon before she managed to get a fire going. Her other decision, as she waited for enough tinder to dry, was that it would be best to stay in one place. With the magic in her head that prevented her from moving far in the 'wrong' direction, searching was not a good option.

With the fire going and slowly building, she dried out larger twigs and branches to add, and the heat finished off the process of drying her out. She stripped off her clothes and let them dry through. In another world she would have been embarrassed and concerned about exposing herself, but there was no one to see her, and it wouldn't take long.

She collected as much wood as she could find before the sun went down, to make sure she had enough for the night. She dressed as the temperature dropped. If she had been Yenteel perhaps she could have made a protection spell to go around her and the fire. But she could not do patterning and, unable to read, she couldn't learn how either. She was not sure that she wanted to even if she had the opportunity.

She lay down close to the fire with her head on her bag and the pile of wood within reach so she could add more without having to move. The exercise of searching for wood had hurt at first, but the aches in her muscles and joints after the flood had mostly gone. Only the one in her head remained and it had decided not to bother her too much, at least for now.

The sky was clear. The stars—the children of Taymar, she had been taught—shone in their perfection. She did not know what her own people called the stars. She couldn't even speak Kadralin. What was the point of all this? Did she really think she was going to find her people? Even if she did, they wouldn't accept her. She knew well enough that just having the same skin colour did not mean that everyone was friends.

There was movement in the grass. She stayed completely still as a *chakik* emerged into the firelight. It was small. Perhaps one of the young. She had seen no sign of any others, it must have become separated from its…pack? Flock? Just as she had. It moved closer to the fire.

Slowly Kantees moved her hand to one of the branches. The creature did not seem to notice her, its attention fixed on the flames. It couldn't possibly understand but perhaps it appreciated the warmth.

Kantees slammed the branch down on its head and her stomach growled in anticipation of food. She hadn't eaten in nearly two days. Just water might sustain her for a while but she needed meat, and this little thing would have to do.

She had never prepared anything like this but she had seen Yenteel gutting animals and knew the basics. She understood that eating the insides was generally a bad idea unless you knew what you were doing, which she didn't. She picked a good-sized flaming branch and made her way to where the river continued to rush past, a man's height above its level when they had crossed it. Wedging the flaming branch between two stones she set to work. Her knife wasn't very sharp but she soon had opened the animal up and washed it out with the freezing water. She decided the scaly skin could stay on, gathered up some mud and packed the animal inside it, then went back to the fire.

She had no idea how long it should cook, and no way of telling how much time had passed. She stared at the ball of clay among the embers as it dried out, blackened, and cracks appeared on its surface. Then the smell escaped. The beautiful, delicious scent of cooked meat. Her mouth salivated.

"Kantees!"

She leapt to her feet as Ulina ran out of the darkness. The young girl threw herself at Kantees and hugged her. Kantees closed her eyes and held the child's body as if it was a lifeline to save her from drowning.

"I saw the fire," said Ulina. "I didn't know who it was, I didn't think it was you because you're not very good with fires. I'm so happy it was you."

She was even happier when Kantees rolled the clay ball out of the fire, hit it with a stone and it cracked open, filling the air with the wonderful smell.

If they burnt their fingers grabbing the juicy meat and stuffing it into their mouths they did not complain even once. It did not make a big meal, but it filled them enough.

Ulina explained that when the wave hit she had been torn from Kantees' back and been dropped a long way away. It was difficult to say how far but as soon as she had been able she had started to come back along the river.

Kantees did not comment on how dangerous it was. This was Ulina, it would take a lot of animal, or man, to bring her down, as long as she had her knife.

"Did you see any sign of the others?" asked Kantees even though she knew what the answer would be.

"Not Yenteel but I think he will be alright," she said and left any comment about Gally hanging. Kantees had the same thought: she could not believe that Gally could survive alone, even assuming that he had not simply drowned. Could he swim? It seemed unlikely, he worked with the *ziri* just as Kantees had. Neither of them had any reason or opportunity. If the flood had dropped her into the water instead of on land, Kantees would probably have drowned.

"I'm sure they'll both be alright," said Kantees.

Ulina looked at her. Kantees expected a comment about being a good liar, or even a bad liar in this case but instead Ulina nodded. "Yes."

Kantees wanted to have them both stand watches through the night, at least that would have been her plan but Ulina slipped into sleep almost immediately and Kantees could not blame her. So she decided not to worry and after throwing the uneaten skin and bones of the little animal into the fire, she lay down herself and was asleep the moment her eyes closed.

The cry of a *sikechak* woke her. She rolled on to her back and stared up. Dawn hung in the sky and the stars were fading while the crimson eye of Colimar, almost full, hung directly above her. There was probably a Kadralin prayer for the red moon, she thought, but she did not know what it would be.

Someone snored.

Kantees frowned. It did not sound like Ulina. It sounded like Yenteel.

She sat up and stared at the two man-shaped lumps lying on the other side of the fire. She shook her head as if she was trying to loosen the illusion and drive it from her mind. But they persisted. Yenteel snored again and then muttered under his breath.

The other was Gally and the two of them looked bedraggled, as if they hadn't dried properly. Kantees built up the fire then looked again as the flames gave better illumination. She couldn't help but smile; for the first time she realised she was happier with these people around her than she was without them. And it wasn't only because Yenteel was a better cook, or because Ulina was the one who could protect her, or because Gally's simple honesty was so much better than the lies she told herself.

When she woke a second time the sky was grey, and the branches she had added in the night had been reduced to ashes. She was the first awake again. Taking care not to aggravate the pain at the back of her head she walked around the camp. She was not too concerned, since she had made it as far as the river yesterday without pain. She just wished that she understood what was happening.

The flood on the other bank seemed to be going down but that was of no real concern since they would not be going back that way. Big chunks of ice were flowing in the water now, rolling and turning as they bumped the bottom. Wherever this water had come from it must have been high in the mountains where everything was only just beginning to melt.

She was worried that those little people with the eels might decide to follow them over the ridge, but even if they did Kantees did not think they would be bringing their vicious pets with them. If they were pets. There was just so much in the world that no one knew about. She had heard tales of the wild, of course, those spaces in between the towns and cities where monsters lurked waiting to kill and eat the unwary traveller, but she had never really believed them. In her imagination the hero had always flown on a *ziri* and the creatures on the ground could never touch them.

And now she was the hero, except she had lost her *ziri*.

She jumped back in horror as a huge mouth full of teeth rose out of the water. Then it turned and splashed back. The back of the creature rose up and its two wide wings spread out on either side. The tip of one wing caught the bank and the whole body slowly turned. It was dead. A dead *sikechak* of huge proportions, its body as long as she was tall. For a moment she simply stared in wonder at the dark, mottled, leathery skin and the cold empty eye that seemed to stare right back at her. It turned and began to move out into the main current once more.

Then she realised.

With a cry she took two steps forward and leapt into the water. The cold seemed to rip the warmth from her. She grabbed at the wingtip. It too was stone cold, but that was a good thing. She felt the bones beneath the surface of the skin and pulled hard. Her effort only succeeded in pulling her towards the dead creature, the opposite of what she intended.

The current tugged at her feet. She grabbed the wing with her other hand and, leaning backwards, beat her feet against the water as hard and fast she could. At first the only thing that happened was that she moved away from it until her arms were at full stretch. The current refused to release the *sikechak*. Finally, she felt the weight of it resisting her. She glanced behind and saw she had come a long way from the bank. If she let go now she might drown in the attempt to get back. The *sikechak* at least seemed buoyant.

They were heading into a curve in the river. Kantees kicked as hard as she could, she might not be able to drag the great thing directly the way she wanted but she might be able to steer it. Perhaps even slow it down as the current tried to carry it away.

The bank drew closer and she redoubled her efforts. Something scraped across her back. For one terrible moment she thought of the eels and believed she might be torn to pieces. Then she realised it was a tree branch, or a root. The tree was almost above her and she was swept under its long thin branches dangling into the water.

She wiggled round and hooked her leg on the root. The current was strong and the beast was large. With her body anchored, the force of the water tried to break her grip but she hung on as it changed orientation and swung in towards the bank.

Taking a chance she released one hand and grabbed one of the long dangling branches. Gripping the end she wrapped it as many times as she could around the wing, as far up from the tip as she could reach. The *sikechak* had claws at intervals along its wing and she managed to use one of those to hook the flexible branch in such a way that it wouldn't simply slip off.

She relaxed as the branch took the strain. All she had to do was hang on to the end so that the turns didn't unravel. The *sikechak* was caught. Climbing out of the water while still holding the end of the branch wasn't easy but she managed it and stood shivering on the bank under the canopy of long branches, with half the wing up on the bank with her. She stood on it to prevent it getting away again, while she decided what to do next.

She knelt down and carefully pulled on the wing and the *sikechak*'s head and body emerged from the water. It was not as heavy as she expected, but it was not light, so she would not be able to carry it.

Her bag was full of water but its contents were unharmed. The dagger was getting blunt but she managed to hack off lengths of the flexible branches and laid them out. There had been pictures of the bone structure of such creatures at her old master's home. It was interesting to see them in real life and to see how the wings folded. Very like a *ziri*.

Using the branches as cords she tied the wings against the body, then awkwardly tied the head with its long and vicious tooth-filled beak. She almost felt apologetic towards the creature. But it would provide enough food for them all for several days. Finally she took one branch, hooked it through the bonds she had made and pulled the thing up on to her shoulders, while its feet dragged along on the ground.

Despite the difficulty of capturing the beast as it floated down the river, she was not far from the camp and it was only a short time later she came into the area around the fire. Only to find them all still asleep.

"I could have drowned and none of you would have been the wiser," she said to no one in particular. She looked at the three of them. She wouldn't kick Ulina because she was only a little girl, while kicking Gally would be unfair because he would think he had done something wrong. So she kicked Yenteel in the leg.

He groaned.

She kicked him again. "Wake up. I've brought food."

That worked. He rolled over, and then just stared at her. She could barely imagine what he might be thinking. Slowly he got up on to his knees and she dropped the wet and bound beast to the ground where it landed with a slap.

"That's a *sikechak*," he said in a bemused way.

"And I'm glad to see you alive too, Yenteel."

He got to his feet. "We saw your fire but by the time we arrived you were asleep. And you did not seem to want to wake up." He grinned. "At least we didn't kick you."

"Is Gally alright?"

Yenteel nodded. "He was very difficult when he couldn't find you but I managed to keep him calm enough."

"I'll have to apologise to him."

"Kantees, if you hadn't shouted that warning we would be dead." He looked down at the flying monster at her feet. "And now you bring breakfast, so I must forgive you for not saving us any of whatever it was that gave off that delicious smell last night.”

“It wouldn’t have been enough for four,” she said. “But I’m sure this will feed man-sized appetites.”

“For a five-day,” he said.

12

They spent the entire day cutting up the *sikechak* and cooking its meat. Yenteel scouted for other ingredients but did not find much beyond some leaves that could be used for flavouring.

Kantees found she could go some distance in different directions without it causing her any additional pain, which had been encouraging. She explored the local area with Ulina and Gally to see whether she was still limited in the directions she could go.

Although she was not as restricted as she had been on the cliff, there were still limits up and down river. She had been moving too quickly at one point and the sudden searing pain knocked her to the ground. Ulina and Gally pulled her back the way they had come and Kantees recovered after a short time sitting down.

This time they tried to map the edge of the pain but the only impression Kantees got was that she was in some kind of tunnel and that, perhaps, it was getting wider the closer they got to the place from which it originated. It didn't seem to make a great deal of sense.

Back at the camp Kantees asked Yenteel about her blunted knife. He searched and found a flat stone then showed her how to sharpen it. The *sikechak* did not carry a lot of fat but they managed to get enough to pour on the stone to help with the process. When they ran out of oil they used water.

Kantees watched as Ulina examined the bones left over. The ones for the wings were straight and very light. Ulina took out her blade and sliced off one of the ends then sharpened it with a few deft strokes.

The girl slammed the bone point first into the ground where it went in a finger's length and stuck there. The girl turned her attention to the others and very soon had a dozen very sharp bones of various lengths.

"What are those for?" said Kantees.

"The big ones are weapons."

"And the small ones?"

She just shrugged. Kantees did not push it. The small ones could be used as weapons as well. After what happened with the eel, Kantees could not object. They all needed to be able to attack.

Yenteel washed the *sikechak* skin in the river and had Ulina cut a scraping tool from a piece of the creature's spine. He gave that to Gally and set him to work removing all the sinew and other bits still attached.

"We can probably make something out of it," said Yenteel. "Or exchange it for food or shelter."

Kantees nodded. Despite the pain in her head, she felt more relaxed now than she had since she escaped from Jakalain on Sheesha's back.

But the reminder of her *ziri* made her heart sink again. She did not know if she would ever find him. Certainly not while she had this pain driving her forward.

By the time they were fully prepared, night was closing in again and they decided to stay another night. It was the longest she had stayed in one place for many five-days.

She wondered how Daybian and Levin were getting on. They would have reached Jakalain by now; she hoped Daybian's father would listen. He was a fair man—even if he saw nothing wrong with owning slaves. Would his experiences with her change Daybian's mind? He wasn't the sharpest sword but he had a good heart. He had never actually forced himself on her, he had wanted her to agree. She pulled a face. *That* would never happen, but then she smiled as she remembered how brave he had been in the cave at Kurvin Port. He was a good friend, even if he was an arrogant lump.

It took them half a day trekking through the long grass to reach the base of the cliff on the other side of the valley. They had gone astray twice and Kantees had run into the wall of pain to put them back on course.

No animal had bothered them but they all carried several of the hastily made bone stabbers tucked into their belts and the rest stored in backpacks. Ulina had been trying to teach Gally how to thrust with the longer ones. He seemed willing to try endlessly but lacked the killer instinct, which meant his thrusts were weak. This seemed to offend Ulina's sensibilities. As far as she was concerned, if someone was going to use a weapon they had to really mean it.

They passed the occasional family group of *lukisa* but none of the males seemed inclined to challenge them. Perhaps they saw people so rarely they were not considered to be a threat. Whatever the reason, they were unmolested for the entire walk.

The incline started gently enough as the grass gave way to stones and boulders, all well-worn and it did not look as if there had been a rock-fall here recently. But Yenteel pointed along the valley's edge to where a tumbled pile of rock stood out black against the green on to which it had tumbled. Even the side of the mountain looked as if it had a fresh wound, revealing bare bleak stone with jagged edges where all the rest was rounded and weathered.

There was nothing like that here. It was all old and weathered with plenty of greenery growing most of the way up, even where the slope was almost vertical.

"How can we climb this?" said Kantees in despair. "You might as well leave me here."

"Don't be silly," said Yenteel. "For a start it's not as bad as it looks, and before we make any decision we must assess the extent of the magic causing your problem."

Kantees did not question his comment about the magic, there

was nothing else it could be, although she had no idea how or why she should be afflicted in this way. There had been no one around to perform a patterning on her, and if it was a creature doing it, well, it made no sense; they only had magic to assist with their lives—usually to help them find food—but this was drawing her in across a very long distance.

As far as she was concerned it must be a patterner.

"What if it was something like a scroll," she said suddenly as they paced the distance between the furthest points she could travel along the base of the cliff. "If I had triggered a trap over in the big river valley by the lake. Can that be done?"

Yenteel did not respond immediately. "It's possible, Kantees. But I don't know how such a thing might work."

"I expect Tenical would know," she said.

"He might, but would he tell you even if he did?"

They reached the far end of her free movement as the pain in her head increased. They had left Ulina and Gally at the other end.

"Just stay there," said Yenteel and he set off at a slow run towards a small tree. He climbed it and used his far-seeing device to focus first on Kantees and then the others.

The day was warm but on this side of the valley the sun was occasionally obscured by the mountains. It wouldn't be until later in the year that it would shine down on them here. But Kantees closed her eyes and listened to the insects. It was a very pleasant quiet.

She heard Yenteel approaching and opened her eyes. He was frowning.

"What's wrong?"

"Nothing."

She looked sceptical.

"No, nothing, it's just confusing. Of course I can't give exact numbers but the distance between the edges here seems almost twice what it was back by the river."

"That's not a bad thing, perhaps it's wearing off."

"Was the pain any less when you got to the edges?"

"No."

"Not wearing off then." He hesitated. "Something else. On the far side of the valley you had no room to manoeuvre at all. Here you have a hundred strides or more. Which is good news for getting up there."

"What does it mean?"

He shook his head. "I do not know." Then he smiled reassuringly. "Let me think about it."

They returned to the middle and called the other two to come back. They ate cold, cooked *sikechak*. Kantees stood up and walked away from the cliff then turned and stared up at it. There was only one point where it became dangerously steep. And even then she could see a line of cracks running up and to the right.

She was most concerned about Gally. He was large and round. He had lost a lot of weight since their escape, and had probably become stronger, but if any of them would have difficulty it was him. From what she knew of Ulina, the girl would have absolutely no trouble at all. She was light, small and, when they had met her in the village near Kurvin Port, the leader had told them how she liked to climb cliffs. Never mind the way she had jumped from *tekrak* to *tekrak* on the Dunor's island.

Kantees smiled as an idea came to her. She called Ulina over and pointed up.

"You can climb this?"

"Yes, Kantees, easily. Shall I show you?"

"Wait, no, I believe you. Fetch a couple of those smaller bone daggers you made, I'd like you to try something."

In the middle of the afternoon Kantees put her foot on the first of the bone daggers that Ulina had hammered into a crack in the cliff face. She gingerly put her foot on it. It did not move. Little by little she transferred all her weight while she clung to the rock with her fingers, then slid her other foot up and across to the next one. Her heart was pounding, the fear of falling was strong but she had to keep going. Not just for her own sake but so that Gally would see that it could be done.

The order of climb had been decided, while Ulina went back and forth across the surface as if she was a strange four-legged spider. Kantees would go first because she was the lightest of the other three and would be able to test the pegs. She was also well aware that Yenteel considered her to be more important than anyone else, so no one else got a chance to break the pegs before she went up.

Yenteel next and Gally last. Gally tried to be brave but his fear was obvious. At Yenteel's suggestion, they spent more precious time cutting the *sikechak* skin from both wings. They sliced them into thin strips and tied the pieces end to end, then plaited them for strength to create a rope. Once the first three were up they would send down a loop of it to Gally for just the difficult bit since it was not very long.

Kantees made it to the top and joined Ulina. Yenteel was slower than Kantees but eventually he made it. They shouted encouragement to Gally but he only climbed a short way before his courage gave out. Kantees was debating what to do when Ulina simply climbed down again, making it look as if she was crawling across a flat surface.

They could not hear what she said to Gally but he started moving again and this time Ulina went ahead of him telling him where to put his hands and feet. He reached the vertical section and Kantees tossed the loop over while Yenteel found a place to anchor it. There was only one small outcrop of rock that seemed solid enough and it was smooth with weathering.

"You stand on it to stop it popping off the top," said Yenteel. "I'll hang on to stop it slipping."

From that point they couldn't see what was happening below. Kantees watched the rope and every time it went slack she would take her weight off it and Yenteel would tighten it. Suddenly, the rope jerked Yenteel's hands to the rock and pulled Kantees' feet from under her. She fell as a cry came from below.

"A hand, Kantees," Yenteel said through gritted teeth. There was blood on his fingers. Kantees grabbed the rope and held it tight. Eventually it loosened again. Yenteel freed his bleeding fingers and Kantees stood back on the rope.

Finally Ulina appeared, along with Gally's two hands. Then he was up on the ledge with them.

"Gally fell," he said. "Very scared."

Kantees gave him a smile. "You were brave."

Yenteel was rummaging in his bag again, Kantees knew he was after his healing patterns. She took the bag from him and, after a moment's hesitation, he let her find what he needed.

"Let's stay here for the night," said Kantees. Being on a ledge above a cliff was not her idea of a good place to rest but it was wide enough to take them all. They did not know what they would discover over the next ridge and she would rather find out when she had slept and was refreshed.

13

They slept lying against the rock at the back of the ledge but it didn't protect them from the rain that started during the night. They just had to endure it and the wind just added insult to injury as it whipped the rain at them horizontally.

Kantees gave up trying to sleep. She sat with her back to the wall and her bag resting on her head in an attempt to reduce the onslaught. It hardly seemed worth it.

There was little to see but she stared out into the wet blackness. Still her head ached. She tried to fathom what it could mean that, as she approached the thing—presuming it was a thing—that was causing it, it became less precise. It seemed unreasonable, if something was luring her in wouldn't it become more accurate? More focused?

She dozed with the question hanging in her mind.

The wind had dropped but the rain continued to fall steadily. The view from the ledge was smudged grey and green with the occasional darker patch that represented trees.

Yenteel's healing patterns had mended his fingers on the outside though they still looked bruised and he rubbed them from time to time. No one said much. The rain dampened any pleasure they might have had from conquering the cliff.

The climb from here was less steep and could be achieved by scrambling over the rocks. Yenteel tried to find the easier routes but it did not help a great deal. Plants grew from crevices and they seemed to thrive. It gave them something else to hold on to and pull themselves up.

They finally reached the point on the ridge where they could see down into the next valley. The rain did not make it easy but from what Kantees could make out, it was a wide plateau. Higher again than the valley they had left. Streams and rivers made darker lines across the surface and trees were common, much to her disgust.

The far side of the plateau where the cliffs rose up again were just shadows in the rain, with the tops of the mountains lost in clouds.

Most importantly, they could see buildings—similar in design to the one by the lake—from which smoke was rising. Kantees' heart beat faster in anticipation that she had reached her goal. Was this the home of the Kadralin? She felt like saying *I told you so* to Yenteel, but decided to wait until they were sure. The mountains had not been good to them up to now.

"How's your head?" said Yenteel.

"Same."

"When we get down to the plain we'll check how much space you have and make sure we're still heading in the right direction."

"How?"

Yenteel smiled. "Some of us have been taking note of the mountains and the direction we've been travelling," he said. "Some of us think that this is not just some random magic and that we are being guided somewhere."

"And when you say 'us'?"

"I mean me." He took out his far-seer and used it to look back the way they had come, then let it drop. "Unfortunately, the rain is a problem."

"We should get on," she said, trying to hide her desire to see who lived in those houses.

"We need to wait until I can establish the correct bearing."

"But the rain might not let up for days."

"Do you want to miss the place?"

Ulina suddenly spoke. "You mean that?"

They both looked at her, she was pointing out across the plateau. At first Kantees could see nothing out of the ordinary, then as she looked back and forth something dark caught her eye. Tall and thin, a black line grew out of the landscape, barely noticeable because of the rain. It vanished as the rain intensified.

She looked at Yenteel who had his far-seer to his eye again, looking at where the line had been.

"Can you see it?" she said.

"Gone," he said but he stayed still with the brass tube to his eye. "Get a stone, Kantees, draw a line that follows the line I'm looking in." Kantees understood and cast around looking for something she could use to make a mark on the ground. But Ulina was ahead of her, she had her knife out and knelt beside Yenteel's feet. Kantees saw what she was doing and went to stand directly in front of Yenteel. On tiptoe she looked along the barrel of the far-seer.

Ulina cut a line in the stone between their pairs of feet.

"Done," she said and the two of them relaxed.

Yenteel and Kantees looked at the line. It wasn't straight and jumped from one rock to another but the overall direction was clear. Yenteel tried looking behind them again but the rain obliterated the view.

"I think it's the right direction," said Yenteel. "It's definitely not the wrong direction."

"I don't want to wait," said Kantees. "We've wasted enough time as it is."

"Wasted time?"

"I lost the *ziri* and we're crawling like babies across the world."

"It wasn't your fault."

"How do you know, Yenteel?"

He shut up.

If she was crying they would never be able to tell with the rain.

She shouldered her bag. "Let's go."

Ulina was beside her in a moment and Gally was only slower because he was bigger. Kantees glanced at the slope before them. Rounded boulders all the way down. Easy to slip on, but not if they were careful.

She set off and did not look behind to see if Yenteel was following.

The descent was much as she had expected, though her foot slipped into a hole and she needed help getting herself uncaught. Yenteel said nothing as he gently eased her foot from the gap between the rocks.

"Thank you," she said as she retrieved what was left of her worn-out shoe that had been left behind. She looked at them all, their clothes were all threadbare, and in some cases torn through. They needed to get some new ones. Perhaps they could trade at this place.

The houses had looked closer when they were on the top of the ridge but it took them until the middle of the day, crossing the many streams that ran through the plateau. There were herds of *lukisa*, far more numerous than the ones below.

Finally, they found a track, which led them to a wooden gate set in a stone wall covered in moss with plants growing from its cracks, looking as if it had been made a hundred years ago, perhaps even more.

The latch on the gate was simple and it swung open smoothly on its wooden hinges. What she found odd was the lack of patterns carved into its surface. That was what people always did. Whether the patterns had any effect or not, beds, chairs, doors, gates, window frames, they always had magic carved into them as protection or curses.

She made a point of looking the gate over thoroughly but there was nothing.

Yenteel watched her. "What is your interest in gates, Kantees?"

"It's unusual," she said. She saw no reason to give him any clues, he was keeping secrets from her, why shouldn't she treat him the same way?

She headed off towards the buildings that could be seen among the trees ahead; there was no sign of any people yet. Yenteel was left staring at the gate.

The track changed to what could be called a road. The surface was stone, though it was old and cracked in places. Again it was reminiscent of the one beside the lake. Not that she doubted these had been made by the same people, no matter that it had been a long time in the past. The one at the lake had been abandoned, perhaps because of the creatures that now lived in the water. This was still in use.

On either side there were paddocks, a couple of *lukisa* in one, the others empty, then a cultivated area with rows of plants. Kantees imagined what it might be like to have a proper cooked meal with vegetables.

The road continued past the houses through a small wood and out into the land beyond. The rain had lifted until it was a drizzle but the trees prevented them seeing any further. Though she was a little nervous of the wood, she assumed it would not contain anything unpleasant since it was so close to this farm. There had been no defences at all, so there was probably little risk here.

A gate opened to a path that led to the door of the building from which smoke rose. The windows were the same as the one by the lake, small rectangles below and long thin ones above. Many of them were blocked by stone or wood. Of the others, the majority contained their glass, but others stood empty.

"What should we do?" said Kantees.

"Knock on the door," said Yenteel.

"Who?"

"You."

Kantees knew he was right but that did not make it any easier. "Better it's just one of us, I suppose," she said. "So as not to be threatening."

"That's what I thought," said Yenteel.

"I will come," said Ulina. "I am only a little girl. I will not scare them."

"That would be their mistake," said Kantees and Ulina gave a little smile.

"A woman and a child seem very safe," said Yenteel. "Gally and I will stand back here, well away from the gate so we don't look as if we're about to rush them."

"They are watching us," said Ulina.

"How many?"

"I have seen five at different windows."

"Then they will have us outnumbered," said Kantees and sighed. "I suppose that's a good thing."

Ulina slipped her hand into Kantees'. "I will not let them hurt you."

"I know. You're a good girl." She looked up at the door again. "Let's go."

She unlatched the gate and they went through. She turned back to Yenteel and Gally who were now sitting on the wall on the other side of the road. She didn't think they looked dangerous, but how others might see them was something else. They had fought the Dunor and escaped. They had survived a night in a ley-circle occupied by monstrous men.

But those had been clear enemies.

Kantees lifted her hand and knocked on the door. This time she was hoping to see a black face, someone that would be a friend. She wanted this land to be a place where she could live and forget the world outside.

Muffled voices engaged in frantic discussion on the other side of the door. She couldn't make out any individual words. Then there was silence until the latch clicked.

The interior was dark and the light from the door highlighted a man. Kantees realised she had been holding her breath and let it out when she saw that he was Kadralin.

He was Kadralin. She felt like shouting it. She had been right. To the depths of the dark with Yenteel and his doubts.

The man was dressed in a coarse woollen shirt, and dark trousers. He stared at Kantees and then his eyes dropped to Ulina. Perhaps there was a slight reaction when he saw her. Perhaps that was her imagination, but Ulina backed away slightly as if she was nervous, and moved behind Kantees.

He said something. The words meant little but they sounded like a question.

"I am Kantees," she said.

The man squinted.

She tried again, touching her hand to her chest. "Kantees." She put her hand on Ulina's head. "Ulina." She turned and pointed to the others. "Yenteel. Galiko."

The man grunted. A woman's voice came from inside. Again Kantees did not understand.

She touched her fingers to her chest again. "Kadralin, I am Kadralin." Almost as if she wanted to convince them, though her skin told them what they needed to know, how could she be anything else?

The woman in the darkness spoke again. The man muttered something angrily back.

Kantees wanted to tell them everything. How she had dreamed of meeting her own people—ones who were free—since before she could remember; since the day she had heard they might exist when she lived in the house of Kevrey in Dakastown. Had her master deliberately said it so that she would hear? He had told her she was a weapon, had this been part of her forging?

She could not allow herself to believe that everything she had learnt was part of his manipulations, so she stood here on the doorstep waiting for her people to invite her in.

Why?

She pushed that down. The why was obvious. She wanted to stop running and she refused to follow the path her Taymalin master had laid out for her.

How can you know this is not the path?

"Please," she said, in part to silence the voice in her head. "May we come in? Is there anyone here who can speak our language?"

Yenteel shouted something. Kantees frowned. She hadn't heard him properly, she couldn't make out what he was saying. She turned. He had come across the road and was standing behind the wall.

Whatever it was he had said, he repeated it.

"You speak their language?" *My language.*

"No, Kantees, but the trader people on the mainland are Kadralin, they have a language that was once Kadralin, mixed with the tongue of the Taymalin. I can speak that, you know it, I have before."

She turned back to the man in the doorway. He had come out

into the light and was no longer paying any attention to Kantees. He spoke slowly to Yenteel. Yenteel replied.

The man nodded and went into the house.

Kantees glared at Yenteel. "You stole it from me."

"I took nothing, Kantees."

"I wanted this, you never wanted it."

"You still have it."

Kantees found herself crying and cursed herself for being so emotional.

"You asked me once why I was with you."

"I asked you a dozen times, you milk-puke." She knew she was shouting but she couldn't stop herself.

He nodded. "My master told me to ease your way."

"You and your master manipulate me just like every other spawn of Taymar. Your skin may be black but your heart is as white as the Taymalin. I've had enough of it."

"But you need me now," he said very quietly.

If she had had anything in her hands she would have thrown it at him.

Yenteel looked her in the eye. "Kantees, the farmer has invited you into his home. Are you going to ignore him?"

"I won't forget this," she said. "And one day I will make you and your master suffer."

He did not say it, but she could see his response in his eyes: *as if I have not already suffered?*

She turned away from him before she felt sorry for him. The man had gone from the doorway and instead there was a woman. She was smiling and holding out her hand. Kantees could not smile even though she felt only gratitude as she stepped inside the room that smelled of cooking, animals, and home.

1 4

It was odd how the farmers seemed out of place in this building. It was not something she could easily put her finger on. Perhaps it was because where there were cracks, old and mouldering, nothing had been done to fix them. That the windows were boarded up or simply left broken where they had no glass.

Kantees followed the woman through the first room that seemed to be used as a dumping ground for old tools, chairs, and tables. It would not be possible to live in here. The kitchen at the back was tidier. There was a fire with pots above, something delicious was cooking. Perhaps the fact they had not had a properly cooked meal for quit some time meant anything would smell good.

Two children, barely toddlers, were playing on the floor and looked up at the strangers. When they noticed Ulina, still at Kantees' side, they stared. A girl carrying a pail entered from the door opposite, she glanced at the newcomers but went to the fire where she deposited the pail and spooned out water into one of the pots.

The farmer's wife turned and said something, pointing to chairs around a table. Kantees took a seat with Yenteel on one side—she ignored him—and Ulina and Gally on the other.

Four wooden bowls were filled, and brought over along with flat bread. There were no spoons or other eating utensils. The smell was good and Kantees lifted the bowl to her lips. The liquid was almost hot enough to burn her lips but she slurped it and the taste exploded across her tongue. It was not that it was a particularly thick broth. But it was flavoursome and was the best thing they had tasted in days.

After she had tasted the food the others followed her lead and ate. Every one of them used the bread to wipe the remaining liquid from the bowl. The farmer, his wife, and the children watched them eat.

Kantees smiled her gratitude.

"Gally?" she said. "Have you got the *sikechak* skin?"

He shrugged the remains of the skin off his back, where it had been tied up with the rope they had made, and placed it on the table. Kantees stood up and looked at Yenteel. "Translate this for me."

"Keep it simple," he said.

"Thank you for your hospitality," she said slowly, as if that might help them understand. Yenteel hesitated and then spoke in the language she so desired to understand.

The man and woman nodded. Yenteel translated their response as, "It is our honour to help travellers from beyond the mountains."

"How do they know we're from beyond the mountains?" she said, concerned that he might have said too much in his translation.

Yenteel just nodded in the direction of Ulina. "And my version of their language is clearly not from around here."

"Alright, now say this: Please accept this gift of a *sikechak* skin."

"You're giving it to them?"

"Just tell them."

"It would be a lot easier to say it was for trade," Yenteel said quietly. "Those are words I know."

But he did as he was told.

Kantees pushed the package across the table. The farmer undid the ties and unrolled the skin. Even though they had used most of it to form rope, the remainder still seemed huge in the room. The children came to examine it, as did the farmer's wife. There was much talking and they seemed impressed.

Suddenly a stream of questions was launched at Yenteel. He answered as best he could and Kantees did not interrupt him, she expected to get a summary when they were done, but Yenteel said two words she recognised in quick succession and she was about to shout at him for daring to call her Kantees of the Ziri again, when everything went quiet.

The farmer and his wife turned their attention to her with a look of what she couldn't deny was fear, and sank to their knees. Their foreheads touched the stone floor in obeisance.

"What have you done?" she demanded, expecting to see a smug look on his face but Yenteel was clearly as surprised as she was. But she wasn't going to give him any benefit of the doubt. "You just had to do it, didn't you? You had to call me that name."

The older girl was also on her knees with her head to the ground. Only the young children seemed immune, and were giggling.

"Their reaction is interesting though," said Yenteel.

"You've scared them out of their wits," said Kantees, her voice rising with her anger.

"You're not helping using that tone."

"One day I might just stick a knife between your ribs."

"You will do whatever you think fit, Kantees, but right now I think we should find out what's going on. Don't you?"

She forced her voice to a more reasonable level. "I'm going to go outside. You talk to them and find out. Don't upset them any more than you already have."

"I will do my best."

"Of course you will, you're here to *ease my way*. Isn't that how you put it?" she said. "I don't trust you, Yenteel, but I have no choice. I can't even tell you not to use that name because you will anyway if you think it suits your purpose. But just remember, no matter how much you think you're doing it for me, the truth is you're doing it for your master and he doesn't care what I want."

He said nothing. She threaded her way round the back of the table and out through the kitchen door with Ulina following, as expected.

· · ·

544

"These mountains are the same ones that I saw from Jakalain but from the other side," said Kantees as she and Ulina stood in the yard outside the back of the farm building. There were a number of other buildings, all of which seemed to hold livestock. *Kelukisa* yowled from one, and they could see the legs of something large shuffling behind the door of another.

Further back was a paddock with three *kichesa* which were probably used for pulling the cart that sat off to one side. Kantees looked up, the rain had stopped and the clouds were tearing across the sky now.

Kantees headed for the corral, avoiding animal droppings. At least the *kichesa* would be tame and they might want to be petted. Ulina walked along behind her, not saying a word.

As they approached the fence one of the *kichesa* rumbled and took long solid strides in their direction. Its scaly tail lifted to balance it. Kantees held out her hand for it to have a sniff and then it approached closer and she rubbed it on the side of its solid neck, feeling the muscles move beneath the green and grey scales.

It leaned down and sniffed her head, its breath puffing through her short hair.

Seeing that there was no danger, the other two wandered over. The smaller one kept stopping to sniff the ground, as if it was pretending it wasn't truly interested in these two new people who had turned up.

"Are they safe?" said Ulina.

"They just eat plants like the *lukisa*," said Kantees. She turned to see that Ulina was standing a short distance away, her hand on the dagger sheath round her neck. "They are used to people. Don't you have *kichesa* at your—?" Kantees broke off, cursing herself. She had resolved never to ask Ulina about her past.

Yenteel had been right and Kantees knew it, had known it almost from the start. The only thing that explained Ulina's skill at bringing death, and her lack of any emotion in doing so, was that she was Farahalek. A child stolen away and trained almost from birth to kill in a thousand ways and without remorse.

"There were *kichesa*," said Ulina. "But they were trained to kill."

Kantees looked at the three animals pushing at her, trying to get her attention and perhaps have her feed them a treat. They were half the size of a *ziri* but though their mouths might be filled with flat teeth for chewing, if they chose to bite they could rip a hand off. Or crush a head.

"Kantees!" Gally called as he came out of the farmhouse. "Yenteel says to come back."

She sighed, grateful she did not have to hear any more from Ulina. She had enough pain of her own, she did not need to carry someone else's.

She turned away from the *kichesa* and Ulina, and headed back to the building. Gally waited for her and then followed her inside. The kitchen was empty of everyone except Yenteel and the farmer. As she entered, the farmer looked away from her and down at the ground. As if he thought she could strike him down where he stood with nothing but a look.

Kantees stopped just inside the door, she had no desire to get close to Yenteel, and really did not want to know what he had discovered. She knew it wasn't going to be good.

"Well?" said Kantees when Yenteel failed to say anything for a long while.

"He's terrified of you because of the name I used."

"I know that."

"And why do you think that is?"

"I'm in no mood for games, Yenteel."

He took a deep breath. "It seems that the *ziri* are not thought of kindly here."

She wasn't sure what she had been expecting him to say, but it wasn't that. "You mean they are wild and eat their *lukisa*?"

"No, I mean the *ziri* are the enemy of these people."

"You're not making any sense."

Instead of answering, Yenteel pulled out his device for calculating the time of the next feeding.

"Put that away," she said. "I'm going to sit down and you're going to explain."

As Kantees pulled out a chair and sat, she heard footsteps behind her as Ulina came into the kitchen.

Yenteel did the same and waved at the farmer to sit as well. He shook his head with a wary glance at Kantees. Yenteel did not try any harder but, with one arm on the table, he turned to face her.

"This happened a long time ago. Urben here doesn't really know how long but it was before the time of his grandfather, so that could be anything from a hundred to a thousand years or more. The people came here. The stories say they were fleeing from invaders who had greater control of the Mother's power than they did."

"Taymalin." She almost spat the word.

"Probably. So perhaps it is a thousand years. It doesn't really matter."

"It matters to me."

Yenteel closed his eyes for a moment. "At that time, the people rode the *zirichasa*, and everything was fine. They found places to live in the mountains like this, there were wild *ziri* here as well. The story is not clear at this point but for some reason the *ziri* turned on the people. At first, because it wasn't expected, the *ziri* succeeded in killing many of the people but then they became organised and fought back. The *ziri* were just animals, of course, so the people were easily able to kill them and succeeded in wiping out most of them until they retreated back into the mountains.

"But," he said, "they still come out of the mountains and attack from time to time. And that's how it's been since then. These people are terrified of the *zirichasa* and will kill them given a chance."

Kantees stared at him. "That … that can't be true."

Yenteel shrugged. "He believes it."

"Did you ask him when the last attack was?"

"A farm was torn apart not far from here a couple of years ago."

"How do they know it was the *zirichasa*? Perhaps it was those eel-men."

"*Ustecalin*, river people," said Yenteel in an almost distracted way. He turned to the farmer and said something. The man stood, went to an alcove and opened a box that was there. The thing he pulled out was bent in the middle but unmistakably a *ziri* feather. It was grey, from a wild *ziri*.

Kantees felt herself grow cold and numb. It was impossible. "I can't believe it," she whispered. "You've seen them, Yenteel, was there ever anything but kindness from the *ziri*? You know they just race. Levin and Daybian, they ride them and race. You've ridden them for days. No *ziri* has attacked a person, neither Taymalin nor Kadralin. You *know* this." She knew she was pleading with him, trying to persuade him, trying to make the story untrue.

"Sheesha has gone, Kantees. We came to this place and he's gone. Looesa with him."

"Then nothing has changed. We have to find them."

Yenteel said nothing. She was not sure if it was because he agreed with her, or because he didn't.

"Urben here is taking a cart to the market tomorrow. He said we can go with him."

"I don't need to go to a market, Yenteel, I need to find my Sheesha."

"If he is in the mountains, Kantees, you can't find him until we deal with the reason why you have such a terrible pain in your head."

She couldn't argue. Suddenly she felt very tired. Lost, as if the world had been ripped from under her and she was falling through nothing.

15

The rest of the day passed in a strange haze for Kantees. It was as if the ground had been ripped from under her. They were given two rooms to sleep in on the upper floor. One for her and Ulina, the other for the men.

There was little furniture, just a table and a pallet on the floor. The blanket they provided was thick wool and kept the two of them warm.

She lay with her arms wrapped around Ulina, unable to sleep and trying to make sense of what she had been told.

She had come here expecting to find her people. She had expected them to be strong, in the safety of the mountains. Over the past few ten-days her belief had been strengthened by the Ziri Towers sited at all the major cities. She knew they were built by the Kadralin and stolen by the Taymalin.

Her people, the ones she believed in, had kept *ziri*. They had bred them and raised them, perhaps they had raced them and that had been usurped by the Taymalin as well.

She had discovered the magic of the *zirichasa*, and that was something nobody had known before. Yet she had seen that trail of gold in the sky a ten-day ago. It had to have been a *ziri* and it had been coming from the direction of these mountains.

There must be people here who still rode the *ziri*.

The farmers were scared but Kantees did not believe the *ziri* would attack a human settlement without provocation.

She slid her arm from under the little girl and sat up, leaning against the cold of the stone wall behind her. Much as she loved Sheesha, and cared about the rest of the *ziri*, she knew they were barely more than animals. Yes, Sheesha responded to her very thoughts. Yes, she could make him fly faster than the lightning. Yes, he was clever, but he was not a person. Sheesha did not have the memory that might make a person hold a grudge for a dozen years only to mete out their revenge when the opportunity arose.

And they did not connive. If there was pain, yes they might remember the cause, but they did not keep that thought in their minds. They did not think about how they might prevent it from ever happening again, they simply avoided it. They lived in the moment. No thought of the future or the past.

She *knew* the *zirichasa*. She had lived with them day and night for so many years. The idea they might attack humans out of some ancient spite was crazy. And if they had, it must be because someone made them.

The thoughts tumbled around her mind. She stood up. The dim light of Colimar made parallel blocks of red on the wooden floor. Dust and dirt clung to the soles of her feet as she padded across to one of the windows and leaned against the wall, peering out.

The fields and trees were shades of grey. The room faced in the direction she needed to go, and the black tower in the distance made a solid blank against the red-stained mountains and twinkling stars. A few clouds floated above, their edges tinged with red, while those near the horizon glowed with white which meant Lostimal would be rising.

Someone was making the *ziri* attack people. That was the only possibility she could accept. Could it be the same someone who had made them turn on the population all those years ago? She shook her head; that seemed impossible—then she caught herself and laughed under her breath. What did *impossible* mean anymore?

She had seen the machines at Cliffedge lifting barges heavier than hills. In just two days she had flown a *ziri* from Dakastown to

Jakalain. She had ridden a *tekrak* that was bigger than a house. And fished a dead *sikechak* from a flooded river so that she and her companions could eat.

No. This was no time for her old ideas of what was usual or likely. If the world did not match her expectations then she must see it for what it was, not what she hoped it would be. But perhaps she could twist its pattern, and make it in the image she wanted.

Was that the height of arrogance? That's what Libbibet liked to say to anyone who thought they might change the way of the world: "A wish can't change the shape of the world, Kantees."

But she already had. The pattern of the world said she was a slave and that her place was with the Taymalin. The pattern of the world said that Daybian could have his will with her, that she lived or died at the will of her master, that she had no possessions.

She had defied that pattern and here she stood. In the land of the Kadralin, in the heart of Esternes. Although some might say, "It's the will of Taymar" or, "It's the will of the Mother".

She sighed. If you couldn't be in charge of your own destiny, were you even alive at all?

In the distance the edges of a mountain glowed white as Lostimal emerged; it was nearly full. Its brilliance lit up the valley, the greys became shades of dark green. The red of Colimar lingered only in the deepest shadows.

Did that mean anything?

Perhaps it meant she should trust herself.

She yawned. Trusting herself didn't always seem a very good way of going about things.

But she could try.

The revelation had exhausted her and, though her head still ached, she made her way back to the pallet, lay down beside Ulina and slept.

She seemed to have barely closed her eyes when Gally was shaking her awake. The light from the windows said it was still night though Lostimal had moved in the sky and, where there had been red bars across the floor, there were now white ones.

"The farmer says it is time to go," said Gally.

Kantees did not argue but slid from under the blanket and shook Ulina.

In a short time they were all in the kitchen where Urben's wife had prepared some porridge which they ate quickly from wooden bowls.

There were two carts waiting outside. Urben climbed up behind the *lukisa* of the first while a man they had not seen before sat waiting with the reins of the second pair in his hands.

Kantees decided quickly and, with Ulina, got up on the first cart. She might not be able to talk to the man but she was not going to let Yenteel fill Urben's ears with more nonsense. She glanced behind to see Yenteel and Gally squeezing on to the second. She looked down into the cart: most of the produce was in sacks and just formless lumps, but there were barrels which smelled of fish.

Urben picked up a stick and slapped the rears of the *lukisa* with a sharp *crack*. They did not react immediately but after a few more hits they started to move. The carts ground their way up the path, out through the gate and on to the road. The paved stone ran out as they left the small wood beyond the farm.

It was still night but the light of Lostimal, even though it was not full, was sufficient to make travel easy enough. As long as they stayed on the track it would be hard to lose their way.

They crossed a wooden bridge that was barely wide enough for the cart and, although it had barriers along each side, they looked frail and she suspected an impact would smash them in a moment.

The carts were slow. As the sun came up Kantees decided she was going to walk for a little while. She jumped down and strode ahead of the plodding animals.

In the distance the tall black tower pointed like an insulting finger at the sky. As she stared at it the pain in the back of her head, that had become such a constant she barely even noticed it, throbbed and sent extra waves of pain through her shoulders and down her arms.

She shook her head and looked away. She stumbled but caught herself and kept walking. She did not want the others to notice. But it confirmed what they had suspected. The tower was the cause of her problem. It was like a candle to night-time insects. She was drawn inexorably towards it, and when she drew close enough it would burn her. That was not something she would allow to happen. She was not some ignorant insect that did not understand that the light which mesmerised them would also consume them.

It was good to stretch her legs. They had been aching from the climb yesterday after all the walking. This helped. The sky remained clear and Lostimal was heading towards the horizon when the sun poured its light into the valley just as they came to the brow of small hill. She stopped to let the cart catch up.

The valley between her and the tower was laid out with streams winding through the fields and dotted with farms and collections of buildings. It was more populated than she had imagined. The river's flood plain where they had arrived had no buildings at all. Perhaps flooding was common and the people had decided it was not worth the effort. If Kantees and her companions had arrived just a day later they would not have been able to cross.

She climbed back into the cart and gave Ulina a hug.

"You stumbled," she said.

"It was nothing." She glanced at the child who was staring back with a knowing look in her eyes. *I did not promise to always tell the truth.*

"It's like the tower in the faraway place," said Ulina, turning her gaze to the black digit.

"Yes, perhaps the *Slissac* built this one too."

"Why not the Kadralin?"

Kantees shook her head. "They may have built the Ziri Towers, but this is too…" she could not think of a word that encompassed the *Slissac* ability to channel the raw power of the Mother's milk, "…too perfect."

Was it here before the Kadralin came? How old were these towers? History said the *Slissac* lived in a distant part of the world where they had enslaved the white-skinned Taymalin before the slaves eventually escaped their masters and fled here.

But if there had been Taymalin and *Slissac* in that place, could there not have been Kadralin and *Slissac* in this one? And if there were, where did they go? And why did they not enslave the Kadralin? There was no tale of that ever happening.

Suddenly she wanted to talk to Yenteel. She sent Ulina off to the other cart and had Yenteel join her.

"You want my counsel?"

"The headache returns when I stare at the tower."

"That's interesting."

Kantees expected him to go on but he didn't. "Interesting? Is that the best you can do?"

"I don't know what's causing this."

"I think it's a light for the night creatures." She half-expected Yenteel to make a joke or deliberately misunderstand her.

Instead he was silent for a while until he finally said, "Does that make any sense?"

"Does it make sense for Sheesha and the others to fly away and not return? Does it make sense for me to be drawn towards this place or suffer pain?"

"You're saying there is a patterning at work here that's affecting you from a distance of at least a couple of leagues."

"Yes, something that affects the *ziri* too," she said.

He looked for a moment as if there was a *but* on the tip of his tongue. The left-hand *lukik* of the team choose that moment to defecate. Kantees closed her eyes as the smell was strong enough to make them sting.

Yenteel gave a choking laugh. "Potent stuff."

The farmer also laughed and said something.

"He says we are unweaned milk-babes if the *lukik* shit seems that bad."

"You can tell him I shovelled *ziri* shit all my life."

"Given their attitude to *zirichasa* I don't think that's a good idea."

Kantees silently agreed.

Yenteel took a moment to gather his thoughts. "But whatever this patterning is it doesn't affect the rest of us, or this fellow."

"But, as you are so keen to point out, I have a connection to the *ziri*, well, to Sheesha anyway."

Yenteel looked at her and then turned to face the tower. "This is smaller than the one in the far south, but it's similar and that one had no effect on you."

"I know," she said. "But I need some sort of protection, do you think you can do that?"

Yenteel sighed. "I'm no patterner, Kantees. I can follow instructions but I cannot create new patterns."

"What about the protective shield you used in the Talamyrth?"

"It creates a ward, yes, but only in the form you saw when I used it before."

"You can't do anything then?"

"I'm sorry."

They fell silent. Kantees glanced at the black tower and winced as pain daggered through her head.

"It's going to get harder for me the closer we get," she said. "The more it fills the sky the more chance I have of seeing it."

"We could cover your eyes."

"It may come to that."

1 6

The landscape crawled by. Walking would be faster.

They had passed a collection of houses where people —every one of them dark-skinned as she was—came out to stare as they passed. There was no emotion in them and as soon as the carts had passed, they just went back into their ancient and patched homes. Nothing seemed to be new.

Farms became more common, and less isolated than Urben's.

Finally, they reached the outskirts of the town. The buildings were all old here too and people watched idly from upper storey windows before disappearing back inside. The streets were busy, though not many paid them any attention, they seemed intent on going about their business. She took pleasure in the fact that every face was some shade of Kadralin. None here were obviously tainted with Taymalin blood.

She shook her head, no, that was not the right way to think. Unfortunately, the shake seemed to re-awaken the throbbing even though she was not looking at the tower. Then Yenteel jabbed her in the arm.

"What?" she snapped. She immediately regretted her tone but was not inclined to apologise for it.

"Haven't you noticed?"

"Noticed what?"

"The noise."

She was about to say there wasn't much noise when she realised that was his point. She stared at the people moving back and forth, carrying baskets, tools, or bundles; they seldom spoke. There was so little sound she could hear the cart wheels grinding on the stone road.

"Folk tales," he said quietly. "Stories for children."

"What are you talking about?"

"The Lord's beautiful daughter cursed by the *Kisharuk* to die—"

"But saved by a powerful sorcerer who cast a pattern that held her, her family and all their realm in sleep for a hundred years," said Kantees. "The Curse of Eftena. Yes, what of it?"

"You asked me to believe in a pattern that could reach across leagues and bend the will of the *ziri*. And," he said, "I scoffed at the idea because nothing could be that powerful."

"You agree with me then?"

"We're looking at it." A sweep of his arm took in everyone around them. He peered round her at the farmer and spoke to him. The man seemed to come awake and replied briefly before returning to his reverie.

"What did he say?"

"I asked him how far it was to go, you saw what happened."

"What did he reply?"

"Not far."

A shop protruded into the main street and the road went around it to the left. Kantees' head was hurting constantly now. As the cart rounded the bend, market stalls came into sight. Crowds moved through it but there was no sound of barkers calling their wares. It was not silent but only the rustling of cloth and a low murmuring disturbed the air.

Until Kantees screamed.

Black stone grew from behind the crowd. Chiselled patterns intertwined up the precipitous walls. At the sight of it, the closeness of it, pain slammed through her head as if she had been attacked with a hammer.

In the eerie quiet of the town her voice bounced off the black wall and struck her back, redoubled. She squeezed her eyes shut from the pain and slammed her hands over them, digging the heel in. The image of the black tower hung in her mind's eye as the pain reluctantly receded.

"Kantees?"

It was a voice she knew but it seemed to be coming from a long distance away. Hands touched her and she pushed them away in terror. She dared not open her eyes, and kept both hands covering them so she remained in the utter dark.

"Kantees, listen to me." Yenteel. "You need to get down from the cart."

"I can't open my eyes."

"Can't?"

"Dare not."

"Pain?"

"You cannot know."

There was a pause. She realised the cart had stopped and the strange quiet of the town continued around them.

"Kantees?"

"It's all right, Gally. I'm all right."

"Kantees screamed. Kantees is lying." He sounded as if he was telling her off.

She gave a short humourless laugh. "The tower makes my head hurt. I can't look at it."

The cart moved as someone climbed up to her left. The farmer was still on her right, he had not moved nor spoken since her outburst.

"I've got something I can use for a blindfold," said Yenteel. "Once that's in place we'll get you down and find somewhere to stay."

"I saw an inn on the road as we came in," she said.

"Yes, but there's one here on the main square."

"I'd prefer one further away from the tower." She tried to maintain a semblance of control in her voice but even she thought she sounded desperate.

"Let me check this one out first," he said as if he were talking to a child. "Twist round to face me. I'll start to wrap this around your head. Remove your hands when you feel it. Keep your eyes shut."

She turned on the cart bench. "You don't need to worry about me peeking," she said as she felt a pressure on the back of her head. A coarse cloth touched the back of her hand and she removed it slowly. No light seeped in as Yenteel wrapped it around the front.

With her both hands free she put one on the backboard of the bench and rested the other on her stomach self-consciously. The blindfold went round her head three times covering from her fore-head down to her cheeks. He was being thorough.

"Can you turn so I can reach the back to tie it off?"

She didn't move.

"Put your hands on the blindfold if you're worried it might fall off."

The side of her mouth twitched in an almost-smile. That had been her exact concern.

Finally the blindfold was tied and she tentatively dropped her hands. It seemed firm enough.

"I'm going to climb down. You slide to the end of the bench then we'll help you off."

She could remember the side of the cart, the position of the footrest, but being unable to see put a terror in her heart. The sudden idea the ground might not be there swept through her. She pushed it away as ridiculous but the uncertainty stayed with her.

She held out one hand and felt Yenteel take a good hold. Then two large strong hands took her wrist and hand on the other side.

"Gally will not let Kantees fall."

She felt as if she could weep. Yenteel's other hand slid up to her armpit and Gally's did the same. They lifted her down. The ground was there when her feet came down. Yenteel's hands loosened and she compulsively gripped both. She was unsteady and the realisation that she might lose her way and her friends swept away all bravado.

"Don't leave me."

Yenteel secured a room at the back of the inn. She had been forced to climb three flights of uneven and creaky stairs. She had felt the presence of the other people around her but, just like the town itself, the place was curiously quiet. But that was not at the forefront of Kantees' mind, she was scared and she could not place the source.

"Tomorrow," said Yenteel, "once you're rested, we will examine the tower in more detail."

Fear wracked her and she could barely understand what he was saying.

"There's something strange here, something that's causing you to have your headaches," he said. "If we leave without solving it, you'll just get them back."

She said nothing. He was probably right but it was difficult to focus.

A small hand pressed against the top of hers. Ulina.

"I do not like this place, Kantees."

She heard a chair scrape against the floorboards. "Let's get the blindfold off."

Kantees panicked. "Is it safe?"

"We can't see the tower from this side of the building."

For some reason she did not trust Yenteel's words. "Gally? Is it safe?"

"I cannot see the tower, Kantees."

"The window looks out on the stables and the place smells," said Ulina.

Kantees jumped as someone touched the back of her head.

"It's just me," said Yenteel.

He pulled against the cloth, jerking her head back, as he untied the knot. Then the pressure diminished as the cloths came away from her skin. Catching on the bristly hair protruding from her scalp.

She said nothing for a few moments, then, "Why is the room so dark?"

"The room is light, Kantees," said Gally.

"That's not funny."

She felt the air move in front of her face and slapped at something there.

"My fingers, Kantees," said Yenteel.

"Open the shutters, Yenteel, please," she pleaded.

Hands gripped her by the shoulders.

"Let go of me!"

She wrenched herself away from the hands but overbalanced the chair and fell back slamming her head against the wood. She rolled on to her hands and knees, scrambling to rise as someone grabbed her shoulders.

"Kantees, stop." Yenteel's voice was not angry, not sharp but pleading, as you might speak to a frightened child.

She pulled away again and stumbled forwards until her shins slammed into something and she fell forwards onto a straw-filled pallet.

And it was black. Everything was black, not a single hint of light. Even if the shutters had been drawn, even on a cloudy day full of rain, there would be light leaking in through the gaps. But for her there was nothing.

"I cannot see," she whispered and then sobbed. "I cannot see!"

Lying on the pallet and facing the wall with her eyes shut she could pretend the dark was just a temporary thing. The day would come, she would open her eyes and everything would be visible once more.

Someone brought them food. She was not hungry but she could not refuse when Gally insisted that he feed her. It was stew and well-cooked though she did not recognise the flavour of the meat. She did not care.

"Use your healing patterns, Yenteel."

He did not respond.

"Yenteel?"

"Sorry, Kantees, I was thinking. Yes, I could do that—" He hesitated.

"You don't think it will work."

"It is intended to deal with physical injury, for use by someone with little skill. It is not a refined spell. I don't know that it will do any good."

"What worse harm could it do?"

She took his further silence as agreement. He bound her head once more and had her lay down again. Feeling him scraping the patterns across the surface was strange and when the chant started she felt a strange tingling in her eyes and across her forehead.

But when he had finished and they unwrapped her eyes she was as blind as ever.

"What does it look like?" she asked.

"Your eyes?"

"What else?"

"They do not look any different." His voice had an underlying strain though he tried to sound unconcerned. "The pattern had no effect?"

"Some tingling."

"Much?"

"No." She sighed and turned her head as if she was looking around the room, but she did not even know how big it was. "Is it still daylight?"

"The sun has gone down."

"I can't smell any candles."

"We haven't made any light."

"Why not?"

"It did not seem fair."

She bit back scornful words. They were feeling guilty for…what? Not having lost their sight as well?

"Don't be foolish."

She heard him get up and move away. Heard the flint clicking as he made a small flame.

"And we could do with a fire in here," she said and suddenly felt her voice was too loud. Though she knew Ulina and Gally were in the room she could not hear them and she felt alone. But she did not want to show weakness, did not want to scare Gally any more than he must already be.

Where is Sheesha?

"Ulina?"

"Kantees?" Her voice came from not too far away, and down. Kantees imagined the girl was sitting on the floor; she turned her head and looked in the direction she thought the child must be.

"Would you sit with me?" She tried to make it sound as if it was something of little consequence. But when the weight of Ulina pressed into the straw beside her Kantees grabbed for the girl's hand, after a moment's groping she found it. Kantees clung to Ulina's cold, thin and tiny fingers as if they were a lifeline against drowning.

"The tower must be the key," said Yenteel. "It was the tower that gave you the headaches, it was the tower that brought us here. It was looking at it that blinded you. Tomorrow we will investigate."

"Have you asked anyone about it?" said Kantees.

"No."

"Wouldn't that be a good idea?"

"I suppose so."

"You suppose?" Kantees raised her voice. "Why not do the obvious thing?"

"I'll ask in the morning."

"Ask now."

"You're not well."

"You think I don't know that, Yenteel?" she shouted and then moderated her voice, forcing herself to calm. "This is an inn. There are people downstairs, people you can talk to. Ask them about the tower. Find out everything you can, let us not go out *blind* tomorrow."

"Try to rest," he said.

His heavy footsteps stomped across the room, the door opened and slammed behind him.

"Why is it such a hard thing to do?" she said out loud.

But neither Gally nor Ulina answered.

She had not believed she would sleep but whether it was the strain of the day or the midnight black of her vision, she did. But it was not dreamless and in her sleeping imagination she could see.

Once more she walked the land from the river to where they had been attacked by the people Yenteel thought a legend. Climbed the hill and looked out across the land toward the tower. But now it reached from the earth to the sky and pierced the heart of Lostimal while Colimar was blood red along its sides.

The terrain seemed to be no barrier as she walked towards it. Her stride ate up the distance and she approached the tower. She grew as she walked until it was almost as if she was flying, until her head broke through the clouds.

She reached out to grasp the tower. It was like a stake driven between sky and earth. For a moment it resisted her until it snapped in two.

And where it was broken, blood poured and rained upon the ground. Curious as to where it flowed from she lifted the broken shaft and looked closer. The falling liquid resolved into the bodies of men, women and children.

Falling and screaming.

With the sudden horror that she had killed them, she flung the tower from her. There was a screech behind her and she turned in sudden happiness as a giant Sheesha stooped down on her to claw at her massive face.

She woke screaming. There was nothing to see. She screamed in the terror of darkness: something clutched her. She fought back thinking it was Sheesha once more. But arms enfolded her and as she gasped for breath she heard Gally's voice in her ear.

"Gally is here. Gally is here. Kantees is safe."

And she broke down sobbing and continued to cry for a while, clinging to Gally.

"Is it day?" she said finally.

"Dawn is coming, Kantees," he said. "There is light at the window."

She strained her ears hoping to catch some sound that confirmed his words. People talking, animals moving, anything. But the town was quiet.

"I am scared, Gally."

"I will look after you, Kantees."

"I know you will."

But you cannot save me from the terror. Not knowing whether it is day or night, or who is here.

The first bird of the morning sounded in the distance. She recognised the sound of *kichesa* snuffling in the stables. The pallet creaked beneath her as she moved. Every sound went some way to help define the world around her. It was far from complete but each one made it more real.

"Is there a stick I can use, Gally?"

"What sort of stick?"

"One I can hold in my hand, something with which I can strike the ground. Hit the walls."

My world will be small. Only as far as I can reach but I will know it is real.

"Gally can fetch one, Kantees, but Gally must let you go."

"Here," said Ulina. She sounded grumpy. A small hand grabbed hers and thrust something into it. Kantees felt the rough bark.

"Thank you," said Kantees. "I'm sorry I woke you."

"Woke the whole inn and half the town I expect," said Yenteel from a short distance away.

Kantees felt the stick, it was not comfortable in her hand but it would serve. She waved it in front of her—and struck something.

"That's me," said Ulina.

"Sorry."

"Where I came from those who were so afflicted did not live," she said.

"I am glad we are not there," said Kantees. And she realised it was the truth, despite the fear, despite the prospect of darkness, she would prefer to be alive than not. Though perhaps she might not feel that way in the future.

"Yenteel?"

"What?"

"Tell me what you discovered about the tower."

He groaned and she could almost hear his joints as he climbed to his feet.

"Did you drink much?"

"Not a great deal. This is a strange place, Kantees. Never mind that you have been blinded by a black tower simply for looking at it."

"What do you mean?"

"They have a potent brew, an ale strong enough to knock out a *lukik*, and they drink it here in huge quantities. Until they pass out, but there's no carousing, no singing. They all simply drink until they put themselves into a stupor."

"But did they talk?"

"Hardly at all."

"But you asked?"

"I believe this is my story, Kantees?"

"Sorry."

"I doubt it." She heard a chair scraping across the floor. "I said you would have woken the inn and the town with your screaming? I doubt it." There was the sound of him groaning as he stretched and then the chair creaked as he sat in it. "I managed to catch one or two between surliness and oblivion. But they told me little except that the tower is alive and they have to feed it."

"With people?" said Ulina.

"Maybe little girls," said Yenteel.

She snorted. "I will kill it first."

"You might anger it with your little knife. I don't think even you could kill it."

"Did you learn anything useful?" said Kantees.

"Neither of the men had heard of it making anyone blind before—the townsfolk are all fine."

"And so are you."

"Just you with the headaches and then the blindness."

"What else?"

"I asked about the *zirichasa*." He stopped there as if unwilling to continue.

"And?"

"I'm sorry, Kantees, if you thought the people here might be like you with the *ziri*, or at least ride them. They don't. It was the most emotional response I got out of the men I was talking to." He stopped again.

"Just tell me."

"They're scared of getting eaten."

"That's ridiculous."

"You don't know anything about wild *ziri*, Kantees, perhaps they do like eating people, they certainly might consider taking a child."

"I would defend myself," said Ulina. "But I wouldn't kill a *ziri*."

"I don't believe it, Yenteel. There are stories, Kevrey knew them, the Kadralin at Jakalain knew them. The Kadralin flew the *ziri*, that's how it always was. Even Romain said so."

"This is the reality."

She heard someone moving about in the inn below them. A door opened and slammed shut in the courtyard.

"Let's have some breakfast, then I want to go to the tower myself," she said.

"This problem hasn't interfered with your desire to be queen," said Yenteel.

She did not know if he was being serious or trying to lighten her mood. But just being able to talk for a while had made her feel better and for that little time she had not thought about her affliction.

Breakfast was procured. But she was scared to eat because she was unable to see the plate or what was on it, and the others would see her. In the end, Gally fed her. Kantees clung to the mug of thin watery ale as the only thing she could control. Her mood became more dismal.

It was still early when she was guided carefully down the stairs. Gally had even offered to carry her but she refused. The idea of both of them taking a tumble—perhaps with him landing on top of her—did not appeal. So he went down first while she followed holding his shirt with one hand and the banister with the other.

Gally was very apologetic as he ran her into a chair but he learnt how to guide her. In the end she hung on to his arm. It was at the moment they left the inn and stepped into the damp air of the street she realised she had not put on a blindfold.

"You're looking right at it now," said Yenteel. "I think it's done its worst."

Yenteel had said her eyes looked normal, and she could feel them as they turned left and right to the sounds, and as if she was trying to see her environs. But she still felt self-conscious, as if the fact she could not see meant there was something strange about her.

So she just focused on the stick and held it ahead of her, moving it back and forth. It caught on the ground more than once when she let it drop. She was not sure it helped but it made her feel as if she was doing something for herself.

She knew when they passed along a tight alley because of the way the sound changed and she was able to tap the wall to her left.

"The tower seems to be completely encircled by houses," said Yenteel. "It's almost as if they don't give it any consideration at all."

They left the alley but the same path continued, the gravel and stones beneath her feet had not changed. Then they stopped.

"What's happened?" said Kantees.

"Nothing," said Yenteel. "We're here. There's a slope up ahead of us, not even Ulina's height, grass growing on it and that goes right up to the tower. Smooth and black like the other. No question it was made the same way. It tapers slightly just like the other, too. I'd like to see the top."

"I'd like to see anything." When Yenteel did not respond, she realised it had been a cruel thing to say. "Sorry."

"You have nothing to apologise about, Kantees. Mine was a poor choice of words. Still, this one is different to the other tower."

"Different how?"

"The other one was circular. This one has straight sides, well, this side is straight."

Kantees thought about it but it was all so far out of her experience she could not imagine what that meant. "What do we do now?"

"You could try touching it."

She hesitated, then nodded.

Gally tugged at her but she disengaged her arm. "No, Gally, I'll do it myself."

Using the stick to find the bank she edged forwards. She knew she was probably being excruciatingly slow as far as they were concerned, but she did not want to trip. Being unable to see was exhausting, as she tried to fill in what she was missing by straining her other senses. Carefully she edged up the gentle slope with the damp blades of grass brushing against her legs.

The stick struck a hard surface; using it to balance she moved up a little further and stretched out her hand. She expected to touch cold stone, perhaps moist from the morning dew or rain.

What she felt made her whip her hand away in a moment.

"Why didn't you tell me there was mould on it?"

Kantees could imagine Yenteel leaning forwards. "There's no mould."

"Have you touched it? It's cold and spongy. Sticky too."

"It's stone."

"Touch where I touched."

Yenteel's sudden exclamation of revulsion told her what she needed to know.

"You can't see it?"

"I can," said Ulina. "When the light catches it."

"Gally sees."

Still silence from Yenteel.

"There is something there," Gally continued. "It's all round. It goes off this way and round the other."

Kantees edged back and this time was grateful for Gally's support.

"We are being watched," said Ulina in a voice that barely carried to Kantees' ears.

"Who?"

"More than one. Some from windows, they think I cannot see them moving in the dark. And two from the street at the other end of the alley."

"Threatening?"

"I see no weapons."

"What do you want to do, Kantees?" said Yenteel. He still treated her as the leader despite her infirmity.

"Why are these people not blind, Yenteel? Why are you not blind?" She asked the questions in anger but as she said it realisation washed over her. "Why did our *ziri* leave? Why are there no others here among the people who used to understand them? Why would a *ziri* attack a farm? Why am I the only one affected by this thing?"

"Because," said Yenteel, "you are almost *zirichak* yourself."

Ulina hissed. Gally laughed.

"Don't say it, Yenteel," said Kantees. Inside she could feel a bubbling laughter. It felt wrong and out of place, she desperately wanted to hold it in but it would not be denied. She held her mouth closed as she choked on the hysteria that threatened to consume her.

"Is Kantees ill?" asked Gally worriedly.

She clasped his hand in an effort to reassure him, not daring to open her mouth. She coughed once and burst into raucous laughter.

"Kantees?" said Gally. "What is wrong?"

But she could not answer. She doubled over as she was wracked with laughs that forced their way from deep inside. Every lie she had told, every time she had denied Yenteel's words, every moment she had pretended nothing was different. They poured out of her.

Then she heard Yenteel roar with laughter.

Gally's grip on her arm tightened and she knew they were

scaring him but she was helpless against the flood of release. Her breathing was ragged and she had trouble breathing in against the involuntary wracking of her laughter.

"I'm … all … right."

Then Ulina started, a quiet giggle that sounded so strange. She could not recall hearing Ulina laugh before, she was always so serious—just the same as Kantees.

And finally Gally. A strange laugh that caught in his throat as if he was uncertain of it, as if he feared it.

Kantees ceased to resist the emotion bubbling up from within. So many years of fighting, arguing, secretly denying everything she was told, relying only on herself. Now broken because without these people who laughed with her she could only die.

The passion burned away. The laughter broke up and evaporated like mist in the morning sun. And she felt as if the weight of her entire life had been ripped away. She was light-headed but knew that was because she had not been able to breathe properly.

The others stopped too but they could not have experienced the release she felt.

She sighed and patted Gally's hand.

The world was still black but somehow it was less oppressive than it had been.

1 8

"Better?" asked Yenteel.

Kantees nodded and then realised she did not know if he was even looking in her direction. "Yes, Yenteel, I am improved."

"They say laughter is a good medicine."

"I was not expecting to taste it here." When he did not respond she continued. "Ulina? Are the people still watching?"

"They are," she said. "And there are more of them. The ones at the windows are no longer hiding in the dark but stare openly."

"Those are not the ones we need be concerned about," said Kantees. "What of the more secretive ones?"

"They remain, and continue to peek." She made a derisive noise. "They are very unskilled."

"One wonders," said Yenteel, "what it is they expect to see."

"Something happen to us, of course," said Kantees. "Who builds a town so close to a ley-circle?"

"They did at the other tower."

"I see the power of this one below us, and when the mother feeds it there would be more than enough to twist those who live nearby." Kantees could almost feel the questions building in Yenteel's mind. "Ask no questions now. We did not meet the people

572

who lived at the base of the other tower. Perhaps they would be quiet like those here, perhaps not. But the answers to all my questions are here."

"What do you want to do?"

"We will find the way in," she said.

It did not take long. With Yenteel in the lead, Ulina in the rear and Gally guiding Kantees they made their way along the first length.

"It's not a square base," said Yenteel as they turned a corner. "But this side is straight too. It has either six or eight sides I think."

"Why would it be different?"

There was silence.

"Yenteel?"

"I'm thinking."

"I cannot see you think."

"I'm sure it would be truly miraculous if you could."

"I'm more interested in the destination than the path."

"I have no idea, but the same effect can be achieved by different patternings. Just a different way to channel the power of the Mother."

"Arrogance," said Kantees. "Thinking one can force the Mother to one's own will."

"There are arrogant people in all races, Kantees; Taymalin, Kadralin and, I expect, *Slissac* too."

"If the story of Taymar is true then that is a certainty," said Kantees.

They reached another bend. Kantees was only aware of it because she tried to go forwards while Gally pulled away from her. She found it hard to rely on him, not because she didn't trust him, but because their relationship had always been the other way around. She had been the one who looked after him.

But she had not lost sight of what she had learnt from her laughter, and tried to simply trust instead of being in command.

"Still no entrance," said Yenteel.

But Kantees knew they were getting closer. She could feel it. From inside the tower she could sense the pull. It called to her—to part of her—it drew her in. It told her that great pleasure waited for her.

"What about the mould?"

"There's more of it," said Ulina. "It covers the whole surface now."

"And our audience?"

"It grows."

"What of the secret followers?"

"I can't see them any more, too many other people."

And Kantees realised she could hear them. They did not speak. Silence was a way of life in this place. But she could hear them breathing and the rustling as they moved, as well as the footsteps and shuffling as they followed.

Yenteel spoke again. "Are we going to our deaths, Kantees?"

She was tempted to treat the question with levity but there was concern in his tone.

"No," she said. "Whatever it is, it wants me. If you can't feel it then it is not for you."

They took another turn. The sound from the otherwise silent crowd was oppressive now and Kantees could sense the anticipation. The feelings from the tower were somehow reflected in the people around them. It reminded her of the lusts and passions that exploded when there was a great feeding, but all held in check waiting for something to happen.

"I see the entrance," said Yenteel. "It's halfway along this side, and there are six sides. The skill in the making of this tower is astonishing," he said. "The grass that grows to its edge seems completely normal. Yet this place must have a feeding at least once per year. The people too. Untouched."

"They are not untouched," said Kantees. "But it's not the tower that has done this, it's what's inside."

They came to a halt.

"I shall go in alone."

All three of her companions cried "No" at the same time, which made her smile.

"There is a hunger here," she said.

"Then you must not go," said Yenteel.

"It is calling me alone."

"Gally will go. Gally will be eaten instead of Kantees."

Kantees shook her head. "It's difficult to explain but I am sure it doesn't want to eat me. This is something else. But it doesn't want you, it wants a *ziri* and I am the nearest thing to that. If I don't go in, I will be trapped here blind and unable to leave because the headaches will afflict me until they send me mad or kill me. It is both a lure and a stick. It says I will find pleasure inside, while beating me if I refuse to go in."

"This is not good," said Yenteel. "The tower may prevent the Mother's milk from creating abominations beyond its walls, but that is precisely what you will find inside."

"I know."

"I will come," said Ulina. "I will kill any abomination."

"Except this one," said Kantees. "I may not know what it is, but it is either very large, or there are very many of them. Too many, or too big even for you."

They did not argue any longer. Though she could not see the crowd Kantees found their presence to be disturbing. She could not imagine how much worse it must be for her friends. Like a wave that hung above, threatening to engulf them at any moment.

"No more arguments," she said. "The sooner I begin, the sooner I'll be back."

She hugged each one in turn. She cared for each in their own way, even, much to her surprise, Yenteel.

"I will not be long," she said as if she was telling Sheesha she was leaving the eyrie to fetch something from the lower floors.

"Be careful," said Yenteel.

"I cannot see," she said. "You cannot imagine how careful I am going to be."

"Take my knife," said Ulina.

For a moment Kantees was tempted, but shook her head. "I cannot take a weapon," she said. "If I did I might be tempted to use it."

Gally said nothing but she heard him sniff as if he was crying.

"Show me to the entrance, Gally."

It became cold and damp inside the tower almost immediately. She imagined the darkness came down just as sharply but, since she could not see, that was not a concern. She touched her stick to the ground. It did not seem to have the mould on it. With great care she moved forward, rhythmically moving the stick to the right, touching it to the floor in front of her and then beating to the left. She would simply have to hope the passage remained tall enough she did not bump her head.

One short step at a time she moved forward. The first stretch was narrow and she felt she was moving through the wall of the tower itself. Certainly to maintain such a height they must be very thick. Her stick came up against a barrier in front and, poking around, she discovered the passage turned right. It occurred to her, too late, that she might not be able to find her way out. But she did not try to remember her route, just followed the way laid out for her. If she survived, she would find the way.

If it had been unnaturally quiet outside, she strained to hear anything beyond the tapping of her stick and the brushing of her soles on the stone beneath her feet in this place. The silence alone was oppressive. At least, in this place, she could pretend the darkness was simply because she had not brought a light.

She came out into an open area and the power of whatever lived in this place overwhelmed her. She staggered forward into a wall covered in the same slime she had felt outside, but so much thicker, and she thought she felt something inside it, long and thin like sinew. As she pressed against it a burst of light exploded in her head and pain ripped through her. She fell to her knees, ripping her hands away. The light faded and with it the pain.

She placed her hands flat on the ground with her stick pressed beneath her palm. She inhaled the dank air in long exhausted breaths. The place reminded her of the path through the World's Pattern in its strangeness but if she ever walked that road again she would not fear it, and would welcome it compared to this place.

The World's Pattern was life but this place seemed to leech the life from her. It grasped and clung as if it wanted to consume her, and yet it would not. It held back. It had other plans.

"I will not reach the end of this on my hands and knees," she said out loud. The sound of her voice did not echo but died away as if it too had been consumed.

She got back on her feet. The power still pressed in on her but she could bear it. It had only been the shock of it, and the pain from the slime that had brought her to her knees.

There was nothing left for her to do but keep moving inward. She tried to imagine what this thing could be, what distortion of the Mother's Milk had caused this monstrosity. Did it change every time there was a feeding? Or simply remain what it had become? Perhaps it had learnt to bear the magic in the same way she could tolerate its power.

The warped men in the Talamyrth must remain sufficiently human to continue to live and breed but they probably understood the danger and kept away when the power of the Mother poured down into their ley circle.

She was forced to turn left. Her stick did not click against the walls now, it touched only the ooze that coated it. But the floor remained clear.

Perhaps the tower itself, focusing and controlling the magic did something to it that meant the abomination did not change. She shook her head. She had no way of knowing. She suspected that even the most learned patterner of the Taymalin would not be able to answer it. Perhaps those who built the tower could.

Then the stick struck something in the middle of the passage. She came to an immediate halt. She willed her eyes to work but even if they had, she doubted there was any light in here. Where her lack of vision had brought her to tears before, now she found it frustrating.

Using the stick she tapped at the barrier to find it reached only to her waist in height, seemed thinner than it was long, had a curved shape and, she gave it a poke, was firmly attached to the floor. There was space on either side of it and, if she was careful, she should be able to round it without touching the walls.

But she wanted to know what it was, she did not want to leave something dangerous behind her.

There was only one way she would be able to do that. She went down on one knee and edged towards it. Finally she was close enough to stretch out her arm and touch it with one finger. It was smooth but ridged. Tiny bumps like waves and the whole surface like frozen ripples. It was hard but not wood and not as cold as you might expect stone to be.

Her tapping had not been wrong about the overall shape, she used all her fingers and even her palm as she gained confidence. The thing did not possess a single straight edge. It was all curves, like something alive. But this was not alive, and she was sure it was not going to hurt her. She knocked against it with her knuckle and it made a dull noise as if it was hollow.

It was thin, she had not been wrong about that either, and the top ridge suggested it was made of two pieces that might be prised apart.

And that was when a memory of her life before Jakalain came to her. In her master's house on the sea at Dakastown, among all his strange and wonderful collection, there had been an area set aside for those things collected from the sea. And she had often touched them, the sea urchins with and without their quills, the skeletons of fish, and the collections of seashells. The most uninteresting of which, next to the huge spirals, had been the one he had called a clam. A pair of curved and ridged shells joined to make a perfect seal.

Just like this.

She jerked her hands away.

The sailor who had brought the clam shells, though they were barely a hands-breadth across, had spoken of ones bigger than a man that lured prey into their mouths and shut up tight on them. Her master had suggested the man was exaggerating but he was in earnest.

Kantees did not for one moment—and had not then, because she was young—disbelieve the sailor. Here was one, though why it should be high in the mountains in a tower a dozen leagues or more from the sea, she did not know.

It might be dead.

When she tended to Sheesha at Jakalain, they rarely saw the harvest of the sea but sometimes the races were at Dakastown or Kurvin Port. And Sheesha loved to eat the shellfish. She never needed to open a shell for him, if he could not crack it with his teeth he would dash it against the stone floor until it broke open and he could feast.

She concentrated on her memories. Given a choice, like any animal, he would eat the fish first because they required the least effort and were swallowed whole. But then he would attack the clams even though their shells were tougher than most.

And she had no idea what that meant and she did not much care for shellfish.

But here was a giant clam in a place it should not be. Was this the abomination?

Perhaps she would learn by going deeper. It was certainly what she felt she wanted to do. She shook her head. No, it was *not* what she wanted to do but it might be what the power that pressed in on her from all sides desired. And if that was the case, she would, perhaps, be safe, at least until she reached her destination.

19

———

She slipped carefully past the inert clam, avoiding contact with the walls as well. The slime that coated everything except the floor also confused her since that did not seem to be anything to do with a clam.

But she moved forward. If there were any other doors or entrances to rooms and passages, she was unaware of them. The walls continued to be covered by the slime, perhaps any alternative routes were blocked. It gave her the strongest impression she was being guided to one specific location.

Another, smaller clam blocked her way. This one was as inert as the first but its angle made it more awkward to pass.

Hunger grew in her belly. It took her a few moments to realise that feeling was not normal. She did not know how long she had been moving—though she had been going very slowly—so a feeling of hunger was not a complete surprise. It became more of a surprise when the desire to eat increased to the point where she felt she would eat almost anything.

She knew it must be the magic of the creature but knowing that did not make the hunger pangs any less potent.

The effect made her feel as if she was tearing in two. The thinking part of her looked and observed. It analysed what the magic was doing, but it could only do it because that part of her that was more *zirichak* was fighting to escape. It was plain to her now as she stood in darkness, perhaps it was she who was the abomination after all. The *ziri* inside wanted to rip open and devour the delicious shellfish in front of her.

It wants me to eat it?

She might be able to stand to one side and analyse, that did not mean she understood.

Have I got any choice?

Could it want to poison her? She shook her head, no, there would be much simpler ways to kill her if it wanted to. It had blinded her, how easy would it be to drop her down a hole, or into the mouth of an open clam?

She squeezed past this one and moved on. There was another clam, smaller again, only coming up to her knee. Then two more that were barely bigger than Gally's hands. The power was beating down on her so hard now it was hard to think. The *ziri* in her was desperate to eat and she needed all her concentration just to hold it in check.

A burst of light and pain drove her to her knees again. This time it did not let up and it was a while before she realised her hand was in a puddle of slime on the floor. She wrenched it away but the aching in her head took a long time to die away.

Eventually her head cleared sufficiently for her to think about moving on once more. She reached out and put her hand down—straight on top of a small clam. Convulsively she yanked at it. It ripped away from the floor and the *ziri* part of her took over. She shoved it as far as it would go into her mouth and clamped down.

Her jaw hurt from the effort and it made no impression. She grabbed it again and smashed it into the stone of the floor. And again, and again. She turned it a little and hit it down again. A piece of shell broke off, flew up and scratched her cheek.

It was working! Using both hands she pummelled the ground with the edge of the shell. More bits flew off. She felt a crack form across the length of one side. Again! Again!

It shattered and something slimy slipped out across her fingers. She jammed it into her mouth and swallowed convulsively, choking as bits of it got stuck and broken shell tried to go down too. She forced it down with a feeling of elation and joy at having succeeded.

She felt it slipping down into her stomach and the desperate hunger faded.

Rationality returned and the horror of what she had just done took over.

She shoved two fingers into the back of her throat in an effort to make it come back up. She coughed and retched, but her body was stubborn and held on to the meal it had been tricked into eating.

"Why?" she shouted but her voice fell flat. The intense oppression of the magic of the creature that lived here lifted slightly.

Was that it? The compulsion to go deeper was gone. The need to eat had all but vanished.

She found her stick and whipped it to the side where it struck the slimy wall. It made a dull slapping sound but there was no other reaction. The creature, if it was just one creature, was too big to even notice.

There was nothing left to do but leave. She had done what the creature wanted and she had not even seen it. Because there was nothing to see, and even if there had been she was blind.

She made it to the second clam blocking the way before pain wracked her stomach. Her muscles cramped and she doubled over in momentary agony. She gripped the walking stick compulsively as she fell to her knees on the cold hard stone. For the briefest moment she wondered if it had deliberately poisoned her after all, but the pain dissipated almost immediately. She climbed to her feet once more and stood straight. A thought came to her, and where the need to eat had been from the outside this one was from within: She needed to leave, to fly from here. This time Kantees suppressed it. She was not an animal.

It had made her eat and now it wanted her to do something else. Perhaps if she had been a *ziri*, the command would have been simple and clear. If she had been only an animal she would not question it.

She was tired of being manipulated, whether it was by a human, or a monstrous sea creature that did not belong in the mountains.

But her refusal brought back the pain. So she stumbled in the direction of what she hoped was the exit, tapping the floor and walls as she went. She did not realise how fast she was moving until her thighs slammed into the rough surface of the first clam. She cursed it with the name of the *Kisharuk* and edged round it.

Her thoughts were confused as she tried to sort her true intentions from those being forced on her by the monstrous abomination that occupied the tower.

She tasted fresh air and breathed it deep. It did nothing to clear her head but she blinked as something moved in front of her. She stood stock still.

Her eyes were open but what she took for light did not change as she placed her hand across them. Even when she blinked the greyness did not alter. She turned round and the light, if it was light, seemed to come from behind her. Except that it was still visible. As if she had eyes in the back of her head.

The drive within her coalesced on the grey light. That was the place she must reach, just as the tower had been the lure before. Whatever was in her now could see the light and was showing her. She turned once more and faced the sullen greyness.

It was just another untruth. Her life was filled with them but this one would punish her if she did not follow it. She took three steps forward and ran into the stickiness of the wall. She realised she had dropped her stick. Another reason to curse this place.

Unwillingly she used the wall as a guide, tolerating the cold damp unpleasantness of it until it dropped away from her and she needed to turn left to stay with it. The grey lure was still in the same direction, she was not approaching it directly but she was still moving toward it, so there was no retaliation from the thing that possessed her.

The air moved against her cheek and she thought she heard someone talking. And came to a stop.

What could she tell Yenteel and the others? Gally wouldn't understand. Ulina might dive into the tower to take on the creature. She shook her head, she couldn't tell them the truth, only Yenteel. But what could she say? That it decided it didn't like her and sent her on her way? Gally would accept that but Ulina wouldn't.

The ache in her stomach intensified. She had been standing still too long and the creature didn't like it.

Tell them nothing. If they have nothing to react against there will be no excuse for rash actions.

"Your life is filled with lies, Kantees of the Ziri." She said the words out loud expecting them to echo but they fell flat and dead against the softness of the slimy walls. She took a step forward to alleviate the pressure within.

"I will have to sleep, monster," she said. "You cannot drive me forever."

"Kantees?"

Yenteel's voice sounded as if his head was wrapped in *lukisa* wool.

"I'm here," she called back. "Don't come in. I'm on my way out."

The wall seemed to be heading in the direction from which his voice had come so she followed it until she felt the sun's warmth on her skin and almost fell as Gally wrapped his arms around her. The air was filled with the susurration of a hundred silent men and women breathing.

"What happened?" asked Yenteel.

"I can't talk about it now," she said, trying to sound commanding, as if she knew what she was doing and was in control. "But—" How could she say this without it sounding bad? "—I need to keep moving. The thing that was pulling me in is now driving me away."

She could not see the day, it was as lost to her as it had ever been, but she could see the grey glow that seemed a very long way off. She pointed. "I have to go that way."

The ache was already growing so she unwrapped herself from Gally and addressed him. "Gally, you must guide me as you did before. That way." She pointed again. "Let me hold your arm."

"There are many people, Kantees," he said as she took hold of him.

"Ulina, you must clear the way for me if they do not move."

"Should I kill them?"

"No, but threaten, perhaps a pinprick if you must. Let us not provoke them unnecessarily—"

Even though they will do nothing, she thought. They do not understand what is happening even though they have been here for so long not a single one of them, not even the oldest, will have seen what has just happened before. Perhaps they have seen *zirichasa* lured inside only to emerge a while later and fly off. Never a person.

"—but I do not think they will be any problem."

"I will fetch our belongings then," said Yenteel. "Walk slow, Kantees, so it is easier for me to catch you up."

"If you can find something to ride," she said. "I would appreciate it."

"I'll see what I can do."

She heard his footsteps depart.

"We must move," said Kantees and then directed a thought to whatever it was inside her. *What's the point of hurting me if it prevents me doing what you want?*

It did not answer but the pain eased as she headed towards the grey light it put into her mind.

They had left the town and were heading out into the fields when Yenteel finally caught up with them. She knew from the thump of padded reptilian paws he had managed to acquire at least three *kichesa*.

The animals padded past at a trot.

"Can you stop?" asked Yenteel, his voice coming from a position some way above her.

"For a while," she said. "How did you pay for them?"

"I didn't, they were donated."

Kantees flopped down where she was. The ground was damp but she didn't care. She pressed her hand into the mud and imagined what it must look like. Would she one day forget how things looked? Would she press her hand into mud and be unable to imagine it squeeze out between her fingers? That possibility scared her more than the fact of being unable to see.

"Donated?"

"Yes."

"You didn't pay for them?"

"No."

"How long before they notice?"

"I have no idea but I don't think they'll be giving chase."

"Why not?"

"It's not in their nature."

Kantees frowned. "What do you mean?"

"You saw them. They're barely more than *lukisa* themselves. They don't care for the places they live in, make no repairs. They don't talk unless they have to and they go through the motions of survival, but I think Ulina could have struck down every single one of them in the crowd that watched and not a single one would have lifted a finger to stop her."

Kantees was silent.

"They won't be coming but, in the meantime, we have three healthy rides."

Kantees put out her arm and Gally was there in a moment, helping her to her feet. She brushed the drying mud from her hand. "Let's get moving then."

With help from both Gally and Yenteel she got up into the saddle of the animal. It wasn't like a *ziri*, it was more like riding piggy-back with the *kichek*'s head directly in front of her.

"Ulina, you ride with Gally."

"I want to ride with you. We always ride together."

"This is different, and I have a special task for you." The girl did not argue—perhaps her interest was piqued—so Kantees continued. "That's the direction I need to go." She pointed. "I want you two to scout ahead and make sure there's nothing in my way because if there is a barrier I won't be able to stop for long."

"Should I remove the barrier?"

"Only if you can easily, or with Gally's help."

"If the barrier is a person?"

"Don't kill anyone unless you are threatened." Kantees could almost see the disappointment on the girl's face. "And Gally is in charge."

"What?" Ulina almost screeched.

"Gally is in charge because he's older."

"But—" Ulina stopped and Kantees was very glad of it. Gally

had little enough self-respect and did not need to be told he was not fit to be a leader. He believed that completely. Kantees was not entirely sure this was a good idea but she needed to get the two of them away so she could talk to Yenteel.

"Gally is in charge, unless there is fighting and then you are in charge."

"Yes, Kantees."

Gally rumbled his agreement although she could tell he was not happy about the responsibility.

"Off you go then, and quickly, I cannot stay in one place for long."

There was the creak of straining leather as Gally got into the saddle and then some grunts as, she assumed, Ulina climbed up with him. After a couple of goodbyes there was only the sound of *kichek* pads going off into the distance.

"Can you guide my mount, please, Yenteel?"

Moments later they were on the move too, but at a slow plodding pace.

"So what really happened?" he said.

It did not take long to recount the details of her experiences in the tower.

"Clams? Really?"

"That's what it felt like," she said. "And *zirichasa* really like them —to eat, I mean."

Yenteel did not respond for a long time until finally he said, "There are insects that plant their eggs in another animal."

"Yes."

"I suppose something could allow itself to be eaten to do the same."

"Yes, the pain I had shortly after eating."

"The host doesn't usually come out of it very well."

"I know."

They both fell silent.

"But the fact it's driving you in a certain direction might mean something."

"Of course it means something," she snapped. "And I doubt it affects what's going to happen to me in the end."

"There must be something we can do."

Kantees shook her head. "I wish there was. I mean, I hope there is. But right now all I can do is follow the light in my mind."

"I'll think about it."

"Sorry, I was angry."

She heard him snort with laughter. "I'm not sure I could be as calm as you are if I had been blinded and then potentially impregnated by a monster clam."

"There's no point in falling apart."

"No," he said. "But people don't always think logically when things become impossibly difficult."

"I suppose not."

The sun must have gone behind a cloud because the warmth went from her exposed skin. A sudden gust whipped across her head. She could even feel the hairs on her scalp now. She needed to have it shaved off. Perhaps she could trust Ulina to use her knife; Kantees did not like the feeling of the bristles on her scalp.

"What are we going to tell the children?" said Yenteel.

"Nothing," she said.

"I agree not telling Gally, but Ulina isn't stupid, she knows there's something wrong."

"When has there not been something wrong, Yenteel?" If I had ignored Sheesha that night my life would be so much simpler.

But now she was lying to herself and she knew it. If she had not flown Sheesha and raised the alarm, the raiders would have taken Daybian. Then they would have come back for her when they realised they had got the wrong person. And there would have been nothing to stop them. She would have ended up on the island of the Dunor where they would have either killed her or persuaded her to work for them. Her train of thought stopped and she squinted as if trying to see the truth.

"I don't know why the Dunor wanted me."

There was a notable hesitation before Yenteel answered. "They knew there was someone who could control *ziri*, obviously. I expect they wanted to see if they could use that skill either directly or perhaps even copy it."

"Or they simply wanted to stop me."

"Or that," he said. "When you catch up with them you can ask them."

"I wish Daybian was here." The words slipped from her mouth before she could stop them.

"Levin too," said Yenteel as if he had not noticed.

"Yes, both of them."

"Tenical?"

"Only if he's piloting the *tekrak*," she said. "Other than that he's not worth much."

"He might have a better idea of what to do about your problem."

He might.

They made good progress heading roughly to the north and west. To fill in the silence that came between them, Yenteel took to describing the surroundings.

"We're on a track."

"I can tell."

"There's a small river and we're alongside it."

"I can hear it."

"What you can't hear are the clouds, the hills or the fields."

"I can smell *lukisa* dung."

"That's on the road, I think they must have driven some into the town in the last couple of days," he said. "There are fields close to the road, wheat and some small green plant with a bulbous body."

"Like the *tekrasa*?"

"A lot smaller, even smaller than the migratory ones, and they don't have a fire-tube."

"That wouldn't be useful if you were permanently rooted to the ground."

"Unless you planned to engage in warfare against your small green neighbours."

The idea was so ridiculous that Kantees could not help but laugh. "Perhaps they might join forces against the humans that come to uproot them in the autumn," she said. "And send out emissaries to seek assistance from all the other green vegetables."

She fell silent. Unfortunately, it felt all too similar to what had happened, except she was the victim.

"I'm sure we'll find a way to deal with your problem."

She hesitated and then lifted her chin. "What else can you see?"

And so it went on. Yenteel describing what was in the distance, the low hills with *lukisa* grazing on them—

"I told you there were *lukisa*."

—to the broken-down but still occupied farm buildings. They crossed and recrossed the river, sometimes there were wooden bridges, and other times through wide fords where her feet and ankles got wet.

Yenteel warned her they were coming up on Gally and Ulina.

"Is there a problem?"

"Not that I can see."

Kantees considered how people took that phrase for granted. She couldn't see anything at all and if he lied to her there was nothing she could do about it. She had to trust him.

It had been barely a turn of Lostimal since that night in Jakalain. As a keeper of the *zirichasa* she had an eventful life, but compared to this she might as well have been sleeping like Eftena.

They stopped and she listened as Gally told them that there had been nothing dangerous and nothing to stop Kantees from moving towards the place she had to go.

He said all this before she had even managed to climb down from the *kichek*. Her legs were stiff and she held on to the reins as the only thing solid and stable in her world.

"Gally does not know how to care for *kichesa*," he said very seriously.

"They're a lot like *ziri*," said Yenteel.

"They have no feathers," said Gally.

"No."

"They do not fly."

"No."

"They eat grass and not meat."

"You see," said Yenteel. "You know a lot about them."

Kantees could imagine the puzzled look on Gally's face, he would not understand Yenteel's word games.

"Yenteel is playing, Gally," she said. "But he is right, they both have their riding tack and I expect it's very similar."

"It is a bit the same," he said.

"You need to look after it the same way. And the—" She stopped and looked up with her sightless eyes.

A golden line traced a path above her and off to one side. Somehow she focused more closely on it and it resolved into two. It was as if a steady hand was drawing across the blackness of her mind.

She pointed up. "What's that?" Though in her mind she already knew the answer.

"It looks like *ziri*," said Yenteel. "Flying fast." But he did not sound certain.

"What's wrong?"

"They're below the clouds."

"Of course, you wouldn't be able to see them otherwise." Kantees concentrated as if she could somehow force herself to see them. After all, if she could see their trail, why not the *ziri* themselves?

"The clouds are low and they aren't *zirichasa*."

One moment they were heading past and away. Next they changed direction sharply. Kantees could only agree with Yenteel, no *ziri* could alter course when using a pattern to fly so fast.

Something else could fly like a *ziri*.

"They're coming our way," said Yenteel, his voice suddenly nervous.

A small hand grabbed Kantees' wrist and dragged her to the side. Unable to see the terrain, and surprised, she stumbled and fell. The reins of the *kichek* were jerked violently from her hands as she came down on her knees, and Ulina pressed her into a lying position. Kantees barely managed to get her hands up in time to prevent her face smashing into the dirt.

She could still see the bright lines as they extended down from the sky towards her.

A growing whistle filled the air and something went past. She could feel the buffeting wind and the *kichek* snorted. The paths of light in her mind diverged and each curved round and back towards them.

"What are they?" she called.

"*Melinasa*," hissed Ulina from somewhere higher than where Kantees lay helpless. *Melinasa*? Those birds they had found with the Farahalek assassins?

The trails stopped in her mind. They must have ceased to use the pattern and reduced to normal flying. Ulina grunted.

A moment later there was a shrill squawk that cut off. Moments later one of the trails started again and the *melinak* climbed fast, turning away from them as it did so. Heading back the way it had come.

"They found us," said Yenteel.

"I got one," said Ulina in a voice that implied she had failed for not killing them both.

There was a pause. "It will be dinner," said Gally.

Kantees climbed to her feet and stood unsteadily. She knew the others were around and the *kichesa* stood nearby but without something to hold on to she felt lost and vulnerable. But she did not want to appear weak.

"What do you mean 'they found us'?" But she did not really need an answer. It seemed the *melinasa* could be used for more than just carrying messages. "It's my fault."

"Your fault?" said Yenteel.

"I don't know how but I don't think they had seen us until I tried to see them better."

"See them better?"

"It's hard to explain, but just like I see this grey light I have to travel to, I could see the trail of their magic. I tried to look more closely, to see what they were. I thought they might be *ziri*."

"You were hoping it was Sheesha," said Yenteel, his voice very close now. She desperately wanted to reach out and cling to him, instead she just nodded.

His arm went round her. "I understand."

"We'd better get moving," said Kantees. Her heart sank as she realised she could not escape her past. "We can't afford to wait until the Dunor catch up with us."

They sent Ulina and Gally on ahead once more after Kantees gave them, as best she could, the direction of the glow. She was not sure but it might be forming into something.

"We'll be reaching the foothills by the end of the day," said Yenteel, and told Ulina not to go in but wait a short distance from them. There was no telling what lived in the mountains, apart from wild *ziri* and *sikechasa* capable of carrying off a whole *kichek*, not to mention a man or small girl. Ulina did not say anything about being able to look after herself this time.

They mounted up and set off at a steady walk. Over short distances Yenteel would have the *kichesa* trot which they seemed to like, but Kantees found it hard to maintain her seat if there was too much bouncing. She couldn't see the terrain to know when there would be dips or rises.

"The *melinasa* can do the same trick as the *ziri*," she said during one of the periods when they were walking.

"So it seems."

"The *ziri* I thought I saw, before we rescued Daybian, it must have been a *melinak*."

"Is that important?"

"No."

I pinned my hopes on it being a ziri. *I told myself it proved there were Kadralin riding the* zirichasa *here in the mountains. I am here because I wanted to believe it. I wanted it to be true.*

Yenteel said nothing as they trotted for a while. "Do you think your ability to see patterns is caused by the thing inside you?"

Kantees hesitated. Her old distrust of Yenteel surfaced, caused by his need to make her into something that she wasn't. She had never wanted to be Kantees of the Ziri. He had wanted her to become a symbol and that is exactly what had happened. But a symbol of what?

"I'll tell you, if you tell me who your master is and the real reason he sent you."

"All right," he said finally.

"You first."

It started to rain. She felt the drops falling on the bare skin of her head and arms. It soaked into her clothes and made them heavy. It hissed as it landed on the fields around them.

"I'm from an area near the Thousand Mouths, south of Faerholme. I grew up free. I worked in the map-makers guild where I learnt to read and draw. I was going to be properly apprenticed when Master Florian visited."

"Who's he?"

"The Grand Master of Patterners."

Kantees was unimpressed, every trade had a guild, and every guild had its grand master. And patterning was a skill like any other, it could be learnt even if you lacked the natural talent.

Yenteel apparently gave up waiting for a reply and continued. "I don't really know why he singled me out, he had been talking to others in my guild, perhaps they said something. So I was summoned into his presence, and he offered me a job."

"You're not a patterner."

"No, and I said as much. 'That's why I asked you' was what he said."

"What sort of job?"

"It doesn't have a name, I don't think, but I was to perform tasks for him. I thought he just meant being a servant, getting food, perhaps carrying messages, that sort of thing. You might call it envoy but it was less official and I have no rank in the Patterners Guild. I was part of his personal staff."

"And you said yes rather than be part of a proper guild, even though you're Kadralin."

"I spent my life working with maps, Kantees. I wanted to go to these places not just draw them. Visit the cities I had painstakingly copied. See the mountains, the lakes and the people."

She would like to see the mountains, for a moment her lack of sight tore at her. She did not think she had given any visible sign but then Yenteel quickly said, "Sorry."

She pulled herself together and stared at the grey light ahead of her. "It doesn't matter. Was this your first task?"

"Oh no, he started me on easy things."

"Like fetching food?"

"He never asked me to do that," said Yenteel and she could tell he was smiling from the tone of his voice. "But he did want me to deliver messages. Short distances at first, then a day or two of travel. Then long distance using a patterner's path."

"I suppose he didn't have to pay, being the Master."

"He always paid."

"Well, that was decent of him."

"You don't sound as if you think much of him or my job."

"He's not Kadralin, is he?"

"It's not the same on the mainland as it is here."

"No, you said, the Kadralin aren't slaves."

"They're not."

"But do they have any power, Yenteel?"

He paused. "You sound like you want to start a revolution."

"Oh, don't worry about it, I'm just a blind slave girl, what good am I?"

This time he stopped talking completely. Kantees knew it wasn't his fault but it was just another way the Taymalin ruled and held the Kadralin down. *We were here first.* But there was nothing she could do about that.

"I'm sorry," she said quietly as the two *kichesa* plodded through the downpour. The air had become colder too and she felt as if they had been gaining altitude although she had no reason to think it. She took a deep breath. "So, this Florian sent you to find me?"

"He did. He told me there was someone at Jakalain who was a *Fahain* of the *zirichasa*, and that I must make sure she stays safe and is allowed to grow."

"A what?"

"*Fahain.*"

She waited for further enlightenment.

"It's a *Slissac* word for someone who is a natural master of patterning."

"And he knew I was a girl?"

"Yes. Master Florian is the most powerful patterner in all the world, as far as I know."

"Throws lightning bolts? Summons monsters? I'm surprised he needs you."

"His knowledge of patterning is beyond anyone, that's why he's the Arch-Mage."

"And that's it?"

"That's it."

"Why didn't he come himself?"

"He had other matters to attend to."

"I haven't been safe."

"Safer with me than without," he said. "But you have been allowed to grow."

"I think he's just another arrogant Taymalin. A meddler."

"You're not the only person to call him that."

They rode on in silence for a while. The rain poured more heavily for a dozen breaths and then blew away, leaving them dripping. The *kichesa* did not seem to mind one way or the other.

"Your turn," said Yenteel.

"Since I am supposed to be *Fahain*, do I need to? You have it all worked out. It was you that chose to call me Kantees of the Ziri wasn't it? Not his idea."

"That was my idea. Yes."

"Why?"

"You're not the only person who thinks the oppression by the Taymalin is bad."

Anger roared up from her belly. "So you thought it would be a good idea to turn me into a symbol of freedom? You did it because you wanted to prove a point? With no regard for what it would do to me? Someone of your own race?" She paused only to take a breath. "In fact never mind that I am Kadralin, you would abuse *anyone* just to be right? It does not bear thinking about. I thought you were my friend."

"I am your friend."

"No, you are only here because some Taymalin patterner told you to come, and you choose to trample on what few freedoms I have claimed for myself, for your own ends. That is not a friend, Yenteel. It seems my mistrust of you was entirely justified."

"If you are *Fahain* then you are the person to lead our people."

"You presume too much! And look about you! We have no

people! They are *lukisa* in the thrall of a monstrous abomination—
that is using me, just like you!"

"I believe in you."

"You can be eaten by the *Kisharuk* for all I care. In case you
hadn't noticed, I'm blind."

"'The hero is forged in the flame of chaos.'"

"*Zatek* dung. Don't quote that bastard Taymar at me. This is all
his fault."

"It was the *Slissac* who enslaved the Taymalin and created the
Kisharuk."

"So they escape their slavery and the first thing they do is
enslave us. They learnt a lot from their previous masters."

Yenteel stopped talking.

2 1

_____

cold wind sprung up as they arrived … somewhere. Yenteel had not bothered to describe their surroundings as they passed through them. It made the journey tedious. But it was over for now. She could smell the smoke from a damp fire and the welcoming voice of Gally was a relief from the silence.

"Gally and Ulina stopped where Yenteel said we should," he said as he helped her down from the *kichek*. Her legs were stiff. "Gally gathered the wood and Ulina made the fire. The *melinak* is roasting."

Kantees forced herself to smile but she did not know if Gally was looking so she thanked him, though her voice cracked as she did so. Her scalp itched and she ran her fingers across the bristles.

"Can you shave my head, Ulina?"

"Yes, Kantees." She was close by.

"I'll see what we can have with the bird," said Yenteel.

He seemed distant and did not project the usual familiarity. Kantees pushed aside the guilt. He had no right to do what he had done. He had destroyed what little life was her own. She chose not to remember she had promised to be more honest with herself, nor the fact that if he had not come to Jakalain, she would be with the Dunor even now.

"Anyway, it's nonsense," she said.

"What is nonsense?" said Gally.

Kantees cringed. She could imagine the faces of Ulina and Gally, one frowning, the other bemused. She had not intended to say the words out loud but somehow, being without sight, it gave her the impression she was on her own. "Nothing."

So she sat on a log facing the fire and letting the flames warm her. Something flickered in the dark of her blindness: A sliver of light that moved and weaved close to her head. Kantees jerked away at first but Ulina put her hand on Kantees' shoulder and held her still as she used the little knife and attacked the bristles. The slick blade slid across Kantees' skin, and she could see it, just as she had seen the potent patterns of the *melinasa*. And she watched it moving around and across her head—feeling it at the same time. Since the magic of the knife could pierce metal without hesitation, the growing hair presented no barrier whatsoever. Ulina had Kantees turn to bring the fire's light on a new area and it took very little time for Kantees' scalp to be smooth once more. She sighed with relief.

What did it mean that she could see strong patterns, or perhaps intensely focused ones? She directed her attention to the grey patch that remained her goal. It was brighter than it had been.

"Are Lostimal or Colimar in the sky?"

"There are clouds," said Ulina.

"Not at the moment," said Yenteel in a dull unemotional voice.

She heard him rummaging in his bag and there was a pause. "A feeding is due tomorrow around sundown but I don't think that will be here." He paused again. "And another one on the next day, though a little earlier."

Kantees could not help herself. "So soon?"

"The paths of the moons are complex but if they have two intersections without much time between, the locations will be far apart."

"If someone can devise a machine for predicting the feedings, why can they not predict their locations too?"

Yenteel was silent for so long after her words that she thought he had chosen not to answer. It was long enough for her to notice the beginnings of a headache. The thing inside her would not let her be; how was she supposed to sleep?

"There are such devices," he said at last. "The patterners have them."

"Taymalin patterners."

"Yes, but..." this time she was sure he paused for dramatic effect, "...the circles themselves know and those who are sensitive can feel the changes."

"Kadralin?"

"I expect so."

She tried to sleep. Perhaps she did doze for a short time but the nagging thing inside her grew in intensity. The night was cold and she did not want to get up. How could they possibly travel through this terrain in the dark? She laughed at herself. She was always in the dark now, and she had to rely on the others for everything.

Perhaps the night was nearly through and the dawn was beginning to paint the horizon with grey. But she knew in her heart it was not the case. The air tasted dry and the ache in her head was such that she knew she would not be able to sleep. Her destination glowed in the distance. Was it a ley-circle? Or some other site of power? What drew the thing within her to that place?

Where was Sheesha? She felt the cold trail of a tear extend across her cheek as she lay on the hard ground. Why had he abandoned her?

In the quiet she could hear the other three breathing. Gally's exhalations were deep and long, Ulina breathed more quickly, and lighter. Yenteel's she could hardly hear at all. There was little to distinguish him from the quiet bubbling of the brook nearby.

She sat up and pulled the blanket closer around her. It had often been colder than this in the Ziri Tower when she tended Sheesha, but never had she felt so alone.

"How is your head?"

Yenteel's voice made her jump even though he had spoken very quietly. It crossed her mind to ignore him but that would be childish.

"It hurts."

"Do you need to move on?"

She wanted to say no. She did not want to inflict her illness on anyone else. But this was not something she could lie about. In the end she said nothing at all.

After giving her enough time to respond, she heard him climb to his feet.

"I'll be a moment," he said and stumbled away from the fire. She was not embarrassed by him having to relieve himself, at least he did not have to have help finding somewhere private.

He returned a short time later. "Shall we leave the others behind?"

"Gally stays with Kantees," said another voice.

Kantees sighed. Everything she had ever done just added more guilt.

"We won't be able to travel fast," she said. "You could just stay here with Ulina and catch up in the morning."

"Gally can sleep anywhere," said Ulina. "Even on the back of a *kichek*."

"What about you?"

"Let me ride with you, Kantees, and I will keep you safe so you can sleep."

Yenteel sighed. "I'll just stay awake for everyone then. But there's one problem."

Kantees turned in the direction of his voice, a sudden fear in her heart. "What?"

"*Kichesa* can't travel by night, especially not in this cold."

She sighed with relief. *Is that all?* But it was true, they were just big lizards, they hated the cold, and getting them to move at night was very hard. The *ziri* had feathers to keep them warm, and she knew from experience that night-flying was not a problem for them.

"I can't stay still," she said. "I'll have to walk."

"Then I would suggest that I accompany you," said Yenteel, "while Gally and Ulina look after the animals. They can follow on with the dawn."

Kantees did not like it. She felt she was abandoning them, but there was little choice. She was not sure whether they could make enough speed to outrun the pain inside, but it was better than remaining still.

It had not even been a single day since she had been inside the tower. They could only have travelled barely three leagues, four at most, from the town, and the tower would still be visible behind them—for those who had the eyes to see.

Rather than walk side by side, Yenteel had her walk directly behind him holding on to a rope that he tied to his belt.

"This way," he said, "if I manage to find a deep hole and tumble inside you can just let go. And there is no risk of you falling into one on your own if you were by my side."

In truth it made no real difference to her. Since she could not see him who cared which direction he was from her? Besides, the ache really was turning into pain and she needed to be moving.

They did not speak for a long time. Yenteel kept up the best pace he could moving, as far as she could tell, along the track they had been using. She had no way of telling how much time had passed and she dozed on her feet as she stumbled along behind her guide and the pain diminished to a dull ache.

She came awake abruptly as she walked into his back. "Sorry."

"No need."

"Why have we stopped?"

"Can you indicate the way we need to be going?"

The glow of her destination was clear enough, which reminded her of something she had almost thought about earlier that night, but her thoughts were like a river of mud. She couldn't place it.

"Which way, Kantees?" he said with more than a hint of annoyance in his voice. She knew she couldn't blame him, he had been awake most of the night.

"Where are you?"

His hand came down on her shoulder and she shrunk away. He removed it.

"No, it's all right, I was just surprised." She lifted her arm. "Just rest your hand on my forearm—or can you see it?"

"There's little enough light, Colimar is making a bad show between the clouds."

She focused on the greyness in her mind and concentrated on

where it seemed brightest. Carefully she turned until she was sure her hand was pointing in the right direction. It was very difficult to tell.

"Unfortunately that's as I suspected," he said.

"What?"

"The path we've been following is turning to go along the base of the hills. We have to go up but there's a large wood in the way."

Kantees groaned.

"I am aware," he said. "All the luck we've ever had with woods has been bad."

"Is there no way around?"

"It's difficult to tell in the dark."

"Well, if there's no choice."

"I'm sorry."

"So am I."

"It's not your fault, Kantees."

She took a deep breath. "I mean I'm sorry about earlier."

He said nothing for a while, then: "I'm not sure you have anything to apologise for." There was another long pause. "Let us save that for daylight, we need to move on."

"Perhaps we don't," she said. "The pain has diminished, perhaps we can get some rest here. If we move off the track Gally and Ulina won't be able to find us."

There was another pause though not as long. Yenteel laughed to himself.

"What's funny?"

"Oh, I was nodding in agreement."

2 2

The air was even colder when Kantees came awake once more to her throbbing head. But she had slept and she had not dreamed. She realised it was strange that half of her was warm though the cold wind slid across her newly shorn scalp. And the part that was warm was pressed against something softer than the ground.

For the briefest moment she thought she was lying with Sheesha. Then she realised it was Yenteel. She had fallen asleep the moment she had settled in the dry gully he had located just off the track. The sides protected them from the wind and even a boulder was a sufficient pillow.

She lay there enjoying the brief moment of warmth but then he stirred as if waking. She was about to push herself up when she saw a bright streak above her, slicing through the darkness of her mind's eye.

"Don't move," she hissed. "*Melinak.*"

She did not know if he had even been fully awake but she felt his body tense.

The line did not change direction, and streaked away until it faded from her view. Not that she had any idea of how far that stretched for such a creature.

"It's gone."

"I suspect we would be safer in the woods," said Yenteel.

"Against them seeing us, yes," said Kantees. "But what of other creatures?"

"Who can say?"

"I think I attract them."

"A jinx?"

"Perhaps it's my magic."

"That would not be a very useful ability."

Kantees pushed him away and sat up. It was strange. She heard all the gossip and the lurid tales of what went on between men and women. She knew the details of what one did with another—had even seen it in the beasts. Sheesha himself had been taken to breed with females.

She knew all about it and, the way the women spoke of it, there was a desire that consumed them, like a fire in dry kindling. And they would nod at her and she would pretend she understood what they were talking about. But she did not. She lay here with a man and there was no heat in her heart, nor her loins. Not even the smouldering of damp moss.

She had never felt it.

She heard him sit and then stand, his boots crunching on the gravel.

"How is your head?"

"Tolerable for now," she said. "How does the wood look?"

"Point the way for me."

She did so.

"Is that directly towards your destination?"

"As well as I can judge." Being unable to see your arm meant it was hard to be precise about it.

"You said it was a glow, is it a single point of light or is it spread out?"

"Spread."

"Can you indicate the limits on either side?"

She tried. He was silent for a while.

"The wood seems to be the only route if we go direct."

"And going round?"

"Perhaps it will not take us too far out of the way."

She heard the distant sound of thumping feet. "They're coming."

"Excellent, we shall break our fast. If we have time."

"We have time."

Kantees did not think she had ever heard Gally sound so relieved. As they ate dry biscuits from Yenteel's bag and washed them down with cold water, Gally kept saying how glad he was that they had not been lost. So she hugged him until he stopped. And then she hugged Ulina even though she doubted the girl would admit she needed it. Then again, Kantees was not sure whether it was for Ulina's sake, or her own.

"I believe I also deserve a hug," said Yenteel.

"I will decide when hugs are deserved," said Kantees.

"As you wish, Mistress Kantees."

Her anger flared like wild magic. "Do not *ever* call me that again!"

"I'm sorry—"

"I am no one's mistress!"

And then she burst into tears. Ulina grabbed her around her waist while Gally's massive arms engulfed her head.

She forced the sobs back down inside and shook the two of them off her. "We need to move. My head hurts."

They packed up in silence, mounted the three *kichesa* and set off.

"There's a river running through the middle of the wood," said Yenteel. "We could follow its course."

"That's still going through the middle of the wood."

"It will be faster than going round."

"No."

He did not argue again. They forded what she supposed was the river he had mentioned. It was not deep, but seemed quite wide.

"We could probably do with catching something to eat," said Yenteel.

"No stopping near the wood."

"There's no need to be quite so fearful."

"We nearly died twice in woods."

"Third time's a charm."

"That's what I'm afraid of."

Time passed and she could feel them climbing. And there were no trees, as far as she could tell, but she was not comforted.

A pattern of three straight lines appeared in her mind somewhere to the north of them.

"How far are the trees?" she hissed. The delay in response was too long. "How far?"

"Five hundred paces?"

"We have to get under them, now! *Melinasa!*"

There were no more questions. One *kichek* pounded away while hers suddenly lurched forwards, twisted to the left, and increased in pace. "Don't lead it!" she shouted. "Run!" And with that she jammed her heels into the flanks of the animal. Its casual trot became a headlong run.

Terror flowed through Kantees as the creature thundered across the ground. She knew it wouldn't allow itself to crash into anything, it was not stupid, but careening headlong was terrifying, especially when she had no idea what was coming, except that it involved trees.

She had to half stand in the stirrups so she was not shaken from the saddle, but ducked low behind the *kichek*'s head to avoid branches. They crashed into the trees, among snapping undergrowth, and branches that caught and tried to pull her off the animal's back. Her clothes ripped.

She yanked back on the reins and tried to bring it to a halt. Reluctantly it did so. She slid from its back, still holding tight to the reins, and crept under its neck to provide more shelter. The *melinasa* might see some people, they might see a *kichek* but they wouldn't see her.

The gold streaks were still coming their way but the whole flight into the trees had not taken much time. But if they had been seen, the *melinasa* still might not have changed direction. Yet. They were going to fly directly over anyway.

Then, to her utter amazement, another streak of gold came into view, and where the spying birds were tiny, this was massive. Like a broad stroke of golden paint across the sky. It curved upwards, seemingly intending to intersect the path of the three lines. The lines came to an abrupt stop and moments later, so did the wide band of colour. She shook her head, not understanding.

"*Ziri!*" shouted Gally in delight from some distance away. Moments later she heard the unmistakable sound of wingbeats that made the air shudder. More felt than heard.

"Hush, Gally, wild *ziri* will eat you."

But she knew the thrill, desperate for it to be Sheesha. The loss and the separation from him flooded through her and a wave of grief took her. Even as the *ziri* above them made a meal of the *melinasa*, she slumped to the ground and wept for her lost love.

A thin line of gold awoke in her mind once more, skimming away from them.

And then all was quiet again. And Kantees prayed there was nothing in the woods that would eat them.

"They're gone," said Yenteel from nearby. She had heard the slow thump of his *kichek*'s pads on the leaf mould beneath the trees.

"The *ziri*?"

"Yes."

"One of the *melinasa* got away."

"Perhaps it didn't see us."

"Perhaps."

"Gally did not see Sheesha," said Gally. It seemed the *kichesa* had managed to stay close even among the trees. Which reminded her that they were still in the woods.

"Is it getting dark? Is there any mist in the trees?"

"No, Kantees." Gally's voice sounded confused. Kantees closed her eyes, even though it made no difference. She needed to be more careful with the way she dealt with Gally. Her lack of sight did not give her the right to hurt him.

"Sorry, Gally, did you recognise any of the *ziri*?"

"Gally did not look too much, Kantees, because Gally must hide from the *melinasa*."

She realised he was feeling guilty because he *had* peeked. "That's all right, Gally, it was important to check. Are Yenteel and Ulina still here?"

"I am here," said Ulina. "Yenteel has wandered off. He does not fear the woods."

Kantees resisted the temptation to say that was because he was an arrogant fool. "His *kichek* is still here?"

"Yes."

"Let's get out of the trees then, he can find us when he comes back from whatever he's decided to do."

She was still holding on to the reins of her mount and realised that she could orient herself with the glow from her destination, and also how the slope ran. They had been climbing with the glow to her left at an angle. So if she had the up-slope on her left and the glow slightly behind, she would be heading out of the wood. The fact she could manage that on her own gave her considerable satisfaction.

"This way," she said, and gathered up the reins of the *kichek* and managed to remount without assistance. If she walked she could easily bump into a tree, but mounted she was safe from that embarrassment.

"Kantees?"

"Yes, Gally?"

"There is much firewood."

"Leave it, Gally. We need to get back into the open as quick as we may, there's no telling what might be lurking in this place."

Her plan went well, though an encounter with a leafy branch reminded her that she needed to keep her head low. But she could feel the change around her as they left the trees behind.

The glow behind her eyes was stronger now, they must be close. She did not want to wait for Yenteel, but neither could she abandon him.

"I see him," said Ulina. "He's carrying something."

"What?"

"Looks like a bird."

"He is holding a *melinak*," said Gally with conviction.

Kantees dismounted. This was probably going to take more time than she wanted.

"Tell me when you think he will be able to hear my voice without me shouting."

There was a long pause until Ulina said she thought he would be able to hear her now.

"What are you doing wandering off without telling anyone? I was in half a mind to leave you behind."

"I saw it come down, the *zirichak* who caught it just dropped it."

Kantees nodded. "They are tasty. I might forgive you."

"It's not dead."

"And you brought it here? To me?"

"It can't send a message back, Kantees, it must go back with its information."

Kantees knew she had been told that but it did not stop her being annoyed. Besides, what was to stop some clever Taymalin from concocting a pattern that could work from a distance? They might be looking at the four of them even now and preparing to send armsmen after them.

She did not think the Dunor would stop at anything in their attempt to locate her. After all they were already combing the mountains for her using these creatures.

"If we're not going to eat it why did you bother bringing it back?" She hesitated. "Why didn't the *zirichak* that caught it just finish it off and eat it?"

"We may never know the answer, Kantees, but I didn't bring it here for that. I want you to have a look at it."

"Is that a joke?"

"No."

All the time he had been speaking she could tell he was getting closer. She got the idea he was going to shove the *melinak* in her face. She stepped back and bumped into her *kichek*. "Keep that thing away from me."

"Seriously, I want you to look at it."

"*I'm blind,*" she hissed.

"Obviously, but in your blindness you seem to have developed the ability to see powerful patterns."

"Changes."

"What?"

"They are changes in the World Pattern, that's what I see. I think."

"Can you explain what you mean?"

She sighed. "The World Pattern is always around us. If I could see it, I don't know, perhaps it would be like having eyes that worked but it's even in the air we breathe so perhaps it would all be a blur or a fog."

Yenteel said nothing so she continued. "But if something disturbs the World Pattern, makes it change in an unusual way? I can see that.

"How long have you known?"

"Since you asked me the question."

He went silent, almost as if he had forgotten the creature he held in his hands. She wondered if it was bleeding. She heard its feathers rustle in a sudden movement. A sound that reminded her of Sheesha when he moved in his sleep.

"How can you know what the World Pattern looks like?" said Yenteel.

"I didn't say I did."

"Yes, that's just what you said."

"I know what I said, Yenteel, and I did not say that."

"Not literally, no, you did not use those words, but you said you see changes in the World Pattern. How can you know whether it's a change if you don't know what it's like in the first place?"

She stared at where she thought he was standing but was fully aware she might be staring just over his shoulder, or at his chest. It was difficult.

"I don't really see the point you're making." Which was a lie and she jammed her fingernails into her palm as punishment.

"Look at this *melinak*, Kantees."

"I don't know where it is."

"The *melinak* is in pain, Yenteel," said Gally suddenly. "Kantees, it is hurting."

Kantees felt uncomfortable. "You're right, Gally. Either put it out of its misery, Yenteel, or heal it. You have the skill."

"You want me to heal this thing that's spying on you?"

"It's not the *melinak*'s fault. Heal it and I will do as you ask. Otherwise you may as well wring its neck now and we'll roast it. We could do with another decent meal."

23

Yenteel grumbled about the conditions placed on him but they found a hollow that provided some shelter where they could make a camp. It was midday before they had organised themselves enough for Yenteel to perform the healing pattern on the creature.

In some ways Kantees was sorry he had agreed. She thought of roasted *melinak* again was pleasing. But if they healed it, they would not be eating it.

She could not help directly but suggested they bind the creature's wings, just to stop it flapping about in an effort to escape. It was a technique they would use even with fully grown *ziri* if they were badly hurt—they could do themselves more damage in their panic.

"His wing is broken," said Gally as he helped Yenteel bind the creature. "He has been bleeding from his body. Many feathers are lost and one eye is gone." He sounded so matter of fact as he described the injuries. Kantees could only imagine how it would look on a *ziri*, how it would be if it was Sheesha who had received those injuries.

"Give him to me," she said and held out her arms.

"Gally has tied his beak. He cannot bite."

But he did squirm, at least a little, when he was laid in her outstretched palms. She brought him in close but just let him rest against her. Poor thing must have been in terrible pain, and confused. It did not need a healer or a special power of the mind to know that.

She closed her eyes and tried to focus her attention on the bound beast in her hands. She did not know what she was looking for, she did not know what Yenteel thought might happen as she did this. But she knew that something like this belonged to the art of the healers. It was not a knowledge that had been written, or drawn, or that she had overheard her old master talk of back in Dakastown.

But it was something she understood nonetheless; she had seen healing patterns at work, and listened to what Yenteel said. How can a healer put something right in a pattern if they do not know how the pattern should be in the first place?

Did that mean they always fully understood the life patterns? No. That did not make sense and it was not something spoken about. No, that was not it. It was a natural order to the World Pattern, or just the pattern of a *melinak* wing. These things were the way they were because it was right for them to be so. And if they were broken or damaged, then they were simply wrong. A healer could sense a wrongness and knew how to put it right.

She felt Yenteel gently marking the cloth they had used to bind the animal.

What did it mean then that a pattern could be used by someone as unskilled as Yenteel? Someone without that natural talent? And what did it mean that a patterning could be woven into the fabric of a scroll in such a way that its power could be released by any person with the key?

She did not know for certain but she suspected that these Taymalin patternings were simply a way to force the patterns of the world into a semblance of normality. That they too were "wrong" but simply better than what existed.

There was something Kevrey of Tander had said many times, usually when he was annoyed at one of his customers "Chaos is easy. Order is hard." She had never really understood it until now.

She tried to do as Yenteel had asked, she "looked" at the creature. He probably thought she might see something in the same way that she did the streaks in the sky. But there was nothing.

Until he started the chant. She almost dropped the *melinak* as the explosion of light overwhelmed her. Yenteel could not pause though he must have seen her reaction. She appreciated that degree of calm and control, she doubted she would have managed it.

After the initial flood the light diminished, or perhaps she simply became used to it. But that in itself gave her pause. Would a flash of power like that be visible to wolves and others like them?

The shape of the *melinak* in her hands now became obvious. The magic of the healing was not focused only on the animal's injuries, it pervaded its entire body with no differentiation. She could not tell if it was changing anything but had to assume it was since Yenteel had done it before successfully.

Then she saw Yenteel. His hands were clearest as they glowed with a golden light. That power flowed like a stream from the rest of him. The pattern shaped the healing and drew its strength from him.

Yenteel finally stopped his chanting, but the power continued to flow, though it was fading. How did he know when to stop? Did it matter? She had never asked a healer but then, before now, it had not been something she even thought about.

"Let's get something to eat," said Yenteel and she heard him stumble away. The magic had drained him.

Gally took the *melinak* from her.

She sat down where she was and thought about what she would tell Yenteel when he asked her what she had seen. Perhaps the truth.

They ate. Yenteel questioned her and seemed satisfied with her answers but she knew he had a thousand more that grew in number the more he found out.

"Why do you have to know all these things?" she asked in exasperation as the questioning continued. "Why can't you just say 'This is the way it is and I am content'?"

"Because you never push for answers and more answers, Kantees," he said.

She frowned and bit into a biscuit.

"I am what is called a Natural Philosopher, Kantees."

"So you ask endless questions, and there is no answer to most of them."

"True, but how will I ever learn without asking? The world has a natural order, and I want to know what that is."

"I think you and my old master would have got on very well," she said. "Though he, at least, made money from his knowledge, which seemed a great deal more complete than yours."

"That is my loss," he said. "The Brothers and Sisters of Taymar do not favour those who ask questions like mine."

"I can understand why, it's irritating."

As she expected, he questioned her about what she had been able to perceive as the pattern took effect. In the end, she told him everything since she could think of no reason why she should lie.

After they had eaten, she said she wanted to move on again, the driving power within her was once more making itself known. She was sure they could reach the destination before nightfall.

It did not take long before they were mounted again and heading up the slope. Kantees worried about the *melinak* that had got away. And worried about the one Gally now cared for, what would it do once it had fully recovered? Gally had presented it with some biscuit which it had snapped at and eaten. He announced he thought it also ate meat because it had sharp teeth like the *ziri*. It really did seem to be a smaller cousin, the fact that it could weave the pattern that allowed it to fly fast only confirmed it.

But would this one go flying back to its masters when they released it? It was just an animal, it did not understand help and betrayal. Although that made her think of Sheesha, perhaps he did not think he had betrayed her by abandoning her.

Had he been caught in the trap of the creature in the tower? Had it infected him too and forced him to fly somewhere? The ability to fly would have saved her a great deal of pain.

Her *kichek* came to a stop as the ground flattened. They must have reached the top of the ridge behind the wood. The glow was much stronger now, below her and slightly to the left, and was changing from grey to gold.

"*Ziri*," said Gally.

"What?" she said in sudden desperation. "What *ziri*? What are you seeing, tell me."

"A tower, Kantees, not so big as the other one but the same, *Slissac* not Kadralin. And *ziri* flying round it."

"*Ziri*?"

"Lots of them."

"I can see twenty-three," said Ulina. "Different sizes, their colours are mostly black, grey and white."

"Wild *ziri*," said Gally.

"Is there any blue? Any gold?" asked Kantees, trying to keep the desperation from her voice.

"We can't go down there," said Yenteel.

"That's where I have to be," she said. "If I don't go the pain will increase until I cannot bear it and it drives me there anyway."

"They'll tear us to pieces."

"Gally will go with Kantees."

Not for the first time, Kantees felt as if her heart would break. Gally was braver than any Taymalin hero, and the most loyal of anyone she had ever met.

"No, Gally, I need to go down there, but you don't."

"Gally must help Kantees."

"I don't want you to be hurt."

"Gally does not want to be hurt, but Gally must guide and protect Kantees from the wild *ziri*."

She hesitated, she knew him well enough to know that when he got an idea in his head it was difficult to dislodge it.

"Kantees never did bring a gift back from Dakastown in exchange for Gally's coin. Gally must protect Kantees until she gives him the coin or a gift."

She broke down in tears again. He was right, she had broken her promise but he had said nothing about it until now. He was a better person than she was. She sniffed and rubbed at her eyes.

"You can come to help me cross the land between here and there. It won't do any good if I fall down a hole."

"Then Gally will not get his present."

"No." She did not laugh but stopped to clear her throat which was choking up again. "But when we get close you must stop. I do not want you to be eaten by *ziri* because then I will have no one to give a gift to."

Her argument was ridiculous but it seemed to make an impression.

"Gally will stop when Kantees says."

24

*Y*enteel gave her a backpack and she took some water, biscuits and her *chilafrah*. Even that was blank to her inner eye, though Tenical had claimed it was a powerful artefact for storing magic.

Yenteel had described the terrain in more detail. They had topped a ridge which led down into a valley with a river moving from left to right, he suggested it might flow round and down into the plateau they had just left. Beyond the river was a cliff which, he said, was pock-marked with caves and behind the cliff were the mountains. The tower had been built close to the cliff and the river flowed around it on this side forming a natural defence.

"The tower is built with six sides, black stone and tapering to a flat top. It's just like the one in the town, but smaller, the way Gally said."

"It's built on a ley-circle," said Kantees.

"Probably."

"I was not guessing."

"I see," he said. "There will be a feeding soon but there is no moon in the sky and from my observations it will be happening very far away from here."

"But another one tomorrow."

"Yes, there's no way of knowing where that will happen."

"There is a way of knowing," she said, "you told me."

"Which is not something we have at our disposal."

They made short goodbyes and with Gally leading her, the two of them set off down the slope. Ulina had not argued and not asked to come with her.

Kantees' mind wandered as they descended into the valley. Through long grass in some places, and rocky screes in others, where she had to cling to him to avoid falling. She was not sure if he was taking her by the best route or simply going in a straight line but she was not going to query or criticise his choices.

This might be the end of her tale. Those people who had learnt her name and called her Kantees of the Ziri would find she never returned. Would she slip into the legends? Would her struggle in the wilderness become a story told by firelight? Perhaps she would inspire the enslaved Kadralin to rise up and break their chains.

But she was not a fool, she knew where that would lead. They would try to kill the Taymalin, but not all of them were bad and it would be a crime committed in her name. She did not think she wanted to be worshipped by murderers and cursed by victims.

Then again, if she were gone and her pattern dispersed, she would know nothing of it, so why did it matter? Except that it did. She felt guilt for a future that had not even happened. Perhaps she would simply be forgotten and life would just go on the way it always had.

The only problem with that argument was the Dunor. If they were not stopped they would kill Taymalin and Kadralin alike, and bring their armsmen-carrying *tekrasa* and soldiers with the flying devices to every realm. They would usurp the power of every Taymalin lord that opposed them, and that meant Jakalain.

If she failed here, who would stop the Dunor? And, if she escaped this trial, who said she would be able to prevent their rise? Why was it up to her anyway?

She sighed heavily. It was the Dunor themselves who had made it about her. And her old master, Kevrey of Tander, was a fool. He had sent her away to protect her, for which she was grateful, but he did not know what he had done by allowing her to learn about the world.

It seemed he had not realised she was more than the sum of his oblique teaching.

She could see strong patterns – changed patterns. Perhaps she had always been able to do so, but it was only the loss of her sight that showed it to her. It was hard to think of becoming blind as a benefit but it had at least taught her this about herself if nothing else.

Finally the ground seemed to flatten out and she assumed they must be at the valley floor. Yenteel's description had given her little more than a sketch for her imagination. She could hear the river now, along with birds calling to one another. The glow in her mind's eye was there in front of her, changed now from grey to only gold— the power of the Mother's milk.

Then a sound she had not heard in what seemed a long time and yet was barely more than a seven-day ago. The call of a *zirichak*. It boomed a challenge across the valley floor and echoed off the cliffs. Others took up the cry until caller and echo became a single raucous shout that echoed forever.

"Have the *ziri* taken flight?" she asked.

"No, Kantees."

Gally was standing beside her. She turned and directed her eyes to where she thought he might be. "I'll go on from here alone, Gally."

"There is a river."

"Does it look deep?"

"Some places."

"Is there a ford?"

"Gally thinks he sees one."

"Take me to a place where the tower and the ford will be in a straight line. I can see where the tower is—" not a complete lie "— so if I walk towards it I will cross at the ford."

"Gally should go with Kantees."

"I do not want you to be eaten by wild *zirichasa*."

"Gally does not want Kantees to be eaten."

"I won't be."

That answer seemed to reach the limit of his ability to argue, though she hated herself for lying once more. But how could she allow him to do something that would only get him killed?

"Besides," she said, "who knows how to look after the *melinak* except you?"

"Gally will find the place for Kantees to start."

And they might not eat me, she thought. It did not seem logical that the creature would drive her to this place if the only thing that would happen was that she would be eaten—and the creature's egg along with it, if that's what it was. That was not a good plan.

But I am not a ziri. She could not disagree with her own argument but the hope that she could survive this was the only thing that kept her going. No matter how unlikely it seemed.

In the tower at Kurvin Port she had thrown herself out and down the cliff. Had she truly thought she would rather die than allow Trimiente Hamalain to harm Sheesha? It was true she would rather die than that but there was always the thought inside that one would not die.

And she had not, because Sheesha had saved her. Perhaps blind luck would save her now. She snorted at the phrase.

"Is Kantees all right?"

"I'm fine, Gally. Are we close?" They had been walking with the tower glow on her right and she hoped that Gally had properly understood what she was asking.

"This is the place, Kantees."

She turned to face the glow. "And the river ford is in front of me?"

"Yes, Kantees."

Now all she had to do was start walking and leave the last of her friends behind.

"Goodbye, Kantees."

"Gally…?"

"Yes, Kantees."

"Let me embrace you."

The sound of his feet shuffled on the gravel and his huge arms went round her. She stretched as far around him as she could and rested her cheek against his chest.

"Thank you, Gally."

"Why do you thank me, Kantees?"

"You have been a good and loyal friend. I can trust you and that is the most important thing I know."

She could feel his rumbling voice through her skin as he spoke.

"You can trust Ulina, Kantees."

"I know."

"And Yenteel."

"Do you trust him Gally?"

"Yes, Kantees, Yenteel is clever and wise. Gally knows about *ziri* more but Yenteel knows more about other things."

"I think you are wise, Gally."

"Thank you, Kantees."

She held him for a few moments more but she could feel him becoming restless at such a powerful show of emotion. She let him go and reoriented herself to the tower.

Carefully she took a few steps forward, it was just gravel here as far as she could tell.

"Wait, Kantees!"

She stopped abruptly as she heard Gally come up behind her.

"Yenteel said Gally must not forget but Gally almost did forget then Gally remembered."

"What is it?" She almost feared to know but instead of saying anything further Gally thrust a thin branch into her hands.

"Yenteel said that Kantees would not let Gally go to the tower. Yenteel told Gally to give Kantees this stick so Kantees would not fall down a hole."

"When did he get the stick?"

"Gally saw Yenteel carry it from the trees with the *melinak*."

"Mother's milk! I hate him."

"Kantees hates Yenteel?" said Gally in a worried tone.

"No, Gally," she said quickly. "Not really hate, it was a kind gift, I was just surprised because I did not see him bring it from the woods."

"Kantees is blind."

"Yes." *I hate him because he knew I would do this on my own and would need a stick to help guide me. It seems I am very predictable.*

"Is that everything he said, Gally?"

"Yes, Kantees."

"Good, then I shall go, be sure you stay this side of the river."

The stick was a good length and not too heavy so, as she moved forward, she was able to touch the ground ahead.

The *ziri* started up their cry again and it echoed across the valley, as if they were heralding her hesitant approach.

25

The gravel continued underfoot. Every now and then there were large boulders which she went around rather than attempt to step on or over. There was no telling what was on the other side. The sound of the river increased in volume and she felt its spray.

The warmth of the sun was on her back. She had not asked Gally what time of day it was but perhaps it did not matter.

The surface of the ground changed, there seemed only to be boulders now. This might be a ford but that only meant the depth of water was not too great, and the current should not be enough to carry her away. It did not mean it would be easy.

She knelt down and used her hands to feel the rocks. They were wet with spray from the river but they seemed to be flat. Not only that but she could feel a gap that ran straight into the water. It was less than a hand's-breadth in width. These were flagstones that had been laid deliberately.

Perhaps the people who had built the tower had made a flat surface through the ford to make it easier to move carts. She stood again and placed her left foot on the stone. It was solid and it was, as her hands had found, quite flat. Though she must take care not to slip.

She brought her other foot up and tested further in. She could feel the water pressing against the stick's tip but the surface seemed to continue flat as she suspected. She shuffled forwards.

A downdraught hit her from behind followed by a crunch in the gravel. It was not enough to knock her off balance, but she knew a *ziri* had just landed behind her. It grunted and the pitch suggested it was a juvenile. Probably just curious but if it decided she was food it would still be big enough to take her arm off with one bite.

She had never dealt with wild *ziri* but she had heard stories. They were predators after all, and they would kill to eat if they could get away with it. A juvenile was small enough that a person might be something dangerous to tangle with. It would keep its distance for now.

Unless it realised she was blind, in which case she would be easy meat.

She kept moving. The *ziri* probably had a pool where they bathed, but they did not like to get too wet because once water-logged they could not fly. That Sheesha had rescued her from the sea had been a testament to his loyalty.

If only he were here now. She did not doubt he would be able to dominate any wild *zirichak*.

The water was up to her ankles when another *ziri* landed behind her followed by squawks and throaty growls, probably for the best position to watch this strange creature crossing the river.

Thankfully the surface of the ford under her feet remained smooth and solid, although the water was now around her calves. The current was quite strong and the water icy cold.

Then her stick went down a hole and she almost stumbled forward. The resistance of the water around her legs helped her retain her balance even while it threatened to pull her feet from under her. She could only assume the water level was higher than usual. They had already experienced the flooding on the plateau, this was probably part of the same melting of snow and ice in the mountains.

Setting her feet apart for better stability, she investigated the hole. It was not wide, no more than the span of two hands, but it was deep and cut into the stone as far as she could reach in either direction.

She could not imagine why it was there but this was not the time. Carefully she stepped over it and continued. It seemed the groove was at the lowest point of the ford because now she was heading up a gentle incline and the water level decreased.

The breath of wind from a *ziri*'s wings hit her from the front and multiple crunches of gravel came from in front of her. She stopped for a moment. And listened to the squawks and grunts of the animals now in front of her. At least one of them was a full adult and the younger ones were making submissive noises.

She could stand here in the water until one of them decided to attack. Or she could keep moving. Of the two options waiting for death while her feet froze in the water was the least appealing so she started up again, shuffling forwards, beating the ground ahead with the stick.

Then she was out of the river and she could smell the unpleasant breath of more *ziri* than she was able to count. The glow of the tower was directly in front of her and, she guessed, so was one of the adults. She was so focused on the creatures surrounding her that she failed to notice the end of the flagstones and, as she stepped forward, the ground was not where she expected it to be.

She lurched forward until her foot landed hard on the gravel. She gave a little cry and flailed with the stick, trying to keep her balance. The stick hit something soft and yielding.

Around her there was uproar as the more distant animals grumbled and shrieked in tones that were both familiar and alien. And in that moment something grabbed the stick and tried to wrench it from her hand. Convulsively she gripped harder and was pulled forwards.

"You can stop that right now!" she yelled at the top of her voice.

There was momentary silence. Her face was stung by wind-driven gravel as several of them must have taken off. She recognised fear in some of the calls—that would be the juveniles—defiance in others.

The one that held her stick still gripped it, but she hung on. While it was holding on it was not biting her, and as long as she presented a strong face it might still be uncertain whether tackling her would be a good idea. For the briefest moment it loosened its grip and she managed to whip it out of the *ziri*'s mouth.

She could tell this was a big one, fully grown so probably male.

When Kantees was eleven years old she had been taken to the ley-circle at Dakastown. Her master, Kevrey, had not told her why. The mere idea that she should accompany him was unheard of. She was just a slave. He had not even told her she was being sold to Jakalain, but why would he? Did you tell a *kichek* when it had been bought?

Something had gone wrong and a young male *zirichak* had got loose. Its wings were still bound but it could run. Kantees had been walking a few paces behind her master when there was an uproar behind her. She turned to see the young *ziri*, still much bigger than her, coming directly toward her at a run.

She did not jump out of the way but waited for it. At the time everyone had said that she had been lucky and the *ziri* must have calmed down just in time. But Kantees had always known that was not the truth. The *ziri* was Sheesha and in the moment of their meeting, something had happened between them.

And here she was facing a wild *ziri* that she could not even see. But she was older now, she knew so much more of the *zirichasa* themselves, and now she knew much more about herself.

She spread her arms. "That's enough of this."

She could still feel the creature's hot breath on her. With a simple snap of his jaws he could have taken her head. But he did not.

Time dragged out. And nothing happened. Around her she could hear other *ziri* moving, occasionally snapping at one another, grumbling and making squeaking noises. These were signs of contentment.

Then the one in front of her grumped and she could hear it sit back on its haunches and felt the wings fold in. It had decided she was not a threat.

Kantees of the Ziri, she thought humourlessly.

• • •

Kantees dropped her arms gratefully, they had been getting tired. She looked around in her mind's eye for the glow of the tower, or perhaps it was the ley-circle beneath the tower but, for a moment, she could not see it.

She frowned. The glow had diminished even though she was now almost on top of it. She moved forward and heard the *ziri* shuffle out of her way.

Using the stick to make sure there was nothing difficult to get over she moved ahead, toward the remnant of the ley-circle's magic glow. If she was able to perceive changes in the World Pattern what did the glow mean? And what did it mean if that glow was disappearing?

She kept moving. As far as she could tell the sun was gone from the sky and the air was becoming chill. Around her she could still hear the rustling movements of countless *ziri*. Wild *zirichasa*, she reminded herself, creatures that would treat people as food given half a chance.

But not her.

The stick hit something at ground level. Another large stone. She poked higher up to judge whether she could go over it, or be forced to go round it. But the stone was big. Awkwardly she dragged the end of the stick upwards along its surface. At least her own height.

Reaching out, she placed her hand on the cold stone. It was perfectly flat. The kind of surface that could only be achieved by the hand of man—or *Slissac*. Or one of the other intelligent races that kept themselves to themselves and avoided humans. She could not blame them.

It seemed she had reached the tower.

And the glow of the ley-circle was almost gone.

She could not understand it. How could the power of the circle disappear? But why did anyone think it was a constant? Even those who supposedly knew about such things, the patterners and the followers of Taymalin, she had never known them speak of it. Not that she knew many, but even Kevrey, a man who trod the line between knowledge and blasphemy, had never spoken of anything like this.

What if the strength of the ley-circles changed all the time? After all, when they were fed by the moons their power must be far greater. And no one was ever really clear as to whether the feeding truly came from the moons, or if it went the other way. That particular argument was one that did exercise those who thought about such things.

Had she discovered the truth?

A cold wind blew past her and through her threadbare clothes. She shivered. Did this tower have a door like the other? Carefully she traced her way around it. Until she reached an opening. No door but at least it would protect her from the wind. But what was inside?

The grump of a *ziri* sounded behind her as she hesitated in the doorway. She froze for a moment and then turned slowly to face the sound.

The *ziri* snuffled. It was barely any distance from her and she could smell its breath.

A low growl rumbled from the *ziri*. She almost cried out but did not want to scare him.

"Sheesha?"

He grumped again.

Did he not recognise her? It must still be light and even if he could not see her he must be able to smell her. That was why he was snuffling.

"Sheesha," she said again, making her voice clear so he would know her properly.

But there was no familiar response. He continued to snuffle at her.

Then she knew what it was. Whatever that thing had put into her, Sheesha could sense it and it made him wary.

The glow from the ley-circle beneath her feet had gone completely, whatever power the place had possessed, it was all gone. But her scalp prickled as if one hundred needles were being poked into it all at once. She rubbed her hand over it in case something was touching her but found nothing.

Sheesha growled. She knew the sound, there were other *ziri* who raced that Sheesha simply did not like and he would growl at them.

She did not know if he thought they were threats or he was simply warning them away. She tried to imagine that Sheesha was making the noise to warn off other *ziri* nearby but in her heart she knew the truth. The growl was for her.

She was not the Kantees that Sheesha had known.

The prickling sensation in her scalp extended down her back, and across her arms and legs. It was almost as if something was attempting to pull her into the tower. She held her hand tighter against the stone but it felt like ice.

I need to get away from the tower.

She took a step forward and the intensity of Sheesha's growl increased. Reversing direction, she stumbled backwards as the pull from the tower increased.

What is this?

She flailed with one hand, trying to grab the edge of the doorway, and missed it. She toppled backwards and fell inside.

Blackness. So deep the darkest night would be the brightest day.

She tried to cry out Sheesha's name but no sound left her body. The raging torrent of utter darkness tore through her. It took everything from her. She could not move. She was not even sure she had a body. All she had was thought, and the strange sight that allowed her to perceive the World Pattern.

But there was no pattern here. Only a flood of chaos without structure and without design. Everything it touched was ripped apart.

Chaos is easy, order is hard.

But she was not ripped apart. Though she could feel the onslaught striking at the edges of her being, and even eroding part of what she was, it built back in other places. She focused on the rebuilding and it went faster. More quickly than the chaos tried to take her apart.

Chaos is easy, order is hard.

She could feel her strength coming back as she concentrated.

And she felt her body. She felt the stone beneath her, more than that, she saw it. This chaotic flood that poured down on and through her was not affecting the stone of the tower. Turning her attention to it she could now see the patterns within it. The strange patterns that responded to and focused the chaos. Directed it where the builders had wanted it. Patterns that reminded her of Ulina's knife.

Order is hard.

She was already exhausted by her journey and the lack of proper food. This strange feeding was taking the rest of her strength. If she did not get out, the part of her that was Kantees would be stripped away and gone forever.

She forced herself to roll over but did not waste time turning round, instead she backed her way out from the tower on all fours.

The Taymalin patterners must know about this was her one thought as her head came free of the cascading unpatterned chaos. Apart from the prickling of her skin it was as if nothing had happened. The *Slissac* who built this tower had known, the Taymalin's pattern lore came from the *Slissac*. They knew and they told no one.

It was as Yenteel had said. There was a feeding somewhere far distant. Kantees knew exactly where. At a ley-circle on precisely the other side of the world from here. Perhaps the chaos filled the gap left by the feeding, if it went upwards to the moons. Or perhaps it balanced the power that came down from the moons into the circle. She did not know. But she did know they were balanced.

Sheesha growled viciously behind her.

"Shut up, Sheesha. I'm thinking."

And Sheesha fell silent.

2 6

"Kantees."

She thought she was dreaming. She opened her eyes but if she had hoped the chaotic magic of the tower had somehow changed her condition, she was disappointed. Beneath her, the glow from the ley-circle had been restored. As far as she could tell the circle itself was some distance underground but the tower prevented it from distorting the terrain around it during a feeding.

"Kantees." The voice hissed quietly again and a small hand came down on her forearm.

"Ulina?" Kantees placed her other hand on the girl's and gave it a squeeze. It was quiet and the only sounds of sleeping *ziri* were a long way away. They had gone back to roost in the caves. Even Sheesha.

"Yenteel wants to talk to you."

"You shouldn't be here, it's dangerous."

"You are not dead," said the girl. "And I am very quiet."

Kantees could see the girl's tiny blade moving with her. And there was something special about the sheath as well—there would have to be for it to be able to contain the blade. She knew now the blade had, in some fashion, been forged to bind the raw chaos into its structure.

"Let us go."

Kantees stood up and felt the stones beneath her feet. Despite the hunger she felt fresh, wide awake and her mind was clearer than it had been in a long time. As if she had been shriven.

Order is hard.

Ulina took her by the hand and led her along the path. The water of the river was freezing, but she relished it. She had realised the groove down the middle was to allow the passage of water during the height of summer when the river become no more than a brook.

It was obvious now.

Ulina turned off the path, they crossed a grassy area and stopped. Kantees found herself engulfed by Gally hugging her so hard it hurt. She did not protest and allowed him to express himself in the only way he knew how.

When he was done, she found his hand and gave it a squeeze. "I'm happy to see you too, Gally."

"Shall I hug you, Kantees?" said Yenteel.

She smiled, though she knew it was night and he probably wouldn't see it. "If that is what you want to do, Yenteel, I will not protest. I will even embrace you in return."

To her surprise he did, and she returned the favour as she had promised. He did not cling for as long as Gally had done.

"I didn't think you would survive," he said, there was a crack in his voice. "When you faced down the big male, my heart was in my mouth."

"I had just had enough of their behaviour," said Kantees.

"It almost looked as if you were welcoming death."

"It seems I have never done that," she said, and if he did not understand what she meant she did not feel inclined to explain herself. "You interrupted my sleep, I would like to get as much as I can. I think we will have a busy day tomorrow."

"Shall we move back to the ridge?"

"That would be a waste of time. Here is as good as anywhere, safer probably, after all what predator would invade a *ziri* fortress?"

"Yes, but what prey would sleep there?"

"I am not prey, Yenteel. Things have changed."

She woke to the smell of roasting meat and sat up abruptly. In the far distance, the ley-circle in the town, beneath the big tower, was glowing brighter. She was right.

Moments later came the sound of Ulina's light footsteps. "Kantees, Sheesha and Looesa are here. They are behaving themselves and seem happy."

Kantees climbed to her feet, overbalancing slightly on the uneven ground. "Bring me to them."

Ulina took her by the hand and led her a short distance. Then Sheesha growled.

"Kantees, Sheesha does not like you," said Gally from a short distance away.

"He doesn't like what the clam put inside me. I'm infected and he smells it."

"Does that affect your plans, Kantees?" said Yenteel from the other side, it seemed she was the last person to rouse.

"No," she said firmly. "If either of you is holding them let go now and back away."

"Why?" said Gally. "Kantees must not scare Sheesha and Looesa."

She was surprised at his defiance, but pleased. He needed to learn to be independent, especially now that things were going to change.

"I will not do that, Gally, but we must be allowed to ride, so I must persuade him."

"It might help if you told us what you're planning, Kantees," said the reasonable voice of Yenteel.

"That's easy," she said then stopped and looked up. Her mind's eye showed streaks of golden light coming across the sky. "You didn't kill the *melinak* for food, did you?"

"No, of course not." Yenteel sounded hurt at the suggestion.

"Good. I think I'll be needing it later."

"But it will return home to tell the Dunor we are here."

"I hope so but not yet. Unfortunately, those will." She pointed into the sky.

"Gally will ride Sheesha and he will eat them," said Gally.

"No need," said Kantees. She visualised the big male that had threatened her yesterday and indicated the food flying through the sky. Within a handful of breaths, first one then two more golden arrows shot upwards from the caves in the cliff.

"Kantees?" said Yenteel.

"We must keep this place secret from the Dunor."

"But what did you do?"

"It doesn't matter. You said there will be another feeding today?"

"Yes."

"I know where it's going to be."

"How?"

"That would take too long to explain just now, but we will be returning to the town and that's why we need the *ziri*.

"Ulina, guide me closer to Sheesha."

"He doesn't want you here."

"I know but he must carry me."

Once more the girl took her hand and brought her slowly down the slope towards the river. In the distance there were calls among the wild *ziri* and she could hear them launching into the air, no doubt more of them going after the *melinasa*.

She could hear Sheesha's breathing and a low grumble from deep inside. The sort of sound he made when he was uncomfortable with a situation that was not an outright threat.

"Move away now, Ulina. Just in case he gets upset." *Not that I want that to happen.*

So she talked to him. He had heard her voice for almost his entire life, from that first day when he had stopped in front of her, already taller than she was, and fully capable of killing her. Nothing had changed.

She talked in a low calm voice describing how they met; the races they had been to; the time he had won; and when he had lost; she talked about Daybian. She talked about anything, while Looesa lay quiet behind Sheesha, and above them the wild *ziri* screeched and tore at the bodies of the *melinasa* they caught.

Every now and then she took a small step forward until she could feel his breath on her face. She had hoped he would settle enough to lie down but he remained alert and upright. It was not that she feared he might harm her, she thought he knew her well enough to avoid that, but could she overcome the fear he had of what was inside her?

It was a strange relationship the clam creatures had with the *zirichasa*; at once being their prey, and the way the clam reproduced itself. The World Pattern conjured a lot of strangeness in the form of animals and plants.

Kantees lifted her hand. "Want me to give you a scratch behind the ear, Sheesha? You know you like that, when's the last time someone did that for you? Just let me touch you."

Sheesha roared and reared. Kantees ducked.

"Sheesha, be good!" shouted Gally. "Sheesha, be good! Be good!"

Everything stopped except for the sound of Gally pounding up to them at full speed. Still shouting angrily at Sheesha.

Sheesha went still and all Kantees could hear was his breathing, ragged and fast. Kantees stepped backwards a few paces, then turned away. Gally stopped shouting and whispered to the *ziri* so quietly Kantees could not make out what he was saying.

She slumped down. All the energy and purpose she had gained in the night leeched away, leaving her more hopeless than she had ever been. As long as she had not been trying to achieve anything more than find her own people it did not matter what success or failure she had. But now, when she felt she had a true goal, to be rejected and thwarted by the only one that she ever really trusted.

A hand came down on her shoulder and she jumped.

"You never did tell us your plan."

"It involved getting back to the other tower as fast as possible."

"But that would cause you pain. It might kill you."

"It's the only way to deal with this once and for all."

"I see." He went silent for a short time but did not remove his hand from her shoulder. "So if there was a way to get a *ziri* to carry you?"

"They won't do it," she said, her voice almost breaking. "You saw what happened."

"Yes," he said, "but you didn't."

"I do not think much of your manners."

"I was not being rude, Kantees, nor trying to hurt you by reminding you of your condition. I was stating a fact. You could not see what happened, you only know how Sheesha reacted." He gave her a moment to absorb what he had said then continued. "I was watching both last night and just now."

"What do you mean?"

"It's true, both Sheesha and that male yesterday did not like you."

"They wanted to kill me."

"No, Kantees, they were scared of you."

"It amounts to the same thing."

"Not quite," he said gently. "The females and smaller males barely reacted to you at all. Looesa was perfectly relaxed and you weren't far from him."

"What are you saying?"

"I don't pretend to know what's going on inside the mind of a *ziri*, I don't know if they are like *lukisa* but those have one male in charge of the herd. Sometimes another male will arrive and try to take over—are *ziri* like that?"

"I don't really know, Yenteel. We only look after the tame ones. All I know is that, sometimes, the males at a race will try to face off."

"I know that when I called you Kantees of the Ziri, I was trying to manipulate you, and the people around you—"

"You were right, though. I know. But don't get cocky, I'm still not happy about it."

"I promise I won't."

"Liar," she said, but not in an unfriendly way. "You're saying they see me as a rival, but how does that make any sense? I have always been just Sheesha's keeper and he was always happy with that."

"The thing inside you," said Yenteel. "It must do something, either physically or perhaps some sort of pattern, that sends the message that you are a big dangerous *ziri* and too much of a threat to fight."

"I'm forcing them to give way to me." Then she gave a short laugh. "And I thought that male backed down because I told him I was fed up with his interference."

"Perhaps that is what it was," said Yenteel—though Kantees thought he was just trying to make her feel better. "It doesn't matter. Sheesha is even more confused just because he does know who you are but you're also this other thing."

Kantees nodded. "You're saying that I could fly Looesa?"

"No, I was going to say that Sheesha probably just needs time to adjust."

"That's no good," said Kantees. "We have no idea how long that might take. We need to get moving as soon as we can." *And we don't know how long I've got before this thing eats me.*

She reached up with her hand and Yenteel helped her to her feet.

"When's that next feeding due?" She could see the ley-circle in the distance pulsating.

"Not too long."

She nodded thoughtfully. "We have to get there just before it starts. If we're too early or too late, the pain will be too much." *And I will die.*

"You're judging the pain against your plan?"

"I have to rid myself of this thing, Yenteel, can you make me a healing pattern?"

"We have tried that."

"This will be different," she said. "I just need you to draw it and give it to me. I will do the rest."

"Who's going to do the chant?"

"Please, Yenteel, just do it and do it quickly, we don't have much time."

It was at that moment she heard Gally shout. "Kantees! Look!"

2 7

"What's happening?" said Kantees in desperation.

There wasn't an immediate response, then Yenteel spoke. "A *tekrak* just came over the cliff."

Kantees cursed herself, of course, one of the *melinak* from earlier must have got away.

"Do they see us?"

"Two brilliantly coloured *ziri* with a group of people in a grassy field? Yes, they see us."

She thought quickly. "Yenteel, get the pattern drawn for me. Please very quickly." She heard the distant roar of the *tekrak*'s fire-tube. "Gally! You ride Sheesha."

"Gally rides Sheesha?" He sounded both scared and excited.

"Yes, I want you to just keep circling round the valley, don't get close enough to the *tekrak* for them to shoot you with arrows."

"Gally understands arrows, Kantees."

Of course, they had already been in a fight for their lives with Farahalek when they were flying the *tekrak*. Kantees, Sheesha and Ulina had arrived late to that fight. They had won the day then, they could do it again.

"They have men with those wings dropping down towards the tower."

"What are the *ziri* doing?"

"They don't look happy but they aren't attacking yet."

"Ulina?"

No answer.

"She's gone," said Yenteel.

Kantees already knew what the child would be doing. "She'll be after the men in the tower."

"The *tekrak* is not coming this way," said Yenteel. "If they can secure the tower their patterner can make a path back to Watching Gate or somewhere else."

"We need to move now, at the very least to provide a distraction for Ulina."

They would have to assume Yenteel's theory was right without testing it but she knew what she needed.

"What do you want me to do?" said Yenteel.

"What's happening at the tower?"

"The ones that have already landed have taken up a position in the tower. They keep peeking out but they're scared of the *ziri*, I think."

"What about the *tekrak*?"

"Looks like it's manoeuvring to land on the top."

"The *ziri* won't see the plant as any kind of threat. We must stop them opening a path…" She hesitated, being unable to see made this so hard. "Yenteel, we'll go on Looesa."

It took a few moments for him to use one of his bandages to create the healing pattern which he rolled up and gave to her. She pushed it into her bag, next to the *chilafrah*. She stared towards the far tower and the increasing glow of the ley-circle.

"Gally is on Sheesha," he said as he took her by the hand.

Kantees waved in the direction she thought Sheesha was.

"They're up."

"I hope he stays out of trouble," she said.

"You demand a lot of people, Kantees."

"I'm only asking him to stay away."

"And he wants to protect you but you won't let him," he said. "And for me, I don't want to get into fights but you insist on putting me in harm's way."

"There and I thought you were sent to protect me as well."

"I wasn't planning on being at the centre of a battle."

"Don't worry, you probably won't be."

As predicted Looesa did not object to having Kantees ride. It still felt odd to her. He felt different. Awkwardly she slid back as far as she could to allow Yenteel up in front of her. She put her arms around him and pressed her cheek against his back.

It was terrifying to be aboard a *ziri* and not to be in control. Not only that but to have someone so incompetent in charge.

Then she laughed inwardly at herself. She had been riding a *ziri* for as long as Yenteel. But she had spent half her life around them, and it was those years that made all the difference. Looesa lurched upwards, his wings pushing the ground away from them. Kantees wondered if sitting this far back was as uncomfortable for the others as it was for her. The bones in Looesa's back were poking into her and very uncomfortable. Kantees did not want to put saddles back on the *zirichasa* but perhaps they could compromise with a cushion.

She tried to relax as Yenteel turned Looesa to the right. With a great effort she let herself lean only as much as Yenteel did, followed his motion as much as she could. No matter how wrong it felt. She knew he was just doing it wrong, he was not in tune with the *ziri* in the way she was. It was almost as if he was thinking about every move, trying to get it right, trying to match the motions—when all you had to do was just feel the beast and understand what it was doing.

"Change of plan, Yenteel."

"Really?"

"Get me into one of the caves."

"An empty one?"

"What good would that do?"

"You want me to drop you off in the cave of a wild *ziri*."

"Yes."

"I don't think that's a good idea."

"No, I'm sure you don't, but you aren't the one who's blind. You aren't the one who's probably destined to be food for a hatchling shellfish. I know what I'm doing."

"I'm not so sure."

"Just do it."

"Do you have a preference?"

"I can't see."

"Sorry, I forgot."

She chose not to respond to his sarcasm.

"I'm not even sure I can persuade Looesa to do it."

"Just come in along the cliff face, make a quick landing. I'll drop off, and you can fly away almost without a break."

"Let me try it once first."

"Just do it, Yenteel," she said and then added more gently. "I trust you."

She wasn't sure whether his failure to respond was because he didn't believe her, or because he was worried about it but she felt Looesa's speed increase. If she had even managed to see a fraction of the valley, she would have an idea of where they were. Instead she had to guess and trust Yenteel. Her only reference point was the ley-circle and they were moving away from it.

"Which way are we going?" she said finally as the air grew colder.

"I'm heading upstream," he said. "Then I'll turn and come down along the cliff. I saw a few big caves where the lip sticks out. I'll aim for one of those. Don't get off the wrong side."

"And the right side is?"

"The left."

"We seem to be going a long way."

"I wanted to look at something."

"We need to get back otherwise Ulina is going to try and kill them all by herself."

"I haven't forgotten."

She was about to order him to go back when she felt Looesa change direction in a tight turn and accelerate.

"I saw what I needed," said Yenteel.

She hoped they had not spent too much time on this side trip just to satisfy some idle curiosity.

"The caves are coming up," he said. "I'll count you down to one." She felt him instruct Looesa to slow by leaning back. The *ziri* responded well, though he did not have the precision of Sheesha—though that might have been a lack in Yenteel.

"Jump on the left," repeated Yenteel. Kantees adjusted her position, moving back a little and bringing her legs up. She gripped the back of Yenteel's tunic. "Three-two-stop! No!" She managed to stop herself though she was now standing on Looesa's back and holding Yenteel's tunic.

"Next one … three-two-ONE!"

She hesitated for a fraction of a moment in case he changed his mind again. Looesa's talons scraped on a rocky surface and their speed dropped almost to nothing. Kantees launched herself forward, past Yenteel's left shoulder, pushing herself off from Looesa's wing. She came down with a crash on stone that smelled of *ziri* shit. "Be careful!" was Yenteel's parting cry as *ziri* claws scraped on the rocks and she felt the blast of wind as Looesa took to the air again.

"I must be crazy," she muttered as she pushed herself up. Her knees were badly scraped and her palms burned. She wiped them on her shirt and adjusted the pack she wore. There was little in it apart from a knife, flint and kindling, and the *chilafrah*. And the rope she needed. She did not know how the magic worked but she thought the chaos of the—what would it be called instead of a feeding? The draining? Other choices involved juvenile male humour. Whatever it was called, she suspected the *chilafrah* would probably have given up whatever magic it might have acquired.

Something grumped and snuffled. The sounds echoed through the cave.

Kantees got to her feet. She could feel the wind at her back so she knew she was facing more or less into the cave. It would not do to walk off the edge. The *ziri* in the cave would see her outline clearly but, if Yenteel was correct, she should be perceived as a dominant male.

She heard human shouts below and a scream that did not sound like it came from one of her friends. Ulina had probably done something unpleasant to one of the armsmen. Kantees did not think she would ever get used to the idea of an assassin-child.

But there was little time to waste. The *ziri* had not attacked her outright so that was a good sign.

Kantees took halting steps forward, allowing a short space between each one. The *ziri* moved, giving Kantees a better idea of where it was. She did not approach it directly, but also did not want to give it a chance to escape. She had the rope out and the loop wide, though she did not want to use it.

Instead she began to sing. She was not good at holding a tune but that had never bothered Sheesha, and Kantees had liked to sing before her world had changed. Since then she had not had much of a chance. So she took it now.

They had spoken about the Curse of Eftena the other day, so she sang the ballad of the Sleeping Girl and the Prince of the Dark. Her voice cracked on the higher notes but Kantees didn't care, she was sure the *zirichak* was settling. The males crooned when they were about to mate, so perhaps this was the same sort of thing. Kantees seemed like a male, and she sounded a bit like one. That meant this *ziri* was, conveniently, a female. Males were notoriously hard to manage, that's why they preferred to bring them up from an egg in captivity rather than find young ones in the wild.

The breeding process had also accentuated the colours. Not that it would have made any difference in this dark cave. Kantees caught herself—she didn't know whether the cave was dark. Though it probably was. It didn't matter.

She moved closer still, still aware of the noises from outside, including screeches from Sheesha—she was certain it was him. She pushed worries about what was happening from her mind and focused on the *zirichak* in front of her.

Kantees could hear the *ziri* breathing. Females were quite docile during mating but could snap at the male. This was a fully grown female as far as she could tell. Kantees reached up and moved her hand behind where she thought the animal's neck should be.

Feathers.

Kantees pressed her hand in and felt the female shiver. But there was no snapping and no growl. So far so good.

Kantees stroked the neck gently and stepped closer. It felt good to be so close to a *ziri*, to be stroking the feathers, to breathe in the scent. The *ziri* moved her head and Kantees froze. Then found herself being sniffed in return. Kantees resumed stroking and the *ziri* continued to relax.

The *ziri* was going to panic when Kantees tried to get on its back but if she could get the rope round its neck just so that she did not fall off. Kantees had never tried to break a new *ziri* into riding, it just wasn't the way things were done at Jakalain. Those bred in captivity were given harnesses and saddles to wear from a young age, and weights increased slowly so that when the final day came, they were used to it.

But she had heard stories.

The interruption of the stroking had meant that the *ziri* became impatient and pushed herself against Kantees. She smiled, it reminded her so much of how Sheesha behaved, it seemed the wild *zirichasa* were little different to the tame ones.

So Kantees scratched, stroked and crooned as the *ziri* became even more demanding. The animal settled lower, lying on the ground to receive the attention of this strange male. Kantees dropped the rope over the neck and reached down to get the end so she had it fully encircled.

If the *ziri* noticed it gave no sign. Kantees gave herself a count from ten to one as she moved carefully but steadily along the neck to the wings, dragging the loose loop of rope and scratching as she went. The *ziri* gave no sign of alarm, perhaps expecting to be mounted—but not in the way Kantees intended.

Kantees reached the count of two and felt the position of the wings, they were spread loosely, as they would be just in advance of mating. Giving a silent apology for the betrayal she was about to commit, Kantees took firm hold of the feathers and pulled herself up on to the back of the *ziri* as fast as she could. She found the ends of the rope and twisted them around her hands, and tucked her legs under the wings.

There was a moment when Kantees thought the *ziri* had not noticed what she had done.

Then it bucked. Shook itself from side to side. Twisted its head to try to snap—Kantees was ready for that one and gave a sharp kick with her heels. The *ziri* launched itself forwards, but the rope held Kantees firm. And then they were in the air. They dropped like a stone with the cold wind blasting through Kantees' thin clothes.

But Kantees was airborne! It was all she wanted. She was on the back of a *ziri* and flying. As the *ziri* pulled up to avoid dashing herself into the ground, Kantees was jammed firmly into the animal's back. There was a jerk and a screech from the *ziri* as it did hit the ground, just for a moment before the powerful wings bore them up again—it was not used to the extra weight and misjudged the dive.

It flew up almost vertically as Kantees hung on to the rope, and gripped with her legs. Thankfully she was still in that position when the *ziri* decided to flip over to dislodge the creature that clung to her back. Kantees did not fall.

Then came a careening ride as the *ziri* flew back and forth, changing direction, climbing and diving, anything it could to get Kantees off her back. But she could not maintain that for long, and finally was flying straight. But if Kantees thought it was over, she was wrong.

The *ziri* landed to resume the bucking and twisting. Kantees was grateful it didn't decide to roll, that would have been very painful. Having failed again, the *ziri* took to the air again, but Kantees had limited time. She needed the *ziri* under control.

This was the part she was not sure about. She knew she and Sheesha had some kind of connection, but she had assumed that had come about from being with him for almost every moment of the day and night for years.

If that was true, this would not work. Even though it made no practical difference, Kantees closed her eyes and rested her hands on the animal's neck. She concentrated and imagined that her pattern was mixing with the *ziri*. That they were not two but one. They were the same, and that Kantees' desires were the *ziri*'s desires.

The ley-circle was now behind them, and a good distance away. Kantees wanted to go back there.

The *ziri* seemed to pause in the air then continued in the same direction.

Kantees growled in annoyance and tried harder but she felt what little connection she had achieved slipping away.

Chaos is easy— "Go away, Kevrey," she muttered. "You also said patterns do not respond to force."

And what is making an effort if not force?

"You think you're so clever."

She relaxed again. It was hard, she was aware she was not present for whatever was happening at the tower. All her friends could be dead by now, and she could never survive alone in this world without her sight.

But she must relax, she could do nothing about what was happening without a mount she could control. She let her legs go loose, and relaxed her grip on the rope. The *ziri* did not try to throw her off. Kantees lay back between the powerful wings that beat and stopped, beat and stopped. Memories of Sheesha came to her mind, he liked to play, she hadn't played with him in so long.

The sound of distant thunder rolled over her and was gone.

Sheesha loved to fly—even before she had stolen her first ride with him, she knew his love for being in the air. To him it was perfection. That thought stuck to her and she realised it was true for this *ziri*, that it was true for all *zirichasa*. Flight was the one truth of their existence.

It was her truth as well. If there was one thing that made them the same, it was that.

The thought that she really must return to the ley-circle crept through her mind. The *ziri* banked hard but Kantees was safe between her wings. As the *ziri* accelerated Kantees hooked her legs under the wings and pulled herself into a sitting position. The rope was gone, fallen to the earth somewhere behind them, but Kantees knew she wasn't going to need it any more.

28

The power of the ley-circle was a beacon and although she could not see what was going on, she was able to circle it. There was something different about how everything sounded. There were *ziri* in the air but the sound of the river was much stronger than it had been before, had it broken its banks?

She could hear no sounds of fighting, no screams of armsmen. Had she been gone so long the fight was over? If it was, where was the *tekrak*? Kantees knew her *ziri* would not fly into the thing, but if there were armsmen with bows, Kantees would never see them. Which brought her back to the fact there was no sound of fighting.

Then she smelt it. There were times of the year when everyone went into the fields to kill the migrating *tekrasa*. They had to be allowed to land, and their fire-tubes go out. Then they were chopped up, releasing the gas they made to lift themselves.

Sometimes people would do that too soon and the fire-tube would ignite the gas, the result was an explosion and a pungent smell of something gone bad. That was what she could smell. Someone had set the *tekrak* afire, the thunder she heard must have been the thing exploding.

The top of the tower would be empty—if there were no

armsmen on it. But if the *tekrak* had exploded, those inside would be dead.

She pictured the tower, or at least a smaller version of the tower in the town, and made sure she meant the one right by this ley-circle. The *ziri* seemed to understand and descended directly into the glow. Kantees recognised the change in wingbeats and braced herself as the beast touched down.

Unwilling to be stranded on top of the tower, Kantees did not dismount. She hoped the others had seen her. But for a while, all she could hear was *zirichasa* calling to one another from all directions, and the river swirling and splashing in a tumult—quite unlike the way it had been.

"I suppose I should give you a name," she said to the *ziri* and stroked the feathers of her neck. "Tabata." Kantees nodded to herself. "She was a great racer though I never saw her. She was Sheesha's dam and came from Otulain. Though I suppose you'll just go back to being a wild *ziri* when it's all over here."

The air thudded with the wingbeats of a big *ziri*.

"Kantees is riding."

"Gally! What's happened, where's Ulina? And Yenteel?"

"I am here, Kantees," shouted Ulina from a short distance away —not the same direction as Gally's voice. "Is your *ziri* safe?"

"I don't know, I think so, but perhaps you should stay back for now." There was no telling whether Tabata would decide to attack or not, though Kantees did not think she would. "Gally, is Sheesha hurt?"

"Sheesha is strong, Kantees. Sheesha was kind and let Gally ride like Kantees."

"What do you mean?"

"Gally flew the golden pattern on Sheesha." His voice was ecstatic—and so it should be. Even Levin had not been able to do that but then he was only Taymalin. "How far did you go?"

"Gally did not go far but bad *melinasa* had come with the men. Sheesha ate them while Ulina killed soldiers and Yenteel made the river big. Then the *tekrak* was a big fire."

Another set of wings came down on the top of the tower.

Kantees did not think it was as big as Sheesha, they were getting crowded here.

"Yenteel?"

"Kantees," he said. "I see your plan worked."

"My plan?"

"You ride a wild *ziri*."

"And you thought that was my plan?"

"It's not?"

"I wanted to ride Sheesha," she said. "What did Gally mean, make the river big?"

"You're not the only one with plans, Kantees. That flood down on the plateau happened when the ice broke in the mountains. Our little detour up the valley was to see whether the river here was also dammed."

"And you undammed it?"

"I did, with the help of Looesa and a little patterning." He sounded very pleased with himself. "Ulina kept the attackers inside the tower—I don't think they realised what was happening until the water was on them."

"Then I cut their *tekrak* open," said Ulina. "I didn't know it would explode."

Kantees was on the verge of telling Ulina she shouldn't have done something so reckless, but it seemed she was not familiar with how *tekrasa* worked, and besides, Ulina would always do dangerous things.

"The feeding is almost on us," said Kantees. "We have to move. Ulina, please ride with Gally." She urged Tabata to turn around, and she did so. Kantees pursed her lips. "Do not be surprised at anything that happens, just follow me."

"I gave up being surprised a long time ago," said Yenteel.

Kantees gave Tabata the gentlest of kicks and she tumbled over the edge. They swooped down, gathering speed, then Tabata stretched her wings. They caught the air and the dive mutated into a fast climb.

Once again using the well of energy beneath as her centre, Kantees had Tabata fly in wide circles. Then she focused herself. She must not use force, she must use what she learnt in the taming of Tabata to stretch out and encompass the flying beasts around her.

She closed her eyes and held out her arms as if they were wings. The *zirichasa* worked together, and when they employed the patterns to fly fast there was just one that was in charge. The others flew with them and obeyed them. Even when flying normally the *ziri* flew in exact positions.

Of course, Tabata was not the most powerful *ziri* in the valley but, as Yenteel had shown her, Kantees was. Even if it was only because of the thing living inside her.

"Kantees!" It was Yenteel's voice from behind and to the left. "Looesa and Sheesha have moved into positions behind you."

It was working, but only with the *ziri* that she had known all her life. Though they were submitting to flying behind a wild animal they had not even been introduced to. She needed the others, she needed them all.

What did the *ziri* want? They were lazy, mostly they wanted to eat and to sleep. Unless it was to fly and hunt. Well, she was offering them an easy hunt, and probably more food than they would eat in a five-day. They should all join the hunt.

"Taymar's teeth!" said Yenteel. He did not sound happy.

"What's happened?"

"I've been moved down the hierarchy," he shouted. Kantees was not sure exactly what he meant but he sounded further away.

"That male you faced off yesterday, he's taken my place on your left, I'm now directly behind in the third rank."

"How many in the formation?"

There was a pause. "About fifteen."

Kantees grinned and encouraged Tabata to climb and make wider circles.

"More joining," shouted Yenteel.

"Where's Sheesha?"

"Sheesha is here," said Gally from her right. "Sheesha and Gally and Ulina are more important than Looesa and Yenteel."

"That is true," said Kantees.

She felt as if she was growing, as if she could feel each additional *zirichak* in the formation, as if she was becoming them.

"Formation is changing shape," shouted Yenteel. "It's not a flat arrowhead any more, it's like …" Clearly a comparison failed him.

She turned her head. "The pointed roof of a round tower with me at the top and the rest spreading out behind in all directions."

"Yes!" This time she could tell he was completely bemused. How could she possibly know?

"How many?"

"I don't know…" he shouted back.

"Forty-three," shouted Ulina.

The time had come. The only *ziri* left behind were those too young or too old to hunt.

Kantees had only seen the tower in the town in quick glimpses, but she knew where it was. It was plainly visible to her mind's eye now, its glow brightening in the distance. They had only the smallest time left.

She pointed Tabata in the direction of the town. They drew power from the tiny ley-circle below and, behind the blindness of her eyes, Kantees watched her whole world turn to gold.

The distance of perhaps ten or twelve leagues was traversed in the time it took to count three fingers.

She wondered what it must have been like to see the vast golden patterning of the *ziri* come storming up from the horizon and flash across the town. Perhaps the people were too numbed by the influence of the abomination that infested the tower to really notice. But it did not matter, they were not the target.

Zirichasa loved to eat these creatures, they were a delicacy— and this time they would be a feast. Whatever patternings were used to keep the *ziri* away, Kantees had blasted through them. This creature, or creatures, did not think fast. It barely thought at all.

When the golden magic dropped Kantees stared down at the restrained power of the ley-circle and brought to mind the creature. It lay there on the surface and there was more of it inside. Enough to feed the entire flock of *ziri*. Just waiting to be eaten.

A pain shot through Kantees' head. It was starting.

She launched Tabata down. She felt her control breaking down as increasing numbers of the *ziri* caught the scent of their favourite food and launched themselves out of formation, wanting to get at it first.

Kantees envisaged the entrance and hoped Tabata would get the idea—it was just a cave like any other. A *ziri* would not be afraid of that.

As they hit the ground Kantees saw the ley-circle flare then subside. The feeding would happen at any moment. Kantees suppressed her instinctive fear of being near a feeding. The *Slissac* tower would channel the power and prevent it from causing abominations. The rooms inside were also untouched, whatever the tower did, nothing outside or inside was affected.

This abomination had survived in the tower for countless years. The people had lived around the tower with no harm.

I hope I'm right. If I'm not either the feeding or the pain will kill me.

She could hear noisy eating all around her, and a slightly echoey sound that told her some of the *ziri* were already inside. She urged Tabata forwards as a knife seemed to slice from temple to temple, and she suppressed a scream.

"Kantees! The feeding is due."

She focused through the agony. "I know, come on!"

"Inside?"

She did not have the energy to answer and just pushed on, keeping her aching head low as Tabata made her way through the corridors. The ley-circle flared again and again. Kantees realised she could see the walls. Their substance seemed to form a barrier to the raw energy of the patterns.

The pain in her head was pure agony now and she was having great difficulty keeping her attention on Tabata, but the *ziri* seemed happy enough to keep going.

A flash of white light illuminated the corridor. For a moment, through her pain, Kantees thought that she must be able to see again, but realised it was the power of the feeding. It always flickered before the raw energy formed the column of brilliant burning white light that joined the land to the moons.

She was here. At the centre.

The ground hit her hard as she tumbled from Tabata's back but the pain of the fall was nothing compared to the hammer pounds in her head. She did not know what was driving her, as she crawled towards the pillar of dazzling white at the heart of the tower.

Hand-over-hand she dragged herself across the floor to the light. Somehow, she managed to get herself to her feet as her head felt as if it would explode. Perhaps it really would. She fumbled in her bag and located the rough material of the healing pattern. She pulled it out and stretched it out, holding it in position around her head.

She focused on it as best she could through the agony. As she wavered before the light, it came to her that it was very cold. Like ice.

It flickered.

Now, she thought and fell forward into the brilliance of the Mother's Milk.

29

"Drink this."

An arm reached round behind her shoulders and pulled her into a sitting position, then a wooden cup pressed to her lips. She was not sure what she was expecting but it was water, tepid and tasting as if it might have been in a bottle for days. She took several sips, which showed her how thirsty she was.

She could smell *ziri* shit but, opening her eyes, she could see nothing. Beneath her was smooth stone, below that was the settled glow of the ley-circle. Whatever the *Slissac* tower did during the feeding, it did not affect the ley-circle itself.

Her body seemed to have little strength, and her head was tender. But there was no pain.

There is no pain.

"How are you?" said Yenteel.

"Alive," she croaked.

"Does it hurt?"

"Everywhere." She felt him tense as if he was ready to fetch a *ziri* to carry her back to the other tower. "But not in my head."

She took a deep breath.

"How did the plan go?" he said.

"Did we win?"

"The abomination has gone," he said. "Eaten. Clever you."

"The *ziri*?"

"Mostly gone, though they left some gifts behind."

"I can smell them."

"How are your eyes?"

"Is there any light?"

"Some."

"Still blind then."

"May as well take that blindfold off, how did that work?"

"All right, that part of the plan would not have worked."

"Nobody wanted to disagree with you, but no, it was crazy," he said, "flooding the valley, now that was genius."

"It was clever."

He tried to untie the cloth but failed, in the end he just slid it off her head. She rubbed her eyes.

"I can see the ley-circle below us," she said. "And I saw the feeding."

"No one will ever believe I was inside a tower when a feeding struck and I lived to tell the tale."

"The ley-circle flares when a feeding is coming."

"That's how you knew?"

"No, that was just before."

"So, how?"

"I could feel it."

"A true Kadralin then."

"If that's what Kadralin can do," she said. "I don't know. Perhaps it's just something Kantees of the Ziri can do."

"As well as tame wild *ziri*," he said.

"That too."

"And lead a hundred *ziri* across the sky in a golden pattern and into battle."

"It wasn't a battle, it was just food. And there wasn't a hundred."

"That's what the story will say." He shifted his position. "Can you stand?"

With his help she got to her feet though it felt as if all the strength had been drained from every part of her body. Lights flickered inside her head.

"My backpack."

There was a pause until he thrust it into her hands and she swayed uncertainly. "Are you all right?"

"I got flashes when I stood up."

"I'll carry you."

"No—" But it was too late. She felt like a child and was angry at herself for not being able to walk unaided. Then the flashing started behind her eyes again as he walked and bumped her along. Shutting them helped.

His boots crunched over something, she hoped it was clamshell. She hated the creature that had been here, for what it had done to her.

The air became clearer as they approached the exit and she took a deep breath.

"Stop at the door," she said.

He did and let her down. "You're pretty heavy for someone so scrawny," he said but he didn't let her go entirely and made sure she was able to stand.

She took a deep breath. Being free from the pain, and even the threat of it, was a tremendous relief. Lights flickered and blurred in front of her, moving back and forth as she swayed a little in the cold night air.

Night?

She turned her face upward. Pinpoints of light swarmed above her, then blurred as her eyes filled with tears.

Trying to keep her voice steady she said, "Tell me it's night, Yenteel."

"What?"

"Night, tell me it's night."

"Yes, it's night."

"And the sky is clear?"

There was a pause. "You can see?"

"I can see." Then her voice was lost in the sobs of joy.

She thought her encounter with Ulina and Gally might give her bruises. His delight at her being able to see again was enthusiastic, even Ulina could not suppress her pleasure and kept holding up different numbers of fingers and insisting Kantees count them.

That's revenge for my lies, Kantees thought but she did not mind at all. She was happy to count them as it confirmed the truth, and she no longer had to hold down the hope she had felt the whole time.

They sat in a corner of the inn where they had stayed that first night. Kantees ate slowly, relishing the real food and the ability to use the utensils on her own. The place seemed noisier than it had been before, as if the death of the abomination had lifted a weight from the minds of the townsfolk, every now and again there was even laughter.

But it did not take long before Kantees became restless. She got up from the table, the others stood too.

"I'm going for a walk," she said.

"We'll come," said Yenteel.

"No—I…I need to be alone."

"Kantees wants to talk to Sheesha," said Gally.

She laughed and put her hand on his shoulder. "Yes, Gally, I need to see him, find out if he has forgiven me."

"Sheesha is strong," said Gally. "Sheesha knows there is nothing Kantees has done wrong."

Kantees did not say *I hope you're right* aloud.

The night was very cold and illuminated only by the dim red light of Colimar—already on its second pass since the feeding. The world was black shadows edged with blood.

She walked between the houses and stared up at the vast black tower. She shook her head, the *Slissac* had tried to tame the feeding —but where were they now? It was a lesson the Taymalin would not learn. The Kadralin had never been under the thrall of the *Slissac*, but they had suffered because of the Taymalin. Did that mean that if they rose up they would become like their masters?

Did the victims always become the oppressors when given the chance? How could you stop that?

She shook her head and focused on getting round the tower to the entrance without tripping. It was strange how she did not fear it, even when she stood at the entrance and stared into the inky blackness. Perhaps it was the smell of *ziri* that drifted out that comforted her, even *ziri* shit. After all she had lived with that smell most of her life.

She listened to the gentle breathing of a *ziri* at the first doorway she came to inside. It wasn't Sheesha, at a guess she thought it might be Tabata. Kantees was surprised at that, she had expected the female to go back with the others once they had finished eating the abomination.

An animal snorted in its sleep and Kantees smiled. That was her Sheesha. Homing in on the sound she found him in another room. Of course she couldn't see him but then she had plenty of experience of that—but not with him. It struck her that Sheesha had not known she was blind, the *ziri* had run away before they reached the town. And had not wanted to acknowledge her yesterday.

Everything had been caused by the creature that had lived in this place. Or creatures. She had not been able to get a clear idea whether it was one or many.

It didn't matter, it was gone now.

Sheesha had little interest in the past, everything for him, like all *ziri*, was in the now. He probably wouldn't even remember that he had been scared of her.

She hoped that was true.

"Sheesha?"

Nothing.

"Sheesha."

He made noises with his mouth and she heard his tail flop heavily. He really was sound asleep. Then he grumped which was a sound he only made when awake—though it seemed a very sleepy grump. And then he yawned and she could smell his breath. That creature certainly was not good for his digestion.

"Your breath smells, Sheesha."

Grump.

"Can I come in?"

Silence—which meant nothing, he just wasn't very talkative in the middle of the night, and who could blame him. Taking short careful steps she moved into the room. She should have brought a candle but these few days of blindness had already broken her of so many habits.

"Where are you?"

He made a long grumbling noise which allowed her to identify where his neck and head probably were. Kantees got down on her hands and knees, then crawled slowly towards his head. At least she wanted to give him a chance to back away if he did not want her.

Suddenly his head came down solidly on her back, grinding her knees and forearms into the ground. Then he rubbed his chin back and forth as if he was using her as a scratching post.

"Ow," she said without much conviction. She was used to it. Sheesha could be very selfish.

She rolled to the side and sat up. In the dark she found his neck and scratched between the feathers. "You've probably picked up some nasty parasites by playing with those country *ziri*. They don't look after themselves the way I looked after you."

Grump.

"Don't pretend you liked being away from me."

Grump.

"Well, I enjoyed being away from you too. You're just a pain and a drain on my life. You know, women of my age are usually married with children."

Grumble.

"Yes, well, no, I am not interested in that, but that is not the point. If I was, you would be in my way."

Silence.

"No, Daybian does not count. I certainly have no interest in him. He wanted to force me."

Grump.

"I know what he said, but I also know what men are like. And, as I said, I have no interest in anything of that nature."

Sheesha burped noisily.

"You're disgusting," she said without any malice. "No, girls don't interest me either, since you insist on asking, though I think that is a very personal question."

Sheesha laid his head in Kantees' lap and licked his lips. Since his head was much larger than her lap, licking his lips involved much of what she was wearing as well which pulled on his rough tongue. She idly scratched the top of his head between his eyes.

"You've forgiven me then?"

Quiet grump. She gave him a shove and stood up. "Don't you dare try to go to sleep on me." Using her hand to guide her she walked along his body and gave him a kick. He rolled over and curled round.

Kantees climbed under his wing and with his heart beating slowly in her ear and the susurration of his breathing she fell asleep in a single breath of her own.

30

*L*ight broke through from the front entrance of the tower, reflected from the smooth walls and floor, and illuminated the room she was in with grey light.

She crawled from under Sheesha's wing and sat on him. He was awake but clearly had no intention of moving. Considering how much he and the rest of the *ziri* had eaten the previous day she doubted any of them would be moving at least until tomorrow.

The Dunor were still after her and their setback at the other tower would not stop them for long. She might have a few friends, one of which was a murderous child, and some *zirichasa* but the Dunor had hundreds of patterners, armsmen and the Farahalek.

What the Dunor wanted, as far as she could tell, was complete control of the lands of the Taymalin. Piecing together what Levin and Daybian knew, some of the noble houses had got together and decided they wanted everything. They must have some powerful patterners on their side, one's that had discovered how to control the big *tekrasa* and could use the *melinasa* for more than just sending messages the way the Farahalek did.

If it were not for the fact they were after her, she would have let them do what they wanted. She had no interest in what the Taymalin did to one another.

She paused. *I really should stop lying to myself.*

She cared. About Daybian and his family, about Levin. The Hamalain were part of the Dunor, and they were very unpleasant people. She would like to see the disgusting smile of Trimiente Hamalain torn from his face, she'd like to see *him* shovelling *ziri* shit.

But that meant she had to do something. And it meant she couldn't stay here. The first attack had not been well-conceived, but the Dunor would be gathering their forces against her and if they attacked this town there was nothing Kantees could do. She must draw their attention away from this place as soon as she can.

She heard Tabata hiss just as a shadow moved in the dim light.

"Gally means you no harm, *ziri*."

There was no further sound apart from heavy footsteps.

"In here, Gally. I'm with Sheesha."

His outline appeared at the door. "Kantees is well?"

"Kantees is very well," she said. "And so is Sheesha and the other *ziri* but they have eaten way too much and will be useless for another day at least."

"Yes, Kantees, and Gally has had his breakfast but Yenteel wanted to know if Kantees was hungry."

"Very hungry." She slipped from the back of Sheesha, who grumbled for a moment and then rolled over with his back to them.

Instead of heading straight out into the light, Kantees checked the nearest rooms. She hesitated at the door to Tabata's room, then went inside. Gally hung back.

"Tabata," she said loudly enough to get the attention of the wild *zirichak*. "This is Gally, he knows as much as I do about the care of *ziri*."

Tabata opened an eye and looked around. Kantees gestured for Gally to come closer, he walked over in slow steps, not walking directly at the *ziri* but towards the wall nearby. Kantees smiled, even she hadn't done something that sensible. When he was close he turned to face the *ziri*, but again not directly and he knelt down.

"Gally says hello to Tabata." He looked up. "That is a good name, Kantees."

Tabata eyed him and sniffed, then closed her eyes.

Gally stood, turned away and headed for the door. Kantees followed him out.

She ate slowly but cleaned the plate that was piled high with cooked meats, bread and butter. She was taking a long time over it, so Gally and Ulina, who had already eaten, left.

"This food is a lot better than it was a couple of days ago," she said between mouthfuls. She looked out at the room. People were talking animatedly with a lot of hand waving and gestures. An old man in the corner had a stringed instrument and seemed to be trying to get a tune out of it. Kantees did not think he was doing a very good job.

"The whole town's changed," said Yenteel. "There was an argument outside earlier, people just stopped to watch it. They were even hanging out of the windows to see what was happening."

"That creature must have been doing something to them."

Yenteel nodded. "I still don't understand how it could even survive. I asked someone how long it had been there and he didn't know what I was talking about. As if they did not even know it was there."

Kantees waved her knife to show she heard him but her mouth was full of the delicious food. They fell silent until she had finished and leaned back. There was a weak beer to wash the meal down. She drained her mug.

"How do they feel about *ziri* now?"

"No one seems to want to bother Sheesha and the others in the tower, but I'm not sure they were aware of the others. They flew off as soon as they had finished eating."

"The tower concentrates all the power of the feeding into a single column right in the centre."

"You saw it?"

"Fell on it."

"And you lived?"

"Not even growing an extra arm or turning into a clam."

Yenteel studied her hard. "You have changed though."

Kantees shrugged. "Has my hair turned white?"

Yenteel took a moment to get the joke then threw back his head and laughed out loud.

"You *have* changed," he said. "The other Kantees was not really one for humour."

She gave him a serious look. "I think we need humour, Yenteel, for what's coming—that's if you want to stay with me. I can't make you, of course."

He sobered. "Well, I have other orders that say I stay with you anyway, so we can bypass that question. What are you going to do?"

"Let's find Gally and Ulina," she said getting to her feet. "This involves them too. And I don't want to repeat myself."

Yenteel was right about the town, it felt completely different to before. The sense of slowness and apathy had been replaced by energy and emotion. The streets were busy and people went about their business with enthusiasm. Her biggest surprise was when she saw someone outside their house with the door off, making repairs to it.

The most noticeable thing before had been the lack of maintenance. When things broke or became unusable they just left them.

"I suppose this will stretch right across the valley."

"Perhaps even further, we have no idea how far the abomination had managed to spread itself. I can't imagine this is the only valley of Kadralin in the mountains."

Kantees nodded and they walked on in silence, just watching and listening.

When they found Gally, he was underneath a cart, lifting it on his back so that someone could replace a wheel. Ulina was idly cutting slices of stone from the wall around a well. They joined her and sat watching the work.

It did not take long but by the time it was done there was a small crowd of about twenty people watching Kantees. Gally came over, stretching his back and grinning from ear to ear.

"Gally helped!"

Kantees smiled too. "Gally did. You helped very well. No one else could have done that except Gally." If it had been possible for his grin to widen, Kantees was sure it would have. "We have some serious talking to do," said Kantees. "But I don't think we can do it with an audience." She inclined her head in the direction of the people watching them.

"Perhaps you'd better talk to them first," said Yenteel.

"Why me?"

"You're the leader," he said. "And it's you they've come to see, I imagine."

"I don't have time for this."

"Make time, Kantees," said Yenteel sternly. "You need to talk to them."

She frowned at him but the new Kantees was less argumentative.

"You'll have to translate."

She took a breath and turned towards the crowd with a smile on her face. It had not been a genuine smile when she started but she saw their faces, and every one of them was Kadralin.

But a town of Kadralin. Her people. This was the place she had set out to find, and she had succeeded. Eventually.

It took barely twenty paces to reach them but by that time she had transformed and could barely contain the emotion within her.

"Hello," she said, taking in their faces—wrinkled and smooth, some hair black and some white, youth and age. "My name is Kantees—" for the briefest moment she hesitated, "—Kantees of the Ziri."

~~ This story is concluded in BATTLE DRAGON ~~

Book 4: Battle Dragon

ISLE OF ESTERNES

1

"Gally must go with Kantees."

"And me," said Ulina. "You promised. And I have saved your life, you owe it to me."

Kantees sighed and felt very uncomfortable. Why had she promised to take Ulina wherever she went? And what was this nonsense about owing a life?

She glanced at Yenteel who was standing a short distance away by the door to the *Slissac* tower but he just shrugged unhelpfully. She had decided to talk in here because it was the only place in the town where they wouldn't be overheard, and where she would be able to mount up and simply leave, with Yenteel.

But only after she had persuaded the other two to remain behind. She had known that was not going to be easy.

"Galiko, Ulina, this is very important. The Dunor will send armsmen, and probably *tekrasa*, to attack this valley in an attempt to capture or kill me. I have to make sure that doesn't happen."

Ulina put her head on one side and the light from the candle reflected in her hard eyes. "That does not make sense, Kantees. You could take us. That would still save the valley."

"Gally has to stay behind because I have a very important task for him. You have to stay to protect him."

The big man shuffled a little. "Kantees. Gally is not clever but Gally is not stupid. Kantees does not want Gally to be hurt, and Kantees thinks Gally will do something wrong."

"No!" She caught herself, she shouldn't shout at Gally, that's what everyone else did. "No, Gally. That's what I used to think, but then you asked Sheesha to fly like a golden arrow and he did. Not even Daybian or Levin could do that. Only Gally." Which meant, according to Yenteel, that Gally was also *Fahain*, but he hadn't been part of the prophecy.

Gally cheered up being reminded of that.

"The Dunor attacked Jakalain to steal away Daybian because they thought he was the one with the power over *ziri*. Since they discovered their mistake, they have been trying to get to me. They must not find out that Gally can make the *ziri* fly fast, because then they will try to kill or capture Gally as well."

She stopped so that he had time to process this information. It took less time than she expected; as he said, Gally was not stupid.

"The Dunor must not know about Gally."

"No."

"We will not tell them, Kantees."

"No, but that's why I need you here. It's very important for you to stay here."

"Why, Kantees?"

"These people, Gally, the monster that lived here made them fear the *zirichasa*. It drove the *ziri* away but our people, the Kadralin, we fly the *ziri* and I want you to teach them."

There was another long pause. "Gally must teach the Kadralin to fly?"

"Yes, Gally, you must do it."

"That is a very important job."

"That's what I said."

"And you want me to stay with him so nobody treats him badly," said Ulina.

"And to make sure they listen to him," said Kantees. "I don't suppose there will be many who want to ride the *ziri* even though the creature is gone, they haven't had any experience for a long time. They will be scared."

"Gally will teach them to ride," said Gally firmly. "But Gally does not have a *ziri*."

"You can have Tabata," said Kantees. "Because the *ziri* must learn to trust the people as well. Tabata has learnt and you can bring others here."

That idea took hold. "Kantees wants Gally to break wild *ziri*?"

Kantees smiled. "I do." She looked up at Yenteel. "Fetch Looesa."

"I'm not riding with you on Sheesha?"

"No. Two *ziri* can fly faster than one with two riders."

He had never been happy riding and muttered as he disappeared into the dark. Kantees gave a silent call to Sheesha who came up behind her. Kantees knelt down to hug Ulina and, though she wasn't expecting it, the child hugged her back.

"Do not be killed, Kantees."

"I'll try not to be."

Then Kantees stood and hugged Gally. "Be strong, Gally, remember that you know more about *ziri* than anyone in this place. And if they are not careful, they could get themselves hurt, you are the one who knows."

"I will teach them, Kantees."

Yenteel returned with Looesa in tow. They had packed food from the inn earlier in the day and together they moved out into the open air. It smelled of spring which came later this high in the mountains.

"What about the other towns and villages?" said Yenteel.

"What do you mean?"

"The abomination spread its seed elsewhere."

"They'll have to wait."

There was a large crowd of townsfolk gathered. It reminded Kantees of that first time she had entered the town, but unlike the eerie silence then, now they talked among themselves. There was still some confusion about who she was but they understood that, in some way, she had saved them.

There were some ominous mutterings about the *zirichasa*, but nobody did anything threatening. Besides, most of them had never seen *ziri* up-close, and the size of their mouths, filled with sharp teeth, was intimidating.

Sheesha and Looesa flattened themselves to the ground so that Kantees and Yenteel could mount.

That should help Gally, she thought, *and imprint the idea that the* ziri *would obey.*

Then two pairs of wings beat hard and they were in the air. Kantees took them around the tower a couple of times, climbing all the time. Then she waved to Gally and Ulina, and to the townsfolk. She set a course to the west and, using the power from the ley-circle, Sheesha and Looesa took the golden path, with the town dwindling into the distance as if it was a stone dropped into a well.

And that should really impress them, she thought.

There was something lonely about travelling with neither Ulina clinging to her waist, nor Gally on Looesa. It was not that she disliked Yenteel, they had managed to mend their differences, or perhaps more accurately, Kantees now accepted the way he had manipulated her and was willing to use it to achieve her ends.

But there was not the closeness she felt for the others. It was a shame.

There was little blue showing in the sky but the clouds were high and they did not need to get above them to avoid the mountains. Kantees watched the landscape rolling by. Between the mountains and the high ridges were plenty of green valleys, some of them as large as the plateau they had left behind—with columns of smoke rising from small groups of huts, and even larger settlements.

She had been right, her people lived here in the mountains. They were not merely a legend. But how many of them were still under the sway of the children of the abomination? She could not be sure and, from time to time, she felt the insidious lethargy they emitted. But the *ziris'* speed was enough to drive them past almost before it took effect.

There were no more of the *Slissac* towers, at least not in this direction.

She intended her first stop to be the ley-circle of Watching Pass, because the sooner she could alert the Dunor that she was no longer at the plateau, the better for Gally and Ulina. Unfortunately, she wasn't entirely sure how to get there.

When they were over a particularly rugged area, she had Sheesha drop to normal speed and found a ledge where they could safely rest.

She slid from Sheesha's back on to the broken mountainside where plants tried to gain a hold in the cracks. They startled a thin raggedy creature that galloped off along the increasingly steep slopes. It seemed oblivious to the danger of falling and was as sure-footed as a *kichek* on flat ground. Some sort of *fenichak*.

Yenteel pulled out his far-seeing device and scanned the peaks about them.

"This is very central," he said.

"Central?"

"It's the middle of nowhere."

She gave a half-laugh, since that was all his contrived humour deserved. "If you could see the Watching Pass from here, I would be happier."

"We've been heading in the right direction, broadly."

"That's the problem, though, isn't it? Without detailed maps we can't know where it is, and we don't even really know where we are. Who needs maps when they can travel by Patterner's path, or a river?"

"Sailors use the stars to guide them."

"Not at all helpful, Yenteel."

"It's something you might want to consider for the future, though."

"I thought perhaps you might want to take up your old profession."

He gave her a sidelong glance. "Are you trying to lure me away from my master with the promise of cartography?"

"I would not stoop so low as attempting to manipulate you."

He raised an eyebrow then went back to scanning the horizon.

"Perhaps we should just go straight to Kurvin Port; if we spend too much time trying to find Watching Pass just to let the Dunor know where I am, we might as well not bother."

"I can't decide for you, Kantees," he said.

She sighed. Her plan had seemed very simple, carrying it out was another matter. She stared at the sky, they still had much of the day remaining and could make a lot of progress. Even this short stop had lost them several leagues of travel.

"Let's move on," she said.

They mounted once more and the *ziri* threw themselves off the ledge rather than expend energy taking off straight up. But Kantees wanted height, as much as they could get without running into the clouds.

They climbed slowly and the mountains dropped away below. The world turned into a map, just as Gally had said to her before. Streaks of colour went through the rocks and, in places, through entire ridges and slopes. In Garbalain, Kantees had heard men talk about veins of ore, perhaps that's what they meant. The valleys were in shadow, some greener than others, filled with trees. Streams ran together to form rivers and they ran into lakes that reflected the grey sky.

In some cases the rivers ran into deeper valleys and continued to grow. Some ran off to the north where, in the far distance, she could see the shimmering green of the great plains where they had spent a day. Other rivers went off to the south, where the only prospect was more mountains.

Abruptly Kantees turned Sheesha. If those rivers went anywhere it would be to the wide valley on which the Watching Pass stood—and even if they did not, they would eventually reach the coast somewhere close to Kurvin Port.

All she had to do was follow the rivers. She allowed Sheesha to descend once more, gliding silently on the air, with Looesa slightly behind and to the right as usual.

The valley of the river she chose wound between the mountains in a channel it seemed to have carved for itself. At one point it poured out into a valley filled with trees and grass, and a lake of enormous size. She hoped it was not a dead end. The valley curved to the east and as they rounded the slope, she saw the lake ended in fog.

A deep and thunderous roar echoed off the steep mountain

slopes on either side as they approached the cloud. She had Sheesha climb as they shot out beyond the edge of the water that cascaded away and down in a tremendous waterfall. The land dropped away precipitously all around them as if it had been cut with a knife. And in front of them lay a flat green plain, with a wide river meandering along its length as far as the eye could see.

The mountains began again on the far side, perhaps five leagues away.

"Is this it?" she called out to Yenteel.

"I expect so."

The last time they had been in this valley it had been night. The time before she had been tied up in the gondola of a *tekrak*, and she had not been paying a great deal of attention to the landscape.

"Can you see a ley-circle?" he asked. She knew he was referring to the ability she had discovered when she had been blinded by the abomination. She had not really tried to use it since her sight returned but she closed her eyes and tried to concentrate.

There might be something off to the right, along the valley, but she could not be certain.

"Perhaps," she shouted back but in the end it didn't matter. Kurvin Port lay to the west and that was the direction they needed to go.

She suggested the change of direction to Sheesha, as well as an increase in speed.

He obliged.

2

As they sped along the valley, Kantees had Sheesha descend as well. She was not sure which would be better: at high altitude they would be able to see things clearly, but would themselves be more likely to be seen; close to the ground they might be surprised by what they encountered, but so would the Dunor.

"Go across the river," called Yenteel.

She turned to see him pointing to the south.

"Keep your distance from the ley-circle."

She had just about decided that he had made a good suggestion when their future was decided for them.

They were approaching a line of low hills that came down from the mountains and lay across their path. Sheesha had gained altitude to go over them when one of the giant *tekrasa* came into view almost directly ahead on the far side of the hills.

Immediately, Kantees encouraged Sheesha into a climb.

"Don't you want them to see you?" said Yenteel.

Kantees frowned. Avoiding them had just been her first instinct. As they flew upwards she saw the *tekrak* was tethered and a group of armsmen were gathered at the base around a small fire.

The one facing in the direction of the *ziri* stood up and pointed.

"They've seen us," she called back.

"They might just think we're wild *ziri*," said Yenteel.

Fine.

At her thought, just as they were passing over the *tekrak*, Sheesha dived again and twisted until he was pointing back the way they had come, and flew directly over the armsmen. If they had been as surprised as Kantees, they were getting over it and she could see them reaching for their bows.

Kantees urged Sheesha faster. The *ziri*'s wings beat hard against the air and they shot forwards; they were heading in the wrong direction now but she just wanted to get beyond the reach of the bows.

As Sheesha went into a climb she looked back. They were not far enough, as the arrows were loosed. Kantees watched them arc upwards then Sheesha changed direction sharply. The arrows whistled by harmlessly but the next volley was already on its way.

Although it would draw on his personal energy Kantees asked Sheesha to go very fast. For a moment the arrows hung in the air, coming directly towards them. Then a wall of golden light grew between them and the armsmen were vanishing into the distance.

Kantees let them fly north like that for a few breaths and then slowed once more. It was easier to change direction at a slower speed. They came down on top of one of the hills. The *tekrak* was a blob in the distance. Kantees dismounted.

"Good idea of yours, Yenteel," she said, trying to suppress the anger she was feeling.

"You didn't have to do it."

"No, you're right, I didn't."

"They noticed us though."

"Yes, they did."

"Looks like the Dunor have decided the Watching Pass is no longer safe from you. I think you should take that as a compliment."

"So, should I continue past there or just go straight on to Hamalain?"

"I'm not sure whether you want my opinion, Kantees, what if it leads you astray?"

She closed her eyes and swore on the Mother's milk.

"Please tell me what you think, Yenteel."

"I think that it will be a day or so before that patrol gets to report back to their seniors. Even if they get the *tekrak* moving right away, it's going to take time."

"So if I want to stop the Dunor from attacking the valley I still have to go to Watching Pass."

"But now we know they are on the look-out for you."

"So this was not a bad thing that happened, it was a good thing."

"Well, it wasn't a bad thing," said Yenteel.

"We still don't know how far the pass is."

"No, but you should be able to sense the ley-circle as we approach it, shouldn't you?"

She shook her head. "I don't know."

Yenteel smiled. "Well, we'll find out."

Something golden flashed across Kantees' mind leaving a trail behind it. She jerked her head up and saw it in the sky. The two images overlaid one on the other.

"Or they'll send a *melinak* to their masters with a message explaining what's happened," she said.

"Or they could do that," agreed Yenteel. "That changes things a little."

"It means they will be ready for us," she said. "With bowmen no doubt."

"What do you want to do?"

Kantees sighed, the situation was unfortunately all too obvious. "I still have to convince them I'm no longer in the valley. We'll keep going."

"South of the river?"

"No," she said. "We'll continue as we are."

Yenteel nodded. "I think you're right."

She gave a humourless smile. "Let's hope they don't manage to kill us."

"I'm in favour of that."

Once more in the air, Kantees adjusted their height until she was sure they were out of bowshot range from the ground. She did consider going even higher, in case of *tekrasa*, but if she followed that logic, they might as well be flying in the clouds so as not to be seen at all.

However, the fact that she had been able to see the *melinak* trail with her pattern-sense as well as her eyes helped her confidence. It meant she had not lost the ability when her sight returned. She just needed to concentrate.

They continued to follow the northern border of the valley at normal flying speed keeping an eye open for other patrols, whether on foot or in the air. She did not think the Dunor would deploy the flying armsmen as they had at the big *Slissac* tower, simply because they only seemed to be able to fly down.

She kept calling it *the Dunor* as if that was a thing in itself. But she knew from what Levin had said it was cabal of Taymalin houses, aligned with powerful patterners. It was not a single entity, it could be in many places at once, and those who controlled their armsmen were probably not those on their inner council—or whatever they chose to call it—they would not do things directly themselves.

Which led to the question of where the Dunor might be hiding. She could not think of them as anything else but cowards hiding in the background.

Her thoughts were interrupted by a glow in the distance which she recognised at once as a ley-circle. Without further thought she asked Sheesha to go fast. The *ziri* accepted and within moments they were accelerating. Kantees reached out and touched the power of the circle. Sheesha drew on it and the air became a golden shroud.

This time Kantees tried something new. Up to now she had simply accepted the patterned speed for what it was. As if Sheesha could either use it or not. This time she urged him faster, even as the power of the ley-circle grew in her mind she channelled even more to Sheesha, and the golden light changed. It intensified and turned white.

Fewer than fifty man-heights from the ground, it became a blur below them. Kantees had to focus forward to see anything at all through the blazing light.

Her worst fears were realised when she saw a net of *tekrasa* around the ley-circle, just like the one which Kantees and her friends had broken on the island. But this time, it was just her and Yenteel.

But Kantees was not planning to fight, her plan remained the same. The Dunor needed to be told she was no longer in the valley. She asked Sheesha to reduce speed and, as they rushed towards the ley-circle—with the sun low and shining through the flying *tekrasa*, she brought them back to normal flying.

"Do we have to get close?" shouted Yenteel to make his voice carry over the blasting wind of their flight.

"They have to know it's me!"

"We could just send a messenger."

Kantees angled Sheesha so they were flying up the valley instead of toward the ley-circle. More importantly, they were out of range of any arrows shot from the upper tiers of *tekrasa*. There were barns and cold stores this side of the ley-circle.

Below them armsmen were running about, some attempting to shoot, others simply shouting, though their voices barely reached the *zirichasa*.

"What now?"

"Have you got any patterns for making fire?"

"No, I have a flint for that. Why?"

Sheesha curved in a wide arc and returned along the valley at an easy speed.

"I was thinking that if we had some oil we might be able to set things alight."

"You want a dragon for that," he called back. "One that breathes fire."

Kantees laughed. "Silly legends."

"Trouble ahead!"

She turned to see the protective pattern of *tekrasa* had broken up and were heading in their direction, with their flame tubes roaring —but they moved too slowly to be a threat. Most of them were to the left while some of them were climbing and were already well above the *ziri*.

Kantees was relaxed, it looked as if they were trying to bottle the *ziri* but, at her urging, Sheesha simply adjusted his direction and slid to the right on angled wings.

The hills were higher in this direction and they had to climb.

The *tekrasa* were moving in, they might manoeuvre slowly but in a straight line and given time they could manage a good speed. But there was no danger, they could always go back up the valley and the *ziri* were just about at the top of the hill—

A horn blared a single note from somewhere ahead of them. Two dozen armsmen stood up at the crest of the hill, bows fully drawn.

Fear overwhelmed Kantees. Time slowed. She stared at the death in every arrow.

Slower to rise than the others, one man stood at the end of the line. He had no bow. There was something about him she recognised. There was no time to say where she knew him from. She saw him breathe in deeply.

Her silent command to Sheesha flew faster than arrows but the *ziri* needed time to gather the power.

Bowstrings quivered. Golden light formed about Sheesha and Looesa.

The ground dropped away.

Sheesha screamed and the gold flickered, then became firm again.

Moments later they were far above the ground and a long way from their foes. Kantees could feel something was desperately wrong but Sheesha kept forcing himself onward, burning the air with golden light.

"Stop, beloved," Kantees whispered. "We are safe."

It lasted a few moments more, then the golden light faded away.

Sheesha fell from the sky.

Kantees hung on desperately as he tumbled through the air and the world spun out of control. Every now and then she caught sight of Looesa and the panicking face of Yenteel as they followed the falling *ziri*.

"Sheesha," she whispered.

The ground was getting closer while the river flashed in and out of her vision. And the sky mocked her.

"Sheesha, please."

She was crying with her arms wrapped round his neck and legs tightly braced against his wings.

Sheesha!

At the last moment his wings stiffened and caught the air. They stabilised for a moment then plummeted into the river.

3

The cold was a shock. The force of the impact tried to wrench her from him, but she clung to his neck.

She was under the surface, surrounded by the rushing and thundering water.

Sheesha rolled over, dragging her deeper. Above she could see the shifting image of the sky and, against it, the silhouette of Looesa. Then a cloud of something dark and red blurred her vision.

Sheesha!

He stirred again.

Kantees, with her lungs burning in her breast, worked her way along his neck to his head, keeping a firm grip. Then she pumped her legs, attempting to force him up and out.

A submerged boulder hit her shoulder, driving the breath from her in a cloud of bubbles. She braced against it with her feet and pushed upwards still holding tight to Sheesha's neck.

She broke the surface and pulled in a painful breath. Sheesha's nostrils opened and he too took a breath. But nothing stayed still and the current was dragging his body past the boulder and downstream. She wouldn't be able to hold him here and she couldn't see the riverbank or anything protruding above the surface.

A shadow went over then a rope hit the water in front of her.

She snatched at it without thinking and looked up. Looesa was hovering, beating his wings hard and fast, he wouldn't be able to maintain that for long.

"Sorry, Sheesha," said Kantees as she wound the rope round his neck just as the water carried him away. She hung on and was dragged out into the open water again.

The rope tightened as Looesa awkwardly pulled away. Each beat of his wings tightened the rope and threatened to pull it from Kantees' hands. She was barely managing to keep her head above water, though the rope was pulling Sheesha's head up. Kantees was terrified it might also be strangling him.

Then Sheesha stopped moving with the current. Looesa pulled once more but the only effect was for him to get dragged downward. He landed, sending up a fountain of water. He didn't disappear but stood in the river covered almost to his body. Kantees managed to get her feet down on to shifting sands, but for her it was up to her neck.

Yenteel jumped down, holding the rope, and Kantees felt it loosen around Sheesha's neck. She pushed through the water to his head and lifted it, driving her feet into the sand. He was still breathing. But now she could see the water staining red with his blood.

Yenteel arrived. "There's a sandbank in this direction. We just need to get him on to it."

"You take his head, I'll pull his body."

Together they wrestled the water-logged *ziri*. Every heave bringing Sheesha barely another fingers-breadth up the shallow beach. They were getting nowhere, even with Looesa trying to help by shoving from the rear.

They gave up. Kantees located a log that had drifted on to the bank and managed to prop it under his head to make sure he could breathe. Yenteel found the arrow in Sheesha's chest, and then a second in his abdomen.

Yenteel did not need any prompting from Kantees. Once they were sure that Sheesha was safe he set about preparing the healing patterns.

"We can't take the arrows out yet," he said when he saw

Kantees' face as she stared at the shafts. "He's not strong enough, they will be barbed and will cause more damage."

"You're going to heal him and then hurt him again?"

Yenteel looked at a loss. "I don't know, Kantees, I am not a healer. I can only do what I think is the right thing." He hesitated. "It might not be."

She nodded in resignation. She understood and this was all her fault. She had been over-confident. She thought that on the back of a *ziri*—on the back of Sheesha—she was impregnable. When in truth she was just an ignorant slave who had managed to delude herself into believing she knew what she was doing.

The sun had sunk below the mountains but the sky was still bright. They were sitting ducks if the Dunor armsmen turned up in their *tekrasa*.

Kantees sat in the water and held Sheesha's head as best she could, as Yenteel found a way to make the patterns he needed on wet feathers.

The chant was becoming all too familiar, she had first heard it when it had been Yenteel himself who had been hurt, on their escape from Jakalain. There had been too many injuries, too much pain in the service of her goals. She was tired of other people getting hurt for her.

And now Sheesha. She brushed a tear from her cheek, not that it made any difference. She was wet through and there was no prospect of that changing in the near future. Even if they managed to save Sheesha—*when* they saved Sheesha—they would still be stuck on a sandbar in the middle of the river with no shelter and little enough food.

Looesa could hunt and they could individually ride out to fetch firewood and other things they needed, but that would mean attracting more attention to themselves.

"Kantees?"

She realised Yenteel had stopped working the pattern and for a desperate moment thought Sheesha must have died. But his breath still rasped in the back of this throat.

"What's wrong?"

"These are very poor conditions."

"You can't give up!"

"I wasn't going to give up, Kantees, but I don't know how much good I can do. These are bad wounds and he's already lost a lot of blood."

"I know—" *And my heart is breaking.*

"I want to try something. This place has no power and Sheesha can't help, have you got the *chilafrah*?"

"Tenical drained it when he conjured the path." *And I haven't told you about the opposite of a feeding.*

"There may be something left, anything would be an improvement on what I have now, but—" he stared at her "—I think I was wrong about the arrows, we need to get them out at the same time as the healing. And I can't do both."

Kantees nodded as if the task was a fitting punishment for her stupidity. "You want me to do it."

"I wouldn't ask if it wasn't important."

"No, you're right, I got us into this situation."

Yenteel looked as if he wanted to say something but then swallowed it. "The *chilafrah*?"

She crawled out from under Sheesha's head and made sure he could breathe properly before fumbling in her backpack and pulling out the carved stone wrapped in a rag.

"I don't know how we'd get anything from it even if it does have power."

"We'll just put it here next to where I'm making the pattern," said Yenteel. "If it can provide more power that will be good. If it doesn't, we've lost nothing."

Kantees stared at the arrow sticking unnaturally from Sheesha's chest. She forced her tears down and focused on the fact that this was her fault. Yenteel had laid cloths marked with the patterns across the feathers—all still bright blue and gold.

"Don't you need to be closer to the skin?" she said.

"It would be better."

Kantees nodded. "I'll do it."

She took hold of a feather near the arrow; she held it close to its base and tugged. It resisted, so she pulled harder until it came free. Again and again she pulled away the bigger outer feathers and then the smaller softer ones until she had cleared a patch around the arrow where dried blood stained Sheesha's skin.

"Is that enough?"

"I'll make it enough."

Yenteel gathered up the cloths he had been using and stuffed them back in his bag. He redrew the patterns on to Sheesha's skin using charcoal. Then he placed the *chilafrah* beside the marks he'd made.

"If you can see the pattern working," he said, "you'll know when and how to remove the arrow."

"All right." She adjusted her position and grasped the arrow shaft with both hands.

Yenteel placed his hand on her arm. She did not trust herself to speak and just gave a nod of her head.

Yenteel started the chant again. Kantees closed her eyes, trying to see the patterns.

Chaos is easy, order is hard...

She relaxed and let the patterns come to her. It was as if they were far in the distance but as Yenteel chanted the light grew. Soon she could perceive the lines that made up Yenteel's markings and, in some fashion, she could understand them. They were crude but all she could do was watch, she could not interfere or change what he was doing.

The patterns imposed themselves on the intricate life pattern of Sheesha. The lines of it were infinitely thin and complex, patterns within patterns. In a flash of understanding, she recognised how the crude patterning of Yenteel's charcoal marks, though on a gross level, matched with the pattern of the living flesh, and she saw how the one was intended to reinforce the other and to manipulate it.

The glow became stronger and the echoes of Yenteel's pattern drove deeper until it encountered the broken flesh and the arrow that pierced it.

Now, she thought, and pulled.

Where the arrowhead lay, the pattern structure collapsed and waves of distortion like a curtain fluttering in sunlight, or the ripples on a lake, moved out from the centre.

You're hurting him, she thought but it had to be done.

As the arrow ripped from Sheesha's flesh he shuddered, and she wept. But she did not stop until the arrowhead came free. She felt Yenteel's chanting become more forceful as if that would help—he did not understand that was not how it worked.

She dropped the arrow in the water and placed her hands over the wound in an attempt to staunch the blood that oozed from it. Her own hands became part of the healing pattern and she focused once more on the wound deep inside. Yenteel's pattern pulsed with energy, perhaps the *chilafrah* was not completely dead. Sheesha's flesh followed the pattern that was being enforced on it and she could see the underlying structure conforming and binding.

Yenteel stopped but the power of the *chilafrah* continued to pulse through the lines he had drawn. Kantees withdrew her hands and opened her eyes. The wound was fresh and pink but it was sealed. She lifted the *chilafrah* away and the power subsided.

"Almost like what happened back in the Talamyrth," said Yenteel. "It did not need me to maintain the pattern. It just kept going."

"We know where that road goes," said Kantees. "It never ends well."

"But for a healing pattern?"

"No," said Kantees. "Fire is a good servant but a bad master. That is what the Taymalin always forget."

"I doubt it's only a failing of the Taymalin," said Yenteel.

"Sheesha has another wound," said Kantees. This was not the time for philosophical arguments.

They wasted no more time and stripped the feathers from around the second arrow. Yenteel carefully inscribed the patterns, they placed the *chilafrah* and began again.

This arrow was not as deep but Kantees still cried as the pain of its extraction flowed in waves through her friend. It was over quicker. This time she gratefully tossed the arrow into the river.

After checking Sheesha once more and making sure he could breathe safely, she stood up and surveyed the area for the first time.

It was just as Yenteel had said. They were on a sandbar in the middle of the river. There were a few bushes that had taken the chance of rooting but they would be gone on the next flood. Kantees was not sure the sandbar itself would survive long either. But that was unlikely to affect them, long before that a patrol from the Watching Gate would find them and it would all be over.

They may have fixed Sheesha's injuries but she had no idea how long it would take for him to wake up, or how they would feed him, or how long he would need to recover. *Zirichasa* that were badly injured in races were often gone until the next season, sometimes they never returned. She knew that some families would simply kill their *ziri* if it was too much trouble to look after them—especially if they were female. At least a good male could still breed even if it could no longer race.

"What are we going to do?" she said.

4

They spent what remained of the day getting Sheesha further up on to the sandbar and out of the water. She hoped they were not hurting him but it was impossible to be sure. Riding Looesa, Yenteel had gone across to the south and found some logs which, he insisted, would work like wheels.

"Don't go near any woods," she had said, "and stay close to Looesa; if there's anything strange, get out of there. And stay close to the ground. Trust Looesa."

He had accepted all her instructions amicably and assured her he had no intention of getting into trouble, or killed.

It took three trips to get the logs. Kantees hacked at them with her knife trying to make them as smooth as possible—wishing she had Ulina's knife—while Yenteel was fetching the rest. Then they manhandled Sheesha on to the first one and harnessed Looesa to Sheesha with the rope. Looesa wasn't happy about it but submitted after a great deal of cajoling from Kantees. She suspected that if it had been Gally making the request Looesa would have allowed it immediately.

So with Looesa and Yenteel pulling, and Kantees placing the logs, they finally managed to get Sheesha onto the sand. Water drained from his feathers but he remained wet. Kantees did not dare make a fire, they were exposed enough as it was. There was little point making a sign that any of the Dunor armsmen would be able to see.

"With a bit of luck they won't have realised Sheesha was hurt," Kantees said, more to settle her own fears than allay any that Yenteel might have.

"I'm sure they would have found us already if they thought that," said Yenteel. She knew he was right but it did not make her feel any safer. Her foolishness had put them in the most dangerous position they had ever been in. They were as vulnerable as a *sikechak* drunk on fermented berries.

"There are a couple of options," said Yenteel. "We might be able to make a raft and just float Sheesha downstream."

Kantees pulled a face.

"Or I find a farm and persuade the owner to help us."

"Or they just kill you and Looesa. Or play along while they alert the Dunor."

"Well, if you're going to reject all my suggestions…"

He fell silent. Kantees leaned back against Sheesha's back, having assured herself she wasn't putting any pressure on his wounds. She stared up at the clear sky and watched the stars coming out. There was a glow in the east where Lostimal was due to rise, she would make the night almost like day with her white light.

So much for her plan of heading back to Jakalain and launching an attack against the Dunor. If only they knew where the Dunor were. Not just that island, although with Tenical, they would be able to get there again. The first time, they had got past the ley-circle guards and to the island by pretending she was a prisoner and her captors were working for the Dunor. If you pretended you knew what you were doing and that you had the right authority, most people would accept it as the truth.

A piece of a plan came to her.

But she must not be overconfident, look what that had done to Sheesha. But there was a difference between overconfidence without a plan, and desperation with one. After all, if she needed to get to Jakalain as fast as possible and Sheesha could not carry her, then perhaps she would have to carry Sheesha instead.

. . .

Next morning she outlined her plan.

"This is a crazy idea," said Yenteel as he looked out across the wide valley with the far-seer.

"I know," she said. "That's why it has a chance of working. Nobody would do this."

"I can see one," he said finally. "It's about two leagues away in the direction of Watching Pass."

Kantees clicked the flint over the kindling at the base of the fire they had built. She looked up when it caught and small flames flickered.

"Go on," she said, "get out of here." He climbed up on Looesa's back. "And stay low—at first."

"I understand the plan."

Kantees didn't reply, she was busy blowing the embers and bringing in slightly larger twigs. She waved her hand at him, then felt the blast of Looesa's down beat as he took off.

The fire caught thoroughly and Kantees put a couple of damp branches across the flames. They steamed and smoked in a satisfying way. She hoped no one in the *tekrak* patrol would ask a very important question.

Sheesha was breathing more strongly now although, as far as she could tell, he had not woken up. She hoped he would stay sleeping through what was about to happen because it might be inconvenient if he woke at the wrong moment.

Kantees carefully poked her head around Sheesha's wing to see if she could see the *tekrak*. It was already much closer, it must have seen the fire immediately and set off this way. Moving slowly and staying hidden she laid herself out beside the fire, next to Sheesha.

She imagined what the armsmen would think—what she hoped they would think: a dead *ziri* lying on a sandbar, a body next to it, someone who had managed to light a fire but nothing else.

Clearly no threat. They might scan the area for others but they would see nothing. "Left for dead" is what they would think, after all, that's what they would do.

She heard the roaring of the *tekrak*'s fire-tube and then it went silent. There were voices above her but she could not make out the words. They did not sound as if they felt threatened.

This would not be a *tekrak* carrying a full complement of armsmen. This was just a patrol. There would be the patterner, and three, perhaps five, armsmen. Then they would drop a rope, or perhaps a ladder, and two of them would climb down. That was her problem, she had no direct way of dealing with two armsmen. But hopefully she would not have to.

"See anyone else?"

"I can see what you can see."

"No one else?"

"Obviously."

Kantees groaned, it was a sound she had become used to making when she had been afflicted by headaches. She knew how to make it convincing.

"Well?"

"After you."

"Check the damn *ziri*."

"You know what they say, never poke a sleeping *zirichak*."

"Very funny. The thing's probably dead, look at it."

"In that case you can poke it."

Kantees almost swore. But at that moment a *ziri* shriek filled the air and there was a crash from above them. Kantees jumped up from behind Sheesha. The two armsmen had already turned away and were looking up.

The massive bulk of the *tekrak* filled the sky above them. But it was not hanging there motionlessly—it was shaking and shuddering as if something big was crashing around inside the gondola.

The front of the gondola tilted down and Kantees saw the terrified face of a patterner, with the shape of Looesa directly behind him—for a moment she was worried the *ziri* would kill the only person that could control the flying plant. But then Looesa turned away. He tore a hole in the side of the gondola as Yenteel appeared at the patterner's side.

The men on the ground were armed but thankfully not with bows. But they drew their swords as Looesa exploded from the side of the structure and took flight.

Kantees picked up the rope and found the end as she climbed over Sheesha's neck. Above them Looesa turned in the air, seeming as if she balanced on the tip of one wing for the briefest moment, before tipping over and plummeting earthward. The men were transfixed at his approach, faster and faster.

Kantees threw the loop of rope over the head of the armsmen on her left. Put a foot in the small of his back and yanked hard. He cried out as he fell, his partner turned to look just as Looesa flashed out of the sky and grabbed him by his shoulders.

He screamed only once.

Kantees pulled the rope tight around the armsman's neck but it was too thick to strangle him. He was much bigger than her, and his struggling threatened to throw her off. She let go with one hand and jabbed the heel of her foot into his neck repeatedly to keep him distracted while she pulled out the dagger.

The weapon was blunted from chopping wood but she slammed it into his neck. He cried out, though it barely even drew blood. She hesitated at the thought of cutting his throat with a blunt knife. Then, behind her, Sheesha made a noise that sounded like pain, and she remembered what they had done to him. The knife went in again and again. He was trying to pull away but then she hit something important and blood spurted.

She kept hacking until she was certain he would never move again.

"Kantees! Grab the rope!"

She lay on her back panting and exhausted. She had never killed anyone in so personal a way and it had drained all her energy. The body was lying on her leg.

"Kantees! Are you all right?"

She opened her eyes and blinked against the brightness of the clouds. The *tekrak* was drifting out of her vision. Sitting up she saw the anchor rope dragging across the sandbar. To be honest she had not really thought past the fight, though she knew that managing the *tekrak* with so few people was going to be a problem—they should not have been in this position in the first place. And wouldn't have been if she had not been so stupid.

"Kantees!"

She waved to shut Yenteel up and pulled her leg out from under the dead armsman. She was not steady on her feet but made it to the rope and grabbed it. She looked round for Looesa but he hadn't returned. But there was Sheesha.

Kantees turned and pulled the rope tight against her shoulder. She leaned forwards until she was angled precariously and stepped towards the unconscious *ziri*. It took a lot of effort but once the *tekrak* had begun to move, it kept going.

"I'm sorry, Sheesha," she said as she looped the rope around his chest and tied it off. Unfortunately, he was the heaviest object on the sandbar. She turned and waved at the gondola. Now she could see that Yenteel had a knife to the throat of the patterner, it would not aid his concentration but would make sure he did as he was told.

They needed to get Sheesha into the gondola and get flying before the patrol was missed. For the time being she simply let Yenteel get the patterner to force the *tekrak* to the ground.

Meanwhile Kantees stripped the armsman of anything useful— which amounted to everything except the clothes close to his skin— then she rolled him into the water and watched him float away. There was still no sign of Looesa, or the other armsman. Kantees suspected Looesa might be eating him. Allowing *ziri* to eat people was not recommended, it was suggested that if they got a taste for human flesh, they would turn on their owners.

There was nothing she could do about it now so there was no point worrying.

The gondola crunched to the ground. Kantees tightened the rope on Sheesha then hurried over and climbed on board.

"This is Pellyn of Otu," said Yenteel, the omission of the family honorific—Otulain—indicated that Pellyn was no longer bound to the family. "Pellyn has been cooperating so far, but I think that's because I have a knife at his throat."

"I noticed you were doing that," said Kantees. "Does Pellyn understand what's happening?"

"He knows we've killed the armsmen and we have a vicious *ziri* on our side."

Kantees did not mention that she had no idea where Looesa had gone. "Looesa is eating one of them," she said instead. She moved to lean against the side of the gondola near the front. "Pellyn, I am Kantees of the Ziri—" he flinched "—and I think you've heard of me. You also know, I expect, that I and my friends destroyed several *tekrak* on the island of the Dunor, and stole a prisoner from under their very noses."

He said nothing and stared straight ahead.

"Have you heard that story?" she said and Yenteel poked him in the back with the point of his knife.

"I've heard it," said Pellyn, he was big and had a voice to match. They would need to be careful, this man was not like Tenical who had been grateful to be rescued. But they had no choice, if they did not use the *tekrak* to get out of here they would be caught soon enough.

"Pellyn, this is a dangerous situation for all of us. My friend and I because the Dunor want to capture or kill us. And for you, because we have nothing to lose and if you become a problem, we will simply kill you and continue without the *tekrak*."

Yenteel poked him again.

"I understand what you're saying."

"Good, because I really don't like killing people, but if I have no choice I will not hesitate. Do you understand?"

"Yes."

And that was the best they could do for now. While Kantees kept a knife at Pellyn's back, Yenteel dragged the gondola across the sand as close to Sheesha as possible. Then went round, driving mooring spikes into the ground and tying the vehicle down. Once that was achieved, they found some thin rope to hobble Pellyn, then the three of them together manhandled Sheesha into the gondola. That he was lighter than a ground animal of his size was no benefit since he was huge, but he was drier now so they weren't moving water as well.

Pellyn seemed fascinated by Sheesha. He was nervous at first but he grew in confidence. Kantees kept a close eye on him to make sure he did nothing wrong, instead he seemed to be feeling Sheesha's bones, skin and feathers. As soon as they had succeeded in manoeuvring his bulk through the hole Looesa had made, Kantees insisted Sheesha was put right to the back. They broke down wooden benches to make space and kept them for firewood.

Kantees helped Yenteel tie Pellyn to a strut and away from his station for controlling the *tekrak* though she was fairly sure he couldn't do anything without using his hands or voice. So she gagged him as well.

"Sorry," she said without any conviction, "but we can't take any chances." Pellyn gave no sign and she was sure he was simply waiting for an opportunity to fight back.

Where is Looesa? She cursed herself for making a habit of losing *ziri*. And scanned the skies looking for him.

"Why don't you just call him?" said Yenteel quietly in her ear.

"What do you mean?"

Yenteel glanced at Pellyn and then spoke even more quietly in her ear.

"Your connection with the *ziri* is obvious, Kantees, why don't you just call Looesa and tell him to come back?"

"I don't know how to do that, or even if it would work."

"Obviously not, but you won't know until you try. I'll stay here with our guest."

Kantees nodded and went out on to the sand once more. She was sick of it and the way it shifted beneath her feet. The fire she had made was still smouldering so she kicked it apart and sent it splashing and hissing into the water. Then she walked out to the far end of the spit and looked out across the flat plain of the valley. To the south and the north the mountains stood like the walls of a mighty fortress.

She had no idea where to start. So she imagined the *zirichak*, imagined the pattern of his feathers, his mouth and teeth. His eyes.

"Come, Looesa," she said into the wind. She pictured the sandbar and the image of Looesa arriving so that they could head away.

The old words, she thought, did they have power? The creatures had been named by the *Slissac*, the Taymalin had brought those names with them and the Kadralin had adopted them too.

Surely we used our own names? Or do we use those names because they are closer to the patterns that make the creature itself? The *Slissac* for all their pride and hubris—which, if the Taymalin stories were to be believed, had finally brought them down—had understood patterns far better than either the Taymalin or Kadralin, because they had lived in the world so much longer than the rest.

A shadow moved in the distance. It was travelling low and fast. It might not be Looesa so she did not want to take any risks and hurried back to the gondola. The roots holding on to the gondola were beginning to move, she had seen that before, it meant the *tekrak* might let go. They needed to put Pellyn back in his seat and let him work his patterns to keep the huge plant under control.

She looked back, it was a *zirichak*, and it was Looesa. She sighed in relief but did not relish the prospect of an *I told you so* from Yenteel. It seemed that she could call a *ziri* from a distance. It was a good thing to know, and she wished she had known it before.

But perhaps she couldn't do it before.

5

There had been a discussion, quiet but heated, between Kantees and Yenteel about how to organise the trip, which had been followed by the question of what route they should take, though that was easier to resolve.

Kantees had wanted to stay close to Sheesha in case he woke up and wondered where he was. Yenteel had pointed out that it would be better if someone was riding Looesa and that since she was the best rider it should be her. In the end she had given in because she knew he was right. And with Yenteel being male, Pellyn might think twice about attacking him, as opposed to Kantees.

The choice of route was certainly not what Kantees wanted but she could not deny it was the best option. They could not stay in the valley because of the chance of being discovered; and there was no point in travelling further west to Kurvin Port since the news that she was no longer in the mountains would have been delivered just as she wanted. Their ultimate destination was Jakalain, so that was where they would go.

That meant flying south and east, over the mountains and into the northern parts of the Talamyrth.

"We don't have to fly into it," said Yenteel. "We can just stay on the mountain slopes to the north and follow the line to Jakalain."

She couldn't disagree since it was the fastest route. That did not mean that she had to like it. "That loathsome place nearly killed us twice over. In one night."

"And now we know not to go near that ley-circle."

"Woods and forests are dangerous."

Yenteel looked as if he was suppressing a desire to argue, and just said, "We'll stay clear but right now we need to get as far away from here as possible."

On that they both agreed which was how she came to be flying on Looesa's back, high above the plain below, with the *tekrak* a dark lump below. This too was their plan. The *tekrak* was slow, compared to the *ziri*, and would stay close to the ground so that it was less obvious. At high altitude she would be able to keep an eye out for trouble.

The day was moving towards night and the ground was rising out of the plains into the low slopes of the mountains, behind them was a village, barely more than a dozen houses but on a clearly marked road. Kantees had spotted it and gone down to get them to change their course. Now they were following a large tributary into a valley.

After one more look behind to make sure the *tekrak* wasn't being followed, she urged Looesa into a fast dive. The *ziri* appreciated the speed after spending the day idling along.

Kantees shot down between the mountain slopes looking for somewhere they could make camp for the night. The giant plant needed a place to put down its roots, they needed a good supply of water but the place should also be defensible. And no more than five trees in a group—any more than that constituted a threat as far as Kantees was concerned.

The tributary wound along the valley floor in a smaller imitation of the great river in the valley behind them. There were plenty of woods which Kantees frowned at but further in, as the land rose more sharply, she came upon an open grassland where *kelukisa* ran panicked at the sight of the *zirichak*. The place she found was not perfect, the ground was not flat, but it fitted her other criteria and the presence of *kelukisa* meant there was food for humans and *ziri* alike. And a single tree to which they could tie Pellyn, once the *tekrak* was firmly rooted for the night there would be nothing he could do.

Having found what she was looking for, Kantees flew back downstream and encountered the others just as they were entering the valley. A few shouted words told them the news and she flew back to await them. After dismounting she sent Looesa off to hunt and bring something back. On previous occasions the *ziri* had returned with food for those who remained behind. She was not sure if the humans counted but Looesa would want to help Sheesha.

Kantees gathered wood and stones to prepare a fire. She was very pleased when she succeeded in getting it well lit by the time the *tekrak* emerged from the bend in the river. Unlike the sandbar this place had anchors for the ropes and they had the gondola landed quickly. The second stage, getting the *tekrak* to release its grip and then land and root was more difficult with just the three of them, but they succeeded and soon had the beast staked to the ground so that it couldn't lift off again.

Pellyn cooperated though he remained sullen and uncommunicative. Kantees was not surprised and wondered whether he thought he'd be able to escape with the *tekrak* because by tomorrow it would take a ten-day to get back on foot—assuming he could make it across the mountains. He looked more competent than Tenical ever had but going through this terrain on foot would be very difficult.

Looesa returned with food and did not object when Yenteel hacked off some pieces and placed them next to the fire pierced with sticks. She assumed Looesa must already have eaten because he let her take the remainder into the gondola to where Sheesha lay. The hind leg of what had probably been a *kelukisa* was still bleeding and she managed to get most of it into Sheesha's mouth. Sheesha was still unconscious but something about the meat made him gulp and swallow. He had been without food or water for longer than a day.

Kantees searched the gondola until she found a bucket. In the river she rinsed it out and carried it back half-full. The meat was still in Sheesha's mouth, but she was sure it was more closed than it had been, as if he had tried biting down. The good news was that it provided a safeguard against him biting her hand off as she poured cup after cup of water into his mouth, even going as far as to put her hand right inside to make sure the liquid hit his throat.

His body shifted and one wing lifted and shook as he gulped on the water. She picked up the bucket and poured all the remaining water into his mouth. The sound of his swallowing gave her hope. She fetched another bucketful and he managed to drink most of it until he finally crunched through the bone and his mouth shut.

He took a deep breath and sighed. Kantees put her arm around his neck and hugged him. Though he did not wake up even once during the entire process. Somehow she could feel that he was asleep rather than unconscious. Looesa climbed into the gondola and curled up next to Sheesha. Kantees smiled.

She finally left the gondola and looked up.

The sky was clear and filled with twinkling stars. There was no sign of either moon although they were surrounded by mountains so they might not have been visible anyway. The air was cold but she did not mind, Sheesha was on the mend.

One thought led to another and she wondered how Gally and Ulina were getting on. At least they would be safe now, the Dunor were not interested in them.

She closed her eyes and breathed in the mountain air. It was scented with wood, flowers, the smoke from the fire, and roasting meat. She opened her eyes once more and looked for Yenteel, he was sitting by the fire but what drew her eye was Pellyn.

He was beyond the fire and tied to the tree as she and Yenteel had decided. But he was watching her, the light of the fire reflected in his eyes. He was dangerous, she knew that. He was faithful to the Dunor and would be entirely happy to bring her back to them. Once Sheesha was able to fly again they would simply leave him behind, she held no particular malice toward him, but nor did she feel any obligation to help him. Let him try to fly more than a day alone with the *tekrak*. He would have to force it to fly through the night if he wanted to get back to his home in a reasonable time because once they landed he would lose it to the wild and have to walk.

Or he would carry them all the way to Jakalain and let the lord decide how to treat him.

Let the Taymalin deal with their own.

Keeping her back to the mountain, and Pellyn where she could see him, Kantees sat by the fire, its warmth made her realise how cold the night was getting.

"How's Sheesha?"

"Better, I think."

"Good."

Yenteel handed her one of the speared pieces of meat.

"Do we know what it is?"

"Does it matter?"

She shrugged and ripped off a sliver, trying not to burn her fingers. It was juicy and flooded her mouth with flavour. The food in the town had not been this good. It occurred to her that she had no idea what its name was. Perhaps even the people who lived there had forgotten.

"*Kelukisa?*"

Yenteel was in the middle of a mouthful and grunted his assent while nodding.

"Have we got enough for Pellyn?"

"Plenty," said Yenteel wiping his mouth on his sleeve.

"We need to lose him as soon as we can."

"I know but have you got any idea how soon Sheesha will be able to fly? Let alone carry you? He's going to be very weak after this."

"Can't we use the healing patterns again?"

"We can but there's a limit to how much they can do. The power from—" he glanced at Pellyn "—your *present* pushed the pattern as far as it can go, I think."

Kantees glanced at her backpack lying on the ground near the fire.

Yenteel sighed then shook his head. "I don't see there's anything we can do other than what we've planned. We keep him tied up when he's not needed and make him fly us to where we need to go. Just make sure you keep that *object* close and don't let him see it."

Kantees glanced across at the huge bulk of the *tekrak* rooted into the soil down the slope from them. Like everybody else, Kantees had only ever been aware of the migrating hordes of *tekrasa* that crossed the skies in spring and autumn. But those were tiny compared to this, even the largest was no longer than man-height.

"Yes, all right," she said. "I wonder what would happen if someone used my present to control a *tekrak*?"

Yenteel turned his head towards the dark bulk.

"I was in the south once where they were constructing a new palace. They had an arrangement for lifting stone blocks up the side of the wall they had built. But something went wrong, perhaps one of the ropes was worn through, anyway the stone fell a short distance before a second set of ropes and pulleys caught it."

"And they stopped it from falling any further?"

"No, the power of the falling stone ripped them and their supporting mechanisms apart and splintered the entire gantry to little more than firewood. The whole thing was destroyed. Killed five men, one cut clean in half by a whipping rope."

"Horrible."

"It was."

"Your point?"

"I suspect that if you put too much power into one of those flimsy gasbags you would probably rip it to shreds."

"You could just have said that."

"Stories stick better than mere facts. They give you somewhere to hang your knowledge."

"But a knowledgeable mage might be able to strengthen the patterns of the creature so that it was not pulled apart."

"Perhaps. It would be a very precise area of study."

"Not unlike healing though."

"Perhaps not."

They fell silent and Kantees stared into the flames and watched them flicker and play in the dark of the night. She was aware that Yenteel got up after a while and went to where Pellyn was tied up.

He returned a short time later but by that time she was curled up in front of the fire.

"Don't you want to sleep with Sheesha?"

His words seemed to come from a distant place.

She tried to say *not yet* but the words came out in a mumble. Yenteel did not push the point.

6

It was full light when she woke. There was cold meat to eat and some biscuits that remained of their meagre food rations from the town.

Pellyn did not look as if he had slept well, but considering he had been tied up, that was no surprise. Kantees found that she felt very much better, though a lot of that was due to Sheesha showing some signs of recovery.

When she went to check on him, she found him curled up as if he were simply sleeping with Looesa beside him—that he had moved during the night made her very happy, as did the fact that she could not find the middle piece of the leg of *kelukisa* anywhere. He must have finished biting through it and swallowed it. She smiled down at him and did not disturb him.

Once they had finished clearing the camp, they set about getting the *tekrak* back on top of the gondola. At least this time they could use Looesa to some extent. He had done this before and did not object to the looped harness being put around him to stop the *tekrak* from floating off into the sky.

"Do you ever name them?" she said suddenly to Pellyn. He seemed as surprised at being asked the question as she was at asking it.

"It's not like your *zirichasa*..." He hesitated as if he was looking for a word to use for her and rejecting each one as he thought of it. She could imagine his choices, none of them complimentary and several that might result in violence against him. "It's just a plant, it does not think, it only knows light which is life, dark which is death, and the desire to move."

"They know pain," said Kantees.

He looked sceptical and she chose not to enlighten him about seeing a *tekrak* react when it was hit by flaming arrows.

Yenteel however did not see any reason to stop. "Armsmen name their weapons. Sailors their ships. They are completely inanimate. I knew a hermit who imbued life and names to every rock in his cave. They even had personalities."

"That is not our way."

"Everything has a unique pattern, why would you not give it a name?"

Pellyn sighed as he pulled on his rope and they slowly dragged the *tekrak* up the slope. "There are some that name these creatures. They are laughed at by the rest of us."

"I can believe it," said Yenteel. "I have more sympathy for those willing to recognise life and individuality."

"It's a plant," said Pellyn. "It does not think. It has no name."

Yenteel ceased baiting the patterner for which Kantees was grateful. It was bad enough they had him prisoner, it seemed cruel to taunt him as well. She decided that if ever she had a giant *tekrak* for her own, she would give it a name. It would do no harm, even if the thing itself did not appreciate it. But perhaps it would anyway, she knew there was more to the patterns of life than the simple structures that made the physical forms.

Despite his tiredness—and the taunts of Yenteel—Pellyn was a competent patterner, perhaps better than Tenical, not that she was any judge. He soon had the *tekrak* winding its roots firmly around the structure of the gondola and they were ready to lift.

This time Kantees was more reluctant to leave Sheesha but it was still the best choice to have her riding Looesa. She waited until Yenteel had Pellyn tied in his chair at the front of the gondola then released the ropes and threw them up to Yenteel who stowed them.

Their previous journeys with these beasts had given them plenty of experience and they knew what to do. She wondered whether that surprised Pellyn, or whether he simply didn't care.

She took off with Looesa in a blast of beating wings. Looesa might be smaller than Sheesha but he was still powerful and fast. It was his smaller size that worked for him in the races: he could turn faster than the bigger *ziri*. He seldom won, but he had always placed well, the crowds loved him, and that had made him a valuable mount.

Lord Jakalain had more or less forgiven her for stealing the *ziri* since she had now rescued both his sons. The clothes she wore were a gift from him and his lady, though they were suffering from the treatment they got being part of her life. She needed a new set, perhaps they would be supplied when she returned to Jakalain.

She had Looesa climb above the mountaintops and headed back towards the river until she could see across the plain. There did not seem to be any sign of pursuit, no troops on the ground and no *tekrak* in the air.

That either meant they had not yet found out their patrol was missing, or that they had chosen not to pursue. The latter option did not please her, but neither would visible pursuit. There was no point worrying over things you could not control, she decided, and headed back.

She overtook the *tekrak* and circled it a few times to make sure everything was all right. Nothing appeared to be amiss so she set off again, this time looking for a route through the mountains that would not require the *tekrak* to gain too much altitude. The ones that migrated might go very high during the day, so the big one was probably capable of it, but it was more likely to be spotted so staying low was preferable.

It soon became clear it would be impossible to achieve her aim. The mountains continued to rise the further south she went, until even the valleys between the ridges were filled with snow and everything was white. In one valley she spotted several big *sikechasa* wheeling in small circles. There must be something close to dying and they were waiting to finish it off.

Despite the cold, she had Looesa climb higher until even the mountains were far below. The sky was clear but the sun offered no warmth. Its light gleamed blindingly off the snow-covered slopes, peaks and frozen lakes. One odd thing was a line of peaks all with their tops broken and jagged. Nearby were great bowls of rock, their edges were cliffs but some were deep enough to have running water, lakes and grassland.

To the north lay the green and brown of the river plain, with more mountains beyond. All of it leagues away. To the south, the mountains piled up as far as she could see until, on the far horizon, she thought there was a dark line that might be green. The Talamyrth.

She had no way of knowing how far it was but comparing the distance behind to the river it must be at least two days travel for the *tekrak*. A shiver went through her. It really was cold up here. If she had been wrapped in the golden power of Sheesha she would not feel it.

Was it just Sheesha who could trigger the magic?

Kantees looked at the back of Looesa's head, his colouration was different to Sheesha, he had more green and yellow than gold mixed in with the blues. She was aware of the lineage lines, Looesa and Sheesha were barely related.

Kantees leaned down and patted Looesa's neck.

"Can you do it too?" she asked him aloud. And Looesa made a rumbling noise that Kantees felt rather than heard. She smiled at the way the *ziri* liked to pretend they were talking. It was something Sheesha did too, and Kantees wondered whether they in some way thought they were human. "Let's try."

She and Sheesha had first discovered the ability when he had been diving very fast. Looesa already had plenty of height for an attempt—Sheesha's had been from a much lower altitude.

Making sure everything was secure Kantees signalled Looesa to dive. The *ziri* arched his wings into the glide position and angled his neck down. His body followed. The blast of frigid air tore through Kantees' clothes, chilling whatever parts of her had remained warm. But she did not care, there was nothing better than this.

She leaned forwards and stretched her arms around Looesa's neck as they flew faster and faster. She could barely look ahead but she knew Looesa would not collide with anything. She willed him on faster, and he steepened the dive. They were falling out of the sky. She felt him folding his wings in closer to his body.

Come on!

The terrain below was rushing at them but she could not tell how far it was. She was sure they could not be getting close yet. Turning her head to the side she watched as the mountain peaks rose up around them as if they were growing.

Golden shards of light flickered around Looesa.

"Yes!" Kantees screamed as the world turned gold. Looesa pulled out of the dive in a long curve that ran them parallel to a snowy ridge for a fraction of a second, which vanished behind to be replaced by mountain peaks flashing past. She encouraged Looesa up just as another mountain rolled beneath them.

She could not let this go on. And the gold light flickered off, the cold air battered them both as his speed dropped, and they were flying once more. Kantees took a deep breath. Without a ley-circle nearby the fast travel was too exhausting for a *zirichak* to maintain for long.

But she had done it—Looesa had done it. They had done it.

It was not just Sheesha who had the power. Like the *melinasa*, it must be inherent in all the *zirichasa* but the little *melinasa* seemed to be able to do it as a matter of course, where the *ziri* needed someone to unlock it for them. Someone like Kantees of the Ziri.

She hated Yenteel for that name. She hated him more for being right even if he hadn't known the truth when he started it. That just made it worse.

Now all she had to do was find the *tekrak* again.

The world around her was all the same, endless ridges, peaks and valleys, all in white, with only the occasional one deep enough to be green at its floor. She was forced once more to climb to the frigid altitude where she could see the green horizon of the Talamyrth, it looked a little closer but that could just have been her imagination. She turned Looesa so it was at her back. To the north she could see the plain but that was significantly further away, however she could make out the river they had followed to bring them into the mountains. As long as she headed for that she should come close enough to the *tekrak* to be able to spot it against the snow.

It was soon after she passed the range of broken mountains and deep bowls that she saw the giant plant's black shadow sliding along the side of a mountain, moving forward and back as the slope changed. The *tekrak* came into view as she passed another peak, and she urged Looesa into a descending spiral that intercepted the course of the *tekrak*.

Yenteel waved as she came into a position alongside. Pellyn was pushing the creature as fast as its fire-tube could drive it, flying between the taller peaks. It appeared to be more or less on a southerly course. A side gust pushed her in toward the *tekrak* and its gondola swung away and then back. Kantees remembered how the pattern-created wind on the tower had blown the attacking *tekrak* far away, assuming it had not forced it down, or even ripped it apart.

They were not as sturdy as a *ziri* but they could carry a great deal more, and for longer.

"It's going to be four or five days," she shouted.

That got her a glower from Pellyn. He looked even more tired and strained. Flying a *tekrak* under these conditions must be hard. They were not very manoeuvrable and he would have to be constantly thinking ahead, as well as dealing with the crosswinds that could come at any moment.

It was no consolation to Pellyn but if there had been another route, she would have been happy to take it.

"How's Sheesha?"

"He's still asleep."

Kantees nodded, more for her own benefit than Yenteel's.

"I'll find somewhere to put down," she called across. Yenteel gave her another wave as Kantees commanded Looesa to climb again.

In the middle of the afternoon they were on the ground and the *tekrak* had been removed from the gondola and rooted next to a stream. She had chosen one of the deep bowls because they seemed to have no exit and she thought they might be safer from surprise attacks.

There were a few trees near the lake at its centre but not in numbers that worried Kantees. The valley floor was covered in grass being grazed by small herds of *kelukisa*-like creatures. They were even smaller than the usual ones and their coats were very shaggy. Perhaps it was these the *sikechasa* were preying on.

There were flowers too, red and yellow ones in their thousands.

But the place smelled. Kantees had no idea what it was and she had not noticed when she had first scouted but there was the lingering scent of rotten eggs. It was not strong where they were but it was constant.

Yenteel was as much at a loss as she was. Pellyn simply shook his head when asked if he knew what it was.

Considering the variety of dangerous creatures they had encountered, Kantees was uncertain whether she had chosen a good place after all.

"We have Looesa," said Yenteel. "And I could set up a ward."

Kantees shook her head and then realised he was smiling. "There's no ley-circle here so I suppose we would be safe from it working *too* well," she said.

"And it wouldn't last long."

Pellyn snored.

"Shall I tie him up?" said Yenteel.

"Let him sleep," said Kantees. "At this rate it's going to take a five-day to get across these mountains. I'd rather he was sufficiently well rested that he could fly all day. He's not getting out of here without our help."

She sent Looesa off to hunt then headed into the gondola to check on Sheesha. He had changed position since had last seen him but was still curled up. She sat on the deck with her back against the hull and watched him, idly sharpening her knife on a flat stone. Looesa was a good *ziri* but he could never replace Sheesha in her heart.

Yenteel got the fire going and after a while Looesa returned with the remains of a *kelukisa*, enough for them to eat and some to force Sheesha to take into his mouth. Kantees wasn't sure the meat would stop Sheesha from closing his mouth this time, so she used a piece of planking from the deck to prop his mouth open while she poured water down his throat. She was pleased to note his responses were much quicker. He even opened his eyes at one point but they didn't focus.

Kantees sat down next to Yenteel while the meat cooked.

"Why have you decided to make war on the Dunor, Kantees?"

She stared into the flames and said nothing for a while. "They made me into a criminal."

"You were a slave and, if you told the story truthfully, it was Sheesha who made you break the law—and you could have refused him if you had chosen to."

"You weren't there."

"I was there, I just didn't see what happened since I was locked up in the cells."

"That's splitting hairs."

"Well, if that's your real reason, it's not a very good one."

"What does it matter to you?"

"I'd like to know why I'm risking my life."

"You don't need me to answer that," she said. "It's because you chose to follow the orders of a Taymalin patterner—and all because you wanted to see the world."

Yenteel shrugged. "Fair enough."

"All right, so answer me this: is it lawful for a group of Taymalin families to wage war on others?"

"They aren't supposed to," said Yenteel. "They have an agreement, the Great Concordance, signed by all the major families about seven hundred years ago. It established the country boundaries for Faerholme, Taltia, Tirnia, Umran, Tenya, Mirriasmia, Raertane and Dirdin, and a council as arbiter of any disagreements between the families."

"But the Taymalin countries have kings, don't they?"

"Originally the most powerful families within the countries, yes. There had been fighting between the Royal families for two centuries with very few breaks. Alliances made and broken, all of them jockeying for position. It was Etrebus of Tanderlain in Faerholme who was the first to declare himself king of all the families that supported him. The others followed suit and the warring just got worse.

"Eventually the Arch-Patterner at that time stopped it by commanding all in the Patterners Guild to stop supporting anything associated with war."

Kantees gave a short laugh. "So the patterners made war possible, I might have guessed."

"A lot of patterners were killed because of their refusal, others ignored the command because either they didn't want to die or were perfectly happy supporting their lords' goals. Yes they stopped it but it still took several years. Armies can still march and fight, they don't have to travel by ley-circle. The Arch-Patterner kept increasing the range of his ban until no trade moved by ley-circle, even the Healers Guild stopped providing services to the war-mongering families.

"Eventually the Arch-Mage called a Conclave and the kings and the major families sat down and worked out the Great Concordance. They have the Conclave once per year, moving it around among the families, and the families get together and have a fair and an opportunity to raise any issues between them. Grievances are resolved. There is no need for war among them."

"So the Dunor are breaking their Concordance."

"It wouldn't be the first time it's happened. Mostly it's Tirnia though, they've been encroaching on neighbouring land. It's always the Tirnians."

"You didn't mention Esternes in your list of countries."

"Esternes is part of the Kingdom of Tenya."

"I see." She did remember some of this from her old master but politics was not what most of his customers were interested in. "So the Dunor are breaking the Concordance."

"What's that to you, Kantees of the Ziri? I didn't think the activities of the Taymalin houses was something you had any interest in."

"I—I feel responsible."

It was his turn to laugh. "For what? None of this is your doing."

"Yet the Dunor want me," she said. "Because I am Kantees of the Ziri." She glanced over at where Pellyn lay, he was still asleep but she dropped her voice anyway. "I made Looesa travel fast today."

"It's not just Sheesha then."

"All the *ziri* must have it in them, it just doesn't manifest as it does in the *melinasa*."

"But Levin could not even make Sheesha do it."

She shook her head. "I don't know why. I don't even know why I *can* do it."

"That's probably not important," he said. "But the fact that a trained rider can't do it on a *ziri* that knows how to, is good news."

"Is it?"

"Can you think of any other reason the Dunor want you?"

"But how could they even know? They were after me before I had even escaped from the Jakalain." The prospect of Dunor armsmen riding into battle in a golden streak was not something she wanted to think about.

Yenteel poked the fire and checked the meat. He sniffed the air. "Is that smell getting worse?"

Kantees tested it. "I don't think so."

"Just me then." He gave a piece of meat to her.

"You're avoiding the question," she said after testing the meat and deciding it was too hot to eat. "How did they know?"

"The same way that I knew to come and find you, in the same place."

"That is also not an answer."

He sighed. "Have you ever heard of the Revered Malea?"

"Sounds like a Sister of Taymar."

"She is, and has been for many years, the most senior Sister in Faerholme. And she is known for her visions."

"Visions."

"You don't sound impressed."

"I'm not."

"You should be, it was a vision of hers that led me, and the Dunor, to you."

"So she's the one I have to blame?"

"Kantees, it was one of her visions that drove the Dunor to you ten years ago. Your old master decided to move you and look where that got him."

"They didn't find me then, why did they give up?"

"Visions are unreliable, and Malea had also had a vision that showed the daughter of a Duke leading an army against a terrible invader. The girl in question was only five at the time," he said and shrugged. "It was ridiculous, of course, and people can be fickle. Your master saved you by getting you out of the way."

"But they came back."

"There were two parts to the vision, the second part pointed to Jakalain but not until a couple of moon-turns ago."

Kantees frowned. "How did Kevrey find out about the vision in time to sell me to Jakalain?"

"My master told him."

"Your master knew who I was all the time? That's how you knew it was me and not Daybian?"

Yenteel did not reply but sniffed the air again. "That smell is definitely stronger."

7

Kantees couldn't disagree this time. "We'd better find out what it is," she said. "Do you know of any strange creature or abomination that smells of bad eggs?"

"No," said Yenteel as he stood up. "But that doesn't mean there isn't one. The whole point of abominations is that they are random."

"That is not encouraging."

The light had faded and the air become frigid. The cliffs towered all around them and she got the impression that they had somehow grown taller. What had seemed at first to be good defence now felt like a prison.

Kantees tried to throw off her sense of foreboding but it seemed to be tied to the smell which was strong enough to make her stomach turn.

Yenteel took a burning branch from the fire and held it aloft. The light it gave was weak and ineffectual. The snow on the edge of the eastern slope shone white.

She pointed at it. "Leave the branch, Yenteel, we'll have Lostimal in a little while. Besides it's worse than useless and if we do meet anything it will know exactly where you are."

"Most creatures are afraid of fire."

"Or enraged by it."

He didn't reply but laid the branch back in the fire.

"We'll take it slow," she said, "and we'll have light before you know it."

"Or we could just wait until we have the light before we move."

"Are you scared?"

"Any sane person would be scared at this point, Kantees."

She shrugged. "I'm glad I am also sane then."

"I find it strange that I wish a little girl was here right now," said Yenteel.

"Ulina would be useful."

The curved edge of Lostimal emerged above the cliff and bathed this side of the bowl in its silver-white light. It was enough to even cast a shadow. The ground grumbled.

Kantees stared at Yenteel. "Is there a ley-circle here?"

"Can you see one?"

She took a deep breath and focused, though she already knew the answer. "I can't see one but the ground groaned."

"I heard it."

The smell of bad eggs got worse. Kantees stared around, half-expecting to see some huge monster stalking them—but there was nothing. No movement, just the smell.

"The ground belched," said Yenteel. "Or farted."

Kantees stared at him, she thought he might be hysterical. "The ground is not alive, Yenteel."

They stood silent for a moment waiting for something to happen, but the only change was the increase in light as more of Lostimal appeared. It wasn't full but only a small piece of it was missing. It was almost as bright as day though everything appeared in blacks, whites and greys.

"Come on," she said finally. She turned away from the fire and headed down towards the lake. She heard Yenteel's boots crunching on stone until they reached the grassy area. She stopped where she could see the whole of the bowl as she turned on the spot.

The silver-painted rocks stood out against the deeper shadows slightly further round from where they had made camp. She spied what looked like the red of a campfire—except it was too big. Her old master had received reports of giants from time to time, he had always rejected them, but perhaps he was wrong: a giant might make a fire that big.

But that made no sense, they would have noticed a giant when they had arrived.

Which was when she saw the head of a giant rising up from their camp. It took her a moment to clear her mind of the idea of giants because that wasn't a giant's head, it was the *tekrak*. Panic hit her as she realised she was watching Pellyn escape with their only means of transport.

"Yenteel!" She pointed.

"Bastard!" screamed Yenteel. He threw his knife as if he had the range, which he did not, and as if the knife could have made any impression on the *tekrak* even if he had hit it. Which it wouldn't.

Frantically Kantees tried to think of what to do, she even tried to reach out to the *tekrak* and control it.

Then she stopped.

Yenteel continued to shout and rage. His voice echoed off the cliff walls. She let him.

The fire-tube of the *tekrak* exploded into life and its roar echoed around the stones. Unhindered by the weight of the gondola the creature accelerated away from them, rising all the time. She couldn't see Pellyn and guessed he must be in the roots which were in shadow. It would make his ride uncomfortable.

Yenteel's anger was finally exhausted and he went quiet. They continued to watch until the *tekrak* breasted the cliff in the north and disappeared from their sight. The last they saw of it was the flame.

Kantees took a deep breath and turned away. "Let us see what this fire really is."

She walked up the slope, listening out for Yenteel but he did not move. She stopped and turned.

"Come on."

"Kantees."

"Yes?"

"Pellyn stole the *tekrak*."

"It was his to take."

"We're stuck here." When she did not reply he continued, "Why aren't you angry?"

"I am angry at myself for not agreeing to let you tie him up. I'm angry at my naivety in thinking he wasn't listening to our conversation while pretending to sleep. I am annoyed at my foolish assumption that he needed the gondola to fly. None of that will change anything," she said. "But, frankly, I am glad he's gone. He might have decided to try to kill one of us, he might have succeeded. We had to spend all our time on guard against him. No, Yenteel, we're better off now he's gone."

"He'll bring the Dunor down on us."

"We have three days minimum. And that's assuming he does not lose the *tekrak*, or simply die in this attempt. The gondola would be a problem for him but the lack if it means he can just force the *tekrak* to land and root. That's good for him. But he has to fly at night which must be exhausting since the *tekrak* will not be happy. He'll be so exhausted the chances are he will lose control anyway. And then he has to be able to find the right place again.

"We have Looesa, and Sheesha is improving, given complete rest and plenty to eat, I'm sure he'll be ready to fly in that time."

"And if he isn't?"

"It's not like you to be such a pessimist, Yenteel."

That stopped him.

"Come along, let's investigate this glowing red fire."

Yenteel said nothing more and followed her up the slope. The light of Lostimal revealed the ground broken by cracks. At first they were almost nothing but they increased in size and length as they approached the red glow. Until finally they stood at the edge of a wide gash in the rock and the redness shone beneath them. Heat poured upwards, and with it the terrible smell.

"A fire mountain," said Yenteel.

"But old," she said. "So old and tired that all this life has grown up inside it. And all it can do is grumble and make unpleasant smells."

"I've known old people like that," said Yenteel, and Kantees laughed.

"It's a family of them," said Kantees. "I saw them when I was scouting, a dozen mountains without peaks. And even more that look like this, great bowls filled with life."

"That's good, I don't think we would want to spend any time next to a young one."

Kantees yawned. "Let's get back to the camp and, in the morning, perhaps we'll move away from this place."

In the light of morning, when they had woken fully and eaten, Kantees' idea of moving the camp was obviously not going to happen. They had no way to move Sheesha. The smell was constant but usually not too bad. It depended on the direction of the wind.

Kantees took Looesa up and scouted back into the north. Even using Yenteel's precious far-seer she did not see Pellyn. It meant nothing either way. He could have lost the *tekrak* or he could simply be out of sight. She did not dwell on it.

What did concern her, at least a little, was whether these fire mountains really were dead, or just sleeping. In the end she flew over every single one she could find. There was only one that looked as if it might overflow. It was easily identifiable because its rim, which should have been covered in snow, was bare. Kantees could feel its heat as she drew closer. Looesa was not happy about it and she did not force him. However, this one was a good distance from theirs.

Looesa hunted and the poor *kelukisa* had nowhere to run. Still, a diet of only meat, no matter how succulent, soon palled and their stock of biscuits was gone. Yenteel looked for roots they could eat and came back with some very unappetising choices.

But it was that afternoon that Sheesha woke properly for the first time.

He lifted his head and made an odd barking sound almost like a *zatek*. It was plaintive and, to Kantees, seemed like a plea for help. She had been by the fire but when she turned her head at the sound and saw his raised head, wobbling and uncertain, she gave a little cry of her own and rushed to him. Flinging her arms around his neck and crooning to him.

She shouted for Yenteel to fill a bucket of water and, when he brought it, Sheesha drank it all. It took another three bucketsful before his thirst was quenched.

Looesa had immediately flown off and returned a short time later with an entire *kelukisa* but, by this time, Sheesha had dropped his head and fallen asleep again. So Kantees gutted the animal and disposed of the entrails. Yenteel had been using his knife to unthread some of the rope and proceeded to hack into soil close to the lake. Kantees did not ask what he was doing.

In the evening Sheesha woke again and consumed the entire carcass Kantees had prepared for him.

Later, the night air was filled with Sheesha's snores and Kantees could not have been happier.

The following morning Sheesha tried to get up. Despite her happiness in seeing him wanting to move, the way he staggered and kept collapsing back on to the ground had her in tears again. She desperately wanted to help but he was just too big. One misstep from him and he could crush her. Nor was it like waking up in the morning when all you needed was to stretch and everything worked properly. He did not improve as he moved.

He eventually made it out of the gondola. Lying flat he stretched his wings to their fullest extent and the tips shook as the muscles stretched. Carefully and slowly he folded them back into his body and pushed himself up so his head was held high and he looked around. Kantees could see his nostrils working.

"We don't like the smell either," she said. Sheesha lay down again, heavily as if stretching his wings had exhausted him.

"His lordship is up and about I see," said Yenteel coming up from the lake. Several large fish dangled from lines he had made. "Fish is good for those recovering from illness. But we get to keep one for ourselves. I'm getting very tired of *ziri*-caught *kelukisa*."

If Looesa was insulted he didn't comment, he just lay on a rock slightly above the camp where he could see everything. Kantees was pretty sure Looesa had his eye on the fish as well. Perhaps he too was tired of a constant diet of grazing animal, though she wasn't sure a *ziri* was really that picky, in her experience they would eat almost anything if they thought it was food.

Yenteel dropped one of the fish by the fire and then glanced up at Looesa. "This is not for you."

Kantees grinned. "We'll make a Ziri Keeper of you yet, Yenteel. Talking to your charges is the first step along a path from which there is no return. Although it's when they reply you need to worry."

Yenteel went over to where Sheesha lay flat but wide awake—and why should he not be, he had been asleep for two or three days.

"Open wide," said Yenteel dangling one of the fish in front of Sheesha's nose. The great mouth expanded and Yenteel threw the fish in, keeping his hand away from the dagger-teeth. Sheesha couldn't eat with his lower jaw on the ground so he lifted his head and they watched as his neck flexed, swallowing the catch whole. He came back down with his mouth open again. The process was repeated twice more.

Kantees glanced back at Looesa who stood up on his back legs, spread his wings and launched into the air. She thought for a moment he might be going for the fish by the fire but he flew over them with long lazy wingstrokes, and headed down to the lake.

He flew low over the placid water, causing ripples from the breath of his passing, and landed on a rocky outcrop on the far side. Moments later he had manoeuvred himself into a position right on the edge by the water with his neck in an arch and his snout almost touching the surface.

"Looesa has gone fishing," said Yenteel.

"I've never seen them do that," said Kantees. "Was he watching you?"

Yenteel shrugged. "Perhaps it's something wild *ziri* do, and he just needed reminding."

Sheesha had fallen asleep again.

"Can I look at the *chilafrah*?" said Yenteel.

"Why?"

"Curiosity. Boredom."

Kantees couldn't argue with that and pulled it from the pack and handed it over.

"You can't see its energy?"

"No."

He turned it over in his hands. "I wonder what it's made of."

In the evening they ate *kelukisa* again, this time cold because Looesa did not make any fresh kills. Instead he stayed at the water's edge until at least mid-afternoon. Every now and again Kantees would catch a movement out of the corner of her eye and see him pulling a fish from the water—or sometimes not—and stretching his head and neck upwards to swallow it down. She commented to Yenteel that he was eating every single fish he caught.

His disinterested answer amounted to: "Perhaps he's hungry."

But it turned out that wasn't the situation. When Looesa finally decided he'd had enough he launched himself into the air. Kantees watched him climb a good distance over the lake, although he seemed sluggish—*too stuffed to fly*, she thought—then glide back into the camp to land right in front of Sheesha.

Then he emptied the contents of his stomach on to the ground. Kantees screwed up her nose, first at the sight, quickly followed by the smell which was even more pungent than that from the crack in the burning mountain.

To make things even worse Sheesha woke up and ate everything Looesa had thrown up.

"That's interesting," said Yenteel.

"Interesting? It's horrible."

"Not at all, Kantees." He gave her a piercing stare. "I always forget you've had a very sheltered upbringing."

"I was a *slave*."

"I know. I suppose I'm slightly surprised you didn't pick this up from your time with Kevrey."

"What are you talking about?"

"It's very common for certain types of animals to feed their young by collecting food like that and partially digesting it for them. But," he said, "only their young. This seems unusual."

"That Looesa is providing food for Sheesha? He did that before with the *kelukisa*."

"True, and for us too. I wonder if wild *zirichasa* do that, or whether it's you."

"Me?"

"You obviously have an influence on their behaviour, and feeding your people is a thing you would do." He stared at Sheesha and Looesa and then back at Kantees. "Definitely you."

"It could be you," she said but she wasn't even convincing herself.

"I'm insufficiently caring."

8

After eating, Sheesha had crawled back into the gondola. This time Kantees went with him but she did not curl up under his wing; she bedded down a short distance away and was lulled to sleep by the soft sound of his breathing. Just as she had done all those years in the tower. It made her feel safe.

The following morning Looesa delivered another stomachful of fish while Kantees and Yenteel ate the last of the *kelukisa*.

"You might want to put more food for us as an idea in Looesa's mind," he said. "I've been hungry before and I do not relish the prospect of it happening again."

"We need to move," she said. Three days was the maximum she had given before she thought Pellyn might have managed to return to the Dunor and have them send someone after them.

They might even use *melinasa* to track them down, and that would mean even less time.

"Only if Sheesha can fly," said Yenteel.

"Tell me something I don't know!" snapped Kantees.

"I know you're worried but we can't force him to heal faster or gain in strength."

"Then you think of something," she said. "I'm going to scout around and see if I can find somewhere else we can hide, perhaps close by but just not here next to the gondola that anyone can see from above."

Yenteel nodded. "I'll give it some thought." He glanced at Sheesha soaking up the sunshine by lying flat with his wings stretched out. "He doesn't look in any hurry to fly."

Kantees said nothing, she was still annoyed, and climbed onto Looesa's back. Sheesha opened an eye and watched them as they took off. Perhaps she could make him jealous enough to at least try to get into the air—but if he was too weak flying might do him harm rather than good.

Looesa went over the edge of the top of the cliff and Kantees was hit by the cold again. Their little valley was warm and so cut-off from the world, it was as if that was the only place that existed. Flying now, above the snowy mountains, she was reminded of what was happening in the real world. She wished she could pretend it didn't exist and hide away forever but that was not something she could do. There were friends out here who were in danger.

Friends? Daybian and Levin, Taymalin lordlings, were they really friends?

She was unable to deny it. They were friends just as much as Gally, Ulina and Yenteel.

With Looesa at a good height and travelling slowly she studied the landscape. Once past the fire mountains there were no green valleys that she could see even though spring was well advanced in the lowlands. Winter was still in control here.

If the worst came, they would have to hide in the snow. She turned back and took her time exploring the valleys much closer to the ground and found some caves that might work—assuming there was nothing dangerous lurking inside them.

It was at that moment a golden streak shot across the sky. *Melinak.* She was close to a cave and urged Looesa toward it. At this height perhaps Looesa would be taken for a *sikechak*, especially since there was just one of him and he was low.

Kantees did not know how good the eyesight of a *melinak* might be. All she could do was trust to hope. The cave entrance was large enough to take a *ziri*. And she slipped off Looesa's back the moment he was on the ground. The golden trail had not changed direction. Then she caught a glimpse of another one further to the east.

They were searching and the forces of the Dunor would not be very far behind. If Pellyn was with them they would easily find Yenteel and Sheesha. And they could be used for bargaining and persuading her to do as they wished.

The cave was dark and Kantees was reluctant to go any further in. They were hidden as long as they stayed just inside. She sniffed. The air seemed clean enough, if there had been something unpleasant in here there would be a trace, and Looesa did not seem unsettled.

Kantees focused on the *melinasa*. The closest one continued in the same direction, heading south, so had missed them. Kantees tried to stretch her pattern-sense but whether she succeeded or failed she did not know. Either way she could not find anything that stood out in her mind.

One day perhaps she would have time to explore her new sense when she wasn't being threatened and chased. Her life had been so much simpler when all she had had to worry about was Sheesha—but that was old ground and the other path lay only in the direction of the Dunor. The one she had taken might be narrow and difficult but for now, at least, she was still free.

Both of the *melinasa* had disappeared from her view. They would probably be back but for now she could move without being seen. She could not perceive any *tekrasa* with her sense so she should just stay low and move slowly. If she had any chance of rescuing Yenteel and Sheesha it would be through surprise.

Except Sheesha would not be able to fly.

Kantees shook her head as she remounted. There was no point worrying about that until it happened.

Looesa dove from the edge of the cave and followed the snow-covered cliff down. His speed increased and as they approached the valley floor he extended his wings fully and went up the other side like an arrow. Kantees had him turn parallel to the cliff and keep climbing until they were just high enough to head over the next ridge and down the other side.

So it went. Kantees kept herself tuned to her pattern-sense just in case the *melinasa* returned, while Looesa went up the slopes, over ridges and down into the valleys, staying as close to the ground as he could at all times.

The first sign of something amiss was when they topped a ridge and Kantees saw a *tekrak* floating above the edge of the mountain side of her fire mountain. In a moment of panic she commanded Looesa to change direction.

If her legs had not already been hooked tightly under his wings she would have fallen off as Looesa simply flipped over backwards with his head and neck leading the way in a graceful arch. Moments later they were plummeting back into the valley. Kantees remembered to breathe.

Of course, Looesa was known for being manoeuvrable, that was what made him a great racing *ziri* despite his size—but his riders were usually strapped in.

They fled along the base of the valley, Kantees hoping to put as much distance as she could between her and the place where she might have been seen. They had only been there for a fraction of a second, the men aboard would have had to be looking directly at the right place. But people saw movements, and they might investigate.

The glittering ice of a frozen waterfall caught her eye. Near its base she saw a dark area and guided Looesa towards it. Beyond the huge pillars of frozen ice there was a cave and before she could stop him Looesa pulled in his wings and shot between them, pulling up for landing—which would have gone well if the floor had not been a sheet of solid ice.

Looesa slid forwards, but back-winged hard. His talons slipped out from under him and he landed on his behind jarring Kantees with the shock. They were brought to a halt by the stone wall on the opposite side. Looesa grunted and Kantees swore by the Mother's milk.

But at least they were down, and hopefully hidden from any investigation by the men of the Dunor or their *melinasa*.

Kantees dismounted carefully but her shoes still slipped on the ice. Taking slow sliding steps she made her way to the wall of the gallery and used it as best she could for support. It too was smooth and glistened with ice but it helped a little.

After the third time she fell, Kantees gave up walking and slid cautiously on her behind to the opening to peer between the pillars and sheets of ice. The view was distorted but she was sure she would see a *tekrak* even if she missed a *melinak*.

Looesa made an oddly plaintive noise and Kantees looked round. The *ziri* was lying on the ice as if he was scared of any attempt to stand up.

"Don't be a baby," she said. "It's only ice." Then she told herself off for being a hypocrite, the ice was a real problem and she was just as scared of falling over as Looesa. "Just stay there. It will only be a little while to make sure there's no pursuit."

She watched and waited while her feet froze. There was no movement outside: neither the slow churn of a tekrak nor the high-speed streak of a melinak. On the opposite cliff, a spur of shadow pointed upwards. It moved slowly across the face and Kantees saw a crack in the cliff in its path. "When it gets to there," she said to herself and waited.

"Come on," she said when her shadow had almost reached the target she had set for it. "No need to wait any longer. If they were coming they would be here."

There was no sound from Looesa. She turned and looked. His eyes were shut. Asleep. "*Chakik* droppings," she muttered. "Why do I have to come to you?"

If Looesa had been one of the scaly ancient creatures she would have been more concerned. They didn't like the cold. *Kichesa* could barely tolerate it at all and were almost useless in winter. She understood that horses were fine with it, and easier to train. Many of the rich Taymalin were cultivating herds over on the mainland.

But a *ziri* was feathered. Underneath the big outer feathers was a layer of smaller softer ones that kept them warm.

As she was thinking this she slid her way to where Looesa snored. She would have shouted but the sounds they made echoed forever in this ice tunnel and she couldn't shake the idea that there was something lurking in the dark. If there was, she did not want to wake it up.

She gave Looesa's head a shove and he opened an eye.

"We're going."

He lifted his head and peered at the light.

"Come on." She shoved him hard. He opened his wing a little but refused to get up. "You're not serious? You're scared of falling over on the ice?" She got a look of reproach for that. "Fine."

Using Looesa for support she dragged herself to his rear-end, jammed her foot into a crack in the wall and pushed. She was surprised when he moved a little. "Ha!" With redoubled effort she put her shoulder into it and he slid forward an arms-length. With her support sliding away Kantees fell on her face. She swore.

But her efforts seemed to have given Looesa an idea; rather than attempt to get up he dug his talons into the ice and pushed. He slid forward. Another push, another slide. He was already close to the edge, he adjusted his direction and headed for a gap.

"Idiot!" Kantees shouted, forgetting her own concerns about monsters in the dark. She got down on her stomach and followed his example, although having differently-jointed knees made her task harder, but she slipped after him.

She slammed into a wall of translucent ice as Looesa went over the edge. Through the distortions she saw him disappear down, and then shoot up and flip around, eventually coming to a landing on a large rock at the base of the frozen waterfall.

"Show-off," she muttered and worked her way along to a gap. The fall beneath her was precipitous and ended in a frozen pool of ice. She did not have the ability to take flight. This had not been her plan, she was supposed to be riding him as he launched himself into the air from the edge.

She focused on him and gave him the very firm idea that he needed to come back into the cave.

Looesa resisted. He did not like the ice.

Kantees insisted.

Reluctantly the *ziri* took to the air and circled round a couple of times. It was not a great distance from here to the other side but Looesa was not constrained. Eventually he sighted on the cave and, much more slowly than the first time, flew at the gap. He also aimed much higher and, as he slipped through, he blasted the air with back-beats to kill his speed and touched down lightly.

And slipped over.

Kantees did not laugh out loud but worked her way to him and climbed on his back.

"Let's go."

The prospect of sliding over the edge, even on a *ziri*, filled her with dread. It was not far to the bottom but it seemed Looesa had already thought of that. Using his talons to push he built up as much speed as he could over the distance.

They went over and Kantees' stomach was left behind for a moment. Then Looesa flipped out his wings, caught the air and beat hard. The ground was coming at them fast. Then the opposite cliff was their enemy. Looesa banked until he was sideways to the ground and as he began to slip through the air, he turned in that direction and flattened out. His wings hitting the air like a drum. They gained altitude with the cliff flashing past just to their right.

Kantees let him continue in this direction along the tight valley as the walls closed in but had him slow so that they wouldn't come on an enemy without warning.

Moments later they went over the ridge and Kantees scanned the horizon. With nothing in sight, she had Looesa set down just below the top of the ridge but on the side away from their destination. Kantees pulled Yenteel's far-seer from her pack and realised it felt strangely light. She remembered she had left the *chilafrah* at the camp. Her heart fell, not only had her friends probably been captured but she had lost that as well. Would her failures never end?

Perhaps she could get everything back.

Perhaps.

Lying beside a rock for cover, she scanned the rim of the fire mountain. The *tekrak* she had seen before was gone and there was no sign of life. She was fairly sure she had escaped detection but every minute she wasted made the situation worse.

But without certain knowledge she had no idea what she was up against, or even if they were still there.

The sky was still perfectly clear and crystal blue. If there had been clouds she would have risked flying over the top at high altitude to see what was happening but that choice was not available.

She climbed back down to Looesa and mounted. He launched into the next valley. Kantees had him fly out and round in order to come in to the fire mountain from the west. If she had been in charge of the Dunor's men she would have kept the *tekrak* above the rim and, if they had another, have it patrol at low level round and round. But she saw no evidence of either.

Looesa mounted the western slope and she had him land just at the point the snow ended. Then clambered the rest of the way to the rim. Small lizards sunbathed on the bare rocks; they slithered from sight when Kantees disturbed them. There was even a hum of insects.

All else was silence.

Mounting the last few lengths on all fours and taking care not to disturb the stones, Kantees made it to the top. She got down on her stomach and slithered forward like a snake until, finally, she could see down into the bowl.

The lake was as serene as ever. The *kelukisa* grazed on the open grass. A haze drifted up from the broken area next to their camp where the burning mountain exuded its noxious fog. Creeping forward a little at a time Kantees could finally see down to where their camp had been.

The remains of the gondola was there. Their untended fire still smoked a little.

No Dunor. No Yenteel. No Sheesha.

The place was abandoned. She was too late. She sent out a call to Looesa and he arrived moments later coming to rest next to her. She jumped on his back and he went into a fast steep glide, staying close to the ground. He shot past the camp, reached the lake, flipped around and flew back to land just short of the camp.

Kantees jumped down. The fire was down to embers. She went into the gondola to see if there was anything she needed, and to see if, by any chance, the *chilafrah* had been left behind. She did not find it.

She went back to Looesa, and prepared to set off after the Dunor. On Looesa's back, she gave one last look and almost gave the order for him to take off.

But something wasn't right.

She looked at the gondola again … then the fire … then further and higher at the haze over the mountain's burning rocks. She dismounted again and headed round the curve of the bowl, then up towards the rocks. She sniffed. The air did not smell of bad eggs.

For a moment she thought she was a fool for being suspicious simply because the air did not smell but then she saw a pattern scratched into a rock. It looked familiar. She went over to it and ran her fingers across it. There was no question it had been freshly made, the lichen had been scrapped off and bits of it fell away when she touched it.

She could see the cracks that led down to the fire but could not feel any heat from them. She reached her hand closer and it came up against something solid in the air. Yenteel's warding spell!

But how was he holding it? The *chilafrah* might still hold enough power to keep a ward in place.

Kantees grabbed a stone and scratched at the pattern on the rock. Moments later it was completely obliterated and a puff of pungent gas flooded out, making her choke, and the heat from the mountain warmed her skin.

If one breath of this air was enough to make her choke what had it done to Yenteel and Sheesha?

Despite the poisonous air she pushed on. Where were they?

"Yenteel! Sheesha!"

Someone groaned and the sound seemed to come almost from her feet she stepped forward again and tripped over someone. It was like seeing someone emerging from fog, except instead of grey they were a shadow against the colour of stone. And now she saw Sheesha as well, lying flat, his chest heaving.

The air was still thick with the gas. Kantees summoned Looesa and commanded him to mount a rock and beat his wings to help clear the air. She rolled Yenteel over, even though his body looked strangely stone-like, he felt normal. He was clutching the *chilafrah*. She ripped it from his hands and threw it as hard as she could towards the camp. She did not care if it shattered.

9

"Remind me never to invoke patterns when I have an endless supply of the Mother's blessed milk available. It never turns out well."

"I'm just glad you're not dead."

She had propped him up against a boulder after which he had promptly thrown up. Sheesha she really couldn't do anything about since she couldn't move him. But the air had cleared and he was breathing normally, lying on the stones. Kantees sent Looesa off with the bucket in the hope the *ziri* would understand what was needed.

"It's my fault," she said. "If I hadn't been so cautious, I could have been back sooner."

"And run into Pellyn and his friends? That would not have ended well, they might have stayed around even longer then we really would have been dead." He coughed again. Kantees glanced over at Sheesha, his eyes were slitted and she thought he was watching.

"You had a pattern to disguise you?"

"We had almost no time," he said. "I saw the *melinasa* going over. I barely had time to cast the blending pattern before the *tekrak* came over the rim. I tried to grab everything that we wouldn't leave

739

behind to give the impression we'd gone, then got Sheesha up on to the rocks.

"They landed by the lake and sent armsmen up. Their caution was my chance. I found the *chilafrah* so thought I might be able to keep two patterns going while they were searching. I managed to get a simple protective pattern in place. I wasn't even sure it was going to work." He cleared his throat painfully. He was probably talking too much. "It worked too well. Again. If it hadn't been for the mountain's farts, we would have been fine."

"It was a clever idea to leave that symbol outside the pattern so I could break it when I arrived."

"What symbol?"

They were right next to the boulder so she pointed to the scratched-out symbol.

"That was outside?" She nodded. "It wasn't supposed to be, I told you I was in a hurry."

Both of them went silent thinking about the possible alternative outcome.

"It didn't happen," said Kantees. "I got back in time, and you're alive and so is Sheesha."

She shrieked as freezing water poured down her back accompanied by the thump of Looesa's landing. "Idiot," she hissed as she stood and turned round. The bucket hung from the *ziri*'s mouth. He was looking down at her slightly cross-eyed. She couldn't suppress the laughter but carefully lifted the rope handle from between his teeth.

"Thank you, Looesa."

Quickly she climbed the slope to where Sheesha lay. "Open your mouth."

Sheesha did as he was told and Kantees poured what was left in the bucket—still more than half full—down his throat. Then she dampened her sleeve with the dregs and wiped his eyes which she thought must be stinging because they looked bloodshot.

"Can you move?" she said to him. "Let's get down from here."

He was shaky and Kantees was concerned about the gaps into the heart of the mountain so she led him by a more roundabout route.

"Perhaps Looesa could get us some fresh meat?" said Yenteel.

"Good idea." Kantees waved at the waiting *zirichak* who turned and pushed himself into the air. He gained height as he headed for the pastures to the north of the bowl.

Yenteel frowned and using the boulder for support, climbed to his feet. He let Kantees and Sheesha go past and followed them down to the camp.

"I'll get the fire going," said Kantees. The embers at its core were still hot. She piled on some tinder and blew. The flames sprang up. She added larger twigs and placed a log at one side. The *chilafrah* was lying among the stones beside the wooden frame of the gondola, she fetched it and put it in her bag. "I'm not leaving this behind again."

"It saved our lives."

Kantees noticed Yenteel was staring at her. He hadn't done that for a long time.

"Yes, I know, it saved your lives and I'm glad for that. But if things had gone differently the Dunor would have it."

"Yes, I know."

He continued staring.

"What?"

"When did you teach Looesa to fetch water?"

It was Kantees' turn to stare.

"Or use his wings as a fan?"

Kantees opened her mouth but no sound emerged.

He turned to where Looesa was returning with a whole *kelukik* hanging from his talons. "Or have him fetch us food with just a hand wave?"

"I—"

Yenteel shook his head and held up his hand to stop her. "Don't make excuses, Kantees."

She closed her mouth and watched almost as if she disbelieved what her eyes were telling her as Looesa flew over and dropped the *kelukik* on the other side of the fire where the blood from its torn-out throat soaked into the stones.

Looesa headed back towards the lake and the small promontory from which he had fished the previous day.

"It just happened," she said weakly. "There wasn't time."

"And you didn't think."

"No."

"That's always been your problem, Kantees, you think too much."

Anger flared in her. "And being rude has always been yours."

He shrugged. "I have never pretended to be anything other than what I am. Love or leave me."

"I certainly don't love you."

"But you haven't left me."

"I thought we were talking about me."

"You indicated that wasn't a suitable topic for discussion."

"You're impossible."

"True."

"And you wonder why your master always sent you on missions as far away and as difficult as possible. I'm sure he's hoping you'll never come back."

"He doesn't care if I come back, Kantees."

"Oh," she said. "You're better off without him then."

"He only cares that I succeed in my mission."

Kantees fell silent. She suddenly didn't want to argue any more. It was always just a waste anyway, pointless.

"Entertaining though," said Yenteel.

"Are you reading *my* mind?"

"No, just your face, you're really not very good at hiding your thoughts and emotions. That's why it's always so painful watching you when you're thinking."

"You're trying to anger me again."

"Sometimes it seems as if it's the only way to get you to the truth."

"Oh? And what truth are we trying to reach this time?"

He held up his hands. "I have absolutely no idea, that's what makes it so much fun and so interesting. I push and prod, you explode and then, when the dust settles, progress has been made."

"And that's how it works, is it?"

"Not today."

They fell into silence again. Kantees looked across the lake at where Looesa stood hunched over the water. Yenteel went over to the dead *kelukik* and proceeded to skin it. It took a lot of effort, their knives were too blunt after all the use and misuse they were getting. Rather than just sit there and watch Yenteel, Kantees checked Sheesha who was sleeping again, then headed up towards the area where the gases from the heart of the mountain leaked out.

The stones were smooth and looked as if they had been like this for a long time. The way that stones in a river were worn small and flat. The heat from inside the ground was a constant surprise, she could not imagine how these mountains could stay so hot for so long.

Old and dead fire mountains, a long time ago they would have belched their insides across the land. What she could see deep inside these holes would have poured out. The World Pattern seemed infinite in its variety. But there was no ley-circle here nor anywhere close. She supposed that Yenteel would be able to explain that, how the movements of Lostimal and Colimar always missed some parts of the world.

She sat on the warm stones and looked out across the lake and pastures. Up at the cliffs of the rim surrounding them. This was a peaceful place. She could hide here forever.

But people needed her.

She took out her knife and tried it on the rock. The surface was very rough but seemed hard. It wasn't going to make the blade smooth but it might get a better edge to it. Almost anything would be better than now.

Yenteel must have noticed what she was doing because he came over.

"Is it working?"

Kantees ran her thumb gently along the disappointingly uneven surface, then offered it to him hilt first. "What do you think?"

He tried it. "Better than this one. Here." He handed her his in exchange. It needed cleaning.

"Thanks."

But Yenteel didn't return to his task. "You're controlling them more effectively, with more refinement."

"I don't control them, Yenteel."

"Poor choice of words. You know what I mean."

"My desires seem to get across better."

"Better? You made Looesa fetch water in a bucket."

"I asked him to."

"That's just playing with words, Kantees."

"Whatever you want to call it, Yenteel." She took a deep breath and dispelled the anger that was building inside her again. "Looesa had already shown he wanted to help Sheesha, he brought food without being asked. This time he just helped in a different way."

"And what would you call him fanning his wings to dispel the gases? When did he do something similar to that before?"

"In the Talamyrth," she said with a certain smugness.

It took him a moment to remember how she had got Sheesha and Shingul to beat their wings to stir up the air to prevent them from being suffocated. But Kantees did not need Yenteel to say that she was clutching at straws and, thankfully, he didn't.

"What happened when you were scouting?"

"Nothing much, I couldn't find anywhere else we could easily stay. I saw the *melinasa* and then the *tekrak* so I hid in an ice cave with Looesa. Then we flew back."

"And there was nothing different about that?"

She thought back. "Looesa didn't like the ice and I had to insist on him coming back for me."

"You insisted."

"It's not wise to annoy someone who's holding a knife, Yenteel."

"It's too blunt to do any damage."

"I can sharpen it."

He just looked at her with his head on one side—which, even more annoyingly, reminded her of the way her old master Kevrey looked at his less bright clientele.

"Yes, all right, I made Looesa do what I wanted. Happy?"

Yenteel gave her a low bow and went back to skinning the *kelukik*.

Looesa returned with a gut full of fish which he dumped in front of Sheesha. Yenteel had built up the fire and now had chunks of the *kelukik* roasting. The remaining pieces he threw to Looesa who caught and swallowed one at a time.

Kantees finished sharpening the other knife and came down and sat by the fire. It was another sunny day and it wasn't cold but the fire made it better anyway.

Yenteel took his place opposite and watched her through the flame and smoke.

"How long until Sheesha can fly?" he asked.

"I don't know."

"Kantees, of the two of us here, you are the one who has spent their life with the *ziri*, you are the one who knows best what a *ziri* can do."

She looked across at Sheesha. "After this set-back? Another two days before he's ready to even try, then he'll have to get his strength back. Another two or three days after that?"

Kantees shook her head. "It'll be nearly a ten-day since we left the town before we even get out of the mountains." She felt her eyes moistening as if there were going to be tears. She wiped them away before they even had a chance to form. "It's almost as if the World Pattern is against me."

He gave her a measured look. "You don't really believe that."

"Don't I?"

"You could live your life just giving in to the pattern," he said. "Or you can change it."

"If I had given in to the pattern I would already be dead," she said. "I've been over this a thousand times in my head. The pattern was set before I was even born. Everything I do is a battle against it."

"There is no plan, Kantees, the pattern doesn't think. It's just everything doing what it does in the world."

"What are we then?"

"We're magic."

She frowned at him and glanced at Sheesha eating his way through the pile of half-digested fish. It was not a pretty sight but at least she didn't have to shovel what came out of the other end any more. "I don't know what you mean."

"Sheesha gets shot by arrows—" she shot him a sharp look, "—and what would have happened if they had gone untreated?"

"He would have died," she said. "But he wouldn't have been there if not for me."

"I'm coming to that. So we healed him. We used a Taymalin healing pattern to repair the damage to his pattern quicker than it would normally happen, so that he didn't die while his body recovered."

She hesitated. "There's something you don't know."

His teeth shone from the wide grin he threw her. "Kantees, there are a world of things that I do not know. I have no illusions about that. But if you have something useful to tell me then I will gladly listen."

The strange little speech put her off her stride. "It's about the healing pattern—it's not very good."

"What do you mean?"

"It's like the difference between a scholar's writing and a child scratching a picture in the earth."

"I thought you couldn't read."

"I *can't*. But I am not stupid and I often saw Kevrey's writing as well as the occasional words at Jakalain. That writing was always small and neat. Compared to the scratching of the symbol you did to make that protection pattern."

"I know you are not stupid Kantees. You're saying that the patterns I'm using are not as complex as those they try to heal."

"No ... I mean, yes, that's what I'm saying."

"How do you *know*?"

She had not wanted him to ask that question but once she had started on this road, she knew it would be coming. "Because when you were healing Sheesha I could see it."

"You saw the patterns?"

"That's what I said. Are you hard of hearing now?"

"Just clarifying to ensure I am understanding what you are saying," he said. "How could you see a pattern?"

She shrugged. "I have no idea, but I could see that the healing pattern could not do any more good by the time you had finished. It's clever, I suppose, in its way. It allows you to channel the Mother's power and mend the actual pattern, but it's like—" She stopped because she simply could not think of a way to explain it.

"Like?"

Kantees was surprised at the passion in his voice, he was desperate to understand what she had seen. This was him being the 'natural philosopher' she supposed. The one who wants to understand everything about how the world works.

Kantees took a half-burnt stick from the fire and went up to where the rocks were exposed and flat, closer to the fissures in the fire mountain. Yenteel followed like a *zatek* hoping to be fed. Perhaps she could feed him with the knowledge he craved.

She found a stone as wide as her arm was long, and drew a big circle on it with the stick.

"This is a pattern."

He said nothing and she had to look at him to make sure he was listening. He nodded. She scratched four smaller circles inside the big one, trying not to overlap them.

"This is the same pattern," she said, "if you look closer." She chose the new circle nearest her and drew four smaller circles inside that. "It's still the same pattern."

"But looking even closer."

"Yes." She chose one of those and inscribed four more inside that. They were very poorly made because she was running out of space and the stick was not good for drawing at that size. She looked at Yenteel.

"Every pattern is composed of smaller patterns and those of even smaller ones and so on until…"

"I don't know. Perhaps it goes on forever."

"You're telling me that if the outer circle was damaged it would also affect the ones further and further in, but the healing patterns only change the biggest one."

Kantees was surprised at the clarity with which he had understood what she was trying to communicate. It would have been very difficult to convey in words. "Yes, that's what I was trying to say. They're not circles, they're much more complicated and changing constantly."

Yenteel was nodding. "That all makes sense."

"Does it?"

"Yes." He stopped staring at the circles and looked at her face. She did not understand what she was seeing in him but he was happy.

She dropped the stick. "So much for that. It doesn't change anything. Everything I want to do, it's just impossible. I feel like I'm swimming in mud."

He gave her a smile that could have been interpreted as condescending but she didn't think he meant it that way.

"You *are* swimming in mud."

"I thought you were going to be encouraging."

"Kantees, the World Pattern does what it does. The creatures that live in it do whatever their part of the pattern says they should do."

"If you're expecting me to be happy I think you're going about it the wrong way."

His grin got wider. "I said we're magic, that we're patterns, and we are. But we have the power to choose not to follow the course the World Pattern lays out for us, that's our magic. That's why you feel like you're swimming in mud, you're fighting the World Pattern. Anyone who is worth anything does that, you don't want to follow the path that's been laid out for you. You have your own ideas and you make your own choices.

"This is a battleground, Kantees, for everyone who has discovered they have freedom of choice." He paused to take a breath. "You're remaking the World Pattern and that takes strength, and persistence."

Kantees pursed her lips. She wanted to say something but she could not think of anything.

So instead she returned to the fire. Sheesha had finished eating and gone back to sleep. Looesa was sunning himself.

Kantees realised she had been frowning for some time and forced her eyebrows to relax. Yenteel came and sat opposite again but she didn't want to see him just now.

"I need to think," she said, almost like an apology, then got up and set off to walk around the lake.

I O

Kantees' introspection did not end when she returned to the camp that day, nor the next day. Or even the next. Yenteel's words had got under her skin and she found herself re-evaluating so many things that had happened in her life.

What she disliked was the idea that so much that had happened had been due to her own actions. It was impossible to blame others, or the World Pattern, as if that simple knowledge that Yenteel had given her was changing everything she had ever known. Except it was worse than that; she knew it was not distorting the past but giving it truth and clarity which, in some ways, made it even more unbearable.

The weather had held out those two days but on the third the wind changed and clouds rolled in from the west carrying rain.

They cleared out the gondola and used what they could find to block up the windows. It was not cold but the rain, when it came, was persistent and driven at a flat angle by the wind. Looesa still fetched food but stayed under cover in the gondola along with Sheesha.

The big *ziri* had slept for most of the last two days, but come the third he seemed finally to wake up properly. He had never liked the rain but being cooped up in the gondola was not to his taste.

Kantees did not issue him with any instructions and he took to spending time outside repeatedly stretching his wings and beating them, as if he was building up his strength again. She found herself questioning everything: was it her decision? Was she changing the World Pattern? Was Sheesha capable of sufficient independent thought to make changes to the pattern or was everything he did dictated by what was natural to him?

"There is nothing I can do that does not modify the World Pattern," she said finally to Yenteel.

They were sitting round the fire they had brought inside, while the rain thrummed on the roof.

He just nodded.

"I am responsible for my every action."

He looked at her though his face seemed almost void of expression.

"The bigger the change, the stronger the resistance."

He nodded again but said nothing.

"And the only failure is giving up."

At that he gave a small smile. "I haven't heard that one before."

"But you have heard the others?"

"I went through it myself, in my own way."

"Your master told you that secret and it changed your life?"

"Something like that."

"Am I supposed to become as cheerful and carefree as you are?" *And willing to spend the night with anyone?*

"I don't think so," he said. "You're just you. I'm just me. We aren't the same."

"Well that's good news, I think I'd hate being you."

"I'd hate you being me too."

She sniffed at him then stood and went to the entrance that Looesa had made and leaned against the side looking out at Sheesha. "I've liked these few days," she said. "There have been parts of it I could have done without but these few days of quiet have been relaxing."

Yenteel came over too but stood on the far side, careful not to get too close. *He knows I am not comfortable with familiarity and he never pushes.*

After a long moment, he asked, "Can I ask you a personal question?"

"As long as you stay over there and don't presume you'll get an answer."

"Fair enough," he said and stared out into the rain for a few moments before turning back to her. "Do you prefer Daybian or Levin?"

"Prefer?"

"Which one are you more attracted to?"

Oh. She weighed her answer. "Neither."

"You like them equally?"

"It depends on what you mean by like. Most of the time I don't hate them. You want to know if I'd be willing to bed them, I suppose?"

Yenteel shrugged and then laughed at himself. "Yes, of course, that is what I want to know."

"I don't want to bed either of them." Then she became suspicious. "Or you."

He held up his hand as if denying that thought. "You prefer girls?"

She was shocked for a moment then remembered who she was talking to. "No, Yenteel, I do not prefer girls. Can I ask what this is all about?"

"Just curious."

If it had been anyone else, she would not have believed them, but this was Yenteel and she did accept he might ask purely out of curiosity. She decided to be completely honest, because there was that thought that bothered her from time to time, Yenteel might be able to help.

She put on her bravest face. "Can I tell you something I have never told anyone?"

"In confidence? Of course, Kantees." He spoke the words without his usual insouciance.

"It's something I noticed and I have worried about…" She hesitated. "I … I find that I am not attracted—in *that* way, you know—to anyone. I never have been." She had offered herself to Levin but that was for his sake, not hers, and she was glad he hadn't taken her

up on it. "I thought perhaps there was something wrong with me."
She prayed he wouldn't laugh, or make a joke.

He sat back down by the fire and poked it so sparks went up to
the ceiling which was now covered in soot from the smoke. They
should probably make a hole.

"Honestly, Kantees, it is not something I've experienced and it is
a difficult thing for me to understand—being me." That was almost
a joke but it was at his own expense and he was simply making a
point. She was under the impression he would have relations with
almost anyone given a chance—that sergeant at Jakalain, and
Lintha, of course.

"There is something wrong with me, then," she said. "I knew it.
I always felt different."

"Ha, everyone feels disconnected, Kantees. That's certainly not
just you. I think I might be able to help but I can only explain
through my own experience."

"But you're the complete opposite of me."

"I am, but that makes us the same. If everyone else is somewhere in the middle, I'm at one end and you are at the other. Don't
think I never worried, Kantees, there are men who prefer men,
there are women who prefer women, but both? I thought I was
strange and unnatural for a long time."

"What changed?"

"I realised I was just me."

"Are we the only ones?"

"No. Definitely not."

"But how do you know?"

"I'll accept that it's easier to spot someone who will lay with
either a man or a woman," he said. "But when I lay with a man,
people assume I am a man who likes men. When I lay with a
woman, they assume the other. They don't see a man who likes
both."

She shook her head. "Your experience has no bearing on mine,
Yenteel."

"I haven't finished. Let us suppose there was a woman like you,
and that she was the daughter of a farmer, what would happen to
her?"

Kantees said nothing.

"What would happen to her, Kantees?"

She shrugged. "She would be married off and would be expected to go to her husband's bed."

"What choice would she have?"

"None."

"And she would look like one of so many other women unhappy in the matches made for them. Nothing different about her. What about a Sister of Taymar, what if she was like you? She would spend her life free of a man's bed and no one would even think it odd. Or it could be a Brother, or a farmer's son."

Kantees nodded with some reluctance. "And a slave makes the match dictated by their master. Or is simply forced by anyone in the house. I understand what you're saying."

"I doubt you are alone, Kantees, but if someone is different in their affections—or lack of them—they are difficult to see." He snorted. "They might as well have a blending pattern cast on them."

"You're not as funny as you think you are, Yenteel."

"Yes," he said, "I am."

It rained all that day, and Kantees was shocked awake in the night by thunder. It occurred to her that winter had truly broken, even here. The rain would wash away the snow and melt the ice. Not that it made any difference to their situation.

She stared into the glowing red embers of the fire, listening to the rain and distant thunder rumbling between the mountain slopes. Sheesha and Yenteel both snored while Looesa's breath whistled in his muzzle.

Tiredness seemed to have abandoned her and she was wide awake. She didn't want to move but got up anyway and went to the opening in the wall of the gondola. Above the cracks to the fire mountain's interior the rain glowed with red while steam jetted up in spurts.

Lightning momentarily illuminated the bowl in a flash of brilliant whites and dense black.

"What can I do?" she said into the pouring rain. The only way to stop the Dunor from chasing her was to defeat them so thoroughly they fell apart.

Yenteel had said they were breaking the Great Concordance but that there was no one to enforce it. Only the other Taymalin kingdoms could do that which was why the Dunor were moving in secret. Only a handful of people knew what was happening, and no one was going to believe a runaway slave. They might believe Daybian and Levin but perhaps not. Kantees knew people did not like to face the truth if it was ugly. She was one of them—had been.

But the Dunor desperately wanted her because some Sister of Taymalin had foretold that she would exist and would have some sort of power over the *zirichasa*. If the Dunor could fly the *ziri* fast like the *melinasa* they would be unstoppable. The giant *tekrasa* gave them power and strength to invade but just one *ziri* had defeated dozens of them.

They wanted the *ziri* because of the speed and agility with which they could attack. No castle could stand against them in sufficient quantities. The vision had identified her as if she was the only one who could do it. But Gally had succeeded as well.

It seemed that prophecies did not know everything.

She yawned.

It was what Yenteel had been talking about with the World Pattern. She had already changed everything, because she had run away from Jakalain, because she had rescued Daybian, because she had survived the abomination, its blindness, and its effort to procreate.

She and the Dunor were far beyond any prophecy or vision now.

She went back to her blanket, and covered herself. With her head resting on the *chilafrah* wrapped in a cloth she went back to sleep.

The rain had stopped by morning but the clouds were still scudding at speed across the sky. The sun tried to break through from time to time but always there were more clouds to roll in and prevent it.

Kantees broke her fast with fish they had cooked the previous day. Yenteel was trying to build up a stock so that they could travel more quickly. Sheesha seemed almost back to his old self but had not tried to fly. Kantees wanted to be away. Looesa preened himself and then launched himself into the air as he had done every day to fetch fish for Sheesha.

"No, Looesa!"

It was almost as if the *ziri* had struck a wall, he snaked his head back and did one of his extraordinary turns which resembled falling out of the sky. He landed light as one of his own feathers and stretched his head in Kantees' direction, turning it a little to one side as if he was asking why.

"No more fetching food for Sheesha. He's lazy. He can get his own."

Looesa gave a grunt as if he understood and accepted her explanation. He lumbered back up to the camp and curled up outside the gondola in such a way that he could see what happened. Kantees climbed up on to a rock above the camp where she could see most of the bowl laid out.

"Sheesha!" she called and when his head popped out through a window of the gondola he looked so comical she laughed. The head withdrew immediately as if he was hurt. "Come out here!"

The gondola rocked a little as he made his way to the large hole and pulled himself out on to the stones. He looked at Looesa, paused for a moment to sniff the ground where Looesa had unloaded the stomachful of fish the previous day. Then he looked across at the lake.

"If you want some breakfast you can get it yourself, you lazy lump," said Kantees. She pointed out across the bowl at the lake.

Sheesha eyed her for a moment then looked at Looesa again but the other *ziri* had closed his eyes as if to avoid becoming part of this argument. Sheesha looked back at Kantees.

She conjured a picture in her mind of Sheesha sitting on the rock that Looesa had used and snapping fish from the water. Then she gave the picture to the *ziri*. Sheesha shrieked in defiance.

"Get it yourself!"

Sheesha stared at her and bared his teeth. For a moment Kantees' certainty wavered, as she was reminded of how he had been when she had been infected by the abomination's egg. But she looked him in the eye anyway; Sheesha held it for a moment and then turned away. He moved into a better position to take to the air and stretched his wings.

He held them there, as if he hoped Kantees would relent at the last moment.

Then he pushed himself up and forward with his legs, beat his wings once, and was airborne. He drifted in a long glide down the slope, slowly picking up speed. Then he hit the flat and was out across the lake. Kantees swallowed her fear as the idea that he might fall into the water filtered into her mind. But she did not need to worry.

Sheesha gave one lazy beat of his wings and gained enough height to cross the lake to the other side, but he didn't stop. Wing-beat on wingbeat he kept heading towards the far wall of the bowl, climbing as he went.

Another fear struck Kantees, that he might run away again.

Sheesha changed direction to fly parallel to the far wall and each wingbeat carried him higher. Just before he reached the rim he turned inward again and floated out into the air above the grass-lands below. Kantees smiled, he was so powerful, and so majestic. How could she have thought he would do anything foolish?

Just as she had that thought, he dipped his head, folded his wings almost into his body and plummeted out of the sky. Moments before he hit the ground the wings whipped out again and he came down hard. Kantees launched herself down the slope, ready to leap on Looesa and get to Sheesha as fast as possible.

But the gold and blue *ziri* launched himself from the ground once more, with a *kelukik* in his talons. But he did not bring the animal back to the camp, he flew to Looesa's rock and proceeded to eat his prey in full view of everyone else.

"That *ziri* would make a very bad husband," said Yenteel.

"And I'm the one who's married to him."

1 1

Sheesha returned to the camp, lay down along the length of the gondola and fell asleep. The effort had exhausted him and Kantees knew they would need to stay at least one more day.

She took Looesa out to scout the way south again, because without the *tekrak* they would be able to travel faster. Even if Sheesha could not manage long distances at first.

Since the rain, the landscape had changed completely. The pillars of ice that made up the frozen waterfall where she and Looesa had hidden had broken, and shattered pieces were melting at its base. There was still snow on the upper slopes but, in the valleys, water tumbled and poured in great torrents as the ice melted.

The amount of water was a problem, there was nowhere to set down in the valleys she passed over but she kept heading south until she thought she had gone as far as Sheesha could easily manage in one day. There was no sign of the Talamyrth, the weather was too murky for that. In the end she had identified the tops of a few ridges and some small ledges where they might land and make camp for one night.

They headed back.

. . .

Yenteel had the fire burning intensely as he cooked what appeared to be three *kelukisa* carcasses.

"I don't think Sheesha wanted to be outdone," said Yenteel. "He's been circling the rim all the time you've been gone except for picking up these three."

"He can feel that I want to get going," said Kantees. "Perhaps he knows he needs to build up his strength." She looked at the *ziri*, once more fast asleep. "How many times did he fly round?"

"I didn't count," said Yenteel. "Thirty or forty perhaps."

"Good, we'll leave tomorrow. First light. Looesa, bring fish for Sheesha then eat."

Looesa launched himself into a low glide—copying what Sheesha had done the previous day.

"Sheesha ate another one of these all by himself."

"Well, if he's not hungry that's fine but I want them fed tonight and ready to fly in the morning."

I'm not waiting a single day more.

Next morning the air was much warmer than it had been, though it was still cloudy and the sun was not in view. Sheesha had eaten the night before, as had Looesa and they were both ready to fly. Yenteel had dumped all the cooked meat into a bag because they had nothing to wrap it in. But if things went to plan, they wouldn't need to rely on it for more than a couple of days.

When has anything gone to plan? Kantees shut down that thought as it formed. If things went awry, she would improvise until she was able to make a new plan.

But she did change something.

"I'll ride Sheesha," she said. "You take the food on Looesa."

"I thought you were concerned about Sheesha's strength."

"I was, and I am. But both of us on Looesa is not good."

"He's taken two fully grown men, and you're not even close to Daybian's weight."

"I know, but I'll be better able to judge Sheesha's strength if I'm on his back."

"Why don't you just say that you can't bear to be away from him for a single moment longer?"

She sighed. "Because it's selfish." At that moment Sheesha's huge muzzle came down on her shoulder and he slobbered on her cheek. Kantees shoved at him but failed to shift him. "And he wants me to ride him."

"You may be selfish, Kantees, but I believe Sheesha may be jealous."

Kantees gave up. "Let's go."

Behind her Sheesha nestled down to the ground to make it easier for her to mount. It gave her a strange feeling of satisfaction as she climbed on between his wings with her legs on each side of his neck. Sheesha lifted himself up, pushing against the ground with the elbow joints of his wings.

Kantees checked that Yenteel was also set then gave the command for Sheesha to launch. If the *ziri* was having any difficulty he hid it well. They were in the air and powering across the lake within moments. Sheesha spiralled upwards. They passed the rim of the fire mountain and the other peaks came into view. Kantees checked below and saw Looesa following. She took a bearing on the gondola—without the slightest concern that she would never see it again—and Sheesha headed south.

The change in the weather had wrought something strange in the valleys: they were all filled with mist. Kantees was at a loss to understand it but it was as if they were flying above clouds, with the mountaintops and ridges poking up or closing through the white fog that lay everywhere. It was almost like flying across a white sea filled with islands.

It was not a problem, she had not intended to fly low since that would require more effort on Sheesha's part. She really wanted to go fast but she doubted Sheesha would have the strength to maintain it, even if he was able to achieve it in the first place. It was too soon to try.

Instead, to save his strength, she had him glide as much as possible. It meant they travelled slower but his health was the most important factor. Not that he seemed to be having a problem. She had checked his wounds before they left. They seemed to be well-healed on the surface at least, and she knew the arrows had not penetrated too deeply. The healing pattern had performed its task well enough and perhaps, with the aid of the *chilafrah*, the best it could possibly manage.

But Sheesha would be scarred all his life. The Dunor might want the power to fly the *ziri* at their magical speed but once they were flying at normal speed they were just as vulnerable to an arrow as any creature. And they could not carry armour like a fighting *kichek* because they would not be able to fly. No, she thought, *zirichasa* were not good for attacks against well-defended positions, that would be a job for *tekrasa*.

The day wore on and Kantees became concerned. They had probably passed all of the landing places she had noted on her scouting trip the previous day. Sheesha needed to rest but the sea of white continued below them. Now they seemed to be following a river of fog, it was on the move following ridges and peaks on both sides. More of it flowed over ridges and down to join the main path.

She supposed that if it was behaving like a real river then this was a valley heading south and it probably had a river at its heart. But they could not go down into it because they would be flying blind and could run into anything: trees, low hills, even *Slissac* towers. And if they made it through that they might land in the river itself.

Or they could land on a ridge.

Like that one.

Kantees turned Sheesha towards the peak that barely broke the surface of the fog sea. Jutting out from it was the beginnings of a ridge that quickly plunged out of sight. Moments later Sheesha and Looesa settled on the bare rock. It was not flat but it was the best they could do.

"It's as if the world has turned upside down," said Kantees as she dropped from Sheesha's back. "I've seen fog on the ground from the Ziri Tower but…" Her words trailed away. The fog seemed to lap the ridge they were on like water.

Yenteel said nothing as he dismounted and pulled open his pack. Kantees went round to Sheesha's head and gave him a stern look. "Are you all right?"

Sheesha grumped.

"What does that mean?" said Yenteel between swigs from the water bottle.

"I have no idea." She studied her *ziri*. "I can't see anything wrong."

"Can you *feel* anything wrong?"

"No."

"How much longer can they fly, do you think?"

"Looesa could manage the rest of the day, I'm sure."

"And Sheesha wouldn't let Looesa appear stronger than he is?"

"I can't let him damage himself again, especially not for something like that."

She stared out at the strange landscape and the moving surface of the upside-down cloud filling the valley. A shape seemed to form in the surface of the cloud. "What's that?" But as she said it the shape vanished.

Yenteel turned to look.

"It's gone." Kantees stared at where the movement had been.

"What did it look like?"

"I—no, it was nothing. My imagination."

Unfortunately, her imagination did it again. It was as if the fog formed into a moving arced shape that rose from the surface and then dipped down again.

"That nothing?" said Yenteel.

Another one rose up and disappeared. Like sea creatures coming up through the water and then diving back down again— yet they were made from the fog. It might have been the first one again because it was further along the flowing mists, but when it rose again there was another one a short distance behind it, and then a third to the side.

Moments later the surface of the fog was being broken again and again by the arching shapes as they moved downstream.

Kantees stood transfixed. More and more appeared, some much closer but all seemingly heading in the same direction. Then one reared out of the water close to them and she realised how huge it was, four times the length of Sheesha—and that was just the part she could see. The whole surface of the fog between them and the far side was now filled with them, rising and falling in complete silence. The smooth white of their backs—which seemed to be made of the fog—reflected the light.

And then the numbers reduced, and they disappeared. One final arching back in the distance lifted from the fog and then sank from sight. Nothing remained, it could just have been a dream.

"Did I imagine that?" said Kantees.

"Only if I imagined it as well," said Yenteel. "And, before you ask, no, I have no idea what they were."

"Tahulin," she breathed.

"Ghost patterns? That's a story for children."

"What would you call them then?"

Yenteel shook his head. "Whatever you say."

"Don't be grumpy, Yenteel, they were wonderful."

"I particularly appreciated the part where they didn't try to kill us. I think that's the first time."

She realised she was still staring at the surface of the fog. And tore herself away. She noticed the *ziri* seemed completely unmoved, as if it had been nothing to them at all. She grinned to herself. "I've actually seen Tahulin."

"Are we planning on staying here the night?" asked Yenteel.

"Let's give the *ziri* a chance to recover and we'll move on. This fog has to end some time."

"And if it doesn't?"

"I was thinking we might land through it."

"I realise I'm not very knowledgeable in these matters but that strikes me as a dangerous idea."

"We may not have a choice. But can you check your device, is there a feeding due any time soon?"

"What's that got to do with it?"

"Bear with me."

Kantees turned her attention back to Sheesha and went through the checks she had learned to do when he was racing. Running her hands along his neck and back to make sure there was nothing out of place. Similarly the leading edge of his wings, then checking and straightening his flight feathers—some longer than her arm. Finally his legs and tail. The familiarity of the routine relaxed her and it had the same effect on Sheesha who lay flat and accepted her examination without any complaint—though he looked round when she did the same to Looesa. *Definitely jealous.*

"The next feeding is in a three-day," said Yenteel finally. "Except it might be two days, or four."

"I thought this process was accurate."

Yenteel looked awkward. "It is completely accurate."

"So?"

"I've lost track of the days."

It hadn't occurred to Kantees, for her the passing days did not amount to much. There had never been much need for her to be aware of the day of the year with any precision. To be able to specify the day, and even time, for a feeding you would need to know what day today is.

"That's plenty of time," she said.

They ate some of the cooked meat and then launched into the air again. Once more following the fog-river, Kantees hoped they might catch up with the Tahulin but she doubted they would see them again. Ghost patterns was what some called them, but Tahulin was the old word, as if they were a race of thinking creatures, set apart from the animals.

She remembered that Kevrey considered Tahulin to be completely made up. He did not think they could exist, but Kantees had heard a storyteller who said the Tahulin were a race that had been wiped out by the *Kisharuk*, the monstrous being let loose by the *Slissac* in their arrogance.

Kantees frowned. Of course, most people didn't think the *Kisharuk* was real either. Just a monster used to scare children when they wouldn't go to sleep.

But if the Tahulin were real, why not the *Kisharuk* as well? Or its opposite, the *Kalamuk*?

The afternoon slid away and there was still no sign of the fog ending. Kantees looked at the sky. The cloud cover was complete and the warm wind from the west continued to pour across them, stirring up the surface of the fog.

She closed her eyes and concentrated. For a long time there was nothing but then she caught the hint of a glow. A ley-circle somewhere ahead of them. Hopefully a small one, which would mean it was relatively close.

With a single thought she had Sheesha change his course, she did not need to look to know that Looesa moved with them. She opened her eyes. They were no longer following the river but heading into an area where many more mountain peaks rose through the white mist.

"Kantees?" shouted Yenteel.

"I know what I'm doing." *Probably.*

The ley-circle must be a small one, because it quickly moved to a point below them. Kantees set Sheesha into a slowly descending spiral. She knew she was making a lot of assumptions but they were reasonable ones. Most ley-circles were either on the surface, or close to it—those that weren't were usually below ground. And they were almost always in a flat open area, at least in her experience.

If they kept the spiral tight above the ley-circle, and only descended very slowly, they should land safely.

"Wait!" called Yenteel again.

"What?"

"Is this a ley-circle?"

"Yes."

"Land over there." He pointed at a low peak.

Kantees was a little annoyed he had interrupted her plan but she did as he asked.

"You should have shared your plan," he said pulling his bag from Looesa's back. "I can help." He searched around for a moment and selected a fist-sized stone.

Kantees looked at the failing light. "We don't have a lot of time."

"That's why you should have told me," he said. "Now hush, I need to concentrate."

He pulled out the small book that contained his list of patternings and selected a page. Using charcoal, he drew a complex set of patterns as small as he could on the surface of the stone.

"All right," he said. "When we get back to the circle, let me activate this pattern before we go down."

"What does it do?"

He grinned. "Let's see how you like secrets, Kantees."

She huffed and remounted Sheesha. She barely gave Yenteel time to get in position before launching off the side of the mountain.

A short time later they had re-established their position above the ley-circle. She could even feel Sheesha almost filling up with it. She did not say anything to Yenteel but he had got the message and was busy with his stone. It flashed with light and he dropped it into the fog.

For a moment its brilliant white flare lit up the mist but it sank rapidly out of sight and disappeared.

"That should last until we get down. We'll be able to see the ground as we approach."

Kantees signalled Sheesha to begin his descent and she had to force herself not to hold her breath as they moved from the open air into the murk.

From above, the mist had looked bright and ethereal. Inside it was just like any other cloud: dark and damp. The temperature dropped and she was soon shivering.

1 2

It was impossible to tell how high above the ground they were. The glow from the ley-circle, inside her head, increased so she knew they were still on target but it was so dark she could barely see Sheesha's neck more than an arms-length from her.

"Kantees?"

"I'm here."

"Thanks."

She had never been in any doubt that Looesa was still flying in formation with Sheesha, but Yenteel needed the reassurance, it seemed. Somehow she found that pleasing, he was so self-assured most of the time, to the point of being irritating.

Then she realised she could see the silhouette of Sheesha's whole neck and his wings. There was light below. She peered down but it was just a sourceless brightness. Much more intense than the stone Yenteel had dropped but they knew what effect the proximity of a ley-circle could have on these simple patterns.

Kantees could not ask Sheesha to descend any slower, they were barely dropping even now. So they kept heading down while Kantees stared into the steadily brightening abyss. She realised there was something wrong with the ground and the light a moment before Sheesha landed in water.

She leapt off Sheesha's back and the freezing water went over her head. But instead of fighting her way back up Kantees flipped down head first and pushed herself towards the light. The water bubbled and pressed into her ears. Kantees focused on the light below her and kept swimming down.

The stone Yenteel had enchanted lay on bare stone. This was unquestionably the ley-circle—it glowed all round her—so nothing was likely to be living here. She grabbed the stone, got her feet under her and launched herself upward as her desire to breathe became a concern. As she headed up she could see the shape of Sheesha swimming awkwardly in one direction. She knew *ziri* floated but they did not like to be in water.

This was not going to happen. They had been through too much.

She broke the surface to see Looesa turning in the air above them. He must have reacted quickly enough when Sheesha hit the water. Good. Kantees breathed in a gulp of fresh air.

"Kantees!"

"Which—way—land!"

There was a pause and Looesa went over and away on her left. "This way."

Kantees told Sheesha to move and struck out with an awkward one-handed stroke of her own while she held up the blindingly bright stone. The air was still thick with fog but there seemed less of it this close to the ground. Finally she saw where the water became stone. She and Sheesha pulled themselves out and dripped in the freezing cold. Looesa landed a short distance away.

The immediate vicinity of the ley-circle was bare but there was a low wall about ten paces from the water. She dragged herself over to it and lay the stone down where it would illuminate what they were doing. Her teeth were chattering and she could barely talk as Yenteel came over.

She let him wrap one of their threadbare blankets round her though it did seem to improve the cold. Sheesha shook himself and water went everywhere. Kantees made him lie down and went to curl up under his wing. He would stay warm and she needed him.

He preened a little but not enough to disturb her. A short time later Sheesha lifted his wing and Kantees, who was beginning to warm up, saw Yenteel standing there, a silhouette against the light of the stone.

"Not your best idea," he said.

"We're—on—ground," she said controlling her chattering teeth.

"Granted. I have some news that is good and some less so." Her silence prompted him to continue. "There aren't any woods nearby for you to worry about. There's no wood to make a fire. The stone looks set to glow forever in this place, but it doesn't give off any heat."

"Sheesha—warm."

"Well I'm glad you're happy. Here's some food." He passed her a couple of handfuls of roasted meat. "And I'll see you in the morning."

Sheesha dropped his wing as Kantees wrapped her arms around the meat as if it would give her warmth.

Sunlight filtered between Sheesha's feathers. Kantees opened her eyes and blinked at the brightness. She was damp but not cold. She stood up and pushed the *ziri*'s wing out of the way. There was not a shred of mist or fog. The sky was filled with scudding cloud but the sun seemed to find a way between them and its light was warm on her skin.

The pool in the centre of the ley-circle had ripples blowing across its surface but it was calm enough to clearly reflect the sky. Sheesha snored. She looked back at him, he was probably exhausted after flying all day and ending up in a freezing pool of water.

Looesa was missing but Yenteel had found some wood after all and was busy trying to light it.

"Do we need a fire?"

"It's the principle."

"Is it?"

"Honestly, Kantees, I have no idea how we're doing this."

"Doing what?"

"Surviving."

"I thought I was supposed to be the one with all the doubts."

"Yes, well, last night must have been the last straw for me. I may have travelled but that ley-circle might have been the end of me."

"You don't know how to swim?"

"I never had the need. If Looesa hadn't reacted fast enough I could be drowned now."

"Or shot with an arrow, or tortured by the Dunor, or eaten by an abomination from the Talamyrth. Or any one of a dozen deaths. You're the reason we survived most of them, Yenteel. You think you don't know how to live in the wild? I don't know *anything*. I even have trouble starting a fire. If I had been on my own, I would have died through my own ignorance. I needed you, Gally, Ulina, even Daybian and Levin."

"Well, right now, you've only got me. And I have no idea how we're going to manage."

Kantees looked at the sky. Then the snow-topped mountains surrounding them. Then back at Yenteel. "You don't need to manage. We're on the move and in less than a five-day we'll be at Jakalain. With food cooked by other people, proper clothes, fires lit by other people, and you'll have the pick of the male and female staff for night-time assignations."

"You make it sound like paradise."

She smiled. "Let's face it, Yenteel, compared to this anything would be paradise."

"It would." He laughed. "It probably would."

Looesa returned a short time later with half of something Kantees did not recognise. The carcass was dumped in front of Sheesha's nose, at which point he woke up and consumed it in a couple of swallows.

"I sometimes wonder if the food even touches the sides on the way down," she commented as she and Yenteel chewed their cold meat. Strangely, the fire improved her mood. The light wind and sunshine dried her out and she ran her hand over her scalp. It was slightly bristly again, she looked forward to the next head-shave from Ulina and her wicked little knife.

Kantees allowed some time for *zirichak* digestion to process their food and they set off again.

"I'm going to leave the stone here," said Yenteel.

"Why?"

"Because one day someone is going to come past here in the evening or early morning, and they'll see the light. They'll wonder who made it."

"Won't the rain wash the patterns off eventually?"

Yenteel looked thoughtful then moved the stone to a small natural alcove in the wall. "Now it'll last longer."

Kantees shook her head. "I don't understand."

"I want my life to have some meaning into the future."

"Even though no one will know who made it—assuming it's ever discovered—and will care even less?"

"You have no appreciation of the future, Kantees," he said as he climbed up between Looesa's wings.

"Your mood didn't last long."

"That was a good speech you gave me," he said. "I appreciated it."

They took to the air and Kantees turned them south again.

The dark green of the Talamyrth came into view shortly after the sun had reached its highest point, and not long after that the mountains gave way to hills and the flat green of the monstrous forest was laid out in front of them.

Kantees shivered. She might make an unnecessary fuss about there being murderous creatures in any size of woods they happened to encounter. But in the case of the Talamyrth, there were monsters and of that there was no doubt whatsoever.

Nothing would make her fly over that expanse of evil trees, but they did not have to. Once they were through the mountains they turned east and followed a line between trees and hills.

When they had come this way from Jakalain it had not taken more than a day for them to reach the eastern edge of the Talamyrth—and they had made the mistake of trying to fly over it. It had taken another full day to do that, though she had not yet discovered the *ziri*'s magic. So at Sheesha's reduced flying speed Kantees thought they probably had two more days of flying ahead of them. Though it might be less.

Now they had descended from the heights of the mountains the air was decidedly warmer, and she appreciated it. Sheesha seemed to be managing the flight well enough though Kantees suspected he would keep flying until he fell out of the sky just to prove he was the strongest. It was a common thread among the males she had encountered.

Which led her to think about the man who had followed her from Cliffedge down towards Dakastown, and then it struck her. He was the man she had recognised in charge of the armsmen who had sprung the trap at Watching Pass. So, he was trying to capture her before, but who was he?

She shook her head. It didn't matter who he was, because she now knew without a doubt he was part of the Dunor. It came to her with sudden clarity: *he has been studying Sheesha and me*. Perhaps he had tried to catch her in the town but when that failed he must have realised he was up against something stronger than he first thought. A slave girl on a stolen *ziri*? How difficult would someone like that be to capture?

Much harder than he thought. So he'd followed and watched.

There was something that had happened in Dakastown, she thought hard, the attack by the Farahalek had been awkward and the Farahalek had not followed up. From what she knew of them, though mostly hearsay and rumour, they would not have assumed she was dead unless they had seen her body, and would have made sure that any possible escape was prevented.

The attack had almost killed her and Levin but when they survived, and were easy targets, no Farahalek had turned up to finish the job. The Dunor did not want her dead. Perhaps this agent of the Dunor had stopped the attack. It was thin reasoning but it made a kind of sense.

So this man had seen her fighting for her life with Sheesha and with Levin.

She had flown back to Jakalain but he could have used a Patterner's path and been there before her. But then the other Farahalek had been attacking the *tekrak* carrying Yenteel, Gally, Levin and Tenical.

Why would they be trying to kill her on the one hand and merely capture her on the other?

It was difficult to understand what was happening—but from what she now understood, the Dunor was a group of powerful Taymalin houses. What if they didn't agree on the right way forward? Perhaps some of them wanted to kill her while others wanted to catch her.

This man who had followed her had learnt enough about her that he had managed to set a trap that had almost been successful. He recognised that she was stupid—no, not stupid, just inexperienced and that she did not understand what she was up against.

Well, each encounter that she survived taught her something new. He may have been learning about her, but she had a better understanding of the Dunor too. And she knew things about the *ziri* that would never have been discovered if they had not pursued her.

It was always the same in the stories, acting on a prophecy was always the thing that brought it about. That was the lesson of every tale the storytellers told.

Did that mean she was the hero? She smiled. No, she was no hero, she had been running away the whole time. Daybian wore the mantle of hero far better than she did. She found that she was quite looking forward to seeing both him and Levin again—and that was quite surprising.

They reached the eastern edge of the Talamyrth at about the same time that Kantees thought they'd better find somewhere to camp for the night. A river, bloated with the melting winter snow, emerged from the hills so she turned the *ziri* and headed into the mountains, intent on having a good distance between their camp and the forest. She wanted nothing sneaking out of the dark wood to attack them.

There was a tall scarp cutting through the hills marking a significant increase in height. The swollen waters of the river thundered over it. Kantees nodded in satisfaction, that should provide a definite barrier to abominations from the forest.

Then there were lights. Kantees stared at the large village, it might even be called a town, that lay in the valley carved by this river. The rushing water lapped at a bank constructed to protect the buildings and dozens of people were busy in the dwindling daylight, shoring it up and dropping buckets of mud on to sections that were being eroded by the flood.

Some looked up as the *ziri* went over. One or two dropped what they were doing and ran towards the buildings, but most of the others went back to work. Kantees directed Sheesha to head for the higher ground on the other side of the town, where the buildings were dry.

They set down outside the town. Lights burned in the houses and she could hear constant shouts, as well as the roaring of the waterfall. She told Sheesha and Looesa to remain, then, with Yenteel she headed towards the river.

"What are we doing?" he asked.

"Helping."

"I thought you wanted to get to Jakalain."

"Yes, of course, but we have to stop for the night anyway."

A man ran past them, glanced their way, then just headed towards the river at a faster pace.

"Taymalin," said Yenteel.

"Some of my best friends are Taymalin," said Kantees. "And yours too."

They stepped out from between the last row of houses. The ground was sodden and planks of wood had been set on stones to provide footing out of the river. In the dying light of the sun behind them, the huge expanse of the river lay before them, almost at their eyeline. Only the mud bank was higher, and only in places.

Kantees looked around until she saw someone standing on the hull of an upturned boat. He became suddenly very animated and pointed at a place upstream. Kantees looked and saw water slopping over the bank. Some groups were simply trying to keep the mud bank high enough to keep the water out. They were the ones running about frantically with heavy buckets—they must be gathering the mud from somewhere.

A smaller number of men were working to put in poles on the water-side of the bank. As a more permanent form of barrier, but it was slow work and they were still fighting the flood as they did it. Kantees could not see how they could win this fight.

"We can't help here," said Yenteel. "We might as well just grab a mud bucket and start running."

"You've always made a protective pattern in the form of a circle."

"What?"

"Why do you do that?"

"Because you always want to protect yourself from attacks on all sides. What's the point of a gate if there's no wall?"

"What if the enemy was only ever going to come from one side?"

Yenteel was not a fool. "Is there a ley-circle here? I couldn't do it on my own. I don't even know if it will work in a line."

"There is but it's not close, we have the *chilafrah*."

"And the fact that every time we've used a pattern with too much power we've nearly killed ourselves?

"This is different."

"It always is."

With that she headed along the boards upstream with Yenteel following like a *ziri* in formation.

They reached a place where the natural height of the land kept the water at bay. This was where the construction of the mud bank began, but here it was solid and there was no one working on it.

"If the power in the *chilafrah* fails we will achieve nothing."

"We'll have tried," said Kantees. "And that's better than doing nothing."

Kantees pulled the dark unimpressive cube from her backpack while Yenteel found something to inscribe the patterns.

"A nail," he said with considerable pleasure. "Better than a stick." Then he stared at the ground as if he was at a loss.

"Just start the pattern," said Kantees. "When you finish the sequence, activate it and we'll see what happens."

It took him a couple of minutes to get the sequence down, scratched into the rock and soil. He shook his head and looked at where the ground turned into mud. "I can't see how this is going to work."

"One thing at a time, Yenteel, these people need our help and if this works they'll be able to use all their people to put in stronger defences."

He nodded. "Yes, sorry." He focused on the pattern and chanted quietly. A light burgeoned at his end. It flickered along the pattern like a flame across wood that was not ready to burn but it gave him more confidence and he chanted more loudly. From Kantees' angle, the air above the pattern looked as if it had turned to glass with a blue-green tint.

"It's working," said Yenteel with considerable surprise. He reached out, the wall colour intensified where his fingers touched. He ran them along it, shaking his head. Then he turned and grinned at Kantees. "You were right."

"So far. Step back, I'm going to see if the *chilafrah* will help otherwise this will be a very short-lived wall." Kantees placed the unimpressive lump of stone against the end of the pattern. Nothing happened. "Perhaps there's nothing left," she said.

"No, something changed." He reached out again. The wall flared where he touched and he snatched his fingers back.

"Did it hurt?"

"Tingles."

"Well, I hope that's all," she said. "Start on the next sequence. If you make the patterns larger, you'll be able to cover more distance."

Yenteel set to work, cautiously at first in case the wall moved with the patterns as he drew them, but the wall did not extend.

"This is the moment of truth," he said as he finished the last one in the sequence.

Kantees was well aware that if the new section did not somehow link to the previous one their effort would be wasted. But while she was worrying over what might go wrong, Yenteel had started his chant and moments later they had a new section of wall. Yenteel touched it tentatively and confirmed it was as strong as the first section. They had merged.

"I'm going to stay with the *chilafrah*," said Kantees. "You work your way along—" *and we'll hope it works just as well on mud,* "—and if anyone wants to talk to you, just send them to me."

Yenteel took a deep breath and set about inscribing the next group of patterns.

Kantees stood up and put her foot on the *chilafrah*. No wonder Tenical had said it was worth a kingdom, with this you could take the power of a ley-circle with you. And it would make you the target of anyone who coveted it.

Yenteel rapidly finished the next section and was already into the mud. She could see that he had taken her advice and made the symbols larger, and more stretched out too. That would probably work better on a soft surface.

Every now and then water from the river would splash up and where before it would have landed on the ground, now it was hitting the barrier and sliding down it like rain. She was a little concerned that the wall might become unstable and fall over. She just did not know how these things worked.

Their work was attracting attention.

People were stopping to stare for a moment then going on with whatever they were doing to help save the town. There was a lot of trouble further down where the mud wall had been breached and water had flooded through, eroding the wall even more as it went.

Kantees hoped they would be in time.

As she expected the man who had been standing on the boat and giving instructions was heading her way through the gloom. He wasn't running, but he was moving fast.

"You, Kadralin! Who are you and what are you doing here?"

She had rehearsed her reply to the expected question. "I am Kantees of the Ziri and I am trying to help you save your town from flooding. I and my patterner are building a wall of protection the river cannot penetrate. That will give you enough time to build stronger defences without having to keep the river back."

He stared at her for a moment. When he spoke again his voice was considerably less abrasive. "Will it work?"

"It's already working." She pointed at Yenteel who was a good distance away now and the wall glowed softly in the darkening night.

"Why?"

"You're asking that now when you should be making plans to use this respite?"

"I need to know. You are Kadralin, and you ride the *zirichasa*, why would you be a friend?"

"You needed help. I am giving it."

He did not seem convinced but did not push it. "Can we help your patterner?"

"He needs to mark the patterns but mud is not a good surface for that. Flat stones, or wood at intervals would speed his progress. And if you have a patterner among you, they could also work. In fact it does not even need to be a patterner, anyone who can create the likeness of the symbols being used."

He nodded. "I will find women for that work, the men are still needed for shoring up the wall." He took three purposeful strides back towards the town then stopped and looked back. "Thank you."

"Thank me when it's done."

13

$\mathcal{I}$t happened exactly as the man said. While the men continued to keep the wall in one piece and block the breach that had been made, first one then more women arrived; most scoured the town to find found flat items that could be drawn on, while six others spent their time copying the symbols Yenteel was drawing.

The process reached the stage where there was a constant supply of surfaces, the symbols were being drawn, one woman carefully arranged them in order and made sure an even number of each were being created. She supplied Yenteel who simply placed them, chanted a few times to activate the pattern and the wall grew longer at a remarkable pace.

The night became completely dark but the wall provided its own illumination for the women to work by. Kantees had no idea how much strength the *chilafrah* could provide but there seemed to be no sign of it diminishing. She had been certain that Tenical had drained it, but now it seemed as strong as ever. The effect of the wall was becoming more pronounced, it was now into the worst affected area and water was sloshing against it on one side but from the very happy reactions of the townsfolk and the way they worked even harder, she guessed the water was not getting through.

They had not been able to dig under the wall of protection when they had been trapped by their own spell in the ley-circle in the Talamyrth, it must go down a distance as well as up. Though, in the Talamyrth, the protective wall had reached so high the *ziri* could not even fly out of it, here it seemed to peter out at perhaps twice the height of a man. Perhaps the *chilafrah* was not as strong as a ley-circle after all.

The wall reached the breach. The river curved a little and it was at the bend that it had broken through, but that meant Kantees could see. The men were still working to repair the hole and there was some heated discussion between them and Yenteel—and the woman assisting him—as the work stopped. The man in charge got down from his boat and went to join Yenteel and the workers.

In the end they ceased their work and allowed Yenteel to place the next set of patterns. Water was flowing through the gap but Yenteel chanted a few times. The wall sprang up and Kantees saw the water flow up the side of it as if it was surprised it couldn't get through, then it settled back and stayed on its own side.

Yenteel continued to build beyond the breach until the natural riverbank was tall enough to resist the river alone. An old woman brought Kantees a mug of something warming.

"Thank you."

"I have never seen such a thing."

"Neither have we."

Kantees turned her attention back to the wall and two more segments had been added already but she could no longer seen Yenteel. It seemed he had stopped. The men who had been trying to fill the breach were now hard at work bringing stones and wood round to the river side to build up the defences.

"You have given us service unbidden," said the woman.

Kantees shook her head. "I couldn't ignore your plight, it would have been inhuman."

"There are many that would have passed us by."

"And others that would help, I'm not special."

"You're a Kadralin flying a *zirichak*," said the woman, her voice was low and carried power. "That was never a good omen in the old days. Your people raided the villages, farms and even the town itself."

"These are new days, mother," she said carefully. "The Kadralin of old have been punished for their crimes and the right to ride the *ziri* was stripped from them. That is why they have not visited you in many years."

The old woman nodded, which was a relief because Kantees had only been guessing, but the woman stayed silent, expecting more.

"I am Kantees of the Ziri. I have freed my people from their bondage, and it is my pledge that the old days will not return."

"I hold you at your word, Kantees of the Ziri."

The woman walked off into the dark with Kantees staring after her. The conversation had unnerved her though she had not felt any malice from the woman. Just doubt and suspicion, which was bad enough.

What have I just done?

She asked herself the question but she had a good idea of the answer. She had just taken responsibility for the behaviour of all the Kadralin in the mountains. Her people. She was relieved when she saw Yenteel walking along the inside of the wall, half of him lit by the eerie blue-green light of the protective wall. He was grinning.

"We did it."

She smiled. "We did."

She glanced down the river again and the men were still hard at work driving stakes into the mud.

Yenteel touched the wall again, it sparked at him. "Ow."

Kantees shook her head. "Why did you do that again?"

"To convince myself that it really worked." He turned his head and looked back into the dark. Kantees thought she could see someone there, lurking, or perhaps waiting. "They said it was your idea to have people making the symbols in advance so I just had to place and activate them."

"I did suggest it. I thought it might make the process go faster."

"I've never heard of anyone doing that."

"It seemed obvious."

"The Taymalin patterners wouldn't do that."

"Too arrogant?"

"The pattern is their creation. They don't like sharing."

"That's good to know."

Yenteel looked over his shoulder again.

"Someone waiting for you?"

"Yes, but I thought I should come back."

"Who is that?"

"Her name's Ithamel."

"Not one of those heavily muscled men?"

He stared at her. "I think you're teasing me."

Kantees grinned. "Was this the one doing the sorting out of the symbols?"

"She's a healer."

"And you're in need of some healing?"

"Can't go amiss."

"I don't mind, Yenteel, you don't have to ask my permission."

"I thought you might want company, it's a bit lonely out here."

"It's surprising who comes by."

"Hagata, the wise woman. Ithamel saw her."

"Didn't you want to bed her instead? In case you were given new and precious patterning scrolls?"

"The night is long, Kantees. There's always the chance for two," he said. "And perhaps a young muscled ditch digger."

"Go and be healed, Yenteel."

Instead of turning away, Yenteel turned to face her directly and bowed.

"Stop it. What's that for?"

"You, Mistress Kantees of the Ziri. I believe you may be one of the finest people I have ever known, and—" he stood up straight before moving closer, "—I have known a lot of people."

"You're an idiot."

"A word to the wise, Kantees, you will have to learn to accept the service of others."

"I'm nobody."

"You can go on thinking that, but you cannot behave that way."

"Just go."

"Are you sure you aren't interested in healing?"

"Not with you, and certainly not with her and you!"

"I'm sure I could find some young and well-muscled fellow who would serve."

Kantees put her hand gently on his shoulder. "Don't. Not even as a joke."

"Sorry. But bear in mind what I said."

"About the healing?"

"About accepting the service of others. You've made a difference here."

"Changed the pattern?"

"Aye, yes, definitely changed the pattern."

Kantees came to the conclusion that while Yenteel might not have found a 'young man' for her, he and the woman had made some suggestions. He understood that Kantees did not want to leave the *chilafrah* and that it would be a long time before the repairs to the bank were complete, and it was not long before more women arrived.

The first few carried the makings for a fire—presumably from their homes since it was bone dry—and it was soon blazing. Then came hot drinks and food. It was the best food Kantees had eaten in many a five-day and she ate until she could not eat any more. The women did not speak to her or look her in the eye. Their attitude reminded Kantees of the way servants always behaved to their masters and mistresses. But she did not ignore what Yenteel had said. She was on a new path now where every step was a change in the World Pattern. She let them treat her as someone important because that was what the new path demanded.

Someone brought a chair and she sat with her back to the wall, over the *chilafrah* and face to the fire. She thought of Sheesha and Looesa on the edge of the town.

She stood up and summoned them.

Most of the women fled, some with screams, as Sheesha and Looesa touched down, their wings causing the fire's flames to stream out sideways and roar with heat, scattering sparks. For the benefit of the women who stayed, mostly younger ones, Kantees went over to

Sheesha and stroked his snout. He settled on to the rock with Looesa a little distance behind him.

Kantees scratched him and then put her arms around his neck. The way he smelled was comforting, reminding her of all those years in the Ziri Tower when she had no concerns beyond making sure he was clean and ready for the next race.

When she was a slave.

She turned back to the fire. Three girls—she thought of them as younger even though they were probably her own age—stood off to one side in deference but they did not have to speak for Kantees to know what they wanted.

Kantees beckoned to them. They hesitated, of course, because who would not when faced with such a monster. He could bite them in two if he had a mind to do it. But Kantees knew his mind and Sheesha just wanted attention. He was as vain as any male.

One girl, blonde hair twisted into a ponytail, was bolder than the others and stepped forward. Kantees stroked Sheesha's neck, showing that she must go with the lie of the feathers. Kantees stepped back and kept one eye on the *chilafrah* and the other on the girl. Perhaps this hadn't been the best idea.

The girl approached to where she was within biting distance of Sheesha's sinuous neck. Then the girl bowed almost as if she was letting herself be a sacrifice if the monstrous beast wanted her. Sheesha turned his head and sniffed at the girl's hair. She trembled.

"His name is Sheesha," said Kantees. "Tell him yours."

The girl stood slowly. Sheesha did not move and she was face to face with him. When she spoke her voice wavered. "Lord Sheesha, I am Helka, daughter of Ithamel, daughter of Hagata."

Kantees could not believe this was a coincidence—but did it need to be? If power over the patterns ran in this family perhaps Helka was drawn to the *ziri* for that very reason?

"He likes to be stroked, Helka, like any male no matter how strong or mighty."

The girl smiled briefly and took a tentative step to his side and placed her hand on the small feathers where they first emerged from his skin and ran it backwards. Kantees could see she was being so careful he probably had not even felt it.

"Also, like any male, if you are too gentle he does not even notice."

Helka stroked harder. Sheesha turned his head to move her hand further round.

"He has an itch, scratch gently."

The other two girls giggled, and Kantees could see why. No matter how big and fierce Sheesha looked, when he wanted to be scratched he was like the most docile *kelukik*.

Kantees gestured for the other girls to come forward. They also bowed and introduced themselves—Marla and Jynolee—referring to the *ziri* as "Lord Sheesha". Kantees told Looesa to move forward and he came up beside her, slightly back from Sheesha. With one girl on each side of Sheesha's head Jynolee changed to the other *ziri* after Kantees introduced him.

Satisfied that no one was going to get eaten, Kantees went back to the chair where she could watch what was happening and make sure the *chilafrah* was not disturbed.

Both the *ziri* were now lying down with their neck and head along the ground. The girls had become confident enough to lean on them though none had dared to get astride. Kantees was satisfied with that.

The first one, Helka, finally stepped away from Sheesha and came up to Kantees. She stood a respectful distance away and bowed.

"Lady Kantees of the Ziri…"

Kantees bit down her urge to tell the girl to just use her name. "What?"

"My grandmother said you ride the *zirichak*."

"That's right."

"My grandmother said Kadralin would come from the mountains riding the *zirichasa* and attack the towns and villages, stealing and killing the Taymalin. We are trained in bow and knife to protect our town and our honour."

"Your grandmother does not lie." *I don't think she's lying, but stories grow in the telling, it might be an exaggeration.*

"But you helped us."

"I am not from the mountains though they are my people. As I explained to your grandmother, the Kadralin who lived there had their ability to ride taken from them and they have been punished. That was long ago, these are new days and things have changed."

The girl paused as if she was weighing her words. "How much have things changed, Lady Kantees?"

She's sly, I can see where this is going. "You want to know if you can ride the *ziri*."

The expression on her face was everything Kantees needed. The girl nodded dumbly as if she had no idea how transparent she was in her thinking.

"It is possible. Send your mother to me in the morning and we will discuss it."

1 4

───────

$\mathcal{S}$ometime around midnight a man had come to tell her they had finished their work and that she could erase the pattern. For a moment she had wished Yenteel was there but he was no doubt enjoying his time of "healing".

Kantees simply reached down and separated the *chilafrah* from the wall. The pattern collapsed and vanished. The night became darker but she could hear the water sloshing along the bank. She hoped their work had been successful because otherwise they would have to rouse Yenteel.

Someone brought oil lamps and they checked the length of the bank. Then they went back into the town and the place became quiet. Kantees left the warmth of the fire and found sleep under Sheesha's wing.

She eventually woke to the sound of activity in the town. Talking, shouting, someone singing a work song. Even laughter. More than the sounds were the smells. Cooking fires, and bread dominated; it reminded her of Jakalain. Especially surrounded by the smell of Sheesha.

Kantees pushed his wing out of the way and climbed out on to the stony ground. The day was bright though a high layer of cloud blocked the sun. Now that she could see clearly, the buildings along the riverbank were store houses with wide doors. Even as she watched, some men were pulling a boat from inside one of them. She took a moment to look at the bank and could see all the new construction further along. It looked sturdy with trunks driven deep into the mud, but men were still working on the inland side adding more rocks.

At least she had given them a chance to protect themselves.

Looesa was lying a short distance away, wide awake, while children stared at him and one of the girls from last night prevented them from jumping all over him or pulling his feathers. She had certainly overcome any fear of the beast. Unlike Helka, who was very clearly of Taymalin descent, this one—Kantees finally remembered her name was Jynolee—had darker skin and features that hinted of some Kadralin ancestors.

The marauders had done more than simply raided. The idea that perhaps the Kadralin were not the perfection she had imagined them to be was difficult to deal with. And it was only because of the abomination they had not continued to raid.

Kantees knew her promise that nothing like that would happen again was not the best idea. She doubted the plateau of the *Slissac* tower was the only place in which the Kadralin lived, even if it was most likely to be the centre. What right did she have to make these promises?

She sighed and stared at the rushing water and then back at the buildings of the town.

The people in the village must have noticed she was up because a small group of women arrived carrying various plates and bowls including a bowl of steaming *tasa*, Kantees could smell it before anything else, an aroma pungent enough to clear the head of any congestion and clear the body of tiredness. Drink enough of it and its smell came out of the very pores of the body.

Kantees could take it or leave it, which was just as well because it did not come cheap. Which meant the townsfolk were doing her an honour by bringing her a bowl of it.

A table was produced, she was asked which direction she would like to face, and when she chose the town that seemed to please them. In truth it was because there was so much activity going on there it would be far more interesting than facing the water—and with all the noises behind her she would worry about being surprised by someone.

But it was an arrangement that seemed to work for everyone so there was no reason to worry.

If Kantees had been hungry for the last few five-days it took almost no time at all for her to become completely full, washing each mouthful down with *tasa*. She could not eat all the breads, pieces of roasted meats and fried fat. When Yenteel arrived a short time later—looking tired but relaxed, and much cleaner than Kantees—he ate what was left. The women withdrew to a polite distance out of earshot.

"Did you sleep well?" she asked, simply because he had, as yet, said nothing.

"Eventually."

Kantees gave him her best withering look but he just grinned. She changed the subject. "Did you find out what this place is called by any chance?"

"Riverrush."

"Good name," she said glancing at the unending water pouring past them, then at where the men were working on the boat. They had turned it over and were applying something to its body. It did not look as if they intended to take it out on the river. "Are there patterns for boats?"

"Of course," said Yenteel, "but like most of these things, they're meaningless. People inscribe what might or might not be a proper pattern but even if they have the skill to activate it, it doesn't last. It's like a promise. Easily broken."

"Unless they have a *chilafrah*." Kantees glanced at her backpack.

"It's a powerful thing."

"Dangerous."

He gave a grim smile. "Mostly to whoever holds it."

She saw Yenteel staring at the girl looking after Looesa.

"Who's she?" he said.

"I would appreciate it if you left her alone."

"I never go where I'm not invited, Kantees."

"Her name's Jynolee, a friend of Helka."

"Oh, Ithamel's daughter, yes I met her this morning. There's another daughter, Marta."

"And how did they feel about their mother spending the night with you?"

"I didn't notice any ill feeling. Nor from Hagata. They rule this place."

"Not the man we saw?"

"Loren. Yes, he's in charge. They call him the townmaster. But he doesn't do anything without consulting with the women first."

"Wise fellow."

"Helka wants to ride the *ziri*," said Yenteel.

"I know."

"And?"

"I think Jynolee will be better at it." Kantees looked at how the girl was with Looesa, confident and relaxed, even nudging him to move—and he obeyed. "But I'll take Helka too."

"She's ambitious, sees you as a rung to gain power."

"She's mistaken about that," said Kantees.

"Name the *Kisharuk*…" muttered Yenteel.

Kantees turned her head to see the women, Hagata, Ithamel, Helka and Marta. Seeing them all together the resemblance was clear. "Marta's the younger sister?"

"She is."

Kantees stood as they approach and all four bowed.

"Greetings, Kantees of the Ziri." At that moment there was an outbreak of loud giggling from the direction of Looesa. The *ziri* was allowing one of the very small children to slide down his neck, with Jynolee holding their hands. Kantees smiled. Definitely, Jynolee.

She summoned Sheesha, and the giggles turned to little screams as the big *ziri* got up on to his back legs and stretched his wings so far they went over the top of Looesa's playmates. Then he shook himself and waddled over to stand behind Kantees.

"Good morning, wise women of Riverrush."

Hagata kept her eyes on Kantees but the other three kept

looking up at Sheesha. He was such a show-off. Marta did not look happy.

Kantees turned. "Lie down, Sheesha."

He did as he was told but arranged himself so that his head lay along the ground next to her.

Kantees looked over to Looesa. "Jynolee! Take Looesa up the hill behind the town. He will become hungry soon and want to hunt. Just let him go."

"Yes, Lady Kantees."

Ithamel spoke quietly to her daughters who followed the *ziri* and the laughing children who chased after him, jumping over his tail. And occasionally landing on it. Kantees was impressed with how good he was being.

"Do you want me to go, Lady Kantees?" said Yenteel.

"No," she said and then added more quietly, "Don't let me say anything stupid."

"That might be hard."

"I could have Sheesha bite off your head."

"I will do my best, Lady."

Again she was forced to accept the title. This was the path she had chosen, and every step reinforced it. If she accepted the changes, she must accept the consequences.

He indicated the chair and had her sit down while the other women stood. Kantees felt as if she was holding court just as the Lord and Lady did at Jakalain.

"Lady Kantees of the Ziri," began Hagata. "My granddaughter has asked that she may travel with you that she might learn to ride the *zirichasa*."

"She said she wanted to ride," said Kantees.

"She is a bold girl," said Ithamel. "I hope you were not insulted."

Kantees wanted to say that, as a runaway slave, how could she possibly be insulted. But those were not words she could use. "Of course not, Ithamel. We are women, we do not need to be easily insulted like men; our honour goes beyond the opinions of others. She asked me because she is ambitious, and she thinks I am a path she can use."

"You understand her," said Hagata. "That is good, yet you are still willing to take her?"

"I am willing for her to travel with me, if you are willing to let her go, but I cannot promise the path she has chosen will lead where she wishes it to go."

"She will do better with you than remaining here where she chafes against barriers she can neither see nor break," said Ithamel. "And it will be a boon to her sister."

"Will you protect her honour?" said Hagata.

"I cannot promise that," said Kantees. "She is a woman and will make her own choices. Nor can I promise to protect her life. My path has always been one of danger and those who accompany me are not shielded from it."

Hagata nodded. "The world is dangerous."

Kantees noticed Ithamel was looking at Yenteel, but she could not decipher her expression.

Ithamel turned back to Kantees. "Can you, at least, promise to protect her from those in your retinue?"

Ah. "I can do that. And I will promise to do my best on the other matters."

Ithamel nodded. "And where will you go, Kantees of the Ziri?"

"I am returning to Jakalain, and from there I cannot say where I will go."

"When do you plan to leave?" said Hagata.

"The *ziri* must feed and digest," said Kantees. "I had intended to be in Jakalain by nightfall but I do not think that will happen now. Perhaps we may impose on the hospitality of your town and stay another night, then leave as soon as we have broken our fast in the morning?"

It was Hagata who responded. "You and your patterner have provided us a great service, Kantees of the Ziri. If you chose to spend a ten-day, no one would begrudge you."

Kantees stood up, the women made their goodbyes and departed.

"Of course, I wouldn't touch the girl," said Yenteel.

"I know."

She sent Sheesha off to find some food, and encouraged him to search a good distance from the town. She didn't want the two of them scaring the locals, or eating their livestock. The hospitality might become strained.

With Yenteel in tow, Kantees wandered up through the town towards the fields on the slopes. She could see the power of the ley-circle lurking there. The people they came across bowed, or curtsied, or simply looked scared and ran. It was a new experience for Kantees, though she had had a hint of it in Dakastown when the cart-driver had recognised her.

"Do you really want another day's delay?" said Yenteel.

"Not really, but another day of rest would be good for Sheesha and we would just end up camping in the mountains. It's safer here, and we can make up the time tomorrow."

"And the food is good," said Yenteel.

"I'm sure you won't object to more healing."

Yenteel laughed. "I find Ithamel's healing to be very much to my taste."

The quality of the buildings improved as they moved away from the river and up the slope. She guessed the town must be home to several hundred inhabitants, probably with farms and villages stretching out around it. Yet it was cut-off from the rest of the world despite the local ley-circle. There had not even been a flicker of interest from Hagata or Ithamel when she had mentioned Jakalain. If she were to guess, Kantees suspected Riverrush was not tithed to any major house. It was simply forgotten.

"Is there a feeding soon?" she asked as they left the buildings behind. A group of children played a game of catch-me around a small clump of trees. Jynolee was sitting in the grass looking out towards the mountains. Kantees smiled. She knew that look, and somehow she doubted Helka would ever stare that way after the *ziri*.

"Just missed one," said Yenteel, looking up from his device.

"Do we know if any big ones are due?"

"Spring usually produces one or two major feedings at the larger circles in this part of the world."

Kantees nodded. "I wish we knew where."

"Does it matter?"

"It might."

The glow of the ley-circle lay off to their left, somewhere over the ridge.

Jynolee had noticed them. She jumped up and brushed off her skirts, then hurried down the slope. She bowed as she approached.

"Lady Kantees, Looesa has gone into the mountains to feed."

"You like the *ziri*?"

Jynolee looked down at the ground and held one hand tightly in the other. "I do. I mean, I was scared at first but Looesa is so gentle and he likes to play."

Kantees smiled. "He does, and it's been a long time since he had the opportunity. I am glad that we came to your town."

The girl looked very serious. "We are honoured by your visit, Lady Kantees."

Kantees turned in the direction of the ley-circle and headed towards the low ridge. Yenteel and Jynolee followed.

"Do you get many visitors here, Jynolee?"

"We have a fair once each moon-turn, the farmers and traders from the land around come to the town."

They reached the top and Kantees paused. The slope rolled down into a set of fields striped with different crops. A set of standing stones marked a circular boundary but she could not see a clearly defined ley-circle within it.

"Does anyone travel the patterner's path?"

Jynolee did not respond. Kantees turned to look at her. "I am so sorry, Lady Kantees, I do not know what that is."

"A magical path between ley-circles?"

Jynolee looked no wiser. Kantees frowned and the girl took a step back as if she was threatened. Kantees forced herself to smile. "I'm not angry, Jynolee. I just thought everyone knew about the patterner's path."

Kantees turned to look at the place where the ley-circle should be. The glow was there but … no. She concentrated and found the glow of the circle originated above the ground. She shook her head, then walked forward keeping her mind's eye on the power she could see.

By the time she reached the outer marker, a worn and ancient stone like a giant's thumb, she could see the ley-circle was at least four man-heights above the ground. She had heard of this.

"The circle is above the ground?" said Yenteel.

"It is." She pointed then turned to Jynolee who was staring at her in mute astonishment. "When there's a feeding, the mother's milk stops up there?"

"You can see it?" breathed Jynolee.

"Yes."

If Jynolee had been impressed with Kantees before, she now gave the impression she was in the presence of a goddess.

"Does the mother's milk stop up there?" Kantees repeated.

Jynolee nodded.

"Fascinating," said Yenteel. "The plants all look normal, there's even grass growing underneath."

Kantees walked further in until she was directly under the glow. And then wondered if the *chilafrah* was taking in more power. She hadn't mentioned it to Yenteel but it was the fact she wasn't dead that convinced her the *chilafrah* could take in a vast amount of power. When she had intentionally fallen into the Mother's milk at the *Slissac* tower she should have died. It was the *chilafrah* that had saved her. It must have filled with the milk, taking it instead of her. Yes, the healing pattern had been triggered and also worked, but the majority of the power had filled the artefact.

Tenical said a *chilafrah* was like a reservoir. If that was the case then it must be filled and a ley-circle was where that could happen. Perhaps every time she stood in a ley-circle with the *chilafrah*, it took in the milk.

Maintaining the protective pattern last night would probably have consumed much of the reservoir so she had been hoping she might be able to fill it once more here. But she had a feeling she needed to be right in the circle for that to happen.

They had a big ley-circle at Jakalain and that was on the ground. She could use that.

Yenteel had joined her. "Can you feel anything?"

Kantees nodded and turned back to Jynolee who had not come any further than the marker stone.

"No visitors from the ley-circle?"

"No, Lady."

She turned back to Yenteel. "What happens if a patterner's path ends up there?"

"Anyone walking it falls down."

"If they don't know about it," said Kantees. "But Tenical said a patterner must visit a circle before he can open a path to it. They would know they had to be careful." She stared around at the green landscape rising to the browns and greys of the mountains. "Nobody comes here. Nobody knows about this circle."

Yenteel was looking at her. "You have a plan?"

"Just ideas."

15

They walked away from the circle. Kantees felt a tug and glanced towards the mountains to see two pairs of wings heading their way.

"They're back."

The *ziri* came in fast, each was carrying some sort of animal Kantees did not recognise. In both cases the horned head lolled on a long neck. The body was scrawny and the legs long.

"What have they got?"

"*Fenichasa*," said Jynolee, proud to be able to offer her knowledge. "They live high on the mountain slopes."

"The ones I've seen tend to be fatter," said Kantees. "These don't look like they have much meat on them."

"We don't eat them," said the girl. "They live too high up and are very hard to catch."

Kantees decided she needed to ask the question. "Jynolee, do you want to ride the *ziri*, like me? With me?"

The girl stopped walking, then, as Kantees turned towards her, she dropped to her knees. "That would be my dream, Lady Kantees."

"Do you need permission from anyone to accompany me?"

"My father, Lokolo, Lady." Confusingly Jynolee burst into tears.

Kantees opened her mouth but before she could speak Yenteel put his hand on her arm. "Mistress, if I may have a word?"

She frowned at him.

"In private?"

Jynolee scrambled to her feet and, mopping at her cheeks with her sleeve, she moved twenty paces away to wait.

"What?"

"Bride price."

"You're not marrying her."

"But her father will be expecting it. Either the girl is paid for or she spends her days caring for her parents until they die."

"You're saying she's a slave."

"As much a slave as you were? No, but the difference is not great."

"I could just take her," said Kantees. "You've seen her with Looesa."

"She's like you, yes."

"There was no talk of a bride price for Helka."

"Hagata and Ithamel are the wise women of the town, they are not ruled by men, and Helka has a sister to continue after her mother. I think Ithamel is grateful, Helka would not make a very wise woman for the town. They made it easy for you."

"This is ridiculous."

"This is their life." Yenteel glanced at the girl who looked as if she was still weeping. "Now you have mentioned it she will dream of nothing else. If you don't think of a solution, you will have made her miserable for the rest of her life. Assuming she doesn't turn to hate."

Kantees closed her eyes. Why was everything so complicated?

"How do I solve this?" she said. "I have no money. The only thing I own is the *chilafrah*, and that is worth more than a hundred towns like this."

"If it's all you have, what is the girl worth to you?"

"Losing the *chilafrah* would not fit with my plans."

"I thought they were only ideas."

"Shut up, Yenteel."

"As you wish, Lady Kantees." He bowed.

Kantees shook her head and headed up to where Jynolee stood waiting.

"Take me to Hagata."

The room was dark and smelled of herbs and wax. The house was built from timber just like all the houses and, from the outside it looked no different. Kantees doubted the inside of the others looked much like this. Ceramic pots lined the shelves from floor to ceiling, each had an inscribed label. Not that she could read them, for a moment she felt the bitter knowledge that even here in this forsaken outpost of Taymalin, these women could read and write while she could not.

One day she would learn. Until then there were things to be done.

Hagata was not at home but Ithamel was in the kitchen, working dough, and beckoned Kantees to come further in—Yenteel and Jynolee waited outside.

"Thank you for taking time to see me," said Kantees.

"Lady of the Ziri, it is our honour to serve you."

Kantees fought down the impulse to say how little she deserved it. "I need some advice."

"We seldom give advice free but we are in your debt."

"My old master used to say that advice given free was worth all that was paid for it."

"He sounds like an unusually wise man." Ithamel stretched the dough then kneaded it hard.

"He knew a great many facts about the world," she said. "As to his wisdom I could not comment."

"Where did he reside?"

"Dakastown."

Ithamel nodded and slammed the dough on to the board. "I think perhaps the Lady of the Ziri was a slave."

Kantees' blood froze. Ithamel paused in her kneading and looked up.

"Don't be surprised, Kantees, you arrive wearing little more than rags with your head shorn. Then you talk of your old master in a place where the Kadralin are slaves? We may be an unvisited backwater but we are not ignorant."

"What are you going to do?"

"Do? What do you think I should do?"

"I expect you will tell the townmaster and we will, at best, be sent on our way. Or you may attempt to enslave us again, though the *ziri* would have something to say about that."

Ithamel returned to the kneading. "There is a kettle of hot water by the fire, could you bring it here?"

Kantees did as she was asked, using a thick cloth to protect her hand from the hot handle.

"I am sure you are right," said Ithamel. "The *zirichasa* could do a great deal of harm if we attempted to imprison you. But I do not think it wise to hurt you and, since I am a wise woman, I am sure I am correct."

She glanced up and in the shadowy light Kantees caught her smile.

"So you won't tell him?"

"He's not an idiot," said Ithamel. "If he hasn't worked it out already, I'm sure it won't be long."

"What will he do?"

"Nothing."

"Why?"

"As I said, he is not an idiot. And he owes you a considerable debt. You may not think much of what you and your friend did last night—" she paused her hands and looked into Kantees' eyes, "—but preventing the river from overflowing was a tremendous gift."

"We just did what we could."

"Oh, make no mistake, we would not have died from it. Though there was one person lost to the flooding before you arrived. It would have damaged the buildings closest to the river and flooded the fields downriver from us. We could survive that as well but it would have made next winter more difficult."

"I'm sorry we didn't arrive earlier."

Ithamel smiled. She reached out and patted Kantees' hand leaving a floury mark. "You said you wanted some advice."

Kantees had almost forgotten. "Yes, it's about Jynolee."

"She is very good with the *zirichasa*, isn't she? Her father runs the smithy but she is happier handling the livestock than she ever was among the iron and fire."

"I want to take her with me."

"And you have already heard that he would demand a bride price? He is skilled at his trade but that doesn't make him a generous man. The death of both wife and a son who would have followed his tradition made the man bitter."

"Does he mistreat Jynolee?"

"His words are harsh but they are not reserved for his daughter only. He does not beat her but nor will he release her unless he receives what he sees as his due."

"Could he not remarry?"

Ithamel nodded as she worked on the dough. "There are widows available, even unmarried girls who could go to his bed and give him the sons he desired."

"Then why doesn't he?"

"Why does one person do this and another that? Perhaps he is punishing himself." Ithamel glanced up at Kantees. "It's a skill many have."

Kantees sighed. "What do you think I can do?"

"I have no advice, Kantees of the Ziri. You force the World Pattern to your will, so I imagine you will follow your own path. I have given you as much information as I can without betraying any confidences."

"And that is all?"

"You are very young, Lady Kantees, and that makes you impatient. But there is one more thing that I will do for you: I will clothe you so that you do not look as if you have wandered from the mountains like a starving beggar."

Ithamel was as good as her word. Once she had placed the dough in a clay container next to the fire to rise she took Kantees to the upper floor and found her clothes to wear—Kantees was not pleased that it involved long skirts, she was not used to them. When she left

Ithamel's house she found Jynolee gone and Yenteel in conversation with Hagata.

Hagata laughed at something Yenteel said then turned her smiling face on Kantees.

"That looks much better," she said. "Less the waif, and more the lady."

Yenteel looked round and studied her from her toes—encased in sandals rather than boots which had been relocated to Kantees' bag —to the top of her head. He raised an eyebrow at the iron circlet now resting on the bristles of her hair.

"Don't say anything," said Kantees.

"The town is putting together a feast," he said.

Hagata took the opportunity to head for the house but she paused as she came level with Kantees. "You must look the part, Kantees of the Ziri, if you are to convince others." Then she was gone.

"Convince who of what?" Kantees glared at Yenteel. "What have you been saying?"

"Nothing about you."

"And what feast?"

"You're the guest of honour."

Kantees sighed. "This is not me." She lifted the dark red material of the skirts by way of illustration then let them fall. "How am I supposed to ride wearing these?"

"You're only supposed to go to the feast in those," he said. "The crown is a nice touch."

"It's only iron." She took it off and stared at the twisted metal composed of four interwoven threads perfectly proportioned and spaced. She could not deny it was well made, she had to look hard to find the joint. She realised the piece had been made from a single strand that went around four times weaving in and out of itself. She put it back on her head.

"We're wasting time. We should have been at Jakalain days ago."

"You are getting good advice, Kantees, why aren't you listening to it?"

"Ithamel gave me no advice. Just clothes."

"Did she not?"

Kantees shook her head.

"Are you *sure*?"

Kantees found Sheesha and Looesa in the field near the ley-circle. A few remains of their meal—the *fenichak*—bloodied the grass. He was lying out straight, slightly rolled to the side, as he always did when he had eaten well. It relieved the pressure on his stomach. Looesa was the same but asleep, while Sheesha was awake.

She sat down next to his head and leaned against his neck. His scent filled her nostrils and it relaxed her, it reminded her of who she really was—just a *ziri* keeper. Sheesha was the one creature in this world who did not judge her, and she did not judge him. He was what he was.

"Are you strong enough to fly fast now?" she said. Sheesha's only response was to yawn. His breath smelled very bad, it was always the same after he had eaten.

The ground was damp and she felt it leaking through to her skin. "Mother's milk!" She stood and tried to see whether the skirt had been stained. It was darker where it was damp but she couldn't tell if the mark would be permanent.

"This is what I mean," she said to no one in particular. "I was a slave, I don't know how I'm supposed to behave."

"I can tell you, Lady Kantees."

Kantees whirled round to find Helka standing a short distance away. "You heard what I just said?"

"You were speaking very loudly."

"I see." Kantees sighed. "Well, now you know."

"Know?"

"Me, being a slave. You may not want to come with me."

Helka's eyes seemed to brighten and she smiled. "Oh no, Lady Kantees, I do wish to come with you. There is nothing I want more."

"I just said I used to be a slave."

"My mother and grandmother said as much after they met you."

"And you still want to come?"

"Lady, you came to the town's aid unasked and there is to be a feast in your own honour. You ride the *zirichasa*, your man makes patterns of great power and you offer to take me out into the world where I can be more than just another wise woman. Perhaps you were a slave according to the law, but were you ever one in your heart?"

Kantees stared at the girl. Growing up with women like Ithamel and Hagata must have rubbed off. Her mother may not think she would make a good wise woman but the girl certainly knew how to praise and manipulate. And perhaps there was even truth in her words.

"The place we are going is where I was a slave for many years. I was keeper to the *zirichasa*, particularly Sheesha—" his head bobbed up at his name but she ignored him, "—and I stole him away along with Looesa and others, and another slave."

"You cannot dissuade me."

Kantees almost mentioned Daybian and his dubious requests but she had a suspicion the thought of a young lordling would have the reverse of its intended effect.

"Very well, if I cannot persuade you to stay then you can show me how to behave at this feast."

16

he skirt dried out and there was no stain. But that did not make Kantees feel any less uncomfortable. The feast was not like anything that had taken place at Jakalain. It was true she had never even been close to such a feast, but from the top of the Ziri Tower she could see down into the main hall—at least some of it.

At Jakalain there were rows of tables that would be filled with the nobility at the high tables and sufficiently wealthy merchants and their families lower down. Here the feast was in a large barn. There were two lines of tables, one on each side, and Kantees had been seated at one end, furthest from the main door. She sat with the townmaster and his wife, Pasimel, on one side and the wise women, Ithamel and Hagata, on the other. Kantees' chair was raised to put her head on a level with the townmaster.

At a Jakalain feast, everyone would be wearing their best clothes that would cost more than the price of a good slave—while what Kantees wore now would have been thrown out, if it had been owned at all. And that went for everyone else's clothes here too.

Apart from the russet skirt, she had a white linen top edged with embroidered patternings. Over that was a jacket of the same material as her skirt. She could not abide the sandals, her feet got wet, and so had changed back into her boots. They were mostly hidden so she did not think it mattered.

And she had the circlet on her head though the dark metal blended with her colouration so she suspected it was not visible. Helka had suggested they put flowers into it but Kantees refused. Flowers in the hair meant a girl or woman was looking for a husband. If Helka had intended to trick her, she failed there. Though perhaps the girl was only trying to help. It was difficult to know. Kantees had always found it easier to talk to serious older women, not the young ones with their heads filled with lovers and nonsense.

Kantees' head had never been filled with that sort of nonsense.

The meal went well enough. Helka had given her some instruction on how to behave but it had amounted to the fact that everyone in the room would be following her lead. So she had to taste each dish even if she didn't like the look of it, so that the others could eat.

It was torture.

Every time new dishes were brought out the attention of everyone in the place focused on her until she had taken a bite, or a spoonful, or supped the drink. But she muddled through. Yenteel was on the end of the first table to her left and he kept smiling and nodding. He was trying to be encouraging, she knew, but most of his attention seemed to be on the young man next to him. Kantees could guess where that was leading, though she still found it unsettling. She hoped the fellow was either of a similar mind to Yenteel or, if not, that he would not be upset at Yenteel's advances. Kantees did not like the idea of having to break him out of a cell again.

Do they have a dungeon here?

At Jakalain musicians were employed to play throughout the evening. Here there was no music while they ate.

She heard someone say "Tahulin" and glanced round at Hagata who was talking across her to the townmaster's wife.

"I've seen Tahulin," she said abruptly and then felt embarrassed that she had cut in on their conversation.

"You've seen the ghost patterns?" Pasimel had a surprisingly deep voice and was as broad-shouldered as her husband. Her hair was grey and thinning but she carried herself with strength.

"We both have, Yenteel and I." She glanced at where he had been sitting. Neither he nor the young man were there.

"Where did you see them?" asked Pasimel. "If you don't mind me asking?"

"We were in the mountains on a day that was upside-down," said Kantees. "Riding the *ziri* we were high and the sky was clear. The sun shone on snowy mountain peaks and on the clouds below. The air above was warm and below was cold. Clouds filled the valleys between the mountains and flowed as if they were a great river of white.

"We could only land on the mountaintops and my Sheesha was tired because he was recovering from injury. So we set down and watched the cloud rivers. Then we saw them, like great beasts in the sea, rising up to the surface and diving down again. It was the Tahulin, at first just one, then two, then so many they could not be counted and their size was three-fold greater than my Sheesha but they were made from the clouds.

"They swam through the cloud river, heading downstream as if they were travelling to a great meeting of the Tahulin. Some came so close we almost felt we could reach out and touch them. And when they had all passed it was almost as if it had been a dream. But I remember and Yenteel remembers, and the *ziri* remember."

Kantees stopped with the sudden realisation that the entire room was quiet and that everyone had been listening to her. She was engulfed in a wave of embarrassment; she noticed she was sitting forward in the chair so she pushed herself back. She turned to Pasimel and smiled. "It was lovely." Then she hid her awkwardness by taking a long drink of the beer which she had been avoiding. It was very dark and heavy with a bitter taste. She could not imagine why anyone would drink it from choice.

"Thank you, Lady Kantees," said Pasimel. "To think there are Tahulin so close. You must have been blessed by Taymar himself."

Kantees held her tongue. If Sheesha had not been shot with arrows they would not have seen the Tahulin and Kantees would have been content. Besides she was not entirely happy that she might have been blessed by Taymar, but she could not expect more from the Taymalin. Pasimel meant well.

The meal had apparently finished although people were still eating. Some men who she knew had been seated at the tables now had instruments and were preparing themselves in a back corner. Others started moving tables.

Ithamel touched her on the arm. "Lady Kantees, we shall move to the side. The townspeople would like to offer you a dance and some music as thanks. They have little else to give."

Kantees managed to get down from the chair and its pedestal without stumbling. Ithamel took her arm and guided her to the side of the room.

"You're not expecting me to dance, I hope?"

"If you don't want to, nobody will insist," said Ithamel. "Your story will no doubt pass into legend and will be retold with many changes. I expect the storytellers will get rid of Yenteel. It will be the Lady Kantees alone in the mountains…" she laughed.

"Doesn't it bother you that it won't be the truth?"

"What is truth, Kantees? You, a runaway slave, promising to keep the Kadralin of the mountains in their place? Or you, a great power who consorts with the Tahulin promising the same?"

"We didn't consort with them, we just watched them—"

A shadow crossed the fire.

"Lady Kantees, I want a word with you."

The new voice was the growl of someone barely walking the right side of good manners.

Kantees turned and looked up into the glowering eyes of a man who looked strong enough to break her in half. She was not sure whether it was the alcohol but she felt calm, even though this could only be Jynolee's father. The conversation she did not want to have was being forced on her. At least Ithamel was here.

Kantees looked round, but Ithamel had gone.

"You are the blacksmith?"

"I am Lokolo."

"Let us sit down."

That required him to locate two chairs and a place they could sit off to one side of the barn.

"You want to take my daughter away."

"Yes."

"Pay me her bride price and you can have her."

Kantees seethed inside, she did not want to be part of any kind of slavery and this was nothing more.

"I have no money."

He shrugged and sat back as if that was the end of the matter. Kantees turned her head and Lokolo took in a breath; she looked back at him.

He was no longer leaning back but had placed both hands on the table.

"What are you wearing?" His voice was strained even more than it had been before.

Kantees frowned and looked down at her clothes.

"On your head."

"A gift from Ithamel."

Lokolo gave the impression of a boiling kettle on the hearth but whatever emotion he was suppressing, somehow, he held it inside. Why would the circlet make him angry?

Of course.

"I meant no disrespect, Lokolo, I did not realise you had made it for her—" *Though if I had been thinking, who else would have?* "—and Ithamel told me of your sorrow."

"She had no right," he hissed, though the tension in him seemed to dissipate.

"I cannot make it right."

"The all-powerful Kantees of the Ziri cannot bring back the dead? I am surprised."

"Nor would I want to."

"You wish me to live with my grief, and you would take my daughter from me."

Kantees glanced around. It was as if they had a pattern of protection around them. Though the festivities and music were still going on, no one approached within a dozen paces.

"I would not wish that upon anyone," she said. "I will give the circlet back to you."

"I do not want it."

"Then I will return it to Ithamel."

"She has made her feelings clear. She gave it to you."

Kantees thought about Yenteel and his habits—and Ithamel's. "Why not go to her?"

"What?"

"Ask her. Wed her if she says yes."

And it was as if the anger in him simply vanished. "How can I ask her?"

Kantees lifted the circlet from her head and held it out to Lokolo. "Offer her this."

The man shrank back into the chair as if he feared the circle of iron. Then he took it from Kantees, his huge hand engulfing it.

"And I will send you a journeyman blacksmith."

He frowned as if he did not understand her.

"Soon," she said, "the ley-circle of Riverrush will become active and there will be commerce beyond merely this valley and the farms. I must speak to the townmaster about this because there is work to be done before it can happen. And if you let me take Jynolee, I will send you a journeyman who can work with you. Or find an apprentice you can train, if you prefer."

"You would do this, for Jynolee?"

"Does she desire to work in iron like her father?"

"She does not."

"But she likes the *ziri* and they like her. She can learn to ride as I do."

He paused. "Will she be safe?"

Kantees smiled. He did care for his daughter.

"I will not lie, Master Lokolo, the world is a dangerous place and I am engaged in a battle. But your daughter is not required to fight and she will spend her time in Jakalain. She will be as safe there as anywhere. But I was told you are all taught to fight."

"It is many years since the Kadralin came marauding," he said pointedly. "But we do not forget, yes, our young people are taught to fight."

He stood up and towered over her. He kept flipping the circlet in his hand. "I will give you your answer tomorrow, Kantees of the Ziri."

And he stalked away.

. . .

Ithamel must have been watching from somewhere in the barn because she appeared a few moments later with a refill for Kantees' cup.

"He did not strike you," she said as if it were some idle topic of conversation.

"He came close."

"But he didn't."

If she had been watching then she would know that Kantees had returned the circlet. But then, Kantees thought, why would Ithamel have given her the headpiece if she had not had a good idea of how Kantees could use it?

"You manipulated me," she said. "Yenteel used to do that until I made him stop. Don't do it again." Even Kantees was surprised by the steel in her voice.

"As you say, Kantees of the Ziri."

"Well, good," said Kantees. "Now, I need to talk to the townmaster, and I think you should be here as well. This time."

"I will find him," said Ithamel and got to her feet.

"One thing, Ithamel," said Kantees. "Please do not spend another night with Yenteel."

"I believe he has found someone else of interest."

"Forgive me for asking but is it common for you to lie with the people of the town?"

"We do not. In our position it could make things difficult, that's why I took advantage of your man's willingness."

Kantees nodded and without another word Ithamel departed.

1 7

antees slept with Sheesha even though she had been offered a bed. She still felt guilty over his arrow injuries even though they had healed well and he, of course, had completely forgotten them. He was back to his old self and as strong as ever. Nestling beneath his wing gave her strength.

Helka brought her food in the morning, boiled eggs with fresh bread and butter. Kantees told her they would be leaving soon and to fetch her bag—also to have a word with Jynolee. The girl had gone off with a skip in her step.

Yenteel turned up looking tired. Kantees had decided she was not going to ask him about his night, but somehow she could not resist.

"Want to stay?"

He glanced at her. "No."

"But a place that offers such a variety of attractions, it must be tempting."

"Did you leave anything for breakfast?"

"Didn't you get anything this morning?"

He didn't reply and checked her bowl. She had already finished it all.

"There's some dried meat still left in the packs."

He held up his hand as if wanting her to stop.

"Well if you want to eat you'd better get something, we're leaving as soon as Helka and Jynolee get back."

"You paid the blacksmith?"

"I think I gave him what he needed. We'll see, I suppose."

Yenteel disappeared back into the town. Kantees checked her meagre belongings. She had changed back into her old clothes but packed the ones Ithamel had given her. She made sure the *chilafrah* was safe.

Twenty of the townsfolk emerged from between the buildings and headed down to where she and the two *ziri* waited on the rocks close to the river. The place where she and Yenteel had performed their minor miracle two nights before. A fitting spot for the send-off. She remembered Master Kevrey commenting to one of his clients as to how people wanted symbols, and how they made a stronger impression.

This place was a symbol now and she would use it. *Now I am the one doing the manipulating,* she thought. It did not please her.

The group was led by the townmaster and Hagata. His wife, Ithamel and Helka were on one side, the blacksmith and his daughter on the other. Both Helka and Jynolee had packs and wore men's trousers instead of skirts.

Kantees suppressed her pleasure at the triumph. *Chaos is easy, order is hard.* Had Kevrey really intended her to learn all these lessons, or had she just been nosey? All servants listened, secrets were currency, especially among slaves when they were not permitted to own anything.

As the group arrived Kantees spotted Yenteel returning, while stuffing food into his mouth.

The townmaster offered her the blessing of Taymar in her deeds and the Mother in her travels. Why not? In a place so out of touch with the rest of Esternes why not merge both cultures? Her heart told her that Taymar was just a usurper used to justify the theft of her people's land. But the townmaster meant well, so she thanked him.

Lokolo pushed Jynolee forward, unnecessarily since she was clearly eager to get started and came to stand behind Kantees on the bank of the river. Helka kissed her mother and grandmother then followed.

A glint of metal in Ithamel's hair caught Kantees' eye: she was wearing the circlet. Lokolo had certainly wasted no time, nor should he. Perhaps the delivery of his daughter had depended on whether Ithamel would accept the gift this second time. It seemed she had.

Everyone was looking at her expectantly and she realised she had to say something.

"In the name of the Mother, I thank you for your hospitality which has been kind and generous. Whatever guided us to this place, it has been good fortune for all of us."

There was a murmur of agreement among the group, and most smiled. *So far, so good.*

"I am returning to my home with two of your daughters, and in return I hope I will be able to repay everything you have given to me."

Kantees ran out of things to say so instead she glanced at Sheesha and Looesa who roared as one, their voices echoing across the river and bouncing from the cliffs. Those in the party who did not step back, flinched.

The two *ziri* moved forwards—and Yenteel detached himself from the crowd, just swallowing down the last of whatever he had managed to find.

"Helka, you will ride with Yenteel, Jynolee with me."

At a thought from Kantees, the *ziri* lay flat. To Kantees' surprise, both girls bowed to their respective mounts first. Jynolee stood on one side of Sheesha's neck with Kantees on the other.

"Sit on his back between the wings, so his spine is … you know. And move back so I have enough room to sit in front of you. I'll hold your pack."

Jynolee passed it over then straddled Sheesha's neck. "I don't want to hurt him."

"You won't."

Kantees glanced at Helka who was already in place and holding her pack in her lap as Yenteel got in place. The girl sat gingerly then pushed herself back.

"That's fine," said Kantees. She returned the bag and hopped lightly into her place. She hooked her legs under the wings and adjusted her position. She leaned forward and stroked Sheesha's neck. With her head facing toward the river and away from the crowd. "Ready, beloved? We shall give them a show they will not forget." Then loudly to Yenteel, "Ready?"

"Aye, Lady Kantees."

"Hold on to me, Jynolee." Kantees barely felt the hands that touched her hips. "No, girl, put your arms tight around my waist. Move closer if you must. What would your father think if you fell off as soon as we took to the air?"

The girl said nothing but moved closer until her pack was firmly against Kantees' back, and her arms were tight. Kantees looked over to Looesa and saw Helka clearly had no qualms about clinging to Yenteel. But he remained straight-faced without even a hint of the grin she might expect under other circumstances.

All was ready. She spoke quietly to her mount. "Go."

Sheesha stood up on his hind legs and raised his wings for the first beat. The *ziri*'s back was at an alarming angle, Kantees held on with her legs hooked under his wings. Any reticence in Jynolee vanished as she clutched Kantees tighter.

Sheesha crouched, brought his wings down with thunderous power and leapt upwards. They were at the maximum height of his jump as the second beat pushed them higher. And again, they moved forwards, he angled across the raging water. Beat after beat, each driving them a little higher and much faster.

Kantees glanced round to see Helka white with fear on Looesa's back. Clinging so hard to Yenteel, Kantees could only interpret his grimace as one of pain. It gave her perverse pleasure to see it. He was far too smug most of the time.

"Are you alright, Jynolee?" she asked as Sheesha reached a good height above the river and was nearly over the other side. Kantees made him turn upstream, which meant that suddenly it was just air between the riders and the water below.

Jynolee may have been starting to reply but all that came out was a squeal.

"Faster, Sheesha!"

The *ziri* stroked hard with his wings and they accelerated until the cold air streamed across their faces.

"Enjoying it?"

"Lady Kantees, this is the most wonderful thing I have ever known."

Kantees smiled and pushed Sheesha harder and higher. The mountains grew around them. The river below narrowed until it because a gushing torrent between the valley walls. There was a low peak ahead and to the left, Kantees had Sheesha go behind it as he turned back south towards the town once more. She intended to show them just how wonderful the *ziri* truly were.

"There may be magic soon," she shouted behind her. "Don't be afraid."

"I *am* afraid, Lady Kantees, but there is no other place I want to be in this world than with you on the back of Lord Sheesha."

The town was visible a little less than a league away. Kantees was not about to push Sheesha if he did not want to go fast, but the town's ley-circle was powerful enough to give them strength.

She urged him faster.

The angle may have been less severe but the careening descent toward Riverrush reminded her of the fall from the Hamalain Ziri Tower at Kurvin Port. When Sheesha had caught her and they first rode the golden path together.

"Oh!" said Jynolee as flashes of gold appeared around Sheesha. Kantees glanced round to ensure Looesa was in position, as she expected him to be. She could feel him.

Then they were wrapped in a cocoon of golden light. She had hoped to see the open mouths of the townsfolk as they went by, but it was too fast. The town and the river fell away behind them in a heartbeat and, moments later, they were crossing over the Talamyrth with nothing but a sea of trees below them.

Kantees had Sheesha climb and turn into the east. In her mind's eye, she thought she saw a glimpse of the powerful ley-circle in the heart of the forest. It was not a place she intended to visit ever again.

Within a short time Sheesha was flying parallel to the mountains in the north. Kantees pushed him up and they broke through the thin clouds.

Jynolee gasped at the white blanket spread below them as far as could be seen.

"The magic of the *zirichasa*," said Kantees. "Very few people can bring them to this place." She almost said, "Only I," but that would have been a lie.

"Can I do it?"

"Whether it is a gift the *ziri* will only share with a few, or whether it is the rider who brings it about, I don't know. I know only one other who can, and he is Kadralin just as I am."

"You think Taymalin cannot do it?" Her voice dripped with disappointment.

"I would say two things. First, I do not really know, though two experienced riders, lordlings of noble Taymalin houses, have tried and failed. Second, you have Kadralin in you."

"What if I can and Helka cannot?"

"Then that is how it will be."

"Is the other your patterner?"

"Yenteel? No, not him. He does not ride the *ziri*, he is carried, like a parcel."

"He is strange."

"Yes, but a good man, and reliable."

"We're going to Jakalain?"

"You've heard of it?"

"We know the houses but we seldom see any travellers from one year to the next. I cannot even remember the last one who came, I was too young."

Kantees watched the land roll past. They left the Talamyrth behind, for which she was grateful, but now she had to consider Sheesha. She did not know whether he was fully recovered from his injuries, and swift flight was very draining. On the other hand, she was desperate to get back to Jakalain. There was a lot she had to do —if she was permitted.

They crossed a large river that she did not remember from the original journey and as it dwindled into the distance behind them she called for Sheesha to slow.

The *ziri* was becoming more skilled at moving into and out of the patterned flight, so when the golden wall collapsed, they were not blasted by the wind.

Kantees focused her mind but couldn't sense a ley-circle, instead she turned them north into the mountains once more and found a grassy but isolated ledge big enough to land both *ziri* and leave room to move about.

She lifted her leg over Sheesha's neck and slipped to the ground then hugged his head.

"Thank you, Sheesha, you are strong but we shall rest a while so you can gather your strength."

She turned to find Jynolee behind her and saw Yenteel lifting Helka down from Looesa's back. She frowned but when Yenteel stepped away Kantees saw the girl's pale face and round eyes.

Helka saw Kantees looking at her and immediately stood up straight as if she was fine, but she could not force the blood back into her face.

Kantees wondered if she should have warned them in advance, but she had wanted them to be shocked just so that she could see their reactions.

When she had come face to face with Sheesha for the first time she thought she was going to be eaten. And then she had been forced to travel the patterner's path with no warning of what it would be like. The difference was that she at least understood what the magic portal did and had heard stories. These two girls had had no warning of what it was like to fly, and especially not what was going to happen with the swift flight.

If she was going to recruit more riders she would have to think about that.

The Taymalin aristocracy were not going to like that idea.

Helka turned away and threw up. Yenteel wandered over to Kantees.

"At least she managed to hold it in while we were in flight."

"That's something."

Jynolee took a water bottle from her bag and hurried over to help Helka.

"I wasn't expecting that reaction," said Kantees. "Was it the normal flight or the pattern?"

"The pattern. She seemed to be quite enjoying the first part."

"Perhaps it just needs getting used to."

"Perhaps."

Kantees hesitated. Helka was sipping water and spitting it out again. "Should I help?"

Yenteel shook his head. "Leave them to it. A leader can't do everything."

"There's only four of us."

"Start as you mean to go on."

Kantees gave a short bark of a laugh. "That would be fine, if I had the slightest idea what I intended for the future."

"Oh, I think you have quite a good idea."

She gave the sky a hard look. The wind was from the west and bringing a lot of cloud but it did not feel like rain. Still, if the wind was behind them they would make better time towards Jakalain.

"Any idea where we are?" she said. "Or where Jakalain is?"

Yenteel pointed east.

"That's not much help."

"It can't be far," he said, "we covered the distance in the other direction in a day or so."

"Not counting the time spent with you on your back."

She wished she hadn't said it. Yenteel had taken an arrow and they had been laid up for a couple of days, even after he managed to use the healing pattern on himself. But it had been the same—or worse—with Sheesha. Struck by arrows and unable to travel for days. She knew she had to just accept these things might happen, but she did not want to see her friends hurt, especially not because of her actions.

The consequences of doing nothing would be worse if the Dunor succeeded.

"Don't punish yourself," said Yenteel gently.

"That's easy to say."

"Even easier when I'm not the one making the decisions." He grinned at her, so she punched him in the arm.

Jynolee fetched food from the bags and served Kantees with bread, a meat pie and water to wash it down. Being served felt very strange but Kantees forced herself to accept it with grace, even though it twisted her up inside. She did not want to make any other person feel like a slave. She was, however, amused that Jynolee did not do the same for Yenteel. He had to fetch his own.

Helka had some colour back in her cheeks when Kantees had the two girls come to sit with her.

"This afternoon we will arrive at Jakalain and I think I should explain what happened between the Lord and Lady of that place and their sons, and me. How I came to leave and how, though we may not be friends, they will hopefully not try to kill us when we arrive."

That last comment got their attention.

She quickly went over the attack of the Dunor, riding Sheesha, escaping, rescuing the younger son, and then Daybian. She skimmed over the events at Kurvin Port, which they had heard of, and Dakastown, which they had not.

"They should be grateful to you for returning their sons," said Jynolee.

"They are, as I have said, but I don't really know how we'll be treated this time. I did wonder if I should leave you two in the town outside the gates."

"I will stay with you."

"We must go together."

"Very well, then let us be going."

Helka hesitated. "Will we be flying very swiftly?"

"We will not be taking the golden path," Kantees said reassuringly. "It takes a great deal of strength and the *ziri* cannot maintain it for a long time." She hesitated. "I am telling you a great deal of *zirichasa* lore which nobody else knows. Many have seen a *ziri* flying swiftly since I have learnt how to do it, but it would be best if the limits were not well known."

Helka in particular seemed to grasp this. "It is the same for my mother and grandmother, much of what they say is not as magical as people think. But they keep their secrets and everyone thinks they are more powerful than they are."

Jynolee shook her head. "It does not make them less powerful."

Kantees was not interested in a discussion and stood up. "We're going."

Jynolee mounted more easily the second time and Kantees got in front of her. Sheesha raised his head and bellowed, Kantees laughed and gave his neck a solid thump. "Yes, Sheesha, we're going home." Home? Kevrey of Tander was dead and the place she was brought up had been torn down, the valley in the mountains held no good memories yet. Jakalain was the closest thing she had to home.

A quick look to Looesa told her that they were ready.

Sheesha waddled to the edge, and dropped. Jynolee screamed. Kantees smiled and allowed him to gain plenty of speed before asking him to pull up as the valley floor rushed toward them. They were crushed down into his back as his wings adjusted their trajectory and they shot away south weaving along a valley that snaked through the hills.

They burst out on to the plain that stretched out west, south and east. Without instruction Sheesha adjusted his direction until they were flashing across the plain so close to the ground that he had to swerve around the taller trees.

He's showing off, she thought. *And excited about getting back to Jakalain, he's missed it*, she thought. *And so have I.*

The glow of a ley-circle grew in her mind. This was a big one and she knew that it must be the one at Jakalain, located less than a league to the west of the castle. They had been so close, still, a break meant that they would arrive fresh.

The *ziri* topped a low range of hills and Jakalain was there before them, its dark brooding walls reflecting the dull day with not a single window on the exterior. There were armsmen moving on the battlements.

Kantees ordered Sheesha to gain height so that they were out of arrow range. He obliged.

Then she tripled the height again, in case the castle's defenders decided to utilise one of the massive engines she could now see located on the towers. They had not been there two ten-days before when she had last been here.

Jakalain must have taken her warning seriously. Good.

1 8

antees had Sheesha and Looesa circle above the castle while armsmen and servants dashed around below them. They went in and out of the doors facing into the inner courtyard and along the parapets like ants stirred up with a stick. The huge spear-throwing engines had been turned to point in their general direction but nothing had been loosed at them. Kantees also saw that there was construction work going on inside the courtyard though she could not quite see what it was.

"How can anything be so big?" said Jynolee, clearly in awe of what was below them. Her words took Kantees by surprise, it had not even occurred to her that these country girls had never seen anything like a castle. She would probably have felt similarly about the town over the river; the buildings were not much bigger than the ones from her home, but they were mostly built from stone, unlike Riverrush.

Just as well she hadn't seen Kurvin Port and the Hamalain citadel first. Or the waterfall and lifting engines at Cliffedge.

Kantees was about to reply when she spotted a familiar figure climbing up on to the walkway along the walls. "Daybian!" she called out to Yenteel and pointed down. Then she waved.

He had a grin on his face and gestured for her to descend. In return she shook her head and pointed at the weapons aimed at the *ziri*.

It took him a moment to understand but he sent armsmen off at a run to the towers and very soon the weapons were once more pointed out beyond the walls. Though the armsmen who manned them were still looking up.

Kantees accepted the gesture and set Sheesha to descend in a gliding spiral.

It was not long before they set down once more in the courtyard of Jakalain. Daybian must have thrown himself down the stairs inside the wall because he appeared from a door, jumped a new low wall and then reduced his speed to a sedate walk more in keeping with the heir to Jakalain.

There were no servants in the courtyard now but several groups of armsmen—equipped with bows—moved out into view. They held their bows down with arrows nocked but not drawn. Kantees glanced round taking in the building work, it looked as if they were building an inner wall around the entire perimeter.

Kantees hesitated, she was not completely sure what reception she would get but at least Daybian seemed pleased to see her. She lifted her leg over Sheesha's neck and slipped to the cobbles.

"My lord, stay back!"

Kantees recognised the voice of Swordmaster Erang coming from the direction of the main tower. The armsmen parted to let him through. His sword was not drawn but he did not look happy, which did not surprise her.

"Nonsense, Swordmaster," said Daybian. He lengthened his stride and bore down on Kantees, moments later he had her in a tight embrace. "Kantees! I am so glad to see you!"

She didn't know what to say.

"Daybian," was all she could manage at first, then she gathered her wits. Making sure that her hands were clearly empty—for Erang's sake—she reached as far round Daybian's chest as she could. "It's good to see you too." She forced the words out, but found they were true.

Then he took a half step back and let his hands move to her shoulders. "Did you find what you were looking for?"

She gave a gentle smile. "I did but that is not a tale for now."

"No, of course not." He turned and looked round. "Yenteel! Welcome!"

"Sire."

He paused for a moment to take in Helka and Jynolee. "Where is Gally? And the child?" His voice took on a tone of extreme concern. "Tell me they are well."

She gave him a bigger smile. "They were well when I left them among my people in the mountains. They were not in any danger and Ulina was charged with protecting Galiko."

"Daybian, if you'd like to put Kantees down, I'm sure she'd appreciate it."

Kantees smiled again at the sound of Levin's voice.

"I haven't—" Daybian realised Levin was not being literal and abruptly released Kantees' shoulders.

Unlike the Jakalain lordling, Levin did not try to embrace her. Instead he simply bowed. "I am very pleased to see you, Kantees, it is a dangerous world and I could not help but be concerned for your safety."

"But I wasn't coming back," said Kantees.

"I know, and I would have spent the rest of my sorry life wondering what had happened to you."

"Don't mind him," said Daybian, "he's been moping ever since we parted."

Levin looked embarrassed. And Kantees turned back to the *ziri*. Both the women had dismounted.

"This is Jynolee and that's Helka, they're my…" She realised she had at no point decided exactly what they were. "They're my apprentices. This is Lord Daybian and Lord Levin."

Both girls went down on one knee and looked at the ground. Helka managed it more smoothly but she kept peeking up at the two men.

There was some activity over by the Swordmaster and Kantees saw a runner moving away. Erang strode over to them. Sheesha got back up on his haunches and fixed his eye on the armsman. The movement was very obvious and Erang came to a halt a few paces away.

"Lord Jakalain requests an audience with Kantees of the Ziri."

It might have been Kantees' imagination but the Swordmaster almost seemed to choke on the title he had given her.

"Thank you, Swordmaster. The *ziri* must roost and be fed. Are their eyries unoccupied?"

"That is not my concern."

"Sheesha's eyrie is as you left it, Kantees," said Daybian, "and Looesa can rejoin Shingul."

Kantees glanced at the Ziri Tower and then back at the Swordmaster. "Please thank Lord Jakalain, I will be there as soon as I can but I must make sure the *ziri* and my apprentices are comfortable."

At her thought both Sheesha and Looesa dropped their long necks and bodies to the ground again. Jynolee and Helka climbed up. Yenteel hesitated. "Please stay here, Yenteel, I will return." Then she looked over at Daybian who thankfully took the hint.

"Let me assist you." He almost bounded over to Looesa and Kantees heard him give Helka a cheery greeting as he climbed up in front of her. Kantees took her place and the *ziri* launched into the air. Sheesha was always one for making an impression so flew low round the courtyard once before climbing the Ziri Tower.

Kantees was sure the door into the eyrie had not been open when they arrived but it stood wide as Sheesha glided in and came to a comfortable halt on fresh straw. She heard Looesa squawking two levels up and the replies from Shingul.

Jynolee's feet had barely touched the ground before Sheesha lifted his head and bellowed, just to remind all the *zirichasa* in the tower that their king had returned. It was answered by every *ziri* giving voice until the tower almost shook.

Without even a thought Kantees glanced at the riding tack hanging from the walls. She noted it had been treated correctly and reflected the light from outside.

"This is where I spent most of my life," she said to Jynolee who was staring around at the piles of hay bales, used for warmth and nesting by the *ziri*. "My room is just above. You and Helka will have to stay there for now."

"You said we are your apprentices."

"Is that all right? I couldn't think of a better word."

"Lady Kantees, I am honoured to be your apprentice."

Again, Kantees had to force herself not to correct the girl over the name. She understood that if she was to be a leader, others needed to treat her with respect and part of that came from having a title.

"We'd best not keep Lord Jakalain waiting any longer than we need," said Kantees. "Come on."

She headed up the ladder just as Daybian and Helka were descending and so introduced the women to their new room. Even Jynolee was unimpressed.

"This was my home," said Kantees. "If you want to ride *zirichasa* as I do then it will do you no harm to be here for a while. However, you two are not slaves and I think we can arrange for conditions here to be improved." She gave Daybian a hard look.

"Naturally. Proper beds for a start," he said. "Better flooring." He eyed the ceiling which was stained in places from accidents. "Perhaps a better ceiling too."

"Yes, good," said Kantees. "Let's keep moving, you two leave your bags and come along, you'll need to be introduced to the other staff here." Not something she was looking forward to.

Daybian headed for the ladder, the two girls hung back. Kantees thought it was to let her go first so she followed the lordling.

"Lady."

"Helka?"

"Perhaps a change of clothes?"

Kantees looked down at her well-used riding gear. There were the clothes she had been given at Riverrush she could put on. As she opened the bag Helka politely asked Daybian to remove himself. Kantees wondered if Daybian was also reminded of the night when she'd hit him over the head because asking him to leave would not work.

It did not take long and soon they headed down again, finding Daybian on the floor below. After two more ladders they reached the level where the stairs started. Kantees did not give them a tour; while Daybian might be unconcerned about keeping his father waiting, Kantees could not afford to damage what little goodwill she had here, she had only been willing to take the time to change because the quality of her clothes would help.

When they reached the first level above the refectory, they finally ran into Romain. For some reason Kantees was surprised that he had barely changed, she felt as if she had been away for years, yet it was barely more than a turn of the moon. Of course he had not, though she was now a completely different person. The smells in the tower had not changed either and she found those more welcoming than the expression on Romain's face—but Daybian was with her and she no longer feared this small man whose knowledge of *ziri* was limited to maintaining their lives, he knew nothing of their magic. And though he might be of Kadralin descent, she trusted Daybian far more than she ever would him.

"Romain, the Mother's blessing on you," she said moving towards him quickly so that he could not get the upper hand. Unfortunately it also involved taking advantage of Daybian, and the possibility his father might not agree. "Lord Jakalain requests my presence so I cannot spend a great deal of time with you. These are my apprentices, Jynolee and Helka, they are to learn the ways of the *ziri*, but they are not slaves. I cannot think of anyone who would be more experienced at providing that learning than you. You have taught so many, and you taught me." She half-turned. "Do you not agree Lord Daybian?"

"Most certainly, Lady Kantees. You are very wise."

Kantees shook her head slightly, she was glad he had got the point, but she thought he was overdoing it. Typical Daybian.

But if Romain had been intending to say anything, it had gone from his head. He looked at her as if he had never seen her before. And it was true, he had never seen this incarnation.

"We can't keep Lord Jakalain waiting," she said. "My apprentices need food; we have flown far today. They should be introduced to the tower and its staff."

"Mistress?" said Helka. "Did you not also order that Sheesha and Looesa should be fed?"

Kantees did not smile. Helka had clearly seen the game being played here and assessed Romain for what he was. Very clever.

"Yes, I did."

"Make sure the *ziri* are fed, Romain," said Daybian.

Romain finally managed to speak. "Yes, sire."

Kantees turned to the girls. "Romain will guide you and instruct you for now. I will return as soon as I can."

Helka and Jynolee curtsied.

With Daybian at her side, Kantees headed across the refectory towards the exit, knowing that all eyes were on her. So many of the castle staff were still slaves and, to them, she was just a runaway and a thief who had yet to face her comeuppance.

"Where are you going to sleep, Kantees?" Daybian asked as they hurried across the courtyard. "With those girls?"

She ignored him, she knew where that conversation was leading. Perhaps you could admire his persistence but not his ultimate intentions.

"What are the walls for?" She pointed at the work being done. The tallest section had already reached the second line of windows on the side above the dungeons, elsewhere it had been barely started. Now that the fuss of Kantees' arrival was passed there was an army of men and boys at work. It looked like a huge construction project.

"In case of an attack brought in by *tekrasa*."

"Did your father need much convincing?"

"If that original attack had not happened, if people had not seen the giant creature with their own eyes, I doubt we could have persuaded him."

"Swordmaster Erang?"

"He's not a fool, Kantees. He saw the beast the night Jelamie was abducted."

"And the walls?"

"His idea, since the *tekrasa* might bring men directly into the courtyard we have to be able to prevent access."

Kantees glanced up at the windows of the main tower. "They don't have to bring men to the ground."

Daybian followed her gaze. "The window shutters have been reinforced. They look normal from the outside only. Additional barriers can be put in place."

"It's still a weak point."

"Have you become a master strategist?"

"I'm just thinking what I would do."

"Then I'm glad you're on our side."

Yenteel was waiting at the entrance to the main tower with Levin and Tenical. She greeted the patterner with a nod but there had never been any comradeship between them. She was simply glad he had not run back to his former masters.

Two of the household staff must have been watching for them and drew back the doors as Kantees approached.

She was led for a third time into the heart of the building and the room where she had first been subject to the questioning over who had raised the alarm during that night-time attack. The furniture here was different again than both the previous times, now there were several tables set in a circle with pairs of chairs at each.

Lord Jakalain and the Swordmaster stood by one. Daybian went to stand by his father. There was another lord and a patterner who Kantees did not recognise at a table beside Jakalain. Levin and Tenical were guided to another, while Kantees and Yenteel were led to a fifth, that faced the lords. A couple of men she took for scribes sat slightly back from the group. She glanced back at the unknown lord, his hair was grey and he had an aspect of sadness about him; the patterner who accompanied him was surprisingly young, perhaps no more than thirty years, but what she found most interesting was the way he was staring at Yenteel.

"Kantees of the Ziri," started Lord Jakalain, dragging her attention away from the men. "Thank you for attending this council. Allow me to introduce Lord Corlain of Faerholme."

Faerholme? That was on the mainland and not even on the coast close to Esternes.

"I am pleased to make your acquaintance, Lord Corlain."

"This is the *ziri* thief?"

Kantees felt her blood freeze. She did not expect to be treated as an equal but open insults were another issue.

1 9

antees glared at Corlain for a breath as she suppressed every sharp retort that went through her mind, then turned on her heel and headed for the door. Yenteel was ahead of her and had the door open in a trice, she was outside the room before anyone else reacted.

She was breathing heavily as she stalked down the corridor. The sound of several pairs of boots emerged from the room and followed her. Nobody called for her to stop but Daybian appeared at her right hand.

"Turn here," he said in a clipped tone as they passed a passage.

She didn't argue and presently they came to a set of stairs.

"Up," said Daybian. They went.

Eventually he guided them to a room with large windows looking out on the courtyard, it was equipped with various tables and upholstered chairs.

"My mother's day-room, sometimes," said Daybian by way of explanation.

Kantees glanced round to find Yenteel, Levin and Tenical had also followed her. She was grateful but her heart was too full of anger to trust herself to speak. Instead she went to a window and stared out at the activity in the courtyard.

She was tempted to simply call Sheesha and fly off.

But that would achieve nothing.

She turned round to face them only to find they were all still standing. "Can we get something to eat?"

Daybian went to the fireplace and pulled a cord.

"Sit down," she said and waved her hand at them. Yenteel did, but the others remained standing. "Oh for the sake of the Mother, just sit down, stop treating me like I'm someone special, you all know who I really am."

"It's because we know who you really are," said Levin, "that we remain standing."

"Well, I'm sitting down," said Yenteel.

Kantees turned on him. "And who was that man?"

She watched half a dozen facetious remarks die on his tongue before he finally replied. "His name is Bejeren."

"Is he an ex-lover of yours?"

The eyes of the other men in the room focused on Yenteel.

"He isn't."

"Are you *sure*?"

"I think I know who I spend my idle time with."

"Then how do you know him?"

Yenteel looked particularly uncomfortable as he glanced at the others in the room. "I can't…"

"Tell me."

"Kantees, I would tell you but…" He waved his hand at the others.

"You don't want to say you and this Bejeren have the same master?"

Yenteel did not respond.

"I see."

Kantees turned back to the window.

"Perhaps we should forgive Lord Corlain," said Levin.

"Why?"

"He lost his wife in childbirth and the surviving daughter went mad."

"Very sad," said Kantees.

"The girl murdered three servants—two of them at a wedding —and escaped."

"This has nothing to do with me or his rudeness. I was invited to the council."

They fell silent until there was a knock on the door.

"Come!" called Daybian.

"I wondered where you had got to," said Lord Jakalain.

No food then, thought Kantees.

"Lady Kantees, I have spoken with Lord Corlain."

She glared at the window as if her gaze could shatter the glass.

"He wishes to express his apologies for his uncouth attitude and harsh words."

"If he wants to apologise, he can do it in person, not send someone to do it for him."

There was a pause.

"Lady Kantees of the Ziri."

She spun round and faced Lord Corlain; the man, Bejeren, stood at his shoulder. She would have to be careful of that one, and anything Corlain said, if this lackey of the Arch-patterner was whispering in his ear. She returned her gaze to the lord.

"Lady Kantees, I spoke out of turn and was unconscionably rude."

Kantees gave a thought to Sheesha and Looesa. "Yes, Lord Corlain, you were very rude."

"I cannot excuse it."

"But you were also right. I was a runaway slave. I did steal and ride Lord Jakalain's *zirichasa,* all crimes which are punishable by death. I took another slave with me, and assisted in the break-out of a prisoner. On the other hand, I alerted the castle to attack, rescued Lord Jakalain's younger son, and then his older son. And I brought word of the impending attack of the Dunor, giving Lord Jakalain the chance to prepare his defences.

"But let us consider, Lord Corlain, that it was the Taymalin that invaded the lands of the Kadralin and ripped it from them. And here in Esternes, if not elsewhere, we were enslaved. It was the Kadralin that rode and commanded the *zirichasa.* I have taken back what is mine by right of birth."

At that moment, there were shouts from outside and the shrieking calls of half a dozen *ziri* penetrated the room, along with the thump-thump of their wings beating hard to hold them in the air. Since Kantees had her back to the window she could only see the reactions of those in front of her, but that was sufficient. They all took a step back and gasped. More than one hand went to a sword or dagger.

Kantees knew the *ziri* wouldn't be able to hover for more than a few moments but they had done their job. She raised an arm and waved, at the same time ordering Sheesha, and the others he had brought with him, to return to their eyries.

It had all been for show, but the look on their faces made it worthwhile, even Yenteel looked impressed. She glared at the one called Bejeren, daring him to make a comment as he turned his eyes on her with a look of that unfortunately resembled satisfaction rather than astonishment. Apparently she was still playing the game the way they wanted.

"You command them," said Lord Jakalain and Kantees could not tell whether the tone of his voice was excitement or fear.

They had returned to the room set aside for the council and proceeded as if there had been no interruption. There was no repeat of the rudeness.

"There's something I don't understand," said Kantees at a lull in the discussions of defences against the giant *tekrasa*.

"What is that, Lady Kantees?"

"Why is Lord Corlain here? I mean, with all due respect, his lordship is only the second most powerful family in Faerholme and that land is a very long way from here. Why is it just Corlain and Jakalain? Where are the others?"

It was Levin who answered. "You know Hamalain belongs to the Dunor, and we were too unsure of my family. The Otulain are very close to Hamalain. I know my uncle is unhappy with the restrictions the Great Concordance places on him."

"The Garbalain?"

"Rejected our approaches." Levin hesitated. "We know from

Tenical that the Tanderlain in Faerholme are part of the conspiracy. We have attempted to recruit other families but they are lukewarm to our approach. It's not that they don't believe us, some are aware of the Dunor it seems, but they are unwilling to pick a side."

Lord Jakalain stood up. "Those you see in this room are the only people willing to commit to opposing the Dunor. I cannot deny that if they had not kidnapped my sons, I would not be here. I would not even believe they existed."

"Do you have a plan?" she asked.

"We believe the Dunor are not aware Lord Corlain is on our side, so we expect them to mount an attack against us alone. When that happens word will be sent to those families who indicated they might side with us if they can see there is a genuine threat."

"They won't support you if you lose," said Kantees.

Lord Jakalain sat down. "No, they won't."

"And if the Dunor don't attack here but continue to build their forces while turning other families to their side, you lose again."

"We are aware."

Kantees sighed. "Then we must ensure they do attack here and that they are defeated."

Lord Corlain stirred. "And how do you propose we achieve that?"

"Getting them to attack here is easy," she said. "If their spies have not already seen, we must let them know that Kantees of the Ziri has returned to Jakalain. It was me they wanted then, and it is me they want now, whether to learn how I control the *zirichasa* or simply to kill me in revenge for embarrassing them." She paused. "I will be the bait. They will not be able to resist."

A warning horn sounded outside. Kantees recognised the call as the one to indicate a foreign messenger coming from the ley-circle.

Kantees stood up. "I will return to the Ziri Tower. Lord Jakalain, you might tell your household to keep silent about my arrival."

"You think that will stop tongues from wagging?" said Lord Corlain.

"Of course not, it will guarantee they will wag, but secretly and that will give it more credence and importance. When a slave is not permitted any form of possession it is secrets that become currency."

With that she gave them a short bow and left, with Yenteel, Levin and Daybian in tow.

They left the main tower and hurried across the courtyard.

Kantees paused as they entered the buildings at the base of the Ziri Tower.

"Daybian, will your father let you attend the meeting with this messenger?"

"Of course."

"Then please do so, I want to know everything that's said. Your father is a good man but I don't think he would be entirely honest with me."

"You want me to be your spy in my father's house?"

"Yes."

He bowed. "It is my pleasure, Kantees. I owe you my life and that of all my family. I will honour that even if they don't." He turned and headed back across the courtyard.

"Do you need me to do anything?" asked Levin.

"I need you to come with me."

"Where are we going?"

"Up there."

She led the way back through the stone passages and rooms, past the refectory to the stairs leading up the tower.

"I've brought these two girls to ride *ziri*," she said as they climbed. "I don't really know what to do with them. I don't know how to teach them, and I don't have authority here."

Levin gave a short laugh. "You've made a great display of what you do not have."

"And it will come tumbling down like a castle built from cards if I do not get a firm foundation soon."

"Don't the Kadralin here respect you?"

"Why would they? I was one of them and now I'm a runaway and a thief. I'm like them, only worse. And they aren't wrong, Levin, I am them. There's no real difference."

Levin said nothing for a few moments. "Do you want me to teach these women?"

"I don't know. I think I should do it but I don't even know where to start."

They had stopped between floors. Afternoon light filtered through doorways and highlighted the stones worn smooth by a thousand feet.

"What do you want them to be able to do?"

"What I can do."

"You mean make the *ziri* go fast?"

"I don't know if they can do that, but they need to be able to fly first."

"How did you learn?"

Kantees shrugged. "Sheesha made me ride him. I just hung on."

"Did you use a saddle?"

"Yes, at first. I didn't know there was another way back then."

"Well, it seems to me that you should follow the same process."

Kantees frowned at him. "But…"

"What?"

"It's just that I spent years tending to Sheesha and the other *ziri*. I looked after him, shovelled his shit, refilled his water when he kept knocking it over. Fed him."

"So you want them to spend years shovelling *ziri* shit before you let them fly?"

"Of course not, but how much of what I learnt then was important in what came later? How can I know how much they should know?"

"I suppose knowing how to care for a *ziri* is important," he said, "but I never had to clean them. And I can fly."

"You can't make them fly fast."

"You're saying that you think your ability with Sheesha is thanks to you spending years cleaning up after him?"

"Yes? No? I just don't know."

"I don't see the problem. Teach them how to look after *ziri*, teach them how to use a saddle and reins. Get them in the air in a way that they can't fall off. Then teach them how to fly without."

Kantees thought about it for a few moments and nodded. "There's another thing, though."

"More problems for me to solve for you?"

"How do I deal with the enslaved Kadralin and the Taymalin here who only knew me as a slave?"

"I have no idea. I was born with authority in my very bones. Do you need their approval?"

"It would be nice."

Levin shook his head. "I've been here long enough to know that Romain is a complete *jikasak*."

Kantees giggled and Levin grinned. "You don't need his approval, and the younger ones? They'll look up to you because you're a runaway who rides a *ziri* and has come back a hero. They'll want to be like you."

"That just makes it worse; they're still slaves."

"There's nothing wrong with giving people hope, Kantees." Then he stood back from her and stood straight. "Enough of the self-pity and worry, Kantees of the Ziri. You've already done far more than anyone here could achieve."

"Remaking the World's Pattern?"

"It's what we all want to do, some of us succeed."

Kantees straightened up too.

"So, what are your orders, Lady Kantees?"

"I need two young *ziri*—"

She was interrupted by Romain shouting up the stairs as he thumped his way up. "What have you done?"

Kantees looked down at him as he came into view. He was a small man, she realised, not just in stature but in his imagination. It wasn't so much that he knew the rules of how to train the *zirichasa*, it was more that he was the embodiment of them. But not as if they were alive in him, more that he had entombed them within himself. He spoke the law, but there could be no change and they rotted away inside him.

"The *ziri* were in uproar! The ones that could get free flew away. And I know it was you, Kantees, don't you deny it!"

He climbed half the steps towards her but Levin took two steps down and loomed over Romain so he was forced to stop—he could not push past a member of the aristocracy, barely even dared approach him.

"Yes, of course it was me, Romain," she said glancing at Levin but he wasn't looking back at her. The fact that he had taken a couple of steps down meant that she towered over both of them. "I am Kantees of the Ziri. I command them and they do my bidding." Just for effect, she prodded Sheesha to make him roar but he ignored her. Perhaps he was asleep. Never mind. "I am a free woman, and you do not rule me."

"Bow," said Levin.

Romain's eyes flicked towards him, uncertain and scared. "Bow?"

"Make your obeisance to Lady Kantees of the Ziri."

Romain stared at him as if the words had no meaning. Kantees desperately wanted to disagree with Levin and tell Romain he didn't have to bow. She didn't want people to bow to her, not through force anyway, that was the Taymalin way. But she knew she couldn't gainsay him without losing what little authority she had. Damn him.

Then Romain's gaze returned to her. She lifted her chin.

He was old, but he was not infirm though you might think he was as he went down on one knee and turned his eyes to the steps in front of him.

"Thank you," she said, trying to keep her voice hard with a suppressed anger she did not truly feel. "Now, you interrupted my discussion with Lord Levin but it had to do with you so I shall order you directly. I require two *ziri* who are old enough to be ridden for my apprentices. They can share the mating eyries below Sheesha. They will require tack and saddles for riding. And the apprentices must learn the care of *ziri*.

"I give you authority in that instruction, but that is your limit. You have no other command over them. You will arrange this as your first priority, after you ask Goodwife Leesa to attend me."

Romain did not look up, nor did he rise. "I must get approval from his Lordship. I cannot have my tower turned upside down."

"Lord Jakalain is dealing with matters of state at present," said Levin. "You will do as Lady Kantees instructs for now. You will have your permissions when it is convenient for them to be delivered."

Levin glanced back at her and gave her a nod.

"You're dismissed, Romain," said Kantees.

He rose to his feet and without looking back headed swiftly

down the stairs, making considerably less noise than he had on the ascent.

Kantees realised she was holding her breath and let it out slowly. Then sat on the steps with her head in her hands. "This is not me, Levin."

"I know but sometimes it's necessary."

"I hope that's enough and I don't have to do it again." When Levin didn't respond Kantees looked up at his face. "Well, I hope I don't have to do it often."

"We can hope."

"That's not very convincing."

"I'll try harder in future."

20

The rest of the day went quickly. The pressure she had put on Romain lasted long enough for him to organise the *ziri* for Jynolee and Helka. Kantees checked them first to make sure they were healthy, since she wouldn't put it past Romain to use lesser beasts.

Goodwife Leesa arrived and Kantees, with Helka's assistance, arranged for some new clothes for herself, and riding gear for all three. The Goodwife was a widow, perhaps in her fiftieth year, who now lived in the tower providing repairs and making clothing mostly for the free servants, and the occasional slave who needed it for a special reason. Kantees had never been one of those.

Although Goodwife Leesa was also concerned about providing the services without proper authority, Kantees assured her it would be forthcoming. She required much less convincing than Romain.

"Another thing, if you don't mind," said Kantees. "What would it take to clothe all the staff properly, even the slaves?"

The woman smiled. "A great deal of cloth, needles, thread and time."

After she had gone, Kantees took Jynolee and Helka to meet their *ziri*. It would not resemble her first encounter with Sheesha but that would not be a bad thing.

The mating eyries were arranged so that a male and female *ziri* could be introduced to one another slowly, just in case, so there was a gate between the two main areas that could be drawn back and locked off so it would not open further. Sheesha had been through the process more than once, he was a popular sire and it brought money into the castle.

However, these two *ziri* were both male and born of the same clutch laid by Shingul. The father had come from Hamalain, but Kantees did not hold that against them.

"This is Kotoka," she said as she put her hand out to the red-yellow feathers of the *ziri*. Kotoka was probably only half the size of Sheesha, but he would grow at least another half-length before he was done. "Jynolee, you will look after him." Kantees took the girl by the hand and drew her up to Kotoka's head. "Let him smell you. He will like to be scratched, they all do, but learn what and where he itches most."

The other *ziri* was all blue but shaded from almost black to purple highlights. "Helka, you are responsible for Yuleto, the same applies to you. He will become your friend if you give him a chance. The *ziri* are clever and they will understand you. They may be ruled by their appetites, but they learn and remember. They are more than mere animals. If you look after them they will care for you in their turn."

She stepped back as the two young women stroked and then hugged the *ziri*. Helka seemed the more nervous, perhaps because of her problems with flying. Jynolee expressed a quiet passion that Kantees understood, but she was determined not to have favourites.

Leaving the girls, she went to a window and unshuttered it. Light flooded in but she was more interested in what was happening in the meeting across the way. Who had arrived? Perhaps an emissary from a family that had decided to align themselves with Jakalain? Kantees hoped that was the case.

There was so much to do, and so little time. No, it was not that there was little time, it was that she had no idea how much time they had. There was no way to judge how much she could achieve, no way to decide what was more important.

She heard Jynolee laugh and turned. Kotoka was using his head to push her back towards his wings and got down on his belly.

"He wants you to ride already, but don't be fooled, he's a *ziri*, they always want to fly, that's what he's made for. Unless they're sleeping, of course. He's just being selfish and he thinks he can push you around." Kotoka kept nudging but before Kantees could give any more advice Jynolee shoved him back. His head swung away from her and she took another step forward, shoving him again.

There was a moment when Kotoka raised his head so he was looking down on the girl.

"We're not going out now," she said. "You can just wait." Then she put her hands on her hips and stared up at him. The contest of wills took fewer than ten heartbeats—or twenty, the way Kantees' heart was pounding at that moment. Then Kotoka dropped his head, and slid it over to her so she could rub it more.

Kantees turned to Helka. "Any problem for you?"

She shook her head. "They're like children, aren't they?"

"So I've been told," said Kantees. "But a child that could kill you with a single bite, crush your ribs by sitting on you, or knock you out of the Ziri Tower with their tail by accident."

"Then a firm and caring hand is all they need." Helka turned her attention to Yuleto. "You do as you're told and we can have fun."

"Good," said Kantees. "I expect they've been fed, they don't seem hungry. I'm going to check on Sheesha." She turned towards the door.

"Lady Kantees?"

"Jynolee?"

"Back in Riverrush we played with them."

"Yes." Kantees smiled at the memory.

"Do we play with them here?"

"What sort of thing?"

Jynolee looked embarrassed. "Like a *zatek*, they like to chase after things and return them."

"Do they?"

"You've never played with one?"

Kantees felt her body stiffen with the awkwardness she felt. "I can't say I've ever played with a *zatek*; there are a couple in the castle but…no. The younger *ziri* do chase each other, and fight over food, though it's never serious. These two are beyond that stage."

"Do you mind if I…we…try?"

"No, of course not, but I wouldn't recommend tussling with them."

"Yes, mistress."

Kantees went up the stairs to Sheesha's eyrie. He pretended to be asleep, although she saw him open an eye. Then he caught the smell of the other *ziri* on her and spent several minutes sniffing her while she idly scratched his head.

"Did you want to play when you were young, Sheesha?"

He paused for a moment in his snuffling and bumped his nose against her midriff, as if that meant something important. Perhaps it did.

"I never had a chance to play when I was young, at Kevrey's home. Then when I found you, I think I had forgotten play existed at all." She sighed. "They took more from me than I even know about."

She jumped as she heard Jynolee shout and there was the regular thump of heavy *ziri* feet across the floorboards below. Then there was laughing and she relaxed. There was a pause and Jynolee shouted *Let go you stupid thing*, more laughing and the thump-scratch-thump of a *ziri* using elbows and talons to move faster across the floor. Helka was laughing too.

Sheesha put his head on one side to listen and then bumped Kantees again.

"I'm not going to stop them," she said. "I may not have played with you but they are not me. Their lives have not been mine. They must befriend their *ziri* in their own way." More laughter and now what sound like two *zirichasa* running across the floor. "Sounds like they already have. Well, let them wear themselves out."

She glanced at the hatch that led from the eyrie into open air. She was desperate to use it. She wanted to get out into the open and just fly. It didn't matter where. But she was trapped. It didn't matter who had come, the idea that she was here secretly needed to be maintained so that when the gossips' tongues wagged the lie would be more convincing. Then the word of her presence here would spread faster and it would be believed.

Kantees of the Ziri is hiding at Jakalain.

And the Dunor would not be able to resist, they would have to come, and they would bring all their might so they could crush Jakalain fast and without a fuss. Then they would have Kantees and be able to wring the secret of the *ziri* magic from her.

Kantees shook her head, she would never let that happen. The Dunor had to be stopped and if that meant she would help to protect Jakalain, then so be it.

A bright golden line crawled above the horizon to the south.

Even though she was inside the tower she jerked her head up as if she could see the *melinak* through the walls. She jumped to her feet.

Only the Dunor used *melinasa* as far as she knew. If Ulina was right, they were a Farahalek secret. It would be spying on the castle, perhaps it was timed to arrive at the same time as the emissary. Perhaps it was just a coincidence.

Did it matter if a *melinak* spied on the castle? It was almost a certainty the Dunor had spies here.

Then she heard someone on the stairs. She backed up and turned Sheesha so he would be in a position to attack if needed.

"Kantees!"

She breathed out. "There's a *melinak* coming, Levin."

"Oh, we've had them regularly."

"But they'll have seen everything, why didn't someone tell me?"

"It's all right, Kantees, they don't see anything. Come on, I'll show you."

"Where?"

"Roof."

He headed up the next ladder. She hitched up her skirt and followed.

The *melinak* was almost overhead by the time they came out into the daylight.

"Look around," was all he said.

It took her a few moments to realise that the castle looked exactly as it had always done—which was not how it had been when she had arrived that morning. The spear launchers were gone and looking down she could not see the new walls.

"Blending patterns?"

"You know about them?"

"Long story."

"They were cooked up between Tenical and the Swordmaster."

Kantees did not hide her surprise. "But Tenical is so unimaginative and the Swordmaster so…angry."

Levin smiled and shrugged. "I can't deny it but he was the one who pointed out we needed to keep the defences hidden and Tenical was aware that such patterns existed. They scoured the town and found someone who knew them."

"A Kadralin wise-woman?"

"A thief."

"Oh."

"Yes, well, in exchange for a pardon he revealed his very limited knowledge, and Tenical improved on it, then they employed a couple of scribes and the castle patterner to make scrolls—"

"Ha," said Kantees with a grin.

"What?"

"Tenical has a very low opinion of scrolls."

"Used to have, I think. Anyway, each of the teams keeps one of them and, when alerted, they hide."

Kantees changed the subject. "Who's the visitor?"

Levin's good humour dissipated. "One of my father's men."

"I see."

Levin leaned out over the low wall and stared down the height of the tower. "I suppose I shouldn't be surprised. I mean I don't know if my father is one of those at the heart of the Dunor, but he is in league with them." He turned round and sat with his back to the wall, facing in towards the cone-shaped roof on the tower. "It explains all the visits from Hamalain."

"Deenya?"

Levin looked up at Kantees. "Oh yes, you met her."

"I didn't like her."

"She doesn't like servants, especially not slaves."

"We already knew that Hamalain were part of the Dunor."

"I just didn't see the connection. It didn't even occur to me until today."

"I wouldn't be too upset about it, nobody knew about them until the attack here." *And that wouldn't have happened if it hadn't been for that stupid prophecy.* "Let's call that a good thing."

Levin looked at her more closely, as if he was trying to see into her mind. "You've changed."

Kantees hesitated with the words *not really* on the tip of her tongue. "Yes. It's been an interesting time." She did not offer any further information and he didn't ask. They lapsed into silence.

Closing her eyes and leaning back against the roof Kantees listened to the castle. It was almost as if she had never been away. The voices and the echoes. The pungent smell of the Ziri Tower— of *ziri* shit—with the constant aroma from cooking coming up from the kitchens.

The hatch of an eyrie ground open. Kantees opened her eyes. Only Daybian rode for Jakalain and he was with his father, the only other two riders were on the roof. Then there was a woman's squeal.

Kantees flung herself to the wall and looked over, to see the tail of a blue *ziri* disappearing downward with a rigid figure perched on its back.

"Idiots!"

She dived for the door and went down the ladder as fast she could, one floor then two. She burst into the mating eyrie to see Jynolee mounted on Kotoka just inside the open hatch.

"Stop!" In the moment of panic and anger she poured her order into Kotoka. The *ziri* froze, pulled in his wings and then dropped his belly to the ground. He wasn't going anywhere. But now Kantees could see a man standing silhouetted against the light.

"Romain! What are you doing? Levin, get that *ziri* away from the hatch." Kantees rushed to the hatch and stared out.

"You told me to get them in the air. Even though they are less than nobody and don't deserve it." His voice wavered but there was an undertone of triumph.

"Get back before I push you over!"

She must have been convincing because he moved away fast.

"Kantees, this stupid beast won't move."

She looked out again but she couldn't see Yuleto. "Leave him, you get after Romain and don't let him go downstairs." She turned her attention to Jynolee; the beast was saddled and the girl strapped in properly but she wasn't wearing protective clothing. And she looked terrified—of Kantees.

Taking care to compose herself, Kantees spoke more gently. "Get off the *ziri*, Jynolee, then take him into the other eyrie. I'm sure you can work out how to remove the saddle and straps. Settle him down."

"Yes, mistress."

One problem at a time. If Helka and Yuleto had not been smashed to bits at the bottom of the tower they were probably safe for now. Kantees pictured the missing *ziri* in her mind and tried to instruct it to return to the tower. She added the idea of nice juicy *lukisa* meat waiting here.

She heard Sheesha grumping above them as if he wanted the meat, then she felt Kotoka snuffling at her. Kantees shook her head. Food was the only thing *zirichasa* truly cared about. But Jynolee grabbed the reins near his halter and dragged his head round then towards the other eyrie. Kantees was pleased with that, anyway. Jynolee had learnt that where the head goes the body and tail will follow.

It wasn't long before Kantees saw a dark blob heading towards the tower. It resolved quickly into the blue of Yuleto, he was coming directly into the eyrie. Kantees stepped to the side of the entrance. Being smaller than Sheesha, the *ziri* didn't have to fold his wings in as much to get through the opening and, moments later, the back-wing downdraught set dust and straw swirling around them. The *ziri* landed neatly as Kantees pushed the eyrie hatch shut.

Before it closed, she saw the one thing she did not want to see; a party of men in peacock colours at the entrance of the main tower and looking up at them. She was sure they couldn't make her out beyond being a Kadralin so finished shutting the hatch. But she cursed Romain for being such a milk-puke and herself for being so trusting.

She turned and leant her back against the wall. Yuleto was strutting and looking pleased with himself. Helka's pale face was whiter than usual but she seemed unharmed.

2 1

Kantees stood in the meeting room while Lord Jakalain shouted at her. She did not argue with him and she did not justify, or try to lay blame elsewhere. It was the price you paid for being a leader, she understood that. That did not mean she was going to gloss over the truth. She certainly would not protect Romain.

Finally Lord Jakalain wound down into silence. An awkward silence to everyone there except perhaps Kantees herself. She had been on the receiving end of much worse, and had received beatings for far less.

"I did two things wrong, Lord Jakalain. I did not warn my apprentices to stay out of sight during the visit, and I trusted Romain." She spoke quietly.

"Romain has never liked Kantees, even before," said Daybian. "If it weren't for his skill with the *ziri* he should have been removed a long time ago."

Kantees wished for a moment that Daybian would not try to help her. He didn't even realise that Romain's knowledge of *ziri* was lacking and what little he did know was hidebound. He could not adapt. What she did not need was an outright attack on Romain as a person.

"Romain taught me everything he knew about the *zirichasa*," said Kantees. "If it had not been for that I would not have been able to do what I have done."

"It may not be all bad, my Lord," said the Swordmaster. "It will add fuel to the rumour which we wanted circulated. You saw as much as they did, and that was only the tail of a blue *ziri* flying into the Ziri Tower."

Kantees stared in surprise at Erang, she had not expected support from that quarter.

"Sheesha is blue and gold," said Daybian.

"Which is to our benefit, Lord Daybian, they will not be able to resist if their information contains uncertainty. If an opponent is in possession of all the facts their path becomes clear. They could choose to attack or not attack, and they would know how to prepare." He paused for a breath. "However, in attacking Jakalain now they will be uncertain as to whether Kantees is here—though it remains the bait—and they know nothing of our defences."

"What about spies within the castle?" said Kantees.

"The ley-circle is under firm control. Any spy would have to go to another ley-circle before they could report. And we are protected against the *melinasa*."

"Have you killed any of them?"

"Certainly not, we don't want to give the game away."

"You don't think allowing spies to view the castle without any effort to stop them is not suspicious?"

The Swordmaster did not reply but looked thoughtful.

Kantees looked from Lord Corlain, who had said nothing but had consumed several glasses of wine, to Lord Jakalain.

"I am responsible for my people but in this they did no wrong, the fault was mine alone," she said. "Is there any action you feel you want to take against me?"

Lord Jakalain raised his eyes and looked into hers across the room. She resisted the automatic response to stare at the ground, and met his gaze instead.

"What's done is done," he said. "And you are beyond my jurisdiction. There is nothing to be gained from recrimination, which means this discussion is pointless. What is important, however, is what we have learnt from this emissary of Otulain."

He waved his hand to indicate that Kantees should be seated, so she took her place behind her table with Yenteel beside her.

"They offered a bribe and a threat," he said with barely concealed anger. "If I support the Dunor they will give me a position on their council and even new lands taken from the families that do not join. And if I do not, they will reduce Jakalain to rubble, killing me and my family." He slammed his fist on the table. "They, who have already threatened my family, kidnapped my sons, and tortured my heir, offered me a seat at their table." The fist struck the table again. "Then dared to threaten me."

He sat back in his chair, grabbed his goblet and downed the liquid within it.

"What did you answer?" asked Kantees.

The lord settled back in his chair with a smile that expressed nothing but contempt. "I said I would think about it."

Three days later, in a light drizzle, Kantees stood on the top of the Ziri Tower watching Jynolee and Helka take turns in launching from their eyrie, flying around the outside of the castle walls and returning. It had been going on all morning.

"If I was them," said Levin, "I would be craving something more than these baby flights."

"I flew off to the mountains the first time," said Daybian. "Best day of my life. Out from under the thumb of Romain, and my parents."

"Women are more used to drudgery," said Kantees.

Daybian just laughed. "Says the woman whose first flight saved us all."

"I know what I'm talking about."

"They'll do as you say, Kantees, because of who you are," said Levin, "but don't expect them to enjoy it."

Kantees suspected they might be right but she wasn't going to admit it. But Levin had planted the beginnings of an idea in her head.

"So, are all the lordling riders like you two?"

"You've seen most of them, Kantees," said Daybian laughing again. "What do you think?"

"I think you like your cups too much, you take stupid risks when racing, and a wench as a bedfellow is your idea of a night well spent."

Levin also grinned. "There might be a reason for that."

"You're male?"

"There's always too much responsibility at home," said Daybian, with an almost serious tone in his voice as he looked at the works in progress. The inner walls were growing fast. They weren't thick but no heavy siege weaponry would be dropped in by a *tekrak*. They just needed to stop infantry.

"No responsibility and lots of excitement," said Kantees, "yes, that sounds like you, Daybian."

"Just me? What about him?" He jabbed his finger at Levin.

Kantees shrugged. "Levin stopped growing up when he was twelve I should say." Levin frowned and Daybian grinned. "Of course you, Daybian, never got beyond five." She smiled to soften the insult but Daybian just broke down in laughter.

Helka was coming around for her landing. Kantees stuck two fingers in her mouth and let out a shrill whistle. Both rider and *ziri* looked up. Kantees gestured for them to fly up and land on the parapet beside them.

"Bottle of my father's favourite wine she falls off," said Daybian.

Kantees turned full towards them. "Levin, if you take that bet, I'll make sure Waileth never lets you ride her again." She glanced down at the *ziri* now labouring to climb to their level—Helka had taken the order too literally and not allowed Yuleto to climb more slowly. Kantees turned back to Daybian whose expression suggested he was expecting a roasting. "But I'll take that bet."

It looked as if Helka had realised her mistake and launched Yuleto off to the side, building speed as he climbed more slowly. When they had reached a height above the top of the tower, they executed a good turn and Helka directed Yuleto at the tower. She let him glide in until they were just above the stones. Then the fierce blast of the backwing brought them to a stop but Yuleto's wing caught on the sloping roof and they overbalanced.

"Ha!" said Daybian.

Instantly Helka leaned in, the change in balance giving Yuleto a moment to regain his footing. He brought in his outer wing first and then the inner one.

Kantees looked over her shoulder at Daybian. "You owe me a bottle of wine."

"You don't even drink wine."

"Reneging already?"

Daybian held up his hand in surrender.

Kantees turned back to the *ziri*. Helka had remained dutifully silent as the beast perched precariously on the wall, using both his neck and tail to balance.

"That's enough practice for today, Helka. Tell Jynolee and Romain that we will be riding out tomorrow, the *ziri* must all be fed. And that includes Waileth, Shingul and Looesa."

"Yes, mistress."

In a single smooth motion, Helka leaned to her left, Yuleto took the hint and allowed himself to fall off the tower. Moments later, rider and *ziri* shot out from the tower then into a reverse turn back to the eyrie below.

"She's good," said Levin.

"And looking for a nice lordling to entrap with her womanly wiles," said Kantees.

"Is that right?" said Daybian with sudden interest.

"You keep your hands off her, young Lord Jakalain, your father won't want you marrying a girl from some nowhere town."

"Who said anything about marriage?"

"If Levin wasn't in the way I'd slap you into the Mother's embrace. I said no touching, and I meant it."

"I was joking."

"Of course you were," said Kantees. "Just like that evening of the feeding."

Levin adjusted his position to face his friend. "Would that be the evening you were struck down by a shit shovel?"

"I still wear the scar," said Daybian.

Kantees gave a short laugh. "I didn't leave a scar, I didn't even break the skin."

"You scarred my pride forever, Kantees."

"You deserved it."

Daybian grinned. "Yes, I did."

Kantees and Sheesha flew out to the ley-circle the following morning accompanied by Yenteel on the back of Looesa. The two girls were already far ahead of him in their skill on *ziri*-back but then he had no real interest in learning.

Lord Jakalain had been very accommodating when it came to Kantees' demands on his estate and resources; she was wearing her new riding gear but that was nothing compared to her acquisition of the two, very valuable, racing *ziri*. She suspected his largesse had nothing to do with her, but everything to do with his anger at the Dunor. She hoped she would be able to repay his generosity, and help him assuage his anger.

She set down a short distance from the circle. The whole area inside and around it was cleared of every bit of plant life. Not even a blade of grass showed.

"Lord Jakalain takes the protection against abominations and attack seriously," said Yenteel as they approached a temporary wooden building that housed the usual guards. It was removed during feedings. Further out from the circle were dozens of tents filled with armsmen, comprising Jakalain's regular troops, men from Corlain, and trained levies co-opted into service from the town.

Between the circle and the castle were emplacements of spear launchers in case they brought in *tekrasa* through a patterner's path.

"I hope it's enough," said Kantees, and she was not talking about the abominations.

At the guard-post they were given permission to inspect the circle itself. To Kantees the entire place glowed with power. Yenteel knew why she was here. Tenical would probably have guessed but he had not arrived yet.

Kantees had the *chilafrah* in her pack. She had no real idea of how it stored power, but being in the presence of a concentration of the Mother's milk seemed to work. So all she had to do was be as close to the power as possible.

"You haven't said where we're going," said Yenteel as they wandered across the damp dirt.

"Riverrush first."

"Showing off their daughters on *ziri*-back already?"

"Partly that, mostly so Tenical and Vonand can learn the circle's pattern."

"You're taking the house patterner?"

"Only for as long as it takes for them to build a platform up to the circle, then he'll make a path back here."

Sheesha screeched and the two of them turned to see four more *ziri* flying out from the castle.

"You don't need all of these for that. You could do it and be back by the evening meal."

"Then we're going into the mountains to see Gally and Ulina."

Yenteel gave a slight frown. "More plans?"

"More plans."

She and Yenteel walked back to the waiting group. The *zirichasa* kept beating their wings with excitement, letting out squawks and shrieks. Kantees could feel them all and their emotions were infectious.

The only two people in the group who were not smiling were Tenical and Vonand. Jynolee and Helka stood close together holding the reins of their *ziri*, they were not ready to fly without saddles yet.

Daybian and Levin with Shingul and Waileth stood without speaking but Kantees could see, for them, this was like that time before a race when they waited before heading out to the starting platform. It had been decided that the two patterners would ride with them, partly because the lordlings' *ziri* were larger, and because it seemed more politic. Some modifications had been made to the saddles to make it more comfortable for the patterners sitting behind. Kantees was sure Tenical would rather be in the gondola of a *tekrak*, but it would be too slow.

Kantees and Yenteel approached the group and she thought she ought to say something, but found she had no words. She just smiled and said, "Mount up please." At her thought, every *ziri* lowered itself to the ground. Kantees saw the way Vonand stared at her. He was loyal to Jakalain, but she knew he would not show any such loyalty to her.

Once they were all settled, Kantees mounted Sheesha. She had flown fast with more *ziri* than this but only Yenteel knew about that in this group.

This would be interesting.

She raised her arm, held it for a few moments and then dropped it. They launched into the air. Wings straining against the attraction of the earth. Armsmen came out of their tents to watch them, some of them even cheered as the group climbed. Kantees brought them over the ley-circle and had them gain altitude in a tight spiral. Her apprentices would learn a lot from this journey, she thought.

She looked back. The *ziri* had organised themselves into a formation with Kotoka and Yuleto in the first row behind her, then Shingul, Looesa and Waileth in the back row. She wondered briefly how they decided on the ordering but it did not matter. If the Taymalin lords and patterners felt slighted that was not her problem.

Once they had gained a good amount of altitude Kantees touched the ley-circle and guided Sheesha to feel it. She leaned forward and spoke to him so that no one else would hear. "Come, my beloved, consume its power. We have a long way to go and must get there swiftly."

Then, just as she had in the well of the circle at Hamalain, at the moment they were aimed along the southern border of the mountains, she gave Sheesha the command to move swiftly.

The golden sheath enveloped them in a moment and the ground slipped away beneath them like a fast-flowing river. That would give the troops something to think about, and the spies that were no doubt watching might be horrified at the show of power. She had given up trying to keep it a secret. The Dunor knew about it, that was why they came after her.

"Lady Kantees!" shouted Helka. "This is better than the first time."

Kantees laughed. "Of course it is!"

She heard Daybian give a whoop of enthusiasm. She shook her head, she liked his irrepressible good humour, and she admired his bravery when faced with impossible odds. But she would never be the woman he took to his bed either in or out of marriage. Not that his father would allow such a marriage anyway.

Now that she knew the rough distance to Riverrush, Kantees was more confident in allowing Sheesha to continue flying in the golden light. The distance they had covered at normal speed was a small part of the whole journey.

It was not long before the dark edge of the Talamyrth appeared on the horizon. Kantees adjusted their direction so they ran along its northern border. Then the big river, pouring from the mountains, came into sight and Kantees had Sheesha reduce to normal speed so they could turn upriver.

"There it is!" called Jynolee.

Kantees set the *ziri* into a glide and flew in low over the river with the town on their left. She noted that the new protective bank looked firm and strong as they glided past. The sound of shouts and cheers from the town grew. They flew past the end of the town and turned to come down and land in the same place they'd arrived on that first night.

Only Kantees and Yenteel lacked saddles and they slipped from the backs of their *ziri* and were there to greet the crowds that hurried out from the houses. But they all kept their distance while they stared and pointed, talking and whispering to one another. Kantees heard the names 'Jynolee' and 'Helka' spoken more than once.

Finally, the crowds parted to make a path for Loren the town-master with Hagata and Ithamel. Kantees spotted Jynolee's father just behind them. He might even have been smiling.

The town's three elders stepped beyond the edge of the crowd and went down on one knee. Like a wave the people around them, then those further out, also knelt. Some younger children looked confused.

Kantees wanted to tell them not to bow to her, but she knew she could not.

"Lady Kantees of the Ziri," said the townmaster. "We did not expect you back so soon, but we are happy to see you."

"Thank you, Loren," she said. "Please do stand."

He did so and the rest followed suit.

"We are not staying long," she said. "But I have brought a master patterner who will activate your circle and allow communication with the ley-circle at Jakalain." She turned to Helka. "Please take the patterners up to the circle, and take Jynolee's father." She turned back to the townmaster. "You will need to construct a platform, so the patterners can reach the ley-circle."

Loren gave some orders to his people. The crowd whispered as Helka headed away from the river accompanied by Tenical, Vonand, the blacksmith and a couple of other townsfolk.

"I shall order a feast," said the townmaster.

"Please don't," said Kantees. "I am honoured, of course, but we don't want to distract your people from their work, or consume more of your food than there is a need to. If you can find us a place to wait that will be all we need for now. If the patterners can do their work quickly then we will be gone very soon, if not we may need to stay overnight but we need nothing more than a place to sleep." She glanced at the sky where the clouds hung threateningly. "And perhaps a place out of the rain for the *ziri* and their riding gear?"

2 2

They did not leave that day. The threatened rain hit in the middle of the afternoon and while work went on creating the platform by the ley-circle, it was considerably slower than hoped. The *ziri* successfully hunted and fed, Kantees had been a little concerned about letting the young ones out to feed on their own but her experiences with the wild *zirichasa* suggested they liked to stay together and would return. And they did just that before the rain let loose.

It was now thundering on the roof of the boat house they had been given to stay in. Not as comfortable as Ithamel's home but it was dry, except where the roof leaked. And it was warm enough with six *ziri* sleeping off their meal.

"Do you know how to play *Devil's Bargain*, Kantees?" asked Levin.

She shook her head.

"It will pass the time." He pulled a leather card case from his bag and pulled out the pack. As he shuffled he explained the basic rules about drawing and discarding cards to create a hand that would beat the others. "Serious players bet on whether their hand is the best," he said.

"I don't have any money."

He shrugged. "We're friends, it wouldn't be right anyway. Daybian, can you collect some stones? We'll use those."

"I hate playing for worthless stuff," he said. "Want to play, Yenteel?"

"I don't gamble."

Daybian laughed. "Must be the only vice you don't have."

"I don't have any vices."

Kantees was surprised at the edge Yenteel's voice had. Thankfully Daybian did not respond but concentrated on locating as many pebbles as he could that were roughly the same size. He ended up with fifteen for each of them, and one over, which he kept. "Pays for my work."

"We'll play through a few hands with everyone showing what they have, so Kantees can get an idea of how to play," said Levin and dealt five cards to each and they began. Both lordlings felt the need to explain what they thought was the best play each time— each different from the other—whether to discard (always face up) and pick up new cards to get elements, processions, elemental processions, royal processions, families and feuds. The seniority of suits was complex, with Mother's milk being the best but it could be outranked by other combinations of the five elements. The *Kalamuk* was a bonus in any hand by promoting card ranks, but could be cancelled by the *Kisharuk*. While, on its own, the *Kisharuk* demoted the cards in the other players' hands.

It was enough to make one's head spin.

"I don't think I'm going to learn anything doing this," said Kantees. "Perhaps we should just play properly?"

She felt someone behind her and turned to find Helka and Jynolee watching. "Don't hover."

"You can hover by me," said Daybian. Kantees gave him a hard stare.

Helka laughed. "I think I'm safer here, young Lord Jakalain. My mistress has told us everything about you."

"Everything?"

"And what she has not said, it is easy enough to know. Tales of the lords taking advantage of poor village girls—"

"Shall we start?" said Levin. He dealt the first hand.

Kantees did not bet and tossed her cards in front of her.

"You had an elemental run of three, or a simple run of four," said Levin after he had taken the pot of four stones. "You could have changed a card and maybe improved it even more."

"I'm sure I'll get the hang of it," she said. "Let's play the next cards."

"Hand."

"Play the next hand."

This time she did bet a stone and the two lordlings let her win. She looked at their cards. "Don't do that! You had much better hands than me, I do not appreciate being coddled like a child."

"You want us to play properly?"

"What's the point if you don't?" she said.

"It won't fill up the whole afternoon then."

Kantees shrugged. "Are you saying I'm not your equal?"

Levin grinned. "I value my life, Kantees of the Ziri, I would never even think such a thought. Though I'm not so sure about my foolish friend over there."

"I learnt my lesson before you even met her," said Daybian rubbing the back of his head.

"So you'll play properly?"

They nodded.

Kantees promptly lost the next five hands and all except two of her stones.

"Are you sure you want to do this?" asked Levin.

She frowned. "Deal the cards."

When they came to show their cards, Kantees unhappily dropped hers face up.

"A royal fire and water feud!" said Daybian and tossed his down. "I have a peasant's procession from two." They weren't even compatible suits.

He and Kantees looked at Levin. He grinned and dropped his in front of him. "You win, Kantees, family procession but still only five up."

"Oh," she said and dragged the six stones in front of her.

They played three more hands with Kantees losing then winning until she was up by twenty stones.

Levin looked at Kantees and then Daybian. "We, my friend, have been washed, wrung out, and hung to dry in the summer sun."

Kantees could not suppress her smile. "Another hand, my lords? You still have pebbles to lose."

"You've played before?" said Daybian.

"What else do you think I did to while away the days between races? There's only so much you can do to look after a *ziri*." Kantees picked up the deck, shuffled it and dealt the cards. "But these are much nicer than the ones we had."

The game became tougher because Daybian and Levin started to work together, pushing the bets up when one of them had a good hand. But once Daybian had lost all his stones, Levin could only fight on for another two hands. Jynolee and Helka cheered and laughed.

"Thank you," said Kantees. "I enjoyed that."

Levin nodded. "It was very educational. You could have lost everything early on though."

"Then you would have let me start again."

Daybian sighed. "We would. The outcome would have been the same in the end."

"If you had realised earlier, you could have beaten me together just like you tried to."

"I never doubted you as a leader, Kantees," said Levin with a serious tone. "Now I am more certain than ever that if anyone can make this work, it's you."

"Life isn't a game of Devil's Bargain, Levin."

"Life might not be, Kantees, but I'm not so sure about war."

The door slammed open, a pair of very wet patterners stumbled in, and stood dripping in the entrance.

"Is it done?" asked Kantees.

"The platform will be complete before it gets dark," said Vonand. "I intend to use it as soon as I can. I have no desire to sleep in a cold damp barn when I could be dry and warm in my own bed."

"I agree," said Kantees. "And it will be good for the townsfolk to know that their ley-circle will bring them back into the world." She turned to Yenteel. "I need to send a message to Lord Jakalain, would you write it for me?"

"Do you want it sealed?"

"Please."

He nodded.

Kantees felt it was important to go to the ley-circle to see Vonand on his way, and wait until then to give him the letter, sealed with wax and wrapped in a greased bag to resist the water.

The rain was still falling hard and the way over the ridge to the ley-circle was treacherous. Both Jynolee and Helka accompanied her, as did Yenteel. And, because they did, Daybian and Levin felt they should as well. Tenical felt no such need and stayed in the dry with the *ziri*. Kantees did not blame him for a moment. Their riding gear was proof against water and had hoods so it was not too bad. Apart from being slippery with mud.

They were not the only ones, however, a good number of the townsfolk were also there.

The platform looked far too well-made to have been simply constructed this afternoon. Not only that but there was a considerable amount of ironwork. Clearly the townmaster had been keeping it a secret, the blacksmith and whoever their carpenter was had been working on it since she had left a few days before. It was good to know, especially as Vonand had to prepare a considerable number of patterns on the surface.

"What's he using to make the marks?" she asked Yenteel as the patterner moved back and forth on the platform more than a man's height above them.

"Some sort of wax stick, I think."

"Well-prepared."

"He's not the travelling sort, he probably assumed it would be wet out in the real world."

"He was correct."

Kantees knew from Tenical that preparing a patterner's path took a long time, and the additional wetness must make it harder so the light was almost gone by the time Vonand was ready. He raised his hands and chanted.

"The people are not going to be very impressed when he's done," she said even more quietly to Yenteel.

Nothing changed when Vonand finally gave up the chant and lowered his arms. Sure enough there were mutterings among the watchers. They had probably been expecting flashes of Mother's milk, or fires perhaps. The sort of thing from the tales of great mages battling terrible foes.

Kantees pushed forward and taking care on the slippery wooden steps climbed up. Pulling the package from inside her cloak she passed it to Vonand. "Please deliver this to Lord Jakalain."

"I will."

"How long will the path hold after you're gone?"

"Until I reach the other end. I don't recommend anyone following me."

"No, I was more concerned with guarding it."

"You can take the platform away."

"It moves?"

"It can be let down and rolled away on wheels."

Kantees was even more impressed. They had listened to everything she had said. "Thank you for your help, Vonand."

He gave a short bow, turned round and walked away from her. And vanished.

There were gasps from below. Someone screamed. Kantees faced the crowd. "Please lower the platform."

Back in the boat shed they dried out in front of a fire. The riding clothes kept out most of the damp but to get properly dry she would have to remove more clothing than was acceptable. She tried to see what arrangements they could make to split the men from the women. If this had been an animal shed they might have had hay to pile up. Or just stalls. But then they would not be able to light a fire. Once separated, they could get dry and curl up with the *ziri* to sleep. She was grateful Sheesha and the others were happy to remain out of the rain, damp *zirichasa* would have added smells to the overall unpleasantness.

"We need to have a separate space for men and women," she said finally, defeated by the problem. "We have to get dry."

"Blindfolds," said Daybian.

"I'm serious," she said. "Yenteel, Tenical, do you have any patterns to provide a screen?"

"You want to use magic for something so trivial?" said Tenical.

"No, I don't want to, but we need something."

There was a long silence.

"Lady Kantees?" said Jynolee.

"Yes, I know we need to sort out the other arrangements as well."

"No, I mean yes, we do but I have an idea. Couldn't we put the *ziri* between us? I know they aren't very big when lying down but it would probably be enough. And there wouldn't be any accidental peeking."

Kantees glanced at Daybian fairly sure he would try to accidentally peek. With her clothes damp and rubbing, and no other option she agreed. It had been easier when her clothes were so thin they dried as fast as her skin.

The *ziri* did not seem very keen on moving from the places they had found to be warm but they did as they were told and before very long they had two ranks of three *zirichasa* dividing the shed in half. Kantees could see the men on the other side but only their shoulders and heads. If the three of them on this side stooped the men would be able to see nothing by accident.

They started a new fire in the rear and peeled off their damp clothes; by running a rope from one side to the other and hanging the clothes on that, they blocked the view more completely.

Kantees finally started to warm up in front of the fire.

And then curled up under Sheesha's wing. The tension flowed out of her, another step had been completed. Levin wasn't really wrong about this war being like a game of Devil's Bargain. In fact, she was now playing the Dunor in exactly the same way she had played Levin and Daybian.

But there was one major difference, although she, and Lord

Jakalain, were giving the appearance of being weak and unprepared, there was no telling whether the hand they held was the stronger one. The cards were complex and the way they interacted far more difficult to understand.

And with that final thought, she slept.

2 3

Next day, having consumed as much as the people of Riverrush could persuade them to eat, the six *ziri* launched into the air once more. Thankfully the rain had given up, though the river continued to live up to its name.

Once in the air, the *ziri* adjusted their positions to the way they had been the previous day with Kantees at the point of the arrowhead.

The rain may have let up, but the sky was still heavy with clouds. Kantees debated the right course of action. If they flew above the cloud they could move faster and would be out of sight from the ground, but they would have to descend through it to get their bearings or land. And that could be dangerous.

Or they flew lower but slower, and risked being spotted by some Dunor scout. However they would not fly into a mountain by accident.

Finally she decided speed was more important. This wasn't a day where the clouds were fog in all the valleys, there would be open air once they broke through, and if they were careful in their descent it should be fine.

Decision made, she started the *zirichasa* climbing in wide spirals. The air got colder as the ground beneath them dropped away. They could see the town and the river, then deeper into the mountains and farther out across the plain.

Then everything became damp and grey as they went into the cloud.

Now there was nothing to see at all. The five other zirichasa and their riders behind her were nothing but grey ghosts.

And the cloud went on and on. Colder and colder. The wet seeped through to her skin and she felt as if all the effort to get dry last night had been pointless.

"Will we fly all the way to Lostimal, Kantees?" said the small, cold voice of Jynolee.

"Only to the sunlight."

They fell silent again. Kantees' other sense could still see the ley-circle below them, glowing in the grey. Sheesha's climbing spiral remained over the town, and if someone fell off they would splash into the river. But only she and Yenteel flew without saddles.

The air around them brightened until everything was brilliant white and they burst out into sunshine while the strange puffball clouds became the landscape beneath them.

Jynolee gasped, and Kantees thought she heard Helka swear under her breath. Let her swear, Kantees had not forgotten the first time she had seen the tops of the clouds. It was beautiful.

Unfortunately she now had a problem, they had been turning so long in the clouds she no longer knew which was the right direction and they were so high that not a single mountaintop was visible.

"That way!" shouted Yenteel. She turned to see him holding his device for judging direction and pointing off to their left. She waited until Sheesha came round and launched him in that direction.

The Kadralin town was to the north, she knew that, and not even very far. Certainly closer than Jakalain. They had only taken so long coming south because she had been an arrogant fool.

"Look!" shouted Daybian. Once again she twisted, he was pointing behind them and up.

A stream of black blobs floated across the sky even higher than the *zirichasa*. A glow burned at the rear of each of them. Her heart skipped as she thought it was a huge army of giant *tekrasa* and that the Dunor were a thousand times more powerful than she could imagine.

Then she realised this was a normal *tekrasa* migration and they were not huge. The biggest would be the size of a cart but no more than that. Most of them the size of a *ziri*'s head. Twice each year they gathered and flew across the land, heading in one direction or the other. Descending at night to root and feed. Rising again each morning to fly to wherever it was they went.

It was spring and that was the first season when they flew.

She turned away from them and focused on their journey. Sheesha would be able to fly fast for a short time without a ley-circle nearby. She gave him the instruction and he dived for speed. The clouds beneath them flashed by, they shot through a great billowing tower as the air around them flickered gold, stabilised and became perfectly still as the formation flashed into the north.

She peered down at the clouds, and desperately wished she could see through them, to understand how far they had come, and whether they were even close to their destination.

"Kantees!"

It was Yenteel, she twisted on Sheesha's back. There was no need to take a great deal of care when they flew like this since it was almost as if they were standing on the ground.

"Why are you using your eyes?"

Why indeed?

She shut them and imagined the world around her, she could feel the *ziri* and their golden power. It was not as strong as it had been with the wild beasts, but there had been many more of them. She was looking for a ley-circle, no, she corrected herself. She was looking for two of them, close together, one more powerful than the other.

She stretched out her senses. When they had flown above River-rush, she had been able to feel it all the way up here. The circle at the Kadralin town was far stronger than that.

It was almost a dream. She thought she could lie along Shee-

sha's back, her face to the sky and her mind reaching further and
further.

Two diamonds sparkled in the distance: one to the left and the
other forward and to the right.

She could not recognise them the way that the patterners said
they could but she knew the one in the distant west must be
Watching Pass. The place where she had almost killed Sheesha with
her arrogance. She had him adjust course until they were flying
directly towards the other glow.

She allowed herself a smile as it resolved into two sources, a
small one standing a distance away from the other, but that one
bubbling with golden light like a fire.

"We're returning to normal flight," she called as she ordered
Sheesha to slow down.

A golden line crossed her sight. In the past, these had always
been *melinasa* in the sky when she was on the ground. This time it
was from below, something was etching a golden path from the hot
glow of the ley-circle towards them. The distance from the ground
into the clouds was nothing to a *ziri* flying with magic.

And Kantees had barely a moment to shout a warning before a
golden arrow erupted from the white billows. It ceased to use its
magic in the blink of an eye and where it must have been coming up
almost vertically it was now horizontal, a good distance higher than
they were and powering down towards them.

"Kantees! Kantees! Kantees!"

She felt her face would break trying to express smile a hundred
times too big for it. "Gally!"

The *ziri* was the bland grey and brown of the wild ones, but
Kantees recognised Tabata.

Gally looped around behind the group staring down. "Yenteel!
Levin! Tenical! And Daybian!"

They called back their greetings. Kantees craned her head to
watch him. He stared at the two women, and they gave back as
good as they got.

"Gally doesn't know you," he shouted. "But Sheesha likes you,
so Kantees likes you, and Gally likes you."

Under his control, Tabata floated into a glide beside Sheesha.

"It is only two ten-day since you were gone, Kantees, but Gally has missed you every day. Gally is very happy you have come back. Gally has worked very hard with the people but they are not helpful. They are scared of the *ziri*, except for Marakees and some others. She is very good and she likes Gally. And there was some trouble but Ulina fixed it. You were very clever to ask Ulina to look after Gally. Gally thinks he would be dead because some of the people are very bad, but Ulina fixed it."

"Stop, Gally!" she said with a laugh. "You can tell me all about it on the ground. It was good of you to come to meet us."

"Gally saw your light and he knew it was Kantees."

Kantees absorbed that information as she checked the cloud cover. It was as dense here as it had been the entire journey. There was only one explanation: Galiko could see the golden trails just as she could. She knew she should be pleased but it felt as if she had lost something.

She tried to turn Sheesha but found him unresponsive. Instead he moved into a position behind and to the left of Tabata. Jynolee came up on the right, with Helka, Daybian and Levin in the third rank while Yenteel with Tenical were on their own at the back.

Gally didn't say anything but steered Tabata into a downward spiral just the way Kantees would have done and they descended into the clouds.

There was no rain when they emerged into the dull light. The Kadralin town lay beneath them and came up to meet them. As they approached the *Slissac* tower, the formation changed until they were flying in line. Kantees did not even know how Gally had done it and she was chafing at her inability to control Sheesha—not that he seemed concerned at all. But how could a small wild female *ziri* be senior to Sheesha?

She remembered that Levin had managed to break out of a *zirichasa* formation but Kantees wasn't going to do that, not just to satisfy her…she was not even sure what the emotion was. Sadness?

She saw changes below them: there was a new fence that stretched around the tower, and the ground between had been cleared. And there were some low wooden buildings, no more than sheds, built up against the tower itself and covering the entrance.

Tabata landed lightly and the others followed suit making a colourful line around the tower's base.

Kantees slipped to the ground and took the full force of Gally embracing her.

"Gally is so happy you're here."

And then someone grabbed her hand. Kantees looked down into the dark serious eyes of Ulina. She disentangled herself from Gally and knelt down on one knee, unsure whether the child would want a hug or not. Ulina placed her arms around Kantees' neck and buried her face in her shoulder.

"Hello, Ulina. I am very pleased to see you."

"You came back."

"I said I would."

The hug tightened then she simply let go and stepped back. "Who are these people?"

"You know most of them."

"Can the girls fight?"

"Their names are Jynolee and Helka, they can fight but not like you. Nobody could replace you."

Ulina nodded.

Kantees stood up and looked past the fence, between the buildings. On the surface the place looked the same as it had before, but the changes she had noticed after they destroyed the abomination were accentuated now. The people moved with energy—some of them—and there was the shouting and animal noises you expected in any town.

It looked normal.

"What's this place called?" said Helka.

Kantees opened her mouth and then realised she had no idea. She had never asked and when the people had been under the sway of the creature in the tower they probably hadn't cared.

"Two Circles," said Ulina. "Even though the other circle is way over there." She waved her hand in a generally westward direction. She stared at Helka. "Which one are you?"

"Helka, she's Jynolee."

"Why are you here?"

"Lady Kantees chose us to follow her, so we do. We do what she says."

"Good."

"Is there any food?" said Kantees.

Ulina pulled a face. "We don't have much."

"We have some from Riverrush. We can share it."

"Where's Riverrush?" said Gally. The light of excitement was in his eyes, and Kantees found it hard to understand. He was so different. Though, in other ways, just the same.

"A town to the south, near the border with the Talamyrth."

A woman emerged from one of the sheds, she might have been close to thirty years, or just sixteen, it was hard to tell, and her skin was as dark as anyone here. It was Daybian, Levin, Tenical and even Helka who were out of place. But Kantees reminded herself what Lintha had said about them all being the same. It was a hard lesson but Kantees did her best. After all, Ulina was very pale and Kantees regarded her almost as a daughter.

The woman approached and gave a very low bow. "Kantees of the Ziri, welcome to Two Circles. I am Marakees. I am afraid the people of my town are too scared or too embarrassed to greet you."

"They're bullies and cowards," said Ulina.

"They are lost and broken," said Marakees.

Sheesha bumped Kantees, she turned to face him, idly stroking the side of his face. He bumped her again. "You ate yesterday." He put his head on one side. "Yes, all right, I did make you fly a long way."

"Tabata can show Sheesha where to feed in the mountains," said Gally. "But the others must take off the saddles first."

There was a flurry of activity as the *ziri* were unburdened and then the party were treated to repeated blasts of air from seven pairs of wings launching into the sky.

The shed was as rough inside as it looked on the outside. But there were more than enough tables and chairs to go round, as if it had been prepared for many more people than those who occupied it.

They brought several tables together so they could sit and eat.

Ulina, Gally and Marakees had fetched some stew that seemed to be mostly vegetables, although there were lumps of meat in it.

"Tabata and some of the other *ziri* bring meat if we ask them to," said Marakees apologetically, though no one had complained.

Kantees was taken aback when Marakees sat down right next to Galiko. So close their legs must be touching, she thought. She tried to suppress the impulse to protect him, but he did not seem at all concerned by the woman's closeness.

Marakees was talking again. "After you left, while we were still befuddled by the after-effects of the abomination, the townspeople were happy to help and build these places for the riders of the *ziri*." She sighed. "But that wore off very fast. Most of them don't want to have anything to do with us."

"Do you ride?" said Kantees.

"I have my Aratat." She saw Kantees smiling. "Yes, Gally told me the story after he suggested it. Falling in love with his own reflection in the lake. Very foolish, I don't think my Aratat will do that. But I liked the name."

"What did you do before?"

"My father was a brewer, and I worked with him. The abomination didn't stop people doing what was needed to stay alive. But —" she hesitated deep in thought and memory, "—it doesn't matter."

"Didn't everybody go back to being the way they were before?" said Daybian.

"Nobody remembers what it was like before," she said. "Nobody knows how long it's been like this. It's never been different in my life."

"There might be dates written somewhere—" started Yenteel.

"Nobody wants to know!"

Marakees looked around in acute embarrassment, stood up and bowed to Kantees. "I'm sorry, Lady, I can't do this. There are too many people."

And she was gone. Without a word Gally chased after her.

Ulina took a bite out of one of the pies from Riverrush. "These are the best."

"I should probably go and apologise," said Yenteel.

"I wouldn't," said Ulina. "They'll be in their place by now. Gally knows how to look after her when she gets like this."

"*Their* place?" said Daybian with half a laugh.

"You laugh at them, Daybian, and I'll cut your precious clothes to ribbons."

Daybian shut up.

"But Gally and this woman?" said Kantees.

Ulina looked at her coolly. "Why not?"

Her question did not require an answer and no one dared try for one.

Finally Tenical broke the silence. "What is it you want me to do, Kantees?"

"Learn the patterns of the two circles—or whatever it is you do to recognise them—there's the big one here and a smaller one nearby. Then you can make a path back to Jakalain. I was hoping we might get a few more *ziri* riders here but it seems not. I suppose it was too much to hope for."

"It'll get better, Kantees," said Yenteel.

"I hope so."

2 4

---

*Y*enteel volunteered to ferry Tenical between the ley-circles. He was also aware of the *zirichasa* at the other circle and knew he needed to take care not to aggravate them.

Kantees took a walk around the town with her apprentices, guided by Ulina. Daybian and Levin stayed behind partly to make sure the *ziri* were not disturbed but also because they were interested in exploring the *Slissac* tower.

So the three women and one child set out into the streets. It had not changed since Kantees had been there last and there was not much to see. The people seemed to vanish as they approached.

"I really hoped they would recover," said Kantees as they looked out on another empty street.

"It means they won't be mounting their *ziri* and pillaging the towns in the lowlands, mistress," said Helka.

Kantees could not blame her for the thought but she had not seen what the people were like before. At least they were alive now, and not merely existing. Kantees could not even understand why the abomination had the effect on them that it did. What it did to *zirichasa* made some sense, they wanted to keep the *ziri* away most of the time, but needed them in order to reproduce. The *ziri* would carry their young to a new place, but it had to be at a time that suited the creature.

But why keep the townsfolk in thrall? What would it be like to be controlled in that way for your entire life, then to be set free without warning? The people wouldn't even really know what freedom meant.

"There are stories," she said without any warning, "of slaves who served their masters well. So well, the master offered them their freedom in gratitude. And the slaves would refuse because they did not know what they would do if they were free. It scared them."

"That's stupid," said Helka.

"Sometimes the story is different," said Kantees. "Where, for whatever reason, a slave suddenly finds themselves free. Perhaps their owners were all murdered. Sometimes they would plead to be killed as well, or immediately want to be the slave to someone else."

"Did you feel that way?" asked Jynolee.

"It was different for me," said Kantees. "I made myself outlaw by my own actions. I knew what life was like for those not born into slavery. It was always around me." She sighed. "And I had more freedom than most, both at Jakalain and before that in Dakastown."

Kantees looked at the buildings again, she had expected too much. Even the one person who had wanted to ride was troubled. Gally had implied there were others, perhaps he had been exaggerating because he was trying to impress her.

She turned to head back toward the tower, only to find a large group of men formed in the street a hundred paces away. Some of them carried large sticks and didn't look friendly.

Jynolee and Helka moved ahead of her then Ulina stepped in front of them. Her knife was in her hand.

Kantees pushed past them. "Stop it. You can't fight them."

Ulina looked round at her as if to say that she could.

"You're not going to kill any of them, Ulina."

Kantees faced the mob, they were not moving towards her yet but there were voices among them. Angry, desperate in tone though Kantees could not tell what they were saying.

"I don't know what to say to you!" she called out. "I can't stop you from feeling what you're feeling. Killing me won't change anything."

"We'll have done something." The voice was stilted as if speaking in a foreign tongue. It was just one voice in the crowd but Kantees could not see who it was.

"It wasn't me who did this to you. It was the thing in the tower."

"Now you're the abomination."

That got a rumbling of agreement. They knew the trouble came from the tower, there was still trouble—even if it was different—so it must come from the tower. Some of the braver souls at the front took more paces forward, or perhaps they were being pushed from those behind.

Kantees called Sheesha to come *right now*, as the mob picked up their pace.

There was a streak of gold. Sheesha stopped above them and, with a rapid beat of his wings, turned on the spot facing the crowd, which came to an instant halt. The air filled with *ziri* shrieks as the others arrived. Sheesha touched down beside Kantees and kept up his cries as the others flew low over the crowd, criss-crossing the street.

Kantees stepped forward and instructed Sheesha to have the others fly in circles at a greater distance. Sheesha walked on one side of her, Ulina on the other with the other two behind as the *ziri* in the air drew back.

The crowd retreated as she approached but those at the back stopped those at the front going too far.

"I'm sorry," she said. "I'm sorry that thing was in the tower and it stole your lives. I'm sorry you feel like you've lost everything—" *because that's what it feels like, I know,* "—but that wasn't me. Hurting me won't mend how you feel, and I won't let you do that to me. I am Kantees of the Ziri."

She couldn't tell if her words were having any effect, perhaps they were less tense but it was the fear of being ripped to shreds by *zirichasa* that was really holding them back. She was under no illusions.

"I have come back to help you. My patterners will open the ley-circle. New people will come and you'll be able to trade with them."

"We don't want any new people!"

Kantees nodded. "Yes, I understand that now. I will make sure there are only a few and only those who want to barter and trade on your market days."

The mood of the mob altered a little, though she felt it could still erupt at any moment.

"It's not that I don't trust you…" she said, letting her words trail off. A few of them laughed which, she thought, was the best sign she could get. "But my *ziri* will remain here until the crowd is gone. If that's all right with you?"

The ones on the outskirts of the crowd, who probably felt the most exposed, were quick to take her up on her suggestion. They peeled off and disappeared between the buildings. The ones who made up the new outer edge seemed to feel the same way, and so the mob evaporated. Kantees sent all of the *ziri* except Sheesha back to the tower. The last small clot of men headed off together down a side street, not looking back.

They returned to the tower with Sheesha walking alongside, head high, balancing with his wings. It was a bit like his pre-mating posture, *look at how great I am*. Kantees smiled, it might look good to a female *ziri* but to her it was comical.

"I'm not sure we can even take Marakees back with us," said Kantees. "How will she cope with being in the castle? Perhaps in a battle?"

"You must take her," said Ulina. "If you do not, Gally will stay and if Gally stays you will make me stay too. And I will not."

Jynolee and Helka were very quiet as they sat in the shed later in the afternoon. Yenteel had returned while Daybian and Levin commented on how unimpressive the tower was.

"Nothing of interest."

Yenteel gave them a look. "When you say 'of interest' I take it you mean 'of value', that you could acquire?"

"The place is completely empty," said Daybian.

"I'm surprised you're surprised, considering its age and what was in it up until recently. Then again, given your lack of education perhaps it's not so unexpected."

"I had the very best education."

"Perhaps," said Yenteel, "but did you have the wit to absorb it?"

Daybian looked at Levin. "I have been insulted."

"Are you sure?" said his friend with a straight face.

The room burst into laughter. First at the joke and then at Daybian's hurt expression. Even Kantees smiled.

"There's not much for people like us to do," said Daybian. "Life can get pretty boring."

"People like you?" said Kantees. "Poor little Taymalin lordling, what a sad life you must lead."

His face became pained. Kantees held up her hand. "Say no more, Daybian, there's no warming yourself with a burned-out fire."

Gally came in with Marakees. She had been crying. Gally looked serious.

Kantees still found it hard to credit that either of them would have taken up with the other but then what did she know of such things? Gally was kind and always tried to be thoughtful though he was not very bright—and had that strange way of talking about himself as if he were someone else.

But if he can give Marakees what she needs, what business is it of mine?

"I am sorry," said the woman.

"No need to be," said Kantees. "We met some of the townsfolk, they wanted to be angry at something and they chose me."

"It's very hard," said Marakees and looked as if she might start crying again.

Kantees changed the subject. "We've been discussing what we need to do next. I admit I was hoping we might get some more riders from here. But I can see I was asking too much."

"I think it's going to be a long time before the people here are able to be useful to you, Kantees, or even think that it might be their duty."

"Do you?"

"I know you gave us a chance to live our lives the way we're supposed to. And we owe you for that, but they are all scared, and so am I."

"We'll be leaving in the morning, Marakees. Do you want to come with us?"

Galiko put his arm around the woman's shoulder, his face more serious than Kantees had ever known him. He had changed a great deal in the time here and she wondered how much of that was because of Marakees.

"Can I think about it?"

"Of course."

Yenteel shifted his position, drawing the attention as Marakees and Gally moved into a corner and sat down.

"What's your plan?"

Kantees looked at him through narrowed eyes. She had to remind herself, sometimes, that no matter how much help he had been as the moons turned, he was not working for her. He might be a friend but he had his own plans and aims as dictated by his real master.

"I haven't decided."

"But you do have one?"

"I think so."

"But you're not ready to tell us?"

"No."

She stood up, and everyone in the room did the same. She sighed inwardly and wished she could do away with these silly rules, but it was what was expected.

"I'm going to look at this empty tower," she said.

"I'll come," said Daybian.

"No. Just Jynolee and Helka. We have things to talk about." Daybian gave a good impression of a sad *zatek* but Kantees did not rise to his bait. "We probably won't be long. Why don't you have a think about how the Dunor might attack Jakalain? How would you do it if it was you?"

Gally met them at the door and handed over a lantern which Jynolee took. "Gally thinks Marakees will go. She is scared but Gally will make her brave."

Kantees placed her hand on his shoulder. "You are a good man,

Gally. And very lucky to have found someone who likes you so much."

He blushed and turned away. She watched him head back to Marakees, then glanced at the men who had pulled their chairs around a single table and were already deep in discussion.

"Come on," she said. "Let's see if we can find something that Daybian and Levin could not see."

25

$\mathcal{A}$s they passed the threshold of the tower, Kantees shivered. It was all very well knowing that the abomination had been eaten by the *zirichasa*, and that she had been scoured clean by the Mother's milk during the feeding. But this place held no pleasant memories for her. On the other hand, it had been the place where she had recovered her sight.

The way Daybian had described the place as completely empty, Kantees had got the idea that it would be swept clean. But instead it was littered with bits of shell, and a kind of dry white dust which she assumed was the desiccated remains of the abomination.

The walls inside were as smooth and as black as the exterior but there was almost no echo. Despite the size of it, it felt small.

"I don't like this place, mistress," said Helka.

"You can go back out if you like."

"I didn't mean that."

They followed the main passageway which wound through the building. Empty doorways led to empty rooms; they examined the first few they came upon, then ignored them.

The passage gave out on to a room with six sides, much larger than any of the others.

Kantees recognised it immediately. This was where the

feeding had been focused. There was a hole in the ceiling and below it, in the exact centre of the room what might have been a six-sided table except it had no top. Just another hole leading down.

There was no feeding due so it should be safe here. She could feel the power of the ley-circle beneath her, it was like walking across a fire mountain.

Unlike the other rooms this one had patterns across every wall. Helka went to one of them and ran her hand across it. "I have never seen patterns like this."

"You've seen a lot of patterns?"

Helka hesitated. "No, mistress, not a great many, but my mother and grandmother were skilled in patterning. I was learning too though my sister was more dedicated to the craft. There were things patterns had in common, not always the same, but there were none like this."

"You said it was made by the *Slissac*, Lady Kantees," said Jynolee.

"That's what Yenteel said, and I have no reason to doubt him, he has seen a great deal of the world. Certainly more than you or I, and more even than the lordlings."

"He speaks to you with great familiarity."

Kantees shrugged and then held the lantern up to see down into the hole. It went deeper than the light could penetrate, but Kantees could see the power burning in the depths. She stood up straight again.

"Yenteel knew me when I was still a slave."

"Do you love him?"

"What?"

Jynolee fell to her knees. "I'm sorry, mistress, I should not have said such a thing. Please beat me if you wish to."

"Get up. I'm not going to beat you. I was just surprised. You can ask me anything, I will not be angry no matter how impertinent it is. Just be sure to ask the difficult ones when we are alone."

Jynolee got to her feet, still looking very guilty.

"I don't love him, no, not at all. He is a friend, nothing more." The next questions were obvious so she didn't wait for them to be asked. "And no, not Daybian or Levin." As an afterthought. "Nor Gally, and definitely not Tenical."

The other two laughed.

"There must be some way up," said Kantees half to herself.

They left the room by the doorway opposite, and turned left to find a spiral staircase.

"Have you had any men at all?" said Helka as they plodded up to the first landing which Kantees judged to be about the height of the main room.

"No."

The stairs continued upwards but there was another exit. Kantees went through and they found themselves in a similar room to the one below, including the densely packed patterns on the walls. She stared at the hole in the ceiling for a long while.

"But what about during the feedings?" said Helka. "Everybody who's old enough enjoys that."

"I avoid them."

Which seemed to stump Helka, as if she could not understand why someone wouldn't want to take part in the reckless abandonment of the post-feeding festival. Which was precisely why Kantees stayed away.

They took the stairs again to another room. Kantees stared at the ceiling again.

"Those holes are getting bigger."

"But the room is getting smaller," said Jynolee.

"The whole tower gets thinner towards the top," said Kantees. "So the room getting smaller is to be expected, I suppose. But why are the holes getting bigger?" She tried peering up again.

They took the next three levels more quickly.

Helka had said nothing more and Kantees suspected she knew why. "You don't have to be like me," she said. "Just because I'm not interested in men, in that way, doesn't mean you can't be. I just want to make the Kadralin strong again, free them. I'm not like Taymar."

"You prefer women then?"

This time Kantees was not embarrassed. "No, not that either. I'm just not interested, at all."

The hole in the ceiling, and the floor, was at least twice as wide as it was on the ground floor. Perhaps even bigger, the reducing width of the rooms made it harder to judge.

"It's a funnel!" Kantees said finally.

The other two stared at her so she continued. "The Mother's milk comes down on the top of the tower. The patterns on the roof and the walls of each room squeeze it inward, floor by floor. That's why it doesn't create abominations, and why the town can build all the way up to the circle and be perfectly safe."

"It wasn't safe though, there was an abomination here."

"It must have got inside during a feeding somehow."

Would it be possible to intentionally create abominations? Kantees pushed that thought away. It was not a pleasant one.

"Did you find anything?" said Daybian when they returned.

"Not really, except the whole tower is a funnel concentrating the Mother's milk and stopping it from affecting its surroundings."

Tenical looked up. "There is too much knowledge in these places."

She did not think he was looking for a reply so didn't give him one. The builders of this place, perhaps the *Slissac*, knew far more about patterning than the Taymalin. But if Yenteel was right and she was *Fahain* then she did not need to know. She could touch the World's Pattern without book-learning. Is that why Kevrey had not taught her to read? Had he known? Or would it have been too obvious?

"How are your plans for an attack on Jakalain?" she said.

Daybian looked up in horror and then relaxed. "I don't think there's anything they're already doing at Jakalain that could be improved. The Swordmaster knows his business."

"What about a force of Farahalek attacking with stealth?"

"They would not be able to gain entry without being seen."

Kantees nodded and looked for the child, unsurprisingly she was a short distance away. "How would your people attack Jakalain, Ulina?"

And there it was. If any of them had ever wondered about the girl, Kantees had finally admitted it.

"I do not know how they would do it," said Ulina. "But if I wished to enter Jakalain in secret and I had a *tekrak* and those wings, I would wait until the night was dark and clouded, my patterner would fly above the clouds and I would jump from it. Like a *sikechak* I would descend on to the high towers of Jakalain and no one would know I was there."

"But there are sentries and guards on all the walls and towers," said Daybian.

"I would kill them before they knew I was there."

"Do you think you could?"

Ulina shrugged. "Kantees asked what my people would do."

There was silence. Kantees glanced at the entrance. The day was still light.

"We're not doing any good here," she said. "Back to Jakalain now. Tenical are you able to make a path from here?"

"This is a strong ley-circle, Kantees, but I need to make the pattern down here and the tower is in the way. Its very construction distorts patterns inside."

"Then we'll do what we did before, make it on top of the tower. Gather what you need to make the pattern." She turned away from him. "Levin?"

"Lady?"

"You take him up."

"As you command." The two men headed out of the building.

"Gally?"

"Yes, Kantees?"

"You and Marakees gather your things, you'll have to come with us."

The woman did not look very happy but Kantees had a feeling that was her normal expression, at least for now. Perhaps she would come around in time.

"Gally, do you still have that *melinak*?"

"Yes, Kantees."

"We'll take that along too."

"What do you want us to do?" said Yenteel.

"Check the next feeding and—I almost daren't ask—do you

have anything in your box of tricks that will tell us when Lostimal is dark next?"

He grinned. "We don't need a device for that, Kantees, it's been waning for the last few days, so in the next ten-day."

"Not a moment too soon for us to get back then."

Kantees looked down at Ulina. "Do you really think they might attack at night like that?"

"I don't know, Kantees. You asked what I would do. The Taymalin always think there will be a big battle, but sometimes it's only shadow in the night."

"If you're right, and we have luck, the Dunor won't think of shadows either, after all, they are also Taymalin."

Ulina smiled. Kantees looked around for Jynolee and Helka but they were already gone, as were Kantees' meagre possessions.

Kantees asked Sheesha to come to the door.

She left the building and climbed on his back, lifting Ulina into place before the great *ziri* launched himself into the air. Jynolee and Helka appeared behind her moments later.

They touched down on the top of the tower alongside Waileth. Tenical was busy marking the top of the tower with chalk. Kantees reached into her bag and brought out the *chilafrah*. Two small grey *ziri* emerged with Gally and Marakees; instead of landing they circled the tower, with Tabata in the lead.

Kantees had not had the opportunity to watch the wild *zirichasa* in flight before. They were smaller than the domesticated breeds but showed no strain in carrying their riders. Their smaller size would probably mean they turned faster. The wild ones had to fly almost every day to hunt. They were not inferior, just less gaudy.

Looesa arrived and Yenteel landed awkwardly on the tower. It was getting crowded. When Daybian finally turned up on Shingul, he joined the wild *ziri* only to find himself second place to Gally. Kantees smiled, the *ziri* had their own rules. However she was not going to let Tabata lead this time.

"*Chilafrah!*"

Kantees frowned at Tenical. He was useful but he really had no respect for her and that was annoying. She walked over and placed the cube in his hands. *It isn't that he has no respect,* she thought, *it is that he is simply rude.*

"How long?"

"Are you planning to fly through again?"

"Of course."

"Get them in the air then."

Kantees stalked back to Sheesha, fuming at the man. She climbed up and Ulina settled herself.

Sheesha dropped off the tower to gain speed and then swept his wings down and they soared up. There was a squeal from Helka when Yuleto did the same thing. At least she was strapped in. Kotoka chose to launch upwards, Kantees wondered if that had been under Jynolee's instruction. Yenteel clung on as Looesa took him down and then up.

The *ziri* moved in and formed the arrowhead formation but Kantees told Sheesha they needed to be in line and positions slowly adjusted. There was a flash of light from the top of the tower and Kantees jerked her head toward it. There was nothing for her eyes to see but this time the pattern made a shadowy arc in her mind.

Waileth launched with Levin and Tenical on her back. Kantees led the train of *ziri* towards the top of the tower. A gap opened behind her and Waileth moved into position.

"The *chilafrah!*" shouted Kantees.

Tenical hesitated but, as Waileth came close, he tossed it across. Kantees grabbed it out of the air and gave Tenical a furious look. But at least she had it back. Sheesha accelerated at the top of the tower, it was somehow reassuring to Kantees that she could now see the portal that led into the path.

Kantees realised she had not explained to Jynolee, Helka or Marakees what was about to happen.

The daylight vanished and they were surrounded by the dark of the World's Pattern.

It was too late now.

26

The wings of the *ziri* hissed in the air as they stroked steadily forwards. Leather on the straps creaked. Someone sneezed. A *zirichak* stomach rumbled.

But the tunnel through the World's Pattern had no sounds of its own, and had no echo.

Beyond the small sounds made by the group themselves, there was nothing.

Kantees wondered where the air they breathed came from, was it conjured as part of the pattern making? Was it always here? Was there air here at all, or just something they imagined they were breathing?

You could mistake the lights behind the walls as stars, if you ignored the fact they moved constantly and were all around, including below.

Kantees urged Sheesha to fly faster.

Could he become golden within the patterner's path? Or would it destroy the path? There were tales of patterns interfering with one another and, of course, in those stories the outcome was never good—

They burst into daylight.

The air smelled of Jakalain. The ground before them sloped

away but was covered in tents. Smoke rose from campfires. Armsmen jumped to their feet as the *ziri* exploded into existence above the ley-circle and arrowed to the south and east.

The sounds of the world returned. And this time it was full of shouting men. Sheesha climbed. Kantees could feel the formation changing behind her. A glance at Jakalain showed it was not surrounded by *tekrasa*.

Sheesha shuddered in the air and for the merest moment Kantees thought he had been shot again. But that wasn't it, there was something wrong with the other *ziri*. She looked round and saw Waileth had pulled free. Levin was waving.

"I'll return!" was all she heard before he and Tenical turned away west heading in the direction of Kurvin Port.

Kantees fumed but there was little she could do. With the other *ziri* tied to her in formation she could not go after him. Instead she brought Sheesha round and headed for the castle.

Kantees was not sure whether Swordmaster Erang was avoiding her but it took a further two days before she had an opportunity to talk to him properly. In that time things had settled into an uncertain pattern that almost resembled her life before the Dunor turned it upside down.

She spent time working with Romain and teaching the new riders about looking after their mounts. Sometimes they would ride out and get to know the terrain. Marakees would have kept to herself but Kantees insisted she join them too. It had taken a quiet word with Romain to prevent him making any derisive comment about the wild *ziri*.

Finally, the Swordmaster agreed to talk to her, with Daybian in attendance, and she outlined her concerns about an attack. Swordmaster Erang nodded. "It makes sense they might try a hidden attack but I have the walls patrolled. There are men outside the walls too."

"What if they were killed and the attackers pretended to be the patrol?"

"We have codes," he said. "Your concern for the castle does you credit, girl, but it does not exceed mine. And you do not have the experience that I do in these matters."

Kantees sighed, she knew he was right, but the men of the Dunor—that one in particular who had lured her into the trap and nearly killed Sheesha at Watching Pass—they had experience and they had new tools of war which the Swordmaster was not familiar with.

"We can only do our best," said Daybian. "If the Dunor have a weapon we know nothing about we cannot plan for it."

That conversation had taken place shortly after they had landed and the *ziri* went to their eyries.

It was late afternoon and Kantees now stood in the courtyard. The construction work continued. The new inward-facing walls had reached the third storey in most places. She could feel the tension in the air. The anticipation of the attack everyone knew would come.

"They've built the wall solid across the main entrance. And made tunnels that lead round the edges and come out on each side. Grills allow us to attack anyone coming through. To get into the main building they have to come out into the courtyard, where they will be targets from above, and then re-enter similar tunnels."

"I wish we still had Tenical."

"You hate him."

"He knows the patterns of the ley-circles both at the Dunor's island and that other *Slissac* tower in the south."

She called for Sheesha. Moments later he dropped from his eyrie and landed a short distance away. Not just landed, he judged the drop perfectly and without a single beat of his wings he swooped into the courtyard, angled up to kill his speed and dropped gently to the cobbles. Perfect.

"Going somewhere?"

"Just the ley-circle."

"Mistress?"

Kantees had almost forgotten about her two shadows. Jynolee and Helka waited on her all the time. They wanted to come, of course, but it would take time for them to saddle their *ziri*.

"Yes," said Kantees. "I think the time has come for you to ride without saddles."

Kantees focused on Kotoka and Yuleto, and called them.

They took longer to respond but two brightly coloured *ziri* tumbled from the tower and made a far less elegant landing. Kantees saw they were drawing the attention of the workers.

"Can I come?" said Daybian.

He was like a little lost boy, but Kantees was not about to take pity on him.

"You're home with your family and you are the heir, Daybian, no more running off on adventures for you."

"You sound like my father."

"I hope not. Anyway, no."

Kantees walked over to the younger *ziri* and helped the women get settled. They both put a brave face on it but they were clearly nervous, not being strapped in and not, they thought, having any way of steering their *zirichak*.

"They'll be following me, at least for now," said Kantees. "Just remember to keep your legs tucked under the wings when taking off and landing, or doing anything difficult."

That made them even more worried.

"But I won't do anything difficult, we're just flying out to the ley-circle."

Before they could say anything Kantees mounted Sheesha, only to find Ulina already there. Sheesha beat his wings and launched upwards. Helka gave a cry as Yuleto followed. Moments later they were over the walls and gliding west.

Kantees checked the two women had not fallen off. Helka was looking unsure but Jynolee was smiling.

The road between the ley-circle and the castle was filled with carts going in both directions. Looking back Kantees saw the line heading past the castle and towards the town. Keeping this army supplied and watered needed another army of strong backs, busy cooks and a hundred carts.

Lord Jakalain must be spending a fortune buying food and bringing it in through the ley-circle. Although that other fellow, Lord Corlain, was presumably assisting. Was he taking precautions as well? She did not know a great deal about the country of Faerholme, except that it was both central but surrounded on three sides by mountains.

It took very little time before they were over the encampment. Hundreds of armsmen looked up at them, faces of all shades from pale to dark. Some wearing Jakalain's colours, some Corlain's, and there were others she did not recognise. Kantees knew they probably ought to ask permission to go into the ley-circle but that would cause delays. Instead she aimed for a staging area just to the north of it where there was space to land.

They landed easily. Kantees waited for some officious sergeant-at-arms to arrive and tell her she was not allowed to be here. But, although they received stares from between the surrounding pavilions, they were not approached. Perhaps Lord Jakalain had given orders not to interfere with her plans.

Kantees looked at the circle. Bare earth surrounded by a region where the grass had been burned away as a precaution against abominations. Around it was the palisade for defence in case an attacking force came through the ley-circle. The fence was built in sections and each one was mounted on small wheels so it could be removed when the two moons aligned in the sky and a feeding was imminent.

A collection of barrels stacked three high stood on a wooden pallet where the cart track entered though Kantees did not know whether these were inbound, or being sent out.

"All right, now you need to practice on your own," said Kantees. "You first, Jynolee. Get Kotoka to take off, fly round the ley-circle once and land back here."

The girl hesitated. "How do I steer him without reins?"

"Lean in the direction you want to go. Lean back to climb and forward to descend."

"That's all?"

Kantees thought about it. For her it was different now, she only had to think about what she wanted and Sheesha would respond—even wild Tabata had done what Kantees wanted. But before that, yes, she had just leaned.

"That's all."

"I'll go first if you like," said Helka.

Jynolee's response was to make Kotoka lie down and she climbed on his back. Moments later, with Jynolee's legs tight beneath his wings and holding on to his neck, the *ziri* launched. He had been pointing away from the ley-circle and that's the direction he headed. For a long moment, his direction did not change and Kantees was ready to either send a request directly to the animal or jump on Sheesha's back to recover Jynolee.

Then Kotoka's wings arched into a glide position and he turned effortlessly to the left.

Kantees watched as Jynolee made her mount fly in a straight line past the ley-circle and then turn again, coming round it. Now Kantees could see the concentration on the girl's face. Her eyes focused on the open ground. She leaned forwards. Kotoka got the idea immediately and came down in a blast of air from his wings to alight close to the others.

Sheesha was preening and did not deign to notice.

"That was good," said Kantees as Jynolee slipped from Kotoka's neck.

"You only have to suggest it," she said breathlessly. "Once he knows what you want you don't have to do anything."

"The trick is making sure they get it right."

"My turn?" said Helka. She was already mounted.

Kantees smiled and waved her hand. "Go ahead."

There was no hesitation. Yuleto launched immediately. Having learnt from Jynolee's flight, Helka turned her *ziri* without a moment's hesitation. Yuleto beat hard and climbed fast. His rider pulled him into a tight turn around the ley-circle and then, instead of landing, went out in a wider circle to make a second turn.

Kantees frowned. She knew Helka was keen to show how good she was but she was not following Kantees' instructions.

Yuleto backwinged hard, turned on his wing—which meant Helka's legs were the only thing holding her in place—and drove down to the ground in front of Kantees. He landed hard. Helka either was not gripping strongly enough or the jolt was too much, and she landed face down in the grass.

Kantees walked over and went down on one knee beside her. "Unless you have more information than I do, when I give you an instruction, Helka, I expect it to be carried out just the way I said it."

Helka pushed herself up into a kneeling position but sat back and kept her gaze to the ground. "Yes, Lady Kantees. I am sorry."

"It is good you want to ride well," said Kantees. "Come." She held out her hand and after a moment Helka took it and Kantees helped her to her feet.

"I have been arrogant in the past," said Kantees to the both of them. "And my behaviour nearly killed Sheesha. Respect your mount and respect those around you who deserve it."

She stared at the sky. The day was bright but clouds were coming in from the east. Lostimal was high in the day-time sky. Kantees thought she'd better check with Yenteel to see when the next feeding was due.

"Why don't you two fly back to the castle without me? Take some time and learn how to fly your *ziri*, properly."

"We should stay with you," said Helka, and Jynolee nodded.

"Nothing's going to happen to me here and you need to make your mistakes where I won't see them. There is something I need to do, and besides, I have Ulina."

The two women took their leave and launched their mounts into the air. Their confidence was already improving and it showed in the way their *ziri* responded. A quick glance at Sheesha showed him flat out and sunning himself. Kantees told him he could stay where he was, to which there was no response, and then set off towards the palisade with Ulina at her side.

There was a gate with a sentry post that led from the staging area to the ley-circle, with two armsmen guarding it. She could not imagine it was a very exciting duty, although even now she saw the golden power of a patterner's path forming in the circle.

One of the men touched his fingers to his forehead. "Lady Kantees."

She allowed herself a wry smile.

A shimmering at the circle caught her attention.

"A path is opening," she said.

Both of them turned to look, probably expecting to see carts emerging, but there was nothing. They turned back to her.

"It's there," she said. "They haven't had time to get through it yet." She took a stone from the ground and flung it at the side of the path as she saw it. They followed its flight and saw it vanish.

One of them went into the enclosed sentry box and checked a board. "Food shipments from Corlain are due about now," he said.

Kantees could not interpret the look they gave her. She shrugged. "Can I go through?"

"Of course, Lady Kantees."

She thanked them as they opened the gate to let the two of them through.

"You want to feed your box with the Mother's milk," said Ulina when they were out of earshot of the guards.

"Yes."

"How do you do that?"

Kantees shook her head. "I think I just have to be here."

"You don't have to take it out of your bag?"

"No."

"Good," said Ulina. She glared at the palisade, and the men behind it who stared back. "We cannot trust these armsmen."

Kantees stepped out on to the ley-circle and the dry dirt crunched under her shoes. The exit from the patterner's path did not occupy the entire space but was big enough to allow large carts and waggons through.

"How do you know we can't trust them?"

"There are too many of them. There will be traitors among them. Whatever your Lord Jakalain said about taking care, people will have talked. The Dunor will know about the fortifications, they will know Jakalain is filled with armsmen. There may be Farahalek among them ready to sneak inside."

"That's not encouraging."

"You wanted to know what I would do."

"And what would you do to defend against that?"

Ulina shook her head. "There's nothing to defend against treachery."

Kantees said nothing else but walked around the edge of the ley-circle. Beneath them the raw white power was like a blacksmith's furnace. They walked around the end of the patterner's path, for a moment it was a thin shining line in the air and then it expanded again. Kantees found another stone and tossed it through the portal. This time it did not vanish but bounced on the other side.

"It only has one side." *Kevrey of Tander would have loved to know what I have learnt of patterning.*

"What will happen to the stone you threw in from the other side when the path stops?" said Ulina.

"The patterner who creates the path must also walk it," said Kantees. "So that he doesn't make it stop before everyone is through."

"Is the stone destroyed?"

"I don't know. Perhaps the Taymalin patterners do." *Perhaps Yenteel's Arch-Patterner does.*

"What if you kill the patterner when people are on the path?"

"Perhaps they will die and be absorbed into the World's Pattern."

"And leave no bodies," said Ulina.

Kantees wondered how long it would take for the *chilafrah* to fill with the Mother's Milk.

2 7

There were problems with rank when it came to the evening meal. Kantees had been invited to eat with Lord Jakalain but without any of her entourage. There had been discussions but in the end she had declined, and chose to eat in the refectory of the Ziri Tower.

Daybian had been torn but, in the end, Kantees had told him he could not ignore his parents. He sulked like the child he was.

Unfortunately the meal in the refectory was just as awkward. Libbibet insisted on serving them instead of them waiting in line with everyone else, which meant the staff were bringing food to two ex-slaves, herself and Gally, an escaped prisoner, Yenteel, along with a whole collection of other Kadralin. Only Helka seemed comfortable, as if being waited on was her due.

Gally sat with Marakees, of course, and the fact the 'simpleton' now had a woman attracted stares and not a few laughs; thankfully Gally was oblivious to them. Kantees was sure that Marakees was not similarly blind, and it must hurt.

But the food was good.

"Did Levin say anything to you about leaving us?" Kantees asked Yenteel.

He shook his head as he swallowed a mouthful. "Nothing."

Kantees glanced at Ulina and back to Yenteel. "Do you think he'll betray us?"

"No, of course not. He might not have the puppy-dog eyes, but he's as dedicated to you as Daybian."

"I wish he'd told me what he was doing."

"Perhaps he was worried he might not be able to succeed."

"That's ridiculous."

"It's human."

Kantees fell silent as the serving staff took away the remains of the main course. She tore a piece from her trencher, dipped it in her wine and ate it. Lord Jakalain had sent them a pitcher of it as recompense for her having to eat in the Ziri Tower. She didn't really like it but the others enjoyed it.

There was a clamour of voices at the far end of the hall.

Kantees had her back to the noise and had to turn in her seat. A couple of castle servants, Taymalin, were talking to Libbibet and Romain, they did not seem happy and were waving their hands to emphasise what they were saying.

It took a moment but Kantees realised there was one word they kept repeating: *Fire*.

Romain disappeared up into the tower as Libbibet bustled into the kitchens. Kantees was about to call out but realised Yenteel was already halfway across the floor.

"What's happening?" said Helka.

"Fire."

"In the castle?" said Marakees.

Kantees turned to Ulina. "We may need to fly, get our things."

"Is it an attack?" said Jynolee.

"We'll wait for Yenteel," said Kantees. "But if it is an attack it would be best if we were in the air."

"But what can *we* do?" said Marakees.

Kantees thought about suggesting she and Gally should just flee, after all, what *could* they do? She loved Gally but he had difficulty with complicated situations. And, as it turned out, Marakees had similar problems, if for very different reasons. Then she caught Gally looking at her.

"We don't know yet," said Kantees.

Yenteel hurried back and didn't wait to be invited to explain. "Fires have broken out in the town."

"Fires? More than one?"

He nodded.

"A diversion," said Ulina who had reappeared at Kantees' side holding her bag. "It's the start of an attack."

"That doesn't mean people aren't in danger from the fires," said Jynolee.

"Of course they are," said Ulina. "What point is there if there's no threat?"

Kantees held up her hand. "That's enough." She took a deep breath to give herself time to think. "Yenteel, Gally and Marakees, you go to the town. There may be people who need help. Yenteel you're in charge. Gally, don't use the golden path unless you have to, it would be best if no one else knows you can do it."

The prospect of the Dunor torturing him to find the secret did not appeal.

"If they try to come through the ley-circle they'll have an army to deal with," she said, "but they might try it. I can see a path if they make one, so I'll go to the circle. Helka and Jynolee I want you two up high, circle at a distance from the castle. If you see *tekrasa* coming, return to warn the garrison."

Kantees took a breath and focused on the *ziri* above them, calling them down to the courtyard. "Come on."

They headed out, being forced to use the newly created side passages now that the main entrance did not give directly into the courtyard. Kantees came out into the light just as Sheesha and the other *ziri* touched down. She looked round and realised they had somehow lost Helka and Jynolee on the way.

"Helka stopped to talk to some armsmen," said Marakees noticing Kantees looking back at the dark exit. At that moment the two women appeared carrying crossbows.

"Why…never mind," said Kantees. "Do you two know how to use those?"

"Yes, my lady," said Helka.

"I don't like crossbows," said Jynolee. "But it's all they had."

"The light is fading," said Helka throwing a belt over her shoulder.

"Stay up as long as you can, but don't get lost," said Kantees. "The *tekrasa* don't move fast so a timely warning will be of most use."

They nodded and mounted.

"Count them but don't pick a fight with something you can't handle."

They launched into the air and if either of them replied it wasn't heard.

"I won't tell you not to take risks," Kantees said to Yenteel.

"There's no chance of that," he said with a smile.

Then he, Gally and Marakees were gone.

"What's going on?" said Daybian hurrying over. "Where are they going?"

"Helka and Jynolee are going to scout for *tekrasa*, the others are going to help in the town if they can."

Daybian nodded. "You think it's a prelude to an attack too? Good. I'll tell my father and the Swordmaster what's happening. What about you?"

"We're going to the ley-circle."

"Why?"

"Because I can see when a patterner's path has been formed, before anything comes through."

"I didn't know that."

"It's recent."

"I'll come with you."

"It'll take you too long to get ready," said Kantees. "I'm going now."

Sheesha put his head down as if he'd understood her words and she climbed up with Ulina who chose to stand behind Kantees, with a tight grip on her shoulders. They were in the air a moment later.

Kantees felt strangely alone as Sheesha slipped noiselessly through the twilight air. Far to the west some of the higher mountain peaks were still lit by sunlight, brilliant white with snow. Here the sky was darkening and the mountains were shadows against a dusky sky.

A sea of campfires spread around the dark of the ley-circle. Yet the power of the circle continued to shine—without illuminating anything around it. The difference between her outer and inner view was disconcerting but at least it gave Kantees a clear target. There was no patterner's path that she could see yet.

She had Sheesha move into a circular path out of bow-shot of the ground. Below her the various contingents of armsmen were being formed up and moved into positions around the ley-circle. The castle was alive with lights as they made preparations for the possible attack. And beyond that and to the south she could see the ruddy glow of fires in the town.

Even if they were right and this was the prelude to an attack, the timing would be difficult. The saboteurs in the town would have been told what day, and at what time, to set the fires. But patterners did not know how long their paths would be. No doubt the Dunor would use the best they had but even so it was an uncertain factor.

And if they were attacking from the air as well, they would find it very hard to determine exactly when the *tekrasa* would arrive.

The air above the ley-circle shimmered and an arch took shape. The tension of waiting coalesced into an iron grip on her heart. They were coming and she froze.

"Kantees?" Ulina's voice cut through her fear.

"The patterner's path ... they're coming."

"We must warn the armsmen."

Kantees nodded and managed to direct Sheesha down to the staging area. It was full of armsmen, waiting. Swiftly Kantees adjusted their course to the ley-circle itself and landed just inside it.

"I am Kantees of the Ziri, who commands here?"

"Swordmaster Zagot, Lady."

"Fetch him, quickly."

She glanced at the magic behind her. "Ulina, find something to throw. A stone."

"Nobody will see a stone, Kantees, it's too dark."

She nodded again. The fact she could see the light so clearly made her forget the others could not.

"A torch or lantern then." She stopped then added, "On a pole."

Not knowing how long it would take for the Dunor attackers to walk the path gnawed at her. Her nervousness was making Sheesha agitated. He kept dipping his neck and pushing at her. She tried to calm herself. She did not think she was very successful but Sheesha seemed to relax a little.

A man emerged from the dark, flanked by two armsmen, one of whom carried a lantern.

"I am Swordmaster Zagot. Lord Jakalain has ordered you be given respect, Lady Kantees." From the way he said it she was sure respect was not what he was offering.

"A patterner's path has opened to here."

"I see no one."

Ulina pushed between the ranks of armsmen and handed Kantees a lantern on a pole. Instead of replying to the Swordmaster, Kantees walked across the dirt to the portal and pushed the lantern across the threshold. She breathed a sigh of relief when it vanished.

"Here, Swordmaster, and they will come through from this direction."

He did not reply but was already issuing orders. One thing you could say about these Swordmasters, they might be confident in their own rightness but when they had the proof in front of them, they didn't argue.

Something scuttled out of the patterner's path. Its small head was barely up to Kantees' knee and it ran on its back legs. It glanced up at Kantees as it passed and chirruped.

It took Kantees a heartbeat, then she swung the lantern hard at the creature and sent it flying as the lantern smashed on the ground and the oil exploded into flame. Then she ran hard towards Sheesha. Somebody among the armsmen laughed.

More chirrups came from behind her, something shrieked with pain.

"Ulina! Sheesha!"

But Ulina was already running. Sheesha was up on his haunches and growling. Kantees told him to lie down so they could mount.

Ulina was up in a moment. Kantees reached him as *chakisa* overtook her but Sheesha's constant rumbling growl kept the space around him clear. Kantees jumped up and then sat with a thump between his wings. Just as his head lashed out, a *chakik* screeched, cut short by a wet crunch.

Kantees stared back at the portal as dozens of *chakisa* erupted into view. Sheesha snapped left and right—it kept the space around him clear but the armsmen were in uproar as the little monsters ran into their ranks, snapping and biting. The *chakisa* were not organised into any groups but were attacking anyone who came in reach. Kantees didn't understand, surely the mass of armsmen would scare them? And if not that, why did they not attack in groups the way they seemed to in the wild?

Chaos is easy…

Then the flow of creatures stopped, no new ones emerged and those in the ley-circle followed the rest out into the dark. A glance behind showed the surging and panicked armsmen battling their tiny foes—some men were on the ground.

"Kantees." Ulina's voice wavered with fear. Sheesha sprang into the air before he had even started to beat his wings without waiting for her order. Kantees had never seen him strain so hard, as if he were clawing at the air to gain height. Then she heard the roar and turned to look at the portal. The noise was louder than the greatest waterfall, and made the air shake. A huge dark shadow pulled itself through the portal. The mouth opened wide, filled with teeth as big as Ulina and large enough to swallow Sheesha in one bite, and it roared again. The monster's huge gait carried it across the ley-circle in two paces. Nose to tail it spanned the entire width of it.

This was the reason the *chakisa* dived unheeding into the massed ranks of the armsmen.

Nachak.

2 8

How would you bring an attacking force through a ley-circle when you knew an army lay in wait on the other side? Swordmaster Erang had said they would need shock troops, or cannon fodder.

The Dunor had chosen a different method, though the shock was real.

As Sheesha circled higher, Kantees watched the defending forces fall apart. The hundreds of *chakisa* had been unsettling enough and had done plenty of damage. But the monstrous *nachak* had destroyed any semblance of organisation in the forces intended to defend the circle. The *chakisa* were fleeing from the *nachak* but there must be something driving the monster forwards.

She looked over towards the castle. It looked peaceful. She leaned forwards along Sheesha's neck.

"Fly fast, my love."

Drawing the power from the circle, he flashed gold for a moment. The cold air hit them as the golden light vanished and he backwinged down into the courtyard.

"Get me Swordmaster Erang, now!" Kantees shouted as Sheesha descended to the cobbles.

She did not dismount. An idea was forming in her mind. She was distracted as a *ziri* she didn't recognise landed, the rider was another matter, however: Daybian in full racing gear. Then Waileth arrived.

"Where did you get to?"

"Greetings, Kantees, it's lovely to see you too," said Levin. "I brought some friends."

Kantees followed his pointing finger. Above them were six more *ziri*, shifting in and out of the shadows, but brightly coloured, she recognised a couple of them from the races.

"Some of the heirs are not keen on having some emperor telling them what they can and can't do in the lands they will inherit."

"And they're willing to fight?"

"Races might be fun, Kantees, but they aren't real life."

"Will they follow an ex-slave girl?"

"Rumours about Kantees of the Ziri have been getting about. They like the idea of being part of a legend," he said. "And they all know Sheesha, of course."

Swordmaster Erang appeared and Kantees explained what had happened at the ley-circle.

"A *nachak*?" said Daybian. "I'd like to see that."

The Swordmaster ignored him. "They will set up a defensive position around the circle as they bring in more troops."

"Yenteel says there might be a feeding here in a few days."

"If they have failed to establish their position by then, it will be too late for them anyway. If they have, a feeding will make no difference. The *tekrasa* will be here soon, we must prepare for their arrival." He headed back into the castle.

There were more wingbeats from above as Helka and Jynolee came down.

"I would not have believed it if I had not seen it," said Helka.

"We followed your orders, Kantees," said Jynolee. "We found them almost immediately. I counted fifty-three."

Kantees hesitated. She wanted to say goodbye to Gally and Yenteel but they were not here. And if they had been, they would have insisted on coming. But this was no fight for them, she did not really even want to take Helka and Jynolee.

But I'm willing to take a little girl.

They were waiting for her to speak.

"You should stay, Daybian."

"If you fail then there will be nowhere for me to rule, Kantees."

"And if you die?"

"That's what Jelamie was born for."

Kantees shook her head as if to clear it.

"Do you need me, Kantees of the Ziri?"

Tenical emerged into the light. *Accept the service of others.*

"No, Tenical, but you honour me with your offer," she said. "We cannot have any *ziri* carrying two on this journey, and there'll be a patterner or two at the other end to bring us home." Then she reached into her pack and drew out the *chilafrah*. "Look after this, will you?"

In the past she might have expected Tenical to grab it greedily but instead he hurried over and took it gently from her hand.

"You might find a use for it," she said. "I wouldn't know where to start."

"You do me a great honour."

"Defend Jakalain."

He bowed and stepped back from Sheesha. "I will, Lady Kantees."

"Let's go," she said.

Sheesha spread his wings, beat down and they launched into the air. The others followed.

Kantees directed Sheesha to join the group of lordlings on their *ziri* and listened to their astonishment as their mounts arranged themselves into an arrowhead behind her as the other *ziri* from below arrived and slotted into position.

A glance told her that Daybian and Levin were on her right and left while Jynolee, Helka and someone she didn't know were in the third rank and the others behind them.

Kantees headed them to the north of the ley-circle. It didn't take long to see that Dunor troops were marching through the portal and filling up the space around the circle. Each group brought some sort of defensive wall with them. It was hard to estimate the numbers but they were already in the hundreds. She couldn't see the *nachak* but if it had not already been brought down it would probably be making for the mountains. Its only purpose had been to disrupt the defences long enough that the Dunor could establish their hold on this end. And it had succeeded.

There was fighting already as the Jakalain forces re-organised and rushed the Dunor but if they were pushed back, they became more tightly packed and harder to move. In the light of the lanterns there were already many bodies

I've delayed too long.

There were eleven *ziri* in the group, too many for flying in line, but they could form three columns. Kantees suggested the idea to Sheesha and the *ziri* re-arranged themselves.

The lordlings were once again surprised. Kantees smiled grimly. *They haven't seen anything yet.*

The arch of the portal was still clear before her and she lined up on it then gave Sheesha the instruction to dive. They had flown through a patterner's path before so that was not a problem, but they had been alone, not facing an army coming the other way.

There was only one way she could do this without killing them all—unless the very act itself killed them. It was a risk they had to take.

Someone in the attacking force must have seen them descending faster and faster because there was a ripple of movement and she could see bows being pulled back.

Not this time.

"Now, Sheesha."

Her *ziri* drew the power from the ley-circle and a cocoon of golden light enveloped the entire group. She had a moment to see a face she recalled only too well commanding his men to fire. But they were already wrapped in the protective sheath and moving too fast. In the blink of an eye they entered the portal, even as more troops exited.

Then they were inside. Like a burning arrow through a keyhole.

How Sheesha kept them flying true when there was so little room to manoeuvre Kantees did not know. The path ahead was lit with torches, men marching in, rank after rank, *kichesa* pulling carts, even armsmen leading horses. The Dunor had been preparing for this a long time, perhaps years. Capturing the *Fahain* had been part of their plan, but Kantees upsetting the attack on Jakalain then escaping had not. Kantees alone had disrupted the pattern they were making for the world. They were readying themselves to attack any resisting families—she had forced their hand with Jakalain.

"Look," said Ulina, pointing down.

Below them the marching ranks were being knocked down by their passage. Kantees tried to look behind. It wasn't clear but their flight was leaving chaos in its wake.

That, at the very least, would give Swordmaster Erang more time to take back control of the ley-circle. But if she could—

—They burst into sunlight—the sky was a milky blue and the sun itself, close to the horizon, seemed to lack strength. Kantees made sure Sheesha was drawing power from the new ley-circle and kept going. It was just as well, it seemed the Dunor were planning to take *tekrasa* along the path as well and there were at least ten ready to go. And there were armsmen still preparing to enter the path; she could barely guess their numbers but there must be thousands. They would be settling in for a siege if necessary and would be supplied through the ley-circle, while the castle would be unable to last long.

As she considered those things the *ziri* had flown far out from the circle.

"This is not the same place," said Ulina.

Kantees looked around. This was not a tropical island. The terrain was undulating grassland and devoid of trees. She brought the formation round in a long turn. There wasn't even a town or castle near the ley-circle. Just a huge camp. A big cage stood off to one side with a stockade next to it. The holding pens for the *nachak* and the big *chakisa*. That meant they must have been brought here from somewhere else first.

The *ziri* streaked back towards the ley-circle. Kantees realised she should have explained the plan but the armsmen and patterners could not be given time. Before they arrived, Kantees shouted her instructions.

"Hold off the armsmen. We'll grab the patterner." She hoped it was obvious who was supposed to do the fighting and who would deal with the patterners.

Over the ley-circle, the golden light dropped and they were blasted by freezing cold air—wherever they were, it was not spring. The silence of the magic was replaced by the bellowing of a thousand men and the shrieks of the *ziri*, tense for the fight.

Below them was a big wooden platform, slightly raised from the ground. She could see the portal, touching the boards. This must be a ley-circle slightly above ground-level, like Riverrush and Dakastown. Kantees encouraged Sheesha to land as fast as possible, she wasn't sure how long these young lords would be able to hold off an entire army.

Eleven *ziri* raised their wings into a V-shape and fell on the wooden platform. Sheesha was already snapping at armsmen in the immediate area as he landed. Ulina slipped off and Kantees hit the boards moments later.

"Don't run off, Ulina," said Kantees. "Sheesha, stay close."

The sound of swords clashing, men grunting, *ziri* shrieks and cries of pain dominated.

Someone ran out of the portal, saw the *ziri* and ran at them, sword raised. A crossbow bolt from behind Kantees took him in the chest and he stumbled then collapsed. She looked round in surprise to see Jynolee reloading.

"I said I didn't like them, not that I couldn't use them."

A scream brought her attention back to the portal as Sheesha snapped off the arm of a soldier.

The patterners stood in a group close to the edge of the portal, as Kantees stalked in their direction one of them slipped through the portal and vanished. Ulina ran after him.

"Don't kill him, bring him back!"

Ulina vanished.

Kantees closed on the patterners, but their eyes were only for Sheesha at her shoulder.

"Where is this place?"

They barely registered her words.

Helka and Jynolee stepped into view either side of Kantees with their crossbows pointing at the three remaining men, all in patterner's robes but with extra furs around the neck and muffs for their hands.

"Where are we?" she asked again. "Answer, or my *zirichak* will tear you to pieces."

"Far north," said one of them. "You are the *Fahain*."

"And where are the Dunor?"

"They knew you might come, not here."

The fourth patterner emerged from the portal with Ulina behind him. She had a splash of blood across her face while his held a look of horror. Kantees did not want to know what she had done, but the blood had not come from this man.

"Kantees." A breathless Daybian was beside her. "This is a lot of fun but could we hurry it up? We've lost two already and the odds are not in our favour."

Kantees looked round, the other lords were still mounted and slashing left and right, as the heads of their *ziri* wove back and forth snapping and biting

"I'll be a moment, get mounted, tell them to be ready to ride."

"Thank you."

Two armsmen stepped warily from the portal. They saw Ulina, the battle being waged, and the crossbows now aimed at them. They retreated.

Kantees turned back to the patterners. "The one who is the keystone of this path will come with me. The others can stay here. The one who comes may die. The others will most certainly live." Kantees watched how their eyes flicked one to another. "Tell me or my *ziri* will bite your legs off. You may live but you'll never walk again."

"That one," said Ulina, pointing at the one who had answered her initially. He was older than the others and his hair was white.

The man panicked and dived into the portal.

Ulina chased after him.

"Mount up!" Kantees cried. She was on Sheesha's back in a moment.

Now it was just the *ziri* biting and slashing. A pile of corpses filled the stairs up to the platform making it harder for those behind to approach. The occasional arrow came in from the side but it seemed they were reluctant to shoot in case they hit the patterners— their only route out of this place. But now they were encircling the raised platform and climbing up. Helka and Jynolee were loosing bolts as fast as they could but it wasn't enough.

Kantees turned Sheesha back to the portal to see Ulina emerging, pushing the older patterner before her. This time he was bloodied and he held his arm.

Once he was close enough, Kantees dragged him with both hands and pulled him up and across Sheesha's neck. Ulina was up and stood behind Kantees.

"We're going! Face the portal!"

"They're ready," said Ulina.

They were still on the ground and Kantees had no idea what was going to happen but she had no choice: "Go fast, Sheesha. Right now!"

The shouts and screams of the outside world cut off as if by a knife. Instead, the shattering of splintering wood filled the air, more than one man and *ziri* cried out in pain.

But they were already on the path. Once more streaming along its length. The devastation they had caused on the way through the first time was fully visible. The once-orderly troops were staggering, their ears and noses bloody. More than one *kichek* lay motionless while others ran amok. There were even fires.

Kantees encouraged Sheesha to accelerate, confident now that nothing bad would happen to them.

Below, within the golden cocoon, lay pieces of the platform. And body parts. Whatever had been within the power of the pattern when it formed. The *ziri* were ramrod straight now. Their wings pulled in tight.

Their prisoner was not struggling, he studied the magic around him. Kantees realised this was what the Dunor wanted, knowledge of the *ziri* magic, and she was giving it to him.

Once more they shot like an arrow out into the night, Jakalain was to the right and the two forces still faced off below them. They had not been gone long.

Kantees commanded Sheesha to slow down. The magic went away and the warm familiar scent of Jakalain filled her senses. The debris they had carried with them fell away. At least now she knew what would happen if someone fell from their *ziri* while flying fast.

She turned and climbed.

She felt Sheesha shudder in the air.

"Sorry, Kantees," shouted Levin, "but we need to be down there."

Waileth and four other *ziri* broke free of the formation and dropped away towards the battle. Kantees turned Sheesha back towards the ley-circle. The portal was gone. The Dunor troops would receive no more supplies or reinforcements.

"What happens to a person on the patterner's path when it stops?" she asked the man, not expecting an answer.

Above Jakalain there was a flash of light. A fire-arrow of huge proportions shot upwards and hit something large and dark. It erupted into a huge ball of flame, the gondola beneath it crashing to the ground. The sound of the explosion rolled over them moments later. The light of the burning *tekrasa* lit up the underside of the clouds, and the other monstrous plants that hung there.

Another giant fire-arrow shot away, and another.

The sky was filled with explosions and in the light, they could see the other *tekrasa* slowly turning away.

"I want to kill you right now, patterner, you have seen the patterning the *zirichasa* can do. You have seen the power of the *Fahain* up-close. And I expect you are clever enough to make sense of it. I do not want you to have that knowledge."

Hanging awkwardly across Sheesha's neck he said nothing, though he turned his head towards her.

"But I expect the Lords Jakalain and Corlain will want to question you. Not to mention the lordlings who assisted in your capture. Two of whom are dead, and their families will no doubt want retribution."

He said nothing but she could see she had his complete attention.

"We are flying quite high now. When the lords question you about the Dunor, you will probably try to be loyal. And then they will be forced to resort to torture. And when they have the truth from you, they will torture you more, to ensure that you were not lying. Have you seen the wrecks of men who have had their nails ripped out, their eyes gouged—"

He jerked once, over-balanced and fell silently into the dark.

"Oh dear," said Ulina. "He fell."

2 9

They landed in the courtyard and nobody tried to shoot at them. The lordlings were assigned eyries for their *zirichasa* and taken into the main castle to be treated as befitted their station. Even the bodies of the dead ones had been returned. They had been tied to their *ziri* in the middle of the fight and returned with the rest.

Five of the Dunor *tekrasa* had been destroyed in all, the rest had escaped but Kantees was in no mind to go after them. Let them take the news of their defeat back to their masters.

She just wanted to sleep.

"Lady Kantees."

She groaned inwardly as Tenical strode through the torchlight to where she stood.

He bowed and held out his hand. He was offering the *chilafrah*. She took it.

"Did it help?"

"You saw the fire-arrows?"

"They were effective."

He nodded. "Both their fire and range were supplemented by patternings that would have exhausted any patterner. We kept the attackers at sufficient distance they could not deploy their forces. Your gift was appreciated, and Vonand was quite envious."

Kantees felt there was nothing to be said and, holding the *chilafrah* to her breast, she turned away, stifling a yawn.

She climbed back on to Sheesha's back and, with Helka and Jynolee, flew back to the Ziri Tower. Kantees nestled under Sheesha's wing and they were both asleep before she knew she was comfortable.

"Lady Kantees?"

It was a woman's voice, she wasn't sure whose but she wished they would just go away.

"I'm sorry, Lady Kantees, but Lord Jakalain has asked if you wouldn't mind attending a meeting in the afternoon."

"Yes, the afternoon. Not now."

"It is time for the midday meal. I think you may want to clean yourself, dress and eat?"

Kantees pushed Sheesha's wing out of the way. He was still snoring. She looked out of the open hatch and could see grey rain. The woman was Marakees.

"Midday?"

"Yes, Lady Kantees," she said. "But Lady Jakalain has put aside some rooms for you in the castle, and there's a bath and fresh clothes. And the kitchen has sent up food but no one knew where you had gone, except my Galiko, he knew."

"You and Gally," said Kantees as she pushed herself to her feet. She felt filthy. There had been too much death in the last day.

"Yes, Lady Kantees."

"Please don't say that every time. If you have to, just say mistress. I'm just an ex-slave."

"Like my Galiko."

"Yes. Like Gally, but that was my decision, not his. I'm sure he would have been just as happy living here as a slave."

"Then I would not have met him, mistress. And I would still be in Two Circles, not even a real person there."

"I suppose."

"You bend the World's Pattern to your will, Lady Kantees." She touched her hand to her forehead and bowed.

Kantees frowned. The woman was far too subservient but perhaps that was because she had lived her life under the sway of the abomination. Perhaps she would improve with time. She followed Marakees down and across to the main castle building.

Bathed, clothed in a dress (which felt very strange) and fed, she finally allowed herself to be led to the meeting. She was the last to arrive and the room was already occupied. This time there was a long table with chairs, most of them occupied. At the head were the Lords Jakalain and Corlain, Swordmaster Erang, Vonand the patterner, and that Bejeren. Close to the other end, the chairs were occupied by Daybian, Levin, Tenical and Yenteel while Gally, Marakees, Helka and Jynolee stood with Ulina at the side of the room. Finally, there was the Jakalain scribe with his own table by the window.

They all stood when she entered and waited until she was seated before sitting back down.

Lord Jakalain went through the introductions, though it was unnecessary. "The attack of the Dunor has been successfully repelled," he continued, "and the loss of life on our side was not terrible. The worst of it at the ley-circle, and in the fires."

"Peta of Garbalain and Barald of Summalain were lost in the north lands," said Daybian.

His father acknowledged the interruption with a nod of his head. "Their bodies will be returned to their families."

"They died bravely, fighting the Dunor, Father."

"That story will be told, Daybian, if you will allow me to continue?"

Daybian went quiet.

"The truth of the Dunor and the families, such as we know them, that have broken the Concordance, will be spread abroad as well. It will be made clear that Jakalain and Corlain stood with the sons of those families against these traitors."

"And what will happen to those who joined the Dunor?" asked

Kantees. "What will be done? What about the Hamalain who employed mercenaries to steal away your son?"

"That is a matter for the council," said Lord Jakalain. "The truth will be brought against them."

"And what will happen?"

Lord Jakalain hesitated.

"Nothing, Kantees," said Levin. There was a tightness in his voice. "What he won't tell you is that nothing will be done. Oh, there will be letters of censure written. Perhaps even fines to be paid, but nothing will change. The Hamalain will still rule in Kurvin Port."

"Thank you for telling me the truth, Levin. It is what I suspected." She found she was not angry, nothing surprised her about the Taymalin and their lack of will to act against their own crimes. "And what of the Dunor?"

"You want plain speaking, Kantees of the Ziri?" said Lord Corlain. He still looked tired and worn.

"I think it's best, don't you?" *I was once a liar, and it brought me nothing but pain and hardship.*

"We can torture the men we captured to find the families to whom they belong but Hamalain is the only one we know with any certainty. The others will deny their involvement and we have no proof. The Dunor itself cannot be traced, even if we know it originated among the Tirnians."

"So, in the end, this was all for nothing?"

"We have stopped them, Lady Kantees," said Lord Jakalain. "Without you, my heir would have been taken, perhaps forever, or Jakalain would have fallen. Or some other place. The Dunor would have made its pacts and brought all the realms under its sway and by the time they were revealed it would be too late.

"So, no, Mistress of the Ziri, it was not for nothing. You have preserved our world."

The Taymalin world. I have saved nothing of mine.

She sighed. "Very well, in that case I have but one request."

"Ask and if it is in my power, I will grant it."

Kantees glanced at Jynolee. "The blacksmith of Riverrush is

without wife or heir, and I promised him an apprentice, or perhaps a journeyman, to take over his furnace one day."

"That is not a difficult wish to fulfill."

"Thank you, lord."

"Is that all you ask?" said Lord Corlain.

"There is nothing else."

Lord Jakalain waved his hand at the scribe who gathered up papers and brought them to the table. The lord smiled at Kantees.

"These are papers of manumission, Kantees of the Ziri. I will sign them and that will free you and the one known as Galiko from the ownership of Jakalain." He took the quill from the scribe, who opened the ink pot for him.

"No!" shouted Kantees and leapt to her feet. "Do not sign. You do not have that right."

Every eye was on her, and only Yenteel was smiling.

"I have the right, Kantees," said Jakalain. "I can free any slave I own."

"And do you own me?"

"I have the papers."

"But tell me, Lord Jakalain, do you *own* me? Can you direct my life and my actions? Can you kill me because I am nothing more than a possession for you to dispose of as you will?"

The man stared at her. "I believe if I so ordered it you would die where you stand."

Levin stood up. "I believe you would have to kill me first, my lord."

"And me, Father," said Daybian getting to his feet.

Kantees felt Helka and Jynolee at her shoulders and Ulina squeezed in front of her. Tenical and Yenteel stood as well. Gally and Marakees closed in.

Lord Jakalain held up his hand. "Sit down everyone. I take back my words."

The ones at the table did sit, the others stepped back, but Ulina stayed where she was.

"The fact remains, Kantees, you are a runaway slave and I thought that you would want that to be taken from you."

"My lords—" started Kantees.

Lord Corlain interrupted. "Don't include me in this, Lady Kantees, there are no slaves in Faerholme."

She nodded to him. "My Lord Jakalain, you cannot free me because you do not have the right to own me in the first place. I will not accept your manumission because if I did, I would also accept your right to own me."

"Then you are damned whether I do, or do not."

"But this matter is not about me, lord, nor about Gally, it is about all the slaves in Esternes."

"I cannot free them all."

"That is correct, because no slave owner had the right in the beginning."

Lord Jakalain frowned. "Then what do you expect me to do?"

Kantees' mind raced for a moment and pieces of ideas she had had since she ran away coalesced in her mind, then she smiled. "Give every slave in Jakalain the right to declare themselves free, if that's what they want."

There was silence around the room and then Yenteel burst out laughing. "That, Kantees, is the cleverest thing I have ever heard." There were confused looks on almost every other face. Yenteel looked very smug but this time Kantees didn't mind and let him have the moment. "On the one hand, my lord, it may encourage the owners to treat their slaves better. At a single stroke you destroy the trade because who will buy a slave if they might decide to free themselves. Where there is no demand, there is no business. And, of course, it will spread to the other places in time."

"But if I declare such a law, those who bought slaves will lose money," said Lord Jakalain.

"How many years does it take for a slave to recover the money spent on him or her?" said Kantees. "Five? Ten? You can offer to compensate the owners in proportion to the years the slave has been owned."

"But that might empty my coffers."

"Consider it the price you must pay for being a good and decent human being, my lord. Besides, you won't have to pay anything for losing me and Gally—in fact, none for any of the slaves you own."

Lord Jakalain pushed the papers away from him and sighed. "I hope there is nothing else you want? The hand of my son in marriage plus half my realm, perhaps?"

Daybian looked hopeful. Kantees laughed quietly. "No, my lord, I do not want half your kingdom, nor your son's hand in marriage." She stood up. "I believe I have achieved all that I wanted. At least, for now."

~ The End ~

AFTERWORD

If you enjoyed BATTLE DRAGON, why not write a review on the site you bought it at, or on Goodreads (even both).

That's the end of this tale of Kantees and the *Zirichasa*, but you can read about Lord Corlain's mad daughter (taupress.com/elona).

USA TODAY BESTSELLING AUTHOR
STEVE TURNBULL
ELONA
PATTERNER'S PATH 1